Acclaim for Charlotte Bingham:

'Compulsively readable'
Options

'Irresistible . . . A treat that's not to be missed'
Prima

'A rip-roaring combination of high romance
and breathless excitement'
Mail on Sunday

'Compelling'
Woman and Home

'Heartwarming and full of period charm'
Daily Express

'Her imagination is thoroughly original'
Daily Mail

'Charlotte Bingham's devotees will recognize
her supreme skill as a storyteller'
Independent on Sunday

'As comforting and nourishing as a hot milky
drink on a stormy night. Her legions of
fans will not be disappointed'
Daily Express

www.rbooks.co.uk
www.charlottebingham.com

Novels with Terence Brady:
VICTORIA
VICTORIA AND COMPANY
ROSE'S STORY
YES HONESTLY

Television Drama Series with Terence Brady:
TAKE THREE GIRLS
UPSTAIRS DOWNSTAIRS
THOMAS AND SARAH
NANNY
FOREVER GREEN

Television Comedy Series with Terence Brady:
NO HONESTLY
YES HONESTLY
PIG IN THE MIDDLE
OH MADELINE! (USA)
FATHER MATTHEW'S DAUGHTER

Television Plays with Terence Brady:
MAKING THE PLAY
SUCH A SMALL WORLD
ONE OF THE FAMILY

Films with Terence Brady:
LOVE WITH A PERFECT STRANGER
MAGIC MOMENTS

Stage Plays with Terence Brady:
I WISH I WISH
THE SHELL SEEKERS
BELOW STAIRS
(adaptation from the novel by Rosamunde Pilcher)

THE
ENCHANTED

Charlotte Bingham

BANTAM BOOKS
LONDON · TORONTO · SYDNEY · AUCKLAND · JOHANNESBURG

TRANSWORLD PUBLISHERS
61–63 Uxbridge Road, London W5 5SA
A Random House Group Company
www.rbooks.co.uk

THE ENCHANTED
A BANTAM BOOK: 9780553819519

First published in Great Britain
in 2008 by Bantam Press
a division of Transworld Publishers
Bantam edition published 2008

Addresses for Random House Group Ltd companies outside
the UK can be found at: www.randomhouse.co.uk
The Random House Group Ltd Reg. No. 954009

The Random House Group Ltd supports The Forest Stewardship
Council (FSC), the leading international forest certification
organization. All our titles that are printed on Greenpeace
approved FSC certified paper carry the FSC logo.
Our paper procurement policy can be found at
www.rbooks.co.uk/environment

Typeset in 11/13pt Palatino by
Kestrel Data, Exeter, Devon.
Printed in the UK by
CPI Cox & Wyman, Reading, RG1 8EX.

2 4 6 8 10 9 7 5 3 1

Mixed Sources
Product group from well-managed
forests and other controlled sources
www.fsc.org Cert no. TT-COC-2139
© 1996 Forest Stewardship Council
FSC

*For perhaps the only actor, playwright,
singer and painter ever to train
a winner under Rules.*

IRELAND IN THE LATE 1970s

Prologue

They come upon her one blustery spring morning
with an April tide running up the white sand
shore. She is just standing there, looking out to
sea, still as a statue in a square. She could indeed
have been a monument for all they know as they
slide carefully down the end of the cliff path to
get a closer look at her. There are three of them,
father, son and daughter, the children full grown
into late teenage, the wind from the sea blowing
their long dark hair back from their heads as
quietly they approach her, afraid of scaring her,
wondering when she will sense them and if
when she does she will make a sudden dash for
continued freedom.

Yet even as they approach she stands quite still.
She must hear them, know they are there, but
not a move does she make. She just stands there
still, looking far out to the sea. And now they are
near they see she is pregnant and greatly so. At
first glance it would seem she is about to give
birth there and then, which might explain her
stillness, so they take even more care lest they

should frighten her into delivery. She is astonishingly lovely. Wild certainly, so it would seem, for what else could explain her presence here on this lonely stretch with no one in sight of her and no visible means of reaching the beach unless from round the corner of the cliffs through the seas? Yet she is more beautiful than any wild one they have ever seen before. In fact she looks every inch an aristocrat with her fine head, her perfect limbs and her noble bearing.

They are only a matter of feet away from her now, and at last she turns and looks at them and when she does they can see the past in her large wise eyes. From dark brown orbs there shines a sense of times before, times that seem to stretch back to when everyone was wild and untamed and the gods ruled the land from strange and wondrous kingdoms. They put out hands, not to catch or touch but to make peace, and it seems she has no fear of them for she just keeps looking at them, her eyes unmoving from theirs. The father watches, then says he thinks she wants to be taken and sure enough, when the girl with the long dark hair stretches closer to her, with a last look at the sea she turns herself round and begins to walk towards them.

Yet they know better than to touch her, so they wait to see if they can discover what she wants. The girl turns away as if to walk back down the beach and when she does so she finds she is being followed. They all walk away now with nothing said, no questions asked and no promises made.

The wind off the sea is dying down and the tide has turned and is running out fast so that by the time they reach the head they may walk round it safely without need to climb any path. Soon they are approaching home with her walking easily behind them, her stomach swaying with every pace as if her advanced pregnancy is no burden to her whatsoever.

But what none of them saw, as far as is known, was the man on the beach now far below them, a young man with long wet blond hair and eyes the colour of sea coral. He stands where she had stood and quite as still as she had been, looking after her to where she has gone yet making no move to follow her. He stands in the very edge of the sea, as darkness falls and an April moon rises to shine on waters that stretch into the blue of the night, until there is nothing more to see or hear and finally then he moves, turning and walking back into the sea, away from the life of the land.

Chapter One

New Life

She lay in the deep, dry straw prepared for her delivery. Someone knelt by her head, gently pulling one of her ears; the other one stood by her tail, watching, waiting, smoking his pipe as he did so, well used to such times. Nothing was said. There was silence, broken only by her breathing, which had become deeper, more powerful and urgent, as the foal moved inside her, ready now to be born.

'I'd say we're under orders.'

'You'll be fine. I'm here. You'll be just fine,' the girl murmured.

The mare's head tilted back once as birth began in earnest, nostrils widening, eyes half closing. She gave a groan that caused her to shudder massively, while her flanks heaved with the effort.

''Tis all right, girl,' the man said, bending lower, his pipe still stuck in the corner of his mouth. 'Come on now – you'll be all right.'

'She's not comfortable, Da.'

'I'd say she is not as young as we would like her; 'tis more of an effort, so.'

'Whatever her age, she has the look of the eagle, and the mark of the prophet's thumb in her neck.'

'Whose horse is she, I wonder? A fine mare like this has to belong,' Padraig said, shaking his head.

'She's come out of the sea, so she has. She's a horse of Mananan. She's come from the kingdom under the seas.'

'Whether she has or hasn't, she has to belong to someone,' Padraig repeated. 'A thoroughbred mare like this is not a tinker's donkey. She probably escaped from one of the farms beyond and got herself cut off be the tide.'

He took off his hat to bang it against his leg, before replacing it.

'But don't I know every one of the horses in these parts? She has to have come from much further abroad.'

Kathleen interrupted him. 'This is not going to be easy, Da. Look, the poor mare is never going to do it on her own.'

'There's never any need for the vet, Kathleen. You know that.'

Kathleen shook her head. They were poor, it was true, but not so poor that she could bear to let the mare die, when it was evident the foal was stuck.

'I'll go call Mr Sweeney, Da. He's only ten

minutes away. I'll pay for him myself, so I will.'

'If he's home. And if he's sober, which I doubt, and never mind the payment; didn't he take a mountain of hay from me last year and divil a penny from him.'

'I'll go call him anyway.'

For once the vet was at home. He muttered thickly that he'd be there as soon as he could, and when Kathleen returned to the stable she found things were no better, and said so.

'And no worse, either, girl,' Padraig protested, as he struggled to find the foal. 'The foal's just not presenting itself – not the right way. I'm trying to turn it now.'

The mare seemed to be giving up the struggle. Kathleen could see it in her eye and in the damp dark sweat that had broken out over her skin. She arched her neck, trying to look round at her flanks, but overtaken by another contraction she threw her great head back into the straw and kicked out in a sudden spasm.

'Careful, Kathleen. You don't want to have her catch you. Where's Mr Sweeney got to anyhow?' her father grumbled. 'I'm doing me best here, but it seems a fore leg is stuck. And for the life of me . . .'

Padraig had both hands in the mare now, but all he could get hold of were the unborn foal's hindquarters. If they couldn't turn the foal they knew they were lost.

The vet arrived a quarter of an hour on in slippered feet, the bottoms of his flannel pyjamas showing under the legs of his trousers and the end of a Sweet Afton stuck to his top teeth. He lurched over to Padraig and all but fell to the floor as he bent down to start his examination.

'We need more light here,' he said.

'More light?' Padraig growled. 'The mare's throwing a foal, not a moth, man.'

'More light and some whisky,' Sweeney repeated. 'We're on for a long haul. And some rope, child!' He called to Kathleen as she rose to go. 'We'll have to pull this fella out.'

Padraig saw it was wrong. He knew the rope was on wrong. He couldn't really see how Sweeney had it attached but he just knew the drunken oaf had it wrong.

'Get away, man,' he said angrily, pushing the vet aside.

'No, Da, let me. I've the smaller hands and arms – let me do that.'

'Where is it now, Kathleen?' Padraig asked her as she took his place, and Sweeney collapsed against the wall of the stable, drinking whisky from a half-bottle clothed in brown paper.

'It seems to be round the neck,' Kathleen muttered, feeling the warmth of the foal, feeling it was still alive, still moving.

'God help us all,' Padraig sighed. 'Take it off there, Kathleen – if you can – and you take yourself home, Sweeney. Sure you're a disgrace to your profession.'

But the vet wasn't going anywhere until the

bottle was done. He just eyed his neighbour and drank some more while Kathleen slowly unwound the lethal noose and as her father instructed tied it firmly round the foal's chest.

'If we can ease him round now, child,' Padraig told her. 'If you can turn him now at all – then we can help him out.'

Kathleen prayed as she started to turn the unborn foal. The mare opened her eyes and turned slowly to look, sensing help, even perhaps sensing salvation.

'I think I have it done, Pa,' Kathleen said, the sweat running down into her eyes. 'The head's presenting itself now.'

'Good girl yourself,' Padraig told her. 'Now all we must do is gently ease him out – gently so – and pray to God the mare gives us a bit of help.'

Padraig took hold of the rope while Kathleen tried to guide the path of the foal. She could see the head now through the sac, bent down to the animal's chest, and as she saw it beginning to be born the mother took the very deepest breath Kathleen thought she had ever heard an animal take, and groaned mightily. As she did so, her foal was eased out into the world by loving hands, until it lay by its mother, still wrapped in its caul.

'Is it alive, Da? Please God let it be alive.'

'It's alive all right, Kathleen girl,' her father replied, taking a large handful of clean fresh straw and beginning to clean the newborn. 'By some wondrous great miracle 'tis well alive – and there you are, 'tis a colt, too. A fine chestnut.'

19

Kathleen gazed at the foal, all leg and little else, soaking wet and covered in its birth, the faintest signs of breath barely discernible.

'You sure he's all right, Pa? You sure he's alive?'

'He's alive, Kathleen – don't fret. How's the mare now? Is the mare all right?'

Kathleen went to her head, kneeling down to stroke her head, her ears. 'She's exhausted, Da. She's barely breathing . . .'

'But she is breathing, girl?'

Kathleen bent closer to watch and listen. She counted the breaths and the intervals between them.

'About ten seconds apart. They're deep – and getting deeper. But she's breathing real slow.'

'And wouldn't you, after what she's been through?' Padraig finished cleaning the foal and stood up. 'The mare'll need stitches, Sweeney, though she's not too bad considering. Get up, man,' he said, for the vet was now sitting in the straw. 'Get up and finish the job we have just done for you. For all our sakes, get on with the stitching.'

He went to the corner of the stable and retrieved the vet's bag, while Sweeney shook his head as if trying to get some sense into it. Kathleen stood watching mare and foal.

'How we got him out, girl.' Padraig sighed, shook his head and turned his pipe back the right way round to try to relight it.

'It was a miracle,' Kathleen said quietly. 'We must thank St Francis.'

'Isn't he the man?' her father replied. 'Isn't he just the man?'

As Sweeney set about his work, another miracle happened, a miracle that they both watched, struck silent as always by the marvel, as a creature not yet twenty minutes old somehow and against all odds struggled up from its bed – half up one moment, down the next, on three legs a second later, then down on its knees again – standing all at once and sensationally up on all four and staying up, balancing on a quartet of long, slender limbs that looked as though if someone suddenly opened the door the draught would snap them.

'Would you ever?' Kathleen laughed. 'Will you look at that?'

'He's not over large, even for his age.'

'He's beautiful,' Kathleen said defensively, moving a step closer and holding out her hand for the foal to sniff. 'He's enchanting.'

'Show me a foal that's not beautiful.'

They went outside to take the air, and stare at the stars, to catch their breath, and ever afterwards Kathleen would wake in the night and blame herself for that, for in that time Sweeney, the drunken son of a drunken father, did his worst, and they lost the mare. But for a few minutes – oh, dear God, but for a few minutes – they could surely have saved her.

There was no time for tears, as there never is on a farm; no time even to curse Sweeney. They must do what they could. Padraig ran to the telephone as Kathleen tried to give comfort to the foal who stood looking down at his fallen mother with uncertainty already in his milky eyes, unsteady still on his lanky legs while Kathleen with one arm around him put her free hand to his mouth in the hope that he would suckle it until her father returned and she could boil and cool him some milk. But as soon as he was called her brother arrived, and was at once dispatched to prepare the feed.

By a miracle, and on only his fourth call to neighbouring farms, Padraig located a mare who had lost a foal not half an hour before. He was offered the stricken mother at once as a foster, and knowing the urgency the neighbours had her loaded in their horsebox and delivered to the farm just as Kathleen was trying to interest the foal in a bottle of warm cow's milk.

'Here, girl,' the groom who'd brought the mare across said to her, handing her a tin. 'Himself said you'd be in need of this, in case you've none yourselves. 'Tis colostrum. He always keeps some frozen for just these times.'

The groom had brought another container as well, a much larger one, a packing case from which he produced the skin of the dead foal, helping them to drape their own live foal in it before leading the mare into the next-door stable. Hoping the disconsolate creature would accept the stranger as if it were her own, Kathleen passed a head slip over the nose of her foal and led it to where the foster mare stood waiting, ears back and tail swishing.

22

'Wait now,' the groom advised Kathleen, putting one arm out in front of her to prevent her progress. 'She's a kick in her, this one.'

He had hardly spoken before the mare lashed out, a blow which might well have caught the foal and finished it had Kathleen not been stopped in her tracks. Once the mare had calmed down, Kathleen slowly led her foal to the mare's head so he could be seen. The mare looked down on the strange sight, the uncertain newborn swaddled in the skin of her own dead foal, and slowly flared her nostrils at him. For a while she did nothing more than regard the interloper, making no move to familiarise herself with him, her nostrils still wide, one eye fixed on the creature standing unsteadily by her side. Then at last, as Kathleen was beginning to despair, the mare slowly lowered her nose until it rested on the foal, and left it there. The foal staggered at first under the sudden weight; then, as if sensing something, turned its head to look up at the creature standing over him. The eyes of the two animals caught and held and then the mare flared her nostrils even more and blew gently down at her foot.

'They're met,' the groom said quietly. 'He'll be on her in no time at all.'

So he was, too, helped by Kathleen who went round to the far side of the mare and slipped a hand under the animal's stomach, the same hand the foal had suckled earlier. A minute or so later a soft warm mouth found her fingers, and Kathleen slid her hand slowly back to the mare's teats. First time, the foal refused, insisting on fingers rather than teats, but the next time Kathleen kept her hand just out of reach until the youngster took hold of the mare and began to suckle.

'I'd still give him the colostrum,' the groom advised as he prepared to leave. 'For that's not his own mother's milk. And we all know the meaning of that, so we do.'

'If there's ever a thing we can do,' Padraig said, walking him through the dawn light to the horse-box.

'You can let us know when he's to win his first race,' the groom replied, stopping to light a smoke. 'Which he will. For I see he has the mark of the prophet.'

'He does.'

'So there you are.' The groom smiled. 'Be sure now to tell us.'

The foal belonged to Kathleen. Not that it was ever said. It was simply understood, so much so that from that moment on Padraig was always to refer to the foal in such a way, as in *you'd best go see what that foal of yours needs*, and later *that colt of yours is fooling about in the paddock again*, and even later, as he raced with his companions in the fields, *that horse of yours has come on a stride or two. Will you look at him go, daughter of the house?*

But though he flourished, and filled out well, and strengthened nicely, fed on the good grass that sprouted on top of the limestone, he never grew tall.

'He's not had his mother's milk, that's why,' Kathleen would state when she and her father leaned on the fence and watched the young stock graze. 'Though the mare, God rest her, his mother was a good size.'

'Size isn't all in a horse, Kathleen, until you come to sell it, and then isn't it everything?'

'He could run over timber, Da. If he has any toe, sure he might be a hurdler, who knows?'

'If there was only three more inches to him, girl,' Padraig replied, lighting his pipe, 'he could make us a million, but today all they want is a good big horse. They're not wanting anything but size now – what they all calls *a fine stamp of a horse*. As if any of them has the eye, as if any of them has anything but a chequebook. Chequebook breeding, I call it. You'll be lucky if you find an owner for him, and then only if you give him a case of whisky to go with the little horse.'

'Ah well, if he's too small to sell, then maybe we'll keep him so,' Kathleen said hopefully, hopping up and over the fence to take the colt his afternoon treat of a sliced carrot and calling back, 'You never know – he might win *us* something!'

When he was weaned and turned out, Kathleen fell into the habit of hiding herself unseen in the long grasses of the paddocks, two or three hundred yards away from where he was cropping grass with his companions. She would crawl on her hands and knees to her chosen hiding place, making sure her foal was downwind of her, then lie on her back, waiting. The first time he

25

found her, it took him six minutes by Kathleen's watch. Ever after that, no matter what time of day she hid nor how carefully, he would come in search of her. Rarely did it take him longer than a couple of minutes to find her; the average was a count of fifty.

Kathleen would lie, always in a different place, flat on her back with her eyes closed, waiting. At first she would hear the delicate pounding of his young hooves as he came to look for her. Not a sound would there be from her, until she opened her eyes and found herself being observed by two round brown orbs, after which he would nudge her, buckle his legs and lower himself to the ground to settle beside her. Finally when it was time for Kathleen to return to her work he would walk slowly beside her to the gate, where she would give one last pull at his ears or a ruffle on his neck before letting herself out. The moment she unlatched the gate he would dip his head, kick out his hind legs, turn on a sixpence and gallop off back to join his friends, and one in particular, a pretty little dark bay yearling filly out of a mare owned by the neighbouring farmer. Kathleen watched the friendship grow between the two young horses, hers becoming attached to the filly as if they were meant to be together, never leaving her side, running with her, and grazing by her side. And when one of them got down to doze in the grass, the other would always stand sentinel.

She never put a leading rope on the colt. Instead she would call him at first with a whistle, but soon all she needed to do was appear at the gate and he would come to her. Finally she would arrive at the gate only to find that he was already waiting, more often than not in the company of his girlfriend, whom Kathleen had christened Finoula.

Her brother usually broke the horses. Liam was good with them, but of late he had grown tall and gangly, and with his sudden growth had come a loss of balance. His hands had grown heavy, too; as a boy he'd had the touch of a girl, his father would tell him – *not farmer's hands, boy*, Padraig would say.

'You don't want farmer's hands. A horse is in its mouth. A horse is all its mouth. Would yous like a great bar of steel being banged on your teeth as if ye'd no feeling? Indeed you would not, so keep those hands light – like your sister there. She is holding ribbons, boy – ribbons of silk, not chains like ye're holding there! Lighten your hands and sit through the horse – don't sit on him like that! Sit through him, boy! And when you're thinkin' of stoppin' him, do just that! Think it – don't pull the bit through the back of his head! Sit down – sit back – change your weight now – and easy! Ease him back – *ease him! Sure he'll have no mouth on him be the time ye're done, boy!*'

Padraig Flanagan might not look much on the ground, a short round-shouldered man who limped from a boyhood riding accident, but up on a horse he was a changed man. Flanagan was a part of every horse he rode. He rode from the leg and the seat, and although he'd the Irish habit of a forward foot, once he had hitched his irons up to racing length and perched himself on the horse's withers he was nothing but balance. Then he would ride his work, all the weight transferred down to the middle of his gumbooted feet, the reins clutched double in a bunch behind the horse's neck, his eye firmly fixed through the animal's ears on a point in the middle distance.

'But I want to back him, Da,' Kathleen pleaded. 'Boyo will expect me. He won't want Liam. Boyo won't go for him. I know it. Don't go asking why – I know Boyo and please, please let me back him, Pa, please?'

The colt had always been known as Boyo, since to begin with Kathleen could think of no suitable or indeed possible stable name for him. *He'll come to his name, one day*, she'd reasoned. *If I can't think of a name now it's because I haven't the right one ready.*

Padraig knew as well as Kathleen did that she must be the one to back him, but he also knew that when it came to horses nothing worthwhile ever came easy. He said he'd think about it. Said he would mull the matter over, give it every consideration.

'Very well,' he finally announced. 'Since you've done nothin' but keep at your poor father every day for the past two months about the business of backing your horse, I have finally made up me mind, so I have.'

Kathleen knew better than to prompt her father.

'Kathleen here is too light and too weak, I'd say, Da.'

'And I'd have to agree with you, boy,' Padraig replied with another nod. 'I'd have to agree with you there . . .'

'It's only common sense, Kathleen, seeing that you are a girl.'

'Am I now, Liam? I never noticed.'

'I'd have to agree with you, Liam,' their father continued, raising his voice, 'if you were right and if I thought you might fare better – but since you are not right and you would not do better I have to disagree with you.'

'Ah come on, Da – sure you're only teasing me?'

'I am not so,' Padraig replied. 'I am commissioning Kathleen here to put a saddle across this horse of hers and that is that.'

Padraig was all too aware that Kathleen had already been about the business. He had caught sight of her putting a roller on the colt's back, then following it by gently easing on a saddle; witnessed the horse eating his dinner with the saddle still on him, although as yet ungirthed; seen his daughter from a distance down the field walking the horse in a bridle, then with a saddle on, later with a sack of potatoes slung across the saddle; and finally watched from afar as she carefully tightened the girth under the saddle and let the irons swing loose against Boyo's side, although, to be sure, it was only the way they always did things with the young horses.

So when it came to it, it was as if the horse had always had a saddle on his back, for what with the weight of the potatoes, and much else, when she had finally slowly and carefully swung her right leg over the saddle, having stood in the left stirrup only while her father had taken a light hold on the animal's head, and sat herself down as lightly as she could, the horse only moved an ear. When she felt his calm she nodded at her father, and Padraig let go his hold and stood back, allowing him another chance to take flight, but still Boyo only stood, ears pricked, eyes bright.

'We're going to walk on now, sweetheart,' Kathleen told him quietly. 'I'm going to pick up the reins, I'm going to ease you forward – and we're going to walk on.'

She gave the horse only the lightest squeeze with her legs. The moment she asked him, he moved – not a sudden burst of activity, but a rhythmic, well-measured pace, easing into an elegant walk that took him in a generous left-handed circle round the small railed paddock. Later she stopped him, turned him, and had him walk round on the other rein. Finally she walked him in four diagonals and one straight line, before calling to her father to take hold of his head while she dismounted as gently and carefully as she had mounted.

'That'll do fine for today, young man,' she

said, patting then kissing his neck. [...]
grand.'

Handing her father the saddle he w[...]
to take, Kathleen slipped the bridle o[...]
the paddock, the horse keeping pace [...]
She walked to the main field fifty yards away, and
opened the gate. Boyo followed her, but once in
the field he didn't run off to join his companions.
Instead he stood staring out to the distant hills
and the sea beyond, with a look that reminded
Kathleen of his mother, the day the three of them
had found her on the beach. Then he got down
and rolled slowly and pleasurably in the well of
dry mud by the gate, got up again, shook himself
off and chose as his grazing spot a place not five
hundred yards but five feet away.

Kathleen leaned on the gate and watched him.
She watched him until she heard her father calling.

Padraig was waiting in the yard, smoking his
pipe as usual, and leaning up against a closed
stable door.

'The day is not long ahead when we have to
sell Boyo, you know that, Kathleen?'

'I know that, Da,' Kathleen replied, quickly
picking up the yard broom and beginning to
sweep. 'But not today.'

'We're not here to keep horses as pets.'

'Well, I never. You know, I never knew that.'

'It's as well to remember it, Kathleen. We can
make no preferences, and we are poor people, as I
have always told you.' Padraig took his pipe from

outh and eyed the smouldering tobacco.
very horse we have is born to be sold.'

'There's the matter of his passport still,' Kathleen replied. 'You'd have to have that sorted out.'

'Don't I already have it that?' Padraig put his pipe back in his mouth and drew on it before continuing. 'Not that it need be a real concern of yours—'

'I'd have thought not knowing which stallion bred him and with no papers for the mare it'd be a real concern for us all.'

'Then for your edification I say our neighbour John Slattery has franked the necessary documentation that says the sire was his stallion,' Padraig said, carefully watching his daughter. 'King of the Sea was your horse's sire, and it shows the dam was Mananan's Girl—'

'The mare you had to buy back from the Heaslips?' Kathleen exclaimed. 'But she's as barren as a hill in Greenland!'

'All that's needed is a name on the passport,' her father replied. 'And your Uncle Noel in Ballydehob has verified the document.'

'You never had Uncle Noel do that, Da?' Kathleen asked, wide-eyed.

'I had so. Sure he's a veterinary himself, is he not?'

'He's a vet for small animals, Da!' Kathleen protested. 'He's a family pet man. The only horses he ever sees are on merry-go-rounds!'

'And that's for us to know, girl, and for nobody

else,' Padraig replied firmly. 'It won't be the first time a man's had to go this route, don't you worry. The horse is a thoroughbred, there's no doubt of that, and since he's gelded now there'll be no career at stud to worry about. Sure the breeding's only words on a racecard. What matters is what the horse does, that's what matters.'

'But Da—'

'That's enough of your buts, my girl. We'll have no more on the matter, so be about your work. We have plenty enough on our hands.'

'We're short of chaff, Pa,' Kathleen muttered, eyeing her father as she swept round his feet, trying to get him to go. 'You'll need to cut some more.'

Her father remained where he was and put another match to his pipe of tobacco.

'Mick Finnegan has a horse he can't be backing,' he said, blowing the match out from the side of his mouth. 'His lad has a leg broken, and the horse is getting skittish. I said I'd send you along.'

'Is that right?' Kathleen wondered. 'And will he pay me?'

'I doubt it,' Padraig replied, taking a satisfied look at his now properly lit pipe. 'But sure you can always try axing him, but I doubt he has ever given a girl money, however good she may be.'

Kathleen said nothing more. Her father walked off and she watched him go, his pipe leaving a curl of blue smoke in the air. Sure it was a man's world. They had the paying of everything so they had the say of everything, it seemed, just as it didn't seem fair. She began sweeping the yard as clean as she could get it, wondering what was going to happen and how much longer she would have her horse to herself.

Still, she had time enough. Time enough to enjoy watching her youngster grow and, in bringing him on, time enough to relish their rides on the long empty beaches and their treks up into the hills beyond their small farm, time enough for them to grow so close they became all but inseparable, time enough to watch the friendship between the two young horses grow; and yet she knew somewhere the wheels were already in motion that would bring the strangers across the water in their search for good horses. And when that day finally came, as Kathleen knew that it surely would, then she would lose him, and she also knew that when she had lost him she would spend her spare time wondering where he had gone and what his poor fate might be.

ENGLAND IN THE EARLY 1980s

Chapter Two

Under Orders

'I didn't know you was interested in racing, Mrs D.,' Evie Tranter said, coming to a stop in front of the television and holding her feather duster in front of her as if it were a bunch of flowers. 'All the years I've been coming here, I'd never have put you down as being interested in horse racing.'

'It's just something to watch while I'm waiting, Evie,' Alice replied, taking another look at her watch. 'I know nothing about racing. I've never even been to a race meeting.'

'My Den's never off the track, if you ask me,' Evie continued, her eyes fixed on the screen, sitting herself down in the chair next to Alice. 'And if I was having a bet, he's the one.' She leaned forward to poke the screen with the end of her duster. 'W. Swinburn. My Den says he don't know how to lose.'

The telephone rang, giving Alice an excuse to break up what was obviously going to turn into what Evie liked to think of as one of their nice cosy moments. 'Excuse me, Evie. That might be Christian. To say why he's late.'

As it happened it wasn't her son. It was her solicitor, ringing to remind her that she really needed to return the documents she had been sent, so they could settle her late husband's estate.

'I promise I'll do them and return them straight away, Mr Pimlott,' Alice told him. 'It's just that I have to go to the country today, but I'll take them with me and drop them in at the post office.'

'While I have you on the telephone, Mrs Dixon . . .' The lawyer cleared his throat. 'If I could just run another couple of things past you? It won't take a minute.'

Alice did her best to concentrate on what she was being told but as always legalese bored and baffled her. Everyone knew that the way the law was written was purposely to cheat people of any understanding of what was being done to them. And as her solicitor rambled on Alice stared at the street scene outside, thinking of anything except what he was saying to her, her mind going blank as usual. She watched an overdressed woman walking past the old bookshop opposite with a poodle on a lead and thought that nowadays poodles seemed to have gone out of fashion, remembering the time when a smart woman was rarely seen without a poodle on a lead.

When she and Alexander had first moved into what was then only a two-bedroomed house,

Kensington still had the feel of a village. Walking through Holland Street and the other back streets, they could have been in the country. In those days, friends who lived in Mayfair used to refer to *travelling out* to see them, very much in the way that Alice now thought of going to see her daughter and son-in-law in Richmond. Yet now Kensington had changed so much that even Evie was always giving it as her opinion that you couldn't tell the High Street from Oxford Street. This statement was usually followed by an *if-I-was-you* lecture about Alice's being better off moving out to a leafy suburb where she would be safer and healthier.

Of course Alice knew that Evie was right, that not only Kensington but the whole of London had changed, and of course it would be more sensible to move out, the most sensible move of all being to Richmond, so she could be near Georgina and the grandchildren. But try as she did to interest herself in this most sensible of ideas, Alice finally found against it. It was just too . . . well, *sensible*.

'Told you he'd win, Mrs D.,' Evie announced when Alice had put down the telephone. 'That W. Swinburn. Won by a street. Like I said, never rides a bad race.'

Alice inwardly sighed with relief that the race was now over and Evie could resume her household chores.

'You thought any more about moving, Mrs D.?' Evie enquired, flicking her duster along the line of Alice's favourite set of eighteenth-century prints, as always, and with unerring accuracy, managing to knock each one slightly crooked. 'You was saying about moving out near your son-in-law and daughter, which as you know I think would be no bad thing. It would be no skin off of my nose – I could still do the journey just as easily from Battersea to help you, and it would be so nice for you and Georgina. And those lovely grandchildren of yours.'

'Yes, I do see it would be nice for Georgina, Evie.' Alice looked out of the window again, but this time to see if there was any sign of her son. 'I'd obviously be much handier for babysitting and so on. I do see that. Limitless unpaid babysitting and school runs would be attractive, I can see.'

'Now then, Mrs D.,' Evie chided her. 'That doesn't sound at all like you.'

'That's probably because I'm not quite sure what me sounds like any more.'

'Come again?'

'It doesn't matter, Evie, really.'

Alice turned away. There were times when she thought, *There's lots of life in me still. I'm not going to just give in and become some sort of housekeeper and nanny* – but there were just as many times when she missed her husband Alexander so much, she no longer saw the point in anything. 'I'm just going to make sure I've left everything as I should,' she continued, heading out of the sitting room. 'It's something Mr Dixon always did whenever we went away, and I still can't get into the habit.'

Sammy, her devoted West Highland terrier, who had been sitting perched on the arm of her chair, jumped down and followed his mistress into the kitchen.

'Leftover life to kill,' Alice said to herself. 'Whatever that means, Sammy. But that's not what we want to do, is it? Spend the rest of our life killing time.'

In the weeks following Alexander's sudden death she had nearly been rushed into agreeing to go and live in the basement of Georgina and Joe's house in Richmond. Still stunned by her loss, she had thought it seemed only sensible to be near a married daughter, until her best friend Millie stepped in.

'Too soon to make up your mind about anything, duck, much too soon,' her oldest friend kept insisting.

Alice had to listen to Millie, if only because when Millie had lost her husband many years before, instead of wasting time on self-pity, she had ignored her family's protests and sold the rambling family home, moving to a cottage with a few acres where by sheer hard work, endeavour and determination she had made really quite a considerable success out of producing the kinds of jams and chutneys in which small local country delicatessens revelled – with the result that she was now not just self-supporting, but vaguely prosperous.

'Best of all, Allie, I don't have to rely on someone else. Number one rule of widowhood: whatever you do, don't get in tow with some man, just because you're feeling lonely. You should see the way some of the widows behave. Talk about ravers. I mean, you should see.'

Now, as Alice waited for Christian to give her a lift down to Millie's cottage where she had been invited to stay, she put her thoughts on hold. She would only think about the fun they were going to have.

The telephone rang again.

'I'll bet that's Georgina, Sammy,' she said to the little dog. 'I don't know what it is, but there's something about the way it rings when it's Georgina. It just sounds different.'

'Mum? Hi.'

'I thought it would be you, Georgie. How are you? How's tricks?'

'Why did you think it would be me? I didn't say I'd ring.'

'Sorry. What I meant was I thought it *might* be you.'

'Aren't *you* meant to be in the country?'

'If you thought I was in the country—'

'I just wanted to ask Chris something.' Georgina sighed. 'If he's arrived yet.'

'Do you know something I don't know?'

'How? I just thought I'd ring on the off chance.'

'Meaning you thought I'd still be here.'

'I wouldn't be ringing otherwise, would I?'

'Let's start again, shall we?' Alice said, bending down to stroke Sammy. 'How's tricks?'

'I do wish you wouldn't always say that, Mum. I mean, what does it mean?'

'It's old-fashioned for how's everything, really. How are Will and Finty?'

'Same as they were last night when you saw them. So Chris hasn't arrived yet, surprise surprise?'

'Punctuality is not your brother's strongest suit.'

'He *is* taking you all the way to the country, Mum. That is *seriously* good of him, you know.'

'I know, Georgie,' Alice replied, still stroking Sammy, if anything a little faster. 'And it's very kind of him.'

'I think you should give him something for the petrol. Seriously.'

'I have every intention of so doing, Georgina. I wouldn't dream of not—'

'There's no need to get in a fluff.'

'I am not in a fluff.'

'You called me *Georgina*. You *seriously* only ever call me *Georgina* when you're annoyed. I only rang to speak to Chris, you know.'

'I'll tell him to call you, shall I, when he gets here? Except hang on . . .' Alice said, listening. 'That might be him now.'

After she had let her son in, she left him talking to his sister on the telephone while she ran a last check on the flat and her luggage, telling Evie that she too had best be on her way since she had to put on the alarm.

Finally she found herself standing around

43

waiting for Christian to finish his conversation with Georgina – which seemed to be a very earnest one, judging from all the *seriouslys* being bandied about – before they were able to make a move.

'Georgie wants a quick word before we go, Mum.' Christian waggled the telephone at his mother and handed over the receiver.

'Mum. Look. Can you babysit next Friday? Be good if you could.'

'No, I shall be away. I told you – I'm going away for the week.'

'Couldn't you come back a bit early, though? Like Friday? You know what the traffic's like at the weekend.'

'I'm going away until Wednesday week, actually.'

'O-*kay*,' Georgina continued slowly, obviously determined not to let this one go. 'You could come back up by train. Joe could meet you.'

'Georgina,' Alice said slowly. 'What's happened to your regular babysitters?'

'One of them's got a filthy cold and Joe's seriously off Tina. He thinks she nicks things, mostly his Scotch. Seriously – you could zap back up by train on Friday, no sweat. We've got tickets for this gig then there's a do afterwards—'

'Darling, I really can't,' Alice interrupted. 'I really can't trek all the way up from Dorset just to babysit.'

'Oh, thanks, Mum.'

'I just couldn't.'

'Thanks a bunch. It's not just pleasure, you know. It's business. Joe has to be there.'

'I'm sure you'll find *someone*, darling.'

'And *darling*'s as telling as *Georgina*, Mum. At least it is the way you say it.'

'I'll ring you from Millie's,' Alice finally said after a short pause, feeling herself weakening.

'Don't bother. I'm sure we'll manage. 'Bye!'

Georgina hung up, leaving Alice to stare blankly at the humming receiver.

'What did she want?'

'Wanted me to come back up to babysit on Friday.'

'Man – Georgie really is something else.'

Alice clipped Sammy's lead on his collar. 'Anyway. Sorry to keep you, Christian. We can go now.'

'Mum?' Chris said as he took the bags he had let his mother carry and put them in the back of his Golf GTI. 'I wonder. Can you bung me a ton? Just for my hols? I'll pay you back end of the month.'

'I lent you a hundred and fifty only last month, darling.'

'Yeah . . .' Chris said, getting in the car at the same time as his mother. 'But that was for the rent – I don't have any spending money. And I'm going to look a right dweeb with Dan and Matt if I can't ante up.'

'I don't know what you're all talking about half the time,' Alice grumbled, opening her handbag and sorting through the myriad contents up to and including two Bonios for Sammy. 'Most I can do is fifty – and I want it back at the end of the month.'

'Good as done, Ma.' Chris grinned, pocketing the loot. 'You are such a star.'

Jamming the car into first gear and keeping the brake on, Chris spun the wheels of the GTI then fast-started it into the outward-bound traffic, throwing Alice backwards in her seat before she even had time to do up her seat belt.

'Great wheels, eh?' He laughed. 'Blow your rocks off.'

Clutching the grab handle above her head and Sammy on her knee, Alice found herself wishing that she'd hired a car to take her to Dorset. Not only would it have been safer, but it would have been a lot cheaper.

Christian put a tape in the cassette player.

'Are we going to have this all the way to Dorset?' she wondered as they sat in a traffic jam at the top of the Earl's Court Road.

'Sorr-*ee*!' Christian stared out of the window as a pretty girl in a fashionable bright blue silk dress sashayed by on the opposite side of the road. 'Don't you like The Clash?'

'It is a little . . . how can I say . . . loud.'

'OK. Bit of the old Radio Middle-of-the-road? Yes?' Christian asked, switching to the radio.

'Anything would be better than the whoever they were.'

'The Clash, Mother,' Christian said in his talking-to-old-people voice. 'Just the best punk band of all time, that's all.'

'Oh, we're going to have to go back to the house,' Alice said suddenly. 'I left the television plugged in.'

'You what?' Her son stared at her incredulously.

'I know, I know,' Alice sighed. 'But your father always said you have to pull the plug out of the wall.'

'No way, Mother. Seriously.'

'I shan't enjoy a minute of my holiday otherwise.'

'Ma . . . ?'

'Please?'

With a histrionic groan, Christian turned off at the traffic lights on the Cromwell Road and drove his mother back to her house, where he ran in to pull the plug out for her.

'Oh God, Mother.' Returning, he peered through the passenger window and chucked the keys into her lap. 'It was *off*.' He climbed back into the car. 'For that, I choose where we have lunch.'

'The least I can do,' Alice muttered, doing up her safety belt. 'Sorry.'

'OK.' Christian nodded. 'Music of my choice as well. OK?'

'Whatever you say.'

An hour and a half later, as they were speeding their way west down the hill that leads back up to pass Stonehenge, they both saw that the traffic ahead was coming to a standstill fast.

'Now what?' Christian said, lowering his window to try to get a better view of what was causing the jam. 'There's some idiot jumping up and down in the middle of the road.'

'I do hope there hasn't been an accident,' Alice said, quickly taking the chance to turn the music down.

'I hardly think they've stopped to have a picnic, Ma,' Christian replied. 'This isn't going anywhere. I'm going to take a look-see.'

He hopped out of the car and disappeared, running along the verge. He was back a couple of minutes later, looking grim.

'Just don't look when we get to go past. Some idiot's run over a horse.'

Sitting and sketching no more than a quarter of a mile away on a hillock to the north of the prehistoric stones Rory had no idea of the cause of the accident. It was true that at one point he had noticed a traffic jam forming, but since that stretch of the A303 was a notorious bottleneck for westbound traffic he had thought nothing of it. A little later he had become aware that there might have been an accident of sorts as he spotted the arrival of a police car, but again, given that it was a long straight road, he simply put it down to yet another lethally impatient driver. Soon it started to rain again, so he threw in the creative towel and went home.

He had hardly had time to park his old Land Rover and walk into the stable yard before he knew something was up, and not just from the look on the lads' faces. Normally the yard at

Fulford Farm was a cheery place, underwriting the amiable nature of Rory's father, Anthony, who had been training racehorses in a charming and deceptively laid back way ever since he had left the army. The yard might not be smart – in fact first-time visitors were generally dismayed by the really rather down-at-heel appearance of an establishment where none of the stable doors matched or fitted, tiles were falling off roofs, and every drainpipe seemed to run at a different angle – but a closer inspection would reveal that the horses' beds were clean and deep and the jumbled boxes surprisingly draught-free and spacious, and the tack was spotless. There were no fashionable matching anoraks for the staff at Fulford, where the horses pulled out to work every morning this side of late, attired in a variety of rugs and sheets that looked as if they might just have been snatched from one of the dog beds lined up against the walls of the Guv's far from spotless office, but, more important than anything else, the horses were healthy, and well cared for. Not that this made much difference to the luck of the establishment, which could be described, at best, as being sporadic.

Anthony Rawlins had had his share of national hunt winners, or rather more correctly had once had his share of winners, but in the past half a dozen years his tally had fallen, and the yard still existed thanks mainly to the goodwill and affection of a small but loyal band of owners who would rather enjoy their racing than be part of one of the increasingly impersonal large training yards. Fun had always been Anthony Rawlins's target. He couldn't abide trainers who referred to racing as an *industry* and thought of their owners as *mushrooms* – fed on rubbish and kept in the dark.

The last season had been the worst ever at Fulford Farm, a horrendous six months during which he had lost three horses, one in a schooling accident and two of his most promising young chasers on the racecourse. It had taken more out of him than even he had realised, a fact which had never hit him harder than at this moment.

'It seems the saddle slipped,' Anthony told Rory when his son found him in his office. 'Something must have spooked the mare, because it was very out of character. She might even have been stung, who knows? Anyway, she dumped Teddy, jumped the wire and disappeared into the heart of the plains.'

'It wouldn't have helped if the saddle was still on her.'

'Wasn't on when the lorry hit her,' Anthony replied, lighting another cigarette from the end of his last one. 'Anything might have happened. But God knows how she got where she did. Someone said they saw a horse charging east along the road from the roundabout just past Stonehenge, but if she'd come down the road from Larkhill . . .'

'If she was on that road,' Rory agreed, as his father petered out, 'yes, why hadn't she headed for home? First thing the older horses do – bolt for home. I remember when I came off Ozzy at Larkhill, he headed straight back here.'

'We'll never know. That's horses. They have their ways.'

Moss Daisy, the mare who had just been killed on the road, happened to be the yard's favourite, not only because she had won two particularly competitive handicaps at their local racecourse, but also because of her character. With a saddle on her she had been a street fighter, but in her box and in the paddocks she had been a lop-eared dozy old softie, with an addiction to Extra Strong Mints. Everyone loved her, and now she was gone and her lad was bereft.

'I've told Teddy it wasn't his fault,' Anthony said. 'These things happen. That's racing, as if he didn't know.'

'Did he check his girths before they galloped? I know it sounds like an obvious thing to ask, Dad—'

'He said he did and if he said he did, he probably did. But it happens. It happened to me once in a Members' Race up at Larkhill, just as I was coming to win it.'

'Sure, Dad. During a race it's understandable, but before a gallop?'

'It was an accident, Rory,' Anthony said, cutting his son short. 'And even if it wasn't, it's not going to bring the mare back.'

Of course his father was right. Even if the lad had been to blame, the how and why of the accident was only academic. They both knew there was a possibility that Teddy had failed to check the girths prior to doing some fast work, but then they both also knew that, if that were the case, the lad's guilt would be punishment enough.

'You're looking a bit tired, Dad,' Rory murmured over dinner that evening.

'Hardly surprising, old lad,' Anthony said, pouring the wine. 'All things considered.'

'You haven't had a break in ages.'

'That's because I don't like *breaks*, as you call them, chum. It was different when your mother was alive, but now, what's the point?'

'It would get you away from here, that's the point. You really should get away, just for a few days – fishing or something. You've got a good staff here. And I can keep an eye on things.'

His father regarded him over his wine glass, but said nothing, turning his attention to his food.

'Tell you what,' he admitted finally. 'I was actually thinking of going to Ireland.'

'Horses?'

'That time of year. If I do go, I don't suppose you'd feel like coming? We could put in a few days' fishing first, then amble along and look at some *harses*. Could be fun.'

'Yes, OK. I must admit I've always wanted to go.'

'And you've always refused.'

'Because there were always reasons.'

'One particularly good reason.'

'Don't go there.'

52

'Wasn't going to, old boy. Where angels fear to tread department. So you'll come, then?'

'Of course.'

'It'll be fun. We'll have some fun.'

Anthony went to bed that night feeling a little more cheerful than he had expected, the loss of Moss Daisy being slightly mitigated by the knowledge that he had persuaded his son to come with him to Ireland. Not that he was feeling particularly fatalistic; it was simply something he had been wanting them both to do – before it was too late.

'No need for all that kind of thinking. Mustn't look back,' he scolded himself as he sat on the edge of his half-made bed smoking the last cigarette of the day. 'It's just losing the mare, it's getting to you, making you soggy round the edges. Can't have that.'

It would do them both good, going away. They'd get in some fishing, on the Lee maybe, then take their time driving through Cork where he'd look up old horse friends and introduce them to his son and heir. If anyone needed a break it was surely Rory, after all he'd been through at the hands of his long-time girlfriend, the minx who'd spun him at the eleventh hour, just when they were all set and under orders to go up the aisle.

Anthony had liked Penny well enough, but he'd never trusted her, not for a moment. She was pretty and amusing and had *seemed* devoted to Rory, at least whenever the three of them were together, but there was something about her face in repose that struck a warning note.

'What do you really want out of life, old boy?' Anthony found himself asking Rory, out of the blue, as they were driving to the airport a few days later. 'I know we've talked about it before, but what do you *really* want?'

'You know what I really want, Dad.' Rory tried not to sound embarrassed, and failed.

'I don't have to leave the place to you, you know. I can just as easily sell up, let you have your bundle and go and live in a warm air bungalow somewhere. There's no obligation to you as far as Fulford Farm goes.'

'What else would I do? It's something you've brought me up to do, you and Ma, to take over.'

'Mmm. But. What about your painting? Your drawing?'

'There are an awful lot of people who are a great deal more talented than me.'

'There are even more people who can train better than me, but that didn't stop me.'

'We don't have to talk about this now, you know. It's time to have fun.'

'You bet,' Anthony agreed, as Rory headed the car on to the airport approach road. 'Let the *craic* commence.'

They stayed for five days in an old inn at Glenbeigh in County Kerry where they fished the local river by day and by night. Anthony caught over a dozen good trout and Rory caught his first salmon, a decent six-and-a-half-pound fish which tasted as well as it had fought.

The September weather was soft and full of sunlight, so golden in fact that the two men were loath to leave their small hotel with its semi-tropical garden and wonderful views over the sea and Rossbeigh Strand, and to compensate made a booking for a ten-day fishing holiday the following year. Then they packed their stuff into their hire car and set off for Cork. As they left the weather broke and the first rains of autumn blew in off the Atlantic.

The following morning they found themselves standing for what seemed like an eternity on the edge of an unkempt and rainswept field just out-side the undistinguished town of Cronagh, some thirty miles on from Cork city.

'I'm just glad we had the *craic* up there in Kerry, Dad,' Rory said, zipping his old Barbour jacket up to his chin. 'This is not a place to spend quality time.'

'You'd be surprised, old chap,' Anthony returned cheerfully. 'It breaks out in the most surprising places over here.'

'What does exactly?'

'Life. Life Irish style.'

'Not here, surely? This isn't just a place that time forgot. This is a place it never visited. That town. How about that for dismal? It's got more bars than houses.'

'Wisht, as they say,' his father replied. 'Hold

your hour. You haven't seen anything yet.'

At this point the long-awaited, bedraggled figure of Sean Phelan appeared out of the mists and rain, leading a miserable mud-covered horse for inspection.

'I think you showed me this poor chap last year, Sean,' Anthony told the dealer after a cursory inspection. 'Probably the year before as well.'

'I did not so!' Phelan protested as he tried to pull the recalcitrant horse out of the mud and up on to the patch of weed-covered concrete by the gate. 'Sure I never had this fellow last year, so I did not! If I'd had him I'd have sold him be now. You just take one look at him yourself and see the quality.'

'All I can see is skin and bone, Sean,' Anthony insisted. 'And the same two scars on its knees as it had last year.'

'Scars?' Sean yelped. 'What are you talking about, Mr Rawlins, sir, forgiving your presence? This horse is entirely unblemished!'

'I remember these scars, Sean. Two of them across both of his knees – where last year you yourself said he'd grazed himself getting out of the horsebox.'

'Where?' Phelan began another of his elaborate pantomimes, pushing his rain-drenched hat to the back of his head as he bent down to stare at the unfortunate animal's fore legs. 'Jeeze, would you look at that now – however did he come by those things? Sure he hadn't a mark on him this morning.'

'Is that so?' Anthony wondered mock-seriously. 'So how come I can see old stitch marks?'

'Stitch marks?' Phelan said. 'This is getting worse be the minute. Someone's been at him, that's what they've been, at him, they have.'

The dealer made a mighty show of clucking his tongue and shaking his head in mock shock and dismay at the discovery of wounds inflicted on the miserable horse well over twelve months ago.

'If you've nothing else to show me, Sean . . .' Anthony said with a private wink to Rory, sinking his freezing hands into the deep pockets of his old raincoat.

'This is a grand animal, Mr Rawlins – you'd have to be as mad as a hawk to spin him, the way you are intent.'

'That is a poor old creature, Sean, fit only for one thing. And you're as big a rogue as ever you were.'

'I am not so!' Phelan protested, dropping the horse's leg, which he had been tenderly nursing, and slapping away the half-starved animal on its rump with his hat. 'The thing is you've not got the eye for him. Not for a good 'un, you just haven't the eye, Mr Rawlins, sir, saving your presence.'

'Ah well, Sean.' Anthony paused and mock-sighed. 'Let's just hope my misfortune is someone else's great luck.'

'Ach,' Sean growled. 'Away with ye! You'd have spun Arkle, so ye would!'

'OK, Dad,' Rory said once they were in the car

and out of the dealer's earshot. 'What in God's name brings you to this godforsaken place anyway?'

'Believe it or not, my son,' his father replied, 'I got the Mighty Midge from old Sean Phelan.'

'You're putting me on!' Rory stared at his father in amazement. 'The Mighty Midge? Who won the Cathcart?'

'My one and only Cheltenham winner. He came out of the very same field as that poor old wreck. I always come back here, just in case, in spite of what they say, lightning does strike twice.'

'But it never has.'

'You know as well as I do, old boy. God knows how he bred it, and you know what sort of horse that was.'

'If only he hadn't broken down . . .'

'*If onlys* keep us all in the game. Racing's full of *if onlys*.'

'You said yourself he'd have been a Gold Cup horse.'

'Racing's also full of *might have beens*. Time for a jar,' Anthony decided. 'Don't know about you, but I am *cold*.'

Rory glanced at his father. It was unlike him to complain, and while it had certainly been wet it really wasn't cold.

'You OK, Pop?'

'I'm fine, old chap. Just wet through. It's all right for you young ones, you don't feel it like us old warriors. Now get us to a bar double quick.'

Rory drove them back into Cronagh, pulling

up finally outside a bar grandiosely entitled in red and white neon *Finnegan's Exclusive American Cocktail Lounge*. Inside it was definitely not as advertised, being dimly lit, poorly furnished and fogged with a thick pall of cigarette and pipe smoke. It wasn't particularly busy, although, as Anthony said to his son while they waited to get served, given the number of bars in such a sparsely populated town it was a testimony to the natives' drinking abilities that so many pubs were able to trade at all.

'Soft auld day,' the man next to them at the bar said, with a sideways nod of his head.

'Dirty old day,' Anthony replied, knowing the score.

'Ah well,' his neighbour sighed, sucking at his pipe. 'There's a lot worse to come. How was your pal Sean?'

'Big a rogue as ever,' Anthony said, as if the man's question had been anticipated.

'Trying to sell you that dammety auld gelding again. As if you hadn't seen enough of it.'

Anthony smiled and took a sip of his Paddy Powers. 'Will you join us?' he asked.

'I'll have a John Jameson,' his neighbour said.

'A John Jameson for my friend here,' Anthony directed the tall poker-faced barman.

'Large, Donal,' his neighbour added.

'As if I would not,' the barman intoned, as if saying Mass.

'And from a fresh bottle, too.'

'I have no fresh bottles, Michael.'

'You have so. Under here.' Michael tapped the bar then nodded his head once to underline his point. 'I like my whisky without the water, Donal.'

'And don't I know?'

'So let's have it out of a fresh bottle then.'

'There are plenty of other bars, Michael Doherty.'

'And aren't they all run by your relatives? Now do the decent thing, Donal, and show our guest here your good manners.'

The squabble finally over, the four of them drank, the landlord pouring himself a generous ball of malt from the freshly opened bottle. He charged Anthony for it, but Anthony knew better than to protest, since he knew from experience that there were plenty of free ones in the offing now a new bottle had been broached.

Some time later he found himself being advised by Michael to go to see a very particular horse. Michael had laid his head on the bar with his face turned towards Anthony, and was doing his best to focus on his drinking partner.

'Padraig Flanagan has him,' he said in a stage whisper. 'But shh! No one's to know I'm telling you that.'

''Tis a fine horse Padraig has so!' a voice from somewhere down the bar assured Anthony. 'A man'd have no one at home not to go and see it now.'

'Don't you go sayin' I'm sending you,' Michael said from his semi-recumbent position. 'He'll be thinkin' I'm after the finders.'

'That's finders as in keepers, right?' Anthony wondered with a frown, trying desperately not to let go.

'Finders as in fee, friend,' Michael replied, before rolling off his seat and sinking slowly to the floor.

By now Rory had the flavour too, and was sitting happily smiling at his reflection in the far from clean mirror over the bar. Anthony took him by the shoulder, but it seemed Rory wasn't that keen to move, turning round to his father and putting a finger to an area near his lips.

'Shh!' he advised. 'There are people sleeping here.'

'Come on, chum,' Anthony said, keeping hold of him with one hand and searching for his car keys in his pocket with the other. 'We're off to see a horse.'

'Ye'll not be driving yerselves, so you won't,' an enormous man in a large brown overcoat warned him, taking the keys from his hand. 'Ye're in no fit state to take ahold the wheel. I shall drive to Padraig's.'

'And you reckon you are?' Anthony asked him, trying to draw himself up to his full height but still finding himself a good foot shorter than the giant swaying over him. 'In a fit state to drive, that is?'

'I am not, for I have drink taken,' the giant replied. 'But there's no need for concern on my behalf, man. There'll be no problem if the Garda stop me.'

'I see,' Anthony said, scratching his head. 'And I wonder why would that be, chummy?'

'Because I have no driving licence,' the giant said. 'Now come along, man, and show me to your vehicular.'

Realising he himself was far too drunk to drive, let alone make any sense, Anthony followed the large man out of the bar, dragging Rory with him, and pointed out the red hire car parked immediately outside. His chauffeur nodded and got in the back seat.

'I thought you were going to drive.'

'I am so,' the man replied. 'Where's your problem?'

'I've always found it easier to do that from the front seat.' Anthony opened the driver's door with an exaggerated bow.

'I have not me spectacles, man. I have them lost,' the giant told him, shoehorning himself into the driver's seat with some difficulty, being far too tall for the economy-size vehicle, and trying without much success to get the key in the ignition. Anthony took the ring from him and, after encountering a similar problem, realised they were his house keys rather than the car keys. Finding the right ones in Rory's pocket, he managed to get the engine started, pushed his swaying son into the back, went round to the front passenger seat, slammed the door shut on his coat and nodded to the man hunched over the wheel.

'Full steam ahead, captain,' he said. 'Full steam ahead.'

'You shall have to direct me, man,' the giant said, unable to lift his head properly. 'You'll have to indicate the route for I find it hard to see the road in front.'

'You can actually drive, old man?'

'Indeed I can. I have been drivin' vehiculars since I was a gossoon.'

'Motor vehiculars?'

'All manner of vehiculars. Now then – how are we doing?'

'We are doing fine,' Anthony replied. 'Just fine. But that's probably because we're still stationary.'

The giant crashed the stick into third gear and the car lurched off very slowly.

'You're on the pavement, old chap,' Anthony said, having cleared a patch of condensation off his window. 'Apparently headed for a chemist's.'

He leaned over and corrected the steering in time to return the car to the mercifully empty road.

'That is a sensible thing you are doing here, man,' his driver told him. 'You make sure to do that now if I go a little off beam.'

'Perhaps it'd be better if I did the driving entirely,' Anthony suggested.

'You should have thought of that before you started the drinking,' the giant replied. 'But then you still may, of course, provided you are content to spend the rest of your day in gaol.'

'The rest of my *day*? For being drunk at the wheel?'

'The Garda Milligan has a scorched earth policy

here, man. He comes down like a mallet on drink drivers.'

And so on they lurched in third gear at all of five miles an hour, with Anthony calling the directions from the passenger seat. By a small miracle and some fifty hair-raising minutes later, they arrived unscathed at a smallholding halfway up a hill, most of which was totally wreathed in mist and rain.

'Padraig Flanagan's as ever was,' the giant deduced once he had levered himself out of the car. 'Pray to God he is still alive.'

'Why? Is there a chance he might not be?' Anthony enquired.

'We none of us know when we may be called, do we? Or when we may be spared. Padraig!'

Reeling from the man's enormous bellow, Anthony shook his head and tried to get his bearings, then went round the back of the car to wake his son.

'Padraig! Padraig, 'tis I, Yamon! 'Tis I Yamon and a stranger come here to see The Horse!'

'How tall are you?' Anthony said, gazing at the figure before him. 'Just exactly how tall *are* you?'

'Shorter than the mother, but not the father. The mother is still our tallest.'

'That doesn't precisely answer my question. You must be over seven feet.'

'The mother can open an upstairs window with no use of a ladder. Padraig!'

The summons echoed round the misted landscape like a fairytale ogre's roar. Back the name came at Anthony – *Padraig! Padraig!* – whereupon at about the fourth or fifth echo the small round figure of Padraig appeared, limping his way across the yard and pulling his old battered hat down over his eyes against the rain, then turning his pipe upside down as an added safeguard.

'What is it possessin' you, Yamon? Ye'll wake the whole county!'

'I have a stranger here, Padraig! Come to see The Horse.'

'I'm standing right beside you, Yamon,' Padraig chided him. 'There's no more need to bellow. And how would he know about The Horse?'

'He had heard tell.'

'And I wonder what has he heard tell, Yamon?'

'That you have this horse, so you have. And that he's something special.'

'Which horse in this country isn't?' Anthony asked, with half an eye on Rory who was slowly pulling himself out of the car. 'Every horse I'm shown is something special.'

'It'll be no skin off my nose if you don't want him, sir,' Padraig said, eyeing him up from under his rain-sodden hat. 'I have several interested parties and the horse isn't even advertised.'

'Did you breed him yourself, Mr Flanagan?' Anthony enquired, looking round at the ramshackle yard.

'I did not, sir,' Padraig answered with perfect truth. 'Though indeed he was born here. The mare came to us in foal.'

'Ye'll not be wasting your time, friend,' Eammon,

pronounced Yamon, loudly assured him. 'Padraig here always has fine stock.'

'I certainly don't mind looking, Mr Flanagan,' Anthony said, even though he was more than half convinced he was wasting his time. 'If you want to show him to me, no harm in looking.'

'We'll see,' Padraig grunted, now eyeing both Rory and Anthony. 'First I'd say you're both in need of a cup of tea.'

Nodding sideways towards a small cottage at the top of the yard, Padraig limped off, expecting them to follow, which they duly did, Yamon included. Padraig went straight to the kitchen at the back, calling ahead in Gaelic as he went. Anthony entered the room well ahead of Rory, who was still outside, taking a lot of deep breaths in an effort to clear his head. A girl with her back to Anthony, dressed in a heavy black Aran sweater and a dark green skirt under a white apron, was busy washing dishes in a bowl at the sink. Padraig said something to her in Gaelic that caused her to turn and stare at Anthony in silence. Then, wiping her hands on her apron, she took the garment off, threw it on the draining board, nodded to Anthony and ran out of the kitchen.

'Something I said?' Anthony enquired lightly, struck by the extraordinary beauty of the young woman.

'Don't mind her now,' Padraig said, taking his hat off and slapping it against his leg. 'My daughter Kathleen. She has her days. Don't mind her at all.'

When Rory appeared at the doorway, Padraig invited his guests to sit at the table and moments later had poured them cups of the strongest tea from a pot that was already standing hot on the hob. A tall gangly young man was the next to show, coming in from outside dressed in a short black oilskin and agricultural gumboots. Padraig addressed him also in Gaelic, whereupon the lad nodded and ambled back out into the rain, taking with him a bridle that was hanging on the back of the door.

'Mr Flanagan has a horse he thinks he might show us, Rory,' Anthony said.

'I keep feeling I'm dreaming,' Rory said slowly, blinking his eyes as if to try to focus on the proceedings. 'Am I?'

'Has the horse done anything, Mr Flanagan?' Anthony asked, guiding his son to a chair by the table. 'Has he raced at all?'

'Has he raced at all.' Yamon sighed, then repeated himself loudly. 'Has he raced at all indeed!'

Padraig eyed the big man and poured himself a cup of tea, stirring the sugar in with the stub of his pipe. 'He has so, sir,' he said to Anthony. 'We gave him a couple of runs tail end of the last season. He ran in a point, then in a hunters. At Tramore.'

'And?'

'I was happy enough,' Padraig said with a nod, returning to his tea.

'That doesn't tell me much, Mr Flanagan. How happy?'

'He'd have won his point be a mile,' Yamon said from where he was standing by the door as if keeping guard, his head bowed under the low ceiling, arms folded across his chest. 'He'd have won it be a mile if he hadn't been run out of it.'

'A touch of the might have beens?' Rory wondered, glancing at his father.

'The boys had a hot horse running,' Padraig said, now sucking at his pipe. 'So they ran our fella out at the last with their other runner.'

'Knocked him halfways to Skibbereen,' Yamon added. 'He'd have won be a mile.'

Anthony nodded, pushing his empty teacup away from him and lighting a cigarette. 'And the hunter chase?'

'Sure the lad fell off of him!' Yamon suddenly bellowed, as if still infuriated. 'The lad only went and fell off of him!'

'And I suppose he'd have won that too by a mile?'

'At the very least, man!' Yamon bellowed. 'At the very least!'

'He was twelve lengths clear at the last, sir,' Padraig said. 'And well on the bridle.'

'And?'

'The boy looked round to see where the others might be, the horse jinked, and the boy fell off.'

'Why run him in a hunter chase?' Rory asked, beginning to come to. 'If he hadn't yet won his point? Or even his points, as in more than one.'

'I was persuaded,' Padraig replied. 'That's for why.'

'Who persuaded you?' Anthony enquired.

'I did, sir,' Padraig said. 'He's an exceptional horse, d'you see, and there's a bit of money to a hunter chase while there's next to none for a point.'

'But if he had won, old chap,' Anthony continued, 'he'd have been out of novice class and straight into handicaps.'

'This horse is no novice, man!' Yamon thundered. 'This horse has been here before! This horse has nothing to learn, man!'

'Your man here means the horse would have had then to run straight in handicaps, Yamon,' Padraig said.

'This horse could run straight in a cup race, Padraig!' Yamon insisted. 'Ye could send this horse straight to Cheltenham and live in clover the rest of your days!'

'If we're going to have a look . . .' Anthony said, consulting his watch, mindful that he and Rory had a plane to catch later – a later which was fast becoming sooner.

'Sure you can have a look now all right,' Padraig agreed, opening the back door. 'The boy should have him fixed.'

They all went out into the yard, Anthony lending half an ear to Padraig's imaginative account of the horse's bloodline. It was still pouring with rain, but Liam had set up a course of makeshift jumps fashioned from barrels, boxes, planks and even broomsticks, and was leading a horse already saddled up from a stable.

'In the name of God,' Anthony said in some dismay. 'You're not going to put the horse over these?'

'Of course not,' Padraig replied. 'Sure we'll warm him up first, Liam?'

Liam took his instructions, nodding as he fastened on a riding helmet that was at least one size too small for his head. Then with a leg up from his father he began to trot the horse round the enclosure.

'There isn't a lot of him, is there?' Anthony observed when Padraig had come back to stand beside Rory.

'He only appears that way with the boy being tall,' Padraig returned.

'OK,' Anthony said. 'But you're not exactly tall and I was judging the animal more by you.'

'He must be under sixteen hands,' Rory added, peering through the rain.

'He just walks small,' Padraig assured them. 'He's a different size altogether when he's jumping.'

As Liam began to trot the horse, Kathleen emerged from the stables, a small oilskin-clad figure with her face half obscured by a large man's cap, and leaned with her back against the wall, watching the proceedings. She saw her brother was having trouble getting the horse to trot sweetly for him, but she ignored his call to her. She had little time for those who came to buy their horses, particularly the smart, moneyed ones from across the water.

'He's quite green, isn't he, old man?' Anthony said to Padraig. 'Doesn't seem to know how to use himself.'

'Use himself?' Yamon roared. 'Use himself indeed! Use himself?'

Padraig took his hat off and threw it to the ground, shouting something in Gaelic to his son, who shouted back to him in the same language.

'Subtitles?' Rory looked at his father.

'All I know is *caed mille failte,*' Anthony replied with an apologetic smile.

The more Padraig and his son shouted at each other, the more the horse began to misbehave. It was as if he deliberately wanted to put on a bad display.

'Put him over the jumps now, boy!' Padraig called. 'You have us all bored. Go on now! Have him jump something! Watch now,' Padraig advised his English visitors. 'Now you'll see some form.'

Liam got the horse half straight but it was immediately obvious that the animal was far from settled since he began to prance on the spot and buck when he saw the jumps in front of him.

'Go on, Liam boy!' Padraig shouted. 'Go on! Go on now!'

Liam tried to do as he was told, shortening the reins and kicking the horse on, but as soon as he did so the horse's head came up and he put in a monumental buck that all but had Liam on the ground.

'Really, old chap,' Anthony said politely. 'Thank you, but I think we've seen all we need to see.'

'You have not,' Padraig insisted. 'You'll not go till you've seen him jump!'

Grabbing a Long Tom that was propped up against the shed, Padraig hurried over and cracked the whip sharply behind the horse to try to encourage him to get himself straight and go forward, but its only effect was to make the animal shoot ahead as fast as he could, the suddenness of his bolt causing the ill-prepared Liam to fall off sideways. He managed to keep hold of the reins, but far from stopping the horse he simply got dragged behind it as it charged around the yard, between them knocking over practically every barrel and plank set up for the horse to jump.

'Well, he can certainly bolt.' Anthony laughed. 'And if it was a bolter I was after, old chap, I would look no further.'

'Pull that horse up, boy!' Padraig shouted at Liam as he was swept past them yet again at full pelt. 'What in all the saints' names do you think you're doing?'

But all Liam could do now to save himself was to let go of the reins and slide across the yard to crash into a small shed, which at once began to shake as if on the verge of collapse. Seeing this, Padraig rushed over to the jerry-built structure and shoved a heavy prop against one wall to prevent yet another disaster while the horse went on galloping headlong round the yard.

'I also note he doesn't object to the hard going,' Anthony remarked wryly to his son as the sparks continued to fly. 'So that's something.'

'Someone should take a hold of him, Padraig,' Yamon advised loudly, 'or you'll be paying for a new set of shoes earlier than you wanted.'

But in spite of Padraig's madly flapping arms and shouts of *Will you not whoa there now!* the horse persisted in its wild journey until Kathleen could stand it no longer. Her ardent desire not to see her horse taken from the yard was at war with her wish that her pride and joy should not disgrace himself, and it was pride that finally won the day. Just as Anthony and Rory were about to leave, she pushed herself quickly away from the wall against which she was still leaning and whistled sharply. Recognising the sound, the horse stopped at once, slithering on the wet concrete before turning back to the caller.

'Come here, will you, you crazy loon,' she said softly to the horse as she walked towards him with her hand held out. 'Come here before you do yourself a mischief. Come here and show them what you can do.'

Straightening his tack and calming him almost at once, Kathleen set him right, then, hopping on to one of the few still upright barrels, vaulted lightly and easily into the saddle. As soon as she was up the horse settled, pricked his ears, snorted and began to walk out like a dressage animal. Liam reset the jumps while Kathleen continued her display, now trotting the horse, now extending his trot, and finally cantering him in a perfect collection round the inside of the course.

'You're not really going to ask him to jump on this surface?' Anthony wondered. 'It's not only concrete, but wet concrete.'

'I wouldn't ask a thing of him, Mr Rawlins,' Padraig replied, 'if I knew he couldn't do it.'

'Most of those jumps are at least four foot, Dad, and a couple are even higher,' Rory muttered in amazement.

'Not our horse, old boy,' his father said. 'Ours not to reason why.'

'They're off their chumps,' Rory said, feeling his head beginning to throb. 'But the girl certainly can ride. Look at that seat.'

'I already have.'

They watched, both privately coming to the conclusion, without publicly remarking on it, that now the horse was standing up and moving properly he looked bigger and stronger than he had when he had ambled out of his box as if he was a donkey setting off for work in the peat bogs.

By no means a big horse, nevertheless he now looked nearer sixteen hands than fifteen, and considerably more athletic than before. He had the air of a street fighter, an animal that as soon as it was saddled up and faced with a challenge seemed to change its physical appearance, prepared to take on all comers, to see anyone off. Getting him ready to jump Kathleen gave him one stroke down the neck, rose up in her irons into the jumping position, then gathered him up.

'Go on, fella,' she whispered to him. 'Show them what you're made of.'

Now the horse moved forward with quite a different look in his eyes, tight held and bouncing into the first of the jumps. No one could quite believe what they then saw, not Yamon, not even Padraig, and certainly not the two visitors from England. From a standing start on lethally wet concrete the horse flew round the yard jumping everything in his way with plenty to spare, arching his back and tucking his fore legs well up as he rose. He didn't touch a plank or a broomstick. He simply skipped over the jumps in the style of a seasoned show jumper. Kathleen took him round twice before easing him up and bringing him to a standstill in front of the two Englishmen.

'Well done, Miss Flanagan,' Anthony called up to her. 'And you, little horse,' he added, patting the horse on his neck. 'Well done you as well. That was some display.'

Kathleen nodded her thanks, despite her feelings.

'Would you like to see him pop over a hedge in the field now?' Padraig enquired. 'The ground's a bit sloppy but he'd not mind that. He'll go on anything.'

'He's like a wave when he jumps, man!' Yamon assured them. 'Like a great big wave when he races, overlapping the fences and flowing like the sea itself!'

'I'll take your word for it,' Anthony said, inspecting the horse more closely now, lifting up and flexing each fore leg before running his fingers down the tendons, satisfying himself that the legs were cool as could be and the tendons clean and sharp. 'If you were going to sell him, Mr Flanagan . . . ?'

'I'd be axing you for twenty thousand of your English guineas, sir.'

'You can axe away, old chap, but I wouldn't go anywhere near that sort of figure.'

'If we were in the sales at Doncaster you would have to, sir.'

'But we're not, Mr Flanagan, and if you really are thinking you might sell him, I might offer you ten thousand English guineas.'

'And I'd take not a drop under nineteen firm,' came the reply. 'And I'll not haggle further.' Padraig spat on his hand in preparation of sealing the deal, watched now in horror by Kathleen who in the heat of the moment had quite forgotten what the purpose of this visit might be.

'And I'd not budge over ten and a half, Mr Flanagan.'

'Then we have no deal, sir. And you have missed out on the chance of owning something exceptional.'

'Da,' Kathleen chipped in, sliding down from the saddle and pulling the reins over the horse's head and under his chin.

'This is nothing to do with you, girl, this is men's business,' Padraig said without looking at

76

her. 'Now do your horse good, and that's an end to it.'

Kathleen glanced round at their two visitors, but they were both taking one last look at the horse before he was returned to his box. She said something to her father in Gaelic, but was met with a dismissive wave of his hand.

'Eighteen nine and the horse is yours,' Padraig said.

'Sorry, Mr Flanagan.' Anthony sighed. 'It's a nice enough animal, but not at that sort of money. Now my son and I have a plane to catch.'

'Eighteen five hundred,' Padraig offered. 'And that's it.'

'Thank you but no thank you. If the horse sticks, you can always give me a call in England.' Anthony gave Padraig his card, then shook his hand. 'He's a nice little horse and I'm sure he'll pick up a race somewhere.'

From the look on both Padraig's and Yamon's faces it was as if they had insulted Mother Ireland herself, while Kathleen, with a face like a thundercloud over Dingle Bay, took her precious charge back to his stable.

'Time to mosey along,' Rory muttered. 'If you fancy keeping your scalp.'

With one last nod Anthony and Rory hurried off to their car and made good their escape.

Exhausted by his recent experiences, Anthony settled down to sleep as Rory headed the car for Cork airport, and Rory had to defer the questions

77

he had stored up to ask, every one of which concerned the little horse.

But they didn't get very far before the matter was once again brought to their attention. Just as they were clearing Cronagh town itself, a desperately battered old truck pulled out in front of them and came to a halt. Forced to stop, Rory saw Padraig Flanagan behind the wheel with the giant Yamon sitting beside him, head bent and knees up almost under his chin. Oblivious of the fact that he was causing a minor traffic jam, Padraig got out of the truck and came round to the passenger window of the hire car, on which he rapped his knuckles sharply in order to wake Anthony.

'Fifteen thousand five hundred,' he barked through the still closed window. 'Fifteen and a half thousand of your guineas and the horse is yours!'

Anthony frowned for a moment, then shook his head and instructed Rory to drive round the obstruction and be on his way. Padraig got back in the driving seat of the truck and followed them, sounding the horn constantly.

Forced to another stop ten miles on by a flock of sheep wandering across the road, in his driving mirror Rory saw Padraig hop out from the cab once again to appear at his father's window.

'Ah but you're a hard man, Mr Rawlins,' Padraig gasped. 'Fourteen thousand flat says the horse is yours.'

'I really don't have that sort of money to spare,

old man,' Anthony said firmly. 'Drive on, Rory.'

With the road ahead now clear of sheep, Rory floored the accelerator, leaving Padraig throwing his battered old hat to the ground in despair. Half a mile on, they joined the main trunk road to Cork where driving as fast as he safely could Rory left the battered old farm truck miles behind them.

Reaching Cork airport in plenty of time, they returned their hire car then went to check in. There was a good hour still to spare before their flight, so they went to the café and had something to eat and a couple of cups of strong coffee. Settled at a table overlooking the runway neither of them was aware of the two figures stealing up on them quietly from behind.

'Eleven thousand five hundred, Mr Rawlins, sir,' said Padraig's voice softly in Anthony's ear. 'The very final offer.'

Anthony didn't even look round. He just eyed his son, winked, finished his coffee and yawned. 'Nine thousand seven hundred and fifty,' he said finally. 'English guineas.'

'Ten thousand five hundred.'

'Ten thousand flat,' Anthony replied. 'Not a penny more.'

'Done,' Padraig agreed, and spat on his hand. 'You're a hard man, but a decent one, and I have the papers here.'

Sitting himself down, he produced a bundle of papers including a bill of sale from his top coat pocket, together with an old cracked biro which he handed to Anthony.

'You have yourself the best horse in Ireland.' He nodded. 'Good luck with him now. And may he bring you joy.'

Anthony leafed quickly through the papers then signed the bill of sale.

'Dad . . .' Rory said quietly.

'In a minute, old man,' Anthony muttered as he wrote a cheque. 'First things first.'

'Dad,' Rory persisted.

'Hush now,' Padraig cautioned. 'Your father's busy here.'

Anthony handed the cheque over, then gathered up the sheaf of papers.

'The passport, Dad?' Rory said quietly.

'Rory.' His father looked at him, clearing his throat. 'I do know what I'm doing.'

'The boy's right, Mr Rawlins,' Padraig said, putting a hand to his inside pocket and producing an equine passport. 'I nearly forgot it meself, so I did. There now.' He handed over the document. 'It's been a rare pleasure, and may your shadows never grow less.'

Then the Irishmen were gone, even more suddenly than they had arrived.

'I hadn't forgotten the passport,' Anthony grumbled, suddenly feeling very tired. 'And old Flanagan knew as well I did no passport, no deal. That's just the way it is.'

'But you hadn't – we hadn't checked it, Pop.'

'We heard how he was born back at the yard, and the horse is obviously thoroughbred.'

'I don't remember hearing the breeding.'

'You were probably still six sheets, old lad. By . . . who was it? And what was the mare again? Mananan's something or other. Mananan's Girl, that's it. By some stallion of his neighbour's that I've never heard of – King of the Sea, that's the boy. By King of the Sea out of Mananan's Girl.'

'You won't be able to put that on the racecard,' Rory said, handing his father the open passport. 'You're going to have to put by King of the Sea out of mare unknown. The dam wasn't registered.'

Anthony frowned at him, then studied the passport.

'Well, that's not the end of the world. She'll be in the part-bred register, no doubt.'

'Whether she is or not, Pop, I'm thinking it doesn't exactly bolster the horse's value. If you're thinking of selling him on, or finding an owner.'

'He's a cheap horse, Rory. And even with an unregistered dam—'

'A useless unregistered dam,' Rory corrected him. 'And an equally useless sire, if you don't mind my saying.'

'We should still be able to sell him on, perhaps for as much as twenty. People are throwing money around these days. After all, he is Irish, and all they want at the moment in England are Irish horses.'

'Big, well-bred Irish horses with some form. And what do you mean by *we* should be able to sell him on?' Rory threw his father a droll look.

'Figure of speech, old boy, figure of speech,'

Anthony said, swallowing hard as he felt a pain hit him mid-chest. 'And there's our flight called.'

Anthony suffered his first heart attack on the plane just as they were coming in to land. By the time they got him off the plane and into an ambulance he was suffering a second one. His life, hanging by a thread, was saved only by the speed and efficiency with which he was transferred to the nearest hospital, where he was placed in intensive care.

'Any idea of his chances?' Rory waylaid a doctor at the first available opportunity. 'He's always been a pretty tough character.'

'He'd need to be, Mr Rawlins.' The doctor looked past Rory to someone else coming towards him. 'That second attack was severe. Nine out of ten on the graph, I would say.'

Despite being warned that there was little chance of his father's recovering consciousness that night, Rory stayed at the hospital as long as he could, hoping in some helpless way that if he stayed around so would his father. Finally, in the very smallest of the small hours, he drove himself back to Fulford Farm, the emptiness of the roads giving him plenty of time to try to sort his thoughts out.

On the morning they had left for their trip to Ireland Rory had received a letter informing him that he had won a scholarship to study at the famous Savarese school of art in Florence. Of course he'd applied for it, although with no more than the faintest hope. At nearly twenty-eight years of age he knew it was high time he knuckled down, but he also knew he was getting far too long in the tooth to be a student. Naturally, being well aware that his father wanted him to take over at Fulford, he had said nothing to Anthony about Florence or the scholarship, not even when Anthony raised the subject on their drive to the airport. Now his father's sudden illness meant that Rory was faced with a very real dilemma. Basically, sell up Fulford, or take over.

If his mother Evelyn had not died in a terrible train crash only eight years before, everything would have been very different. They had been such a happy family. His father and mother had been devoted to each other, and because of Evelyn's seemingly everlasting patience and understanding as well as her innate good humour his father had managed his small yard with considerable success, even achieving a third in the Grand National.

But then Anthony's sweet-tempered wife had been killed because some idiot had made a terrible mistake with a set of points, and everything, right up until this present moment, had subsequently gone downhill, not fast, but bit by little bit, unwinding itself; Anthony losing his grip, Rory not on hand as much as he should have been, reluctant to muscle in on a grieving father. Wrong decisions had been made, the farm income had declined, staff had left unexpectedly

83

and, on top of it all, compensation for victims in the rail accident had been interminably delayed because of the usual series of appeals, counter-appeals and counter-counter-appeals in the wake of the official report. Then when the money had finally been paid over, sums that were far too little in the opinion of most people, much of the received capital had to be utilised in helping make good damage already done to Fulford Farm, all of which had added up and brought them to this moment.

He unlocked his father's office door and went and sat behind his desk, in his chair. He had to get a grip. He had to get a grip and make decisions, in case his father never recovered.

First things first, he thought. First he would have to do something about the apparently useless horse his father had bought in Ireland. To buy an undersized and inexperienced horse with no notable breeding, regardless of how much had been drunk, seemed to Rory to be yet another example of the kinds of wrong decisions that had brought Fulford to its current state of near bankruptcy.

He stared round the room at the photos of the old glory days, of fine horses winning their races, of owners being presented with cups, of his mother and father and himself standing smiling beside horse after horse and owner after owner, remembering the good days, the happy ones, the times when the future had seemed safe and secure. Not like now. Now his father lay dangerously and possibly mortally ill, his mother had long been gone, and the yard was all but on its last legs, with yet another owner about to remove two decent horses and the only incomer being an undersized Irish squib. Something had to be done, but what that thing was for the life of him Rory could not imagine.

He could send the incoming animal straight to the sales, of course, but given the provenance of the creature he doubted whether they would get more than two thousand pounds for it. He sighed and scratched his head with a pencil in the faint hope of firing some sort of inspiration, but nothing was forthcoming. He was absolutely sure that his father had no old friend or owner on his books who was looking specifically for a small and underbred horse. Those in the know liked their steeplechasers to be big, athletic and strong enough to do the job, which this Irish horse was most certainly not, failing, it would seem, on all counts. What his father could have been thinking when he finally agreed to buy it was beyond Rory's comprehension – and, on top of everything, at this particular moment when thanks to the wretched government and the latest set of restrictions from Brussels, farming was in such difficulties that Fulford Farm could not support Fulford Racing Ltd, as it had so often done previously.

'If the old man gets better, the way things are we're going to have to shut up shop and buy him a nice little warm air bungalow,' Rory sighed to himself, watching the dawn break. 'Failing some sort of miracle.'

He stood up, and was about to turn off the office light when his eye was caught by a photograph of his mother. She was on her favourite hack, a part Welsh part thoroughbred bay gelding, the wholly delightful old Brown Jack. She was smiling happily into the camera, totally relaxed, as was her horse, the sunlight catching at the sheen of Brownie's coat and the polish on his mother's immaculate black riding boots. Behind them stretched the lush green of the summer paddocks and the light ochre of the cereal fields beyond, the whole a picture of elegant ease, a study of one of the most intrinsic elements of English country life, a beautiful woman on a fine horse in the fold of the countryside.

But there was something else about the picture, something that held Rory back. It was as if his mother was trying to talk to him, to send him a message.

'I must be tired,' he said to himself, as his dog Dunkum stretched himself out at his feet, ready to move back to the warmth of the kitchen. 'I must be imagining things. Photographs do not speak.'

Yet there was something most definitely in his head, and the more he listened the more he heard his mother's pretty voice. *Remember, Rory,* she was saying. *Just remember we never know where our good luck is coming from.*

What good luck? he wondered as he let Dunkum

and himself out of the office just as the stable clock outside struck six, finding himself for once at odds with his mother. He did know one thing: any luck they might be getting would most certainly not be contained in the horse transporter that would shortly arrive at the stables from the Emerald Isle.

Chapter Three

Grenville

By now Grenville Fielding had resharpened every Venus HB pencil in the small silver container on his dark-green-leather-topped partner's desk, trimmed the dirty edges from his Staedtler Tradition eraser, carefully polished with a tissue the gold nib on his Parker 51 fountain pen – a present from his father on the occasion of his twenty-first birthday exactly twenty-five years ago – arranged his ivory ruler in a perfect parallel with the black leather correspondence folder that sat dead centre on the desktop, shot the cuffs of his freshly laundered and ironed dark blue and white striped shirt, and finally adjusted his Garrick Club tie before sitting back to review the day's play.

'Good,' he said to himself after a moment's reflection. 'Highly satisfactory, in fact. Could not have come at a better time.'

To celebrate the new business that had just

come his way, he decided he would allow himself his first gin and tonic of the evening a quarter of an hour earlier than usual, assuring himself that if he drank it more slowly than was his habit, in the end it would come to much the same thing.

'It will come to very much the same thing, Grenville,' he said aloud as he rose to walk slowly to the skilfully distressed Georgian wardrobe that he used as a drinks cupboard. 'As long as we sip – and do not gulp.'

Carefully pouring a double London Gin from a silver-plated bar measure over two large cubes of iced Malvern water and adding precisely half a bottle of Slimline tonic to the Waterford tumbler, he dropped in a thin slice of freshly cut lime and then took the drink over to the window that looked out on to the iron-railed garden reserved solely for use of the residents of the square.

'Perfect,' he sighed, but then quickly stepped back as he caught sight of Lady Frimley walking a pair of small Tibetan dogs in the garden square below, and staring up at his window. When she raised one gloved hand in a vaguely royal gesture, it became really rather too obvious that she had seen him, which meant he was forced to wave back, rather less royally. He even managed a smile.

'She must walk those dogs of hers about twenty times a day,' he said out loud to himself, still smiling down at the woman far below him.

Like so many, Grenville had found out that there was only one drawback to living in a smart

London square, and that was that the place was still filled with so many of the old guard that you were always dodging sherry parties, not to mention invitations to the theatre where one set of crumblies in the auditorium sat enthralled by a cast of another up on the stage, most of whom were seriously trying to remember where they were, or in what play.

But then living where he did also brought its advantages, since many of the old things around him had chosen him as their investment counsellor. Few invested very large sums, all of them having grown understandably ever more cautious with age, but none the less it all added up to something rather than nothing, and the more it added up the happier Grenville became. A few, such as Lady Frimley, had resisted the temptation to invest, but he had high hopes that she too would finally succumb to his lures, although, as he had come increasingly to realise, success was something of a double-edged sword. The greater his number of investors, the more invitations he received to attend very dull dinners, generally held in ancient restaurants and clubs with old-fashioned menus, peeling wallpaper, and inordinately tiresome company.

The previous year, Grenville had actually had to take the decision to try to find younger, rather than older, people on whose behalf he could invest. Recent good fortune had come from the word-of-mouth recommendation of one of his clients, the Honourable Pelham Augustus

Dashwood, to someone he met in the Long Room at Lord's, a moderately charming but singularly undistinguished actor by the name of Jeremy Bell, who had recently amassed a small but satisfactory fortune by way of the deaths of two maiden aunts and a homosexual uncle who had owned a modest brewery. Bell was uncertain as to what precisely to do with his new-found wealth, but as is so often the way with actors, had been unable not to mention the windfalls several times *en passant* to Dashwood, who, by coincidence, had himself come into a certain amount of money as a result of the more than convenient theft of an antique Bugatti racing car he had inherited from his godfather. Dashwood had then kindly recommended Grenville and so Grenville had taken on fresh, rich blood without so much as the raising of a finger.

As it happened, Grenville was a very wise and happy choice, because he really did have the knack of making money in unexpected places. More than that, he had a brilliant sense of timing, of making an investment at just the right moment – and of course, from Grenville's point of view, managing someone else's money was a gift, particularly when it came with no strings attached, just orders to go full steam ahead. The job required a minimum of effort, and yielded a most satisfactory income. Dashwood's faith in Grenville was completely justified, and so he was soon followed by others of his kind, Old Etonians all – or, as they preferred to say, the alumni of *Slough Grammar*, this affectation generally followed by a loud bray of undeniably Etonian laughter. Most conveniently of all, Dashwood's friends still thought it vulgar to talk about their money, and so were more than happy to hand over substantial handfuls of their unearned to be invested by someone they understood from Dashwood was a Chap Like Them, something which, as it happened, Grenville certainly was not. Nevertheless, because Dashwood had made Grenville his investment manager, everyone now thought Grenville was of the same ilk as his sponsor. It was a case of class by association, really.

Now, for want of anything else to do, and because he was anxious to avoid being waved at again by Lady Frimley, Grenville went to the looking glass over his chimney piece and regarded himself carefully.

For someone in his mid-forties, he was good-looking in an unremarkable sort of way. Tall, slim, hair greying a little round the edges, what he liked to think of as honest eyes, hands perhaps slightly too heavy to be those of a patrician, but at least the signet ring was on the correct finger, the little finger of the left hand, and the Asprey's cufflinks in his striped Turnbull and Asser shirt were of a discreet medium size and fashioned from old gold, unlike the overlarge decorations sported by so many of his peers. Looking at his mirrored image he had no doubt in his mind why he passed so easily as a gentleman. He looked like a gentleman.

Yet he had a problem, which he was pondering

once again as he stood carefully sipping his gin and tonic, and this was the fact that in many ways he was now possibly a little too successful. He badly needed some sort of stimulus; he needed to feel energised again because, quite frankly, at the moment he felt nothing at all. That was the trouble with all this achievement. Being fairly wealthy and successful seemed to mean that he now felt less about everything, which was very disappointing. Grenville had always thought that the more you had the more you would feel; he had imagined success brought more colour to your life, yet this seemed not to be the case with him. It had merely brought a feeling of emptiness, as everything in which he invested went up and up, and his clients became so fat and content they ceased even to ask after their investments, and consequently about him. Instead he imagined them all sitting around congratulating themselves on their perspicacity and innate brilliant business sense, ignoring the fact that it was he who had precipitated their success.

'What one needs,' he said to himself, back to idly staring out of the window now that the coast was clear of Lady Frimley, 'what one needs is for something to happen which is out of the general run of things. One *really* needs a chum or two to come in with one on something stupendously trivial, perhaps. One needs a silly situation, instead of a pounds, shillings and pence one. One needs to do something totally frivolous instead of always doing the sensible thing. Ah, yes – yes, but what?'

The fact that he could find no answer to his own question made Grenville feel even more like an old bachelor who had been too busy making money to realise that life was passing him by, not to mention someone whom others had passed by as well. It made him feel unwanted, which in fact he now wondered whether he truly was. Except for the money he made for people, he was not actually needed by anyone, not as a person. If he dropped dead tomorrow the most that his acquaintances would say at his memorial service probably would be that he was *a good sort of chap, splendid with the old lucre, but lived just for his work really. Reason why he never married probably, and had so few close friends – too caught up in his work.*

The telephone rang and the sound brought him out of his long reverie. When he picked up the receiver he heard a voice which immediately brought even further dejection, at once making him feel like a lonely little boy all over again.

'Hello, Mummy,' he said, hoping he had contained his small sigh of anguish. 'How are we today?'

Chapter Four

The Singleton

Lynne carefully crossed her long and elegant legs, hooked a tress of blond hair back over one ear and smiled at her solicitor. He too smiled but with less brilliance, and Lynne was unsurprised to see that he had coloured a little, too. Mr Morgan was a short, curly-haired Welshman much prone to embarrassment. They were an odd duo, but however different their natures might be, between them they had at last got Gerry on the run, so much so that it had now become one of their running jokes, like something out of a British situation comedy: *I say – we've got old Gerry on the run, what?*

Certainly, whenever Lynne entered Mr Morgan's office she was always happy to share their jokes in order to take her mind off the stale and musty smell of the room, as well as off Miss Fanshawe, Mr Morgan's squat, bespectacled secretary who kept peering through the glass partition that divided her office from his. She actually watched them so closely, and with such regularity, that Lynne had come to the conclusion that the secretary thought that she might have some kind of designs on her boss, which added to her amusement.

On this particular visit Miss Fanshawe was at her spying in spades, constantly up and down from her desk to pop into the office wearing her best *Does Mr Morgan need me?* expression. But as it happened Lynne was in far too good a mood to mind if Miss Fanshawe stuck her nose right against the glass partition and left it there. Today was a marvellous new day. Lynne stroked her pale grey cashmere shawl-collared cardigan, which exactly matched her new pale grey T-shirt, thinking that if she now played everything right today really could be the first day of the rest of her life.

She stretched out her legs once more, noticing happily that they shone with that well-known iridescence provided by only the most expensive hosiery, stockings that beautifully set off her pleated white linen skirt and white Victorian-style half-boots. She was just the right mix of expensive clothing and startling good looks, and the best thing of all was that once again she knew it. Small wonder then that Mr Morgan kept feeling his shirt collar as he doodled on the legal pad in front of him.

'But to come to the point, Mrs Fortune—'

'It would appear you've just broken yours,' Lynne said, smiling. The solicitor's eyes had caught her legs and the point of his pencil had snapped on the page.

He laughed awkwardly in acknowledgement and plucked a fresh pencil from the mug on his desk. 'Very good, Mrs Fortune – yes, very good indeed.'

'You know, now everything is being so nicely wrapped up, Mr Morgan,' Lynne said, 'I think I shall miss hearing all about you and Mrs Morgan hitchhiking around the States and visiting sites of special interest, I really will.'

'Oh, you're far too kind, Mrs Fortune.' Mr Morgan dabbed at his forehead with a handkerchief. 'But before we get distracted, I really must come to the point,' he repeated, doing his unsuccessful best to refit the left lens that had just fallen out of his glasses. 'I have to say you have been the very personification of patience, Mrs Fortune, through what has been a very difficult and I dare say often unpleasant time for you.'

While doing her best to look duly grateful as well as understanding, Lynne privately wished that her lawyer wasn't so long-winded. He really had no need because, as both of them knew, hers was a pretty straightforward case. Yet still he droned on about nothing very much in particular, so to escape from the monotony she allowed herself to indulge in a recap of the events via which she had come to find herself closeted in a stuffy, overheated, dusty and dreary office with someone as boring and embarrassed as her solicitor.

                    *   *   *

It had happened when she had gone away for
two days' pampering, not as a self-indulgence but
as the result of a surprise birthday present from
her adored husband Gerry.

> Have some seriously wicked days enjoying
> yourself at the Lakeside, my lovely. Pamper,
> pamper, pamper! And come back looking
> even more sexy – as if that were possible! A
> ton of love, Gerry xxx

So Lynne had turned up for her pre-booked
stay at the Lakeside Beauty Spa, where, after
being toned, massaged, plucked, pummelled,
beautified and coiffured, she finally considered
she'd had enough, not only thinking that the spa
had done everything it could for her but also a
little resentful of the staff's slightly high-minded
attitude. She decided there was too much
emphasis on the body's being a temple and not
enough on life's being a bowl of cherries, the
latter summing up a philosophy to which Lynne
was more than a little addicted. So she decided
to bail out early and return home to surprise her
beautiful Gerry, a man she reckoned was just
about the best and the sexiest husband a girl
could have.
  Full of good and loving intentions she stopped
off in Bath to shop for Gerry's favourite food
– fillet steak, which she'd serve with a Béarnaise
sauce, baked potatoes and a tomato salad with

mozzarella and follow with his addiction, chocolate mousse – as well as flowers, vintage champagne, and an expensive bottle of claret. With all her goodies packed in the boot of her blue sports car, she had driven smartly off home, easing down only when she reached their automated gates and remotely controlled garage doors, driving in as slowly and as quietly as she could in the hope that if Gerry was around she'd surprise him. The house was so designed that she could unload the shopping straight into the kitchen or if necessary into the deep freeze in the garage, yet another of the luxuries and blessings she thanked her darling husband for.

So, having happily stowed away her shopping, delighted to be home and feeling suitably primped and pampered, Lynne had gone looking for her husband, who she thought must be somewhere about because his car was also in the garage. Upstairs, she finally went along to their second-floor bedroom suite, with its brilliant yellow Cole's wallpaper and its balcony overlooking the garden – and surprised him.

He was in bed with her best friend Maddy, and they were all more than a little surprised. In fact it was hard to tell which of the three of them got the biggest shock.

Afterwards she had wished she'd been able to think of something crisp and cutting to say, but all she could do was stare in momentary horror before turning on her heel and fleeing back downstairs, her eyes flooding with tears.

She also found herself wishing she'd made a real scene, but unfortunately making scenes was just as much *not her thing* as finding something witty and crisp to say at moments of distress. She hadn't quite said that to Mr Morgan when he had asked her what her reaction had been. She just said she thought that since the deed had already been committed it was better simply to walk away from it in as dignified a manner as possible, although in fact her departure had been well short of that. During her confusion she had lost a shoe on the staircase, which caused her to slip and fall and slide the rest of the way down to the first floor on her backside. Then she had walked into the doorpost, and finally she had managed to engage drive in her car rather than reverse and put a serious dent in her front bumper before regaining her senses and reversing out of the garage, after which she had driven way too fast back into Bath and checked into a hotel in a quiet part of the city for a very long think. At first her thoughts, predictably enough, had all been the heartbroken *how could he?* stuff, self-pitying reflections that quickly turned to the angry *how dare he!* bit, and finally became quite practical as soon as she realised that there was no use in thinking that a man who had strayed once would not stray again, and at the earliest opportunity.

Her mother had always told her, drink in one hand and a cigarette in the other, that the rule was one strike and they were out. 'Believe me, Linnet,' she'd say. 'Believe me, girl, it's the only way.' And now Lynne – who privately had always thought her mother's creed to be a little unforgiving – found herself agreeing absolutely with this point of view: *one strike and out*. Most certainly did she not want to spend the rest of her life pretending not to notice that Gerry was at it again . . . and again. She'd seen quite enough, up front and very personal, of what infidelity could do to a woman. It had most certainly done it for her poor mother – spelt out in great big capital letters.

Being married to the two-timing so-and-so that was Lynne's father had driven her mother quietly mad, no question about it. Possibly its most useful result had been the piece of worldly wisdom she had passed on to her daughter; it was her tragedy that she had learned it too late to put it into practice herself. A life spent always wondering where a man was and why, or whom he was with and why, or simply whether or not he had just told her the truth instead of yet another lie, had without any exaggeration made her mother paranoid. In the end she had not known which way to turn, whom to trust, what was the truth, or whether there was any security to be found anywhere, which was obviously why she had finally chosen to take what she thought to be the only way out.

'I still don't know why she did it,' Lynne's father kept saying at the funeral.

'You might not, Dad,' Lynne had replied. 'But everyone else seems to.'

'Meaning?'

'Meaning Mum got tired of covering for you, Dad, you know? She just ran out of that kind of energy – always making excuses for why you hadn't turned up for dinner, or were late back for my birthday, or, even missed your son's eighteenth *altogether*, know what I mean? People get fed up with it – worn out, if you'd rather – and it becomes too much. So you decide you can't go on, so you don't. Got it? But don't you worry, Dad. You're on your own now, and here's hoping you find out just what it's like yourself. And who knows? You might end up feeling just the way poor Mum did.'

Then she'd left him to it, all alone – turned on her heel and walked out of the graveyard and into a brand-new life of her own with Gerry.

A brand-new joke rather, she had told herself as she sat privately reflecting in the room she'd taken in the Bath hotel, and not exactly a good one. In fact it was a joke in the worst taste possible because even Lynne, who as she herself well knew was not exactly the brightest bunny on the block, now saw that within a few months of her mother's death she'd fallen into the trap. She had only gone and fallen in love with exactly the same kind of man as her mother had loved, in other words her father. She'd fallen for a two-timing so-and-so who obviously couldn't wait to get her out of the way so he could lay someone else. As she stared out at the hotel's fine gardens below her window, her normal resilience had suddenly vanished, the world turning into just one large room with only her in it, a room with no walls and no other people. She found herself sitting in the darkness of space.

But as the light faded and only the sounds of distant city traffic, punctuated occasionally by the wail of ambulance and police sirens, floated up to her room, she found her centre once again and steel entered her heart.

'Let's face it, Linnet,' she told herself, pouring herself a drink from the mini-bar. 'If and when push comes to get out, maybe it's better to get tough rather than angry. Being angry and staying angry's too bloody tiring.'

Getting tough meant resolving to take her husband Gerry not just for everything he had, but for everything he was even thinking of having. Lynne determined to skin him, skin him so badly that dear sweet little ex-best friend Maddy, she of the innocent eyes and ways and the little girl looks, wouldn't be able to get a postage stamp off him, let alone another pair of Janet Reger silk knickers.

So she had steered Mr Morgan's boat and steered it well, the end result being that her divorce settlement meant Lynne would never have to work at all, at least not in the remotely foreseeable future. The sum settled on her ensured she could not only afford to live, but afford to live very well, enjoying herself in more or less any way she wished. The world was not merely her oyster.

As far as she was concerned, it was to be her playground.

'I have to say I feel that their final offer is really quite generous,' Mr Morgan told Lynne now as she studied the papers in front of her, getting up from his chair and coming round to Lynne's side of the desk as if to go through each point carefully with her, but really simply so that he could be that little bit closer to her.

'Generous, Mr Morgan?' Lynne laughed. 'It's fab.'

Mr Morgan nodded, and then sneezed, whipping out a spotless white cotton handkerchief, which had *Monday* embroidered on it, even though it was now Friday.

'You've done a great job, Mr Morgan, really good.'

'Really?' Mr Morgan replied, putting *Monday* away and looking down at her over the top of his glasses. 'Do you think so?'

'I really do. Straight up.'

'I'm so glad. Thank you, Mrs Fortune.'

'I think you've done such a good job, in fact' – Lynne folded the papers up and slipped them into her bag, shutting it with a snap – '*such* a good job that *I* am going to take you out to celebrate. You were dead right to go for a lump sum, Mr Morgan, really spot on. No haggling and no bargaining, just down and dirty. So come on. A glass of the bubbly certainly beckons.'

She turned and smiled, the first true and heart-felt smile she had given in months.

'It is a little early in the day for me, Mrs Fortune,' Mr Morgan said with a sad smile and a series of quick nods to indicate his regret. 'Still only a quarter to twelve.'

'Yes, well, time to live dangerously, Mr Morgan,' Lynne told him, on the move now and taking his arm. 'Now the harvest is in.'

Leading him past an astonished Miss Fanshawe and a couple obviously waiting for the next appointment, Lynne marched Mr Morgan smartly out of his office and across the road to a wine bar, where she ordered a bottle of their best champagne.

'You know what this means, don't you, Mr Morgan?' she asked him, as she sipped her drink, displaying even more leg than Mr Morgan had seen before, thanks to the height of the bar stools. 'It really means no more worries. It means I do *not* have to think about where next month's rent's coming from; it means I do *not* have to think I'm going to be forced to find me some rich old sod – sorry, I mean bod – some rich old bod to be nice to, just so that I can keep my head above water.'

'No, no – less of the *old*,' Mr Morgan chimed in. 'I feel perfectly sure that you will only attract the best, Mrs Fortune.'

Lynne gave him a quick glance, and then looked away, frowning lightly.

'What I meant to say—' he continued, too late, only to be stopped at once by his client.

'Think nothing of it, Mr Morgan,' Lynne assured

him. 'As I was saying, this settlement, if it's as good as it looks—'

'Which it is, Mrs Fortune. Believe me. It most certainly is.'

'Provided, of course, that Gerry coughs up with the cheque a.s.a.p.'

'They're much stricter about this sort of thing nowadays, Mrs Fortune – he really won't be allowed to delay payment.'

'You have to watch Gerry. He's not someone to take your eye off. He didn't get where he is by playing soppy date.'

'He's certainly been very successful, Mrs Fortune.'

'I'm just surprised he's simply rolled over the way he has. I really thought he'd put up a bit more of a fight. I suppose he's so glad to be shot of me, he doesn't mind paying.'

Lynne sipped her champagne and looked over the top of her glass at Mr Morgan, hoping he might contradict her. He did not.

'You have half the value of the house, you keep your car, you have a generous settlement in consideration of your excellent record as a wife,' he said. 'So, as long as you take the right financial advice, you most certainly should remain more than solvent, Mrs Fortune.'

'OK, Mr Morgan.' Lynne checked her lipstick in her compact mirror. 'Fair dos. And now I think I might treat myself somewhere. After all, getting divorced isn't something you do every day.'

'I don't see anything wrong with that,' Mr

Morgan agreed. 'Provided we don't go too mad.'

'Oh?' Lynne looked at him teasingly, wide-eyed. 'You coming along too, then?'

Mr Morgan smiled shyly back, turned a beautiful plum colour, and walked uncertainly back into the broad daylight of the street to return to his office.

Lynne stared at herself in the mirror behind the bar, all her put-on flirtatious manner gone, a sense of trepidation and muted excitement taking its place. She still had half a bottle of champagne to finish, and by the time she had done that justice she reckoned she should feel ready for the fray. After all, as she'd decided, this was the start of the rest of her life. This was her, herself, by herself.

She drank another glass of champagne and thought some more about the reality of her position. Until this moment there had still been half of her that believed this was happening and half that did not, yet now she knew it was in fact all true, one hundred per cent so. She really was on her own. *By* my own, as she used to say when she was small. *I don't want to be by my own.* Yet now, like it or not, she was indeed by her own, totally and utterly and completely. And because she was alone she knew she would be lucky if she didn't end up as some dreary divorcee with a backlog of hard luck stories about relationships that hadn't quite worked out, tales of near misses, of what might have beens. She knew, champagne or no champagne, that from now on she was going to need all the luck that was going. She looked into the face staring back at her in the mirror behind the bar and saw the former Mrs Gerry Fortune, looking a lot less poised and buffed and groomed than the happy young woman who had waltzed happily out of the Lakeside Beauty Spa, on her way home to surprise her gorgeous sexy husband.

Chapter Five

Back Across the Wather

He sensed the change; smelt it even. It was the tones of the voices of those who came to feed him, to look at his feet, to brush out his coat and mane, to check his legs. And he knew it because wasn't herself coming too often, bringing his favourite sweet things to eat, pulling his ears and resting her face on his neck before kissing him on his nose, the way she knew he liked it. More than that, he noticed that despite all this there were none of the words that were normal to her coming to him. Since he was hardly old enough to put his head over the door he had known it was her coming, for she would sing quietly to him as she went about her work, and ask him all the time, time after time, if he was all right then – which he always was. But not today. Today he was not all right. He was uneasy, walking about in the straw, holding his head away from her, standing at the back of his stable and looking into the corner. He sensed something was up, and not something good. Something bad was about to happen. He understood

...us from the tone of her voice and the sadness in her dark eyes.

'I shall try to come and see you, Boyo,' Kathleen told her horse, as if sensing his trepidation and seeking to reassure him. 'I don't know how, my love, and I don't know when, because it won't be easy, but I'll find a way. I'll think of a way of getting to see you, because if I don't . . .' She fell silent, as if reluctant to spell out the rest of her thoughts. 'You just make sure you're a good boy and behave yourself, Boyo. You'll always be mine, don't you worry.'

She pulled his ears and kissed his muzzle softly and gently.

'At least you'll have your friend Finoula with you,' she whispered. 'Some of the way, at least.'

Which indeed was the case, since their neighbour had sold the young filly who was Boyo's paddock playmate to a horse scout from England, arrangements having been made for the two horses to travel with a large consignment of other bought horses from the area.

A lad came in later, looked in Boyo's manger, then slapped the horse on the neck and asked him why he wasn't eating. In answer the horse just pushed him aside, turning his rump on him, ready with his hind feet. The lad was about to have a go but seeing the way the horse had laid his ears back flat thought better of it.

'Suit yourself so,' the lad said, taking his manger away but avoiding his hind quarters as he eased his way to the door. 'You're the one who's going to get hungry, not me, and you won't be getting much on your travels.'

Sensing something bad, the horse walked his box for the next two hours before finally sleeping. He woke at first light, but it wasn't the dawn that woke him. There were sounds in the yard, the sort of noise that he normally didn't hear until much later in the day. His stable door was thrown open and the tall boy came in, carrying the things they put on his legs when they took him to some different field to jump hedges with others like himself, things to protect his legs in the moving box. So perhaps that's what it was. Perhaps this was another of those times when they went and raced each other in another field somewhere, yet if it was, why was herself so upset? Why had her face been wet? And why wasn't she here now? Why wasn't she here now with him? It was always herself who put these things on him, not this skit of a lad who liked to hit his rump and slap his neck. So why was she not here?

So when they led him out to the moving box with the things on his legs and a warmer on his back he tried to get away. He stood up on his hind legs and gave the moving box a great whack with his fore legs; then he crashed down again and turned and turned and bucked and pulled. The great strip still had a hold on his head collar but he was red in the face and yelling at him fit to burst.

The noise brought herself down. She rushed

out of the house, shouting at the lad and taking hold of the leading rope.

'What in hell do you think you're doing, boy?' she shouted. 'You get him stirred like this you'll never get him in!'

Now he stood still and looked at her, wanting her to tell him why she hadn't been there earlier and why she wasn't dressed to go with him in the moving box the way she always did when they went to another field. But she said nothing. She stroked him, gave him a carrot, stroked him again, and led him silently into the moving box. He went in. He would always go in for her. He would do anything she wanted. So he walked up the ramp and went in, and still she said nothing.

When he was in, she tied his head. He gazed at her, turning both his great brown eyes to her, looking to her for help. Still she said nothing. All she did was suddenly hug his neck, hug it tight, and then she was gone. *Why?* He gave a great cry. *What are you doing? Come back to me! Come back now! Come back! Come back!*

'Quiet!' the strip told him, checking his head rope to make sure he couldn't get free. 'And stop stamping those damned feet of yours!'

Then they led Finoula in. He didn't know she was coming as well, or going, whatever it was they were doing. Where were they going? No one had said where, but the little mare was standing beside him now, her own head roped to a ring, and she looked frightened. She had never been in the moving box before and had had to be manhandled and beaten before she would jib her way up the ramp. Finally she had relented and allowed herself to be installed and tied up, but she was scared. Boyo could see it in the way her eye was, with half the white showing. He whickered at her and she whickered back, but nothing it seemed could stop her trembling.

When they took them out, the horses found themselves in a very big barn. Outside, through the doors, Boyo could see something huge and dark, like another barn but much, much bigger, with enormous doors thrown wide to allow a line of wheeled boxes to enter, which they were doing, slowly, while people in brightly coloured coats waved and pointed at them. The huge barn seemed to be moving very slowly up and down, up and down, and on top of that he could smell and taste salt. A wind was blowing hard, swirling heavy rain about the large barn and drenching everyone who was standing between the two buildings. He and Finoula were made to wait in a small box with rails, with their heads tied and no hay or water, so Boyo stamped and shouted until Liam appeared with a bucket. He stroked his neck.

'It'll be all right, lad. I wanted to come with you all the way and so did Kathleen, but we can't afford that now, so we can't. But I'll see they take care of you all right.'

And then the two of them were put in a big box

with other horses, but all their eyes talked of was fear, and then the big box moved, slowly, and there was a lot of noise outside the big box, the rumble of other boxes, and the slamming of doors. There were raised voices, the smell of fumes and a slow, sickening, rocking motion. Some of the other horses whinnied fearfully, and started to stamp, and someone moved among them tightening their heads, talking to them roughly.

Boyo knew that here was danger, and knew also not to make a sound. After a lot of darkness there was a long, slow shudder and the sound of something deep and low and powerful, a throbbing noise, and the clanging of a bell somewhere, and he could hear the rushing of water. Alongside him the other horses began to stamp and whinny, calling to each other, crying out, *What is happening, where am I?*

Now this new, more frightening box was moving, swaying from side to side, then plunging forwards and backwards. The deep throbbing had become louder and more powerful, while all the time there was the distant sound of thrashing, rushing water.

In the darkness Boyo could see Finoula's eyes grown even larger. She was pulling back on her head collar, whinnying pitifully, her eyes rolling white and huge, half sitting as she tried to break free. Boyo whickered to her; he whickered to show her that she would be all right if she stood but not all right if she went down. They were packed tight in the big box and it was hot and

114

airless. If anyone went down they could really hurt themselves. They had to stand. They had to endure it, to stand together, to keep each other on their feet, although the big box was now dipping and climbing and swaying terrifyingly. The water could be heard now smashing on the sides of whatever huge thing they were in and the journey got rougher and rougher.

The little mare saw his eye, felt his breath on her, and stopped her tugging. Half down and half up she scrambled, her hooves sliding on the wet floor as she tried to get her hind legs up under her. But the box was swaying and plunging so much now that as soon as she was almost up another great drop downwards would make her lose her balance all over again.

He pushed his rump round behind her as best he could, standing there with his own hooves planted as firmly as he could manage. The mare felt his strength and pushed herself back against him, and then was safe, up on her own feet, shoving herself forward and regaining her balance. Her whinnying stopped and her eyes regained their proper look. They all calmed down as best they could, but after a long darkness the plunging and rolling became even worse and once again a panic broke out, and there was whinnying and stamping, neighing and snorting. He stood as steady as he could but it was so difficult now that he kept sliding sideways and almost falling over, his head and neck stretched out as he slipped and then wrenched as he lurched to one side. He had never known a feeling like this. And it was endless; endless, and so dark. Except for the dimmest light filtering in through the filthy windows of their big wheeled box, it was dark, and terrifying.

Some time on, the long and horrifying nightmare ended. The ground stopped heaving, the water stopped rushing, and suddenly there was a great flood of light and noise.

Boyo could hear the other wheeled boxes beginning to move, and finally their big box slowly but surely followed the others out into the daylight. There was still wind and rain, growing louder as the light in their box grew brighter, but underfoot it was firm, and the ground seemed to have stopped moving. In the calm that followed he looked around him at the other horses and saw that they were settling down as well, some beginning to pull at their hay nets even though the hay was dry as dust. He was thirsty too, but there was no water anywhere, just the dry and dusty hay to pick at.

It was a very long day and the wheeled box grew very hot from the heat of all the horses. But there was no respite and no refreshment. Even when the box stopped for a time, there was no water brought, although the dust from the hay was parching. A man came in and they all looked at him as best they could. They tried to tell him they must have something to drink but he ignored them, blowing smoke out of his mouth and nose as he picked his way through the packed box looking at them all. Then he was gone and the door was shut again. The heat built up more and more and to his horror he saw the little mare suddenly stagger and slip even though they were not moving. He tried to help her again, but she was too distressed to respond and fell heavily against the partition separating them. The others sensed the crisis and started to panic but no one came, despite the crescendo of stamping and whinnying. Then the box began to move again, on and on and on.

It was all but dark when the back of the box was finally lowered and a gust of fresh cold air blew in, making them all suddenly shake and shiver as the sweat dried on their steaming bodies. Some stamped again to get their blood running, others bowed their heads as if in hope of finding water, while others just stood trembling in every muscle. The box was full of the steam of their terror before they were all pulled out and led off to a block of stables. All but one. Finoula, his friend. The little dark mare was no longer moving, half held up by her head collar as if that was what had caused her death; as if she had been strangled by it. But she hadn't. She had died from terror, and thirst, and shock, and unable to fall to the floor hung there with her beautiful head twisted grotesquely to one side and her big pink tongue lolling uselessly out of her parched mouth.

As he was led away he heard them dragging her body out and half turned to watch. The man leading him pulled roughly at his head collar but he was so much the stronger that he just pulled the man over as he turned to see the body of his dead friend being towed away behind a wheeled box, bumping and shuddering over the concrete of the strange yard, steam still rising from her skin. The one at his collar tried to pull him on, hitting him round the head, but he just butted him away, causing the man to make a noise and hold his face.

They were all put in a line of draughty stables with only the thinnest of beds to lie on, bedding that had not even been cleaned out after the other horses that had passed through the yard. They all wanted nothing more than to lie down, but the beds were so filthy and poor that most just stood disconsolately, their ears back, their lower lips sticking out in misery, with only half-buckets of lukewarm, dirty water within reach. Later they were given food, but it was old and worthless, dusty nuts that tasted of nothing, and a slab of stale hay chucked on to the floor to see them through the long darkness.

He stood in the corner of his box, resting his hocks against the splintered timbers behind him. He had no idea what was happening to him or why. All his life he had met nothing but kindness. He'd had to stand in the rain and the wind, he'd had to put up with the sun and the flies, but no matter, since every day he was brought into a stable and brushed and washed, and given fresh food and damp hay. And on the fine days they were all put out in a field with sweet grass and clean fresh water in a stream that ran down from the hills. But now all he knew was misery.

When it was light again another wheeled box came for him and two other horses. It took him on a shorter journey to another place where he was taken out alone, leaving his new friends behind. He looked around him. Stables, and the sense of another horse nearby, and a new human standing looking at him.

'There's not exactly a lot of him, boss,' Teddy said after he and Rory had unloaded the new arrival. 'I thought the guv'nor liked 'em tall.'

'He does,' Rory replied, walking round the liver chestnut to take a good look at an animal that seemed a good deal smaller than the one he and his father had bought in Ireland. 'And now he looks even smaller than he did over there.'

'Knowing the Irish they probably sent you another,' Teddy said with a shake of his head. 'And there really isn't a lot to him.'

'He jumps well,' Rory said defensively. 'He can certainly jump. That we do know.'

'He'd need to, boss. He'd need to stay as well.'

'Wash him down, Teddy, and give him a decent feed. The poor fellow looks half starved.'

Boyo shook himself thoroughly, from the top of his head to the end of his thick tail, and then took another look at his new surroundings. That done, he raised his head and shouted as loudly as he could; after a moment, from some distant field, another horse answered his cry. Boyo listened attentively, then gave another loud shout.

Neither Teddy nor Rory could hear any response this time, but Boyo obviously did because he pricked his ears and whickered to himself quietly before allowing himself to be led away for a good hosing down.

Rory watched him walk away, noticing that even in his travel-weary state the horse moved well and easily. He was a long way short of what his father would call match fit, but there was plenty on his quarters, tissue that if Rory and his small team did their work right should soon build up into good racing muscle.

Once the horse was washed down and housed in the box reserved for newcomers – a stable set well apart from the others just in case the in-comer was carrying any sort of infection – Rory wandered back to his father's office. The horse's papers, including his passport, lay on his desk.

'That the new boy?' Maureen, his father's and now his secretary, asked, looking up from her paperwork. 'Not very big, is he?'

'Don't you start,' Rory replied. 'We have to find an owner for him, so as far as everyone here is concerned, he's a fine stamp of a horse. OK?'

'Got it.' Maureen smiled. 'As it happens I like small horses.'

'Then get one of those brown paper parcels out from under your bed, Maureen, and buy him.'

'I wish. What's he called? Is he named?'

'He must be, because they've already raced him. But I can't remember what they called him.'

'Small wonder,' Maureen said, rolling another

letter page into her typewriter. 'It usually takes your father a good two or three days to recover from his Irish trips.'

'Small Wonder would be a good name, but he's called The Enchanted,' Rory announced, having consulted the horse's passport. 'That's apparently his given name, although what is enchanting or enchanted about him has yet to be seen.'

'Let's hope he's just that,' Maureen returned. 'And before I forget, Colonel Willoughby wants you to call him.'

Rory made the call immediately, the colonel being both one of his father's oldest friends and an owner.

'Any improvement, Rory?' the colonel wanted to know up front. 'Do hope so.'

'No change as yet, Colonel,' Rory replied. 'But he's no worse and that's good. I think they describe him as stable.'

'Glad to hear it. Keep me posted.'

'Of course.'

The colonel cleared his throat. 'Now this isn't easy, Rory. I prefer to do these things face to face. But fact is, don't have much option. Betty's fallen ill, I'm afraid, and is going to take a lot of looking after.'

'I'm sorry to hear that, Colonel. It never rains, does it? Has to damn well pour, as my father always says.'

'Absolutely so, Rory. Now, you know as well as I that when this sort of thing happens, one has to clear the deck somewhat. And, as you also know, certain people have been pressing me to sell Hardway Boy.'

'I know, sir,' Rory replied, his heart sinking at the realisation that they were obviously just about to lose the only class horse they still had in the yard. 'But before you do, Colonel—'

'Too late for that, I'm afraid. Don't want to sell him, you know that. We all think he could be a National sort of horse, but it's a question of needs must, and of course Betty comes first.'

'I quite understand, Colonel. If you'll just keep me informed as to when and where, and all that.'

'Naturally,' the colonel replied, and cleared his throat once more. 'And you keep me posted about your father.'

'Damn,' Rory said after he had put down the telephone. 'Damn, blast and every other wretched swear word.'

'I thought something was up,' Maureen said, typing away. 'He doesn't give much away, but there was something in his voice.'

'Not a good day,' Rory concluded. 'Out goes the only class horse in the yard, and in comes an Irish donkey.'

'You never know,' Maureen replied, handing him the letter to sign. 'Strange things do happen, particularly with horses.'

Chapter Six

The Odd Couple

Constance always chose the same ensemble for such occasions: a middle-length skirt in dark grey, black silk blouse with cravat, three-quarter-length black wool jacket and large-brimmed black hat. Looking at her image in the cheval mirror in her bedroom, she was forced to realise that really, give or take a few wrinkles on her hands, she was nevertheless remarkable for her age. She still had a good figure, her eyes were nothing less than brilliant – many remarked on them still – and her complexion was flawless.

Beneath the shade of her deeply brimmed hat she reckoned she could pass for a woman in her fifties rather than one of her real age, which she was far too vain to acknowledge, even to herself. This proved to be no misconception, she was very happy to discover, since the moment she left the house to walk to the bus stop two workmen high up on the scaffolding wolf-whistled at her, and a well-dressed gentleman walking along the King's Road nodded in her direction, or at least she thought he did. No matter. It was a good feeling to think that the opposite sex noticed you at all, and that for a change it wasn't just you noticing them.

The only thing that spoilt her growing good mood was the fact that she had to travel by bus, but since it was very unlikely that anyone else attending the service in St George's, Hanover Square would be taking public transport she assumed it was quite safe to do so, as long as the bus arrived promptly so that no one she knew saw her lingering at the stop.

She sat downstairs towards the front of the bus. It wasn't too crowded, since it was well past the morning rush hour; the conductor gave her a smile, there were riders and horses trotting through the Park, and flowers still blooming in window boxes even though they were now well into autumn. In all, Constance decided she liked the look of London that morning. It was a good place to be, a great city which still had a heart.

She alighted from the bus, and made her way slowly towards the church. It was only as she made her way up the steps that she realised she had forgotten the name of whoever it was whose life and times she had come to commemorate. Nor could she recognise the faces of any of the other people who were now arriving, alighting from taxis or out of very large and frankly, as far as Constance was concerned, somewhat vulgar motor cars.

She gave her engraved visiting card to the man on the door; then, as she always did on these occasions, settled into a seat halfway down the church, the right position for someone titled but not related, an acquaintance of the deceased but not necessarily a close friend. Constance enjoyed memorial services, attending at least two or three a month, carefully earmarking the date of any forthcoming event. She worked from information gleaned from the *Daily Telegraph*, naturally, yet there was something about the congregation gathering for this particular commemoration that bothered her. She knew she had the right day because it was obvious that a service was about to be held. But when she looked about her, as she felt increasingly free to do, she found there was no one there whom she could recognise, which was unusual to say the least. There was always someone who knew her, or whom she knew – but not, it seemed, today.

None the less, she would be able to identify the deceased from her programme – or *dance card* as she called it for her private amusement – just as soon as she had retrieved her spectacles from her handbag. She managed to find them after some initial difficulty, and having held them carefully at the end of her nose so that she did not have to disarrange either hat or hair she stared with some surprise at the name. *How very embarrassing*, she thought. She had absolutely no idea of who the deceased might be. She had never heard of him, in fact, nor indeed of any of the speakers marked down on her card. However, to judge from their names and the general look of those beginning to fill up the seats, the departed perhaps had been somebody from either the world of sport or possibly even the underworld, two things about which she knew absolutely nothing at all and cared even less.

As soon as the service began she found herself quickly able to reject the notion that the subject might have been a gangster, thanks to the innumerable references to scoring the goal of ambition, playing the game of life, and passing on to what was – it was to be devoutly hoped – the final round of a long and distinguished cup tie. All too ghastly for words, Constance decided, but sitting as she was in the very centre of her pew, hemmed in by both gentlemen and ladies carrying considerably more weight than she, she was quite unable to slip away early without causing offence. So she had to sit through what turned out to be a long and extremely tiresome service, with terrible hymns and embarrassing eulogies. As she listened to a large red-faced man in a shiny suit telling singularly unfunny anecdotes about the dead sportsman, Constance decided that, given the nature of a memorial service, in order to avoid total boredom at least a rudimentary knowledge of the deceased was an absolute necessity.

Finally the service began to draw to a close

with 'I Vow to Thee My Country', a hymn that Constance at least knew and could sing. As she did so, she heard a rather fine tenor giving out right behind her, so, when able, she took a discreet peep to see who owned the fine, well-modulated, upper-class voice, hoping as always to see herself staring into the eyes of some handsome grey-haired patrician gentleman with whom she would at the earliest opportunity find something or perhaps even someone in common. Instead she found herself looking at the tall, slim, well-dressed figure of early-middle-aged Grenville Fielding.

'I think we know each other, but from where?' Constance asked at the end of the service, when she found herself lined up in the aisle beside Grenville as they queued to leave the church.

'Ah, yes – well, we live in the same square, Lady Frimley,' Grenville replied, having recognised her immediately. 'You walk your dogs in the gardens, and we have met once or twice at various things – last December, for instance, at the Belvilles' drinks party. They always have such a good party on the Sunday before Christmas, don't you think?'

'Oh, the Belvilles. It was there, was it? How interesting. They're in Eaton Square, of course. I know. And I think you shared my cab back, did you not?'

Grenville smiled politely, although the way he remembered it, it was the other way round, with Lady Frimley getting into the cab he had called, and sitting herself down even before she had asked him in which direction he might be headed, simply announcing that *they would share the cab*.

'Very interesting service,' he heard Lady Frimley continue. 'A close friend?'

'An acquaintance,' Grenville replied. 'I looked after his affairs for a while.'

'I am a complete dunce when it comes to sport.' Constance sighed. 'I don't even do the pools. Does anyone these days, I wonder?'

'Oh, I'm sure,' Grenville said, looking to see if he could spot a fast path out. 'Oop north and that. Old habits, right?'

'He was some sort of footballer, this chap, wasn't he?'

'Indeed.' Grenville nodded. 'Quite a famous one, as it happens.'

'Do you watch football?'

'No. No, it's not *actually* my game, Lady Frimley. Ours was purely a business relationship.'

They were now almost at the book of condolence, a landmark after which, Grenville knew, he could find freedom.

'On to the reception, Grenville?' someone asked from one side of them.

'Thought I'd opt out actually, Charles,' Grenville replied. 'Not really being a *familiar*. Thought I might stroll along to Claridges, and avail myself of one of their excellent dry martinis.'

'My thoughts exactly.' Constance seized the moment and turned to him with a smile. 'Why don't we stroll along there together?'

*   *   *

Constance drank champagne, while Grenville slowly sipped his cocktail, making it last as long as he could. He had already guessed who would be picking up the bill, and he wasn't sure how quickly he would be able to escape.

'Interesting title, yours, if I may say so.'

'An old title, *and* an interesting one,' Constance murmured, looking at him a little more closely now over her champagne flute and wondering as to his sexuality. Were he some twenty or so years older he really would have made the ideal walker. Nicely mannered without being too smooth, good-looking enough but not in a gigolo way, and well dressed without being a peacock. He also looked at people when they were speaking as well as apparently listening to them, appeared to mean what he said, laughed without showing all his teeth, or his gums; altogether he was very what the French called *comme il faut*. 'It wasn't always Frimley,' she continued. 'That is the modern appellation.'

'I always thought Frimley was a town in Surrey,' Grenville said. 'I never knew there was a title.'

'It has nothing to do with Frimley as in Frimley, Surrey. People always make that mistake. It is a medieval title, as I understand it, originally of course spelt entirely differently.'

Taken aback by this apparent non-sequitur, Grenville decided to let it pass.

'The title *hove* from a husband, obviously?'

'Certainly.' Constance sighed. 'It certainly *hove*

all right. Some earldom or other granted during the Barons' Revolt way back when. Long before things began to matter.' She smiled. It was still the smile of a great beauty, which she had indeed once been, and she hoped this was a fact that her new friend appreciated.

'You are having another?' she quickly observed as Grenville summoned a waiter to their table. 'Thank you, then so shall I, thank you.' She nodded at her now empty glass and then at the waiter, while Grenville picked up the order of service he had put down and tapped it on the table.

'I suppose you go to quite a few of these things,' he said, having decided on a change of subject from titles.

'One sees so many very attractive men at memorial services,' Constance replied. 'I do so prefer my men to be grey. They look *so* much more distinguished. Although there were perhaps rather fewer such gentlemen there today, alas.'

As fresh drinks arrived, Grenville once again searched for a safe subject, and found one.

'And how long have you lived in our square, Lady Frimley? It is the most charming location, do you not agree?'

'Our square?' Constance repeated. 'Whose square?'

'I see you walk your dogs in the garden.'

'They are not actually my dogs.'

'But you have a key to the garden.'

'I do have a key to the garden,' Constance agreed. 'The dogs too are residents.'

In spite of another conversational impasse, Grenville managed to smile politely and sip his cocktail, wondering which of them was going to make the first move to leave.

Moments later Charles Danby, the acquaintance who had first hailed him at the service, appeared with drink in hand.

'Ah, Grenville, excellent,' he said. 'I was looking for someone to drink with. Mind if I?'

'Oh. No. No, not at all, Charles,' Grenville said, half rising and immediately and thankfully effecting introductions.

'Are you going to Sandown tomorrow, Grenville?' Charles wondered, after the initial small talk was over. 'It's the opening meeting of the new NH season and my bro-in-law, who trains, as you probably know – he's got a runner. Says he rather fancies its chances.'

'That sounds fun,' Grenville replied. 'First place I ever went racing, you know. Because of course the family home's in Esher.'

'I adore Sandown,' Constance sighed. 'I haven't been there for centuries, but I *have* always simply loved it. I know! Why don't we all go?'

'You don't have to if you don't want to, Allie love,' Millie was saying in a vague voice, turning back from the stove to where Alice was sitting at the kitchen table chopping carrots into neat julienne slices. 'I'll quite understand if you'd rather not.'

131

Carefully side-stepping round not one but five dog dishes of varying sizes, she went to a kitchen cupboard to take out some wine glasses, while from his perch Excelsior, her parrot, made a cracking sound with one of his new satisfactorily overlarge nuts, a bag of which had been a gift from Alice.

'Of course I'd like to,' Alice stated, trying to make the best of a somewhat ancient and wrinkled carrot. 'Why wouldn't I want to?'

She had no absolute idea as to what Millie was actually talking about, but since she rarely did she generally found it best to agree to whatever was being suggested, before Millie forgot what it was that she had proposed. It was their own particular way of going on, and had been for years and years.

'And by the way, you're looking better than ever.'

'Thank you,' Alice replied. 'But I still feel quite tired. In fact this morning when I looked in the mirror I thought I looked so exhausted that . . . well. I think it's when you stop everything that you feel at your most drained.'

'Children are very demanding, duck. Particularly old children.'

'It's really so good to be here, and for you to have me to stay, Millie. I can't thank you enough.'

'Stay as long as you like. It'll do us both nothing but good.'

'How does that poem go? Not waving but drowning? I've been treading water.'

'It's all right, you're out of the water now – and do get out of the way, Simpkin,' Millie grumbled, stepping round a tabby cat who was sitting washing itself on the kitchen floor. 'I'll break my neck tripping over you one of these days.'

'It was my fault really,' Alice continued. 'After Alex died, I had the blinkers on. Charged about like the famous bull in a china shop – so what I got was what I well and truly deserved.'

'You sound like my mother,' Millie laughed. 'After I lost Douglas she was always saying, *You people nowadays – you don't observe the mourning periods properly. Mark my words, you're only storing up trouble for yourselves.*'

'Well, she was right in her way,' Alice replied. 'I know mourning *is* old hat, and the Victorians *did* take it too far, et cetera. But there *was* a sort of sense to it all. A period of mourning *is* sensible. It's not just out of respect to the person you've lost – it's out of respect for yourself and your *own* feelings. Nowadays everyone thinks you should be up and running within a couple of weeks of the funeral.'

'You're absolutely right, of course. As always.'

'It all changed with the First World War when the losses were so huge and came so quickly, there was literally no *time* for mourning. So all the old customs were thrown to the wind, and then when the Second World War came, well – same old, same old, really. Only worse. War isn't just about loss of life, though God knows that's horrific enough,' Alice continued. 'You lose so much more as well, as our parents did; and yet our generation always seems so cheerful. Despite the war and rationing and all that austerity, and bringing up our children with next to no money, as well as looking after our husbands full time, with no time off for good behaviour.'

Millie was about to reply when the parrot interrupted her.

'Hello, sailor!'

'Shut up, you, or I'll turn you into an oven glove,' Millie grumbled. 'Anyway – to get back to what we were talking about. What *were* we talking about?'

'You were saying something about my not having to do something or other,' Alice replied. 'Though don't ask me what it was.'

'Oh, yes. I just wondered if you'd like to come racing tomorrow,' Millie said, removing a cheese sauce from the stove and pouring it over the chopped chicken and ham, before sprinkling it with grated cheese.

'Racing?' Alice frowned. '*Racing?*'

'It's perfectly legal,' Millie reassured her, straight-faced. 'Truly, a lot of respectable people do it.'

'I really know absolutely *nothing* about horses.'

'That goes for most people who go racing, sweetie. Particularly the trainers. Actually, that's why I'm going tomorrow. The Dear Departed had this rather useless horse with this very nice trainer. They were army bods together – and after the Dear Departed handed in his dinner plate I was going to sell said horse, but Anthony, the trainer, offered to keep the horse in the yard at *prix d'ami* which was jolly fair of him. Anyway, said horse is running tomorrow, at Sandown Park of all places. He usually runs at places like Catterick and Newton Abbot, so I just thought it might be a bit of fun. For us both.'

'I really don't know a thing *about* racing, Millie. I'll say all the wrong things, and do all the wrong things, and generally make an ass of myself.'

Millie laughed. 'You don't have to pass an exam at the gate, duck. No one's going to ask you testing questions – such as where would you find a fetlock, or what's the difference between a standing and a running martingale, et cetera. It's not like the Pony Club. There are no tests, and you don't have to go to camp. Besides, I'll tell you all you need to know – *and* introduce you to the excitement of the Tote Double and the Dual Forecast.'

'Heavens above,' Alice said solemnly. 'And to think I was hoping that you might be about to start trying to lead Sam and me astray.'

'Listen up, sugar plum – the Tote Double can lead a nun astray.'

Chapter Seven

A Day at the Races

The following day was bright and dry, with a freshly raised zephyr changing the going on the racecourse from good to soft to good. As always there was a large crowd for this particular meeting, a mixture of visitors from the country and the regular racegoers.

As soon as they arrived Alice found her spirits rising, charmed by the setting of the lovely Surrey course, so well laid out in parkland that it provided possibly the best viewing anywhere in the country. Here was something altogether new and different. Walking from the car park to the course, as the mix of colours and the constant flow of people became a heady kaleidoscope of ever-changing patterns, Alice realised she had quite lost her feeling of being more than a little grey around the gills – or perhaps, almost shockingly, she realised just how grey about the gills she had actually become. Here, she realised, she was stepping into a shower of experiences that promised, over just a few hours, to make her a part of something both exciting and risky.

'Is this right?' Alice asked as Millie headed them towards the members' enclosure. 'I'm not a member, for a start.'

'If you have a runner you get free admission,' Millie explained, picking up her complimentary tickets. 'And I have a runner, remember?'

'This *is* going to be fun,' Alice decided.

'If you can still recognise fun,' Millie agreed, picking up on it. 'You've spent so much of your life making sure everyone else was all right, I bet you've quite forgotten what you actually like.'

'All too true, I'm afraid, Millie. I seem to have fallen right out of touch with myself.'

They had arrived at the rails and were watching the horses being led round.

'Goodness, aren't they a picture?'

'They'll look even more of a picture when you see your pick running up the hill clear of the rest of the field, with your quid about to become twenty.' Millie laughed. 'While on the other hand . . .'

'If the one you picked is trailing in last . . .' Alice said.

'Now looks like a dog, and you can't understand why you liked it. So, no taste in nothing as they say, sweetie, and racing's no fun without a little flutter, so what's your pick of the paddock?'

'I wouldn't know where to begin. Will you help me?'

'Of course.' Millie opened her racecard. 'First race, drop a finger, look at a name you like. Anything's as good as anything else when the sun shines.'

Alice hesitated before she even began to consult her own card. She hesitated because of the money she had been foolish enough to advance to Christian on the way down, and the cheque she had recently handed over to Georgina to help with the children. She hesitated as she thought of the gas bill, the rates, her weekly household expenses; and the more she thought the more she realised that the very last thing she could afford to do was to lose money on a horse, however small the sum.

And yet a second later she thought, *What the heck? This is not a race for the faint-hearted, and this is a one way ticket to ride. Above all, just remember – it's the soul afraid of dying who doesn't want to dance. So do it. Better to do something than to stay grey at the gills. What was it Alexander used to say – yes, 'Follow your bliss.'*

'Yes, of course,' she suddenly said a little too loudly, making Millie turn and stare at her. 'You bet I'm going to have a bet, or else – else I'll never be able. Of course I must have a bet, or else I shall never be able to face myself in the mirror again. OK – so what do we do? Lead on, Mrs McDuff.'

'God forbid a name such as that,' Millie sighed. 'I could not imagine being a Mrs McDuff, could you?'

'I'm beginning to imagine all sorts of things,

Millie, do you know that? Up to and including winning this famous Tote Double thing.'

'You've got a little time yet, sweetie,' Millie informed her, steering her friend towards the Tote. 'First what you are going to do here is buy a ticket for however much you want to put on the horse – or horses – of your choosing. You can back them to win, or come into a place, or both. And the very best of British. I know what I'm going on.'

While Millie bought her tickets, Alice played eenie-meenie-minie-mo with the runners in the first race, coming up finally with two horses.

'You can back them separately, as I told you,' Millie informed her. 'Which I should do, seeing they're both decent prices – in fact why not do a forecast?'

'A forecast?'

'A dual forecast, for them to come first or second, in either order. One never knows, does one?'

Alice duly followed Millie's recommendations even though she was still not sure what they meant, then went up into the stand to watch the race – or rather not to watch it.

'I can't bear it,' she said from behind hands shielding her eyes. 'I didn't know they were going to jump things.'

'Yours is ahead!' Millie yelled at her over the increasing din. 'Yours is only leading – and your other one too!'

'They can't both be ahead,' Alice replied, still not daring to look.

'Oh yes they can!' Millie screeched. 'In fact

they're first and second! Oh my God! You have only got the first and the second!'

'What does that mean?'

'You had a forecast, yes?' Millie laughed, waving the tickets in Alice's astonished face. 'The winner was ten to one, and the second sixteen to one, so chances are you are going to be one rich bunny! Come on!'

Grabbing Alice's hand Millie tugged her all the way down the grandstand steps and back to the Tote, this time to the Pay window, where once the winner was weighed in the announcer declared the Tote dividends.

'What?' Alice cried in astonishment. 'That isn't me, is it? I can't have won that sort of money!'

But she had. The Tote paid out handsomely on the two long-priced horses, particularly when coupled in a forecast, which was how Alice found herself staggering away from the window with nearly two hundred and twenty-five pounds in her wallet.

'But how come it's this much?' she asked Millie in amazement. 'Really? You only put on – what? Two pounds or something for me, didn't you?'

'Two pounds fifty to be exact, duck. One pound to win on horse number seven, fifty pence each way horse number ten, and a one pound forecast the two.'

'Yes, but two hundred and twenty-four pounds?'

'The Tote's not the same as the bookies,' Millie explained in a patient voice, leading Alice off to a nearby members' bar and ordering them both whisky and ginger ales. 'All the money goes into a pool and you get paid out according to how many tickets were on what horse, et cetera. Obviously a lot of people didn't have horses seven and ten in a forecast, because that alone paid out over a hundred and fifty pounds.'

'I still don't understand,' Alice objected, trying to work out how she could possibly have come to win so much money for such a small outlay. 'Are you absolutely sure they've got this right?'

'Absolutely!' Millie laughed. 'In fact I'm so sure, you're going to buy the next round – while we choose the object of your next betting coup!'

Alice won again, this time at fourteen to one.

'I don't think I should bet any more today, actually,' she muttered after she had walked away from the Pay window clutching yet another handful of ten pound notes. 'What do they say? Always stop when you're ahead.'

'Nonsense,' Millie retorted. 'What sort of stuff are you made of, Mrs Dixon? You have the winning touch today, so to stop now would make the gods angry.'

'Seriously, Millie—'

'You can't lose, honey! If you keep betting only a couple of quid on each race as you've been doing, you're still going to come out way on top – so live a little! You're having fun, aren't you?'

'Well – yes. Yes, I suppose I am really,' Alice admitted. 'Yes, I am.'

'So go for it, as they say, sweetie. And have

some more! Now I promised Rory I'd meet him at the saddling-up boxes, and since I have no idea where they are – why don't we ask that chap over there?'

Having been directed to an area adjacent to the paddock proper Millie soon found Rory Rawlins on his way to saddle up his runner. With little or no knowledge of what trainers looked like, other than a very occasional glimpse of one on television, Alice had formed the image of a red-faced middle-aged man dressed in tweeds and one of those heavy military-type overcoats. Instead she found herself being introduced to a young man who had more the look of a scholar or even an artist about him than of a racehorse trainer, a tall, slender, thoughtful and handsome young man, his dark hair worn at a length that showed under the baker's boy tweed cap he sported – instead of the sorts of battered brown trilbies worn by most of the other trainers around them – and his faded tweed coat cut with a decidedly dashing look to it. All in all, Alice decided, if she was going to use one word to describe Rory Rawlins it would be Florentine, and only the fact that he carried a saddle cloth and a racing saddle over his arm, and had a large, old-fashioned pair of racing binoculars slung over one shoulder, suggested what his profession might actually be.

As Millie introduced Alice he nodded at her, and put the saddle and number cloth down on the ground by the corner of an empty box. Then he turned to look at the rugged up horses who were being led round the pre-parade ring by their lads and lasses.

'He's got a bit of a chance at the weights,' he told Millie, his eyes running over the horse. 'Probably best chance he'll ever have. If he's ever going to win, or go close, today might actually be the day.'

'The sooner the better,' Millie replied. 'Otherwise we'll have to change his name to Also Ran.'

'As it happens,' Rory continued, as the horse walked past them for a second time, 'he did a decent piece of work a couple of days ago. Galloped all over Goldenhawk who'd run a horse called Makeshift to a short head at Ascot a week before, and Makeshift's a decent sort of horse. So you never know. Funnier things have happened. And if you're in the betting mood, girls, Harry Jenks's horse is meant to go close in the next, but don't go putting all the housekeeping on it. Might be worth a bit each way. I'll see you in the paddock proper in about twenty minutes.'

Harry Jenks's horse did not in fact win. Under a sterling ride by the amateur Mr Theodore 'Tog' Ogilvy, it just failed to catch the Queen Mother's horse at the post, the two horses battling it out up the famous Sandown hill.

'I followed the trainer,' Millie sighed, tearing up her Tote ticket. 'Idiot that I am. How about you?'

Alice managed to look embarrassed. 'I don't know.'

'What do you mean, you don't know, love? What did you back?'

'I think I might have backed the winner.'

Alice showed Millie her ticket.

'Another winner?' Millie exclaimed, her eyes widening to their maximum as she looked at the ticket and heard the result and starting prices being announced.

'And I put five pounds on it this time.'

'You've not only got another winner, duck, but another long price one! Ten to one? What is it about you today? Come on, let's go and see how much the Tote are paying out.'

The Tote paid out odds of nearly fifteen to one, so for her five pound bet Alice got a few pence short of seventy-five pounds. Millie shook her head and laughed so much when she saw Alice's expression as she collected her winnings that several racegoers stopped momentarily to stare at the sight of two middle-aged women beside themselves with laughter.

'The gods of punting are smiling on you, Alice Dixon – they really are,' Millie avowed as they walked to the unsaddling enclosure so they could watch the horses coming in. They stood by the white rails in front of the weighing room, admiring the winner and the two runners up, the steam rising off them, their mouths flecked with white, their flared nostrils reddened and dilating while their lads expertly swung sweat sheets over their heaving frames, as the jockeys, having already unfastened their saddles, girths and weight cloths and swung them over one arm, tipped their caps to their connections and hurried off to weigh in.

'Time to go and see our horse,' Millie announced as the unsaddling enclosure emptied of people. 'See if they managed to screw all four legs on in the right order, for once.'

Even to Alice's unschooled eyes Millie's horse was an unprepossessing animal, what would professionally be described as a lightly furnished chestnut with big floppy ears and an odd uneven gait.

'That's called stringhalt,' Millie explained as they walked into the middle of the paddock, a space reserved only for owners, trainers and officials. 'Funnily enough once he's cantering it disappears so it doesn't affect his racing prowess at all. Prowess? What am I talking about? Anyway, as a last resort Rory's running him in blinkers for the first time. Not that apparently he particularly believes in the *shades*, as they call them. But you know – any port in a storm.'

'I feel rather self-conscious standing in here,' Alice muttered. 'I mean, I don't really have any business being here at all.'

'Nobody'll notice you, honey,' Millie reassured her. 'They're all too busy pretending to look at the horses, but as everyone in racing knows, all they really talk about here in the ring is who did what, when and with whom.'

Rory arrived, looking nervously round at the opposition with an expression of near doom.

'Cheer up, Rory,' Millie said. 'Silly old horse has got his donkey look on, which usually means he's at the races, doesn't it?'

'At the races?' Alice frowned. 'So where else would he be?'

Rory smiled at her bewilderment.

'*Façon de parler*, Mrs Dixon,' he said. 'Racing jargon. Means he's feeling fit and ready to go.'

'Think he's got an each way chance, Rory?' Millie wondered.

'Don't see why not,' Rory replied, before departing to leg up an over-tall jockey who was standing by the horse, tapping his leg nervously with his whip. 'As I said, he'll never have a better chance. But don't put the mortgage on him.'

Yet in spite of his professed caution, and most unusually for him, Rory himself had placed a large bet to win only, a wager he could really ill afford given not only his own financial position but also the family situation. He knew that should anything happen to his father he would need every penny he had in order just to keep afloat, yet he had placed the largest bet he had ever made on a horse that had always been considered by everyone concerned as a no-hoper. But Rory had somehow convinced himself, the way those who back horses so often do, that the information he had as to how the horse had worked and how well he was in at the weights was enough to all but guarantee the animal's not only coming in first but easing up and still being, as they say, on the bridle. What he really couldn't afford to do, other than actually place the bet, was contemplate losing.

Despite her intention to stop when she was ahead, once again Alice found herself in the Tote queue behind Millie, who was about to put ten pounds to win and ten to place on her late husband's horse, currently at sixteen to one on the Tote.

'What does IRE mean? By the horse's name?' she asked Millie.

'Means that it was bred in Ireland. Or by an Irish stallion.' She looked down at her racecard. 'You fancy number thirteen, do you? The Gossoon? Didn't you see it in the paddock? It's about the size of a milk pony.'

'Does that matter?'

'It'd be better off running at the dog track.'

But Alice wasn't deterred. For some reason or other – and she knew not either – she had quite fancied the burly little horse, so instead of following Millie's example she put her twenty pounds on number thirteen. Then she hurried off to join Millie and Rory on the lawn in front of the stands.

It was a fierce gallop from the off, which made Millie groan.

'Too fast too soon,' she said. 'Always the way in these handicap hurdles. Particularly when Mr Pope has a runner.'

'The difference between hurdles and fences being?' Alice asked, needing reminding.

'Hurdles are much smaller than fences and you can knock them over,' Millie replied, still watching the race through her binoculars. 'Although it's not particularly advisable. But you can do and get away with it.'

'They really are going awfully fast,' Alice observed as the field thundered past them for the first time. 'I never realised they went that fast.'

'Our chap's pulling the jock's arms out,' Millie muttered. 'He's taken a hell of a hold, Rory.'

'He's all right,' Rory muttered from behind them. Too nervous to watch the race, he was staring up at the sky and following what was happening via the commentary. 'It's OK – he likes to front-run.'

And so indeed it seemed, since as they headed for the hill and for home with only two hurdles to jump, their horse Trojan Jack was a good ten lengths clear of the field and still going strong, while the rest of the runners behind had wilted, as was obvious from the desperate thrashing of whips and kicking from their beaten jockeys. The only danger was The Gossoon, who was still on the bridle, going easily, and in between the two last hurdles now starting to mount a challenge.

'Come on, Trojan Jack!' Millie urged, finding herself suddenly in full voice as she realised her horse was probably going to win. 'Come on, our lovely boy! *Come on!*'

Torn between shouting for her friend's horse and the horse moving up so smoothly on the outside, Alice chose instead to keep quiet and watch, which was more than Rory could do. Hearing what he could not believe and then seeing it, he had now turned his back completely

148

on the action, closed his eyes and put his head in his hands.

'Come on, Trojan, my love!' Millie was shouting. 'For God's sake, horse! Come on! *Come on!*'

But it seemed that The Gossoon might have him, so easily was he going, his jockey not having had to make a move other than give one shake of the reins. Coming to the last Trojan Jack was still two lengths to the good, but with the Sandown hill still to contend with the little dark bay had him, and that was for sure, even to Alice's inexperienced eye.

'Come on, The Gossoon,' she said quietly to herself, quite unable to believe her luck. '*Come on.*'

The race was the little dark horse's bar a fall until his idiotic jockey tried to organise him at the last hurdle, shortening up and kicking him into a stride. Consequently the animal half checked, put down, and hit the hurdle hard. Thanks to the blinkers Trojan Jack had been unaware of the horse that had been mounting such a challenge to him, although he must have sensed that he had a fight on his hands, because he stood well off the last hurdle and flew it as consummately as he had flown every previous one, landing running and pulling a good five to six lengths clear of The Gossoon who, although now clearly beaten, somehow remained on his feet.

'He's won, Rory!' Millie shouted, turning to her trainer, who still had his head in his hands. 'You've only gone and done it! He's only gone and blasted well won!'

Rory put up his glasses at last, just in time to see his horse gallop past the winning post with The Gossoon four lengths behind in second.

'I don't believe it,' he said, pushing his cap to the back of his head. 'I just do not Christmas Eve it.'

Millie turned and threw her arms round her trainer's neck and kissed him on both cheeks, while for the first time in what seemed to him to be a very, very long time Rory found himself smiling.

'Amazing,' he said quietly. 'Amazing. Well, well, well.'

'Well done, well done indeed,' Alice said, putting her hand out to shake his. 'What a very good race. Really well done.'

'Thank you,' Rory replied. 'Thank you very much.'

Alice smiled at him, then looked out on to the track where a couple of officials had gathered just by the winning post. She pointed towards it with her hired binoculars.

'I don't suppose it matters that something dropped off just before the post, does it?'

Rory stared at her, hoping he had not heard right.

'Dropped off what?' he asked anxiously. 'Off what? Dropped off the horse? My horse?'

'Yes. I thought I saw something drop off him just there.' Alice pointed to where the two officials were standing, one of them holding something that the other was inspecting.

'Looks as if a weight cloth just dropped off some-one, Rory,' a fellow trainer said, as he began to leave the stands. 'Hope it's not yours, dear boy.'

'And if it is our weight cloth, Rory?' Millie asked, faintly, even though she already knew the answer.

Rory didn't reply. He had his race glasses up again, observing in close-up as one of the two men now held up what was quite clearly a weight cloth for another official who was hurrying to the scene to see.

'It's a weight cloth all right,' Rory muttered, putting his glasses down. 'And I have a terrible feeling that it's Jack's.'

'What difference should that make, Millie? I don't understand,' Alice wondered as Rory hurried off to the unsaddling enclosure. 'Your horse won fair and square, surely?'

'If his weight cloth fell off I think the rule is that the horse didn't finish with the correct weight, which means Jack will be disqualified.'

'Even though he was first past the post?'

'That's the rule, duck,' Millie replied, looking tight-lipped and starting after Rory. 'I'm very much afraid.'

The result was announced over the tannoy. Trojan Jack was disqualified for failing to finish the race with his correct weight which meant that The Gossoon was automatically promoted to the winning spot.

'Oh, that really is terrible luck,' Alice sym-pathised, taking Millie by the arm. 'Come on, let me buy you a very large double something or other.'

'One man's bad luck,' Millie said resignedly. 'It means you won.'

'Oh.' Alice stopped and thought for a moment. 'You mean the horse I backed – The Gossoon? I see what you mean. Yes, of course, I see what you mean.'

'How much did you have on it?'

'Twenty pounds. I think. Ten to win, ten to place.'

'And this from the girl who wasn't going to bet.'

'I'd far, far rather you'd won,' Alice said, pulling a face. 'Talk about turning to dust in your mouth.'

Millie shrugged her shoulders. 'That's racing, Allie. Come on – let's go and collect your winnings and have that double something or other.'

They walked off to the Tote window, and Alice began to search through her chaotic handbag for her purse. 'I don't believe it,' she said. 'I think I've lost the ticket.'

'You can't have done. What about your jacket pockets?'

More searching revealed no winning ticket, just as the results of the dividend were being announced over the tannoy.

'What can I have done with it?'

'Maybe you dropped it,' Millie replied. 'If so, we are going to have to find it. Did you hear what they're paying out? Eleven to one your horse! So we are going to have to find that ticket.'

Millie marched Alice back over the way they had come, retracing their steps up to the place on the lawn where they had watched the race. Alice looked about her at the sea of dropped tickets. 'You'll never find it, Millie. Not in a month of whatevers.'

Millie looked up at her. 'I might not. But you and I might, so you do the lawn while I look on the steps here.'

Reluctantly Alice began sorting through the discarded litter that lay on the grass while Millie started sifting through the trash lying on the steps. As they searched, they were observed by a couple of older gentlemen racegoers who stopped to watch.

'I'll say this for Sandown,' one of them remarked. 'It attracts an altogether better class of bag woman.'

'Thanks for that,' Millie muttered. 'That's all we need.'

'Got it!' Alice suddenly cried.

'You sure?'

'Absolutely. Look!' Alice waved the winning ticket from the lawn. 'It must have dropped out of my handbag when I got a hankie to clean my binoculars.'

After they had walked away from the Tote window, with Alice stuffing into her already packed handbag another large wad of money, they went looking for Rory. They eventually ran him to earth in the trainers' and owners' bar, standing up in the corner staring darkly into a very empty glass.

'Cheer up, Rory,' Millie said. 'It wasn't your fault.'

'Kind of you to say, but of course it was my fault. I saddled him up.'

'Was that what it was? A saddling-up error?'

'The jockey insisted on using his own numnah.'

'That's the thing that goes under the saddle,' Millie explained to Alice.

'I saw it,' Alice returned. 'That sheepskin thing.'

'It shouldn't have been,' Rory said. 'Should have just been a cloth, but Dennis had a fall yesterday and hurt his – whatever that bone is at the bottom of your spine.'

'Coccyx,' Alice said helpfully. 'Least I think that's what it's called.'

'If only,' Rory sighed. 'I shouldn't have let him – then the bloody saddle wouldn't have slipped. And et cetera.' He raised his eyebrows helplessly, which made him look even more tragic, and to Alice even more Florentine. She felt like taking him into her arms and giving him a hug, and then remembered her age.

'Did you have a bet, Rory?' Millie asked, as Alice disappeared to order some drinks.

'Better not go there, Millie,' Rory replied. 'Don't go anywhere near there.'

'OK.' Millie grinned, nodding in Alice's direction. 'But if you need a loan, ask Mrs Midas. She's hit just about every winner so far. If she goes on like this, she'll be warned off.'

'I'm going to need more than a loan, Millie,'

Rory said. 'I'm going to need a miracle. The yard is in something of a mess.'

Alice returned from the bar carrying a tray with three glasses of champagne.

'Not in celebration,' she said. 'In commiseration.'

Millie looked at her friend and decided that this was very much *not* the person she had brought racing. Gone was what she thought of as Alice's startled rabbit look and in its place was an altogether different person. In fact if Millie hadn't been with her all afternoon she would have sworn that her best friend had just fallen in love.

'What is it they say about champagne?' Alice wondered, setting the glasses in front of them. 'I read it somewhere. About the best time to drink it. I can't remember what it was for the life of me. Any time, that was it. The great thing about champagne is that it can be drunk at any time – for anything.'

'Last glass I'll be having for a while,' Rory muttered. 'Of all the things to happen. Wait till the old man gets to hear.'

'How is he?' Millie asked. 'Is he back with us yet?'

'Sort of,' Rory replied. 'I mean he's come round, thank God, and they don't think there's any – any brain damage or anything. There certainly will be if he gets to hear about my performance today.'

'You're being awfully hard on yourself, if I may say so,' Alice chimed in. 'My husband always maintained there are such things as *accidents*, pure and simple. And that the sooner we recognise that fact the better able we shall be to cope with them. It was an *accident*.'

'You're really very kind, Mrs Dixon.'

'Alice, Mr Rawlins.'

'OK, Alice.' Rory nodded. 'And I'm Rory.'

'I know.' Alice smiled.

'The trouble is I compounded the felony – or accident as you so kindly have it – by placing a rather large bet on the horse, with money I simply do not have.'

'I'm sorry to hear that.'

'I said you'd see him right,' Millie joked.

'Of course,' Alice agreed. 'If you really are a bit stitched, Mr Rawlins – I mean Rory—'

'If the seat were hanging out of my trousers, Alice,' Rory said quickly, 'I wouldn't take a penny.'

'I'm serious.'

'I'm sure you are. And so am I.' Rory smiled at her then took a drink of his champagne. 'Of course you could always buy a horse and put it in training with me.'

'Could I?' Alice's frown deepened.

'That was a joke,' Rory said. 'And not a very gallant one either. Sorry.'

'But I could buy a horse, could I? When we've all stopped joking.'

'You won that much?' Rory laughed. 'Sorry – there I go again.'

'Depends how much a horse costs,' Alice said. 'Anyway. What I have in my handbag isn't all I have.'

'Alice?' said Millie. 'Steady.'

'I'm being serious, Millie,' Alice insisted. 'Anyway, this is your fault. You brought me here, and if you really want to know, other than your poor horse losing so unfairly, I don't think I've had as much fun in – well, actually I don't remember when last I enjoyed myself so much.'

'You're not a regular then?' Rory asked. 'You don't do this – go racing – this isn't something you do?'

'This is my first time on a racecourse. And it certainly won't be my last. I'd love to come and see your stables. That's somewhere else I've never been. A racing yard.'

'There are better yards to see,' Rory replied. 'It might put you off.'

'Nonsense. Perhaps Millie and I – I'm staying with her at the moment.'

'If you really want to,' Rory said. 'But as I said, it's not exactly Lambourn.'

'The Newmarket of jump racing,' Millie explained once more.

'Thank you,' Alice said. 'Actually I think it might be rather fun.'

'Visiting the yard?' Rory said with a frown.

'Having a racehorse,' Alice replied. 'And visiting your yard, of course.'

Before the matter could be taken any further a slim, beautifully if traditionally dressed man stopped by their table, putting a consolatory hand on Rory's shoulder.

'Rory,' Grenville Fielding said. 'I say. *Such*

hard luck, really. Of all the things to happen.'

'That's racing, as they say, Grenville,' Rory said, before introducing the visitor to Alice and Millie.

'Sorr-ee,' Grenville said when he realised everyone's attention was being drawn to one of the people with him. 'Yes. This is – this is a *friend* of mine,' he continued, hoping there was enough uncertainty in his delivery to indicate that the person in question was an acquaintance rather than a bosom buddy. 'Let me introduce you to Lady Frimley.'

Constance looked round from one face to another, and as she did so she had the same pleasurable feeling she experienced standing by a nice, warm fire.

'How do you do?' she said as she shook everyone's hand. 'How very nice.'

When Alice was introduced the two women smiled at each other, Constance because she found herself immediately taken by what she saw as the kindness and honesty in Alice's eyes, and Alice because she found herself privately approving of the older woman's style, pleased that at least some people still bothered to dress up when going out for the day, rather than wearing clothes that made them look as though they were living in what Evie always called a Fifth World country.

'I do like your hat,' she told her, after the introductions. 'I wish more people wore hats nowadays.'

'Some of the men could do without them altogether,' Constance replied, narrowing her eyes.

'That ghastly little man Grenville was talking to—'

'A steward, Lady Frimley,' Grenville interrupted with a helpful smile. 'One of the stewards.'

'Got a hat like a scoutmaster's,' Constance continued. 'Looks like an old pixie.'

'My father had a hat very like that,' Grenville told her. 'Used to actually steam it into that shape.'

'Backed any winners?' Millie enquired. 'Alice here has absolutely emptied the Tote.'

'I only ever bet on the Tote,' Constance replied. 'I cannot abide bookmakers. One thing the French have got right. I used to adore going racing in Deauville. But of course France is no longer the same, one just has to face it. You have to say the Revolution was the worst possible thing for the wretched French, you really do.'

'I did tell her to back The Gossoon,' Grenville informed the company. 'With respect of course, Rory.'

'I couldn't possibly back a horse with such an absurd name,' Constance retorted, now seated and fishing out of her handbag a small cheroot which she lit with a large old-fashioned silver table lighter, also produced from her bag. 'I cannot stand all these foreign names they keep giving these poor creatures.'

'I really thought Trojan Jack ran an absolutely splendid race, Rory,' Grenville said, sitting down beside him. 'And how's your father? Rory's father used to train for mine, do you see?' Grenville continued, enlightening the rest of the company. 'They were in the army together.'

Rory put Grenville in the picture regarding his father's current condition, about which Grenville was immediately considerate and sympathetic, assuring Rory that as soon as Anthony was well enough to receive visitors he would be there.

'Actually though,' Grenville said after a moment of further reflection, 'actually this could be karma, or whatever it is they call it. Seeing you here. Meeting you like this, because I was thinking only the other day I should get myself a racehorse. Now the old man's gone AWOL I rather miss having an interest.'

Rory nodded but said nothing. Much as he would like to sell the donkey that had just arrived from Ireland, given Grenville's family background and racing experience he saw little chance of persuading him it would be just the sort of horse for him. Anyway, even if Grenville Fielding were to visit the yard his eye would hardly be taken by an animal that hadn't eaten an oat since its arrival from the Emerald Isle, a self-imposed starvation diet that was beginning to cause everyone at Fulford Farm a considerable degree of worry.

'So how *are* things at the yard?' Grenville wondered, as Rory finished his drink and began to think about leaving.

'On hold a bit, really.' Rory pocketed his race-card and started winding the strap round his race glasses. 'We're keeping things ticking over, but with my father in hospital and not knowing what sort of recovery he's going to make . . .'

'So not a good time to come and have a look-see then. Got you.'

'There's not exactly a lot to have a look-see at, Grenville.'

'Thought you said earlier about some horse or other you'd just brought over from Ireland,' Millie remarked. 'Didn't you?'

'Did I?' Rory muttered. 'Oh yes, that's right. But there's somebody coming to look at him.'

'Really?' Grenville asked, pricking up his ears. 'Got any form, has he?'

'The person coming to see him? Don't really know.'

'The horse, old chap.'

'Not a lot.'

'Unexposed?'

'Sort of. Now if you'll excuse me . . .' Rory made to get up and take his leave.

'Worth coming to take a look?'

'As I just said, someone else is already interested.'

'Even so,' Grenville smiled. 'If someone's already *interested*, someone else might also be interested. Look – I have to come down west on some business, so why don't I pop in and take a shufti? Nothing ventured as they say, eh?' He produced his pocket diary and consulted it. 'I could in fact come down quite soon, as it happens – this business thing being a movable sort of feast. Why don't I call you when I get back to town – when I've sorted out the old diary? Right?'

'We might see you there,' Alice said with a smile, as she too began to take her leave, prompted by Millie who wanted to watch the last race. 'Millie and I are planning a visit to the stables as well.'

'Then why don't we all make a day of it? I should be charmed,' Grenville said, standing and raising his hat to Millie and Alice. 'I shall liaise with Rory here.'

'Nice man,' Alice remarked as she and Millie returned to the grandstand. 'Lovely manners.'

'I thought the woman with him was his mother,' Millie remarked, putting up her glasses to watch the horses at the start. 'He looks the sort of man who'd take his mother racing.'

'Unlike my son,' Alice said with a wry smile. 'The only place Chris takes me is to the cleaners.'

'They're off,' Millie said. 'Last chance saloon.'

The race was won by yet another long shot, a victory greeted in near silence by the few dogged punters determined to see the end of what had turned out to be an expensive afternoon for backers.

'Don't tell me you had it or I shall scream,' Millie said to Alice, consigning her worthless ticket to the litter bin.

'Not exactly,' Alice replied, looking at the slip in her hand. 'Only on that thing you said I should do.'

'The Tote Double? That's been and gone.'

'Oh. Then what's this?' Alice handed Millie the ticket for her perusal.

'The Tote Treble, duck,' Millie informed her, then widened her eyes. 'You did the Tote Treble?'

'Apparently.'

'And?'

'They all seem to have won.'

There were three winning tickets and the Tote paid out seven hundred and ninety-eight pounds exactly.

Coincidentally Lynne had also been to Sandown races. She had been out shopping first, her newly gained money already burning holes in her pockets, and among other items she had bought she was extremely pleased with the outfit she was wearing, a silk dress in a particularly fashionable Matisse blue, with big shoulder pads, and a wide, tight belt, teamed with a particularly outrageous pair of pink shoes. She also wore a well-cut middle brown suede top coat with a pale cream fur lining, which came to just below the knee and was very flattering. When she got to Sandown Park and remembered that this was a jumps meeting, not a flat one, she immediately buttoned up her coat, and wished she had chosen the sort of sensible racing outfit being sported by the other women racegoers.

Happily, since everyone seemed to be caught up in their own little worlds, Lynne seemed to attract little undue attention. However, one man whose attention she most certainly grabbed was

Rory Rawlins, for the good reason that Lynne quite literally bumped into him as he was backing out of the building she was walking past, his arms full of saddles and bridles. Lynne had been looking round at a couple of young men who had given her the full up and downer. The next thing she knew she had knocked someone flying.

'Oh, God, sorry,' she exclaimed, immediately helping the man she had knocked over to his feet. 'I really am sorry.'

'No, no – my fault entirely,' Rory replied. 'I really should look where other people are going.'

'All your stuff, it's gone everywhere,' Lynne said, picking up some of the spilled tack. 'Oh, I just love the smell of leather. I used to think if I had the money I'd have a tack room just for the *smell*. Actually – what the hell.' She laughed. 'I've got the money now, so who knows!'

'Sorry – I have to go and saddle up a horse,' Rory said, retrieving his racing saddle.

'Right,' Lynne replied, standing up. 'That what you do?'

'In between training horses,' Rory replied. 'Or rather trying to train horses.'

'OK,' Lynne said, nodding. 'I'd heard it was a tough job. A friend of ours – well, that's when there was an *ours* – this bloke we knew was a trainer but he found it so tough he took to burglary.'

'Thanks,' Rory said, having now collected the rest of his tack and standing back up. 'That's just the steer I needed.'

'No, seriously. He lives in a huge villa in Marbella all year round now. So it doesn't have to be all bad.'

By now Rory was taking a good look at the beautiful young woman who had just knocked him for six. She was handing him the last piece of recovered tack, smiling and regarding him with a pair of blue eyes that were quite literally the colour of her dress.

'Got a runner then?' she asked.

'Yes,' he said, feeling himself lightly blushing, which was certainly not a habit of his. 'Trojan Jack in the handicap hurdle.'

'Worth a couple of bob?'

'That's what they tell me.'

'Even though you're the trainer?' Lynne raised two perfectly shaped eyebrows.

'Next to owners, trainers are the last to know anything.'

'Seriously. Should I back him?'

'He's very well,' Rory muttered, hugging his tack to him. 'He could go close.'

'Then I certainly shall back him,' Lynne said. 'And if he wins I shall find you and buy you champagne.'

'Date,' Rory said with a nod to indicate he was on his way.

'Date,' she called after him. 'Good luck!'

When she heard the announcement telling racegoers that Trojan Jack had failed to win his race because of his lost weight cloth, Lynne remembered the handsome young trainer and went in search of him, thinking she might buy him a drink to console him. She saw him in the distance by the unsaddling enclosure, but just as she was about to approach him she saw someone else, too – her now ex-husband Gerry, with one arm draped round her now ex-best friend Maddy's shoulders. As The Gossoon was proclaimed the winner, Gerry punched the air, kissed his mistress, and turned in Lynne's direction. Before he could spot her Lynne took evasive action, hiding herself behind one of the large trees that stood nearby and shifting carefully round its great trunk as Gerry and Maddy crossed close by. When they were past, Lynne trailed a safe distance behind them until she saw where they were headed, then she took her dark glasses out of her handbag and set off in the opposite direction.

She could have kicked herself when she realised how stupid she had been. Why wouldn't she bump into Gerry taking Maddy to the races? After all, they had been racing often enough when they were married, so there was every possibility that he would now take Maddy. Had Lynne been with someone else she might possibly have had enough confidence to see her through the afternoon, regardless of whether or not she bumped into Gerry. But by herself she felt exposed and vulnerable, and yet determined not to be put off. She would not, absolutely would not be scared away. Lonely, friendless, but not scared. Besides, it was becoming a kind of duty to spend

Gerry's money, even lose it, and she proceeded to do so on a procession of horses.

Just before the last race she saw them leaving and breathed a sigh of relief, deciding to treat herself to a drink to celebrate their departure.

Rory passed her going out as she was coming in.

'So there you are,' Lynne said when she saw him, as if she had been spending her time looking for him rather than hiding from her ex-husband. 'That was such tough luck about your horse. Maybe I could buy you that drink I promised, even though for a rather different reason?'

There was nothing Rory would have enjoyed more at that moment than to have a glass of champagne with this particular young woman, but whether he liked it or not he had a job to do.

'Thank you,' he said. 'But I have to see my horse loaded and get him home.'

'Oh,' Lynne said, trying not to let her disappointment show. 'Right. Some other time, perhaps.'

'You bet,' Rory agreed. 'Sorry.'

In two minds whether she should stay or go, Lynne found herself hailed by someone else who recognised her.

'Mrs Fortune?' a voice from across the bar called. 'Mrs Fortune.'

When she turned Grenville Fielding was at her elbow, doffing his brown trilby hat.

'I thought it might be you,' he said. 'Grenville Fielding. I had dinner with you and your husband not long ago. Last year sometime. At Cappelli's, wasn't it? I thought it was you.'

With his hat off Lynne just about remembered him from a rather overlarge dinner Gerry and his business partners had thrown in a restaurant to celebrate some company coup or other.

'Sorry,' she replied with a smile. 'There were rather a lot of people there.'

'I sat next to you,' Grenville reminded her. 'We talked about the house your husband was thinking of buying in Provence.'

'Of course. Sorry. It's just that since the divorce—'

'You've got divorced?' Grenville frowned at her. 'I am *so* sorry. I had no idea.'

'It's OK,' Lynne replied rather too brightly. 'It's not as if someone died.'

'No, I am *so* sorry,' Grenville said again. 'I had no idea.'

'Why should you? Hardly page one stuff.'

'Can I buy you a drink, Mrs Fortune? I'm with some people over here, and we'd be delighted if you joined us.'

Lynne glanced over at the man and woman sitting at the corner table and, seeing no danger, agreed. Grenville introduced her to Constance and to Charles Danby before going off to buy more drinks.

'You look very colourful, my dear,' Constance said, lighting a cheroot. 'That blue doesn't look good on everyone.'

'Thank you,' Lynne replied, pleased at being

complimented by an older woman, particularly one as stylish as Constance. 'I like your hat and all.'

'Of course,' Constance said with a regal smile. 'You're acquainted with Mr Fielding, then.'

'Well – yes and no. He's a friend of my ex – least, I think he is. Business friend, that is.'

'Your ex?' Constance puffed her cheroot. 'You are *divorcée, alors*.'

'You got it.' Lynne nodded. 'Hole in one.'

'It happens to the best of us,' Constance said. 'It happened to me all over the place.'

'Right,' Lynne agreed. 'So let's just hope it might also be the best thing to happen to us.'

'I like that,' Constance replied. 'I think I like you, too.'

The crowd was dispersing fast as Grenville returned to the table bringing glasses of champagne for Lynne and Constance, and gins and tonics for Charles and himself, but before the party broke up he discreetly managed to get Lynne's current telephone number while Constance had disappeared to the loo – as she informed the company with a perfectly straight face – to shed a tear for Lady Hamilton.

Chapter Eight

Irishitis

Kathleen had not been herself since Boyo had gone. A restlessness filled her being, and nothing that would normally give her happiness held much interest for her. Her father and brother seemed too human, and the dog too canine. The sea lacked impact without the image of a horse coming out of it, and the skies, whatever their colour, were merely patchwork pieces above her head when she could not hear the sound of her beloved horse cantering towards her. She knew that they had been too close, as an animal and a human being often can be. His feelings had become her feelings, and she knew before he knew it if he was sick. So now, even in her restlessness, she felt that he was ill, and yet she also had no way of knowing whether she was right. If only they had not had to sell him. If they had had just a little more money they would have been able to keep him, but they were poor and every penny counted, so it was inevitable that every horse born on their little farm would always finally be sold.

If only things had been different, Kathleen would often sigh. If only her mother hadn't died so young – if only her uncle hadn't swindled her father out of his inheritance, which small though it was would have surely been enough to pay for rebuilding the yard. If only, if only. If only her Auntie Aileen had wheels sure she'd be an omnibus, she would scold herself. And sure with a big enough *if* you could even put Dublin in a bottle.

'You're not yourself, girl,' her father chided her one morning when he found her sitting at the table with her chin in her hands, her tea undrunk. 'You're looking as pale as a winding sheet. 'Tis a grand morning, so take out auld Batty Boy for a spin. You like riding auld Batty Boy, so you do.'

'Boyo isn't well, Da,' Kathleen stated, not looking at him.

'Ah, and why shouldn't the horse be well? He's gone to a good enough yard, so why shouldn't he be well? You and that horse. You and your imaginings. We've got enough to deal with here without your imaginings. The horse is fine. So now you go out riding.'

'You know what happens to horses when they leave Ireland, Da. You told me so yourself. They often get sick. I know Boyo's sick.'

'And if he is, there is nothing you can do about it from here, Kathleen. They have veterinaries over there, and men of the stamp of Mr Rawlins look after their horses. If a man pays for a horse himself he'll keep it well, so he will. There's no point otherwise.'

'I'll ride Batty Boy out for you, Da,' Kathleen said, fetching her oilskin coat and taking down her boy's cap. 'But only because there's little point in doing anything else.'

It was a fine and breezy day with the rain keeping well off and a weak autumn sun shining down, the distant hills still blue and the valleys green though the countryside was about to give way to winter, yet even though Batty Boy was as good to ride as ever, striding out strongly with his tail held high behind him and his ears well pricked, Kathleen rode with a heavy heart. She knew her horse was ailing.

Every anxiety ran through her. She could see what might happen. The new owner might become so dismayed by the horse's lethargy he would sell him on. Boyo might find himself in some inferior yard where they would do all manner of things to him in order to get just the one race out of him, so they could recover some of the cost to themselves before selling him on to some rundown riding school, or worse.

'There's only one thing to do, Batty Boy,' she yelled to the horse as she galloped him up the grass track. 'He needs me so I must go to him, God help me!'

After she had mucked out, groomed and fed the horses, she found her brother and told him he must look after everything.

'And what am I to tell Da when he finds you gone?' Liam asked.

'You play the dumb one,' Kathleen replied. 'You're good at that. Put back that old cap of yours, scratch your head and say, *Jesus, Da, I didn't know she'd gone anywhere – but if she's gone at all sure she won't be long for she never is*. Anyway, it's market day tomorrow, which is why I've chosen it. So if he notices it won't be till he's home, and when he's home after market he's always late and always drunk, so the chances are he won't know I'm gone till the day after.'

Kathleen smiled at her brother, kissed him fondly and hurried to her bedroom, where she took a small tin box from inside her mattress. Out of the box she lifted her trousseau money and counted out what she would need for the journey, then returned what was left to the box and the box back to the mattress.

'The bus, the train, the ferry,' she said to herself. 'Then a train again and possibly another bus. Then a bus, a train and the ferry, then a train and then the bus.' She regarded the cash she was holding. 'That'll never be enough – not when you account for refreshments and emergencies.'

She withdrew the box again, took out some more money and stared at it.

'Ah, to hell and high water anyway.' She sighed. 'Might as well be hung for the sheep as well as the lamb. And who cares? If Boyo needs me I most certainly don't.'

* * *

173

The train to Cork was overcrowded, and the ferry to Fishguard full of nuns and people returning to what they liked to call the mainland. Kathleen avoided the bars, and sat with the nuns who, when they heard the reason for her journey, offered prayers to St Francis for her little horse. Then, after another two long and crowded train journeys, first to Bristol then on to Salisbury, and finally a taxi ride, Kathleen finally arrived at Fulford Farm.

'I'm looking for Mr Rawlins,' she informed a curious Teddy, who was leaning on his broom when she walked into the yard. 'Would you know where he might be, please?'

Teddy continued to stare for a moment at the apparition before him. Her clothes might be poor, but he couldn't remember ever seeing a more beautiful girl than the one standing staring at him so solemnly.

'You could try the office, miss,' he finally advised, after a small pause during which he wondered if he had ever seen a greener pair of eyes, or a darker and more lustrous head of hair. 'Shall you wish – that is, shall I take you – I mean, show you?'

'You're so much more than kind,' Kathleen replied, picking up her small suitcase. 'Thank you.'

'It's nothing, miss. Let me carry that for you.' He took her case and with a doff of his flat cap and a quick shy smile he led the way to the guv'nor's office. They found Rory sitting staring into space, having just come off the telephone to his bank manager.

'What is it, Teddy?' he asked, seeing just the lad standing in the doorway. 'Didn't anyone tell you it's rude to interrupt a suicide?'

'There's someone here to see you, Guv,' Teddy replied. 'A young lady.'

'Wouldn't make much difference if it was Julia Roberts, chum,' Rory told him. 'Altogether in the altogether.'

'It isn't she, Mr Rawlins,' a soft voice said from behind Teddy. 'I'm quite fully dressed, too.'

Rory looked up and could hardly believe what he saw.

'Miss Flanagan, isn't it?' he said incredulously. 'Miss Flanagan? Surely not.'

'I should have telephoned you,' Kathleen said, her well-prepared excuse at the ready. 'I would have done too,' she lied, 'had the lines not been blown down in a terrible storm.'

'So, what – what can I do for you?' Rory was almost at a loss for words as he stared at the beautiful young woman standing in front of him. 'What are you doing here?'

'I've come to see the horse,' Kathleen replied. 'That's why I'm here.'

'You – you've come all the way from Ireland just to see your horse?' Rory stammered, finding himself reduced to the helplessness he used to feel as a boy when confronted by pretty girls.

'I have, Mr Rawlins. If you've no objections.'

'Nobody from here – nobody telephoned you,

175

did they?' Rory suddenly remembered the new incumbent's present ill health. He turned to his secretary, who was busy at work in the other corner of the office. 'Maureen—'

'No one has called anyone in Ireland from here, Rory,' she replied. 'At least not to my knowledge.'

'No good looking at me, Guv,' Teddy said. 'I wouldn't know who to ring.'

'And why should they, Mr Rawlins?' Kathleen asked, all innocence. 'Is there something wrong?'

'No,' Rory faltered. 'I mean, yes, but nothing really wrong as in the horse being ill. It's just – it's just he's not eating. We can't get him to eat.'

'Not at all?' Kathleen asked, concerned.

'He's barely gone near his manger for a week. Is he prone to this sort of thing?'

'He never left an oat at home, Mr Rawlins. Always got to the bottom of the pot.'

'The vet can't find anything wrong.'

'He wouldn't. The horse is homesick.'

'Homesick?' Rory repeated in astonishment. 'Did you say – did you say homesick?'

'I did so,' Kathleen assured him. 'Do you find that so astonishing? It happens all the time, bringing horses over here. They call it Irishitis. Or rather you do. We don't. We call it homesickness.'

'Really.' Rory half got up from his seat then sat back down again with a deep frown on his face. 'Really.'

'Horses have feelings, Mr Rawlins. Same as

you and me. I wonder if I could see him? I don't have a lot of time. I'd like to be back home again by tomorrow morning, before my father finds me gone.'

Rory shook his head and frowned even more deeply, utterly thrown by this turn of events.

'I can't b-b-believe you came all this way on a whim. J-j-just to see your horse.'

'It wasn't a whim.'

'Well – what-what-whatever,' Rory said, gritting his teeth and closing his eyes against his suddenly returned stammer, an affliction he had thought he was by now well rid of. 'Yes, of course you can see the horse – your horse. Yes, of c-c-c-course you ker-ker-ker-ker—' He stopped and clicked his finger and thumb together, as taught by his therapist. 'Of course you can,' he said slowly. 'I'll show him to you myself. Not that I think you'll learn much by l-l-l-looking.'

'No, Mr Rawlins,' Kathleen replied. 'But he might learn something be seeing.'

The horse was standing in a back corner of his box, facing the wall as if he was a dunce with a cap on his head. Kathleen watched him for a moment from the door, noting how tucked up he was and out of sorts with himself. After a few seconds, as she knew he would, the little horse turned his head slowly to look at her, which was when Kathleen put her hand over the top of the door and held it out, palm upwards.

'Doubt if that will work. He's been refusing treats all week,' Rory assured her.

'I'm not offering him a treat,' Kathleen replied. 'Just my hand. Just me.' She kept her hand outstretched and the horse returned to staring into the corner.

'This is how he's been for days,' Rory said. 'Won't go near anything or anyone.'

'Boyo?' Kathleen called quietly, then spoke to him in Gaelic. Still the horse didn't move.

'S-see what I mean?' Rory said.

'I think we have to be patient, Mr Rawlins. Really we do.'

A few minutes later the horse slowly swished his tail, after Kathleen had spoken to him some more in Gaelic.

'I don't speak any Gaelic so you'll have to help me out here,' Rory muttered. 'About all I know is Aer Lingus.'

'Sure even if you did, you mightn't know what to say to him. He's far from himself, you can see that. Look. Look into his eyes for yourself now – look at his sadness.'

'His – sadness?' Rory repeated. 'Do horses get sad?'

'And why shouldn't they now?' Kathleen chided him. 'The horse is pining. Perhaps if I could fetch him a fresh feed he might just eat. Particularly if I put some of this Guinness in it. I didn't know whether you would have any so I brought some over with me just in case,' she added, taking a bottle out of her overnight bag. 'Might I use your feed room?'

Rory showed her the way, and she prepared

a mixture exactly to her recipe, adding the Guinness last of all.

'He likes a drop of stout,' Kathleen told Rory, carrying the manger back to the stable. 'He always has, ever since he was a nipper.'

As Rory opened the stable door, for the first time the horse turned right round and came over to greet Kathleen. Kathleen at once put up a hand to touch him and to stroke his neck, and when she did so the horse pricked his ears and shook himself thoroughly, as if awakening from a sleep.

'At least he can still walk,' Rory said. 'He's hardly m-moved for a week.'

'He's a sick horse, Mr Rawlins. Think about it. It's a big thing, leaving the place where you're born, being shoved in a lorry and then on a boat – things you know nothing of, with people and horses not known to you. Wouldn't you expect him to get sick?'

The horse now lowered his head slightly, both eyes watching Kathleen. She put one hand up to pull one of his ears. After a moment he took a deep breath and seemed to sigh. Then he shook himself again, slowly at first, but then faster and faster until it seemed to turn into a full-scale tremor.

'That's better, Boyo. You'll be better now,' Kathleen told him as she walked round him and put his manger in the corner holder. 'So now you be a good boy and eat up every last bit, you hear me? Every bit now.'

'Or else,' Rory said, trying to lighten the mood,

'it's s-straight to bed and no ster-ster – no *story*.'

'You may laugh, Mr Rawlins, but it's not funny really, what they like and don't like,' Kathleen said, coming out of the stable, closing the half-door and bolting it. 'Let's leave him now. He likes to eat in peace.'

Rory frowned again, giving her another away-with-the-fairies look behind her back, yet he did as he was bidden, following Kathleen away from the stable. He couldn't, however, resist a look over his shoulder to see how the horse was doing.

'You shouldn't,' Kathleen warned him. 'You'll put him off, I promise.'

'He's eating.'

'He'd rather be left in peace, really he would. And if it's all the same to you, I wouldn't say no to a cup of tea. I haven't had a thing since I changed at Bristol.'

'I don't know wh-what I was thinking,' Rory said, finding to his dismay not only that he had started stammering again but that the blush he had suffered at Sandown was not a one-off. 'In fact, why don't I get you something to eat? You must be ster-ster-ster—'

'I am,' Kathleen said with a smile. 'Not even half starved. Totally.'

Rory nodded and led the way into the house, where he made not only a cup of tea for both of them but a cooked breakfast of eggs, crisp bacon and fried potatoes for Kathleen. She ate in near total silence.

'If you feed your horses as well as you fed me, won't you be winning everything?' she told him when she had finished, gratefully accepting a second cup of tea.

'Yes, but I'd love to know what really brought you over, Miss Flanagan,' Rory said as Kathleen got up and started to clear away. 'And you can leave that, really you can.'

'I wouldn't hear of it,' Kathleen replied. 'The mess you make you clear. And didn't I tell you? I came over to see the horse.'

'Ber-ber—' Rory stopped and scratched his head. 'Because?'

'You'd laugh if I told you, so I won't. Where do you keep your tea towels, please?'

Rory handed her one automatically, then scratched his head again.

'Did you know something was wrong?' he finally wondered. 'You wouldn't travel all the way over here – you'd her-her – *hardly* come all this way and at great expense just to s-see the horse. Would you?'

'Don't you ever have feelings, Mr Rawlins?' Kathleen wondered, turning round and looking at him directly with the brightest pair of green eyes Rory had ever seen. 'Some people do, you know. They have feelings – and that's exactly what I had.'

'A f-feeling? A pre-pre-premonition?'

'I said you'd laugh.'

'I'm not laughing.'

'You're smiling. The overture to a laugh. Yes

181

I had a feeling Boyo wasn't right, and you can make what you will of it.'

'You could have written,' Rory argued. 'If the telephone lines were down—'

'Which indeed they were,' Kathleen said in quick defence.

'I'm just trying to save you money, Miss Flanagan.'

'It's a little late for that, Mr Rawlins. Anyway, I consider it well spent. And talking of that, I have some trains and boats to catch,' she added, glancing at the kitchen clock.

'I think it was mer-mer-mer—' Rory stopped and snapped finger and thumb behind his back. 'I think it was very good of you to come over. I think it was a terrific thing to do.'

Kathleen looked at him with her head on one side, then nodded.

'Thanks,' she said. 'But you see, if I'd written and say you hadn't written back because you thought the horse just wasn't eating and would get over it—'

'Which he would have done, eventually.'

'You can lose the best part of a season, Mr Rawlins. While a horse – while it acclimatises itself.'

'So it was just as well you came,' Rory agreed. 'I really do believe that.'

'OK. Right. Would you ever run me to the station, please?'

'I'll take you back all the way if you like,' Rory offered. 'To F-Fishguard if you want.'

'That's really kind, thank you, but I have my tickets.'

'Let me at least run you to Bristol. Save you that change at least.'

'OK. Right. Thanks.'

Before he left he put his head round the office door to tell Maureen where he was going.

'If anyone rings,' he added, 'tell them I'll be ber-ber-ber-ber—' He stopped and closed his eyes, waiting for the block to pass. When he opened them he found Maureen frowning at him.

'I know,' he said. 'It's just come back. Don't ask me – I don't know. It'll go away again. I don't know what b-b-b-brought it on. Anyway, tell anyone who rings or c-calls I'll be back in a couple of hours. Say three. OK?'

Maureen agreed. After Rory had gone she glanced out of the window that overlooked the yard and when she saw Kathleen waiting for him, Maureen nodded to herself, taking a pretty good guess as to why Rory's long-absent stammer had so suddenly returned.

'I'm sorry about your mother,' Rory said to Kathleen in the car as they began to talk. 'Must have been very hard, her dying when you were that young.'

'Two's no age to be an orphan,' Kathleen replied, but without an ounce of self-pity. 'No, it was hard on everyone. Particularly the da. My father. They were childhood sweethearts.'

'I thought my father would never get over it

– when my mother died. She died in a train accident eight years ago.'

'Jeeze,' Kathleen said, looking round at him sharply. 'Losing someone like that, in an accident – it's unthinkable. Do you have brothers and sisters?'

'I've a sister,' Rory replied. 'An older sister.'

'Right,' Kathleen agreed. 'But nothing really helps, does it? Not that I'd know, because I don't remember my mother. But my brother does and it hit him hard. And now there's your father lying in hospital—'

'At least he's back with us,' Rory said, stopping at some traffic lights beside a cider factory. 'The der – the *doctors* thought he wasn't going to make it, but then they don't know how tough the old man is. Take more than a couple of heart attacks to see him off.'

He turned and smiled at Kathleen but she wasn't looking at him. She was staring far into the beyond.

'I'll have a Mass said for him when I get back,' she said as Rory moved the car off from the lights.

'That's very good of you. Thanks. Really.'

'Anyway,' Kathleen continued, now giving Rory her full attention. 'We got Boyo eating all right.'

'You did.'

'He'll be fine now,' she assured him. 'Did you see he has the prophet's thumb on him?'

'That impression, you mean, on his neck?'

184

Kathleen nodded. 'You know about the prophet's thumb, right? The prophet was said to have marked all the best horses with his thumb, which is why horses with the prophet's thumb always win. Which they do.'

'As long as they don't stop eating again,' Rory returned.

'He won't,' Kathleen told him. 'Particularly if you put this on – I near as anything forgot.'

She produced a tape from her bag, pushed it into the cassette player and turned it on. Moments later the sound of a lyric Irish tenor filled the car.

'Who's this?' Rory enquired. 'And why?'

"Tis only John McCormack, our most famous tenor. I near as anything forgot to give it you. You're to play him this now—'

'By him I t-take it you mean your horse?'

'Your horse, Mr Rawlins. Yes, you're to play him this,' she continued as factually as if she was telling Rory what food to give him. 'You're to play him this continuously and he'll think he's back at home. My father's forever singing John McCormack in the yard.'

'I suppose I'll be lighting peat fires next.'

'Do you have an Irish lad on the place?'

Rory shook his head but more to stop himself from laughing in delight than in disagreement. 'I've a Welsh one,' he said. 'Think the horse will know the d-d-difference?'

'Don't be silly, with all due respect, of course he will.' Kathleen sighed. 'I'm serious now. Horses are no different from us. They miss the sounds of

185

home as well. So make sure he gets a good daily dose of John McCormack and you won't look backwards again.'

Rory just drove for a while, happy enough to be in Kathleen's company and perfectly content to listen to the music of the greatest Irish tenor of all time.

'If you ever want a job over here,' he finally said when the cassette had finished playing the first side, 'I mean I know you're wanted at home—'

'No, I'm needed there, Mr Rawlins. As you know, we're not exactly overstaffed, and I'm afraid I'd be missed. But thanks for the offer, OK?'

'Well, if anything changes,' Rory concluded, 'you know where we are. And where the horse is.'

'Don't you worry yourself now.' She laughed, tossing back her head of lustrous dark hair. 'I shan't ever be out of touch with Boyo. Not ever.'

They heard the train long before it pulled into the station, heralding its approach like a bad guest arriving full of his own importance. Rory handed Kathleen her overnight case, and, noting how battered and worn it was, realised how much she must have spent to come over and see what might be wrong with the horse. 'Can I give you something towards the cost of your journey?' he asked.

'You most certainly cannot,' Kathleen replied smartly. 'Coming over here was my idea, not yours.'

'I just thought it might help.'

'And there's nothing wrong with the thought so you don't have to look so tragic about it.'

'I'm l-looking tragic?'

'As if you're being sent off to war. Now don't forget the music, and don't forget to give me a call if anything else goes wrong,' Kathleen said as Rory held the carriage door open for her.

'I won't,' Rory assured her. 'And I'm awfully ger-ger – I'm awfully ger-ger-ger—' He stopped, half closed his eyes and clicked a thumb and forefinger.

'Me too,' Kathleen said with a smile which through his half-closed eyes Rory missed seeing. 'I'm awfully glad I came over as well. 'Bye now.'

Then she was gone, disappearing into the rapidly filling train, turning to wave to him once she had found herself a seat by the window, then suddenly remembering something and sliding a window open to beckon to him.

'One other thing,' she said when Rory had hurried to stand below the open window. 'He has a very soft mouth on him, and he won't be hit.'

'Right,' Rory called back. 'I'll remember that.'

'Never.'

'Not once.'

He watched the train leave the station, waving once or twice at the girl who could no longer see him and feeling at long last as if all the hurt had now gone from the past, although on the drive back he wondered if it was just the beginning of yet another heartbreak. He put any such thoughts from his head and instead played the second side of the John McCormack tape, listening to the great tenor singing 'Bless This House' and finding his mind straying straight back across the sea to Ireland.

Chapter Nine

Moving On

Millie had decided for them both. They would keep looking at cottages and small houses until they found something near to Alice's idea of where she might now like to live. In the short time she had been staying Alice had already been taken to see the outsides and some of the insides of near twenty properties, but, as she said, there was always a snag.

'They're either right on a road, just under a huge great pylon, slap bang next to a pub, or next door to a quarry,' she had observed.

'Which is why they're still on the market, and stuck,' Millie had replied. 'It's very difficult to find anything round here because everything nice gets snapped up before it's even advertised. We're just going to have to pray to whoever the patron saint of estate agents is—'

'Croesus, perhaps?'

'—or hope that I hear about something before it hits the market.'

But they drew another blank that morning, finding something very wrong with each of the three properties they viewed. On top of that it was pouring with rain, which made the somewhat down-at-heel cottages look even more dismal as well as helping to compound Alice's belief that this was a wild and miserable goose chase.

'Come on,' she finally urged her friend. 'Take us to that nice pub near you and I'll buy us a cheery lunch.'

'You're on,' Millie replied. 'Then after that I'll drive us over to Rory's. He wants to run Trojan Jack again next week at Wincanton, so we might as well go and see how the old horse is. We promised we'd look in anyway, remember? When we were at Sandown.'

Just as Millie and Alice were disembarking outside the Cross Keys prior to enjoying the excellent lunch that was always available in the pub, Grenville Fielding was also about to eat. He was in the bar of the Wellington, one of his favourite lunchtime haunts, a small but smart hotel tucked away in a side street in Knightsbridge just behind Harrods, a venue that suited him not only because it served one of the best lunches in town, but also because it meant ease of shopping. Being a man, Grenville liked to be able to stroll into a store, buy everything he needed and then stroll off to lunch in the immediate vicinity. He had never been able to understand how women shopped. Pell-mell, rushing from one shop to another, and very often back again, never seeming to have a clue what it was they were meant to be buying.

Grenville's way was always to make a list before going on a shopping trip, often taking the extra precaution of telephoning the store in advance to make sure they had what he wanted in stock. It was only sensible. It saved time. It saved boredom. But women seemed to like to waste time; they even seemed to like boredom. Today, however, he had been too excited to visit any of his usual haunts. He was having lunch with Lynne.

He arrived at the Wellington a little early so that he might enjoy a quiet and private early gin and tonic to settle his nerves. Even as he was sipping from his glass in that rather surreptitious manner that lone drinkers develop, he found himself wondering how he had plucked up the courage to ask such a beautiful young woman out. It seemed to him it was as if he had been propelled by some unknown force. It had never happened before. He had never asked someone he had barely spoken to actually out on a date, as it were. After all, they had hardly exchanged more than a few words at the races, nothing more than the briefest of conversations, and yet within hours of wishing her *au revoir* he had found himself picking up the telephone to ask her out.

'I'm sorry, I don't know what you mean? You want to go on a date?'

'No – no, well yes, at least what I was wondering was whether we might have lunch? Pick up where we left off?' He cleared his throat. 'I could help you with your affairs, perhaps?' he added lamely.

'What sort of affairs?' Lynne had asked him, pretending to be shocked. 'A bit fresh, isn't it? I mean I've only been divorced a couple of minutes.'

'No, look, I'm sorry, that's not exactly what I meant.'

'It's all right. I'm only joking.' She must have guessed how disconcerted he felt, because her next words sounded part maternal and part contrite. 'Of course I would like you to look after my affairs, and have lunch.'

As he put down the receiver Grenville found himself smiling in a way, now he looked back on the moment, he might not have ever smiled before, except perhaps when he was given a bicycle on his sixth birthday. She had accepted his invitation, and he knew he was done for, perhaps for ever.

But now she was late.

He tried not to look at his watch. Of course ladies were always late, and he had half expected she might be, because even with his limited experience with members of the opposite sex he prided himself on spotting the sort of person they might or might not be, and he had certainly marked this particular card down as *perhaps a little disorganised*. So he wasn't surprised. Of course not. He just wished that she would arrive.

He stopped looking at his watch, and settled for staring at the clock behind the bar. She was now nearing his maximum patience point, and that was half an hour late. Half an hour was the very longest time he could be expected to remain waiting for a guest.

He ran through the telephone conversation in his head. She had seemed to have accepted his invitation not only readily but happily, so to have been stood up made him feel not only rejected but dejected. It had meant nothing to her.

Someone arrived by his side. A waiter.

'Mr Fielding? A young lady has just telephoned to send her apologies and to say that unfortunately she will not be able to meet you for lunch.'

'I see. Thank you. Did she happen to say – did she happen to say why?'

'No, sir. She simply asked me to convey her apologies.'

Grenville leafed through his diary, found her number, and went to the public box in the hall to telephone her. He got her answering machine. Without leaving any message he returned to the bar and immediately ordered another gin and tonic.

She had been at the doorway of her flat and just about to leave when the panic had set in. It had been as unexpected as a sudden spasm of pain, hitting her without warning as she was just about to pull the door closed behind her. The next thing Lynne had known, she was sitting trembling in a chair with her head in her hands. Later she would vaguely remember making a telephone call but at that moment she could think of nothing other than trying to control the deep and totally unreasonable fear that had her in its grip. She thought she heard the telephone ringing and her own muffled voice saying something as the answerphone kicked in, but she was totally incapable of getting up to answer it herself. All she knew was that somehow she had to pull herself together and try with all her might to return to her previous state of perfect sanity.

She could recall perfectly standing in front of the full length mirror fixed inside the wardrobe to check how she looked before going out; she remembered looking into her handbag to make sure she had enough money and her door keys; she knew she had taken one last look at herself in the small mirror hanging in the hallway and smiled at herself because she thought that she didn't look at all bad, that in fact she really did actually look on top of it all; but that was all. She couldn't remember with any definition at all what had happened after that, in the moments that had taken her from standing at the door of the flat to sitting in a chair, for some reason frightened out of her wits.

Had someone been outside? Had she seen something dreadful or had someone perhaps threatened her and she had fled, banging the front door behind her and locking herself in for safety? She took her hands from her eyes and stared round the room and then out into the hall-way, where she saw that far from being locked closed the front door was wide open. Lynne sat looking at the open door knowing that she should get up and shut it but unable to move, still petri-fied with fear. *But why*? she wondered. Why was she panic-stricken? Was the person she had seen, this someone who had obviously frightened her, inside the flat? But if so, why was the door still open and why was she free? Surely if someone was attacking her or robbing her they would have shut the door and rendered her helpless, instead of leaving her sitting in a chair with an open door in sight? There seemed to be no sense to it at all, no rhyme, no reason. What could have happened to her in the moments between opening the door and finding herself sitting shaking and nauseous in this chair?

After a long time, a length of time that Lynne couldn't possibly quantify, she found she had come back to her senses, seemingly as suddenly as she had lost them. She knew what had hap-pened – she had panicked. In fact, she thought to herself, I think they even have a name for it now. A panic attack. She'd suffered a panic attack, in exactly the same way as the people she had read about only recently in some paper or magazine or other. She had been on her way out to lunch, something to which she thought she had been looking forward, when all at once she knew she just couldn't go through with it. She remembered standing in the open doorway suddenly feeling sick and dizzy and unable to do anything else except go on standing there feeling sick and dizzy. Someone had walked by her to the lift, a total stranger who Lynne remembered had just stared at her, saying nothing. The woman had kept throwing curious glances back at Lynne, still standing marooned in the door of her flat, as she waited for the lift. Then the lift had arrived and the woman had disappeared, which was when Lynne had finally summoned up enough strength to go back inside her apartment and lower her shaking frame into an armchair.

'Come on, girl,' she now found herself muttering. 'Come on – this won't do at all. This won't do one bit. Where were you going anyway? What was it that made you feel like this? You were only going out to lunch. That's all you were doing,' she repeated slowly. 'You were only going out to lunch.'

That was when she remembered making the telephone call. Lynne turned her head to stare at the telephone as if in hope that somehow the instrument would help unravel the next part of the mystery.

'My God,' she whispered miserably as another piece fell into place. 'Grenville. It was Grenville, poor bloke. Oh, poor Grenville. He deserves better than that. No way does he deserve to be stood up.'

Yet there was no way that she could have kept her date, not feeling like this. If by some miracle she had actually managed to get as far as the restaurant she knew she'd have only made a fool of herself, either by bursting into tears or by collapsing, which was not like her at all; but she knew something like that would have happened because whatever had been holding her together wasn't doing the trick any more. The elastic had suddenly snapped and gone.

Lynne spent the next few minutes sitting breathing in and out as deeply as she could, which was something she remembered being recommended in the article she had read about this sort of anxiety attack, and then, once she had all but stopped trembling, she went and made herself a cup of strong coffee.

'Poor Grenville,' she thought aloud once more. 'What can he be thinking? What could I have been thinking? Of all the people to stand up.' She shook her head sadly as she took her coffee back into the living room. She'd been looking forward to having lunch with Grenville, had been flattered when he'd asked her so unexpectedly to have lunch with him after they had met at the races. She'd never gone out with anyone of Grenville's class before and she sensed that he would treat her very well, in complete contrast with the way Gerry had treated her. Gerry had always behaved as if Lynne was the lucky one, lucky to be there, lucky to be part of Gerry's world, to be allowed to share certain moments of his life, and most lucky of all to have been allowed to be Gerry Fortune's wife. There'd been no give and take in their marriage – at least, there had been, but it had always been Lynne doing the giving and Gerry doing all the taking. She sensed that Grenville was absolutely not that sort of man; that he was the very opposite, in fact, which was why she had been so looking forward to their date, particularly because she knew Grenville was the sort of man whom Gerry would take one look at and write off as *a bit of a ponce*.

As she sat drinking her strong black coffee and trying to pull herself together, she reflected on quite how hard she had been hit by Gerry's infidelity. She had felt humiliated, deceived, betrayed and cheated and those, she decided ruefully, were not good feelings. She had loved Gerry. She knew he could be mouthy, and she knew he could get a bit rough sometimes, but when he wanted to be, Gerry could be fun, and that, Lynne decided, was what made his treachery even worse. The fact that they had had fun together. But the fun ended the day she caught him with Maddy, when she finally discovered the real Gerry, a man who could obviously lie about anything and everything. And that meant, to her way of thinking, that when he had said he was having fun with her he might just as well have been lying. And when he had said that he loved her, that he really fancied her, that she was just the greatest and most gorgeous thing on two legs, he could have been lying as well. Everything about him and everything to do with their life together could have been a lie, and if he were to deny it now and tell her to her face that it just wasn't true, who was to say that he wouldn't be lying then as well?

After her divorce had been granted Lynne had felt a sense of euphoria, but that had quickly evaporated and she had found herself starting to suffer from what she understood others called *the come-down*. She'd learned that dealing with a divorce was very like dealing with a death – not of someone but of something, a trust, a love, a union. She had read that when people got divorced the innocent party often went through exactly the same range of emotions that people go through when they lose a loved one – release and a sort of euphoria, the process of depression and guilt, then anger and helplessness before they start to rebuild. Now her own marriage was over Lynne was beginning to see how much truth there was in this theory.

'Fine,' she suddenly announced out of the blue. 'But that's all done and dusted now, and you are certainly not going to sit here feeling sorry for yourself for the rest of your life, my girl. What's done is done and where you are right now you do not want to be. So take a deep breath – and get on with it! You have got to get *on* with your life, and getting on with it starts right here.'

With that she went and repaired her make-up, left the flat, hailed a taxi in the Brompton Road and ordered it to take her to the King's Road, where she shopped almost until she dropped. On her return home, with designer bags full of yet more new clothes and shoes, she poured herself a glass of cold white wine, took several more deep breaths, then made a telephone call.

She also got an answering machine, but unlike the man she had stood up she left a message.

'It's me – Lynne – and please listen. I am terribly sorry about lunchtime, Grenville. But I can explain, and I'd really like to – so look, why don't you let me buy you lunch in return for standing you up, and maybe we can start again. If you don't want to I'll quite understand, fair enough and all that, but if it's all right then give us a ring back and we'll make a date.'

Her phone rang almost as soon as she replaced the receiver and Grenville and she made a date not for lunch but for dinner that very evening.

'You couldn't have come at a better time, actually,' Rory said, when he greeted Alice and Millie in the yard that afternoon. 'As you know, Millie, we generally work the horses in the morning, but the farrier was late this morning – had a shunt in his car – so everything was put on hold.'

'Why does that make this a good time?' Millie asked.

'Because we're just about to work old Jack now, so if you hop in the back we'll go up to the gallops.'

'Just don't forget I have a train to catch,' Alice murmured to Millie as they dutifully climbed into the back of Rory's old Range Rover and took their seats alongside his dog Dunkum, among an assortment of old racing papers, sweet wrappers and much other ancient detritus.

'If the balance of your mind really is still that disturbed, I will try to remember,' Millie replied, giving her a look.

'I'll be back as soon as maybe. I was strong-armed into it. You know that.'

Actually they both knew it. Georgina had rung every day to work on her mother to come back up to Richmond to babysit for her, and finally, as always, Alice had relented.

'Anything for a quiet life,' she'd sighed, giving Millie a craven look when she'd finally had to confess she had conceded. 'You know how it is. If I don't agree, I shall rue it for the rest of the year, or possibly even the century. She'll stop me seeing the grandchildren, or move to Albania, or something!'

'The sooner *you* move down *here*, the better . . .'

'Your horse did a good bit of work two days ago,' Rory now said to Millie, as they drove up the steep track that led to the gallops. 'If he doesn't do anything too stupid this afternoon, I'd say we really should run him again at Wincanton.'

'You're the boss,' Millie said, doing up her coat tightly in preparation for braving the elements on the hill, as Rory slowed the car to a halt. 'Who's that?' She pointed to a tall patrician figure standing with another man, both of them with race glasses hung round their necks. 'Some of your other owners?'

'Someone who rents the gallops,' Rory replied, getting out of the car. 'Trains near by.'

As the three of them walked across to where the other trainer was standing, they heard him calling to his owner.

'Here they come now!' he was shouting, pointing to a line of horses just cresting the hill, still some quarter of a mile from them. 'They'll be coming up and past. Yours should be leading, and if he's not there will be questions asked.'

Everyone watched in interest as the line of horses drew nearer. The air that had been absolutely quiet except for the sighing of the wind became full of the thunder of horses' hooves, a noise that grew louder and louder as the line of galloping racehorses came up to where the five of them were standing and pounded past them, rugs flapping in the wind, work riders crouched over their mounts' necks, reins threaded lightly through skilled fingers, balance perfect, half standing in their irons with their eyes fixed firmly on their chosen point, and then they were gone, the horses' hooves fast becoming a faint and distant rumble.

'Jolly good,' the trainer said, a hand cupped over his eyes to shield them from the afternoon sun. 'Looked good, your chap. Strode out nicely, I thought. We'll go and hear what his lad has to say.'

Sticking a cigarette firmly back in his mouth, the tall, hawk-faced man was about to return to his car, parked just behind him, when he was stopped by a shout from a man coming up fast on horseback.

'Henry?' cried the rider, a small man in riding-out clothes, with an uncovered race helmet strapped under his chin. 'Sorry about that, chum! I sent my string up first because one of yours has got loose and is still about at the bottom of the gallops on the road! Hope you didn't mind!'

Then he was gone, cantering off after his string on his old hack.

Alice stared after the retreating male figures as Rory and Millie turned away, their shoulders shaking.

'I don't understand,' she began.

'It wasn't his string,' Millie replied, poker-faced. 'He was watching another trainer's horses.'

'Easily done,' Rory added, shaking his head. 'When I began helping Dad, I tried to saddle up the wrong horse at Fontwell once. Two greys, couldn't tell a spit of difference between any of them. At least I couldn't. Ah. Here come ours – at least, after all that, I hope they're ours!'

Rory pointed to a distant line of horses thundering up the gallops and raised his glasses to watch the horses go past, all except one which cantered by about a dozen lengths or so adrift of the others.

'Wasn't that Jack?' Millie said, pointing at the straggler who was now pulling himself up, opting to stop and eat grass rather than bother with any more work, in spite of his rider's clearly strenuous efforts to get his head back up off the ground.

'There is a possibility,' Rory admitted. 'He doesn't always put his best feet forward up the hill. A morning glory he is *not*.'

The three of them wandered over to where the unwilling horse was still happily grazing, ignoring all the slaps Teddy was delivering to his rump.

'OK,' Rory said as he came alongside the horse and rider. 'So did he do anything right?'

'Not a damned thing, boss,' a still out of breath Teddy replied. 'Got one of his stay abed days on. Come on, you idle bugger! Stop eating that grass!'

Again, in spite of the directions and reminders he was getting from his pilot, Trojan Jack remained happily grazing, until, unable to put up with any more rib-kicking and rump-smacking, suddenly and without any notice whatsoever he put in a massive buck, ejected his pilot and with a flash of flying hind feet bolted off in the wake of his distant stablemates.

'I think I'll take up rocket science instead,' Rory said, turning away with a shake of his head. 'It has to be easier than this.'

They arrived back in the yard well ahead of the string, which was being walked steadily back from the gallops. Alice asked permission to wander around the yard while Rory and Millie tried to form some kind of game plan concerning the errant Trojan Jack. She declined Rory's offer of refreshment, as she was anxious not to miss her train from Salisbury.

With an anxious glance up at the stable clock, Alice decided to fill in the time before leaving by looking round the top yard. As she walked into the yard she heard the sound of music from somewhere and traced it to a cassette player that was hanging outside one of the boxes. Curious as to who might be listening to this fine Irish tenor she looked into the stable and found herself being stared at by a small lop-eared horse that was standing to the side of the door munching contentedly on a mouthful of hay.

'You like this, do you?' she said, as the tenor began to sing 'The Star of the County Down'. 'This is your sort of thing, is it?'

The horse continued to watch her, still chewing slowly.

'You have lovely eyes,' Alice murmured to him. 'You really do have the most lovely, lovely eyes.'

After more mutual staring the animal slowly laid back his ears and equally slowly curled back his top lip, as if giving her a smile. Alice laughed in delight, taking the expression at face value, whereupon the horse curled his lip back even more, revealing a large expanse of bright pink gum, a sight so comical that Alice found herself laughing even more. The horse immediately disappeared back into the darkness of its box, and Alice stopped laughing, afraid that her laughter had upset him. Not a bit of it, it seemed, since the horse reappeared as quickly as he had disappeared, with a new slice of wet hay which he then proceeded to shake so thoroughly that drops of water as well as loose bits of forage flew all over Alice.

'Where's the party?' Millie enquired from behind her, having come to look for her. 'You found a new friend?'

'Just look at this horse, Millie.' Alice sighed. 'Isn't he lovely?'

'Could be a she.'

'He isn't. He's a he. Isn't he lovely?'

'He's certainly not enormous.'

'Looks big enough to me.'

'Yes, but then you're not exactly tall, ducks. Come on – we have a train to miss.'

'I think there's something rather special about him, don't you?' Alice continued, staying when she should be moving on. 'He's got very wise eyes. And any horse that listens to John McCormack has my vote.'

'Is that who this is?' Millie was looking up at the cassette player. 'I thought it was that man who used to sing on the TV in a cardigan.'

'You have such a tin ear, Millie. But then you always did have, even at school. I wonder who actually owns this fellow?'

'Ask Rory – here cometh the man now.'

'No one owns him,' Rory told them. 'Yet. He's a newcomer.'

'You mean he's for sale?' Alice asked.

'I think I'm probably going to end up having to give him away.'

'Why? Isn't he any good?'

'I don't know how good or how bad he is,' Rory

replied. 'He's a long way off any serious work. He can jump, though. That I can vouch for.'

'So how much would a horse like this cost?' Alice persisted.

'Your train, sweetie?' Millie said, touching her arm.

'Seriously, Mr Rawlins.'

'Rory.'

'How much would he cost, actually?'

Rory looked at her, frowning, not thinking for one second that Alice could be seriously considering buying herself a racehorse, but even so, he knew that when it came to owners he had to watch what he said. If he named too low a price she might repeat the figure to someone who *was* thinking of buying a horse. There again if he quoted too high a price the same thing might happen, but this time it might deter any potential buyer.

'As he stands, that is as an unknown quantity – although he's young so he's got all that going for him, as well as having no miles on the clock – we certainly wouldn't ask anything less than fifteen thousand.'

'Fifteen thousand. I see.' Alice nodded, trying not to look either shocked or surprised. 'But then that's quite cheap for a racehorse, isn't it? Not that I'm thinking of buying one, of course.'

'Alice,' Millie reminded her. 'Not that I mind if you miss your damned train, but just in case you do, by my reckoning it is about to leave the station.'

'I read that some sheikh or another only recently paid over a quarter of a million pounds for a horse.'

'Guineas,' Millie told her in a kind voice. 'And that was for a stallion that had won some rather good races. Now come along.'

'I was only asking, Millie,' Alice protested as she found herself being bundled into the car. 'There's really no harm in asking.'

All the way up to London Alice found herself thinking about the little liver chestnut horse she'd just seen. Not that she herself actually thought of him as being particularly small, since she didn't really know what size racehorses were meant to be, but she did think him odd; this was not anything to do with his conformation or appearance in general, but it most certainly had something to do with his appearance in the particular. It had to do with his eyes, the eyes that had watched her so closely, the eyes into which she had stared and by which she had found herself transfixed.

I know what it is, she suddenly said to herself. *Of course. I know just what it is. He's been here before. He's been here – before.*

The delight of her fanciful notion carried Alice through her babysitting, not that she needed any such mental distraction as far as her grandchildren were concerned. She adored them wholeheartedly, although like so many other women of her generation she privately considered that they were allowed to spend too much time in front of the television. As usual she turned the set off as soon as Georgina and Joe had left the house for the evening, and in spite of Will and Finty's protests she read to them instead. After only a few minutes their tantrums abated, thumbs and sucky blankets went into mouths and they happily listened to nearly an hour of stories before drifting off into blissful sleep. Nothing more was heard of them all evening. Alice checked them before turning in herself, but the two children were still sound asleep.

'What's that tie you're wearing, Grenville?' Lynne wondered, as she finished her smoked salmon first course at dinner that evening. 'Were you in the army?'

'MCC,' Grenville told her, trying not to smile. 'The Marylebone Cricket Club.'

'Really? I didn't know they had a club,' Lynne said with a frown. 'Where do they play? Down the High Street?'

'Oh, very good.' Grenville laughed, seeing it as a joke, while all the time trying to come to terms with the fact that it was actually Lynne sitting opposite him and not some illusion. He had already noted and been pleased to see the envious looks on the faces of several of the other male diners when Lynne had swept into the bar, looking like something that had just stepped out of a fashion magazine.

Maybe not quite Vogue, Grenville thought as he

assessed what she was wearing. *Maybe a little bit more* Cosmopolitan *than* Vogue, *but who am I to criticise?*

'No, the MCC do not play down Marylebone High Street, Mrs Fortune,' he said with a smile.

'Lynne,' she interrupted him. 'Anyway, I'm not Mrs Fortune any longer. I'm back to being plain Miss Faraday.'

'Never plain and Miss is lovely. Just as long as you don't become Ms. Sounds like an abbreviation for miserable.'

'What do you do exactly, Grenville? If you don't mind me asking. I remember you saying you were helping Gerry with something to do with business, right?'

'I'm an investments manager, Lynne. In the private sector. Nothing to do with banks or anything. I work purely for myself, for my clients.'

'You managed Gerry's money, then?'

'I was helping him build a portfolio. But he . . . he didn't see it through.'

'Hope he didn't short-change you. He's pretty good at that. I shouldn't have said that, I suppose. Sorry.'

'You don't have to be sorry.'

'Sorry,' Lynne said, yet again. 'Anyway – you were saying you were going to help Gerry with his car businesses.'

'I was going to help him invest some of the proceeds, Lynne,' Grenville said, remembering how long Gerry had kept him waiting for his cheque, a cheque that when it finally arrived was a couple of hundred short. 'I think he simply decided to put his money elsewhere.'

'Right.' Lynne nodded, and sipped some champagne. 'Actually, I wouldn't mind some financial advice.'

'You have money to invest?'

'I have some money, Grenville. But I don't know about investing it. I quite enjoy spending it.'

Grenville nodded, took his glasses off and in order to buy a little time began cleaning them with the silk handkerchief from his top pocket. He knew plenty of ways to invest Lynne's money, mostly ways that would be highly advantageous to him, yet he found himself resisting for the first time ever.

'For the first time ever,' he said out loud.

'Come again?'

'Sorry,' Grenville said, replacing his glasses. 'Just thinking out loud. No, look – look, if you're enjoying yourself, provided you always leave yourself what my father used to call the rainy-day reserve for the times you may need a bit of money, if I were you I'd go on enjoying myself. After all, as someone once said, this life is not a dress rehearsal. I rather like that. Life's not a dress rehearsal. Rather good, that.'

'That's a bit what I feel now, Grenville,' Lynne admitted. 'I mean I was all over the shop when it happened, the divorce – you know. It was just something I wasn't prepared for. Something I just hadn't imagined happening, fool that I was, and probably still am. But I'm sort of trying to get it together now and everything, and since I have I've started to think sod it – sorry. Sorry. I meant – I meant to hell with it. 'Cos just like you just said, this isn't some blooming dress rehearsal. I don't want to go through the rest of my life regretting not the things I've done but the things I haven't done. Know what I mean?'

'I do indeed, Lynne.' Grenville nodded solemnly. 'As they say nowadays, I hear what you're saying.'

Lynne gave him a shy smile, wondering how she was doing. She hoped she was keeping the ball in the air and convincing the man opposite her that she was one altogether together young woman, and not someone who was becoming increasingly certain that she was busy falling to pieces inside. If she could get him to believe that she was as fine as she knew she wasn't, then there was every chance she would convince herself.

The next morning, while their parents slept in after their late night, Alice got her grandchildren up, fed them their breakfast – which, strictly for her sake, she knew, they ate at the table – and knocked on Georgina's bedroom door to tell her she needed to be taken to the station to catch her train.

'Oh, listen,' a weary voice answered. 'OK if you take a taxi? We didn't get in till three, Mum. There's some money on the hall table.'

'What about the children?' Alice asked. 'They've had their breakfast.'

'Fine,' Georgina called back. 'Just give them each a bag of Cheerios – they're in the larder – and stick them in front of the telly. They'll be fine. Oh – and make sure you pull the front door shut behind you.'

'If that's what you want.' Alice pulled a face. 'As long as one of you is up and about to check them.'

'Mum,' came the familiar cry from the bed-room.

'OK. I have to go, Georgina.'

Having made sure there was something suitable for her grandchildren to watch on the television, Alice kissed them goodbye and took a taxi to the station, praying every inch of the way that no harm would come to them while their parents remained in bed sleeping off their late night. In the train she sat by a window watching the landscape gradually changing from urban to rural, and found herself enjoying the reverse of the feelings she normally experienced on such journeys: instead of leaving home to go somewhere, she now felt she was leaving somewhere to return home.

She thought about her family and wondered how she had come to let herself be persuaded to make such a long and tiring journey just to babysit, knowing perfectly well that Georgina could have easily found someone else. So why, she wondered, had Georgina insisted that Alice come up to babysit all the way from deepest Dorset? There could only have been one reason for the summons from Richmond, and that was that her daughter had *wanted* to interrupt Alice's holiday, just out of pique. She still wanted her mum at her beck and call.

Alice sighed, but it wasn't really a sigh of regret, rather one that could be taken to mark the end of something, a sigh of punctuation, the mark of coming to the end of a particular chapter, or perhaps even a book; and now she had finished that chapter or book she sensed there was a new one on the way.

An eye was looking into hers, a large round brown eye, and in it she could see a land under the sea. The waves were high above her, with a bright sun shining through them, while first one horse then many swam through water which was as clear as crystal with the most beautiful people she had ever seen riding them. They rode bareback and without bridles and now Alice was riding as well, through an underwater palace whose walls were hung with gold drapes and harps and swords that rested in jewelled sheaths. As she rode silently through the ocean there was nothing but a sense of peace and a fine voice singing a song in a tongue she didn't know, yet she thought she knew what the song was saying.

Her horse looked round at her and she saw herself in its eye, young again, a little girl in a gingham dress with her hair in plaits just the way she used to wear it, and on her feet red shoes that sparkled in the sunbeams.

She woke up just in time for Salisbury. People

were already getting up from their seats in preparation for the train's pulling in to the station, but Alice just sat there, remembering the dream, determined never to forget it.

The two days of rain had stopped, so Millie and Alice drove through a rolling countryside warmed by late autumn sunshine, with a strong breeze making the clouds scud so that shadows flitted across the dark green hills. There was no traffic on the long sweeping road that went down into a valley then up and round a long barrow in front of them, so for a while it was as if they had both been transported back to a time when there was just the land, and the sky and the unseen sea beyond the hills. They drove in silence, hushed by the elegant majesty of the landscape.

Finally they found themselves not in Millie's hamlet but in the neighbouring picture-postcard village of Chalfont Magna.

'Hold your horses!' Millie stopped her car as she saw a man coming out of a thatched cottage at the top of the lane. 'I think I know him. Yes I do – and it's just the man we've been looking for – Mike? Michael?'

Seeing Millie becoming involved in talking to her acquaintance, Alice decided to stretch her legs, and take a better look round the village. As she peered over garden walls and the tops of gates it seemed to her to be an idyllic spot if not the ideal one, peaceful and quiet, well away from any main roads and miles from any flight paths.

In fact every property she saw seemed to be just the sort of small house or cottage for which she had been searching, particularly the one she finally found herself standing outside, the one up whose path Millie stood talking to a short red-faced man in a lovat green tweed suit.

'Of all the luck,' Millie said as she rejoined Alice in the roadway. 'The man I've been talking to? He's only the bloke who sold me *my* house, would you believe? And as luck would have it he's just been taking instructions from the man who owns that drop-dead-lovely cottage. Not only that, ducks: no one, but no one else has seen it yet – and what is more and what is best of all, we are allowed to look round it, right now!'

The old stone-built cottage was as lovely inside as it was pretty outside, with plenty of exposed beams, open fireplaces with fine old carved stone surrounds in the sitting and dining rooms, a flagstone-floored kitchen with an Aga, four surprisingly light and airy bedrooms, all of which enjoyed views over the unspoilt rolling countryside, and a beautiful acre of gardens that were laid to roses and lawn.

'You are going to have to buy it,' Millie whispered as they walked round inspecting the outside. 'Because if you don't the next person up the path most certainly will. It is *perfect. Quite perfect.*'

'I'm about to do just that,' Alice assured her. 'Buy it, that is. I think I'd be mad not to.'

'Bonkers,' Millie said with a broad smile,

taking Alice's arm for one more stroll around the gardens. 'And I would give good money to see the look on your children's faces when you tell them.'

'But I'm only doing what they're always nagging me to do,' Alice replied. 'What is it they say? Getting a life.'

'Right on, sister.' Millie laughed. 'Let's hear it for the biddies.'

A brief discussion with the agent and the owner was all that was needed for parties to make their resolutions clear. Alice agreed to buy the cottage at the asking price, and would put down a deposit to secure it as soon as was necessary while she issued instructions to put her London house on the market. On learning exactly what sort of property Alice owned and its location, the estate agent told her his firm's London office would happily handle the sale, since they had a list of buyers looking for houses in that particular part of Kensington.

'Couldn't have worked out better,' Millie remarked as they drove away. 'It was as if it was meant.'

'So all I have to do now is to break the news to the family.'

'Any time, duck. There's no obligation, you know.'

'You're right.' Alice sighed. 'I still think of them as depending on me.'

'While they dread the likes of us depending on them.' Millie laughed. 'So come on – let's go and have a drink to celebrate. After all, it's not every day you get to turn your life around.'

Alice agreed, unable quite to believe the change in her fortunes, while all the time wondering whether the strange and wonderful dream she'd had on the train might in fact have more significance than she thought; that in some way it had told her about this very moment in her life.

Chapter Ten

Himself

Grenville arrived first. Rory found him wandering around the yard looking into the stables, gloved hands clasped behind his back, trilby tilted down to the edge of his spectacles, in the company of the glamorous young woman who had literally knocked Rory for six at Sandown.

'Could do with a few more residents, old man, yes?' Grenville remarked when accosted. 'Not that it's any of my business.'

'Correct,' Rory replied. 'Want to go on to the next round?'

'Seriously, Rory. With the old man laid up – how is he, by the way?'

'Making progress.'

'Good. Good. I'm sorry – allow me to introduce you to Mrs Fortune. Or rather Miss Faraday, as she wishes to be called now.'

Lynne turned round from her inspection of the

horse stabled in the box in front of her and put a hand out to Rory.

'We've met. Hello again, Mr Rawlins. Great yard.'

'Nice of you to say so,' Rory replied, shaking the offered hand. 'But it's not really looking at its best.'

'Long as the horses are happy, that's all that matters. And they certainly look happy enough.'

'To get down to business, Rory,' Grenville chipped in, anxious to get to the point. 'And racing is a business. With the old chap laid up, Rory, you could really roll up your shirtsleeves and get to work here. First of all, you could have an Open Day. You know, let Joe Public in to ooh and aah. Never know what the tide might bring in.'

'With the number of horses we have in training, Grenville, they'd be here for all of five minutes.'

'Do what some of 'em do over at Lambourn, in that case.' Grenville lowered his voice. 'Borrow a few nags from your neighbours and pretend they're yours. Fill the yard and say they're all spoken for, then along comes Bob your famous uncle. Shove a few geraniums about the place, couple of hanging baskets, you can even borrow some staff from your chums, too. Works wonders. Appearances are everything, as you know, old chap. Even if they do turn out to be mirages.'

'Not exactly my style, Grenville,' Rory replied. 'And can you imagine if my father found out?'

'Just a thought,' Grenville said, taking his hat off and carefully removing a small piece of straw from the brim. 'What about this famous horse, then? I like the look of that big bay in the second box.'

'That's not him, Grenville. That's Tiger Talk. And as a matter of fact I'd far rather you saw the horse when he's fitter. He's only just arrived and we're – we're still acclimatising him.'

'Do I hear music?' Grenville wondered, looking round. 'Who's that singing somewhere? Sounds like John McCormack.'

'The lads play the radio when they're doing the grooming and mucking out,' Rory said quickly. 'They say the horses like it.'

'My mother *loves* John McCormack.' Grenville smiled. 'Daddy did as well. But look. Look, now I'm here and since I've come all this way, you might as well let me just have a quick dekko.'

'I thought you said you had to come down this way anyway,' Rory said, continuing to try to stall him. 'I'd quite like a cup of tea, and I'm sure you both would as well, then perhaps I'll give you a guided tour afterwards.'

'I'd love a cuppa,' Lynne put in quickly, sensing that Rory wanted to tread water for a little.

'Of course,' Grenville replied politely, offering Lynne his arm. 'But I really would like to see what you've got afterwards, Rory. Now I *have* come all this way.'

'Teddy?' Rory hissed at his head lad, dropping back as the others made for the house. 'While we're inside, pile the little horse's box as high as you can with fresh straw, and don't ask why. OK?'

221

'He's just had a fresh bed, boss,' Teddy replied. 'I only just skipped him out.'

'That's not what I'm saying, Teddy,' Rory insisted. 'What I'm saying is bulk the horse's bedding up as high as you can.'

'Ah,' Teddy said with a nod. 'I hear you, boss. Gotcha.'

'What one would dearly like is what's known in the trade as a *fun* horse,' Grenville said as they sat having tea in Rory's seriously untidy kitchen. 'A horse that will provide the necessary entertainment without necessarily breaking the bank.'

'Really?' Lynne said, dropping two sweeteners into her mug of tea. 'I'd have thought if you were getting a horse you'd want one with a blooming good chance of winning. Sorry, but I mean that's what I'd want.'

'I didn't know you wanted a horse, Lynne?' Grenville looked vaguely unsettled, as if she had been keeping something from him. As far as he could make out Lynne had only accepted his invitation to come down to the country because she wanted to look at some apartments that were for sale in a large country house that had recently been converted into flats.

'I don't,' Lynne replied. 'That was – what do they call it? A something or other.'

'An hypothesis?'

'If you say so. Who knows what I might buy next?' Lynne looked at Grenville, before starting to sip her tea. 'The world is my oyster, right?'

When they had finished their tea and Teddy had done the bed, Rory took the two of them round the yard and showed them three of the horses he knew the owners were keen to sell. Grenville failed to be taken by any of them, spinning all three for elaborate reasons that smacked to Rory of being straight out of the a-little-knowledge-is-a-dangerous-thing school of equine thought.

Finally, he showed them The Enchanted.

'The Enchanted?' Lynne said, taking an interest for the first time. 'What a great name for a horse. You call him that?'

'He was named that when my father bought him,' Rory said. 'Something to do with some old Gaelic myth or other.'

'The Enchanted,' Lynne repeated, looking over the stable door at a horse that thanks to Teddy's constructive bed-building looked considerably taller than he had before. 'I think that's a winning name.'

'There's not exactly a lot of him, is there, Rory?' Grenville turned back to look at the trainer. 'Hardly an Aintree type.'

'But then he was hardly bought for that,' Rory said defensively. 'Although a horse that won the National just before the last war – Battleship, I think it was – was only just over fifteen hands, my father said.'

'Can we see him out of the box?'

'Yes, of course, I'll have him taken out for you,' Rory replied, unable to think of a good reason to refuse. 'If you go and stand in the school over there I'll have the girl lead him round.'

'What? Over there?' Grenville said. 'I'd quite like to see him led out from here.'

'He's still a little skittish,' Rory lied, crossing his fingers. 'I'd hate to see him take a lump out of Miss Faraday here.'

'He moves well enough,' Grenville observed as Pauline, the most diminutive of Rory's skeleton stable staff, trotted the horse up and past them. 'Gets his hind legs under him.'

'I don't understand. Where else would he put them, Grenville?' Lynne puzzled. 'Bit odd if he got them over him.'

'It's an equine expression, Lynne,' Grenville explained. 'Like the way this horse covers the ground, do you see? For a smaller sort of horse he walks out well and covers a lot of ground. You want a horse that covers the ground well, and picks his feet up, as this chap's doing. He's nice and short-coupled, too, and not over at the knee.'

'All Greek to this lady,' Lynne said with a shake of her head. 'You are speaking complete Greek to me.'

'Let's see him stand up, if we may?' Grenville called out to the lass. 'If you could stand him up just there, please – I'd like to come and pick up his feet, if that's all right, Rory?'

'Your call, Grenville,' Rory replied. 'Just watch the sharp end.'

'I understand that bit all right,' Lynne said. 'Hope you know what you're doing, Grenville.'

'I was brought up with horses, Lynne,' Grenville assured her. 'No worries.'

He went up to the horse, which was standing eyeing him with half-flattened ears. He walked round him twice, nodding to himself, then walked round him twice in the opposite direction. Behind his back the horse kicked out, narrowly missing him.

'Change of rein there, I see,' Rory called out. 'Even a change of leg perhaps.'

'Got a good shoulder on him,' Grenville called back, ignoring the tease. 'Stands into himself well.'

Rory winked at Lynne, who smiled back at him.

'Nice and high in the wither as well,' Grenville continued, bending down to pick up and flex one of the horse's fore legs. When he replaced it he ran one hand down the back of it as he had often observed horse people doing when inspecting possible purchases.

'Find anything?' Rory called out.

'Got plenty of bone as well.' Grenville nodded. 'What's he got, Rory? Seven? Eight inches?'

'Haven't measured, Grenville,' Rory replied, exchanging another look with Lynne, who came over to stand beside him.

'I think he's a smashing little horse,' she said. 'Just gorgeous. Not that I know a thing about horses.'

'Long as you like him,' Rory returned. 'But a little less of the little, if you don't mind.'

'I only mean that affectionately,' Lynne said, taking him seriously. 'I haven't a clue what size a horse should be. I just think there's something about him.' She blushed a little as Rory turned to look at her. 'I mean it. He's got sort of – I don't know what they call it. When a horse looks a bit special.'

'The horse has presence.'

'That's it exactly.' Lynne nodded. 'That's exactly what this horse has got. Presence.' She looked back at the horse and found she was being stared at in return.

'I'd say the feeling's mutual,' Rory told her, nodding towards The Enchanted.

'Is he cantering, Rory?' Grenville asked, still walking round the horse.

'Not at the moment, he isn't,' Lynne muttered, with a sideways smile at Rory.

'He's in light work,' Rory called across to him. 'And he's working fine.'

'And he's really done relatively nothing?'

'Hardly any miles on the clock at all. Run in a point and a hunter chase – both of which he should have won, apparently.'

'Ah.' Grenville nodded, coming to join Rory and Lynne. 'That old that-old. Ah.' Grenville took his hat off, wiped his brow, nodded again, then replaced his hat. 'Fine. No, I think I'll pass on this one, Rory, thanks – if it's all the same to you.'

'Your choice,' Rory said. 'You're the expert.'

'Even so.' Grenville smiled, nodding once more. 'I think I'll pass just the same.'

'Well, if you don't want him, I think I'll buy him,' Lynne said suddenly.

'Lynne?' Grenville turned and attempted a businesslike look. 'What did you say?'

'Hang on, Grenville,' Lynne said, turning to Rory once more. 'Just for fun – if I was to buy him, just for fun, what would it cost me?'

'Lynne?' Grenville tried again, but Lynne wasn't listening.

Rory paused, cleared his throat and looked into the pair of bright blue eyes that were looking into his. Again he found himself between the notorious rock and a hard place. If he said too much he might put her off, whereas if he asked too little away would go the profit all trainers must make when selling on a horse.

'Just for fun?' he wondered, buying a little time.

'Just for fun. How much would a horse like this cost?'

'Fifteen thousand.'

Grenville gave a small but significant whistle while Lynne's eyes widened to the full.

'Fifteen thousand – what, fifteen thousand pounds?' she echoed. 'God, I'm a right charley. I thought a horse like this in a place like this would cost, I don't know – a couple of grand, tops.'

Rory shook his head sadly and heaved a deep sigh. 'It's fifteen thousand guineas. And you could hardly buy a decent riding horse for two thousand now,' he said.

'Right,' Lynne agreed. 'I said I was a charley. Oh

well.' She shrugged and buttoned up her coat as if that was the conclusion of any possible further business. 'A girl can dream, I suppose.'

'There's more than one way of skinning the famous cat,' Rory said lightly, sensing her very real disappointment. 'You could get up a partnership. That's what a lot of people do. Buy a leg, as they say. Find three others to come in with you – to buy the other three legs. That's what a lot of people like yourself do to have a bit of fun, to have an interest, as it were.'

'Really?' Lynne's blue eyes came alight once more. 'I see. You mean sharesville?'

'Sharesville. Precisely. And a lot of people do it.'

'Lynne?' Grenville said in a tone with a distinct warning note. 'Lynne?'

'Go on, Mr Rawlins,' Lynne continued, ignoring her escort. 'So what would that mean?'

'If you were serious,' Rory replied, 'and if you could find three other people, and if, say, I let you have the horse for twelve K, that would be three thousand one hundred and fifty guineas a leg, plus training and racing costs.'

'Which costs will run out to at least a hundred guineas a month per share,' Grenville chipped in. 'So you would have to think *pretty* carefully, Lynne.'

'I think I could afford that, Grenville. Easily, in fact. Particularly since it would be fun, which is something I have been a bit short of recently. Wonder who else would go sharesville?'

Both Rory and she pretended to think deeply; then they both turned to look at Grenville.

'Now wait a minute, one and all . . .' he stammered.

'All that stuff you were saying just now?' Lynne asked him overseriously. 'About how he covered the ground so nicely, and got his legs under him, and stood up to his withers and all, and how he's got these huge bones—'

'We'd still have to find two other people, my dear.'

'But you just said you were thinking of buying a horse. I mean otherwise why did you come down here? You just said you wanted to buy a *fun* horse, wasn't it? Right?'

'Yes,' Grenville said uneasily. 'But I just spun this one.'

'Spun?'

'Said thank you but no thank you, Lynne.'

'We won't hold it against you,' Rory said. 'In fact we'll pretend you never said it.'

'That's right, Rory,' Lynne agreed. 'That's what we'll do.'

'Good,' Rory said. 'That's exactly what we'll do. While if you refuse, Mr Fielding . . .' Rory teased, wagging a schoolteacher's finger at him.

'Right,' Lynne said with a grin, following suit.

Grenville smiled weakly back and nodded once again. He found himself in a dilemma. By now he was so taken with Lynne that the last thing he wanted was to lose the pleasure of her company. Since the horrendously painful experience of his broken engagement to Jane some twelve years earlier he had never enjoyed any sort of medium-term let alone long-term relationship with a member of the opposite sex, and not even a short-term one with a member of the opposite sex as gloriously attractive and glamorous as Miss Lynne Faraday. If he were now to refuse a share in this little racehorse with which she had suddenly become so enamoured, he knew it could easily spell the end of any chance he might have of extending this burgeoning friendship, particularly if she went ahead and formed a partnership to buy the horse, since chances were she might well meet someone else infinitely more attractive and personable than he. Yet as he knew – something of which he now felt properly ashamed – he'd only really brought Lynne down to Rory's yard to try to win a few Brownie points, or in other words to show off, hoping that by airing his knowledge of the horse world but spinning anything Rory might have to offer he would succeed in impressing her.

But now it all seemed to have backfired, and to such an extent that he was going to have to dig deep into his pockets to finance a quarter-share in a horse that he considered had as much chance of winning a race as he had of landing a Hollywood contract.

'Look,' he said finally. 'This is lovely. A lovely idea altogether, but one we should perhaps talk over between us.'

'Why?' Lynne wondered. 'I mean, sorry, but

it's not as if we're contracted to each other in any way. My money is my money to do what I like with, if you know what I mean. No offence and everything, but really, if I feel like blowing it all in one sort of great big spending spree, then the only person I've got to answer to is me. Really, isn't it? Sorry. But you know what I mean.'

'I do,' Grenville agreed, feeling himself beginning to redden under the collar. 'I was only trying to help. Explain all the ins and outs. Owning a racehorse is not as easy as it sounds. Perhaps on the way back to town I can explain exactly all the whys and wherefores.'

'Well of course you can, Grenville, because that's something you're good at.' Lynne nodded seriously. 'But I doubt it'll make much difference 'cos this is something I really think I might like to do. OK? So when you're ready and everything, you promised me we could have a look at those apartments on the way home.'

With one last look at the new object of her affection, who was standing nearby pushing his groom in the back with his muzzle, Lynne said goodbye to Rory and walked off towards Grenville's car. Rory followed them, saw them off, instructed Pauline to put Boyo back in his stable, and prepared to leave for the hospital to visit his father, unconvinced by anything that he had heard. Lynne was obviously a nice young woman at a loose end, and Grenville was clearly besotted with her, but he would talk her out of it on the way to see the flats. Rory was quite sure of it, which, he thought ruefully later, once again only went to show how little trainers know not only about their horses but about those who own them.

Constance Frimley was walking her neighbour's dogs in the square when Grenville finally returned from his day in the country, having dropped Lynne off at her London rental. Contrary to Rory's belief, Grenville had been completely unsuccessful in talking Lynne out of buying the horse, or forming a partnership. In fact the more he had told Lynne about the ups and downs of racing, the more fun she declared it sounded. Even her decision to rent the apartment in the large house she had inspected on the borders of Hampshire and Wiltshire after leaving Rory's yard had not deterred her. On learning roughly what the rent on the large, unfurnished apartment might be on the pretext that a relative of his was looking for exactly the same sort of accommodation, Grenville had hoped the cost of the place might finally dampen her enthusiasm, but since this was not the case he could only conclude that Lynne must have more money than sense. Furthermore, she had given him every indication that if he didn't want to join the racing partnership he would have to expect to see very little of her, because she would be spending so much time on the gallops and going racing. Although that had been more of a tease than an ultimatum, Grenville reflected as he locked up his car in his resident's parking bay, if he wanted to continue to see the gorgeous Miss Faraday it looked as though he would have to declare himself in and put his winter skiing holiday on hold for at least a year.

'Good evening, Lady Frimley,' he greeted his neighbour politely, having every intention to hit and run. 'Bit of a chill about it, alas.'

'Been racing again, Mr Fielder?' Constance remarked, having noticed the binoculars slung over one of Grenville's shoulders. 'Quite the sportsman.'

'No, no, Lady Frimley, been down to my trainer's,' he replied. 'Down to watch gallops – and it's *Fielding*, Lady Frimley. Not Fielder.'

'We galloped, Dick galloped, we galloped all three,' Constance replied vaguely, reining in her two small canine charges. 'We had racehorses, once upon a once. In the dim and distant.'

'Did you now?' Grenville wondered, suddenly interested, seeing a window of opportunity open. 'Do well? Were they any good?'

'Arthur Budge-Thomas used to train for us.' Constance avoided the question. 'Frightfully nice man, if I remember correctly.'

'Hence your interest in the horse, obviously,' Grenville continued, falling into step alongside Constance as, having locked the garden gate behind her, she began to head for home. 'Something that never leaves one, yes?'

'I dare say, if you say so,' Constance replied. 'I find the older I get the less need I have for opinions.'

'True, Lady Frimley, very true.'

They stopped when they reached Constance's front door, and she handed him the two dog leads while she fished in her bag for her key.

'I'm off racing on Thursday, as it happens,' Grenville said carefully. 'A friend's got a runner at Wincanton.'

'Never been there,' Constance said, having located her key. 'Wouldn't even know where it was.'

'Charming course in the west country. Perhaps if you'd like another day out, Lady Frimley . . .'

'Perhaps.' Constance nodded. 'Thank you. But only if you don't drive too fast. You know how I cannot abide this modern habit of driving at absurd speeds.'

'Once again I shall be a maiden aunt behind the wheel, Lady Frimley,' Grenville assured her. 'Shall we say ten o'clock?'

It was raining heavily at Wincanton, sheets of water being driven across the course by the prevailing westerly directly into the faces of any racegoers brave enough to take the grandstands. The less courageous had sought refuge in the bars or were sheltering on the eastern side of the Tote building, trying to catch sight of the horses in the paddock directly in front of them where connections for the first race stood in miserable huddles, some of them occasionally testing the ground with the heel of a shoe or the point of an umbrella. Others, their coats dripping with rain, hunched their shoulders and narrowed their eyes the way people do when exposed to remorseless torrents sluicing down from windswept skies.

Millie and Alice had sought refuge in the owners' and trainers' bar, a charming but ramshackle building packed with trainers in gently steaming Barbours and owners in saturated tweeds. Several badly tuned televisions were broadcasting highly coloured pictures of the action from Wincanton and two other racecourses.

'This is the downside of winter racing,' Millie said. 'Weather like this on courses as exposed as this.'

'I don't mind at all,' Alice replied. 'It sort of adds to the fun, really. It's better than sitting inside staring at the rain pouring down the windows.'

'I forgot to ask you. What news about your house? That call you had before we left – I've been so busy talking about Jack's chances, I quite forgot to ask.'

'Yes, I put it out of my mind as well, isn't that odd? I was so excited about coming racing again. Anyway,' Alice continued, 'it seems they have someone definitely interested and so it's really a case of fingers crossed. I could be moving in a month.'

'And you're really not going to tell Georgina?' Millie smiled. 'I mean until it's a *fait accompli*?'

'I don't really see the point, Millie. It's really got nothing to do with her or Christian. They know something's up, I'm sure, but I'm dashed if I'm going to tell them what.'

'Right on, sister.' Millie laughed, clenching one fist.

'Hello,' Rory said, returning from the bar with drinks. 'Not another outbreak of white power?'

The door of the bar was once more pushed open as three more refugees from the weather came in.

'Here we are,' Grenville announced to Lynne and to Constance, who was still trying to hold an enormous and totally unsuitable picture hat in place even though she was now well out of the wind. 'Soon dry out in here.'

'I'm not sure I know anyone here,' Constance said, looking round the crowd. 'In fact I couldn't possibly.'

'Rory?' Grenville called, spotting the trainer seated at a corner table with Millie and Alice. He led his charges over. 'Well, well, so here we all are again. The Rawlins Racing Club, perhaps we should call it. Mrs Brandon, Mrs Dixon, may I introduce Miss Faraday?'

'I've never been to wherever this is before,' Constance said, sitting down on the chair Grenville had pulled out for her while Millie and Alice exchanged greetings with Lynne. 'I must say the climate is most incontinent.'

'This is nothing,' Rory said, as Grenville went to get drinks for the newcomers. 'You want to try one of the February meetings. There's nothing between here and the Urals.'

'It is a bit pissy, isn't it?' Lynne said, taking off her Mrs Miniver hat and shaking the rain off it. 'I think we should have come dressed as frogmen.'

'I hear you have a runner today,' Grenville said to Millie on his return, producing his racecard. 'Trojan Jack again, yes? Must have a squeak after that good run at Sandown.'

'He'll like this ground,' Rory said. 'Got just enough cut in it. He really doesn't like the soft, not a bit.'

'Might have a little interest then, Rory,' Grenville decided. 'That was *such* rotten luck at Sandown. Now then – how's our horse then?'

'Grenville has just bought a horse,' Rory said in response to Alice's quick look of concern. 'Or rather Lynne has and Grenville might well be.'

'Which horse have you bought?' Alice enquired of Lynne. 'One of Rory's? Please not the one with the big floppy ears who likes to listen to Irish songs.'

'The *very* one.' Grenville smiled.

'Put the sock back under the bed, duck,' Millie murmured, turning to Alice. 'It's sold.'

'Please not?' Lynne repeated, picking up. 'You hadn't got your eye on it, had you? Seriously?'

'Well, yes,' Alice replied. 'Yes and no, really. Yes when I saw him, and no when I found out how much he'd cost.'

Everyone fell silent for a moment, during which Rory finished his drink and stood up to take his leave.

'I'd better go and see how everything is with Jack,' he said. 'Don't want anything falling off him today. If you'll excuse me.'

'You really have bought that horse?' Alice asked Lynne. 'You and Grenville?'

'So it seems,' Lynne replied. 'Actually Grenville's still hovering, but I think he'll come in.'

'He will if he knows what's good for him,' Constance observed, straightening her hat.

'No, no, I'm definitely in,' Grenville said quickly. 'I was just kicking the tyres on this one, that's all, do you see.'

'Whatever *that* may mean,' Constance said.

'It's not all writ in stone,' Grenville continued, trying again. 'So if you really *are* interested . . .'

'It'd be great if you came in,' Lynne said, putting her hand on Alice's. 'I mean it really would be fun.'

'I'm not sure what it would entail,' Alice said, turning to Millie for help. Ever since she had seen the horse she had thought about little else except how it might be possible to buy him, and even when she realised there simply was no practical or indeed sensible way she could do it, she had still been unable to put the idea out of her head. Yet now it seemed there might be a way, although before she allowed herself to get her hopes up she needed to know the nuts and bolts of the situation. The matter had become vitally important to her and up until today she hadn't been quite sure why. Now, as she sat in the warm fug of a bar at a small rural racetrack, she began to understand. It was as if she was beginning to discover herself – the person who had disappeared during her marriage to a man whom she had loved but for whom she had sacrificed the greater part of her personality. But now, today, she felt a stirring in her soul, a reawakening of the person she had once been, of her younger self.

Millie was telling her how partnerships worked in racing and what a wonderful thing they were for small would-be owners, giving them a chance to enjoy all the excitement of owning without having to pay out the sort of money that only big business or the rich could afford.

'Then there are all the extras,' Millie was saying, in conclusion. 'The shoeing, the vet, the insurances, the entry fees, et cetera, but again in a partnership you are only paying a quarter. And if the horse you buy is any good and you want to go on racing it, you take it in turns to have it carry your colours.'

'Your colours?' a wide-eyed Alice repeated, since such a notion had never occurred to her. 'But I don't have any colours.'

'You design what you want, duck, and if they're available you pay an annual fee and they're yours.'

But before any real and businesslike conclusions were made there was Trojan Jack's race to be watched. When they all went to look at him in the paddock Millie remarked that he had one of his cross days on, since he looked moody and restless, swishing his tail as he walked and laying back his ears. Grenville commented that it might well be due to the increasingly inclement weather, to which Millie replied that it was the same for all the horses and none of the others seemed to be minding. There was certainly little confidence in her horse in the market, his opening price of two to one having drifted to nine to four, then to three to one, finally to settle at an uneasy nine to two.

'Not as uneasy as Herr Trainer,' Grenville observed as they saw a rain-sodden Rory scuttling across the paddock towards them, beetle-browed. 'Something amiss, guv'nor?'

'Only forgot to declare the blasted blinkers,' Rory muttered as he joined the party, now up in the grandstand as the horses went to post. 'My own damned fault.'

'What does that mean?' Alice wondered.

'Means he can't wear them, Alice,' Grenville explained. 'You have to declare the fact you want to run your horse in a blindfold. Which would explain why he's taken a walk in the market.'

'A walk in the market?' Alice sighed. 'This is all way over my head.'

'The way his odds have drifted,' Millie said. 'He really should be favourite, given his last run, and the fact he hasn't gone up notably in the handicap.'

'He's now five to one on the Tote,' Grenville said, looking at the show of the approximate Tote odds.

'Why would he need blinkers?' Alice asked. 'I thought only milk ponies wore blinkers.'

'It's meant to make them concentrate,' Grenville said. 'Stop them becoming distracted by other

240

horses. Lot of horses stop racing altogether when they see another horse drawing up alongside to challenge. They simply throw in the towel.'

'Like this one,' Rory said. 'And as if that's not bad enough, our pilot's just taken a bang on the head. Or on what passes for his head.'

'Then he won't be fit to ride, surely?' Grenville said in astonishment. 'He won't pass the MO, surely?'

'The doctor won't have known about it. They were horsing about in the changing room, playing piggy-back jousting or some such idiotic game as played by people with size three hats, and our jock banged his head on the lockers. When I was briefing him in the paddock he thought he was at Chepstow.'

'Can't you get another rider?' Alice asked.

'Bit late now,' Rory replied. 'Trouble is he knows the horse and he also happens to be a good pilot. So let's just hope his wretched concussion is only temporary.'

'I'm sure it will be fine once they're off and running,' Millie said. 'Jack's such an old hand I could ride him round here.'

'Now why didn't I think of that?' Rory said. 'As it happens, it's not much of a race. The two good horses have been withdrawn because of the change in the going, and so if only I'd remembered the blasted shades—'

'They're off, old sport,' Grenville announced, putting his race glasses up. 'And your chap's gone straight into the lead.'

It was a handicap hurdle race over two miles, the same as at Sandown but of a lower standard. This was perfectly apparent because as they passed the stands for the first time, having only jumped two flights of hurdles, half a dozen of the field of ten runners looked to be tailed off already, the two back markers already receiving hefty reminders from their pilots that there was still work to be done.

By the time they turned out of the back straight Jack was still ten lengths in the lead, and cantering, his jockey sitting still as a mouse.

'Bar a fall, Rory,' Grenville announced, glasses fixed firmly on the action.

'Just wait and see,' Rory muttered in return. 'Early days. Jack has a sleeve full of tricks.'

With two flights to jump, breasting the sharp rise in the track, Jack could be seen making his way to the far side of the run-in, his pilot having obviously decided to finish with the help of the running rail.

'Wrong,' Rory announced. '*Wrong move.*'

'He's still five lengths ahead,' Grenville said, watching the horse clear the penultimate flight with ease. 'And going easily.'

'But look at this other horse coming at him!' Rory shouted, slapping his head with his rolled up racecard. 'I told him to come over on the stand rails! To avoid exactly this! Seeing another horse coming at him! Kick him, Derek! Kick him on, for goodness' sake!'

But as he landed over the last flight, even

though he was still a good three to four lengths clear, Jack's head went up as he became aware of another horse at his quarters and he started to look round. Even when the challenging horse was within three-quarters of a length of Jack, he was not really catching him, so if Jack just kept galloping, which he could well have done, so full of running was he, he would still have the race at his mercy. But the moment he sensed and then saw a rival out of the corner of his eye, he simply downed tools. He didn't just slow up and get caught: he all but stopped dead, his tail swishing round furiously and his head sticking up high in the air. The jockey did his best to regalvanise him, kicking him and hitting him, but the horse was having none of it. He simply planted himself a hundred yards from the winning post and let the second horse labour past him, and then the third and finally the fourth, the rest having pulled up. Finally, as if at last completely sure there was no danger from any other passing horse, Jack picked up his bit again and galloped happily past the post, barely out of a sweat.

Rory refused a consolatory drink, excusing himself on the score that he had to go off and shoot the jockey, while the rest of the party hurried back out of the rain and into the owners' and trainers' bar.

'That was dastardly,' Constance said, pressing Lynne's hand. 'Snatching defeat out of the jaws of victory, yes? What hard luck, my dear. Better luck next time.'

'Thanks,' Lynne replied. 'But it's not my horse, Lady Frimley. Sorry. It's Millie's.'

'I imagine you must feel a bit like the Queen Mother when that horse of hers did that silly thing it did,' Constance said, linking arms with Millie. 'The horse that writer chappie rode. Now come along, you need a good stiff drink. Glanville? Millie here needs a stiffie.'

'Of course, Constance, just coming.' Grenville sighed. 'And it's Grenville, not Glanville.'

'As if it matters,' Constance retorted. 'Just get this poor creature a large brandy. Really. Did you ever. The manners of the young nowadays.'

As Constance took herself off to the ladies, Alice sat down by Lynne while Grenville was busy at the crowded bar.

'The horse,' she began. 'There are to be what? Four partners?'

'So I'm told,' Lynne replied. 'And so far there's Grenville and me. So seriously, if you do want to come in, apparently it's three thousand, one hundred and fifty guineas, plus training, and all the bits and bobs.'

'Three thousand,' Alice repeated, more for her own ears than Lynne's. 'Still, that's a bit less than the fifteen thousand Rory was asking.'

'You'd have got him for twelve.'

'I couldn't have afforded that!' Alice exclaimed. 'That is an awful lot of money.'

'Yeah, me neither,' Lynne agreed. 'Well actually I suppose I could, but I didn't think I should. No – no, this seems to be the way to go, right?

We'll have fun. Life's too short, Alice. So maybe let's try and have a bit of fun while we still can, eh?'

'Absolutely,' Alice agreed with a nod. 'After all, and as they keep reminding us, we all only pass this way once. Three thousand, one hundred and fifty guineas. Millie?'

'It's your money, duck,' Millie returned. 'And since it looks as though you've sold your house, and compared to what you're paying for Cherry Tree Cottage – if I were you, why not? Go for it. Why ever not?'

'We'd still need one more partner, to make it viable,' Alice said. 'Will you come in, Millie?'

'I'd love to, but I can't really, angel. Least not while I've still got old Jack to pay for. But really, it shouldn't be that hard to get the last leg. Perhaps Rory will take it, except I don't think so. Not given the precarious state of his business.'

'Hello,' Lynne said with a grin. 'I think Connie's scored.'

The other two women looked over to where Constance now was, having reappeared from the ladies, and saw she was being chatted up by a short red-faced man in a bright tweed suit who was holding an opened bottle of champagne up by way of invitation. After a moment's hesitation Constance allowed herself to be almost frog-marched off to a table in the far corner of the bar.

'Not really her type, surely?' Millie remarked. 'She told me she only likes tall men with silver hair, not short tubby bald oranges.'

'Well anyway,' Alice decided, 'I'm in. You can definitely count me in.'

'Great,' Lynne said. 'Grenville's doing all the paperwork. I reckoned he should look after the partnership since he seems to know all about it. Horses, I mean.' She added a shy smile before raising her glass to celebrate their forthcoming partnership.

'Alice is in,' she told Grenville when he returned with Millie's drink.

'Good,' Grenville said. 'Excellent. But I thought I was going to sharp-end it, as it were?'

'You are,' Lynne replied. 'I just invited her in, that's all. You can do all the dotting and crossing and all that.'

'Here's poor Rory,' Alice said, opening her bag. 'Rory, let me get you a drink – and I insist. What would you like?'

'A large hemlock would do nicely, Alice,' Rory said as he sat down. 'And if they can't do hemlock a brandy and ginger would do the trick. Thank you.'

'Well?' Millie said.

'I don't know what to say.' Rory sighed. 'What can I do to get this wretched horse of yours first past the post?'

'A one-horse race, maybe?' Grenville laughed. 'Find a nice walkover somewhere?'

'I wouldn't be too sure,' Rory replied. 'Knowing Jack he'd find a way to lose a walkover as well.'

'Quickly, one of you,' Constance hissed, quite suddenly reappearing at their table at considerable speed, pursued by her claret-faced, bright-check-suited suitor. 'One of you say you're my husband. Quickly!'

'I think this had better be one of you two,' Millie said with a smile at Rory and Grenville.

'Perhaps I could be your son?' Grenville wondered *sotto*. 'Would that be any help?'

'Darling,' Constance sighed, putting her hand over Grenville's, as her admirer arrived equally hotfoot, bottle of champagne still in hand. 'Have you seen that great big strapping husband of mine anywhere?' She fixed Grenville firmly with her eye and waited, while her beau came to a stop behind her chair, wondering whether or not to pursue his suit.

'When last seen he was just putting some welshing bookmaker to flight,' Grenville replied. 'Not a pretty sight.'

He turned to smile at the small bald man behind Constance, who was now obviously having very visible second thoughts. A moment later he withdrew and hurried away.

'He's gone,' Grenville said, reclaiming his hand. 'All clear.'

'What a perfectly dreadful fellow,' Constance said, straightening her skirt and adjusting her hat. 'Owns supermarkets and wanted me to go up to Blackpool. Imagine.'

'I've always thought it was a pity about Blackpool,' Grenville mused. 'Among the best sands anywhere. Be quite a different proposition in the south of France.'

'Thank you, Glanville,' Constance said, blowing him a little kiss with one gloved hand. 'What's that they say nowadays? I owe you one.'

'And I think I might just have the answer to that, Lady Frimley,' Grenville replied. 'And it's Grenville, remember?'

'Yes, yes. You do make such a fuss, you men. So what is your answer to everything, young man?'

'Let's discuss that on our journey home, Lady Frimley,' Grenville smiled. 'Or may I call you Cynthia?'

Almost caught, Constance looked at him sharply, then saw the smile in his eyes. Opening her bag, she took out her cheroots and lit up once more with the help of her table lighter.

'What you may do, Grenville,' she said carefully, 'is get me a nice large gin and It.'

'Hope you're feeling flush, Connie,' Millie remarked after Grenville had gone to the bar. 'I think your so-called son has plans for you.'

Chapter Eleven

A Sickness

Boyo wasn't at all himself. The day before he had relished every mouthful of his food, but this morning he couldn't even stand the smell of something he generally found delicious. Instead he stood with his head hanging down in the corner of his box, his nose running, giving the odd shiver.

Then he coughed.

'I don't believe what I just heard,' Rory groaned as he did his morning rounds, having just passed by the horse's box and now turning back. 'Don't tell me that was you, matey,' he told the backside that he saw facing him. 'Because if it was, that's all I something well need.'

Drawing the bolt on the lower door back, Rory entered the stable and saw the full manger of food. When he did, he knew the worst.

'Teddy?' he called in despair as he returned to the yard. 'Teddy – fetch the thermometer. This horse is coughing.'

'Never,' Teddy said, wide-eyed.

'No, of course he's not,' Rory replied. 'I'm just joking. You know it's the kind of thing that has me rolling about the yard holding my sides. He's coughing – and he hasn't touched his grub.'

'Typical,' Teddy sighed, dumping his pitchfork in the muck barrow. 'Just as I was getting some condition on him.'

'It might be nothing,' Rory said, without much conviction. 'It might be just a bit of dry food stuck somewhere. Though if it is I'll eat your hat.'

Just when he'd been getting the horse right and ready, Rory mused as he headed towards the office to ring the vet just in case of trouble. Since Kathleen's visit the little horse hadn't looked back. He had put on condition so fast that Rory had been forced to revise his training schedule, curtailing his road work and getting the animal cantering much earlier than anticipated. In fact so well had the horse come on that Rory had even managed to get a good fast piece of work under his belt, and had been well pleased with the result.

And now the little horse was coughing.

When he got into the office he noticed that Maureen had her bad-news look on.

'Now what?' he groaned. 'Don't tell me – someone else is taking their horse away.'

'No. That was the hospital, Mr Rawlins,' Maureen replied. 'They want you to call them.'

Rory bit his lip in anguish, as if to swallow what he had just said. As far as his father's health went, everything was going so well that Rory had simply assumed that any day now his father would be discharged and returned home all but fully mended. But when he spoke to the hospital he learned this was far from the truth.

'It's just one of those things, Rory,' said the doctor, a man with whom Rory had become friends, so much respect had he for the care he had taken over his father. 'These secondary infections catch us all out. We took every precaution we could.'

'I know that, Dan,' Rory replied. 'I know what care you've all taken.'

'The good thing is he was beginning to make such headway that the possibility is he'll be strong enough to resist the infection, which certainly would not have been the case a couple of weeks ago.'

'Can I come in and see him?'

'Of course. We've isolated him, naturally, but there's nothing to stop you coming in and showing him your cheery mug.'

'I'll come in now,' Rory said. 'I just have to call the vet and then I'll be on my way.'

He rang Noel, the stable vet, immediately.

'Yes,' the lugubrious Noel sighed. 'I'm not being surprised here. There is an awful lot of this about, young man.'

'I don't have any other horses coughing,' Rory replied. 'I've isolated him, but I'd like you to come and have a look at him as soon as you can. One good thing – his temp's only half a point over normal.'

'They don't always run a high temp with this thing. And I'll be there as soon as I can.'

'I have to pop over to the hospital to see Dad, but I won't be gone more than an hour.'

Ten minutes after Rory left the telephone rang again.

When she answered it Maureen could barely hear the person on the other end of what was obviously a very bad line.

'I'm sorry,' she said. 'I didn't catch who this is.'

'Leen,' was all Maureen could hear. 'Leen Lanagan. Peek to Mr Rawlins?'

'I'm afraid Mr Rawlins isn't here at the moment. Can I help you? This is a very bad line, I'm afraid.'

On the other end of the phone Kathleen missed that information altogether. This time Cronagh really was suffering the aftermath of a severe storm that had brought most of the country telephone lines down. She was making her call from one of the few lines still available, the one in Finnegan's Exclusive American Cocktail Lounge.

'I was just ringing to see how the patient was,' Kathleen said, raising her voice against the interference that she could now hear. What she didn't say was that the night before she had experienced a very vivid nightmare in which the horse was found sick and starving in a field. It had been such a disturbing dream that, unable to get it out of her head all morning, she had felt compelled to call his trainer, as Rory had told her she could.

'The patient?' Maureen repeated, having heard

that question clearly enough and raising her own voice even more in reply, although misunderstanding the enquiry. 'I'm afraid it's not good news. He's had rather a bad setback and is suffering from a quite serious secondary infection. Mr Rawlins is with him now.'

'How . . . he?' the caller asked, now all but drowned in atmospherics.

'You'll have to repeat that, I'm afraid. This really is a terrible line.'

But all Maureen could hear was appalling interference on the line.

'Hello?' she called. 'Hello?'

But since it seemed she had lost her caller Maureen hung up, thinking that if the woman wanted to know more she would ring back when the lines were better.

'Hello?' Kathleen said in desperation at the other end, hearing Maureen well enough now, but then realising that she herself could not be heard. 'Hello – hello!'

But the line had gone completely dead. Kathleen tried going through her friend the local operator, but could get no joy there either.

'Sure the lines are down all over the place, love,' the operator told her. 'That was a heck of a storm and you were lucky to get that line out at all. I had to put it through on Father Leroy's line.'

The last time all the lines were down after such a storm they had stayed down for nearly a fortnight, all but cutting off the entire area from Cronagh to the Atlantic coast itself. Fearing the

253

same thing might happen again, Kathleen knew what she must do. Somehow or other she would have to cross over to England again and go and see her beloved little horse, who she was now convinced was dangerously if not mortally sick, although how she was going to be able to afford the trip had not yet occurred to her.

Rory was back from the hospital in time to catch Noel before he left.

'I've taken some blood, and I scoped the horse as well, young man,' the vet told him. 'I'll call the moment we have the results. Been making any noise at work?'

'Not a sound,' Rory said, shaking his head. 'He's completely clean-winded.'

'I know it's little consolation, but there really is a lot of this about. Nick Granger's had to shut up shop.'

'Thanks for that, Noel.'

'Keep an eye on his temperature,' Noel advised, closing up his bag. 'You're right. It is only half a point up so it might be just a dirty nose.'

'And pigs might do aeronautics.'

'Not much of him, is there?' the vet remarked with a backward nod of his head as he walked away from the stable. 'Got quite decent quarters, but there's not really a lot of him.'

'Stand by for surprises,' Rory said. 'This horse has got a motor.'

'What were you saying about flying pigs?' Noel returned, getting into his cluttered car. 'Anyway, since he is coughing, I wouldn't go entering him up for a while.'

'Shall I move Boyo to one of the bottom boxes, boss?' Teddy asked, when he heard the news.

'I wouldn't bother, Teddy,' Rory replied, trudging back towards his office. 'If I were you I'd just start looking for another job.'

Certainly as far as Rory was concerned, had today been a fish, as he remarked to Maureen, he'd have thrown it back. Maureen told him about the call he'd missed without being able to enlighten him any further and in return Rory told her about his father.

'He looked better than I thought he would,' he said. 'All those awful tubes and feeders are out, or most of them, at any rate. He's still on a drip because of the infection, and he's also got one of those newfangled oxygen things. But still – he looks a better colour, and he even managed a cheery wave or two. The problem is that they think the infection might have gone to his chest, which is just the place they don't want it to go.'

'I'm so sorry,' his secretary said. 'Everyone's so fond of your father.'

'Right,' Rory replied. 'Me included. And now on top of everything, just as the little horse was coming to hand, he goes down.'

Rory made himself a cup of coffee and then sat at his desk to do a bit of metaphorical head-scratching. First of all he consulted the list of entries he had already earmarked for the horse and wondered whether he should just throw in the towel and forget about them, since if Boyo really did have the cough he wouldn't be seen on a racecourse for at least two months, or whether he should select a few choice entries just in case it was nothing serious. Then there was the problem of how much he should tell the new owners, if anything at all. Like his father Rory believed that owners had a right to know everything about their horses, good and bad, and that they should be part of the decision-making process, because they owned the animals and paid the bills for their keep. Yet because this partnership was not yet fully and officially formed he could see a reason for not letting them know just yet, not because he was afraid of losing them as potential owners but because he couldn't quite see the point since they hadn't yet paid out anything. Then if the horse was found to be suffering from something minor – which Rory still believed was possible since no one else was coughing in the yard – they could simply carry on from where they had left off, which was three legs in and one to go.

In that case, Rory told himself, he would make some select entries, which at least would look good on the cards he would then send out to his new but still nominal owners, and might even encourage someone to buy the fourth leg since as soon as entries were made attitudes changed immediately. It was the moment when reality took over from fantasy.

*   *   *

As it happened, as far as filling the partnership went, reality had all but been achieved, thanks to the sales pitch Grenville had delivered to Constance on their return journey to London from Wincanton. He had used Lynne as his unwitting accomplice, discussing with her how much fun and excitement they were going to have as owners, over-egging the pudding as much as he dared by even going as far as to suggest that if the horse was anywhere near as good as Rory said, he could see them ending up at Cheltenham being presented with some cup or other by the Queen Mother. Since he also made sure that the speedometer never went over forty miles an hour, his sales pitch had of course – just as he had hoped it would – finally proved irresistible to Constance, while his driving speed had – as he had feared it might – totally bewildered not only Lynne but any motorist unlucky enough to get stuck behind him on the narrower parts of the A303.

Even so, by the time they reached Knightsbridge, Lady Frimley had declared herself to be the buyer of the fourth leg in the now perfectly formed racing partnership. Grenville's only remaining concern was how exactly he was going to extract any monies from the most senior partner.

'All my money is tied up in some wretched trust or other in one of those equally wretched islands or other,' she had told him when he invited Lynne and her up to his flat for a celebratory glass. 'It's an utter bore since it only allows one a certain amount of loot at a time, but then I'm such a spendthrift it's probably a very good thing, all told.'

Grenville had pulled a private face to himself, remembering Constance's taxi tactics. Her latest scam, having agreed to come into the partnership, was to promptly delegate Grenville to run her share of the affair, indicating that all telephone calls and any petty expenses incurred should be handled and met by Grenville. So be it, Grenville had privately decided between equally privately clenched teeth, if it meant that they were finally up and running – a situation he desired not because he had ever been really serious about owning a horse, let alone a share in one, but because it would give him free and constant access to his adored Lynne. No more could she threaten him with exclusion: their lives were now going to be permanently intertwined, thanks to their involvement with their new purchase. So if Constance proved to be a late or a bad payer, it was something with which he would have to deal – and most certainly would, because if there was one area in which he could steal a march over Constance it was in the running of any affairs of business. Most of all he knew that if she did prove a thorn in all their sides, or if she did indeed fail to meet her dues, then they would simply dump her overboard and find another sharer, something that he reckoned would not be very hard, provided that the horse when finally in action performed even reasonably. If the animal showed any real potential, the plus point was that they might even make some money buying Constance out.

The following evening he called Rory to tell him the good news.

'You don't sound very happy,' Grenville remarked when he heard Rory's tone. 'I thought you'd be greatly cheered, old chap.'

'I am, Grenville,' Rory replied. 'My apologies. It's my father. He's had a setback.'

Rory explained and Grenville listened sympathetically, saying that if there was anything at all he could do, Rory was to count on him. Touched, Rory thanked him and put down the telephone, feeling terrible. He had just had confirmation from the vet that the horse's blood was wrong, and he had said nothing at all about it to Grenville.

But as it so happened, his saviour was just about to make her way to him, once she had finished with what was to become known as the Cronagh Syndicate.

Those in that small Cork town who had seen The Enchanted run in both his Irish races were convinced they had seen something special, but then such normally is the case in that part of the world, and in particular in the environs of Cronagh, both rural and urban. Now they were waiting for his first run in England, and since they knew that Anthony Rawlins's small racing establishment must be a betting yard (for, as they all asked, how else do small trainers keep in business?) they were ready to note the horse's entries and then to take advantage. In order to get the best price, they knew to a man that it would have to be a well-organised coup, the money to be placed simultaneously with various bookmakers, spot on the dot of the chosen minute of the designated hour because none of them wanted the odds to shorten before the money was down. Absolute secrecy and total discretion were the prime requisites.

'Now something is afoot,' Michael Doherty declared when they were all met late one evening in the back bar of Finnegan's Exclusive American Cocktail Lounge. 'Here we have a horse entered up all over the shop yet not running, so we can only assume our man is waiting for *the right race*. So as soon as we see him declared as a certain runner, that's when we know, and that's when we move in. What would really help of course is if we had a spy in the camp. For not only would we know how the horse is doing in his home work, we'd know well in advance when he was running, and then we could get the money down early.'

'We've no way of tellin' who the work rider is, I suppose,' Napper Reilly wondered, himself a retired jockey and now a small-time bloodstock scout for a small-time British trainer.

'Pity about the auld leg,' Padraig sighed, tapping Napper's prosthetic with his hawthorn stick. 'Or we'd have you on the first boat over.'

'There's someone all too willing to go over,

Padraig.' Yamon spoke up from the darkness. 'And they're family too.'

'God, man,' Padraig groaned. 'Aren't I short-handed enough?'

'Maybe so, but ye'll be looking at poor men for the rest of your days,' Michael warned him. 'Get that streak of a boy of yours to work double for a while.'

Padraig looked at Michael, shook his head, then drained his glass, pulled the collar on his old brown overcoat up round his ears and walked out into the cold night air, knowing that what his friends had said was true and that it was sense to do as he was advised.

When he got home, as if ordained by the gods, he found Kathleen sitting on top of a packed suitcase, trying to squeeze it closed.

'How's this, then?' he asked. 'Off on your travels again, my girl?'

'What travels?' Kathleen was surprised. 'I don't go on travels, Da.'

'So you're off on no travels, then.' Padraig nodded, sticking his pipe in his coat pocket. 'Just like the no travels you went off on before.'

'See, I have to, Da,' she replied after a while. 'I know the horse is sick.'

'You do so?'

'Yes, I do. I really do.'

'But how are you affording it? Sure you can't keep financin' this sort of thing.'

'I still have a bit left in the trousseau tin.'

'You think I'll countenance that sort of

palaver?' Padraig growled. 'What sort of father do you think you have who'd allow his daughter up the aisle in her wedding gown with only some tired old chemise under it? What sort of father would that be? I'll hear of no such thing. So if instead I were to give you your wages for the next month—'

'No, Da!' Kathleen protested. 'You can't afford that. I'll be fine. I'll manage.'

'If managing means standing be the side of the road hitching your skirts I'll not hear of that either,' her father replied, taking a sheaf of notes from the top inside pocket of his trousers and counting some out. 'Sure we made a bit on the horse, so why not invest a bit of what we made? Besides that, you can be of use to us all, girl. And not only in getting the horse right, if you mind me.'

'I'm minding you, Da,' Kathleen said. 'When did I ever not?'

'Just when you get there, when you reach Mr Rawlins, offer him your services but do it for free, saying you have to be near this horse of yours. He'll not refuse you. What sensible man could?'

Padraig handed her some money, then, his pipe back out, lit it, not taking his eyes off his daughter.

'Ah, you want a spy in the camp, don't you?' She laughed. 'You're a wily old article, so you are.'

'We only need to know how the horse is working and when he's entered up, and who better to tell us than she who knows him best? Than she who rides him best?'

'So it's riding him I am now?'

'He's seen how you ride, that young man, and weren't his eyes out on broomsticks? You'll be riding him out in no time.'

'I have first to make sure of his health, Da. The woman on the phone said he was bad.'

'So go see, girl. If anyone can get him right, 'tis yourself.'

Rory was waiting for Noel to arrive when he caught sight of a figure carrying a small suitcase making its way up the long tree-lined drive that led to the farm and the yard. He thought he knew who it was from its size, and from the way it was walking, but then he dismissed such a notion as fanciful or maybe even wishful thinking, for he'd been in two minds as to whether or not to put a call in to Cronagh later in the day, particularly when he had heard the news that the horse was in the vet's opinion definitely suffering from the current equine virus. Not that he thought the call would do any definite good, because the virus was the virus. He had just thought about making the call because he thought he would very much like to hear Kathleen Flanagan's voice again.

Now he could see his visitor more clearly, and he felt a tug on the string of his heart, because unless his eyes and reason and understanding had all completely failed him his visitor was indeed none other than Kathleen.

'Kathleen?' he said, hurrying to greet her and to take hold of her suitcase. 'Do you know, I thought it might be you and, good heavens, it is.'

Relieved of her case, Kathleen straightened herself up and then extended her right hand.

'Look,' she said. 'Look, I was just passing so I thought I'd drop in.'

'You must have heard the ker-kettle,' Rory replied, falling into step beside her, and closing his eyes as the stammer returned – a hesitation that had completely disappeared since he had seen the girl by his side off on the train from Bristol.

'The Irish,' Kathleen said, 'can hear a kettle going on in another county.'

'So,' Rory continued, walking towards the house. 'So you were just passing through, on your way ter-ter-to . . . ?'

'Just on my way through.'

'Of course,' Rory agreed, pushing open the front door with his foot. 'And I'm right on the route.'

'Hello, dog,' Kathleen said in surprise to the large lurcher who was greeting them both. 'I don't think we've met.'

'This is Dunkum,' Rory told her as the huge dog suddenly jumped up to put both front paws on Kathleen's shoulders. 'And if you w-want to know why he's called that it's because of how he likes his teatime biscuits. You'll also need to – to – to *watch* your things, because he's also a full time ker-leptomaniac.'

'I'll do that,' Kathleen agreed, trying to keep

up the pretence of the casual visitor. 'So how's everything?'

'So-so,' Rory replied. 'Unfortunately my dad's not too good at the moment.'

'God, no,' Kathleen said, her face suddenly serious. 'God, now, I'm real sorry to hear that. But he's going to get better?'

'If I have anything to do with it he will.'

'The right and the best attitude to have. And everything else about the place?'

'Your horse isn't too bright at the moment,' Rory said carefully, keeping an eye out for her reaction.

'He isn't working too well? Or what? What exactly?'

'What exactly is – he's been coughing.'

'He has to have his hay well soaked, but then you know that.'

'The hay's always soaked,' Rory replied. 'All the hay. It always is. The vet thinks he's got the v-v-virus.'

'The virus or a virus?' Kathleen wondered. 'I never do understand why vets always call these things *the* virus, as if there's just the one.'

'You can ask him yourself,' Rory told her. 'He'll be here shortly. Look. Look, I was just about to have a drink. Can I get you one?'

He got them both a drink, orangeade for Kathleen and beer for himself.

'I see you have a case,' he remarked as he handed Kathleen her glass. 'Are you staying with somebody?'

'Depends on what's required,' Kathleen replied, raising her glass, determined not to give away too much, reminding herself that, after all, it had only been a dream. '*Sláinte agus táinte*.'

'Your good health, Miss Flanagan.'

'If it's a virus, Mr Rawlins, I suppose you'll be shooting him up with antibiotics, then?'

'I suppose I shall have to do whatever the vet advises, Miss Flanagan.'

'I wonder if I could see the horse, Mr Rawlins? Before I go on, that is.'

'Go on as in passing through, do you mean?'

'I might. Would that be possible?'

'Of – of – of *course*, Miss Flanagan,' Rory replied, clicking finger and thumb behind his back. 'Soon as we've finished our drinks we'll go. We'll go as soon as we finish our drinks.'

'I got you the first time round, Mr Rawlins,' Kathleen said, eyeing him over the top of her glass. 'And I've finished mine.'

Rory nodded, downed his beer and led Kathleen out to the yard.

'I don't see him,' she said, looking at an empty stable.

'We put him in the lower case. Just in yard. We put him in the lower yard, just in case.'

'Has he been coughing much?'

'As far as I know, a horse doesn't have to cough much, Miss Flanagan, to be deemed to be coughing.'

'Sure I know that well enough.'

'He's been coughing enough to cause anxiety.'

Kathleen looked over the horse's stable door and saw him standing the way he always stood when something was amiss, with his head stuck in one corner, his ears flat and his tail tucked between his back legs. Kathleen didn't even have to call his name. The moment she put her hands on the top of the half-door he swung his head round and looked at her.

'He looks well enough, Mr Rawlins,' Kathleen observed. 'Looks the business, so he does.'

'He's a good doer, now he's back eating. Never leaves an oat – thanks to his personal serenader, Mr McCormack.'

'He's eating his bedding,' Kathleen said, having noticed the horse taking a mouthful of the straw on the stable floor.

'Horses do,' Rory replied. 'That's one of their th-things.'

'OK – fine,' Kathleen persisted. 'So where do you get your straw?'

'Off the farm.'

'And is it sprayed, maybe?'

'Maybe,' Rory said with a shrug, followed by a frown as he saw where this might be headed. 'I don't run the farm, and anyway everyone sprays their crops. Don't they?'

'If they do,' Kathleen said, 'they shouldn't give it to their horses as bedding. If they eat it what they get is a gutful of chemicals.'

'Sort of like us, I suppose,' Rory offered somewhat hopelessly.

'Is that the right example, I wonder? With the

greatest respect, I'd hardly take us for yardsticks, Mr Rawlins. Besides, horses have a completely different way of ingesting things and who knows what the chemicals do to them, the poor creatures. We only ever bed ours on straw we've grown or that we know hasn't been sprayed.'

'I was thinking of putting him on shavings,' Rory said out of the silence that had fallen. 'I was thinking of p-putting all the horses on shavings. But with my father in hospital . . .'

'Sure I know,' Kathleen consoled him. 'Isn't it one of those things you can do tomorrow? So now let's see how else he is.'

Kathleen entered the stable. After she had given the horse several long strokes down his neck, put a hand on his muzzle and pulled his ears, she gave him a thorough physical, paying particular attention to the area at the top of his neck and the bottom of his jaw.

'I'd say that the reason Boyo's been coughing, Mr Rawlins,' she said, coming back out of the stable, 'is because the glands in his neck are up. Not desperately so, but they're definitely larger than they should be.'

'So he has got an infection, then,' Rory said, as if that would close the door on it.

'It could just be a reaction, on the other hand,' Kathleen replied, looking at him sideways on. 'To something that's disagreed with him.'

'The point is, surely – whatever the reason – the point is if he does have an in-in-in-*fection* he's going to have to have an antibiotic, which in turn means even if it's a short course we won't get him on a racecourse for at least a month. He can't run, as you know – well, of course you do. He can't run with antibiotics in his system.'

'You could perhaps try something other than antibiotics.'

'Aspirin, perhaps? Have him gargle with TCP?' Rory enquired facetiously, immediately regretting his tone. 'Sorry. What else is there? For horses, that is.'

'If you want your horse racing, I'd try some bryonia,' Kathleen replied. 'I might put him on some ignatia as well, in case he still hasn't quite settled – and I'd certainly take all the straw out of his box and fumigate the whole stable. And before I forget it, his teeth need a rasp as well.'

Silence fell. For a moment Rory just stared at the ground, hating having what he considered to be his incompetence discovered, as well as not knowing what to say regarding Kathleen's suggestion that they try the horse on homoeopathic medicines for whatever infection he might or might not be suffering from. He stuck his hands deep in his pockets and continued to stare at the ground while he tried to work out how to deal with what was being suggested – whether to allow Noel to shoot the horse up with antibiotic, which was the standard and most practical procedure, or to fly in the face of veterinary advice and expect a dilution of some weird herb or other to do the trick.

'If I may say so, one of the main reasons he's

not eating up is because his teeth need seeing to.'
Kathleen broke the silence. 'Has he been quidding?
You know, dropping food at feed times?'

Rory nodded, remembering this was something
he had indeed noticed but not paid much
attention to, thinking the horse's carelessness at
the manger was simply the result of sloppy eating
habits. He coloured slightly at the illustration of
yet another instance of his apparent equine
mismanagement.

'The dentist's due in sometime this week,' he
lied. 'He's been on holiday.'

In another ensuing silence he continued
privately to berate himself for imagining he
could simply take over and run the yard with
as little experience as he'd had so far in training
and managing thoroughbred racehorses. It had
been easy enough when his father was around,
particularly since Anthony always made it look
quite straightforward. Consequently he had
thought all he had to do when his father was
taken ill was follow the daily routine. He realised
now that he had never known for one minute
what the full and proper protocol really was.

'Suppose I did – suppose we did try what you're
saying we should try,' he suddenly asked. 'What
would I say to Noel? To my vet? Who is probably
going to appear in the drive any moment now.'

'You must only do what you think best, Mr
Rawlins,' Kathleen replied. 'But if he does suddenly appear and you still don't know what to
do, just give us a broom and an old cap and I'll

say you're not here. That you had to go back to see your dad maybe, that the horse has stopped coughing and that you want to take a bit of a pull until you see if maybe the old infection will clear itself up.'

Rory took another long look at her, and realised that if this absurdly beautiful young woman with the bright green eyes told him to go and jump off a cliff because it was good for him he'd do it, willingly.

'OK, yes,' he muttered, frowning deeply and staring down at the ground again. 'But if we did – if we were to do this, you know. Where do we get this whatever it is – this homoeopathic stuff, whatever it is.'

'You have a big town near here?'

'We have a city. Salisbury. About half an hour away.'

'Then there's bound to be homoeopathic chemists. And if you're still anxious, let me tell you about the horse of Tim Milligan's that won at Cheltenham this year. He was said to have had the virus but they wouldn't treat him with antibiotics. Tim Milligan said if you do that you might as well put the horse away for the rest of the season. That horse won the Mildmay without going near the antibiotics.'

Rory listened and nodded. He knew what she was saying was perfectly right, not necessarily about homoeopathy, about which he knew less than nothing, but certainly about the effects of a course of antibiotics on a horse. He remembered one of his father's owners who happened to be a doctor saying that antibiotics remained in a horse's system for much longer than people believed or indeed than it showed on blood tests, which was why whenever one of his horses was treated that way he insisted they came out of training for at least three months.

Besides that, what was influencing Rory was the fact that he was starting to feel that he might actually have the sort of horse that, while not exactly projecting the stables into the big time, might well be capable of winning enough races to kick-start Fulford Racing Ltd back into proper business. The little horse that he had initially considered useless, first when his father had decided to buy it and particularly when it had arrived in the yard looking like something on its way to an equine rehabilitation centre, had now caught his fancy, not necessarily because of the little bit of faster work that he had seen but because of the animal's aura. There was not only something businesslike about the animal, but something almost mystical. By now Rory knew the characters, foibles and idiosyncrasies of all the horses in the yard and while he was fond of all of them, including the bad-tempered and dispiriting Trojan Jack, none of them had the presence that The Enchanted seemed to have. And although he was an artist and so blessed with an imagination, Rory knew that his instinct about the little Irish horse had nothing to do with imagination. He was like a star performer, in fact, he had *It*. Your heart raced a little faster when you saw him work.

Of course if the little horse did come up trumps the stable fortunes would take a turn for the better. A winning horse always catches owners' eyes, and since his father always maintained that there was nothing more a certain type of owner liked than to stable-hop in the hope that a new and winning trainer could turn their goose into a swan, every stable winner brought the chance of new owners.

And there was nothing that Fulford Racing Ltd needed more than new owners, unless it were a new *owner*. So the sooner Rory could get the little horse fit and ready to race, the better their chance for survival, and the only way to do that was to take a chance that Kathleen was right. QED.

'You've been away a long time,' Kathleen remarked, as Rory came back to earth.

'Things to think about,' he replied. 'Now you write down what I've got to get from this homoeopathic chemist place and I'll go and get it, because at the same time I can pop in and see my father – and you can do as you suggested, when the vet arrives.'

'OK,' Kathleen replied, with another toss of her dark hair. 'You won't regret it.'

'Guaranteed?'

'Absolutely.'

But as they turned away from each other, both of them knew nothing was absolute, other than real belief.

Chapter Twelve

Fast Work

'I'm moving to the country,' Alice said, closing her eyes and waiting for the explosion on the other end of the telephone line.

'I can't have heard right, Mum,' Georgina said after an ominous silence. 'Did you say you were moving to the *country*?'

'I think that's what I said, Georgie. Yes.'

'You're a townie, Mum.' Georgina sighed. 'You wouldn't work in the country.'

'Oh, I think I might.'

'Come on – you'd be bored stiff in a minute. There's nothing to *do* in the country. Not at your age.'

Alice was on the point of telling her about the horse but managed to button her lip in time, knowing that if Georgina got hold of that piece of information the fun would go out of it all, and it would lead to yet another litany of questions and accusations, such as:

What on earth did she think she was doing?

Had she *completely* lost it?

Did she *ever* think of anyone else but herself?

Like, did she *never* think of her family?

And much as she loved Georgina, which she did with all her heart, Alice couldn't face it.

It had obviously been a mistake to tell her and Joe that she was moving to the country. She should of course have waited until she had actually gone, because that way nobody would get the chance to spoil it, but unable as always to keep herself to herself she had proceeded to spill the beans.

'What about your grandchildren?' Georgina was now wondering. 'When are you going to see them, and them you – stuck miles away somewhere in the country? I suppose we'll be expected to hump all the way down there at weekends, just when the traffic is *really* at its loveliest.'

'Rather than me "humping" all the way up to you when I'm down in the country enjoying myself.'

'Meaning?'

'Meaning exactly that, Georgina. You'll all be more than welcome to come and stay once I'm settled in.'

'Joe's allergic to the country. It brings him out in depressions.'

'That's just too bad. The point is I've bought the cottage and I'm moving in next week.'

'Is this some sort of very late mid-life crisis?'

'No,' Alice replied as evenly as she could. 'It's just something I want to do.'

'You won't last a minute down there. Really, Mum, you're out of your mind. You really won't be able to hack it.'

'So you keep telling me.' Alice stroked the dog on her knee and then eased him to the floor, deciding it was time to end this conversation, in line with one of her new resolutions, rather than let her daughter hang up first, which she always somehow managed to do. 'I have to go now, Georgie dear – Sammy needs a walk. Goodbye, darling. Love to the children.'

Alice was sure she heard her daughter giving a slight gasp just before she put down the receiver, but that was just too bad. She was back to being herself. She'd found her voice again, young Alice's voice, the voice of the woman who had stood up to her parents and everyone else who had tried to stop her marrying the love of her life.

Lynne was also on the move, heading out west ahead in her recently acquired second-hand silver Mercedes SL sports car. All she had awaiting her in her new apartment in Brook House was one single bed and an armchair purchased and dispatched from Peter Jones, but as far as Lynne was concerned that was more than enough. What mattered was that she was making a brand-new start in a brand-new home, and for once she was not going to be rushed and bullied into buying not what she wanted but what someone else did.

Fortunately the newly appointed apartment came already fitted with an expensive kitchen and bathroom and the latest and most efficient form of central heating, as well as something Lynne considered the very height of luxury: a central vacuuming system. She would buy everything else she needed at her leisure, taking as much time as she liked to find exactly what she wanted. She didn't care how long it took her, because after all she only had herself to worry about.

'Blow you, Gerry Fortune!' she said to herself as she moved out into the fast lane. 'Who needs ya, baby?'

Brook House was a very large Georgian house that had once apparently been the country seat of some local earl or other, Lynne had gathered when being shown round the conversion. Then it had become a hotel, and then a girls' public school of doubtful repute, finally being purchased by a developer and turned into what was described as the ultimate concept in modern country living. At the end of the day, Lynne decided after her tour of inspection, what this meant was living in a nice new and very spacious apartment overlooking parkland instead of trying to hack it in a cramped two-bedroom flat overlooking some noisy and generally gridlocked road feeding central London, and for considerably less money. The ultimate concept in modern country living was fine by her. They could call it what they liked – to Lynne it couldn't matter less. What mattered was that it was hers and hers alone, and that she was free.

On her second visit Lynne had met a couple

of people who'd already moved in, and since they seemed about the same age as her, the one fear she had nursed, that she might be moving into some sort of upmarket retirement home, had been quickly dispersed. In fact judging from some of the expensive machinery parked at the front of the large stone-built mansion the very opposite was possibly true.

Singing happily to herself she locked up her Mercedes and gave it an admiring glance, relieved that she had obviously bought the right sort of motor to go with her new home. Then she took the lift to the apartment on the second floor, which as the brochure had put it *enjoyed fine and uninterrupted views over some of the most unspoilt land in west Hampshire.*

'I'm home,' she said to herself as she put a bottle of Dom Pérignon in the fridge to chill. 'I have finally come home.'

Chapter Thirteen

Blaze

Returning to the yard after his trip to Salisbury, where he had managed to find the homoeopathic chemist as well as look in on his father, Rory presented Kathleen with the chemist's bag.

'Interesting,' he said. 'What the Alchemist had to say. Seems every horse he can name has been miraculously cured by one of these m-magic potions.'

'Might your second name be Thomas, Mr Rawlins? You're a born doubter.'

'I prefer to think of myself, if I think of myself at all, as a bit of a realist actually, Miss Flanagan.'

'And where did realism ever get anybody? Into the alcoholic ward, that's where. And I really don't mind if you call me Kathleen.'

'If you call me R-Rory.'

'Thanks, but how could I do that when I'm working for you? How was your father?'

'No better, I'm afraid. But then he's no worse

either, and his doctor says that's a big plus.'

'Tell him he's in my prayers,' Kathleen said, preparing the first dose of bryonia. 'And everyone back home. Make sure to tell him now.'

'I will,' Rory agreed, touched. 'Thank you.'

'OK now,' she said, showing him the medicine. 'We'll go and shoot this into Boyo's mouth, all right? We have to give him a dose every four hours. Without fail.'

'We as in?' Rory enquired, scratching the side of his head and wishing that he could stop feeling like a schoolboy every time he talked to this lovely girl.

'Every four hours, mind,' Kathleen repeated, looking sideways at him. 'From this little syringe, see?'

Rory followed her out across the yard, thinking that now she was back in his life the last thing he wanted was for her to disappear again. But he really didn't know how he could persuade her to stay. There was no money to pay for another pair of hands, and even though she had arrived uninvited he could hardly expect her to stay and work for nothing, particularly since his powers of eloquent persuasion seemed to have deserted him.

'What is it?' she asked out of the blue, after she had given the horse his medicine. 'You've gone all silent again.'

'No. It's nothing. Nothing, Kathleen. No, I was just thinking.'

'No harm in that, I suppose.'

'No, actually I was wondering . . . it doesn't matter.'

'For heaven's sake don't go doing that.' Kathleen sighed. 'Don't go starting something and then not bother to finish. That really is – it drives me mad.'

'You were really passing through, as you called it, were you?' Rory asked, picking up a bit of baling twine from the ground and starting to make it into a cat's cradle. 'You know – when you said – when you arrived that is, this time. You said you were passing through, but that isn't or rather wasn't what you were doing at all. Was it?'

'Does it matter, Mr Rawlins?' Kathleen asked, looking him right in the eyes. 'It's neither here nor there now, is it? What matters is getting Boyo here right, and if my being here helps, then let's just call it providential, OK?'

'Fine by me.' Rory offered her the cat's cradle. 'Know how to do this?'

'Know how to do it?' Kathleen laughed. 'I'm the Cronagh open champion.'

Expertly and deftly she took the cradle of string from him, turned it into the next complex and handed it back to Rory, who almost as quickly played on and handed it back to her. She smiled.

'Misspent youth, Mr Rawlins?'

'Too much time on my own,' he replied, getting stuck on the next move now that he had it back. 'No good. Can't do it.'

He held up the cradle as far as they had got it and raised his eyebrows at Kathleen, who shook her head at him, took the cradle and quickly polished it off.

'Told you I was the champion,' she said. 'It's a hard school, the Cronagh Cat's Cradlers. All-Ireland champions.'

Rory smiled shyly back at her, took the small ball of baling twine into which Kathleen had restored the cradle and pocketed it, finding himself vowing like a child never to part with it ever again, whatever happened.

Kathleen cleared her throat, tidied her hair with her hands and checked the bolts on Boyo's stable door.

'OK,' she said, a word that seemed to Rory to be her mantra. 'Better get back to what I was doing, then.'

Rory said nothing. He just watched her as she began to sweep and tidy the yard as automatically as if she was back home in Cork. He watched her check the water buckets and the bolts on all the stable doors when she was done sweeping, and he watched her as she put her broom away, dusted her hands together and stood with arms akimbo surveying the now immaculate yard.

'I can't offer you a j-j-job,' he said finally, picking up the smallest piece of straw imaginable and handing it to her with a straight face.

'Can't think how I missed that,' she returned, equally straight-faced.

'I w-wish I could.' Rory nodded. 'Offer you a j-job. But we can't afford it.'

'Did I axe for a job?' she said wide-eyed,

thickening her brogue deliberately. 'I don't remember doing so.'

'You just came here to see the horse,' Rory offered, and then immediately regretted doing so when he saw the flash in Kathleen's green eyes.

'I did not come here looking for a job, as you call it, Mr Rawlins,' she all but snapped. 'I have a job at home, as you well know.'

'Sure.' Rory held his hands up in mock innocence. 'You were just passing through.'

Kathleen glared at him, but in truth she was more angry with herself than she was with him. She would have loved to tell him the truth, and not just the truth but the entire truth, because there was nothing Kathleen hated more than deceit, yet she knew she could not, for more reasons than just the one, so she had to bite her tongue and put up with what she saw as his facetiousness. She knew he knew that she had not just been passing through, as she had so lamely tried to convince him, but she knew that even if she told him a bit of the truth, that she had dreamed this terrible thing about her horse, that she had seen him sick and dying and that the dream had been as vivid and as potent as reality, she knew he would just think what she thought they all thought about the Irish, that they were full of nothing but whimsy and away with the fairies. So she put up and shut up, deciding to live in hope that what she wanted so much to happen might indeed happen, and she could somehow manage to stay here at Fulford Farm and look after a horse that although no longer hers would always belong to her in her heart as long as they both should live.

'Of course,' Rory began, twisting the ball of twine round his fingers out of sight in his pocket. 'Of course if you wanted to stay on for a while – see how your horse does – there'd certainly be no objections.'

Kathleen frowned but didn't say anything immediately. She looked past Rory into the distance and tried to work out how best to accept this invitation without making it seem that it was precisely what she had come for.

'OK,' she decided. 'But there's a proviso. If I was to do that – for a while, to see how Boyo does and all – if I were to do that I would have to work for my keep – and for nothing.'

'Yes – well, as I just s-said,' Rory replied, trying to keep the glee out of his voice, 'there wouldn't be any question of m-m-my paying you because there's nothing in that particular ker-ker-ker – *kitty*. You'd be looked after all right. I mean it might look a bit frayed at the edges, this place, but it's very comfortable. And warm. And of course you'd be able to keep an eye right on your horse.'

'Your horse, Mr Rawlins.'

'Fine. *The* horse, then. You'd be able to keep an eye on *the* horse.'

She turned her attention back to him, looking him once more directly in the eyes. Rory met the look and held her eyes with his. Even so, in spite of his determination, he found he dropped his first.

'Done deal,' Kathleen said. She pretended to spit on her hand and offered it to Rory, who took it and held it for as long as he dared.

'OK,' she repeated. 'But when Boyo gets better—'

'Yes.' Rory stopped her. 'If and when, which of course he will.'

'God willing,' Kathleen added. 'So when he does—'

'Let's cross that one when we come to it, shall we? That particular whatever,' Rory cut in. 'So now we've a deal, I'd better show you around and get you s-s-s-settled in.'

As they walked away together, behind her back Kathleen gave Boyo, who she knew was watching, the thumbs-up.

As soon as Rory had finished the full guided tour, including the rooms in a warm and comfortable little groom's cottage at the end of the yard, Kathleen set about her work. First, she saw to her horse, standing him in another box while she took his stable apart, disinfecting every inch of it, changing his bedding over to wood shavings – a supply of which Rory managed to scrounge from a friendly neighbouring trainer until he could get a full delivery – and washing out his mangers with boiling water. Then she disinfected his hay net and all the woodwork including the outside of the doors and windows, before finally giving the horse a thorough wash-down followed by a top-to-tail grooming. When that was done she went to find Rory, who was in his office checking the entries for his horses.

'If you don't mind my asking, Mr Rawlins,' she said, 'how often do you turn him out? Boyo, that is.'

'Well, I don't at the moment,' Rory replied, looking up from his paperwork in some surprise. 'If it's fine on Sundays some of them get run in the paddocks, but being short-handed and nearly in winter now we don't have the time or the m-manpower to clean off mud-covered horses.'

'But he needs to run out every day,' she told him. 'He always has. It's something he's been used to.'

'While he was growing, perhaps.'

'We run ours out even when they're in work.'

'As I just said, Miss Flanagan—'

'Kathleen.'

'As I just said, I don't have the – the – the—'

He knew perfectly well what he wanted to say, but the more he found himself looking at Kathleen the harder he found it to speak.

'I'm sure you could make an exception in his case,' she chipped in. 'It's what he needs. Look, I'll rug him up and I'll clean him off when he comes in. He really won't do good standing in all day like this.'

'We'll try it,' Rory agreed. 'But if anything happens—'

'Nothing will happen,' Kathleen replied, and

finding himself rewarded with a smile Rory at once felt it had been not only the right but the only decision to take. 'Are you expecting someone?' Kathleen went on, having seen something through the office window. 'It seems you have a visitor.'

Rory got up to take a look for himself and saw a battered old yellow VW Beetle with blackened windows and a sawn-off exhaust pulling noisily up in a cloud of smoke and dust at the edge of the parking area. Barely had it stopped before the driver's window was wound down and the end of a cigarette flicked away by the still unseen driver. For a moment no one got out, then all at once the door was kicked open and one hand appeared to be hooked backwards over the edge of the car's roof where it remained while the fingers drummed out a brief tattoo. Finally someone emerged from the interior, a lean, athletic young man in oddly old-fashioned riding breeches, well-worn tan half-boots, an off-yellow anorak over a thin black polo-neck sweater, and aviator-style dark glasses.

The young man stretched, yawned, stretched again, and raising his dark glasses briefly, looked round the yard to see if there was any sign of life. Not yet having spotted Rory watching him from the office he kicked the door of his car closed with a backward shove of one foot then sauntered casually round the yard, peering into the boxes with his hands clasped behind him like a cleric.

Unable to contain his curiosity any longer, Rory stole out of the office and crept up on his visitor until he was right behind him.

'Can I help you?' he said suddenly, hoping at the very least to startle the young man. But far from being disconcerted, the stranger turned slowly round to face Rory, nodded, smiled and held out a hand.

'Mr Rawlins,' he said, in a lilting Irish brogue, as a statement of fact rather than as an enquiry. 'Blaze Molloy. How you doing?'

'Blaze Molloy?' Rory returned, shaking the black-gloved hand. 'Yes? So what can I do for you?'

'They said you might be looking for a rider,' Blaze said, walking on uninvited ahead of Rory to resume his inspection of the horses. 'And since I have meself just moved in near to this very locality—'

'Who said I might be needing a rider?'

'The grapevine, Mr Rawlins,' the young man replied, putting both hands up as if in surrender but continuing his stroll.

'What sort of rider did you have in mind?' Rory called after him.

'Work rider, race rider, stable jockey – anything that's going.'

'I can't afford to take any more work riders, sorry,' Rory said. 'I'm afraid you're wasting your time.'

Blaze went on walking, apparently unperturbed. 'Word has it you bought a nice horse from

Padraig Flanagan,' he called back. 'Might I see him?'

'No, not really,' Rory said, catching up with him. 'He's not receiving visitors.'

'Not well, is he?'

'Had a dirty nose. Nothing serious.'

'Is that him? In the box down there?' Blaze pointed towards the horse's isolation stable and headed there before Rory could stop him.

'How did you know I'd bought a horse from Padraig Flanagan?' he asked when he caught the young man up.

'There's always talk when a horse crosses the water, Mr Rawlins, so there is,' Blaze replied. 'Particularly when it's to a betting yard.'

'This is not a betting yard. At least not when I'm in charge.'

'Rumour always was that your father liked a touch.'

'My father is in hospital at the moment.'

'I'm sorry to hear that.' Blaze turned to him, fixing him with a look of genuine sympathy. 'I hope it's not anything serious.'

'He had a heart attack,' Rory replied. 'And now he has a secondary infection.'

'Then may God help him,' Blaze said sincerely. 'He'll be in my prayers so. Now let's have a look at this horse of yours.'

'I'd rather you didn't disturb him, Mr Molloy,' Rory said.

'Blaze, please,' the young man insisted. 'And disturb him is the last thing I'll do.'

Rory sighed and stood by the half-open stable door while his uninvited visitor cast his eye over the horse.

'Not a lot of him,' Blaze observed. 'But he's got a good backside – and I hear he has a bit of a leap in him. Good legs too. And not far off racing I'd say, either. Long as he's well in himself.'

'I don't need a work rider, Mr Molloy, thanks all the same,' Rory said, closing the stable up behind the jockey.

'I'll ride work for nothing, sir. Not even the petrol.'

'Why would you want to do that?'

'Because I would, because of what I've heard about him,' Blaze replied, now dropping his laconic manner and becoming serious. 'Look, Mr Rawlins – I'll ride all the work you want in return for the ride. The first ride, mind. Just the first ride. I'm not asking for all of them. Let me ride his first race for you, that's all I'm asking.'

'I'm sorry,' Rory replied. 'I don't know anything about you. I don't even know if you can ride.'

'I can ride, Mr Rawlins, and if you let me ride the horse I'll win on him, for sure I will,' Blaze informed him, taking off his sunglasses and regarding Rory with large bright eyes the colour of cornflowers. 'And when I do, you'll want me to go on riding him, I promise you.'

'Do I look like a lemon? I don't know a thing about you, Mr Molloy,' Rory repeated. 'You could be the worst rider in Ireland for all I know.'

'No, he's certainly not that,' Kathleen's voice said behind Rory. 'He's not that at all, Mr Rawlins. They say this is a lad who's really going places.'

Rory turned round to stare at Kathleen and found her staring at Blaze.

'You two know each other?' he enquired.

'I don't know Mr Molloy,' Kathleen said. 'Not personally. But I know of him.'

'Then how do you know his name?' Rory frowned at her.

'I was – I was eavesdropping, I'm afraid,' Kathleen confessed. 'I'm afraid I was born nosy.'

'And you are?' Blaze asked, staring back at Kathleen.

'Kathleen Flanagan. Padraig Flanagan's daughter.'

'So you are,' Blaze said quietly. 'Is that right now? So you are, so you are.'

'I think this is utter – what do you call it? Blarney. Utter blarney. This is complete and utter blarney,' Rory protested. 'So you are – is that right now – yes you are. So you are, so you are.'

'Mr Molloy rides point to point, Mr Rawlins. And hunter chases.'

'Ah, but I have a proper licence this season, Miss Flanagan,' Blaze said. 'I can ride conditional.'

'I can vouch for his riding, Mr Rawlins,' Kathleen said. 'I saw him ride a grand double at Tramore in the spring.'

'But only point to point,' Rory said, becoming slowly aware of how the two were still regarding each other. 'Mr Molloy here is proposing himself to ride under Rules – and n-n-not only that – he's proposing he rides your horse here.'

'No, your horse, Mr Rawlins,' Kathleen corrected him. 'And you could do a lot worse,' she said.

'You won't do better, sir,' Blaze said with a sudden broad smile, taking off his cap and shaking out a head of curling blond hair. 'You wait and see.'

'If anyone else tells me to do that today,' Rory sighed, 'I shall give all this up and take up market ger-ger – *gardening*. Dammit, look – all right. Look, I'll put you up on something tomorrow – but only to see if you're as good as you seem to be saying you are – and when I've seen how you ride work, maybe I'll let you know my decision then.'

'God, now, that's fair enough,' Blaze said. 'God, thanks. God, that'll do me nicely.'

'I should think it is fair enough,' Rory muttered before turning his back. 'And you can leave G-God out of it.'

'So now tell me about yourself,' he heard Blaze saying to Kathleen as they walked away together. 'And how come and God knows why we've never met before.'

'Dunkum?' Rory called to his dog. 'Get in the car, boy – I don't know about you but I need a good long walk.'

By the time Rory had returned from a three mile point on Salisbury Plain, he was happy to see that Blaze Molloy had gone from the yard, just as he was happy to see that the yard was looking altogether smarter and tidier now that he had not only an extra pair of hands at work but hands that belonged to the skilled, devoted and beautiful Kathleen Flanagan. The clocks had long gone back so twilight was already setting in, the yard illuminated now only by the lights from the feed and tack rooms and those on the outside walls of the stables. Rory stopped and looked round him and thought what an oddly pleasing and happy sight it was, a racing yard at the time of evening stables, the horses all exercised and fed and most of them standing dozing happily at the doors of their boxes, or quietly munching a mouthful of fresh hay, while the stable cats stood stretching their backs and yawning in the anticipation of a good evening's mouse-hunting. Tonight all was quiet with not a horse kicking a door, the silence broken only by an occasional snort of equine satisfaction or the sound of one of them shaking itself after a good roll in its bedding. He had always enjoyed evening stables, ever since he was a boy, but now he was actually in charge he found he was deriving an even deeper sense of contentment from walking round the boxes, checking all the occupants and seeing them settled for the evening.

'Strange,' he said to himself as he made his way to the most important box on his round. 'I could be in Florence painting, doing the thing I do best, the thing I always wanted to do – and yet here I am, and really not minding at all. Which is really very odd altogether.'

He looked over The Enchanted's door and to his relief saw that the little horse was at his manger, which he was busy licking clean. The horse cocked an eye at him then returned to his pot-scouring, his tail swishing occasionally as he searched vainly for one last mouthful. Having checked the rest of the yard Rory wandered over to the tack room and found Kathleen there in company of Teddy, cleaning saddles and bridles that now looked like new.

'Want a mug of tea, boss?' Teddy asked him. 'Kettle's just boiled.'

Rory accepted the offer and sat down opposite the two of them, picking up a racing saddle and beginning to clean it.

'This mysterious visitor of ours, Miss Flanagan – Kathleen,' he said, quickly correcting himself as he dipped a piece of sponge into a tin of saddle soap. 'What more do you know about him?'

'No more than I said, really,' Kathleen replied, glancing up at him from her work. 'He's made a bit of a name for himself riding point to point in the south-west – in Cork – and of course he rode in the Foxhunters at Cheltenham this year.'

'Did he finish? How did he do?'

'He was fifth, on one of Red Turvey's runners. I didn't see the race, but they say it was a good enough effort. He led for most of the race and he caught the eye enough to get a mention in the press.'

'And he wants to ride over here now professionally,' Rory said, wondering why. 'Rather than over there.'

'So it would seem, Mr Rawlins,' Kathleen replied, polishing the saddle on her knee. 'But then don't most Irish jocks come over sooner rather than later? There's a lot of opportunity and the pay's better, too.'

'Yes. Yes, that's true – but if you don't have much of a track record getting started isn't easy. Not even getting bad rides.'

'Which is why he's come here then, I'd say,' Kathleen replied. 'Not for the bad rides—' She glanced up again at him, this time with a smile in her eyes. 'I meant to try to get a start.'

'Nothing to do with anything else, then?' Rory asked her, concentrating on cleaning the saddle he had on his knees. 'Or anyone?'

'I said I never met him,' Kathleen said, the smile now gone. 'And I have not so.'

'Fine.' Rory dipped his sponge in the soap again. 'But he thinks I'll just take him on just like that – sight more or less unseen.'

'You said you'd give him a trial. You couldn't have been fairer than you were.'

'I doubt he's much of a jockey yet, though.'

'Why would that be, Mr Rawlins?'

Rory shrugged and smiled at her. 'He still has all his teeth.'

'He has,' Kathleen replied, giving as good as she had just got. 'Which gives him the best of smiles.'

Favouring Rory with a deliberately overpolite smile of her own, Kathleen stood up, hung the clean saddle on the rack and took down another, leaving Rory with nothing except a deep desire to go and kick some furniture.

Chapter Fourteen

The Remedy

There was no doubt about it. Boyo was feeling better. Before, he had been feeling bad. His throat had hurt him and he'd felt as if he was full of dust, as if everything he'd eaten was dust. But now he felt good again, he felt right, so to tell her he went and kicked his stable door many times. Finally he threw back his head and bellowed because he knew this often got them running.

Sure enough, here they came – here *she* came, the one who had found her way here to be with him again. He'd been happy to see her and this time she was here for longer so he made a noise at her, blew at her through his lips, then pushed her with his muzzle because he knew this always made her laugh.

'So who's feeling better then?' she asked him, pushing him back, then running her hands up under his neck and tickling the bottom of his chin. 'Are you feeling all better then, Boyo?

Because you look as bright as a May morning. Come on, let's take you out. Let's put a collar on you and walk you out.'

She unbolted his door and led him out. He stopped when he was in the yard and pricked his ears, hearing something from a distant field, before giving himself a good shake.

'Mr Rawlins?' she was calling. 'He's eaten all his breakfast and the glands in his neck are right as rain!'

The man came over to him now and felt his neck and looked into his eye.

'Can I run him out? Let him have a bit of a blow?' she asked. 'He's been standing in a while so he could do with a blow.'

'His nose is clean,' the man said. 'And you're right about the glands. Just check his temperature, and if it's still normal—'

'Which it will be.'

'Which it undoubtedly will be, turn him out for an hour, and we'll see how he is then.'

Kathleen did as told and checked his temperature, which was, as she had predicted, still absolutely normal; then she rugged him up and took him to the home paddock where she let him go.

He stood until he knew she was safe then turned right round and bolted down the field as fast as he could, leaping in the air twice as he did so. He found the muddiest and the smelliest part of the paddock, bent his front legs at the knees, lowered himself carefully down then fell happily to one side, his shoulder splashing in the thick heavy mud. Once down he lay still for a moment then rolled on to his back, all four legs waving in the air as he tried his best to bury himself in the ground. He fell on to his other side and rolled there as well, then once he was sure he had well and truly covered himself in mud he got carefully to his feet, front legs first then a good push with the hind, shook himself thoroughly, jumped in the air, reared, turned round twice, then walked slowly away to begin grazing, safe in the knowledge that whoever lay in wait in the trees above him would no longer recognise his smell and so would no longer wish to eat him.

Kathleen watched him for some time, seeming to sense the horse's mood and condition, so that when she saw him running, rolling, shaking and jumping for joy in the air she knew he was better. Leaving him to his grazing, she hurried off to continue with her work.

Chapter Fifteen

A Piece of Work

'There's nothing wrong with his foot,' Kathleen insisted as she walked the horse up for Rory the next morning. 'Nothing at all.'

'No, he really was going short last night,' Rory insisted. 'If you'd just trot him up?'

'I put arnica on it!' Kathleen called over her shoulder, having turned the horse away first before trotting him back up to the waiting trainer. 'He must have stood on a stone in the paddocks.'

Rory felt like replying that it had been her bright idea to turn the horse out but thought it a cheap shot so decided against it.

'Fine, but we've been through all that, Kathleen,' he replied instead. 'What we have to make sure now is that he's nice and level. That it's not still bothering him.'

'Well?' Kathleen asked after she had trotted the horse up twice.

'Seems fine,' Rory said. 'As far as I can see he's totally sound.'

'Arnica is great for the bruises.'

'We learn a little every day,' Rory said, lightly, he hoped, but obviously not, he concluded, when he saw one of those quick but dark clouds scud across Kathleen's beautiful face.

'We do, don't we?' she replied. 'If we look and listen.'

'You can put the horse away now, thank you, Kathleen.'

'Think of the saving in vet's bills,' Kathleen called back to him as she put her charge in his box. 'How much is it for a call out now?'

'Enough,' Rory told her, following her into the stable. 'Thank you.'

'So are we on?' another Irish voice asked him from the door of the box. 'Is himself sound or what?'

'How did you know— Yes, wait a minute,' Rory said, turning to regard Blaze. 'You knew the horse— I don't understand.'

'Kathleen here rang me,' Blaze replied. 'She was worried she'd done something wrong.'

Rory gave them both a look before returning to Boyo and picking up and inspecting the hoof that had been damaged.

'If he stays sound, which let's just hope he will . . .' Rory said, cueing a glance between Kathleen and Blaze that he just happened to catch.

'God willing indeed,' Blaze added. 'God willing, yes indeed. That he stays sound, sir.'

'. . . I thought of giving him a piece of work tomorrow.'

'Tomorrow would be favourite, Mr Rawlins. Then we shall see what we shall see.'

'Most pro-pro-profound, Mr Molloy. I c-couldn't have put it better myself.'

'The horse looks grand, doesn't he? He looks well in himself to be sure,' Blaze observed.

'He's still got too much of a belly on him,' Rory muttered. 'But a couple of bits of f-fast work should do the trick. I'll put you up on him tomorrow. See how you get on.'

'Mr Martin along the way has just seen me ride – and he says I can ride for him.'

'So g-go – g-go and ride for him then,' Rory said, ushering Kathleen out of the stable and closing the door behind them.

'Wouldn't I rather ride for you?'

'Mr Martin along the way has over forty horses in training,' Rory informed him. 'You'd stand a far better chance of riding your winners there.'

'Riding winners is not what I'm after,• Mr Rawlins,' Blaze said slowly, fixing Rory with his bright blue eyes. 'Riding good horses is what I'm about.'

'We pull out at nine,' Rory said. 'On the dot.'

'I shall be here be eight, sir,' Blaze said, touching his cap and just before taking his leave smiling just a little bit too long at Kathleen for Rory's peace of mind.

*   *   *

Duly summoned by Rory and alerted by Grenville, the new racing partnership were told to be in the yard at Fulford Farm at 8.45 a.m. sharp, well wrapped up for the gallops. Alice and Millie were the first to arrive, by which time five of the six horses that were to work that morning were already rugged up and walking round the edge of the square of grass in the middle of the yard, the work riders busy adjusting leathers and girths as their charges warmed up under them. As Alice and Millie sat watching from inside their car, Grenville's Jaguar pulled into the yard with the other three partners aboard.

'Morning, all,' Grenville called with a doff of his hat as he emerged from behind the wheel. 'Cold enough for the famous monkeys, I think, don't you?'

'I don't have the foggiest idea what he means,' Alice said *sotto* as she and Millie went over to greet Constance and Lynne, the latter looking like someone going on a *Vogue* fashion shoot in her fur-lined knee-high boots and new suede coat, also lined with sheepskin.

'I know.' Millie smiled. 'But I like Grenville. There's something almost quaint about him.'

'I could do with a hot toddy,' Constance complained. 'And what on earth am I doing here and not in Antigua?'

The women then fell to silence as Kathleen led their horse out of his stable. It was not the sight of The Enchanted that transfixed them, however, but the slim and elegant young man who now appeared from the tack room, ready to mount up.

'Top of the morning to you!' Blaze called, touching his crash hat. 'Let's hope we are going to see something special this morning, ladies!'

'I already have, thank you,' Lynne muttered. 'Who is that bit of eye candy, please?'

'This is our mystery man, Lynne,' Rory said, coming to greet his owners. 'Blaze Molloy, if you would, freshly in from the land of Eternal Charm.'

'I often thought of going to live in Ireland,' Millie remarked. 'Now I well think I might. Talk about the world being bright and gay.'

'I take it that's a reference to his Irish eyes and not his private preferences, Millie,' Alice remarked, also unable to take her eyes off the slim figure in his tight riding breeches and shiny red windcheater.

'You betcha.' Millie laughed. 'But something tells me he bats for our team, Alice.'

'Did one hear right?' Constance wondered, looking in a vaguely accusatory way at Grenville. 'Did someone say his name was Blazer? What will parents think of next?'

'Blaze, madam,' their jockey corrected her as he prepared to be given a leg up by Rory. 'Blaze Molloy, at your service.'

'Most original,' Constance said with a nod. 'But not as good as my great-uncle, who was called Daisy.'

'Daisy, Lady Frimley?' Lynne frowned. 'You

didn't actually have a great-uncle called Daisy?'

Constance sniffed. 'I most certainly did,'

'How on earth did he get to be called Daisy, Constance?' Alice enquired.

'Possibly because his preference was to dress as a woman.'

By now Blaze had swung easily into his saddle and gathered his reins, the little horse feeling good and strong under him, both of them glad to be alive on this crisp, sharp winter morning. 'Let's hope your lovely horse goes as well as he looks, girls,' he said, before moving off to join the back of the string.

'I like "girls",' Constance murmured. 'I wonder if he has a father?'

'How do you think your horse looks?' Rory asked. 'I know he's still got a bit of a belly on him but that's only because he's short of a piece of work.'

'Nothing wrong, I trust?' Grenville enquired in line with his role as the partnership's racing manager. 'Nothing we should know about?'

'No – no, a couple of days in the sick bay with a dirty nose, but he's all better now, Grenville. If you'd like a quick cup of tea or coffee? Let's all have something. It takes them a good twenty minutes to get to the bottom of the hill.'

The party followed their trainer into the house, where they were all greeted joyfully by Dunkum. The lurcher took a particular shine to Lynne's new fur-lined coat, which had to be hung up well out of his range.

'He has a very bright eye, don't you think?' Alice remarked as Rory prepared the coffee.

'The jockey or the horse, Alice?' Lynne said.

'Our horse, Lynne. He looks – well. He looks rather full of purpose, I thought.'

'Let's hope you're right. You want a horse to be a bit of a street fighter,' Rory said, handing round the tea and coffee. 'And from what we've seen so far, Boyo doesn't like being taken on.'

'Not another candidate for the shades?' Millie wondered.

'Heavens no – no, the last thing he'll need will be blinkers, Millie,' Rory replied. 'Listen – soon as someone gets to his quarters he seems to find another gear. All right, OK, so he hasn't done a really serious gallop yet. This is only what I've seen so far, but we'll certainly learn a bit more this morning.'

'They're going to take each other on, then?' Grenville said. 'And in case you're wondering, ladies, what we mean by that is that some gallops are just precisely that. Horses coming up in line and not really racing each other. A serious piece of work should have the horses pitched against each other.'

'Not everyone would go for that though, Grenville,' Rory said. 'There's a theory that if you do that you can leave your race on the gallops.'

'Pass,' Alice said, with a shake of her head.

'Meaning you can cook your horse in before he gets to the races,' Rory explained. 'But don't worry. I'll try – I'll do my best not to let that happen.'

But Rory was a long way from as confident as he was trying to sound. As far as he was concerned this was where push very much came to shove, since in all his time as assistant to his father and during the weeks his father had been ill he had never really had to face the question of how far and how fast to work a piece of machinery as complex as a thoroughbred racehorse. He had seen how his father did it and there were many things about his father's methods that he criticised, but he had never so far had to put any of his own theories into practice. He knew that one piece of wrong work could quite easily spoil the newcomer and ruin his immediate chances, which would mean either a deeply disappointing first run or not running him at all for another month while they struggled to get the animal right again. So, smile as he might, as Rory drove his new owners up to the gallops his heart was well and truly in his mouth.

As indeed was Kathleen's. She too was riding work, having volunteered her services when one of Rory's occasional work riders called in to say he had the flu. She was riding Trojan Jack, with instructions to hit the front two furlongs from the end of the gallop and see if The Enchanted could get anywhere near the canny old handicapper. She knew from Teddy what a rogue Jack could be, but also that when he put his mind to it he could murder the rest of the Fulford string. So if he decided to put his best foot forward this morning Kathleen knew that her little horse would have his work cut out for him.

'Don't go soft on him now, Kathleen!' Teddy called as they reached the foot of the gallops and prepared to go. 'The boss wants to see what the new boy's made of, so you kick that old bugger on, right? I'm going to take him on as well!'

Teddy was riding Alone At Last, a relative newcomer to the stable who having taken time to grow into his frame was yet to race, but was now beginning to show the signs of some ability in his fast work. Now that he had strengthened, instead of looking like a giraffe the big horse looked purposeful and strong, as well as standing a good hand and a half over The Enchanted, who with the tall figure of Blaze in the saddle looked even smaller than he really was. Kathleen took a good look at the little horse, thinking the very same thing, yet noting that under his coat, which now had the beginnings of a real gleam to it, the muscles looked tight and hard.

'OK!' Teddy called. 'Kick on!'

A second later they were off and running.

When she felt what she had in her hands as well as under her saddle, Kathleen suddenly realised she had never ridden anything quite as fit, fast and strong as Jack, who had obviously decided today was going to be one of his good days. They had barely gone half a furlong before he had pulled himself clear into a two-length lead and was seriously motoring, really enjoying having the good turf under his hooves and a flyweight on his back. She heard Teddy yelling at her to take a pull as he got left behind, so she shifted her weight back a little and shortened up, but Jack had hold of the bit and was taking no notice. She tried to take a quick look round but the horse was pulling so much she was afraid of losing her balance and coming off, so she kept her head down, looking between his ears and doing her best to keep him balanced.

She had half expected and certainly hoped that halfway up the hill she might catch a glimpse of Boyo hacking up beside her, but there was neither sight nor sound of him, just the wind howling in her ears and the thunder of hooves on old turf.

'Dear God in heaven,' she prayed. 'Don't let me go beating my own horse now.'

'Here they come!' Rory told everyone, pointing to where the horses were just beginning to come into view – or rather one horse was, a horse that with only two furlongs left to run was well clear of the rest.

'Who is that?' Grenville called, peering at the distant animal through his race glasses. 'God, it's only Jack!' he cried. 'Going like a train, too!'

'It can't be,' Rory muttered. 'If it is, there's a glue factory waiting.'

He'd wanted The Enchanted to lie up so he wouldn't have a lot of work to do if he were to try to catch any horse leading him, but from what he could see it was Trojan Jack first, the rest nowhere, all of them stuck in a bunch some four or five lengths down. Then, as they got closer, with about a furlong and a half to run, he saw The Enchanted in the middle of the group. Blaze had him settled and the horse was moving easily but well within himself, his rider sitting as still as a statue and waiting for the moment, waiting for the time he would press the button and say go – at least so Rory hoped, although in view of how much Blaze seemed still to have under him, hope was growing fainter and certainty fast taking its place.

Jack was still galloping flat out, with no one else apparently making the slightest impression on him. Then, in a second, it was over. Blaze let out an inch of rein, his horse picked up and that was that. The little horse didn't look so little any more as he cut down the leader, ranged alongside and then left him, thundering past his trainer and his owners a good two lengths to the good and still hard held.

The others followed on in a cacophony of hooves on grass, leather slapping, riders shouting and whips cracking, but all to no avail. The Enchanted had murdered them, so comprehensively in fact that the moment he flew past Trojan Jack the beaten horse dropped his bit and slumped from first to last. Alone At Last came out of the pack to finish second, but looked and sounded cooked when Rory got over to where the horses were pulling up.

'Did you see that then?' Blaze grinned down at him from the saddle. 'But if I were you now, I'd keep it under your hat.'

'I just hope no one else is up here this morning,' Rory said with a shake of his head. 'Was that as easy as it looked?'

'That was just third gear, sir,' Blaze assured him. 'It doesn't matter how good or bad the rest of them are, this fella wasn't even in top, let alone overdrive.'

'He's blowing a bit,' Rory observed.

'Sure he is, but then isn't this his first bit of real work? It's a question of how long he blows *for*.'

Kathleen trotted Jack up to join them.

'Jeeze,' she said. 'One moment I saw his head and the next his backside. And this horse is nowhere near race fit.'

'Fine! Thank you!' Rory said, instructing his riders. 'Keep your horses moving, please! Don't let them stand still – particularly in this wind. Soon as they have their breath back, go back to the yard. Thank you!'

'Blaze said he never let the horse down, Mr Rawlins,' Kathleen whispered to him, bending down to him from the saddle, so close Rory could feel her warm breath on his cheek. 'He said he could have picked Jack off from ten lengths.'

'That's good, but it's early days yet, Kathleen, early days,' Rory replied. 'Now keep your h-horse moving, if you would.'

'The little horse really is something other, I tell you,' Kathleen said, before swinging Jack round to catch up with the others. 'Quite something else!'

'Ladies,' Grenville said when the partners

311

and Millie were back in Rory's kitchen where Maureen was in the middle of making them all a fried breakfast. 'Ladies, I am here to tell you I think we have a horse.'

'He certainly looked jolly impressive,' Millie agreed. 'That was some gallop.'

'Was it?' Alice said. 'I say.'

'Absolutely,' Grenville continued. 'I think what we saw this morning was most promising, and I really do think we may have a rather good little horse here. He might well pick up a nice little race somewhere.'

'Less of the little, Grenville,' Lynne warned him. 'This little horse – our little horse – is going to win a lot of races and not little ones either. Any more of that little nonsense and Connie won't be the only one calling you Glanville.'

'OK,' Rory said, coming into the room, having finished his debriefing. 'Now then – look, I don't want anyone to get over-excited—'

'Oh, I don't mind,' Constance interrupted. 'I'd quite welcome it.'

'As you've probably gathered that was a very good piece of work we all just saw,' Rory said carefully, still not quite able to believe what he himself had seen. 'And I'm not going to make any great pronouncements – just this. There are such things as morning glories – horses that beat the birds on the gallops, but then when you get them to the course it's an entirely different matter. I'm not saying this is the case here, I'm really not. No, all I'm saying is we won't know how good or bad this horse is till we get him to the track, and with that in mind and with your say-so I think we should run him in the two-mile novice chase next week – at Wincanton again. It might be a country track but the going's invariably good, the racing's always competitive there so it's not a question of an easy option, and given that the horse looks as though he might have a bit of toe—'

'A bit of a toe?' Alice enquired.

'A bit of toe, duck,' Millie corrected her. 'Toe as in speed. Being a sharp track Wincanton might just suit him.'

'A sharp track?'

'Sharp as in fast, sweetie. A flat galloping track.'

'I thought we were going jump racing.'

'Flat as in level,' Millie sighed. 'There'll be jumps all right, don't you worry.'

'I'm getting there, slowly,' Alice replied.

'We'll give him another bit of fast work before then,' Rory told her, 'as well as lots of long slow stuff, but as he's small and appears to be quite naturally athletic, I don't think he needs a lot of hard work. So if it's all right with the owners – Wincanton it is.'

'What about a school?' Grenville asked.

'They want to send him to school now?' Alice enquired, deliberately wide-eyed.

'School as in jumping,' Rory explained. 'School him over fences. Yes, of course we shall give him a school – I was planning to do that tomorrow provided all is well. Although one thing I do know,' Rory added, remembering a famous rainy afternoon in Cronagh. 'I do know this horse can jump.'

The following day Blaze schooled the horse over the yard's four practice fences, jumping them twice. The first time they let him jump on his own, and he didn't put a foot wrong. The second time they jumped him in the company of two of Rory's neighbour's hunter chasers who were both schoolmasters when it came to jumping birch, and The Enchanted jumped all four fences alongside, straight and true, and most important of all, as Rory noted, landing and getting away from the jumps much more quickly and nimbly than the experienced duo schooling with him.

'You have to fancy his chances, Guv,' Teddy said when they were back in the yard. 'I know these two-mile novice chases take a bit of winning, but this horse doesn't seem to be a novice.'

'It'll be a hot race. Tony Pope's bound to run a couple,' Rory said. 'And I know Captain Timms intends to run a rather smart novice of his, so it's not going to be exactly a gentle introduction. Pope's will go off as if they've been scalded, and the captain's will be able to jump.'

'Nothing ventured,' Teddy said, taking the saddle from Rory, and starting to head for the tack room. 'This fella looks as if he was born doing it.'

'One thing's certain,' Rory said. 'He won't start favourite.'

Chapter Sixteen

Off and Running

The four of them sat round Rory's kitchen table studying the declarations in almost complete silence, as if the list of horses running was some rediscovered masterpiece. Occasionally Rory would click his tongue, or Blaze would inhale and exhale with apparent deep significance. Kathleen sat absolutely still, her lips pursed together so tightly that all the colour seemed drained from them, while Teddy chain-smoked his way through several cigarettes.

'There's no doubt about it,' Teddy said, finally breaking the hush. 'The captain's horse is the one to beat, given the way he trotted up at Ludlow.'

'My father says there's always one to beat, Teddy,' Rory said, waving away a cloud of smoke from Teddy's cigarette. 'If there wasn't we might as well keep all our horses in their stables.'

'But look at the way it's bred, boss,' Teddy replied, tapping his paper. 'This is a class horse.'

'Mr Pope's two have got form as well,' Blaze remarked. 'Both Taunton winners.'

'There's a decent-looking horse from Lambourn, too,' Teddy added. 'One of David Chambers's. The yard's in form and the horse cost a packet at Doncaster sales.'

'Can we discount this unraced fella from Eddie Rampton's yard?' Blaze wondered. 'Isn't your man fond of using the racecourse as a schooling ground?'

'You want to watch what you're saying if Mr Rampton is anywhere in the vicinity,' Rory advised. 'Eddie Rampton's renowned for his short fuse. He's had several head to heads with reporters for hinting that he hadn't run some of his horses on merit recently.'

'He certainly has,' Teddy agreed. 'Eddie Rampton is not someone to cross. Before he took up training he was the stable lads' unbeaten light-weight champion for four years running.'

'His training methods aren't all that tasty either,' Rory added. 'Prone to hitching his horses to his Land Rover with a lead rope and making them gallop flat out behind him.'

'Imagine working for a guy like that,' Teddy muttered, returning to his study of the form. 'Anyway, all things considered, it looks as if it's going to be a hot one.'

'They're quoting our fella at anything from sixteen to twenty to one,' Blaze said. 'I'd say he's going to make some people very happy.'

'And I'd say that just about represents his

chance,' Rory said, getting up from the table.

'Well, I'm going to have a touch,' Teddy decided, stubbing out his cigarette. 'In fact I'm going to have a wallop. Jack left a rather nasty hole in the savings.'

'You're very quiet, K-Kathleen,' Rory said, looking at Kathleen, who was still sitting stock still and had hardly said a word since they had all gathered round the table.

'I know,' she said quietly, swallowing hard. 'I think I have to say I've got what we call at home an attack of the reals. In fact I think I need a breath of fresh air.'

'Good idea,' Blaze said, getting up with her. 'After sitting next to Teddy here, I need fumigating.'

Rory watched the two of them cross the yard and walk over to The Enchanted's box. When he next looked, Blaze had his arm round Kathleen's shoulders and seemed to be talking to her most confidentially. The next time he looked, which he found he had to do, Kathleen had her hand in Blaze's and was walking away with him towards the paddocks.

'Don't they make a pretty couple?' Maureen remarked, handing him some letters to sign. 'They're both of them very good-looking.'

'Who's that?' Rory wondered, feigning ignorance. 'Sorry?'

'Kathleen and your new rider fellow.'

'Do they? I wouldn't know,' Rory said, glancing over the papers he'd just been given. 'I was looking at the skies. Seeing what the weather's doing.'

317

'Don't forget your appointment with your bank manager,' Maureen said, rolling her eyes up to the ceiling. 'You've less than an hour.'

It's a race, Rory kept reminding himself as he drove into Salisbury. *Or rather more specifically, it's only a horse race. And anything can happen in a horse race, and usually does.*

But however much he tried to convince himself that he must treat the outcome of tomorrow's race the same way he had seen his father react to racing's ups and downs – treating both impostors just the same, in the words of Anthony's favourite poem – he could not escape the feeling that he might just have a horse that was capable of winning what looked like a decent novice chase. There wasn't really another animal on the yard about which he could say the same; they were all either exposed handicappers that were capable of running a good sort of race off the right weight in moderate company, or horses that had been weeded out from some smart yard or other as being simply not up to their elevated standards, or promising moderately bred novices such as Alone At Last. There was nothing that excited him the way The Enchanted had done the morning he had got his first glimpse of what this youngster might be able to do. The times he could remember being excited racing were those rare and memorable occasions when along with other racegoers he had witnessed a horse with that special magic – the ability to find another gear and leave its fellow competitors stone cold. Most times, like everyone else, he enjoyed watching good honest horses racing courageously over stiff fences on a fair course. That was the nature of the sport as it was the nature of everything in life. What stopped people in their tracks, what made the hair stand up on their necks, what made them gasp, tingle or become speechless, was witnessing something not just out of the ordinary but quite extraordinary, and however much Rory tried to dismiss the notion, he found he was unable to stop believing that the result of tomorrow's race might actually prove to be a turning point in the fortunes of the yard.

More than anything he wanted this to be so, not for himself but for his father.

If it happens, he told himself as he walked towards the bank. *If and only if it happens, this might just be the tonic you need, Pop.*

'I quite understand your position, Mr Rawlins,' the bank manager told him. 'And please don't think I am not sympathetic to it.'

'Yes, well, you might be, Mr Hawkins,' Rory replied, 'but certainly not the letter from the bank. The bank's letter to my father was most certainly not, not at all. I mean, the bank must know that he's lying in hospital not just seriously ill but he's there fighting for his life, and instead of that – that is, instead of giving everyone a little more time here, the bank is saying it feels it must call in the loan.'

'This is simply bank policy, Mr Rawlins. It is nothing to do with me personally. I have always done my best to find ways of helping your father and his racing business.'

'And in return you've had some more than good information, at least so my father told me, Mr Hawkins.'

'That is neither here nor there, Mr Rawlins,' the bank manager replied after quietly clearing his throat. 'All I am trying to point out is that these orders come from head office, not from me personally.'

'Yes, fine – but can't you put in a plea for special consideration?'

'I have done that, believe me. But while my superiors are naturally sympathetic it must be remembered that this is a bank, not some form of charitable institution.'

'So exactly how long do we have before you come and take the fixtures and fittings, then?'

'It certainly won't come to that, rest assured, Mr Rawlins.'

'You mean you'll accept an IOU.'

'I think we already have that in some form or another, Mr Rawlins. But to answer your question properly, as to how long we can extend the current overdraft facility on the yard itself, I would say we shall be looking at a time scale of four weeks.'

'If you wouldn't mind, because I've forgotten . . . How much exactly does the overdraft stand at?'

The manager turned the sheet of paper in front

of him round so that Rory might be able to read it and pushed it towards him.

When he saw the figures, Rory froze inside. Whatever happened tomorrow or indeed in the next month or even the next six months, there was no way he was going to be able to find the funds to repay the debt his father had run up on the business.

'What about the farm?' Rory asked, when he had got his inner breath back. 'Leaving the racing business aside, if we can – or may— I mean, the farm itself must have a considerable value. More than considerable.'

'Indeed so, Mr Rawlins. And while the bank would have been quite content to take that as collateral—'

'Would have been happy?' Rory interrupted, frowning. 'Would have been?'

'Your father resolutely refused to let us have a charge on the farm in return for what is owed on the racing business. He has consistently maintained that he would rather go to prison than put the farm at risk and thus his family, meaning you in particular.'

Stopped in his tracks momentarily, since he had never realised this had been his father's priority, Rory attempted to marshal his thoughts.

'There must be some way we can use the farm now, isn't there?' he said. 'After all, look, if I am to inherit it—'

'Which I understand is exactly the case, Mr Rawlins.'

'Can't we somehow use it as security? I mean, if the worst comes to the worst—'

'I'm very much afraid that's exactly what would have to happen,' the manager replied, averting his gaze. 'If sadly your father were to—'

'No,' Rory said quickly and firmly. 'Come on now – there just has to be some other way.'

'The only other way would be for you to get your father to allow the bank to take a charge on the farm now. That way the loan would be permitted to stand, for a while anyway. But given your father's condition—'

'I couldn't possibly ask him to do that, not now!' Rory said. 'If he's been that determined to avoid putting the farm up, then to try to persuade him to change his mind now – I mean, can you imagine? For crying out loud, in his condition? No, I really couldn't do that. Really.'

'I understand.'

'Oh, no – sorry, but I don't think you do,' Rory said, beginning to get angry. 'What you want is either to take possession of the stables and everything to do with it, or else – or else you want my father to die, isn't that right? You would rather he died so that I can sign the other part of his life's work over to you – in order to wipe out a debt that compared with what the banks are losing left right and centre with their totally ill-advised investments—'

'I think that's enough, Mr Rawlins, don't you?'

'No I do not, Mr Hawkins. Enough? No, this is far from enough, Mr Hawkins. The money the

322

banks are losing and lending quite indiscriminat-
ingly overseas? That money is their customers'
money, right? But in order to plug the holes in
your boat—'

'I really do feel this interview has come to a
close, thank you.'

'In order to try to balance your books,' Rory
continued, 'what do you do? You start calling in
every measly little overdraft you can find! And by
doing so – by so doing—'

'Thank you, Mr Rawlins,' the manager said,
rising from his chair.

'And by doing so, ruining good little businesses
everywhere through your blasted impatience!'

'Thank you, Mr Rawlins,' the manager repeated
as a security man appeared at the door in answer
to a private summons made moments before. 'I
think in future it would be better for both sides
to conduct this business formally by letter. Good
day.'

Before he left the building, Rory asked to see
the balance on his personal account. He knew he
was in the black not the red, but was surprised to
see the amount he actually was in credit.

Where on earth did that come from? he wondered
as he began the drive home. *I don't have anything
like that sort of dosh.*

The mystery was cleared up when Rory examined his bank statements in detail when he
returned home. The day before they had left for
Ireland, it seemed his father had given instructions to transfer the sum of two thousand pounds

from the farm account to his son's account without saying a word about it. Rory stared at the details on the statement and, knowing his father, became convinced at that moment that he must have known that – as Anthony would put it himself – something was up.

Then he remembered the conversation they'd had over a dinner of delicious freshly caught mackerel and floury potatoes their first night in Ireland.

'You enjoying yourself, old chap?' his father had asked.

'Bit early to say, Pa,' Rory had replied. 'We've only just got back on terra firma. But the omens are good.'

'I meant in general. As in life in general, old thing.'

'Well, yes, Dad. Yes, I suppose so.'

'You suppose so? You *suppose* so?' His father had laughed, but not unkindly. His father wasn't given to unkind laughter. 'You can't be enjoying your life if you only suppose you are. The thing is – what you have to do,' his father had continued, pouring them both some wine, 'you must find and do something you love. Now I know what you want to do and if that's the case you simply have to go do it. You have to do what the man said – find out what you want and do it. I have to tell you that, leaving personal stuff aside' – Rory knew this meant the loss of his mother and the grief that had caused, something his father much preferred not to talk about – 'leaving that aside,

I have to tell you that as far as my wonky old life has gone, I have enjoyed practically every minute of it. I've been very fortunate in doing what I do. I've met some wonderful folk, trained and worked with some cracking horses and above everything I've had *fun*. So now when it comes to it—'

'When it comes to what, Pop?' Rory had interrupted, wondering if there was something his father wasn't telling him. 'What do you mean? When it comes to it?'

'Oh, nothing.' His father had dismissed the question with an airy wave of his hand. 'Just a manner of speaking. What I meant was at this point of my life I can put my hand on my heart and say I really have enjoyed what I've done. That's all. Because I want you to be able to say the same when you reach my age – that you've done what you wanted to do and you have enjoyed your life. That's all.'

'I like working at the yard. Being your assistant.'

'Sure you do, old boy – but that's not what you *want* to do. You know what you really want to do. *I* know what you really want to do – so remember, it's never too late. It's never too late to down tools, say blow it – and bugger off and do the thing that really consumes you. That's all.'

So perhaps his father had known that he was ill, Rory thought, and in order to shore up the defences he'd deposited a sum of money in Rory's account to say to him, in this particular term of trial, *If all fails, old chap, you can always take off now and do your thing*.

That would be his father all over – and because this was what Rory knew and believed, it simply made him all the more determined to make the yard come good, one way or the other, because the yard was his father's life.

The only other thing he was left to wonder about was the fact that he hadn't stammered once during the interview at the bank.

'Are you frit, as they say oop north?' Millie asked Alice as they drove to the course. 'You definitely look a lighter shade of pale.'

'Of course I'm nervous, Millie, what do you think?' Alice replied. 'Don't tell me you don't get nervous when Jack runs?'

'I can hardly bear to look, if it were known, duck. I don't know why we do this to ourselves.'

'If I'd known I'd feel like this I think I'd definitely have had second thoughts,' Alice agreed. 'And this is only his first run.'

'Even so, it's exciting as well, right?' Millie enquired. 'Having a runner.'

'A runner's precisely what I feel like doing.' Alice sighed. 'I must be totally and completely bonkers.'

'Let's take a rain check on that, shall we? At least until after your chap's raced. In a couple of hours' time you might be feeling very different indeed.'

Lynne, Grenville and Constance were already

warmly ensconced in the bar by the time Millie and Alice arrived. It was a cold but dry day, and with the promise of a good card the racegoers were arriving in force.

'Splendid,' Grenville said as Millie and Alice joined the rest of the partnership. 'Splendid – we are all met.'

'Isn't this something?' Lynne exclaimed. 'I am so excited I can hardly think straight.'

'I gave up thinking straight years ago,' Constance said. 'For all the good it was doing me.'

'Well now look,' Grenville said, tapping his hat against his leg. 'Since you ladies are all warm and cosy here, I am just going to pop out to the rails and see if there's an early betting show.'

'He's twenty to one in most papers,' Lynne said. 'And I am most definitely going to have a few quid each way at that price.'

'My money is staying in my purse, since I agree with whoever it was who said it,' Constance remarked, lighting a cheroot. 'Horse sense is the wisdom that keeps horses from betting on people.'

'*Very* good,' Grenville said, nodding and smiling. 'E'en so, and if you will excuse me, ladies, I to the bookmakers.'

On his way to the rails, Grenville bumped into Rory.

'How is the little horse, Mr Trainer?'

'He looks well,' Rory said, hoping to sound nonchalant. 'Travelled fine.'

'I'm off to see if I can get me better than twenties,' Grenville said with a smile.

'Teddy's got him at twenty-five.'

'Then I shall try to match him. See you in the paddock, old man.'

Rory watched the dapper Grenville head for the rails where the account bookmakers had their pitches, wishing that he too had an account. For a moment he thought of asking Grenville to lay his bet, but as soon as he realised he would have to disclose the precise size of his wager he thought better of it. His first intention had been to find a regular bookie with whom to bet, but being a less than novice gambler he was uncertain of the protocol. He had seen on several bookmakers' boards the slogan *No Limit*, but he also knew from past experience – his father's, not his – that some bookies had a habit of welshing on successful large bets, running away from the course before the winning punter could claim his cash, and given his intention Rory could all too easily imagine himself being caught like that. So he knew the best, safest and only way was to bet with the Tote.

But he also knew enough about how the Tote worked to know that too large a bet placed too early could well attract the floating punters, the ones who watched the odds on the Tote shortening or lengthening to see where the money was or wasn't going. The way the Tote worked, the more money invested, the smaller the winning payout, so if he was going to use the Totalisator he was going to have to do so at the very last moment, just before the off. That is, if he placed a bet at all. The way Rory's mind was now working, the closer they got to post time the more absurd the thought of any gamble became, let alone the one he was contemplating.

The Enchanted's race was the second contest on the card and the runners for it were already being led up to the pre-parade ring, so since Rory had supervised all that he needed to supervise at this stage, he took himself off for what he hoped would be a calming walk round the enclosure, preferring to stay out of the bar and away from his owners lest their nervousness rub off on him. On his second circuit he bumped into Alice, who he discovered was also a refugee.

'I didn't realise I could get so nervous over a horse race,' she admitted to Rory as they walked into the Silver Ring to soak up a bit more atmosphere. 'Is he going to be all right, Rory? Please tell me he's going to be all right.'

'Of course the horse will be all right, Alice.' Rory did his best to comfort his ashen-faced owner. 'He's a tough sort and he can jump, so bar accidents of course he's going to be all right,' he added fatuously.

'That's what I mean,' Alice said. 'Accidents. It wouldn't be nearly so bad, I suppose, if there weren't any jumps, but I've just had a close look at those fences.'

'And you shouldn't have done,' Rory assured her. 'You're looking at them from the ground.'

'They're enormous.'

'Because you're looking at them from the

ground, Alice. The horse is much bigger than you, and the jockey's on his back. To them – well, they're like athletes jumping hurdles. This is probably even easier.'

'They still fall, Rory.'

'He won't fall, Alice. No, let's put it more accurately than that – he shouldn't fall because he's a very good jumper. A lot of the horses in the race – remember, it's a novice chase, and believe me, most novice chases are exactly that – for novices, for horses with L plates on – a lot of the horses won't really know how to jump until they've run round here, and even then some will never learn. But our chap can jump, and since we're going to tell Blaze to keep up at the front and well out of trouble, I reckon he will be just fine.'

'I should never have said yes to this, Rory,' Alice said, as dismal as ever. 'It's really making me feel quite ill.'

'Come on, Alice.' Rory laughed. 'I think I'm going to have to force a brandy down you.'

'Best I could get was sixteens,' a puzzled Grenville informed his co-owners as they made their way out to watch the first race, a novice hurdle. 'Something's afoot.'

'News of the famous gallop has leaked, perhaps,' Millie said. 'There's absolutely no reason for him to be fancied.'

'Particularly since he's still only in the pre-parade ring,' Grenville added.

'What difference does that make, please?' Constance enquired, holding on to the top of her hat.

'Means he's still rugged up,' Grenville explained. 'Nobody can tell much when the horses are still rugged up, do you see. No, I think Millie here is right. I think some little bird has sung about his gallop.'

'I can't really watch this,' Alice said. 'My mind's not on it. I think I'll go and see how our horse is.'

'I'll come with you,' Lynne said, taking her arm. 'I must admit I'm feeling a bit Uncle Dick as well.'

While the first race was run, Lynne and Alice watched as Kathleen led The Enchanted from the pre-parade ring into the parade ring proper, where he joined only two other horses, some of the others already being tacked up in their saddling boxes, while the rest remained behind in the lower ring.

'How is he, Kathleen?' Alice asked as the girl led the horse past them for the second time. 'Is he all right?'

'He's fine, Mrs Dixon,' Kathleen replied, as Alice followed her round on the other side of the rails. 'He's actually switched himself off, which is pretty good.'

'How do you mean, switched himself off?'

'He's very relaxed. He's not wasting any unnecessary energy.'

'I just hope he's going to be all right,' Alice said yet again as she rejoined Lynne. 'Have you seen some of the other horses? They're enormous.'

'Size doesn't matter, Alice,' Lynne replied with a grin. 'Least so they tell me.'

'I remember Alex talking about boxing, and he said a good big 'un always beat a good small 'un, or something like that,' Alice muttered, taking some mints from her bag and offering Lynne one. 'I don't know about you, but I've got a terribly dry mouth.'

'Me, too,' Lynne agreed, accepting a sweet. 'What's wrong with us, anyway? This is meant to be fun.'

'I'd rather be having root canal treatment,' Alice said. 'Really I would.'

The roar from the stands told them that the hurdle race was reaching its climax, and within moments the crowds had streamed away from the course on their way either to collect winnings from the Tote or to stand round the winners' enclosure as the successful horses were led in. All except the four racing partners, who now gathered at the entrance to the paddock to cast their eye over the competition in a field of fourteen runners.

'One of Pope's horses has been withdrawn,' Grenville told them. 'Found him cast in his box this morning, apparently.'

'Cast?' Alice wondered. 'I thought that's what sculptors did.'

'It means basically he got stuck lying down,' Millie explained. 'They can jam themselves up against the wall and hurt themselves trying to get up.'

'Anyway, that's one less,' Grenville continued. 'The Chambers horse from Lambourn is also rumoured not to be quite right, but they haven't taken him out. There must be something up because he's certainly gone for a walk in the market.'

'Will that do him any good?' Alice enquired. 'I can't see going for a walk anywhere at this late hour's going to do much good, let alone in some market or other.'

'No, no, Alice,' Grenville said patiently. 'Going for a walk in the market equals the betting market. Look – you can see how his price has gone out.'

Grenville pointed to the Tote approximate odds board where it could be seen that a horse called Put Upon had drifted significantly from three to one out to five to one.

'While our horse is now only twelve to one,' Grenville said quietly. 'I wonder where the money's coming from?'

'Certainly not from me,' Constance assured him. 'My father always used to say a racehorse is the only animal that can take hundreds of people for a ride at the same time.'

Rory was standing in the centre of the paddock talking to another trainer. When he saw his group of owners he beckoned them to come in.

'I'm going to tell Blaze to either make the running or keep up with the pace,' he said. 'The seven pound allowance he gets as a conditional will certainly help, as long as he's up to the job.'

'I remember that bit.' Alice smiled. 'He gets a weight allowance because he's really only an apprentice.'

'Which is what these boys always used to be called,' Rory agreed. 'Until someone invented *conditional*.'

'Hope your belief in him is founded, Mr Trainer,' Grenville said as a line of jockeys now snaked its way into the paddock.

'He knows the horse, Grenville, and he hasn't put a foot wrong in his work so far.'

'He just hasn't ridden in a proper race, that's all.'

'This'll be a picnic after an Irish point to point, believe me,' Rory replied. 'And seven pounds is a lot of weight off this horse's back.'

As Blaze joined them, with a touch on the front of his cap, all eyes including his turned to the horse who was now having his rug removed by Kathleen. The moment she had it off his back, he gave a small buck born from good health and kicked his heels.

'Looks well, boss,' Blaze observed. 'Looks even better than when we boxed him up. Nice and bonny.'

'I like your colours,' Millie said to Alice, admiring the blue and claret shirt and cap. 'Very smart. Are they yours?'

'Apparently,' Alice replied. 'I chose them with the team, and Rory.'

'I think I might redo my bedroom curtains in that blue,' Constance said. 'It's not too bright.'

'You're not to go using that,' Kathleen said to Blaze, pointing to his whip.

'You giving the instructions?' Blaze replied, waiting to be legged up.

'Mr Rawlins?' Kathleen asked, as Rory legged their jockey up.

'He has to carry a whip, Kathleen,' Rory muttered. 'We've been through all this.'

'But he's not to use it,' Kathleen insisted. 'If he does I'll use it on him.'

'Just keep him handy,' Rory said to Blaze, as Kathleen prepared to lead them out on to the course. 'Get him into a nice rhythm and let him enjoy himself. But stay right in touch. If you can't make it, keep up with the pace. They go a fair old clip here.'

'Got you, boss,' Blaze said, making some final adjustments to his tack. 'I'll see yous all in the winner's enclosure!' he called over his shoulder.

'Don't you dare hit him, Blaze,' Kathleen warned him again as she walked the horse on to the exit from the paddock. 'I'm telling you.'

As the runners made their way to post, Rory excused himself and told his owners he'd see them up in the east end of the members' stand. As they hurried off to get a good vantage point to watch The Enchanted on his way down, Rory hurried off to the Tote.

'Little horse is going down well,' Grenville observed through his glasses as the line of horses made their way across the centre of the

335

racecourse and past a fine old stone barn on their way to the two-mile start. 'As if he's been doing it all his life.'

'I feel sick,' Lynne said. 'I think I'm going to have to go and sit in the bar.'

'I'll join you,' Alice said. 'In fact why don't we just go and get legless, Lynne?'

'You'll be fine, both of you,' Grenville assured them. 'This is the worst part, believe me. Now, Captain Timms's horse is favourite,' he continued, training his race glasses on the bookies' boards in the next enclosure. 'Roaring Cavalier at five to four, so they *really* fancy that one – Pope's horse as well – Go Fast Carb two to one, while poor old Put Upon is still going walkies at five to one now and six to one in places.'

'And The Enchanted?' Millie enquired.

'Pretty solid at twelve to one,' Grenville replied. 'Making my sixteens look better by the minute. But who's backing him – and why, I do wonder? And where's our trainer gone?'

The horses were all down at the start now, the last arrivals having their girths checked by the starter's assistant while the starter himself climbed up on to his rostrum ready to call them into line.

'Where on *earth* is Rory?' Grenville wondered again. 'He's going to miss the start.'

Rory was standing alone at one of the Tote windows, the rest of the punters having all placed their bets, as the race was about to start. Rory had the money in his hand, but found himself still unable to do the deed. He was trying to convince himself that because it wasn't his money there really should be no problem, particularly since it had obviously been deposited in his account as his do-as-you-like fund. But then if it was his father's and he lost it all, it would matter. At least, according to the way Rory's mind was working it would – because if he lost it all on one ridiculously chancy gamble there would be no getting out for anyone.

'The starter's calling them into line . . .' he heard a voice announce on the tannoy. 'They're under starter's orders . . .'

'Fifteen hundred pounds to win horse number nine,' he heard a voice saying. He saw a hand pushing the money across the counter and under the glass and the operative's hand taking it. It wasn't until he had the ticket in his hand that Rory realised the voice, the hand and the money were all his. The bet was on – and the horses were off.

'And on the run to the first it's Go Fast Carb already in a clear lead,' he heard the course commentator calling as he ran back to the members' stand and up the steps to join his group.

'And they're all over the first,' the commentator continued. 'Go Fast Carb landing well clear of Roaring Cavalier in second, third Put Upon who jumped it particularly well, and then a gap to So I Gather, Lilac Daisy, Wender, Please Sir and The Enchanted.'

'So much for riding to orders,' Rory observed,

now he had his glasses up. 'He must be ten lengths off the leader.'

'They are going a hell of a crack, Rory,' Grenville replied. 'But the little horse is certainly not being run off his feet.'

'I really can't look,' said Alice's muffled voice from behind Rory's back. 'Will someone please tell me when it's over?'

Out on the course itself Blaze thought he was sitting quite pretty, with his horse settled into a nice regular rhythm, jumping the second and third easily enough and lying nicely in about sixth place on the rails, some eight lengths off the leader, who really seemed to have bolted. He knew what his instructions had been, but once the Pope horse shot off like a bolting hare there was no way he was going to kick his horse on after it and waste all that precious energy. He wanted to keep The Enchanted sweet, wanted him to swing along nicely on the bridle, wanted him to have plenty of time to see his fences and plenty of time to take them in his stride. Already the tactics of the jockey up on Go Fast Carb were apparently rattling several of the novices, two of them crashing out at the first open ditch and another falling heavily at the cross fence. By the time they were turning into the home straight for the first time Go Fast Carb had failed to increase his lead although his jockey was shaking his reins and had given him a couple of hard slaps in his attempt to poach the race, while both Put Upon and Roaring Cavalier were still on the bridle and jumping like seasoned horses rather than novices.

Up the rise into the straight they rode, into the first of three big black fences and past the grandstands, Go Fast Carb's lead now no more than three lengths over the next two horses, with The Enchanted still biding his time in sixth. But Blaze could see that the two horses immediately in front of him were already labouring, finding the pace too hot and the fences too stiff. At the last fence in the straight they lost So I Gather who nose-dived on landing, his spread-eagling fall then bringing down the already beaten Wender whose rider stepped off in mid-air and managed to land on his feet and running, earning a round of applause from the spectators. Blaze saw the first horse fall and swung The Enchanted to the left, not snatching him up but just easing him to the outside of the fence in order to avoid what he suspected might be carnage on the landing side.

'Did you see that, Rory?' Grenville asked. 'The boy rode that fence like a real pro.'

But Rory was not really looking. He could hardly bear to do so. As far as he could see The Enchanted was still just cantering, but given the pace of the contest he knew it simply could not be so and that he must be kidding himself, indulging in more than a little wishful thinking. So, trying not to let anyone in his group notice, he dropped his race glasses, closed his eyes and began to sing a particularly difficult song to himself in his head.

All the field bar one had now safely negotiated the water jump positioned somewhat recklessly just before the turn into the back straight, the faller being Please Sir who dropped his legs in the water and slithered to his belly, giving his jockey no chance of staying in the plate. As they swung round the sharp right-hand bend the horse immediately to the left of The Enchanted failed to negotiate the turn and grabbing its bit swerved out across the track towards the slope that led down to the boundary of the course, consequently running out at the next fence.

'Six gone, six still standing,' Millie remarked. 'They're sure not taking any prisoners out there.'

A weak and watery sun had now come out, shining directly in the eyes of the riders and the horses and making it difficult for them to get a clear view of the fences. Blaze could see fine, but it was bothering two of the leaders who stepped into the bottom of the second fence down the back but somehow managed to get away with it. As for The Enchanted, Blaze didn't need to look for a stride because the horse under him was foot perfect, finding his own distance from the fences as if he'd been jumping all his life and getting quickly away from them on the other side without losing his rhythm. By the time they had flown the open ditch and picked up two lengths in doing so Blaze knew the little horse was going far and away the best of all of those still racing.

Again at the cross fence they lost another horse. Blaze had no idea who it was – all he heard was the crash of something heavy hitting the birch and a yelled expletive as the jockey was catapulted over his mount's head. The Enchanted, on the other hand, had met the tricky fence perfectly, again picking up a good length in the air and landing with ears pricked and still on the bridle. Into the straight now for the last time Go Fast Carb was beginning to tread water and was being reeled in by Put Upon and Roaring Cavalier, who had both now engaged top gear. The Enchanted was lying fourth.

'Time to make a move, I'd say,' Grenville informed his party. 'If we're going to get in the frame.'

'How many more times do they have to go round?' Constance wanted to know, turning her pocket race glasses on some of the more attractive older gentlemen in the grandstand. 'I've quite lost count.'

'This is it, Connie!' Lynne called to her over the increasing din. 'I think these are the last three jumps!'

'I still can't watch,' Alice cried, her head buried in Rory's back, unaware that their trainer also was standing with his head bowed and his eyes still fast closed.

'Hello?' Millie cried. 'He's got a double handful, chaps! He's cantering all over them!'

'I cannot watch!' Alice yelled. 'I cannot *bear* it!'

'You are going to have to watch, duck!' Millie shouted back. 'Your little horse is going like a winner!'

341

'What?' Rory said, now forcing himself to look. 'Bloody hellfire!' he exclaimed when he saw what was happening. 'Crikey almighty!'

Unlike her guv'nor, Kathleen had seen every stride of the race from her perch on the little hill at the end of the grandstand from which the lads always watched their charges, and she had known the outcome of the race as her horse had galloped past her the first time.

Bar a fall, Boyo, she'd whispered. *It's all yours, Boyo – bar a fall.*

As they ran to the third from home the race was now on in earnest, at least as far as the first three horses were concerned. The three leading jockeys all thought the race lay between them, unaware of the outsider who was lying about four lengths behind them, swinging along as if out for an exercise canter, his rider sitting motionless while the three up front were all kicking, changing their hands, throwing their reins at their horses' heads, beating their horses regularly – in fact doing everything in their power to win the race. All three rose and cleared the third last together, followed by The Enchanted still four lengths off, but as they landed Put Upon suddenly slowed almost to a halt, his jockey's silks splashed with blood from the burst vessel the horse had just suffered. The sight of the distressed animal momentarily caught Blaze's eye as he passed it, causing him temporarily to lose his bearing so that when he turned his attention back to the business of the race he found he was all but running up Roaring Cavalier's back end as they ran to jump the second last.

'If that horse falls,' Rory muttered, more to himself than to anybody else, 'God, we are history. He'll bring us down for sure.'

'Get away from him, Molloy!' Grenville yelled fruitlessly. 'For God's sake get away!'

Blaze had seen what was happening in time and if ever his lack of racing experience was to show, this was the moment. Were a jockey to take a pull at this stage and at this pace he could easily unbalance and unsettle his horse, with the result that it might either put down at the fence and so take it by its roots and fall, or simply just panic, balloon the fence and fall on landing. Yet if the rider remained just where he was and the horse right in front of him fell there would be no way of avoiding crashing into it. And the time in hand to make a decision was possibly less than one second.

In the end Blaze didn't do a thing, at least nothing physical. All he did was call out something to his horse, something in a language not known to his rivals, and as soon as he heard the call The Enchanted did the rest. Seeing nothing but horse slap bang in front of him and nothing but hedge beyond that, the horse jumped the moment after his adversary did, but instead of rising in a dead straight line he swung himself to the left in mid-air, not enough to throw himself off balance but enough to land clear of Roaring Cavalier, who as it happened didn't fall but landed well and still running. But The Enchanted landed even better, not crooked and not in the slightest unbalanced, although his evasive action had cost him what normally might well prove to be an all-important length, because as they began their run to the last the little horse was still three or perhaps four off the leading pair, Go Fast Carb and Roaring Cavalier, who were now running neck and neck.

'What's happening!' Alice cried. 'Someone please tell me what's happening!'

'Oh, for goodness' sake, Allie!' Millie shouted back. 'Take your fingers out of your ears and take a look for yourself!'

'And as they come to the last it's still Go Fast Carb in the lead but only just!' the commentator called. 'Roaring Cavalier is right there with him with The Enchanted now beginning to make significant progress!'

The din that had swelled to a roar as both the favourites seemed to have the race between them now died considerably as one of the outsiders laid down what in other circumstances would appear to be a hopeless challenge, with the two leaders still four lengths clear at the last and neither of them showing signs of weakening. But the roars were lessening because of the notable ease with which the unknown and unfancied little horse was racing. He was running so easily that, as every seasoned racegoer in the crowd knew, provided he jumped the last as well as he had jumped all the previous fences, this horse was going to win doing cartwheels.

Blaze knew it, too. As they thundered towards the last he could see the jockey on Go Fast Carb hard at work, giving his mount two sharp ones behind the saddle before he left the ground, while the rider on Roaring Cavalier, who had chosen to come up the rails, was shouting and yelling blue murder for room as Go Fast Carb suddenly swerved across in front of him. The fence was wide open for The Enchanted who stood so far off Blaze thought he was gone and buried and all but closed his eyes. It was the longest and greatest jump he had ever sat on any horse, The Enchanted practically taking off outside the wings and yet landing lengths clear the other side.

A roar went up from the stands when the race-goers saw it, their indifference now turned to genuine admiration and respect as they realised they might be witnessing the debut of a really special animal. A few more strides were all that were needed to silence anyone still doubting, The Enchanted coming away from the last three lengths down on the leaders who were both still racing flat out, catching them both hand over fist, and in a matter of a few lengthening strides, in the time it took for Rory to put his race glasses back up, in that brief moment the battle was won. Blaze didn't even have to shake the reins at his mount. He didn't have to shout at him the way the other two jockeys were berating their brave horses. He didn't have to touch him. He didn't have to do anything more than let out the same amount of rein as he had up on the gallops and the race was over. The Enchanted went into top gear and flew.

'It's The Enchanted now!' the commentator called. 'The Enchanted is simply flying! He's right alongside Go Fast Carb – and he's past him! He's flown past Go Fast Carb and Roaring Cavalier! And to add insult to injury he's putting daylight between himself and the second two! It's The Enchanted by two, by three, by four lengths now, and Blaze Molloy still hasn't moved on him! And on the run to the post it's The Enchanted going away from them still – and it's The Enchanted – The Enchanted wins by six lengths!'

The grandstands were buzzing as everyone began discussing what they had just witnessed, while the little group of those who owned him stood in stupefied silence as they tried to come to terms with what they too had just seen.

'What happened?' a small voice said from somewhere behind Rory.

'He won, that's what happened, Alice!' Rory laughed, turning and swinging her round to face him. 'He's only gone and won! Didn't you see any of the race?'

'Not one bit,' Alice said. 'I didn't hear anything, either.'

'Because she had her ears blocked,' Millie groaned. She turned to her friend. 'I bet you were singing loudly, too, the way you always did at school when you didn't want to hear any-thing.'

346

'He really did win?' Alice said, wide-eyed. 'I mean really? This isn't all a dream?'

'He not only won, my dear Alice,' Grenville said, whacking his leg with his hat, 'he blooming murdered them!'

'Come on,' Rory said. 'You lot have got to go down and lead your horse in. Yes, and there's a cup to be collected too. Wow – yes, this is a very big day, everyone – and oh my heavens above—'

Rory stopped as if pole-axed as he remembered, as he felt the winning Tote ticket between his fingers in his coat pocket, realising how well and truly this would now see the wretched bank and its equally wretched manager off.

'Oh my goodness gracious me,' he said again. 'Right. Yes. Yes – this is really quite a very big day.'

They made their way down the stands, Alice with her eyes full of tears, arm in arm with Millie who was laughing her head off, Grenville still beating himself up with his trilby, and Constance now singing at the top of her voice.

'We've got a horse right here!' she sang. 'And he's a little dear!'

'Of course it's only a novice chase so it could mean anything,' a rather mean-faced military-looking man was saying behind them. 'The horse was carrying seven pound less than any of the others, and for God's sake, have you seen the way it's bred? Or rather isn't? No, I don't think we have to go getting carried away here, do you know?'

'Pooh,' Constance said, turning round to him. 'You're talking twaddle. And you look quite as silly as you sound.'

'Here are the Tote returns on the last race to a pound stake,' an announcement rang out over the tannoy. 'Horse number nine – win nineteen pounds seventy, place three pounds fifty . . .'

The rest of the prices were lost to the group who with the exception of Constance had all backed the horse, Grenville on the rails and Alice, Millie and Lynne on the Tote – and of course Rory as well.

'Eighteen and a half to one, old chap,' Grenville said to Rory. 'And the best I could do was sixteens. So two and a half points better on the Tote – except— poor chap.' Grenville suddenly stopped and pulled a sympathetic face at Rory. 'Of course. Poor Rory. You didn't have a bet, did you?'

'No – no I didn't,' Rory answered with perfect candour. 'I didn't have a bet personally. But my father did.'

There was a terrific buzz around the winners' enclosure as the crowd waited for The Enchanted to be led in. To the side of the pen where the victorious horse would stand was a small dais on which stood a table bearing a large silver cup, while photographers and press hurried back from the course and down from the press room ready to fire questions at the winning trainer and take pictures of the winner.

'I think Constance should accept the cup on

our behalf,' Alice suggested. 'If that's all right with everyone else?'

'Absolutely,' Grenville agreed, although he had been just about to propose that Lynne accept the cup, hoping thus to give an added boost to his chances there. 'I couldn't think of anyone better.'

'Will I have to speak?' Constance wondered, looking round at the gathering crowd. 'I would really rather not, don't you know.'

'You absolutely do not have to speak, Constance,' Rory assured her, still unable to believe what had just happened and afraid to pinch himself just in case. 'Just smile and accept the cup, that's all. Just be your lovely gracious self.'

'I do know rather a good poem,' Constance said as they continued on their way towards the enclosure. 'A very smart lady named Suki, said she liked to mix business with nookie – before every race she'd go home to her place, and curl up with a very good bookie.'

'Oh, I think you must say that,' Millie said. 'You'll bring the place down.'

'Should I really?' Constance asked, wide-eyed.

'Most certainly not, my lady,' Grenville laughed. 'You'll be up before the stewards.'

'I think I'd quite enjoy that,' Constance sighed. 'Oh well.'

They were just in time to see a radiant Kathleen leading in their horse. A great round of applause began and lasted until Teddy had thrown a rug over the winner's quarters and Rory had gone to the horse's head to pat his neck and congratulate him. As is so often the case with horses after they have won, The Enchanted now looked quite a different animal; not only did he seem to stand taller but the look in his eyes suggested that he sensed what he had just done. As he looked imperiously around him he looked altogether stronger and even more purposeful, ears pricked, eyes bright and so full of himself that it took all Kathleen's skill to keep him contained in the small enclosure.

Grenville escorted his fellow co-owners into the pen, hat off and smiling broadly. Alice and Lynne went shyly to join Rory, who was calling them over to the horse's head so that they could all have their picture taken with their hero and their jockey, who was smiling broadly and hugging the horse's neck.

'And Constance?' Rory looked round. 'Where's Constance gone?'

'She's up on the podium already,' Grenville said, spotting her. 'Waving to her subjects.'

After they had all been photographed, Grenville took Alice and Lynne with him to the podium while Rory was besieged by the racing press. A cheerful woman in a large felt hat and horn-rimmed glasses announced her pleasure in presenting the trophy to the winning owners, the cup being accepted on their behalf by a mercifully silent Constance. The presentation was followed by yet another photograph session.

'The last time I saw as many cameras as this,'

Constance remarked loudly, 'I was not wearing anything like as much clothing.'

The party were then finally led away by two of the course's directors, to enjoy a celebratory bottle of champagne in a small back room heavily decorated with photographs of famous horses winning famous races at the track.

'Good race, Blaze,' Rory told his jockey in the weighing room after Blaze had weighed in. 'Well done.'

'Nothing to do with me, boss,' Blaze replied. 'That horse is magic.'

'Got a bit of toe, hasn't he?' Rory said. 'Jumps, too.'

'Did you see the way he took the last?' Blaze asked, his smile replaced now by a serious expression. 'It was as if he had wings on him. Listen now, I could have picked the leaders up any time I wanted to, boss. I never got a feel like it. I never asked him a thing, not once. I never asked him to pick up, I never asked him to see a stride, I didn't even have to ask him to jump round that other horse at the second last. He did it all himself. And when I let out that much rein . . .' Blaze opened his index finger one inch away from his thumb. 'That's all. When I let out that much rein – whoosh. He quickened so fast I hardly even remember the final furlong.'

'He hardly blew after it, as well,' Rory remembered. 'While you have to say the second and third were out on their feet.'

'Congratulations, young man.' A tall, distinguished-looking man with a racing saddle slung over one arm stopped to offer his good wishes. 'That was some performance.'

'Thank you, Captain,' Rory replied. 'Thanks a lot.'

'I never mind losing to a good horse,' the captain replied. 'And that is most certainly a very good horse.'

'Captain Timms,' Rory said. 'You probably don't know my jockey, Blaze Molloy.'

'Well ridden, young man,' Captain Timms said. 'Well ridden indeed. I shall keep my eye on you. And by the way, Rory, did you get the time? A new course record for two miles. Well done indeed.'

'A new course record?' Rory repeated when Captain Timms had left them. 'A course *record*? I thought it was a fast pace, but a course record? It can't be. It looked as though you were easing up at the finish.'

'I was, Mr Rawlins,' Blaze replied. 'Or rather the horse was.'

Kathleen had almost finished washing her horse down when Rory found her.

'I said this was a special horse, Mr Rawlins,' she said, throwing the last of the bucket of water under the horse's stomach to cool him. 'Didn't I say just that?'

'He was certainly d-d-dreadfully impressive,' Rory agreed. 'I don't mean dreadfully. I meant he was certainly – he was certainly – he was – ter-ter-*terrifically* impressive. Wasn't he?'

'Didn't I just say so? This is a very gifted horse, so this is,' Kathleen said, straightening up and looking into her horse's eye before kissing him on one cheek. Rory watched, wishing for the first time in his life that he was a horse, here and now.

'OK,' he said, bringing himself back to earth. 'What have I got to do? Yes – yes, I have to go off and join my owners, but look, what about later? I mean, what about when we get h-h-home this evening . . .'

Kathleen glanced at him then carried on fussing her horse.

'Thanks, but we're all going down the Chequers,' she said over her shoulder. 'Blaze asked me just now. Teddy, Pauline, Blaze and I. After we've done stables.'

'Oh. Right. Fine.' Rory nodded. 'Yes of course, that's fine. Yes. I just – I just wanted to make sure you all had something organised.'

'You're more than welcome to join us, Mr Rawlins.'

'Am I? You mean . . . ? Right. Right, thanks, but no, we're all going out as well. The owners and I. I think I said I'd take them all out to dinner. Something like that. After all,' he added, 'this isn't exactly the sort of thing that happens every day.'

'It most certainly is not,' Kathleen agreed, now turning to look at Rory, to stare right into his eyes.

'But then this is not exactly an everyday sort of horse.'

Before going out to dinner, Rory called in to see his father.

'Any improvement, Dan?' he asked the doctor, catching him just before he went off duty.

'I was going to ring you, as it happens, Rory,' the cardiologist replied. 'I think we might have turned a corner.'

'When?' Rory asked as the two of them walked down the highly polished corridor that led to Intensive Care. 'What, you mean there's been a general improvement in the last couple of days?'

'I would say today, actually, Rory. This afternoon to be exact.'

'This afternoon?' Rory said, feeling his blood change. 'Right. Tell me, yes – why this afternoon exactly?'

'I looked in on your father this morning and he was much the same. Sleeping, as he mostly does, although quite comfortable. But his temperature was still raised – we can't really seem to get it to come down and stay down, not safely, that is. And while as we all know a temperature means the body is fighting the infection, in infections such as the one your father is suffering from, and particularly following several heart attacks, obviously it's not only worrying, it's very debilitating for the patient. Anyway. Anyway, all said, until the nurse called me at – what was it? About quarter past two.'

'Round about the time we were weighing in,' Rory muttered.

'Sorry? What was that?'

'Nothing. No, I was just – it doesn't matter. Go on with what you were saying.'

'The nurse said your father's temperature had dropped down to normal. So of course I went across to see him at once . . .'

'And?'

'And not only was it normal, but the patient was awake,' Dan said. 'His temperature has stayed down ever since.'

Dan pushed open the door to the side ward. Rory's father was sitting propped up on his pillows, looking while not exactly the picture of health considerably improved since the last time Rory had seen him, when he had thought he might lose him at any minute.

'Hi, Pop,' he said, going in.

'Hello, old boy,' Anthony whispered. 'Haven't got much of a Hobson's, I'm afraid. So if you want to hear me, best pull up a chair.'

'I'm sorry to say I've come empty-handed, I fear,' Rory said, sitting by the bed by his father's head. 'I didn't know you were back with us. By that I mean awake and everything.'

Anthony cleared his throat and then put one long-fingered, elegant hand on his son's.

'I had the very devil of a dream today,' he said, barely audibly. 'There was this horse. And it had wings. I was on it, do you see, this flying horse. It had somehow rescued me from the sea, I knew that. It was a very rough sea, and very cold. Then I was on this horse's back and it flew me to safety. The devil it did. It plucked me out of the sea and flew me to safety.'

Chapter Seventeen

Headlines

'Hey, Gerry?'

'I'm in the bathroom!'

'Wait till you see this!'

Maddy stared again at the news stories in Gerry's copy of the *Sporting Life* and the racing pages of the *Telegraph* and the *Mail*. The Enchanted's victory was a major sports story in both dailies.

'You just wait till you see this,' Maddy said, pushing the *Sporting Life* Gerry's way as he came into the kitchen in a white towelling dressing gown, still drying his hair.

'So where's the fire, then?' he asked. 'What's all this about?'

'Get reading and you'll find out, lover.'

Maddy poured herself another cup of black coffee and sat watching Gerry read, coffee cup held two-handed, both her elbows on the table.

'I wish you wouldn't do that,' Gerry said, having glanced up and noticed what she was doing. 'It's dead common.'

'I am dead common,' Maddy replied, remaining exactly as she was. 'Anyway, dead common according to who?'

'You know who,' Gerry replied, sitting down with the paper. 'Bloody hell.'

'Yeah,' Maddy agreed. 'How about that?'

'How long has she had a horse? I mean, it can't be long. We haven't been divorced that long.'

'Well, she's got one now, Gerry. And not only a horse, a winning horse and all.'

Gerry read on, shaking his head.

'"The Enchanted,"' he read out from the *Life*. '"A breeding mystery."'

'Yeah, I know, I read it,' Maddy said, still watching him.

'"The easy winner of yesterday's Markham Novice Chase at Wincanton as far as the stud book goes is a completely unknown quantity."'

'Her mug is staring out at me everywhere,' Maddy complained. 'Look!'

She turned her copy of the *Daily Mail* to Gerry, simultaneously tapping the picture on the front of the *Sporting Life* with a long, manicured, bright red fingernail.

'I mean, look, Gerry!'

'I'm looking, Maddy. I'm looking.'

'"Lynne Faraday, one of the four owners of the debuttant horse . . ."' Maddy read out to him, taking her paper back.

'Debootant,' Gerry corrected her. 'That should be debootant horse, Maddy.'

'Yeah, yeah.' Maddy sniffed. '"Lynne Faraday blah blah blah expressed herself *delighted* with the horse's performance and said as a first time owner she never for a moment imagined herself as being a winning owner. Certainly her part-owned young and unconsidered horse won a fast-run race with considerable authority and without making the semblance of a mistake. The Enchanted has to be one for the notebook and certainly goes on my list as one to follow, as indeed does his lovely co-owner." I mean, that just isn't *fair*, Gerry!'

'What particular part just isn't fair, Maddy?'

'She's got her picture in every blooming newspaper, that's what! It just isn't fair!'

'So what am I meant to do about it, my love?'

'I dunno, Gerry! But I do know something.'

'You do? I'm dying to hear. What do you know?'

'That you are going to have to *do* something!'

'Mum? Is this true?' Georgina was asking Alice on the phone. 'I mean, I am looking at this picture of you in the *Daily Mail* and it says—'

'It's all perfectly true, Georgina,' Alice replied, picking up Sammy's water bowl to freshen it.

'So what are you groaning for, Mum?'

'I'm groaning—'

'I'm the one who should be groaning, Mum.'

359

'I was groaning because I was bending down, dear. To pick up Sammy's water bowl.'

'Just tell me this isn't true, right? Seriously? That you've bought a *racehorse*?'

'Part of a racehorse, Georgina dear. A share in a racehorse.'

'Are you completely out of your head, Mum? Have you totally lost it?'

'Not at all.'

'First of all you suddenly decide to move *miles* away from your family, without so much as discussing it with us, then the next thing we know is you've bought a *racehorse*.'

'A share in a racehorse, Georgina. Do get your facts right. A share in a *winning* racehorse.'

Alice smiled to herself and sat down on the old sofa she'd put under the kitchen window in the cottage, patting her knee for Sammy to jump up. It was a cloudless winter day, and the wonderful views she now enjoyed were lit by a gentle early November sun.

'I honestly don't know what to say.' Georgina sighed down the phone.

'You could try "Well done. Congratulations",' Alice suggested.

'Mum?' her daughter replied in her particularly irritating sing-song way. 'Mum, do get real.'

'Actually, Georgina,' Alice said, 'I think that's precisely what I am doing. Bye-bye.'

Instead of being cross, which she felt she should be, Alice found herself first smiling and then laughing out loud. Now that the little horse had won she was even more determined to stand firm and be free. She was no longer invisible. And she had ended another telephone call by putting the phone down first.

Chapter Eighteen

Back Across the Wather

'There is only one certain remedy for a sore head,' Michael Doherty announced to his fellow sufferers in the snug of Finnegan's Exclusive American Cocktail Lounge in Cronagh, 'and that is to avoid excess in the first place.'

'And if they was to mind you, Michael,' Donal replied, polishing a pint glass with a tea towel decorated with the head of Arkle, 'what would I be doing for a living?'

'And where would we be doing our drinking?' Tim O'Cloughlan asked from further down the bar. 'Perish the thought altogether and have another. That's generally considered to be the best cure-all for this sort of malarkey. Donal? Fill all the glasses again, man, for God's sake now.'

'Let's hope for the sake of all our sanities this is not going to be a regular occurrence,' Padraig muttered, leaning on the bar and holding his head. 'I have a large motorway gang at work in here.'

'This business about a statue,' Eammon pronounced Yamon said from his usual standing position in one corner of the snug. 'Was this a serious thing or was this just a jest?'

'Who said anything about any statue?' Padraig groaned. 'A statue of whom, for heaven's sake?'

'Not of yourself, Padraig,' Donal told him, wiping the bar with Arkle. 'Of that you can be sure.'

'I'm not following you one whit, Donal.' Michael frowned at the landlord. 'If there's any statue to be posted, then I think most certainly Padraig here should be in the running.'

'Whoever heard of posting any statue?' Tim wanted to know. 'Meself I never heard the like.'

A red-faced man with a large powdered nose burst into the snug, shaking his head violently.

'May I never live through such a time again, so help me God,' he announced, collapsing against the bar and resting his head on it. 'May I never bear witness again to the like.'

Donal filled a tumbler with a double measure of John Jameson and put the glass on the bar for the new arrival.

'Will the bank not recover then, Mr Coulihan?' he enquired politely with a wink at the others, throwing Arkle over his shoulder.

'The bank?' Coulihan wondered, standing upright now and regarding his peers wild-eyed. 'The bank indeed? I doubt if the entire Irish economy will ever get back on its feet. I have never seen such a run on our money.'

'Your money?' Padraig muttered. 'And there was I going round thinking now the money belonged to the depositors.'

'Never mind that,' Michael said. 'What about poor old Tobias Tandy? Surely he's the one facing the ruin? All you did is what you always do – give us some of our money back that you've been making yourself even fatter on.'

'The problem with you people is that you do not have a proper grasp of banking in any way whatsoever,' Coulihan retorted. 'There is a lot more to banking than just counting out money, you know.'

'That's the bit you enjoy, Mr Coulihan,' Donal said, with a nod. 'The rustle of all them new green ones sent down from Dublin. I've seen the expression on your face.'

'Tobias is never ruined now, surely?' Padraig said, concerned. 'I'd never forgive meself if Tobias was done out of it.'

'He's a bookmaker, Padraig!' Michael said fiercely. 'He's there to be done out of it!'

'He was in and out of the bank like a hen on fire,' Coulihan told them. 'For him to meet his obligations to his customers, sure the bank had to take a charge on his shop.'

'What he means is Tobias had to cancel the charge he has on the bank,' Michael said with a broad grin. 'Isn't that so, Coulihan? Wasn't it yourself that had the very worst of times this last Cheltenham?'

'Mr, if you don't mind, Michael Doherty. That

is if you want me to go on cashing those rubber cheques of yours.'

'And did you have a bet, Mr Coulihan?' Yamon bellowed from the back of the snug. 'They say you took the twenties!'

'I'd have been no sort of financier not to have done so, Yamon,' Coulihan replied. 'I could hardly call meself any sort of banker if I'd eschewed such an investment opportunity.'

'Padraig here is suggesting we put up some sort of a statue to your man,' Donal told Coulihan. 'Your man with The Horse, this is.'

'I couldn't but agree.' Coulihan nodded. 'There's astute trainers, there's very astute trainers, and there are the inspired ones, and your man over the water falls well and truly into the latter catechism.'

'Hadn't we all been sitting here watching and waiting for The Horse?' Michael asked rhetorically. 'Waiting to see him properly declared and entered, for then we knew he'd be off.'

'We all knew he was off,' Padraig said with a nod. 'Helped be word of the daughter who kept us regularly posted about his work.'

'She said his first piece of fast work scorched the turf,' Michael said, dropping his voice to a whisper. 'She said she'd never seen the like. Said he buried the rest of the string and wouldn't have blown a candle out after it.'

'What was the worst anyone took, I wonder,' Coulihan said, holding his now empty glass out for a refill.

'The twenties you had, Mr Coulihan,' Michael said. 'Sure we all had the thirty-threes.'

'All except himself here,' Tim said with a nod to Padraig.

'And what price did you get him at, Padraig?' Michael enquired. 'Did you do better than our thirty-threes now?'

'Maybe I did and maybe I did not,' Padraig said with a careful nod of his throbbing head. 'Let's just say I had him backed at extremely good odds to win the very first race he ran in.'

'So they'd be longer than ours, so.'

'They'd be considerably longer,' Donal said, handing the bank manager his fresh drink. 'So if the Irish economy needs boosting, you'll know whose bed to be looking under.'

Chapter Nineteen

The Morning After the Day Before

Grenville went to collect the morning papers, which he gathered were left in a large box inside the main front door of Brook House. Since there seemed to be no one else about he thought it perfectly safe to do so in the large white towelling dressing gown that he had found hanging behind the bathroom door. Padding barefoot down the polished wooden stairs he found himself singing to himself with happiness, something he very rarely did – something in fact he couldn't remember doing for far too long a time.

'I've got the world on a string, sitting on a rainbow,' he crooned. 'Got the whatsit round my doodah – what a world, what a life – I'm in—'

'Fielding?' a voice from behind interrupted him. 'Grenville *Fielding*?'

Grenville stopped dead in his tracks, his moment of unbridled joy spoilt. He knew the owner of the voice without even having to turn round to identify him.

'Barrington,' he intoned. 'Montague Barrington, I do declare.'

'I say,' said his investment client, 'I say, Grenville, what on earth are you doing in this neck of the woods, eh?'

Grenville slowly turned about, putting a polite smile on his face. 'Just visiting actually,' he replied lightly. 'And you, old chap?'

'Got an apartment here. Had quite enough of SW3, thanking you kindly. Thought I would take me to the country instead. I like the casual look, Grenville. Very *soigné*.'

'Just getting the daily rag,' Grenville replied, pulling his borrowed dressing gown more tightly round his midriff. 'If you'll excuse.'

'I'll come along with you, dear boy,' the portly Montague told him, falling into step alongside Grenville as they crossed the large marble-floored hall. 'L. F.,' he commented, noticing the monogram on the dressing gown's top pocket. 'Undercover, are we? Jolly good. Or are those the initials of some hotel you nicked the robe from? Eh? Right?'

'Belongs to a friend,' Grenville explained.

'Oh I say.' Montague smirked. 'Oh I say, I say, I say.'

'So you just said,' Grenville remarked. 'Look – tell you what, if you're around later, perhaps we might have a drink, yes? But at the moment—'

'At the moment I should think so too,' Montague

cut in, giving Grenville an over-suggestive wink. 'What? I should say.'

'Which is your apartment, Monty? I'll come and take a drink off you lunchtime, if you're around.'

'Good thought, Gren, but I'm off shooting all day. But should you be around this weekend, I'm in apartment six. *Ciao*, Casanova!'

Relieved to see him go, Grenville found himself puzzled by why he should have felt so embarrassed, as if he'd been caught doing something he shouldn't instead of something of which he should be proud. He could only put it down to his mother's prevailing influence on his life. Fond as he was of his mother, he resented her still constant interference in and regular criticism of his private life and affairs. But because his parents had divorced after his father had been found *in flagrante* with his secretary, Grenville felt sorry for his mother and so had remained loyal to her, even though she had never met his kindness and understanding with any real kindness or understanding of her own. Worst of all she was a purely dreadful snob, an affectation that had been directly responsible for the ruination of several of the young Grenville's love affairs, most particularly the termination of his engagement to the charming, sweet and pretty Jane Denton, whose only failing was her family's modest beginnings.

As Grenville padded back upstairs with the newspaper tucked under his arm, he wondered what his mother would make of the young woman with whom he was now – as he liked to think of it – *associated*, and when he thought of it he literally stopped to think about it, halfway back up the polished wooden staircase. And to his joy he realised he didn't care what she thought.

Better than that, he told himself, *I won't even ask her what she thinks because I won't even introduce her to Lynne. Or rather I might not*, he decided, re-forming his thoughts as he continued on his way. *And even if I do decide to take Lynne home to meet her, it will not matter a single jot if she tries to make any of the usual sort of trouble. Not a jot.*

'Grenville?' a sleepy voice called from the bedroom as he let himself into the apartment. 'That you?'

'It's only me,' Grenville called back to reassure her. 'Like some coffee? I thought I'd make some coffee.'

'OK,' Lynne called back. 'I'll be up in a jiffy.'

Grenville put the newspaper on the table, and went to tidy up his makeshift bed on the sofa, taking the quilt Lynne had given him and stacking it neatly with the pillow on top of the pile of his immaculately folded clothes on a nearby chair. After straightening the creases out of the sofa he plumped up the cushions, squared the bright-coloured Scandinavian rug in front of it, and finally pulled the curtains back at the sitting-room windows, flooding the room with pale winter sunlight. Before going to the kitchen to make the coffee, he stood for a moment admiring the apartment, once again finding himself surprised by his reaction, since never for a moment had he thought he would end up approving of such a Spartan style of interior décor. As far as furnishing and design went, he was a dyed-in-the-wool traditionalist, preferring brown furniture to white, chintz to single bright colours, and portraits of ancestors to geometric abstracts. Yet Lynne had chosen to decorate and furnish her new apartment in the sort of style he would have thought would be anathema to him, and he found himself admiring it.

The decoration and furnishing were only in the initial stages, with the walls freshly painted in what Grenville thought would probably be described as a subdued white. The sofa and armchair were large, modern and upholstered in single-coloured tweeds, the chair in an Etruscan red and the sofa in dull ochre. Two of the walls were hung with large, bright and beautifully executed landscapes, one of mustard fields, the other of pale mountains shrouded in a light mist. The bathroom was furnished with a large modern tub fitted with oversize chromed taps and its window fitted with handmade American-style shutters, and the large modern kitchen dazzled with clean lines and an abundance of worktops.

'All so very uncluttered,' Grenville observed to himself as he made his way to the kitchen. 'Rather like the way one hopes one's life is now going to be.'

'I'm sorry about last night,' Lynne said to him as they sat drinking their coffee in the sitting room, Lynne in her pyjamas with a cashmere sweater pulled over the top and thick white ski socks on her feet, Grenville still in her dressing gown. 'Really I am. Sorry.'

'There is nothing to be sorry about, Lynne,' Grenville assured her. 'Absolutely. And do stop apologising for everything.'

'Sorry,' Lynne said, pulling a face.

'Lynne?'

'No, I am sorry about last night,' she insisted. 'I had far too much champagne and everything—'

'You were celebrating. We all were.'

'I know, but I did – I had far too much.'

'You mean nobody else did? I didn't?'

'Yeah – but then you sleeping on the sofa and everything. Did you get any sleep?'

'I slept like a top, thank you, Lynne. Like a top.'

'You got a hangover?'

'I could have a coffee or ten, certainly.'

'Me too.' Lynne sighed. 'That was some party. I didn't make a fool of myself, did I?'

'Depends how you define that,' Grenville replied, pouring some more coffee. 'If you think being totally delightful—'

'Me?'

'Totally delightful,' Grenville assured her. 'Funny, interesting, wonderful dancer—'

'Course, we danced, didn't we?' Lynne groaned in recollection, head in hand. 'Back at Rory's.'

'And sang.' Grenville laughed. 'Though not me, you'll be happy to hear. A foghorn in distress is infinitely more musical than yours truly. You sang, Rory sang—'

'He was at the piano, wasn't he?'

'Pretty fair too, on the old ivories. Constance was the star of the show, however.'

'I remember that all right. She was marvellous.'

'Yes,' Grenville said thoughtfully. 'Yes, she was, wasn't she? Mysterious old thing, isn't she?'

'I'm really fond of Connie,' Lynne said. 'I think she's had a really tough life.'

'I don't really know anything about her life. She seems to have married quite a lot.'

'So she says. I think she's probably rather lonely. Which is why this is good.'

'And she was obviously once a bit of a looker,' Grenville remarked. 'Wouldn't you say?'

'I'd say she still is, Grenville. Just because she's older doesn't stop her being beautiful.'

'No,' Grenville agreed, such a thought never having occurred to him before. 'No, I don't suppose it does.'

Lynne put down her coffee cup and leaned across to touch Grenville's hand.

'Sorry you only had a sofa to sleep on,' she said. 'As you can see, I've hardly really started furnishing this place.'

'It's very nice, you know,' Grenville replied, pretending to look round him at the apartment to take his mind off the warm hand that was resting on his. 'I really like this plain, uncluttered look.'

'Why *did* you sleep on the sofa, as a matter

of interest?' Lynne asked him, frowning. 'No, I didn't mean to ask that. Sorry.'

'You really must stop apologising for yourself all the time,' Grenville told her, patting her hand with his. 'You have nothing to apologise for.'

'I don't apologise for myself all the time, do I? Really?'

'I'm afraid you do a bit, yes.'

'Do I really? Oh. Sorry.'

'You really have nothing to apologise for. You're a wonderful girl. You're bright, you're funny, and you're – you're really very pretty.'

Overcome, Lynne stared at Grenville for a moment, then dropped her eyes.

'And you dance quite beautifully,' Grenville added.

'And you're a . . .' Lynne began, 'you're a real gentleman.'

'Why, Lynne,' Grenville said, his whole face brightening. 'Why, Lynne, what a very nice thing to say.'

'Well you are, Grenville,' Lynne assured him. 'I can't tell you how nice it is to be with some-one who treats you – well, who treats you with respect. I can't tell you what it's like. It's so – I don't know. It's so different. It makes you *feel* so different.'

'Thank you.'

'I mean, a lot of men might have taken or tried to take a bit of advantage last night or something,' Lynne went on. 'You know, your horse wins, you have a lot of champagne, you party and dance

374

and everything. A lot of people would have tried to take advantage.'

'Lynne—'

'No. No, you really don't have to explain, Grenville. All I want to say to you is thanks. Really. You're such a nice man.'

She smiled so sweetly at him that Grenville could no longer help himself. The next moment they were kissing and only a short time after that Grenville found to his delight he would no longer be sleeping on the sofa.

Alice was also nursing a sore head, the first one she could remember having since Alex and she had drunk too much champagne on the night of their silver wedding anniversary. In the belief that a hangover shared was a hangover slightly spared she had telephoned Millie, who she thought might also be suffering since they had all insisted she come to the party as well, reasoning that if it hadn't been for Millie Alice would never have met Rory and they would never have formed the partnership.

Millie had thought it an excellent idea to share the hangover and had the iced and spiced Bloody Marys all ready and waiting in a large glass jug when Alice turned up with Sammy and a box of home-made spaghetti carbonara from her deep freeze. After a couple of drinks and a restorative lunch the two of them sat in front of a roaring log fire while the November winds lamented round the grey and cold landscape outside, with Sammy and all of Millie's dogs, two pugs, a bearded collie, a rescued mongrel and an oddly self-assured whippet, sleeping peacefully at their feet.

A ringing telephone woke them from the sleep into which they had both fallen.

'It's Rory,' Millie told Alice, handing her the receiver. 'He rang earlier because he couldn't find you – you'd obviously left already – so I said you were coming over here and he said he'd ring back. I forgot to tell you. He wants a word with you.'

'Not bad news, I hope?' Alice asked when she got on the phone. 'The little horse is all right?'

'He's fine, Alice,' Rory replied. 'Didn't Millie tell you? He's come out of his race really well.'

'No, Millie didn't tell me,' Alice replied, giving her friend the mock evil eye.

'I didn't tell you because I thought you'd like to hear it for yourself,' Millie excused herself quickly.

'I'll talk about plans for the future in a minute,' Rory said. 'But first I have to tell you what's happened.'

'Something has happened.' Alice all but groaned. 'I thought you said the horse was all right?'

'The horse is *fine*, Alice.' Rory laughed. 'He's eaten up, had a run out in the field, and at the moment is having a total body massage from the lovely Kathleen. No, what I have to tell you, although it concerns the horse, is nothing about his health or fitness. And I'm obliged to tell you about it although I hope I know what your answer will be.'

'Yes? So?'

'I had a call. Someone wants to buy the horse.'

'What?' Alice said, astounded. 'But he's not up for sale.'

'Who's not up for sale?' Millie mouthed. Alice turned her back to her, flapping one hand at her friend to try to stem further interruptions.

'Why should anyone think they can buy the horse?' Alice wanted to know.

'This is the sort of thing that happens in horse racing,' Rory replied. 'People see a winning horse, particularly a young winning horse, and out come the chequebooks.'

'Well, he's not for sale,' Alice said. 'At least my leg most certainly isn't.'

'I'm relieved to hear that.' Rory laughed. 'After the agony you went through during the race I thought you might be glad to get rid of him.'

'Nonsense,' Alice reproved him. 'I've never enjoyed not enjoying myself more. How much did they offer?'

'Do you really want to know?'

'Just for the record.'

'Fifty thousand.'

'Fifty thousand guineas?'

'Fifty thousand guineas.'

'That's more than four times what we paid for him.'

'That's what people will pay for a winning horse. A special horse.'

'What has everyone else said?'

'Grenville said no, Lynne of course said no, and Constance said something I can't repeat.'

'Suppose one of us wanted to sell?'

'By the terms of your contract, if you couldn't come to an agreement then the horse would have to be sent to the sales,' Rory told her. 'But since none of you want to sell . . .'

There was silence from Alice.

'Alice?' Rory pressed her. 'Are you having second thoughts?'

'Of course not. I was just wondering who on earth had the cheek.'

'No sale, my love,' Gerry reported to Maddy later in the day. 'Went as high as I dared, but no takers.'

'So what are you going to do, Gerry?' Maddy demanded, pouring herself another glass of champagne. 'You're not just going to sit down on this, are you? Because if you are—'

'Yes, my love? If I am, what?'

'Never you mind. Just don't expect *me* to be around while you do.'

'While I do what, lover?'

'Sit down on it, that's what, Gerry!' Maddy yelled at him. ''Cos if you are, I am not!'

'All this just because Lynne got herself a bit of a horse?'

'This is not all because of that at all, Gerry! Look – I'm a model, right? Not far off the top, neither, and I do not want some nothing and nobody

378

knocking me out of the papers, right? Got it? I mean, who does she think she is anyway? Poncing around all over the place mouthing off as if she's just won the bloody Derby or something!'

'All right, all right,' Gerry said, holding up both hands. 'All right, all right!'

'No it is not bloody well all right all right, Gerry!' Maddy all but screamed back at him. 'You told me when we got together I could have everything she had and more, right! So go get it, Rover! I want everything she's got and more!'

Gerry shook his head and went out to stare at his new BMW coupé, wondering why women couldn't be more like cars, beautiful yes, sexy certainly, but under your control, with your foot on the accelerator and your foot on the brake. It was at times like this, and in Gerry's view recently there had been a few too many times like this, but it was at times like this that he began to miss Lynne. Lynne might have been a bit boring and a little too compliant and even dutiful as far as Gerry was concerned, but at least she wasn't given to these sorts of you-just-wait rages, the terrible spoilt tantrums that Maddy was beginning to throw all too frequently. But it was too late now, he thought to himself as he walked round his gleaming red car, idly kicking its wheels. There was no going back now. Lynne and he were divorced, a settlement had been made and Maddy had well and truly moved in, in more ways than one.

Maybe the fact that he hadn't married her

yet was what was making her so mouthy, Gerry supposed. Or maybe it was all to do with this hormone thing he was always hearing about; maybe it was just her hormones playing her up at her time of the month or whatever. What did he know and how was he to know? He was just a bloke and, like so many of his mates, he admitted that women were more than a bit of a mystery to him. When they behaved the way Maddy was behaving they became totally inexplicable. Worst of all, he realised as he walked slowly back into the house, the reason didn't make the slightest bit of difference, because life would in no way return to normal till Maddy got what she wanted. And if she didn't get what she wanted, Gerry was beginning seriously to dread what might indeed happen to him. After all, not only wasn't he getting any younger, what was worse, he wasn't growing any new hair.

Chapter Twenty

Kicking On

The horse was due to run next at Huntingdon.
Rory was astonished at how well his charge had
come out of his first race, which even though he
had won it with ease had been run at a track-
record-breaking pace. Yet the horse had come
home, eaten up every oat that evening, slept like
a baby and run out in the paddock next day with
the sort of energy that made Rory think he could
have raced again that very afternoon.

'I see they're running Fly The Flags,' Grenville
observed on the morning of the race, when he
called the trainer before leaving for Cambridgeshire. 'Quite a useful novice, I gather. He's won
his first two races by healthy margins, beating
some other half-decent novices into the bargain.'

'Yes. I asked Dad about him, now he's sitting up
and reading the racing papers—'

'He's that much better, is he?' Grenville interrupted. 'I'm so glad to hear that.'

'Thanks, Grenville. Anyway, what the old man said – I think I should stop calling him that, actually – what my father said is that his connections have always seen him as a Cheltenham horse and so far nothing he has done has made them think of reconsidering.'

'So the little horse will have his work cut out. Fly The Flag's owned by some Yank or other, correct?'

'The some Yank or other, for your information, isn't just any Yank or other. He has six horses with Geordie Mainstone,' Rory informed him. 'He also owns the runner-up in last year's Grand National and—'

'Of course he does,' Grenville ad-libbed. 'I've been a bit out of touch since Papa bolted. We used to race all the time.'

'Eddie Rampton's running one of his hot hopes as well, and he doesn't send them this far if he hasn't had a good touch.'

'And you don't think the increase in distance is going to bother the little horse?'

'Don't think so. According to our pilot, our fellow hasn't just got toe but stamina as well.'

'Yes, right, Rory – but untested stamina.'

'No – no, that's why we decided to try him out over two and a half miles, Grenville. Huntingdon's a flat track like Wincanton – another fast galloping track – so it's not going to ask too big a question of him.'

'Fine,' Grenville replied. 'Right. Jolly good – see you at the track, then.'

As he hung up the phone, Rory could almost see Grenville tipping his hat on the other end of the line.

In spite of having bought herself a nice low-mileage second-hand Renault 5, Alice did not feel sufficiently roadwise to drive herself all the way to Cambridgeshire from Dorset and so had persuaded Millie to drive her there – not that her friend needed very much persuasion.

'It's very flat, Cambridgeshire, isn't it?' Alice observed after they had motored a dozen or so miles into the county. 'Alex always said it was murderers' country.'

'The Fens are worse,' Millie replied, 'Lincolnshire particularly. I don't think I could stand living in a flat county. How are you feeling, duck? Getting the wobbles yet?'

'Nowhere near as badly as last time. Although I must admit to feeling slightly nauseous.'

'The horse must have a good chance.'

'Perhaps we should have called him that,' Alice continued. 'Slightly Nauseous. On the other hand, I don't think so.'

'I don't think you can change a horse's name once it's registered,' Millie told her. 'At least, if you do – if indeed you can – I do know it's considered the most frightful bad luck.'

'Even if we could and we wanted to, I couldn't possibly change his name. I've always felt sure the horse was called The Enchanted because that's exactly what he is.'

'An enchanted horse, indeed,' Millie mused. 'Certainly looked like it at Wincanton. And today perhaps he'll look even more so.'

'Rory says it's quite a hot race.'

'If he's a good horse he has to beat good horses,' Millie said. 'And here we are – we've arrived.'

It was a mid-week meeting, but due to the quality of the racing there was a good crowd, despite the rain that had now begun to fall, accompanied by a biting east wind. After Alice had picked up her complimentary owner's tickets, she and Millie walked out on to the course with the first race only five minutes from the off. Alice's increasing nervousness was allayed by the good-humoured atmosphere, the vibrant colours of the jockeys' silks and the elegant beauty of the thoroughbreds parading in the paddocks. As arranged, they met up with Lynne, Constance and Grenville just outside the weighing room, then went and had a drink to refresh themselves after their long journeys.

'Right,' Lynne said, opening her racecard, after they had all sat down at a table. 'Let's see which ones are going to make us rich today then.'

'A man I knew once, can't remember his name,' Constance said, 'he was a reformed gambler who always maintained that the only people who made money from following the horses were the ones with a brush and a shovel.'

'You're full of those things, aren't you, Connie?' Lynne remarked. 'Full of equine bon bons.'

'Bons *mots*,' Grenville said, helping her out.

'Thank you, sweetheart,' Lynne replied, putting a hand on his, and cueing an exchange of looks between Alice, Millie and Constance.

'Trouble was, that's about all he ever did say,' Constance concluded. 'He was the most frightful old bore. And totally bald, which made it even worse.'

'Rory tells me the word is out for Fandangle, another west country horse, in our race,' Grenville said. 'Won easily a couple of weeks back at Devon and Exeter from a big field of novices, including two Lambourn hotshots.'

'You've seen Rory already, have you?' Alice asked.

'We have indeed,' Grenville replied. 'He said the little horse is very well and travelled up fine. But I'm afraid he *will* be favourite.'

'He's favourite in about eighty per cent of the papers,' Millie said, having consulted the tipster's table in the *Sporting Life*. 'I must say I always hated it when Jack was favourite. Seems you're there to be shot at, instead of just another runner.'

'That's racing.' Grenville sighed. 'Time to go and look at our runner, I'd say.'

The Enchanted started at an even shorter price than forecast, finally going to post at six to four on, four pounds on to win six, in spite of the fact that this was only his second race in Britain and he came from a small and what was largely regarded as an unsuccessful west country yard, was trained by a novice assistant trainer and was ridden by a conditional jockey who was having only his second ride in England. Yet throughout the race there was never really a moment's doubt in anyone's mind that the horse was going to win. This time, with no front-running Pope horses entered, Blaze jumped his mount off in front and let him lead the rest of the field the merriest of dances. Three fences out he was an easy twelve lengths clear of the chasing bunch, who were all quite obviously beaten horses, and the race was his bar a fall.

'I've warned Blaze about the last two fences here,' Rory said, as he watched his horse cantering into the straight, with Alice once more hiding herself behind his back. 'They've just rebuilt them and they're very stiff. Dad had a horse here at the opening meeting who took one heck of a fall at the last.'

'Thanks for sharing that with us now,' Grenville said, his large race glasses trained firmly on The Enchanted. 'He's coming to the last now.'

They all held their breath, particularly as having nothing to race against the horse was seemingly beginning to idle, but closer inspection revealed Blaze sitting as still as a fox watching chickens, his eyes only on the last fence, his hands still full of horse. The nearer they got to the fence the more he felt his mount regain his rhythm, putting down foot perfect and still on the bridle with ears pricked, not touching a twig of the formidable black wall of birch, and landing still full of running. This time, having taken a quick look after clearing the last at the distance between them and the rest of the field, Blaze eased his horse back and they passed the post at almost a walk.

'He's only done it again,' an incredulous Grenville said, as the cheering that greeted the little horse's victory began to abate. 'And if anything, even more easily.'

'Blooming heck,' Lynne said, grasping Constance by the arm. 'Two in a blooming row.'

'What else can you expect?' Constance replied. 'With such distinguished owners?'

'He didn't really win again, did he?' A white-faced Alice had finally emerged from behind her human shield. 'This is getting ridiculous.'

'This is getting unreal,' a none the less delighted Rory said. 'Seriously. Come on – let's get down and lead him in.'

'Thanks, boss,' Blaze said, when he'd been congratulated by his trainer, full of smiles and positioning himself for the team photograph. 'And didn't I say he'd stay? He could have gone round again. And again.'

'Very well done, if I may say so,' a tall and distinguished-looking American said to all the partnership met to greet their returning hero. 'If I may intrude on your celebrations, I just wanted to say I thought your horse ran a simply marvellous race. If you ever feel like selling him . . .'

He had a smile on his face which was reflected in his large blue eyes as he teased them, standing hatless with his hands clasped behind his back and his silver hair blown by the stiffening wind.

'How very kind,' Constance replied at her grandest. 'But I doubt that you could afford him.'

'I doubt that too, ma'am,' the American replied. 'Though I sure would like to own him.'

'The only way you'd be able to do that,' Constance told him, 'would be to marry one of the owners. Or perhaps all three of us.' She turned to her fellow partners and opened her eyes very wide.

'Mr Lovell,' Rory said, entering the conversation rather hastily, having dispatched Blaze to weigh in. 'If I may – can I introduce you to everyone? Everyone, this is Mr Lovell who owns Fly The Flag.'

'I thought your horse ran a very decent sort of race,' Grenville said, after they had all been introduced. 'Ran on to be second, I believe.'

'He certainly did, Mr Fielding,' Harrington Lovell replied. 'He ran a very good race and he came home sound, which is what I always pray for. But he couldn't hold a candle to your fellow. Not a lot of him, I dare say, but what there is is all heart and class. So my congratulations – and who knows? We may cross swords again some time. I very much hope so. Ladies.'

And with a small half-bow and another smile he took his leave.

'What a very nice man,' Constance observed. 'I think I shall go and marry him.'

'Not a chance, Connie,' Lynne said. 'You're far too young for him.'

'Lovely old world manners,' Alice remarked, looking after the departing American. 'I do like that.'

'My turn to buy the champagne, I say,' Rory said, handing Grenville some money. 'Even if it isn't I'm buying – I'll meet you in the bar after I've made sure Kathleen hasn't forgotten about his dope test.'

'Kathleen said it took him twenty minutes to do a wee at Wincanton,' Lynne informed the rest of the party as they made their way to the bar.

'I trust you're talking about our horse and not our trainer,' Constance remarked.

Harrington Lovell was at the bar when Grenville went to buy the champagne. 'Why don't you let me do that, Mr Fielding?' he suggested. 'I had a good wager on your horse so I feel the need to celebrate as well.'

'I have an even better idea, Mr Lovell,' Grenville replied. 'Why don't you come and join us? I gather from the young lady at the bar here that the winner's champagne is on the house, which might make the offer even more attractive.'

'That's very kind of you, Mr Fielding. I would certainly appreciate the company.'

'I gather you make it a habit to come over here to see your horses run,' Grenville said as they sat down at their table.

'Whenever it's possible I do,' Harrington

agreed. 'As a matter of fact I would live in this country if I could, I love it so much.'

'And your family?' Grenville wondered. 'Are they Anglophiles as well?'

'Sadly my wife died some six years ago and my family have all long flown the nest. Only thing keeps me home are my dogs.'

'You like dogs?' Alice chimed in. 'How many dogs do you have?'

'Far too many, ma'am.'

'Alice, please.'

'Far too many, Alice. Two Lhasa apsos, that were my wife's originally, a French bulldog, a Standard poodle and two mongrels, both rescue jobs and consequently my friends for life.'

'Perhaps you're a little like me then, Mr Lovell,' Constance said, lighting a cheroot. 'The more I see of dogs the more I wish I was one.'

'You want to be careful there, Connie,' Lynne whispered. 'That sort of remark could be whatever. You know. Mis-whatever.'

'Misconstrued?' Millie said helpfully.

'If you say so,' Lynne agreed cheerfully. 'I doubt I could even spell it.'

'And I agree with you, Constance,' Millie added. 'When I see how spoilt my dogs are, I think you're exactly right.'

'Your very good health, everyone,' Lovell said, raising his glass of champagne. 'And health to your quite magic little horse, too.'

*   *   *

Blaze found Kathleen coming out of the dope box with her horse. They said nothing to each other about the race, because they did not have to. All they did was exchange smiles, smiles perhaps a little longer than those they would normally give each other, and share a big, long, strong hug, which Rory happened to see on his way to find his horse. Unaware of him, Blaze then wandered off to watch the next race, and Kathleen went to prepare her charge for his return journey while Rory hung back, then turned and wandered back to the bar.

'Another drink?' Grenville mused, offering Rory a refill from a fresh bottle of champagne.

'Not for me, Grenville,' Rory said, putting a hand over his glass. 'I have to drive.'

'Jolly good,' Grenville replied, topping up the glasses of all those in the rest of the party who weren't going to get behind a wheel. 'Now what is it they say? Keep yourself in the best company and your horses in the worst, yes? Or is it the other way round? No – no, I think that's the right way round, and if so, and *à propos* of the fact that I don't know your exact thinking—'

'I don't know my exact thinking either – in fact I'm usually the last person to know what I'm thinking,' Rory agreed. 'But it might help if I had the slightest idea what you were on about, Grenville.'

'Plans,' Grenville replied, taking off his spectacles and carefully cleaning them on a spotless white handkerchief. 'Plans for the little horse.'

'Now then. OK. It's not that I think he should run against the rubbish because that's not going to get us anywhere.'

'But if you're thinking what I'm thinking, Rory—'

'Sorry – one thing at a time, Grenville. What I was going to say was it might be a bright idea to keep away from the grade-one tracks and the more – how shall I put it? – the more spotlit races. Keep a low profile, in other words.'

'Then you are thinking what I'm thinking.'

'Just keep a low profile,' Rory repeated. 'Until we know exactly what sort of horse we actually have.'

'Gotcha.'

'And I think we should certainly run him over three miles next time. Blaze said he wasn't in any way cooked, and finished full of running.'

'Can anyone else join in this?' Alice wondered. 'Or is it boys only?'

'Of course, Alice.' Rory moved his chair slightly away from Grenville's and turned to Alice. 'All we're doing – we were only discussing the next race.'

'Yes.' Alice nodded. 'Well, I know we're not exactly *au fait* with all that stuff, the distaff side as it were,' she added, indicating Lynne, Constance and herself. 'But we do have something to say, and the point is that if you two are hatching some sort of plot to enter our horse in the Grand National you can forget it—'

'Alice—'

'Seriously, Rory.' Alice overrode him. 'Because that's what we've been discussing, the three of us, and Millie, while you two have been talking. And the Grand National is over our dead bodies.'

'Mine too. I couldn't agree more,' Rory assured her. 'Not that it would be on even if we thought it was a good idea, because the horse is still a novice, and the National is no place for novices. Even so—'

'Even when he's not a novice,' Alice insisted. 'None of us want him ever to run in the National.'

'I couldn't agree more,' Grenville said. 'Too many good horses get injured in the National, and usually through no fault of their own. So you mustn't worry, Alice, because that was not what we were discussing at all, I do assure you. We have our eyes on something quite different.'

'Grenville here has his eyes on something quite different,' Rory said with a frown. 'I prefer to look not quite so far ahead. I'll send you all a list of suggested entries in a day or two, but now if you'll excuse me I have to hit the road. My father's coming home from hospital tomorrow, and I have to make sure everything's in place.'

'That's wonderful news, Rory,' Millie said. 'When did he turn the corner?'

'After Wincanton, would you believe?' Rory said. 'After the horse's first race.'

*   *   *

Since they had come such a distance to see the race, now their horse had won again none of the owners was in any great rush to get home, so they all decided to stay and enjoy the rest of the excellent racecard. The feature race was a three-mile handicap chase, the betting for which was dominated by Insider Trading, a big grey horse from Eddie Rampton's yard ridden by Sandy Bridger, his retained jockey, a man with a reputation as formidable as the trainer's.

'Think I should have a flutter?' Lynne asked Grenville as they stood at the paddock rails watching the sharp-faced jockey receiving his instructions from the pug-nosed, broad-shouldered Eddie Rampton. 'It's not much of a price.'

'I think that's because it's considered one of those nailed-on certainties, my dear,' Grenville replied. 'If I were you I'd go for something a little longer priced, some little each way chance.'

'Who's that dreadful-looking villainous type in the Al Capone hat?' Constance wondered, pointing at Rampton who was now turning round to face their group. 'He looks as though he should be carrying a gat.'

'Careful,' Grenville warned her, dropping his own voice as he thought he caught a glare from the trainer while quickly lowering Constance's accusing finger. 'And I'm sure Nanny told you how rude it is to point.'

Having both decided to back Whistlestop, one of the rank outsiders, Lynne and Alice hurried off to the Tote with Millie while Constance and

Grenville made their way to their appointed spot in the grandstand. By the time the others finally found them, the race had started.

'Did you get my bet on, Millie dear?' Constance enquired.

'Certainly did, Constance,' Millie said, handing Constance a Tote ticket. 'Two pounds each way number seven.'

'You've had a bet, Constance?' Grenville asked in surprise. 'You the great anti-gambler? You who said no one ever put enough on a winning horse?'

'Just a smokescreen, young man,' Constance replied, putting her ticket in her bag. 'I have a whole multitude of hidden vices.'

'Number seven,' Grenville said, looking at his racecard. 'Piper Aboard. No chance.'

With two miles of the three completed, Insider Trading was lying second and going easily, his jockey already looking around for any sign of danger.

'The way he's going, five to four looks generous,' Grenville remarked, as the favourite ranged up alongside the now struggling leading horse.

'Thanks for that,' Lynne said. 'I could still have made a packet. And where's blooming Whistletop, girls? I thought we were going to get rich.'

'In your case rich*er*, dear,' Constance said. Then, startling them all, she suddenly called at the top of her voice, 'That's the one. Come on, Piper Aboard! Stuff that great big grey carthorse!'

Most people in the immediate vicinity smiled or laughed, all except naturally the horse's bull-necked trainer, who was standing right in front of Constance, who having heard Constance's exhortation turned round to stare at her with a considerable degree of menace.

'Pipe down, you silly old woman,' he commanded.

'I most certainly will do no such thing,' Constance replied. 'Not even if you say please.'

For a moment those witnessing this brief but pointed exchange believed that Eddie Rampton was about to add to his notoriety by hitting a woman in public, so dark had become his countenance, but the call of the racecourse commentator drew his attention back to the race, much to the relief of those in Constance's party.

'And coming to the second last it's now Piper Aboard who's laying down the challenge to Insider Trading, on whom Sandy Bridger is now hard at work . . .' the commentator called.

'He's hitting that poor horse far too much,' Alice remarked, an observation which earned another look of consummate fury from the animal's trainer. 'That is just awful.'

'And Piper Aboard and the favourite Insider Trading rise at the fence together! And land together – neck and neck!' the commentator continued. 'And if anything Piper Aboard has got away from the fence the better!'

'Come on my horse!' Constance yelled. 'Come on my lovely little horse!'

'Somebody should shoot that jockey!' Alice insisted. 'Surely he's not allowed to hit his horse like that?'

'He'll be up before the stewards don't you worry,' Grenville whispered to Alice, not wanting to incur another fit of rage from the man in front of them.

'My horse has done it! He's only gone and done it!' Constance cried, whacking Grenville on his hat with her rolled-up racecard. 'The carthorse is estuffadoed!'

Everybody nearby held their breath waiting for the inevitable eruption. But it seemed that the notoriously short-fused trainer was far too taken aback both by the performance of his hot favourite and the behaviour of some mad punter behind him to do anything other than give Constance yet another drop-dead look.

'And as they approach the last it seems Piper Aboard has got the favourite's measure!' the commentator called. 'He's drawn a length clear now and at the run to the fence he definitely has the measure of Insider Trading, who in fact might even be beaten into third place by Whistlestop!'

'Whistletop!' Lynne shrieked. 'Come on, my son! Come on Whistletop you beauty!'

'And as they land over the last it's Piper Aboard clear by three lengths from the fast tiring Insider Trading – with Whistlestop closing on the favourite now – and passing him easily – it's Piper Aboard increasing his lead to four to five lengths now, with Whistlestop running on in second, two lengths ahead of Insider Trading who's in danger of being caught on the post by Catzoff – and Catzoff just catches the favourite on the line to snatch third place!'

'We won – we won!' Constance carolled, waving two triumphant arms in the air. 'My little horse won!'

'Will you shut up about your wretched little horse woman!' Eddie Rampton finally warned her, turning to face her. 'Some of us do this for our living!'

'I do *hate* bad losers,' Constance groaned. 'It's only a race, chum – it's only a silly old horse race.'

'Get me out of here,' Eddie Rampton rumbled. 'Before a terrible tragedy occurs.'

'Oh pooh!' Constance sighed after the thick-set retreating figure. 'What a dreadfully rotten sport.'

'Yes indeed Constance,' Grenville agreed, taking her arm to lead her off in the opposite direction. 'But he is absolutely not someone to cross swords with.'

After the three women had collected their winnings from the Tote they walked past the unsaddling enclosure where to judge from the sound of raised voices it seemed that Eddie Rampton had not yet regained his composure. Grenville tried to chivvy his party through and past the confrontation but Constance was having none of it.

'Don't be such a spoilsport Grenville,' she said,

detaching herself from his arm, 'I want to hear what Al Capone is sounding off about now.'

Rampton was addressing the small company of racing journalists who had gathered around him to learn his thoughts on the race.

'It is a perfectly disgraceful situation,' he announced loudly. 'Certain trainers run their horses in handicaps not on their merits. We all know this for a fact – that they do it to get the weights down when their horses are fly weighted then what a surprise! They trot up in handicaps such as this. And no one says a bloody thing. No one.'

'Except for you, Eddie,' one of the braver scribes suggested.

'The horse that won today hasn't even been placed for eighteen months, he's getting a stone and a half from my horse and you saw the result!'

'Isn't that what handicaps are for, Mr Rampton?' another journalist wondered. 'To give horses such as Piper Aboard a chance to compete favourably with higher-rated horses?'

'When horses are run on their merit it's a level playing field,' Rampton replied in no uncertain tones. 'When they are not, it's a bloody travesty.'

A heavyweight man with what looked like visibly high blood pressure pushed his way through the throng.

'I hope you are not suggesting I've not been running my horses on merit!' he asked in a west country accent. 'One of the reasons my horse hasn't won for eighteen months is because he was swallowing his tongue.'

'Too right he was, Peters,' Rampton growled. 'More's the pity you don't follow suit.'

'We tied his tongue down today, you oaf,' the other trainer replied. 'Hence the improvement.'

'And you never thought of doing that before? Don't take it, pal. You're not doing yourself any favours here. Now bugger off before I make your nose bleed.'

With that Rampton pushed his blackcurrant-complexioned rival out of the way and stormed out of the enclosure, passing right by Constance and her group. 'And as for you,' he said, stopping briefly to eye Constance. 'Don't you *ever* be fool enough to stand anywhere near me on a race-course ever again!'

'Not unless you have full police protection,' Millie murmured as they made their way back to the bar. 'What a sweetie.'

On their way to the bar, they passed a short, thin-faced man with sleek oiled-down hair and darting eyes, dressed in a double-breasted pinstripe suit, standing gossiping with a small crowd from the county set just past the unsaddling enclosure. Suddenly noticing Constance, he stopped and stared at her, then looked sharply at her again.

'Sylvia?' he said, breaking away from his associates and pursuing her.

Constance, who had been idling along at the back of her group with Grenville, grabbed

Grenville by one arm and began to hurry him forward.

'Quickly, Grenville,' she urged. 'You're being the most awful Mr Slowcoach.'

'Sylvia Topsham?' her pursuer repeated, now almost alongside Constance. 'It is you, isn't it?'

'It most certainly is not,' Constance replied haughtily, hurrying on even more quickly. 'Now go away at once. I have no idea who you are.'

'You mightn't know me, Sylvia,' the man insisted, following on, 'but I think I know you all right. You're Sylvia Topsham, aren't you?'

'Grenville,' Constance muttered, dropping Grenville's arm and preparing to flee forward. 'Get rid of him. Lose him. See him off. I mean it.'

'Look here,' Grenville said, placing himself between the rapidly departing Constance and her pursuer, 'I'll be most obliged if you will stop pestering my mother.'

'Your mother?' the man said with a frown, stopping in his tracks.

'My mother, precisely,' Grenville assured him. 'My mother, Lady Frimley, who for some reason you mistakenly believe is someone else, apparently.'

'Lady Frimley, did you say?' the man repeated, raising his eyebrows. 'Your mother. Apologies. OK – sorry, but I could have sworn—' He stopped, looking in the direction in which Constance had now disappeared from view. 'Excuse me,' he said, and left.

Grenville waited and watched to make sure

he did not double back in pursuit of the obviously distressed Constance before going after her himself to make sure she was all right, but although he looked everywhere he could find no trace of her. None of the others appeared to know where she had gone to either, although Millie thought she had seen her hurrying away, hand on hat, towards the owners' car park. Grenville went there at once, happily to find Constance all but hidden behind his car.

'Constance?' he called in bewilderment. 'Constance . . .'

Instead of replying or greeting him, Constance simply put a finger to her lips and remained where she was, stooped low beside the passenger door of Grenville's Jaguar.

'What on earth is the matter?' Grenville enquired, begging the question.

'Please open the car,' Constance hissed at him. 'And then please take me home? Please?'

Too much a gentleman to refuse, Grenville opened up his car, went to find Lynne, explained the situation to her, and returned with her to the car park.

'Right,' Grenville said, starting the car. 'London first, everyone.'

'I don't care where you take me,' Constance muttered from the back, sitting down in her seat with her face turned well away from the window.

'I thought you wanted to go home?'

'And I said I don't care where you take me,'

402

Constance repeated. 'As long as it's away from here.'

Grenville frowned at Lynne beside him as he backed out of his parking space. 'Sorry,' he murmured. 'You'll be awfully late home.'

'It doesn't matter,' Lynne said quietly. 'I can stay in London tonight and take the train home tomorrow. Long as that's all right with you.'

'Yes, yes of course,' Grenville said quickly. 'I should have suggested it. Sorry.'

'You really must stop apologising for yourself all the time, Grenville,' Lynne teased him, putting a hand discreetly on his knee. 'You really have nothing to apologise for. Nothing at all.'

On the road now and headed south, Grenville glanced in his driving mirror to see Constance slumped down even further in her seat, a handkerchief held to her face.

'There's something the matter,' Grenville said *sotto* to Lynne. 'Perhaps if we stopped and put you in the back . . . ?'

As soon as he could safely do so, Grenville pulled the car off the road and Lynne slipped into the rear seat.

'It's OK, Connie.' Lynne took one of her hands, leaving Constance to dab at the tears on her face with the other. 'Listen, if you want to talk, I'm here.' Constance just shook her head. 'Look – something's upset you, and that's terrible. I mean, on a day like this. Of all the days to be upset . . .'
Still Constance tried to tough it out, shaking her head again and clasping her handkerchief even

more tightly to her mouth. 'Did someone say something to upset you, darling? Or what? Why don't you tell us? It'll be much better if you talk about it. Honestly.'

'It was something that happened long ago,' Constance whispered, glancing red-eyed at Lynne over her hankie. 'And if I told you, you'd only hate me.'

'I couldn't hate you, Connie,' Lynne assured her. 'Don't be daft. I love you.'

'You wouldn't. Not if you knew. Not if I told you.'

'Was it anything to do with that man at the racecourse, Constance?' Grenville asked from the driving seat. 'The chap who thought he recognised you? As a matter of fact I thought I recognised him from somewhere.'

Connie nodded and carefully wiped her eyes with her handkerchief.

'He's that gossip columnist johnny,' she said. 'And he did recognise me.'

'Sylvia – what was it?' Grenville frowned at her image in his driving mirror. 'Sylvia . . .'

'Topsham,' Constance replied. 'My married name. I was born Sylvia Barton, which was my professional name as well.'

'Professional?' Lynne asked. 'Professional as in what, love?'

'I was an actress,' Constance replied. 'Before you were born, dear, so don't worry.'

'Sylvia Barton,' Grenville said to himself. 'You were more than just an actress, Connie. You were a bit of a film star.'

'A bit is about right, Grenville, dear.' Constance sniffed. 'Rank School of Charm.'

'What's that when it's at home?' Lynne asked.

'The J. Arthur Rank studios, just after the war, dear. Made all those British films, and put a lot of us girls and boys under contracts. Trained us up the way he wanted us to go. I was what was called a Rank starlet. Which is not quite what everybody called us – as you can imagine.'

'You were in some rather good films, Connie,' Grenville said.

'Didn't have much to do with making them any good, dear. I was there purely as decoration.'

'Yes, but even so, Connie,' Lynne continued, with a reassuring smile, 'I don't see what's so dreadful about being a starlet. I mean that's hardly going to make us hate you, is it?'

'You are so sweet, Lynne,' Constance said, squeezing her hand. 'I've really grown terribly fond of you.'

'I told you, I love you too.'

'Very American,' Constance returned, trying to smile.

'Doesn't matter. I happen to mean it.'

'It's got nothing to do with my being an actress, you're quite right,' Constance continued, beginning to recover her composure. 'It was my marriage. Or more particularly one of the men I married. You're too young to remember, sweetie – you probably both are. It might just ring bells with Grenville. One of my husbands happened to be a somewhat notorious fellow called Andrew Topsham.' She waited for the expected reaction but all she got was silence from both Grenville and Lynne.

'See?' Lynne exclaimed after a moment. 'Nothing to us. Not a thing.'

'Andrew Topsham,' Grenville said slowly. 'It does ring a bell somewhere or other. Yes.'

'Let me save you the trouble, dear,' Constance said. 'He was a spy. Cold War jobby. He spied for the Russkies.'

'Red Andrew, of *course*,' Grenville exclaimed. 'Defected, didn't he? Sometime in the early sixties, if my memory serves me.'

'I met him just after the war. He'd had a rather good war, so I was told, if there can be any such thing, which I very much doubt. He was frightfully well connected, knew all the right people, terribly dashing, but – well, a little peculiar I thought, but we won't go into all that. Anyway, the point was he worked for Intelligence, or *in* Intelligence or whatever they call it, but all the time he was stealing stuff for his Red friends. He got out, defected, and left me behind, high, dry and stranded. The so and so had implicated me as a sort of red herring—'

'I remember now,' Grenville said. 'It's all coming back to me.'

'I thought it had gone away,' Constance sighed, turning to stare out of the window at the rain-lashed winter landscape flashing by. 'I was finally given the all-clear, but of course you know what they say about mud. It does stick, you know. By George it does. So they advised me to go on holiday, a long holiday, which I did. I went to a friend's in South Africa, a chum from the Rank school of little charmers who had married really rather well and lived out there until a few years ago. Met someone there, as it happened, and got involved. An absolute beast of a fellow who went in for a lot of beating up. Wouldn't think it to look at him. Looked like an angel, sweetest little baby face and lots of curly blond hair, and drank himself to death.'

'Lord Frimley, perchance?' Grenville wondered, giving her a smile via the driving mirror.

'Sir Peter Frimley, as it happened,' Constance replied. 'Don't laugh, dear, that really was his handle, though don't ask me. So I took his title since I thought that was the least he owed me and back I came, thinking the dust must have settled by now, because I was frightfully homesick, don't you know. Pretended we'd been wed. It worked because no one remembered me, not as Lady Frimley. They hadn't a clue. All washed up and long forgotten.'

'You obviously haven't lost your looks, Connie,' Lynne said.

'Obviously not,' Grenville agreed. 'Hence the tripe hound's recognising you.'

'For the life of me I don't know how,' Constance said. 'As a girl I was raven-haired and now I'm grey as a ghost; a little shrunken, invisible old woman.'

'Oh yes?' Lynne laughed. 'I've seen the heads still turning.'

'Pooh,' Constance said, but with a half-smile.

'Anyway,' Grenville said. 'So what if he thought he recognised you? It's all over. Dead, gone, buried.'

'You know the papers, dear.' Constance sighed. 'They'll dish it all up again. Red Andrew's scarlet woman and all that nonsense. I really don't want it all dragged out of the cupboard yet again.'

'We'll take care of you,' Lynne assured her, linking her arm in Constance's. 'We won't let the illegitimates get you.'

'I do hope you won't,' Constance said quietly. 'I think it would finish me. Just when everything was at its very best, too. Do you know something? I think this is the first time I've ever had any fun, first time I've been really happy, since I was a gel, as we used to say in those days. This is the very first time in such a long time I've felt really happy.'

Before they began their own journey home, Alice and Millie treated themselves to some tea and cake. While they were enjoying their refreshment, Alice noticed Harrington Lovell looking at her occasionally from his own party across the room, but thought little of it until, after Millie had disappeared to the ladies preparatory to leaving the course, she found Harrington standing at her table, hands clasped behind his back and inclining himself forward as if he wished to speak confidentially.

'Alice,' he began. 'Forgive the intrusion, and I'm

not quite sure how to put this without seeming too forward . . .'

'You're not intruding at all,' Alice assured him. 'Would you like some tea?'

'No thank you.' Harrington gave a cautious smile. 'No, what I really wanted was to know – well. How can I best put this? I wondered when you might be racing your horse again.'

'Why's that, Mr Lovell?'

'Harrington, please. Or better still Harry. That's what all my friends call me.'

'Sorry. Of course,' Alice said. 'Why do you want to know when the horse is running again? Do you want another bet?'

Harrington laughed. 'No. No, the reason I wanted to know is because I'd like to know when I might see you – you all – again.'

Alice looked up at him quickly, and found to her interest and surprise that her heart was suddenly beating a little bit faster.

'To be truthful, I don't know,' she said. 'Rory's sending us a list of entries later in the week.'

'I see.' Harrington nodded, not knowing quite how much further to go, before deciding to cut his losses and leave. 'In that case, best thing I can do is to keep an eye on the racing papers,' he said, straightening up. 'Or have my trainer let me know.'

'Of course,' Alice agreed. 'Except now I'm curious,' she added. 'I don't mean to be rude—'

'I doubt very much whether you could be, Alice.'

'But since you have horses of your own, I was just wondering why you were so keen to see ours running.'

'It isn't your horse I want to see, Alice.' Harrington leaned forward again. 'Actually it's you.'

'Oh,' said Alice, finding herself unexpectedly on the back foot. 'Oh. Oh, I see. Or rather I don't. I don't see.'

'I'd like to say because me Tarzan, you Jane,' Harrington replied. 'Except I think I'm a bit too old now for that to sound convincing. So let's just say it's a man–woman thing, Alice. I've enjoyed meeting you, and now I find I would like to see you again. That is, provided it's all right with you.'

'It's perfectly all right with me, Harry. I've enjoyed meeting you as well. Very much.'

'So,' Harrington concluded, straightening himself to his full and still impressive height as he saw Millie making her way back to the table. 'To the next time. To our next time.'

Then he was gone.

'So what do I spy here?' Millie said, collecting her things off the table. 'Got yourself a heavy date, sister?'

'Never you mind that,' Alice replied, getting up to leave. 'That was just horse talk.'

Even so, as she left the bar, Alice couldn't resist one last glance over her shoulder, and, when she looked, she saw that apparently Harrington couldn't resist one either.

Chapter Twenty-one

Best Laid Plans

Rory was sitting studying the Racing Calendar with his mind on entries when Kathleen walked into his office. He had been doing his very best to keep his mind off the subject of Miss Kathleen Flanagan ever since it had become obvious to him that she and Blaze Molloy were an item. Up till now, he had been managing the task better than he thought he might, using what little free time he had in trying to make his convalescent father as comfortable and happy as possible. He was surprised but pleased to see that Anthony seemed more than happy to watch the activity of the yard from the warmth and comfort of an armchair in the drawing room, and to catch up on all the news at drinks time over a weak whisky and water, rather than try to take back hold of the reins.

There was concern, however, over the exact condition of Anthony's health, Dan having told

Rory privately before sending his patient home that in an ideal world he would have the sort of heart surgery that currently was only being practised in America, and at a price. As it was, they had done everything they could and would continue to do so in order to keep their patient up and about, as Dan put it, which Rory took to mean they would do everything possible to keep his father alive and well enough to enjoy life for as long as they could. That was all that was said, because on their side of the Atlantic that was all that could be done.

But now Kathleen was standing on the other side of Rory's desk, looking even more beautiful than ever, Rory thought, if such a thing were possible. Being at Fulford Farm obviously suited her for since she had come to work in the yard everything about Kathleen seemed to have become more exceptional; her skin gleamed, her eyes shone, her hair looked more lustrous, her figure even shapelier, and her personality was ever more vibrant. It was as if she was in training herself and blooming under her new regime.

Despite all this, Rory wanted her to disappear from his life, while with all his heart he wanted her to stay, because he knew from the bottom of that same heart that he could have no chance with her, not since the arrival of the handsome, laid-back and highly talented young jockey Blaze Molloy. It seemed every time he looked up or turned round there they were, deep in conversation, Blaze with an arm draped round her shoulders, or Kathleen just smiling across the yard at him as she went about her work, or the two of them in deep and private debate on the course, or celebrating their horse's win with their peers, while the only time he himself spoke to Kathleen in any depth was when they needed to discuss matters concerning Boyo. Every time Rory thought he might try to dig a little deeper, either someone or something interrupted them, or Kathleen excused herself on the pretext of having to do something to or with her precious charge. So Rory had resigned himself to an existence that now included a seriously unrequited love.

'We have a problem, Mr Rawlins,' she was saying, her cap off, gently tossing back her head of long dark hair. 'He's off his food.'

'Since when?' Rory asked, getting up immediately. 'He's been eating up everything. So when did this start?'

'He started picking at it yesterday, and now today he won't go near his pot.'

'Right. Fine. I'll come and have a look,' Rory said, thinking that although going to stare into the horse's manger was hardly going to work the oracle, at least it would afford him some time with the object of his affection.

'What I was wondering was why you'd changed the supplier,' Kathleen remarked as they crossed the yard. 'I'm sure you had good reason.'

'Changed the supplier?' Rory stopped and looked at her. 'I don't understand what you mean.'

'It wasn't the usual corn merchant who

delivered the last lot of fodder,' Kathleen told him. 'The man said someone had rung him and transferred all the stable orders to his firm.'

'I don't understand,' Rory said again, his brow furrowing. 'We had a new supplier and no one thought of mentioning it?'

'You weren't here, Mr Rawlins,' Kathleen replied, looking as though she were mortally affronted. 'It was the day you were collecting your father from hospital. And since it was exactly the same food we'd been having before, no one thought anything of it. Anyway, Pauline said it was all in order, that there'd been some problem or other with the last people, and so we never thought another thing about it.'

'Pauline? But it isn't really Pauline's – look, we'd better f-f-find Pauline, because I don't like this at all. I certainly never authorised any such change – not m-me.'

'But Pauline's not in. Didn't you know? She's been off for a couple of days, and she called this morning to say she was still unwell.'

'Why am I always the last to know any – it doesn't matter. Forget it,' Rory muttered, hurrying now towards the feed room. 'How many feeds has B-Boyo had? From this famous new delivery?'

'You don't think—'

'I th-think a lot of things, but first things f-first.'

'He's only had supper last night and breakfast today from the new stuff, because I don't like waste and I thought we should finish the last consignment first. It's just the way I was brought up.'

'Ker-ker-ker – *quite* right too, Kathleen,' Rory said, inspecting the new consignment of fodder. 'You might just have saved the day.'

Noel took the foodstuff away for analysis, having thoroughly examined the horse and found nothing apparently amiss with him, although as a precautionary measure he also took away a blood sample and a specimen of the horse's droppings for analysis. After Noel had departed, Kathleen insisted on giving her charge a purge as well, assuring Rory that the mixture she intended to use was purely herbal and would leave no unwanted medicinal traces.

'Obviously you think it was doped with something,' his father observed at drinks time. 'Although if someone's keen on stopping the horse, wouldn't they wait till nearer the time of his next race?'

'Well, yes, I suppose so, but this could be – couldn't it? – one of those slow-term drugs you were on about,' Rory replied. 'Something they might simply want to get into the horse's system, that works insidiously; some sort of dope that – you know, something that might slow him up a bit on the gallops, but not sufficiently so for us to get worried.'

'But then when you get him to the races—'

'There was that horse you swore was stopped

415

end of last season? One of Dick Anderson's up at Haydock? And then it went and dropped dead in the paddock after the race.'

'Lovely thing to do to an animal,' Anthony observed. 'Nice people.'

'And that chap you know – the security guy from the Jockey Club,' Rory continued. 'Didn't he tell you there was this new stuff coming in from Scandinavia that left absolutely no trace? That it was worrying them all sleepless?'

'How long before you get the result?'

'Twenty-four hours, tops. Noel's giving it priority. And can you believe they got at Pauline, of all people? You just can't tell with people.' Rory shook his head in dismay and poured himself another beer.

'And she's done a runner, you say,' Anthony said.

'Well, of course. Could be anywhere by now. Who'd want to do this anyway? We're not exactly a big betting yard or anything. Bastards.'

'We don't know what they've done yet, old chap – if anything,' Anthony remarked, holding up his own glass for refreshment. 'But it wasn't very subtle, was it? Somebody's going to remark on the change in the food merchant sooner or later, sooner more likely than later. And the moment they do, end of story.'

'They probably thought that with me in charge nobody would bother to remark on it. Not the sort of thing anyone would get past you.'

'Don't be hard on yourself, Rory. You're doing

well, so don't beat yourself up – there's no need.'

'I forget to book the dentist, I left the horses on contaminated straw when we'd discussed putting them on shavings, I let Kathleen turn the horse out in the paddock – we were lucky to get away with that one – and now someone's sending us unauthorised fodder.'

'Rory?' his father interrupted. 'You've had a lot on your mind, and I wasn't here.'

'I can't have been paying that much attention when you were here, can I?'

'You've also trained a horse to win two races.'

'I've also got a horse who's won two races.'

'What is this about anyway?' Anthony asked. 'This isn't like you at all. So what is it about?'

'It's about me thinking I could just take over just like that and manage, Dad, that's what this is about,' Rory replied. 'Instead of thinking what I was doing. Instead of asking for advice. I should have asked for advice instead of just going ahead thinking training horses and running a yard was . . . was – I don't know. Child's play.'

'That isn't what this is all about at all, old chap. You've got something on your mind.'

'I've got a stable full of horses on my mind, Dad, that's what. And if Kathleen hadn't brought the subject up, this latest thing – the change in supplier – it might have gone unnoticed for days. Maybe the others thought with the way things have been – with the way they still are, actually – maybe they thought there'd been some problem or other over the bills, let's say, and if so they might have been too tactful to mention it.'

'What did our regular suppliers say? Mortons? I take it we're back with them?'

'Mortons told me someone had rung a few days ago cancelling the order but without any explanation.'

'A woman?'

'A man, oddly enough. Pauline's contact, presumably. And yes – I put our order back in place.'

'Makes your hair stand on end,' Anthony said, draining his glass. 'The lengths people will go to stop a horse.'

'People as in bookmakers?'

'The poor old bookmakers,' Anthony said wryly. 'They get to carry the can for everything. This sort of thing can be down to anyone, you know. A rival. A soured ex-owner. An embittered bloodstock agent – the racing world is full of people carrying grudges, real and imagined. Let's wait on the tests. Maybe they'll give us some sort of indication.'

'Maybe they will,' Rory agreed. 'Now if you don't mind, I think I'll take Dunkum out for a bit of a walk.

He took the lurcher for a long walk round the farm, trying without success to sort out his head and his heart. He hated both making a fool of himself and being made a fool of, so he resolved at least to put a stop to both of those, determining to ask for advice when in doubt and not to say yes to anything equine when he either meant no or just don't know. Horses were an unknown quantity even to the most experienced of trainers, so to Rory, who considered himself well and truly still an apprentice in the craft, it seemed absolutely vital that every decision regarding the yard must be thoroughly discussed and not arrived at on the wings of some whim or other. He would make lists, he would have charts, people would have specific tasks delegated to them, and nobody would do anything without the properly considered consent of both him and his father.

As for his affairs of the heart, he would really have to stop mooning about like some lovesick schoolboy and simply realise that Miss Kathleen Flanagan was spoken for, and that even if she was not he could think of not one good reason why he should ever be of the slightest interest to her. Besides, even if her heart did not fully belong to Mr Blaze Molloy, it was certainly given long ago to the little horse who was now the star of the yard, and not for one second did Rory imagine that even were Kathleen free she would find either time or reason to take the very slightest of interests in someone as incompetent and as diffident as he.

'All we want to know is what we're meant to do about Christmas, Mum,' Georgina was saying on the telephone. 'It's not a lot to ask.'

Alice felt like reminding her daughter what

they and everyone else were meant to do at Christmas, but resisted the temptation.

'I'm not sure what I shall be doing yet, Georgie,' she replied instead. 'Our horse is meant to be running somewhere on Boxing Day, so I'm not making any hard and fast plans till we know where.'

'It's not exactly as if we're seeing a lot of you at the moment,' Georgina continued inexorably.

'I know, love, but what with moving and everything . . . Once spring comes, and summer, then you must all come down.'

'But what about Christmas, Mum?'

'You're more than welcome to come down here, I told you that.'

'All of us? Plus Christian *and* his new girl-friend?'

'He's got a new girlfriend?'

'Not in touch, then?' Georgina sighed. 'Yes, he's got a new girlfriend who if anything is even more frightful than the last one – and they are an item. Yes? So all of us coming down would be a little out of the question? In your cottage, Mum? Do get a little bit real. No, much the best if you come up here to Richmond.'

'When I know where the horse is running, and if he is—'

'I hear he won again,' Georgina cut in. 'Thanks for telling us.'

'I didn't know he was going to win!' Alice laughed. 'And can you imagine if he hadn't won? And I'd told you to back him? Can you imagine?'

'As it happened Joe backed him, but at pretty miserable odds.'

'He *was* favourite, darling. Anyway. Let's discuss this as soon as I know my plans this end.'

'Mum?'

'Georgina?'

'Nothing.'

But Alice was getting stronger. She still managed to hang up before her daughter.

Rory and Maureen had just finished entering The Enchanted up for several good-looking races on the great feast of National Hunt racing otherwise known as Boxing Day, when the telephone rang.

'Noel,' Maureen said, holding the receiver out to Rory.

'Noel? I thought he was meant to call yesterday,' Rory said with a frown, taking the phone. 'Noel?'

'Yes, I'm sorry for the delay, Rory,' his vet said on the other end of the line. 'We all wanted to be absolutely sure before we made any pronouncement, but the feed was definitely tampered with, no doubt at all.'

'Right. Really? With what, Noel?'

'Steroids,' his vet told him. 'There are definite traces of steroids in the food, and if anyone had gone on using this food – and why the hell shouldn't they? – there'd have been enough there to show up in any dope test.'

'Which of course means . . .' Rory said, trying to remember the exact rules.

'Automatic disqualification, Rory, and not just from any new race,' Noel reminded him, 'but from any races recently won.'

'Nice,' Rory said. 'End of the horse and nice for the yard. We can't get any winners, so we give them steroids.'

'It's a bit of an amateur plan,' Noel said. 'Yet one that just might have worked. There are a lot of yards where this sort of thing could well go unnoticed until too late.'

'One month's supply of fodder. And by the time the change in corn merchant is noticed, it could well be too late. The race could have been run.'

'That's possibly a very good horse you have there, Rory. So be vigilant.'

'As of now I am riding shotgun, Noel.'

From then on security became of paramount importance. Kathleen, Teddy and Rory took it in turns to sit on watch during the nights, and no one was allowed into the yard without advance permission. All gates were kept locked and Dunkum roamed freely in the role of watchdog.

'He might be as kind as a saint,' Rory told Kathleen, 'but the bark is quite off-putting.'

'What else can go wrong, Mr Rawlins? Whoever it is, they're up to right mischief, I'd say.'

'We've hardly caned the bookies,' Rory replied. 'His first race he was any price. If you ask me, the money that shortened his odds all came from your homeland.'

'Tell me something that would surprise me.'

'And all right – he was favourite for his second race, but it was hardly a hot betting race. No, this is about something else altogether.'

Oddly enough, Rory might have put two and two together and made a decent stab at four had he read the racing papers more carefully that morning instead of getting some of the more important news second-hand from Maureen when he returned to his office.

'There's still plenty of it about,' Maureen commented, looking up from the *Sporting Life* she was reading at her desk. 'The favourite for the King George, My Pal Joey? He's been sold for what they call an undisclosed sum.'

Rory stopped and looked at his secretary, who was back to reading the paper again, sticky bun in hand and a mug of coffee beside her.

'Who'd want to sell a horse like that?'

'One of those offers you can't refuse, maybe?'

'He's also ante-post favourite for the Gold Cup,' Rory said. 'Who'd sell a horse like that? Mind you – yes. Yes, there were rumours that the present owner wasn't at all well. So maybe . . . no, I don't know.' He shook his head. 'I still don't get it. Think I'll go and see what the old man makes of it.'

'"The deal was brokered by bloodstock agent Roddy Downes,"' Maureen read, '"on behalf of Mr G. Fortune." As in G for good, I imagine.'

But when she looked up Rory had already gone.

*　　　*　　　*

There was more bad news on Christmas Eve. When Rory came down to the yard at first light he found an agitated Kathleen waiting for him.

'Not the horse?' he asked quickly, seeing the expression on her face. 'Please tell me there's nothing wrong with the horse.'

'There's nothing wrong with the horse, it's all right, Mr Rawlins,' Kathleen assured him. 'But there's plenty wrong with his jockey.'

Blaze had been set upon. It was as simple as that and yet just as baffling. Kathleen, Teddy, Teddy's girlfriend Julie and Blaze had gone as usual for a drink at the local after evening stables, a safe and friendly pub that was even more so than usual because of the time of year. Everyone had been full of peace and goodwill towards their fellow men right up until the moment the three from Fulford Farm and Julie wished everyone a Merry Christmas and walked out into a starlit night, whereupon three men in balaclavas and anoraks had set about Blaze, and only Blaze. Teddy, who was brave but only a lightweight, was soon dealt with, felled by a single punch, leaving Kathleen and Julie to scream blue murder as the hoodlums went to work on Blaze, but because everyone was singing 'Hark The Herald Angels Sing' at full volume in the bar, no one heard their shouts for help.

Blaze could look after himself but only up to a point, and by the time Kathleen had run back into the bar and brought half a dozen of their racing friends rushing out to help, Blaze was on the ground and being given a serious kicking. The cavalry soon saw the thugs off and then the soberest among them drove Blaze to Salisbury General Hospital, where they found he had a split lip, a broken nose, and severe bruising to the ribs and back where he had been kicked. When Kathleen had left to come back to the farm Blaze was still waiting to be X-rayed.

'There'd been no sign of bother inside the pub?' Rory asked.

'Not a bit of it, Mr Rawlins,' Kathleen told him. 'It had been the very best of nights. They were lying in wait outside, pure and simple. Waiting to do him over. But why? Everyone loves Blaze. You couldn't meet a sweeter man.'

'Yes,' Rory said, preferring to avoid the subject of Blaze's exemplary character and concentrate on the aftermath of the affray. 'He's not going to be fit to ride Boxing Day, then.'

'Now we don't know that yet, Mr Rawlins,' Kathleen said quickly, with obvious concern. 'He's as tough as old boots, Blaze, and if he can ride, sure he will, he will.'

'There are other jockeys, Kathleen.'

'You said yourself – I heard you, Mr Rawlins, talking to Maureen – what a lottery getting a jockey was on Boxing Day. How many meetings are there?'

'Far too many,' Rory retorted, knowing that all the decent jockeys would have long been booked for the best rides over the holiday.

'You don't want to go trusting some untried lad

on Boyo, I know you don't,' Kathleen persisted. 'I'm sure Blaze will be fine, Mr Rawlins. He has a whole day to recover.'

'I won't put him up if there's any doubt about his fitness, Kathleen,' Rory said. 'I'd rather not run the horse.'

'But you have to!' Kathleen insisted, before immediately recovering herself. 'I mean, the poor owners, Mr Rawlins. They'd be mortally disappointed, so they would.'

'That's not why you said I have to run him.'

'That's all I meant.'

'Hmm.' Rory looked at her, then shook his head. 'We'll wait and see how the lad is,' he decided. 'Your precious Blaze.'

As soon as he said it he knew he shouldn't have, since it sounded churlish and childish even to his own ears. Kathleen said nothing. Nor did she smile; nor did she frown.

'Thank you, Mr Rawlins,' was all she said, at last, before hurrying off to do her duties.

When Blaze appeared in the yard the next day, he looked as though he'd been acting as a punchbag for a heavyweight contender. Besides a thick lip he had two black eyes, and his nose, although apparently mercifully not broken after all, was heavily strapped across the bridge. In spite of his battering, however, he was his usual jaunty self, although he must have been feeling a long way from good.

'You're not expecting to ride tomorrow, are

you?' Rory said the moment he saw him. 'Surely not.'

'I am indeed, guv'nor,' Blaze replied. 'This is not as bad as it looks. Believe me.'

'But how does it feel? That's the important thing,' Rory said. 'If you've any cracked ribs—'

'Devil the one. I'm a bit black and blue, but sure I'm all in one piece.'

'I think I'd rather put someone else up, even so. Just in case.'

'Tell you what, boss,' Blaze said, following him across the yard. 'See how I do riding work this morning. Put me up on old Jack since he's not running over the holiday, and I'll give him a blast. The both of us will know after that, particularly if you put Kathleen up beside me. She'll tell you right enough.'

'Isn't she a little biased?' Rory said sarcastically, then immediately kicked himself.

'In favour of the horse, Mr Rawlins,' Blaze said with the best smile he could manage through his swollen lips. 'She won't let me near him if she thinks I'm not up to him.'

So to the gallops they all went and Blaze passed the test with flying colours, giving Jack such a good ride he won the gallop. Afterwards Rory insisted on Blaze's schooling one of the younger horses over the practice fences to make sure he was as confident jumping at racing pace as he was just galloping, and again there seemed to be no visible chink in his physical armour. Finally, since by chance Dan had dropped in to

427

have a Christmas Day drink with Anthony and to check up on his well-being, Rory got their doctor friend to give Blaze a quick physical to make sure he really was fit enough mentally as well as physically to ride.

'He might not be a very pretty sight at the moment, Rory,' Dan told him when he had finished his examination. 'But there's absolutely nothing to make you think he can't ride the horse. He's a very strong and very fit young man, which is probably how he walked away relatively unscathed.'

'OK, buster,' Rory told Blaze in the yard. 'You're on. Now go away and have a quiet – and I mean quiet – Christmas Day. And a happy one.'

'Happy Christmas to you as well, boss,' a delighted Blaze returned. 'And God bless you.'

Rory watched as Blaze hurried off to find Kathleen to tell her the news. She was just finishing grooming Boyo, and after she had put her box of brushes and combs away in the tack room Rory saw her making for Blaze's car. He'd thought of asking her to have Christmas lunch with himself and Anthony, but had not, because Kathleen had volunteered the information that Blaze and she had been invited to spend Christmas Day with Teddy and Julie at Teddy's parents', so once he was sure all the horses were fed and watered he took himself back into the house to have his Christmas lunch with his father.

*   *   *

In the end, Alice had gone up to London to spend Christmas Eve and Christmas Day with Georgina, Joe, Christian and the new girlfriend, Sofia, at Georgina and Joe's house in Richmond. Her daughter and she cooked lunch on Christmas Day and the whole event passed off happily and peacefully, with no anxieties being aired, and no quarrels being picked between brother and sister as they usually were when all the family were gathered. The only bone of contention arose when Alice was helping Georgina clear up the debris of lunch and tea, while the men were doing their best to dispose of the endless amount of decorative wrapping paper and cardboard boxes that now littered the sitting room.

Somehow, right out of the blue and without prompting, Georgina had managed to turn the conversation to her greatest ongoing preoccupation, the matter of her children's school fees. There was no direct request for help, just a long conversation full of hints and bewilderment.

'I just don't know what we're going to do, Mum,' she kept saying. 'Joe ran up the latest projections on the cost of privately educating two children the other day and *it was horrific*. I just don't know what we're going to do.'

'You could send them to state schools, Georgie,' Alice said, carefully drying the set of cut-glass Waterford wine glasses she and Alex had given their daughter as one of her wedding presents. 'You were saying the other day that there are some good state schools in this area.'

'There were, Mum,' Georgina sighed. 'You should see them now. They are *huge*, and it's pretty obvious children like ours are not particularly welcome. Anyway, the feeling's quite mutual really, after what I've been hearing about what goes on in these places. Last week one of the teachers was so terrified by her class that she barricaded herself in her office and wouldn't come out.'

'Then in that case you're going to have to find schools you can afford,' Alice said, with perfectly good common sense. 'Other people manage, so I suppose you and Joe are going to have to do the same.'

'Great,' Georgina replied. 'While you go and blow all the money Dad earned doing a job that finally killed him on some stupid racehorse.'

'That's enough, Georgina dear,' Alice said, folding up her tea towel now she had finished drying up. 'I don't think this is the sort of conversation we should be having, particularly today of all days.'

'When else are we going to have it?' Georgina demanded. 'We don't see anything of you nowadays.'

'Georgina.'

'Do stop calling me Georgina.'

'I don't see why. It's the name we christened you.'

'You only call me that when you're cross.'

'So you're forever telling me,' Alice replied. 'But let's just get one thing straight, shall we? I

430

have only just moved to the country. I'm hardly even settled in. When I am, then from the spring onwards we can see as much – or as little – as we like of each other. And as for blowing all the money you say your father earned, for your information your father and I always saw the money he earned as being our money – not his, ours. That was your father's idea. As it was that when . . . when he was gone, any money he left me should be mine to do with as I pleased. We used to joke about it. He was always telling me to shock everyone by going on a round-the-world cruise, or buying a fast car, or a wardrobe of brand-new clothes – *Anything you like, Alice*, he used to say. *But for God's sake, Alice, make sure you enjoy the rest of your life, because you've earned it. All you've done all your life, he'd say, is work, work, work – for me, and for the kids, so you just promise me you'll do what you like, and have a good time.'*

'Yes,' Georgina said, her mouth tightening. 'But that – that was just Dad. The last thing Dad would really have wanted was to see you squandering all his hard-earned on a racehorse.'

'You know that for a fact, do you?' Alice queried. 'I see. Then all I can say is that obviously you knew your father a lot better than I did.'

She went to her room and quietly packed her things. She had intended to stay over until the morning, leave early to avoid the traffic and drive straight to the races. But all of a sudden she was filled with an enormous longing to return to her cosy little home in the west, to light a fire, open

431

a good bottle of wine, and dream of what might or might not happen on Boxing Day. She waited till all was quiet downstairs, with the adults sleeping off the effects of their lunch and tea, and her grandchildren sitting mesmerised by some traditional Christmas Day movie, before stealing outside to put Sammy and her belongings in the car. Then she wished everyone a fond but quick goodbye, resisted all protests against her leaving already, and drove off into the peaceful Christmas night.

Grenville took Lynne home for Christmas to meet his mother. This was something on which he had not been overly keen, but owing to his feelings for Lynne and the feelings she had for him it was something that he knew he would have to do sooner rather than later. He warned Lynne what his mother was like, and although Lynne said little in return it worried her and Grenville saw that it did so.

'It doesn't matter, Linnet.' Grenville smiled, feeling strangely proud of the pet name he had given his beautiful girlfriend. 'It really does not matter one jot, tittle, whit or scrap. It's simply a formality.'

'I know, Grenville, you're sweet and I'm sure it's all fine,' Lynne replied. 'It's just I'd much rather have Christmas with just you. *Chez* me.'

'Me too, dearest girl. But one has always felt one should have Christmas at home, especially since the old man went AWOL.'

So he drove them to Esher, to his mother's house, which was situated at the end of a lane well away from the town and the main road, a small but very pretty redbrick Queen Anne house Grenville's grandfather had lived in before bequeathing it to his only child, Grenville's father. Since Grenville's father's disgrace, as it was known in the family, his mother had been granted custody of the house in which she resided and over which she presided like a Victorian matriarch. As small as her son was tall, Catherine Fielding was famous for the sharpness of her tongue as well as her arrant snobbery, and as a consequence had an exceedingly select circle of friends, a company of like-minded people who saw modern life as a shocking disgrace, particularly the change in social and moral values, which they all considered – and not particularly privately – to be the beginning of the end of civilisation as they had known it, and a terrible waste of all the lives that had been sacrificed trying to preserve it.

Her only weakness was her son, Grenville, whom she had always considered to be something extraordinary, in spite of an extremely average career at school and the attaining of a less than distinguished university degree. To her Grenville was simply a late developer, like so many brilliant people in life, and once he achieved a certain seniority he would come into his own. For the early part of Grenville's life such an indulgent maternal attitude was nothing but harmful, spoiling the child by giving him an inflated sense of his own ability and worth.

Fortunately his father was an altogether stronger character, and besides taking the wise decision not to send Grenville to Eton, which he himself had hated, while he remained married to Grenville's mother he did at least manage to teach his son some of what he considered the more masculine virtues and interest him in some manly pursuits. Terrified that his son might turn into a mother's boy, he made sure Grenville went to boarding school from the age of seven, and when he was a teenager encouraged him to take a healthy interest in the opposite sex, something of which Catherine Fielding most certainly did not approve.

'So why exactly are you taking me to meet her, Grenville?' Lynne asked him on their way there. 'If what she thinks doesn't matter a dot, whittle, scrip or scrap, then why are we doing it instead of getting legless at home and watching *The Wizard of Oz*?'

'It's just a formality really, Linnet,' Grenville assured her. 'Don't worry your pretty head. We'll just put in an appearance, have lunch and then take off back to yours.'

The one thing of which Grenville was sure was how pretty Lynne looked that Christmas Day, dressed in a black and white silk and wool dress worn under a beautifully cut crimson velvet jacket, her hair piled expertly on top of her head, and her long elegant legs clad in a pair of black silk stockings, one of the gifts he had bestowed on her. He was happy to see her looking so elegant, because he knew that yet another thing his mother was picky about nowadays was appearance, taking every chance she could to pronounce that people simply did not know how to dress any more.

'Ah, Mummy,' Grenville said on finding his mother sitting waiting for them in the drawing room, ostensibly working on a sampler on her knee.

'Grenville, dearest boy,' Mrs Fielding replied, remaining seated while Grenville came over and kissed her on the cheek. 'I was beginning to worry.'

'Quarter to one, you said, Mummy,' Grenville said, tapping his watch. 'Quarter to one on the dot.' He hated still calling her Mummy but knew that if he tried anything else all he would get in return was a severe dressing-down.

'I am sure I said quarter past twelve, dear,' Mrs Fielding replied with a small shake of her head, before turning to regard Lynne with a pale smile. 'Good. And you must be Anne,' she said, offering a hand vaguely.

'Lynne, Mummy. This is Lynne.'

'It's my great age, Grenville, darling boy.' Mrs Fielding sighed. 'Things just go. Names particularly. I lie awake at night going through my address book in my head. I'm on the Gs at the moment, and not, I have to say, doing all that brilliantly. Do forgive me, *Lynne*.'

'It's fine, really, Mrs Fielding,' Lynne replied with a quick reassuring look to Grenville. 'You can call me whatever you like.'

'I do so like your jacket, *Lynne*, and such a – such a nice *bright* colour,' Mrs Fielding continued smoothly. 'Have you been to cocktails somewhere on the way?'

'No, no.' This time it was Grenville who gave Lynne a reassuring look. 'No, of course not, Mummy. No, we came *straight* here.'

'I find everything so confusing nowadays, don't you, *Lynne*? People do such different things. In such different ways. Shall we have some sherry, Grenville? Traditional, isn't it, sherry at Christmas? Ever since you were a boy. The first time you drank it you must have been . . . eight, yes?'

'Eleven actually.'

'And you got terribly squiffy. Then you were sick after lunch. There's only the three of us, I'm afraid, Lindy.'

'Lynne,' Grenville corrected her.

Lynne smiled. 'I don't mind Lindy. Lindy's fine.'

'Most of one's friends are dead. Or losing their minds. Alas. The perils of great age. It will come to you, my dear, just as it will surely come to me.'

'Let's talk of something more cheerful – Christmas and all that,' Grenville said, pulling a small face.

'What was that you said, Grenville? I missed it.'

'Nothing, Mummy – nothing at all,' Grenville said hastily. 'Do you need any help in the kitchen? Sprouts need doing or something? Can we do anything?'

'Mabel is here.' Mrs Fielding gave a little laugh then rose from her chair to accept the sherry Grenville had poured for her. 'Mabel is here and everything is in hand.'

'Mabel?' Grenville frowned. 'I thought you'd – I thought you'd dispatched Mabel.'

'Did you?' His mother stared and then smiled slightly at him. 'Mabel is undispatchable, Grenville dear. You know that as well as I.'

Grenville tried to put on a brave face, and failed. The thought of Mabel's dreadful cooking filled him with gloom. She had been his mother's housekeeper since time immemorial. Food inedible, Mabel unsackable, it all contributed to the general atmosphere of immutability in this house where nothing that needed changing was ever changed, and no discussion wanted or allowed either.

'Perhaps Lynne and I could go and give Mabel a hand?' he suggested, hoping it might still not be too late to salvage something of the lunch that was being prepared.

'Oh, no, really, Grenville, darling. I hardly think that's necessary. Of course if Lynne here would like to go and help . . . ?'

'No, I think we should both go,' Grenville suggested, finding himself defying his mother for the first time in as long as he could remember.

'Take Mabel a glass of sherry and wish her the compliments of the season, yes? And since it's Christmas, in the spirit of Christmas we could also see if she needs a hand.'

'I see.' His mother regarded him without even the semblance of a smile. 'Very well. But please do not be long. I shall stay here by the fire. By myself.'

Grenville rolled his eyes privately to Lynne as they left the room, and Lynne grabbed his hand as soon as the door was closed behind them, kissing him quickly.

'Stop looking so tragic,' she whispered. 'You said yourself it didn't matter and it doesn't. So come on, let's go and get old Mabel tiddly.'

Mabel needed no help. Grenville and Lynne found her in the kitchen singing an incomprehensible carol with a nearly empty bottle of Fine Old Tawny open on the table. Happily they were just in time to do a rescue operation on lunch, Grenville pouncing on the sprouts before they turned to water, taking out the potatoes and sausages before they went quite black, and managing also to salvage the turkey before it was reduced to the size of a quail, removing it from the oven and wrapping it in tinfoil while Lynne concocted what smelt as if it was going to be a most delicious rich gravy. Leaving the Christmas pudding to steam gently and Mabel likewise, they repaired to the dining room where Grenville carved and Lynne served what was, while not the best Christmas lunch they had ever eaten, most certainly a more than serviceable one.

'Do you see now, Grenville?' Mrs Fielding asked her son after sampling her food. 'You do see what I mean about Mabel?'

'We saw exactly,' Grenville replied urbanely. 'All to the good that you dispatched us to the kitchen.'

'So,' Mrs Fielding continued. 'And what are you young doing for the rest of the holiday, might I ask?'

'We're off racing tomorrow,' Grenville replied. 'Lynne and I have shares in a horse that's running—'

'Perhaps you would like to come with us?' Lynne put in, to Grenville's surprise.

'Not on Boxing Day, I don't think so. The crowds are simply frightful. In more ways than one. They most certainly do not consist of what I would call true racing people.'

'It would still be fun. This horse we have, he's really rather promising.'

'Perhaps some other time, Grenville dear. I was thinking we might go to Royal Ascot this year, for Ladies' Day. Have you ever been to Ascot, Lynne?' Mrs Fielding enquired, slowly turning to gaze at her.

'Not really,' Lynne replied. 'I mean not Royal Ascot. I've been to Ascot, but only to ordinary Ascot. Not Royal Ascot.'

'I think I understand what you mean, thank you.'

'I don't know whether I could now, anyway,' Lynne continued, after taking a sip of her claret. 'Don't they still have some rule or other about divorcees?'

Grenville took a deep breath and stared up at the ceiling.

'And that might concern you perhaps?' Mrs Fielding asked. 'Are you saying that you, personally, are divorced?'

'I don't know whether it's actually possible to be divorced *im*personally, Mummy,' Grenville chipped in, hoping to create a diversion.

'I was divorced only a few months ago, actually,' Lynne admitted.

'I see,' Mrs Fielding said. 'I see.'

She took a sip from her wine glass and looked away from Lynne, as if it would be improper to go on addressing her directly.

'A lot of people get divorced nowadays, Mrs Fielding,' Lynne said. 'And a good thing too, if you ask me.'

'Really?' Mrs Fielding sniffed. 'I wonder why you should nurse that particular sentiment? I personally have always believed in the sanctity of marriage and, please God, I always shall.'

'Yes, I'm sure,' Lynne replied. 'But all that left the men free to do just what they wanted, right? Which is not always such a good thing.'

Mrs Fielding tapped the mahogany table in front of her and shook her head. 'People of my generation never believed hurting the children helped anything. And as for airing one's marital difficulties in the divorce court, just try to imagine the effect on one's family.'

'I can understand that,' Lynne agreed. 'Luckily, in my case there are, or rather were, no children.'

Mrs Fielding looked at her. 'And had there been?'

'Maybe it would have all been different, who knows? The last thing I would ever want to do would be to hurt my kids.'

Mrs Fielding dabbed her lips with her linen napkin. 'I see.'

'Lynne was the totally innocent party,' Grenville said carefully, mindful of the dangerous ground they were still on. 'Her husband was flagrantly unfaithful.'

'Grenville,' Mrs Fielding warned him. 'I have just said I do not wish to hear about it. As I have always believed in the sanctity of marriage—'

'Even though Papa was serially unfaithful and left you to run off with another woman?'

'Grenville?' Lynne pleaded quietly.

'Whatever your father might or might not have done, Grenville—'

'There's no might or might not about it, Mother,' Grenville insisted, brave enough now to dare a change of address.

'Grenville? I can look after myself, sweetheart,' Lynne said to him. 'It's OK.'

'Whatever your father *might* have done, Grenville,' Mrs Fielding persisted, 'it remains something between your father and me. It was certainly something he and I would never have wished to have resolved in the divorce court.'

'Mother—' Grenville started, now determined to see his mother off for the first time. But seeing the look in his eyes Lynne hastily put a hand over one of his and came in quickly.

'Your mother is absolutely right, Grenville,' she said. 'Marital difficulties should if possible be sorted out between the partners, not by a lot of greedy lawyers – particularly when there are children involved.'

Grenville was about to disagree but, seeing the look of kindness in Lynne's eyes as well as the small warning frown on her forehead, he pulled back from the brink.

'Of course, Lynne,' he said quietly. 'Sorry, Mother – that really was uncalled for.'

'That's perfectly all right, Grenville dear,' Mrs Fielding replied, now sensing the understanding as well as the love that Grenville and Lynne shared. 'I was probably speaking somewhat out of turn myself.'

'So now it's my turn,' Lynne said, taking a deep breath. 'To speak out of turn, as it were. The point is, Mrs Fielding, although I'd far rather you and I got on, Grenville is my real concern, and I don't want anything to spoil what we feel for each other. You see I love your son, Mrs Fielding. He's just about the kindest, sweetest and gentlest man I have ever met and I really do love him very much, OK? Just in case you've got it wrong – which I'm sure you haven't, but just in case. And you see, I don't care what anyone is or was or whatever because what matters now is what's in the future because that's the only thing we can really affect. We can't change the past but we can care for the future. OK? That's all.' She smiled. 'Sermon over.'

'Thank you.' Grenville took her hand. 'I feel the same – exactly the same – about you and about everything, now that you have put it so well, which I most certainly could not have done.'

'It's all that matters,' Lynne said quietly. 'You said so yourself on the way here – you said it didn't matter what anyone might think and all that, and I really go along with that. We just have to follow our star and feel what we really feel. Life's too blooming short.'

During the silence that ensued Grenville looked first at Lynne, then at his mother, then back to the woman he loved.

'Happy Christmas,' he said, raising his glass. 'Happy Christmas to us all. I have a feeling this is going to be one of the best Christmases ever. If not the very best.'

'Good,' Mrs Fielding said after a moment spent carefully wiping her mouth on her napkin. 'Now I do hope you two are not dashing off somewhere – at least not until after the Queen's speech. Then of course there's the Tree. Mabel and I went to a lot of trouble decorating the Tree, or rather, truth to tell, I spent a great deal of time redecorating the Tree after Mabel had finished ruining it.'

Grenville and Lynne laughed quite genuinely

at her observation, a reaction that pleased Mrs Fielding no end.

'And then,' she continued, 'after that, perhaps we might play a game. Monopoly – or Cluedo, maybe. We always so used to enjoy playing Cluedo.'

'Me too,' Lynne agreed. 'Colonel Mustard in the conservatory with the candlestick. I think it's my all-time favourite board game.'

'I rather agree,' Mrs Fielding said. 'I never really tire of it.'

'Whereas with Monopoly,' Lynne observed, 'someone's always got a hand in the bank.'

'Then Cluedo it shall be, Lynne,' Mrs Fielding decided. 'And now if you'd like to pour us all some more of this excellent claret you brought, Grenville, I'd quite like to finish my equally excellent lunch.'

Chapter Twenty-two

Lost in the Furze

Rather than reveal that their pilot had been the victim of an unprovoked physical assault, Rory had already excused his appearance before Blaze came into the racecourse paddock. The jockey, he explained, had suffered a riding accident.

'Taken a bit of a bashing off someone else's horse, but he's all right now, passed fit to ride.'

And in fact, thanks in part to Kathleen's powdering down the black and blue bits, other than the thin strip of plaster across his nose, as he stood taking instructions from Rory, Blaze did indeed look nearly, if not quite, himself.

'It's a good field, but not the strongest,' Rory told the owners and their connections, as they gathered together just before the race. 'That's what my father says is the good thing about racing on Boxing Day. Too many meetings and not enough horses to go round.' He stopped before going on. 'Where's Connie?'

'She couldn't come,' Lynne said quickly. 'We'll explain afterwards.'

'Rory?' Grenville said, bringing a well-dressed woman to the fore. 'I don't think you've met my mother.'

'Mrs Fielding,' Rory said, taking off his hat and shaking her hand. 'How do you do?'

'How do you do, and good luck with your horse, Mr Rawlins. I have heard great things of him.'

'Fingers crossed.' Rory smiled before turning to Lynne. 'Is Connie all right, Lynne?'

'Not really,' Lynne told him. 'I mean – sorry – she's not ill or anything. At least she's not sick. She's just not quite herself. We'll tell you later.'

Once an oddly quiet Blaze had been legged up by Rory they took their places in the stands to watch the race.

'They're difficult fences in the home straight, so be warned, everyone,' Rory said, taking his race glasses out of their leather holster. 'You come uphill off the bend and the camber's tricky. Tips towards the rails. The fences are pretty stiff, too, and claim quite a few fallers, particularly when the horses are tiring.'

'Thanks for that, Rory,' Alice said. 'I wish I'd stayed in bed now.'

'They're off and running,' Rory muttered. 'Good luck, everyone.'

Blaze had intended to try to make it all as instructed, but two of the fancied runners, the favourite and joint second favourite, stole a march

446

on him, their jockeys forcing him off his preferred berth on the rails as they waited for the starter to set them off. Blaze had barely finished the turn he had been instructed to take on his horse when they were off. In no time, The Enchanted was a good ten lengths down on the leaders, but seeing the scorching pace they were setting, and remembering what Rory had told him about the two hills he would face on the course and the fact that the going had been declared as good to soft, he decided not to waste any petrol by taking off in pursuit. There was plenty of time. The important thing was to get his horse jumping in a good rhythm, which he had done by the time they had jumped the third fence.

The two leaders were still ten lengths or so in front, but the rest of the field were well bunched, and judging from the conversation between the jockeys round him no one was particularly worried about the situation, confident that as the race developed they would be able to close the gap at will. Blaze felt the same, remembering that when he had walked the course that morning he had been surprised at how long the run without fences was when the field left the back straight to descend downhill towards the home stretch and the final four jumps. It seemed there was plenty of time to make up ground, and since it was all downhill he kept The Enchanted cantering along with the rest of the field, heading them by about a length, perfectly happy at the way his horse was going and jumping.

It was only when they reached the top of the hill to turn into the back straight that Blaze's best-laid plans began to go astray. Coming to the last fence along the back, an island fence with a drop on landing, and with the leaders now only half a dozen lengths at most in front, in an effort to pass him in the air the horse alongside The Enchanted suddenly jumped sharply to the left, going through the top of the birch and cannoning into his horse.

For a moment it seemed they would be knocked out of the race as his horse lost all momentum, knocked sideways by the impact of his rival, but somehow – and Blaze would never know how – The Enchanted managed to get his front legs untangled although he landed almost on his nose. Instinctively Blaze slackened his reins and sat back, giving the horse every chance of recovery, but as the horse pitched on landing his head came up and back, and hit the jockey in the face.

Blaze could see nothing except a wall of red. His head felt as if it had been chopped in half by a meat cleaver and his mouth filled with blood. At that moment he wanted nothing more than to fall off the horse and roll to the ground, but that option was out of the question. Not only had he a race still to ride, he had a race to win. So he shortened his reins, took a lot of deep gasping breaths, closed and reopened his eyes several times in an effort to clear the fog and got himself balanced again in the plate, aware only of what was now the distant noise of the race and the vague shouting of the jockeys round about him.

It all seemed a hundred miles away from where he was, but then as the intensity of the pain faded a terrible giddiness set in. He could see now all right, but what he saw was blurred and very far away. What he could see was a field of small blurred horses galloping in the distance while the ground seemed to be falling fast away in front of him. He was running downhill.

I'm going down the hill and there's something I have to remember, he told himself, shaking his head and taking one hand off the reins to wipe the blood from his nose. *But I have plenty of time to get Boyo back in the race because we have to go round again. And if we have to go all the way round again, then we have the time, Boyo. I have time to get my head back, I have time to settle my horse, and I have time to make up the ground – next time round. Good. Good. I make up the ground next time round.*

He settled his horse back at the head of the chasing group as they turned into the home straight. Still thinking he had all the time in the world, he didn't ask his horse, instead letting him bowl along in the same rhythm and at the same pace, as they approached the first fence in the home straight.

'What the hell does he think he's doing?' Rory suddenly asked himself and his group as they stood up in the stands watching. 'They're going for home now and Blaze is just sitting there.'

But even in what he realised afterwards must

have been a semi-conscious state Blaze could not help being aware of the activity around him as they ran uphill to the first fence in the straight.

'Where's the fire?' he shouted to a jockey busy beginning to go to work on his horse. 'Haven't we to go round again?'

'Do as you please, Paddy!' the jockey shouted back. 'But this is where we get off!'

It was then that he finally got the picture. Now he understood what all the shouting and the beating and the kicking was about – this was it. This was the finish. No going round again, not for him, not for anybody. He had the last line of fences to ride and after that was the lollipop. Way ahead of him they were already gone for home. As he landed over the fourth from home he could see vaguely the leaders heading for the next fence, half a dozen or more lengths clear of him, and racing hard. But The Enchanted had landed perfectly yet again, passing two of those racing alongside, horses who were visibly tiring, so he knew he had them beat, but not the ones in front, not yet. He let out more rein than he had ever let out before and sat and pushed – and pushed, shaking the reins at his horse's head but never touching him with the whip. All he did was shake the reins, call to the horse and sit. He'd change his hands if he must, but he'd not hit him – don't hit him – he remembered that – don't hit, just sit, and ride him, ride him, ride him! Before he even had to change his leading hand he felt the horse responding to his urgings. He felt the horse coming alight. He felt him flying.

He could also hear a sudden and almost overwhelming wall of sound, a roar from the grandstands as the racegoers saw what was happening.

'He's left it too late!' Rory shouted, watching as the horse flew the second last fence, passing the horse lying in third who was still a good eight lengths behind the two leaders, who were locked in battle on the run to the last fence, both of them still racing although both of their jockeys were hard at work. 'He's left it far too late, for crying out loud!'

'Please tell me he hasn't!' Alice yelled from her hiding place behind his back. 'Please tell me, please!'

'He hasn't!' Lynne shouted back over the cheering, watching transfixed as their horse continued inexorably to close the gap, coming to the last fence with Blaze still just pushing at him with his hands and his heels. 'He's catching them hand over whatsit! Look, Alice! You've got to look!'

'I can't!' Alice cried. 'I'd have a heart attack!'

'Come on, Enchanted!' an astounded Grenville heard his mother shouting, and turned to see her waving her rolled-up racecard in the air. 'Come on Grenville's horse!'

Out on the track Blaze thought he saw a stride before the last fence and was just about to ask the horse to put in a big one when the horse beat him to it, jumping once again, just as he had done in his last race, from practically outside the wings as he soared into the air and over the top of the black birch without disturbing a twig. There was a huge gasp from the stands, followed by a roar as the racegoers realised that what they were witnessing was a singular performance by what was definitely a singular horse.

After landing over the last The Enchanted ate up the ground and the six lengths' difference between himself and the two leading horses. All at once they were no longer alone, but being passed.

'He's done it!' Lynne yelled, jumping up and down in her excitement before throwing her arms round Grenville and knocking his hat to the ground. 'He's done it, everyone! He's only done it!'

It was an unforgettable sight.

And that would have been exactly how it finished had not something else happened, something that would stamp this race even more indelibly on its witnesses' memories. No more than fifty yards from the post and now easily five lengths clear of the beaten horses, Blaze eased both himself and his horse back and in that moment his heroic effort abruptly ended as suddenly a wall of darkness fell about him and he passed cleanly and entirely out.

Everyone watched aghast from the stands as just yards from the post the winning horse lost his pilot, the comatose Blaze falling sideways from the saddle to the ground, his feet mercifully coming free from the irons, leaving his triumphant horse to gallop joyfully past the winning post with an empty saddle.

They carried the bloodstained jockey on a stretcher to an ambulance that had been rushed up to the winning line. 'His poor old face was just covered in blood,' Kathleen told Teddy as he held the horse's head while Kathleen washed him down. 'It was awash with it. He must have taken some sort of bang out there in the country somewhere.'

'If only he could have hung on till he'd passed the damned post,' Teddy growled. 'If only he'd just hung on somehow.'

'If he got a crack in the face out in the country, Teddy,' Rory pointed out, having joined them for a few seconds to see the little horse, 'Blaze did wonders to stay up that long, let alone ride the race he did. Now I have to go and explain to our loyal owners what happened – then I'm off to see our pilot.'

A few minutes later, looking at the concerned faces surrounding him, Rory realised he was one very spoilt trainer. These owners, this bunch of anxious people, only wanted to hear about Blaze and the little horse; there wasn't a mention of their disappointment.

'Our little chap won it anyway,' Alice said, after a small pause, because she knew from everyone's faces that she was speaking for them all. 'I think that's pretty obvious. So it really doesn't make any difference.'

'Other than the fact that we're out of the money. Come on, I'll buy you all a nice strong consoling drink before I chase after the ambulance.'

'What do you think actually happened, Rory?' Alice asked when they had all repaired to the owners' bar.

Rory shrugged his shoulders, handing round the drinks.

'Bad luck, that's what happened – jockey injured, stayed on brilliantly, lost consciousness as he came up to the post. Fell off. Bad luck. That's racing.'

'Which is something I must speak to you about, if I may,' Grenville murmured.

'Can it wait till I've got back from the hospital?' Rory asked, already making for the door.

'Of course, yes. I mean no – if you could wait just a second.' Grenville dropped his voice. 'It's just that I got an unofficial timing from a chum of mine who's one of the stewards here, and it appears they're all talking about it. It seems that was the second fastest time ever posted here.'

'I know what you're thinking, Grenville: the same as you were thinking the other day when you phoned me. So you know what I'm thinking too. Same as I told you the other day. Big dreams and small horses don't mix.'

'I know, I know, Rory. But this hadn't happened then. I mean, by any standards that was a remarkable performance, regardless of the fact that the jockey finally fell off.'

'The horse is only a novice, Grenville,' Rory

replied, putting his race glasses back in their holster. 'He was also only carrying around eleven stone today, with Blaze's allowance taking another seven pounds off his back—'

'I know, Rory, I know.'

'In the race you have in mind he'd be carrying twelve stone with no allowances. If Blaze rides him in a Grade One the horse carries the same weight as the others. But the real point is, they're both still novices, Grenville, The Enchanted and the boy. Speaking of which, I have to dash off to the hospital – so if you'll all excuse me?'

With a doff of his cap, Rory was gone.

'He's not going to, is he?' Lynne asked, joining Grenville after Rory had left. 'He won't, will he?'

'All it is is an entry, that's all.' Grenville sighed as they headed back out on to the course. 'Just an entry, Linnet. We don't have to do more than just enter the little horse.'

'Yes, but you could tell by the look on Rory's face that he doesn't think it's a good idea, honey.' Lynne slipped her arm through Grenville's and smiled up at him.

'We're the owners. We pay the bills.'

'Rory and his dad – they know all about these things.'

'And we're learning.'

'You more than anyone, Grenville. You're becoming a little bit of a turf expert,' Lynne teased him affectionately. 'My own little walking, talking *Sporting Life*.'

Grenville shrugged. 'It's only an entry. At this

stage of the proceedings there are going to be all sorts, shapes and sizes entered. So what does it matter? There's no risk to putting a horse in for a race, is there?'

'Yes, but be honest, Grenville. You don't think he should be just an entry, do you? You think he should run.'

Grenville looked down at Lynne, and smiled.

'Chances like this do not come round twice, Lynne,' he said. 'Believe me, they don't.'

As he headed for the car park, Rory reconsidered the conversation he'd just had and shook his head. He knew perfectly well what Grenville was thinking, but it made no difference. He had no intention of going down that path.

'Mr Rawlins?' he heard a familiar voice call from behind him. 'Would it be all right if I came to the hospital with you? I've done Boyo and Teddy's going to box him up. So would it be all right if I came along with you?'

Looking at Kathleen it was perfectly clear to Rory that he could think of nothing he would like more.

'You're not suggesting Teddy drives the box back alone, Kathleen, surely?'

'He's got Julie with him,' Kathleen replied. 'They'll be perfectly all right, because if anything happened Julie knows the ropes. She drives George Clement's horsebox, after all.'

'In that case, hop in. I'll be glad of the company.'

'As long as you don't mind,' Kathleen said, suddenly sounding a little shy and looking up at Rory from underneath her fringe. 'I won't jaw on, or anything. Leave you to your thoughts, and all that kind of thing.'

'You can jaw on as much as you please, Kathleen,' Rory replied, unlocking the car. 'As I said, I'd be delighted.'

He opened the passenger door. Kathleen was about to step in when she saw the inside spilling out towards her, a forest of old racing papers and racecards, sweet and chocolate bar wrappers and empty plastic water bottles.

'Right,' she said as Rory got in beside her. 'Since I forgot to give you a Christmas present, to make up I shall spring-clean your car for you.'

'It really isn't necessary—'

'It really is, Mr Rawlins,' Kathleen assured him. 'This is not a car anyone civilised would drive. It must be a health hazard, and we're not even at the hospital yet.'

When they arrived they learned that although Blaze had regained consciousness he was still not making much sense. The doctor in charge told them there should be nothing to worry about, since this was a fairly common symptom of concussion, but even though there appeared to be no fractures they were keeping him in for observation.

'Can we see him?' Rory enquired. 'Just to say hello?'

'Of course – but no excitement, please,' the

doctor added after glancing appreciatively at Kathleen.

When they approached the bed the figure in it looked pathetically small, as if Blaze had been shrunk by the ambulance service.

'Blaze,' Rory said, raising his voice, as the eyes barely opened. 'We just thought we'd look in and see how you were.'

'Hi there, Blaze,' Kathleen said, bending over the figure in the bed and kissing him gently on the forehead, which apart from his eyes was about the only non-bandaged part of Blaze's handsome face. 'Haven't I told you before, this sort of thing just isn't funny?'

Blaze stared at them, trying to focus his eyes.

'How's my horse of Mananan come through the race?' he enquired. 'And didn't I tell you he could fly?'

'He's come through the race just fine,' Kathleen said, with a quick glance up at Rory, who was standing on the other side of the bed. She took one of the jockey's bruised hands in hers. 'They said no excitement now.'

'The horses of Mananan . . .' Blaze murmured.

'You certainly took a terrible smack in the face, you poor lad, did you not?' Kathleen said quickly. 'They're keeping you in until you're fit for a pretty girl to look at without screaming.'

'He doesn't know about the horses, though,' Blaze said, looking at Rory with eyes that Rory could swear had changed colour from the last time he saw them, although being a man he was never too certain of the colour of people's eyes. 'You don't, do you, Stranger?'

'This isn't a stranger, Blaze,' Kathleen said. 'This is Mr Rawlins now. Mr Rawlins trains the horse you were riding, doesn't he?'

'There was a kingdom below the sea, once,' Blaze muttered. 'A long time ago there was a kingdom . . .'

Kathleen nodded down at the bed, worried. 'He really shouldn't be talking, Mr Rawlins,' she murmured. 'So tiring for him. I think we should leave him, so.'

'Of course we must, Kathleen,' Rory agreed. 'And just as I was enjoying the story too.'

'The horses belonged to Cuchulain, the god of the sea,' the voice from the bed continued. 'It was said they were once the waves on the sea which was why they could go over anything . . .'

'We'll come in and see you tomorrow, Blaze.' Kathleen nodded briefly at Rory, indicating that she thought they should be heading for the door.

'The horses had endless power and they would weep tears of blood if one of the warriors was killed. Cuchulain's horses were immortal and possessed a divine knowledge of Fate,' the voice from beneath the bandages continued.

'As Kathleen just said,' Rory told Blaze, following her to the door, 'one of us will look in tomorrow. You just get better quickly. And completely.'

'Some of them – some of them were sent from the kingdom,' Blaze went on, speaking in snatches. 'Some of them – some of them left

459

Mananan to be sent out from the sea, and when they reached the shore . . .'

"Bye, Blaze,' Kate said, easing Rory out of the door before her.

'Once they were ashore they took the earthly form and went into the world to perform all manner of wonders.'

'See you tomorrow.' Kathleen shut the door on Blaze and his ramblings.

'They went forth into the world,' Blaze went on, now quite alone, 'to do wondrous things, to do the magic that would make the people understand, love and worship horses. Those were the wondrous horses that were from Mananan, the horses that have come down to us to this very day.'

'What was all that stuff about horses of Manahan or wherever?' Rory wondered as the two of them walked out of the hospital.

'Mananan,' Kathleen corrected him, looking away across the car park. 'He's obviously still concussed.'

'Horses that could weep tears of blood and had – what was it? Had a divine knowledge of Fate,' Rory mused. 'I just loved that. A divine knowledge of Fate.'

'I hope he's going to be all right, Mr Rawlins,' Kathleen said, changing the subject, zipping up the front of her anorak and tossing back her head of long black hair. 'I really do hope with all my heart he's going to be OK. He took a right old knock, so he did. I don't know how he stayed on as long as he did. Yes, well, I do actually. He stayed on because Blaze Molloy is something special. Something very special. At least I think he is.'

'You do? You think so?' Rory said, with a quick glance at her across the roof of his car as he unlocked the door.

'Of course,' Kathleen replied. 'Don't you?'

'Yes, but it's different for me. By that I mean, yes, I think he's . . . he's special, but perhaps in a d-different way.'

'You're a man,' Kathleen said, waiting to be let into the car. 'You're bound to see it differently.'

Rory frowned, got into the car and opened the passenger door.

'What I meant was I think he well might be an exceptionally talented young jockey,' he continued, settling into his seat. 'While what you th-think of him—'

'What I think of Blaze was firmed up the moment I saw him, Mr Rawlins.'

'Really?'

'I think he's already very special. Yes.'

'Yes, I see. As far as riding g-goes? Or – or . . .'

'Or what, Mr Rawlins?' Kathleen asked, looking round at him with what seemed like genuine bewilderment on her beautiful young face.

'Well,' Rory muttered, firing the ignition. 'You and Blaze – n-n-not that it's any of my business—'

'If you say so, so then it isn't.'

'I don't understand what you mean by that. I was being p-p-polite.'

'Of course you were,' Kathleen agreed. 'And I was being polite as well.'

'L-look,' Rory grunted as he drove out of the hospital car park. 'How this all started – I was simply wondering—'

'Then don't, if you'll excuse me. Wondering usually leads to the wrong conclusions.'

Rory took a deep breath. 'You like Blaze.'

'Of course I like Blaze. Don't you?'

'Of course I like B-B-B-Blaze!' Rory returned, banging two clenched fists on the steering wheel.

'Be careful now,' Kathleen warned him. 'I don't think you saw that bus.'

'I saw the b-b-b-bus. *I saw the bus*, thank you.'

'Not that it's easy driving in this rain – and in this light.'

'I was simply trying to establish . . .' Rory tried yet again. 'All I was wondering was in what *way* you – you know . . .'

'Sorry?' Kathleen frowned and looked round at him again. Rory glanced back at her, taking his eyes off the road, and a car hooted angrily at him.

'Careful—'

'It's all right. It's all right, I s-saw him,' Rory replied, eyes back firmly to the front.

'All you were wondering was . . . ?' Kathleen prompted him.

'It doesn't matter,' Rory replied with a shrug,

feeling that he had tied himself completely in knots. 'It really d-d-doesn't matter.'

'OK,' Kathleen said brightly. 'Then if it really doesn't matter, we won't bother going on with it, so.'

'Kathleen . . .' Rory groaned.

'It's OK,' Kathleen replied, looking quickly away out of her window. 'No worries.'

'Kathleen.'

'Really, Mr Rawlins. No worries at all.'

'I do wish you wouldn't call me M-Mr Rawlins.'

'I work for you, Mr Rawlins,' Kathleen replied, still looking out of her window. 'I couldn't possibly call you anything other. It wouldn't be fair on everyone else.'

'One day, maybe,' Rory muttered.

'Of course,' Kathleen agreed politely. 'What will be.'

Unable to think either of how to reanimate their conversation or of anything fresh to say, Rory lapsed into silence, as did Kathleen, both of them wondering at their failure to connect, Rory ascribing it to Kathleen's obvious interest in Blaze and Kathleen to Rory's equally obvious lack of interest in her. Finally, unable to contain himself any longer yet still unable to think of quite what to say, Rory shook his head and turned briefly to her, to find her sitting staring down at her hands, which were clasped in her lap.

'OK,' he said. 'So. Penny for them.' Kathleen looked up at him, a worried expression now clouding her beauty. 'Penny for your thoughts.'

'I was just thinking I really shouldn't have done this,' she replied. 'Gone to the hospital. I really should have gone back in the box with Boyo.'

Sensing they were now on ground where the very angels might fear to tread, since once again his companion had turned herself away to look out of her window on the dark landscape flashing by, Rory sighed quietly to himself and put a music cassette in the car radio, drowning himself and his private consternation in the sound of Arthur Rubinstein playing the Chopin ballades. Finally, as they had all but reached Fulford Farm and the tape had finished playing through the first side, Rory ejected the cassette and tried one last and different approach.

'This is really *à propos* of nothing in particular, Kathleen,' he began. 'J-j-just a completely general enquiry – but when you came here, when you agreed to work in the yard, did you put a t-time limit on it?'

'Why do you ask that?' Kathleen asked quickly, thinking that she must somehow have displeased her employer and he was now wondering whether to ask her to go. 'Have I done something wrong?'

'No.' Rory laughed, although his mood was a far from happy one. 'No, of course not. You do everything right. Just right. No, no – I was just wondering what your plans were.'

'In truth I'd hoped I'd be able to stay as long as I was needed, Mr Rawlins. But if you'd rather I

464

went – that is, if you feel that I'm *not* needed any more—'

'No, I didn't say that, K-K-K-Kathleen—'

'Sure I've done what I came to do, Mr Rawlins, so you'd only be right,' she said as the car turned in at the top of the long drive down to the yard. 'We have the horse fit and well, he's winning his races, you've staff enough now – and anyway, my father's at me to go home all the time so really it would be best all round if I were to go back as soon as is convenient.'

'This is entirely your call, not mine,' Rory replied, now parking the car at the yard gates. 'What do you really want to do?'

'What do you really want to do, Mr Rawlins?' Kathleen asked in return, turning a pair of now dark and troubled eyes on him. '*Really.*'

'That's neither here nor there, K-Kathleen – what I really want to do. We're talking about y-you here.'

'Is this what you want?'

'Is *what* what I want?' Rory shook his head, finding himself unable to cope with the way the conversation was going hither and thither, sensing a subtext but unable to quite make sense of it. 'I really c-c-can't follow this.'

'I don't think this is what you want at all,' Kathleen said quietly. 'Not one bit of it.'

'Are we talking in general terms here? Or are we being specific? What I was asking—'

'And what I was meaning, if you'll forgive the interruption, was that I've always sensed you're

465

only marking time. But then that's me being previous and that I mustn't be, so forgive me.' She smiled at him, almost formally, then opened her car door. 'I'll be gone as soon as is convenient – and thank you, Mr Rawlins. It has been great, but as they say, all good things . . . Thanks, anyhow.'

Then she was gone. He watched her walking into the yard then breaking into a run as soon as she was through the gate, hurrying to Boyo's box to make sure her horse was safe and sound and had travelled home all right. She shut him up for the night and walked quickly off to her quarters, with Rory still sitting in his car watching her. He hoped she might stop and turn round, the way they often did in films, to take a look back, and if she did he would be out of the car, running into the yard and taking her up in his arms – but that was not the way it happened. Life was not like the movies, Rory told himself. Life was far more prosaic, harder, less forgiving. In real life people did what Kathleen was doing now – continued to walk to their destinations without a stop, a pause or a backward glance.

Anyway, as far as Kathleen Flanagan was concerned, Rory decided that he was hopeless – or rather perhaps that *it* was hopeless. Kathleen Flanagan quite obviously loved another, so as far as his own aspirations went he might as well try to catch a moonbeam, or light a penny candle from a star.

*　　　*　　　*

'Yes, well!' Anthony Rawlins shook his head and laughed when the two of them had finished watching the video tape Rory had brought back from the course of The Enchanted's race that afternoon. 'Good heavens, it's hard to believe it's the same little horse we bought that day when we were both tight!'

'I was the one who was footless, Dad, not you.'

Anthony smiled. 'Forget about beware the Greeks when they bring you gifts. More to the point would be to beware the Irish measure, my son.'

Rory took the tape out of the video player. 'Well, you've seen the videos of his other two races, so what do you think?'

'I have to say – with a certain amount of caution, naturally – that I can actually see what the excitement is about, Rory.'

'When you think that this is only his first season and that was his third race. His third *proper* race . . .'

'It's a race often won by younger horses, old man, there's that in his favour,' Anthony said, holding up an empty glass to be refilled. 'The point is, you don't want to run him at Cheltenham, but your little quorum do. It's the usual dilemma with trainers and owners. A race like the Gold Cup can ruin a young horse, as we both know.'

'There'll be plenty of other chances, Dad, God willing.'

'I always used to think that, you know,' Anthony replied, sipping his whisky and water.

'Until I was persuaded to run Starlight Fleet in the Schweppes at Newbury. He was ten pounds out of the handicap. Didn't think he had a hope. I told the owner the selfsame thing. The horse was young, he hadn't many miles on the clock, and there'd be plenty of other chances, I said. But the owner stuck to his guns and you know the rest of the story.'

'He sluiced home by a distance.' Rory looked rueful as he remembered.

'Which is exactly why we trainers don't like running our horses out of the handicap. It makes it look as though you haven't been running them on their merit.'

'The Gold Cup isn't a handicap, as you well know, Dad.'

'Same point. For weight, read class.'

'What you're saying is if owners insist on running their horses—'

'Then you must run them,' his father replied. 'Or make it look as though you will. You do at least have to make the entry. What you can do then is try to advise them against it. Talk them down slowly, use reason and gentle persuasion, and ninety-nine per cent of the time the owners will come round to your way of thinking, because at the back of their minds they know or they think you know best.'

'But if they don't come round?'

'Then you have to run. The owners own their horses. The owners pay the bills. So the owners have the right to say where their horses run.

Remember dear old Eileen Nesbitt? When she had her horses here, she insisted they only ran in televised races, when in fact they were barely out of egg and spoon class. But since her health prevented her from racing and she wanted to see them run, the only way to do that was to run them in televised races. It was agony for me, old man – can you imagine? Time after time they'd trail in last, if they finished at all, so that was *very* good for one's reputation, I don't think. For a while I was a complete laughing stock. But there you are. They were her horses, and she paid the bills.'

'Point taken. Now come on, time to eat. We have a mass of turkey to finish up.'

'Rory?' his father said as he followed Rory out. 'I do appreciate what you're doing, you know.'

'Oh, nonsense. I'm not doing anything.'

'Yes, but sooner or later, and preferably sooner,' Anthony insisted, putting a hand on his son's shoulder for support, 'we're going to have to make some other sort of arrangement.'

'Everything in due course,' Rory said, holding the kitchen door open. 'That's what you always say – everything in due course. Now come on – we've got some rather good burgundy to finish off.'

The following morning it began to snow. At first it snowed only in light flurries, but by mid-afternoon when Rory was sitting in the office with Maureen preparing the entries and catching up with his paperwork, the fall had become a blizzard.

'I do hope we're not in for a freeze-up,' he said. 'My father always says this is the curse of racing at this time of year. You get your horses right just at the time winter decides to kick in.'

'Luckily it's a level playing field, Rory,' Maureen reminded him. 'At least it is this time round because apparently, according to the news, the whole country's blanketed.'

'Sure,' Rory sighed. 'But some of the rich boys in Lambourn have got covered canters so they can at least keep their horses moving, keep them in work. You know what our gallops get like here when it snows. Talk about north to Alaska. And who on earth's that?'

Rory rubbed some of the condensation off the window and stared at a small figure battling its way through the blizzard, one arm held up face high in protection against the snow. He got up quickly from his desk and hurried outside.

'Hello?' he called. 'Who is that?'

'No, please!' a small female voice answered him. 'Please don't worry! It's only me!'

As soon as he was outside and got a better look at their unexpected visitor Rory thought he knew who it was, yet he could hardly believe his eyes when finally he helped Constance out of the storm and into the warmth of his office.

'What on earth . . . ?' He came in behind her, closing the door. 'Connie, what are you *doing* here?'

470

'Don't even ask,' Constance replied. 'This is not a day to remember.'

On her way down to stay with Lynne, Constance had missed her stop. Lynne had invited her because, having read the rehashed stories in the newspapers concerning Red Andrew and his once equally suspect wife, anticipating her friend's imminent distress, she had telephoned Constance at once and offered her refuge, an invitation that Constance had gratefully accepted, only to miss her stop at Andover. It had begun to snow heavily in London long before the weather hit the west, so by the time Constance was able to get off the train at Salisbury, the next stop down the line, the services had been so disrupted by the snowstorms that all trains in and out of the capital had been cancelled.

Unable to get back to Andover by rail, Constance had tried to get a taxi to take her, but to no avail, all drivers flatly refusing to take the risk of driving anywhere other than within the city itself. Panic stricken, and after a moment of not knowing what to do, she remembered that Rory lived close to Salisbury. She decided to try to get herself transported to Fulford Farm, which she imagined to be only a short hop from the city. Again every driver she asked to take her there refused, advising her to book into a hotel until the weather cleared. Constance was about to throw in the towel and find a room when a local lad in a large truck, overhearing her dilemma, offered her a lift since Fulford Farm was on his own way home.

'I couldn't telephone you to warn you, because the queues at the public telephones were right round the block,' Constance explained as Rory took her soaking wet overcoat to hang it over the Aga in the kitchen, and then filled the kettle for tea. 'And the lad who brought me here was quite understandably anxious not to delay any longer than was necessary.'

'He didn't bring you all the way down here, surely?' Rory asked. 'Even with four wheel drive I doubt if he'd have got back up again.'

'I walked from the top of the drive,' Constance said, in a forlorn voice, standing with her back to the Aga. 'I got utterly lost twice.'

'You poor thing,' Rory said, putting a cup of tea in front of her. 'Well, I'm afraid you're not going to get to Lynne's today and I doubt very much if you'll make it tomorrow either. In fact, according to the forecast, we could be snowed up here for a good few days. So I hope you've brought your toothbrush.'

'I've just been reading all about you in the papers,' Anthony told Constance when Rory took her through to the drawing room, once she had defrosted.

'Oh, please, don't,' Constance groaned, putting her hands to her face and sinking into an armchair by the fire. 'The very reason for my flight.'

'Nonsense.' Anthony laughed. 'Water under the bridge. Besides, you don't want to take any notice of these gossip columnists. No way to earn

472

a living, I always say. Not what I'd call a proper job, more an improper job.'

'Can I know what you're both talking about?' Rory asked, throwing some more logs on the fire and earning himself a hard stare from the dormant Dunkum in return. 'What exactly was in the papers?'

'Here,' Anthony said, fishing out from under himself a well-squashed tabloid. 'In the diary.'

'You really don't have to,' Constance muttered. 'I would much rather you didn't.'

'Nice picture of you, though,' Anthony said in admiration. 'You know, I think I probably saw all your films.'

'They were hardly my films, Mr Rawlins,' Constance replied. 'You mean the films I passed through.'

'Far too modest, Lady Frimley.'

'Do call me Constance.'

'You're far too modest. *The Lady Returns*, for instance. You had a very decent part in that and gave a very decent performance, too. Saw it again only the other day.'

'Did I?' Constance frowned. 'I don't remember.'

'I was madly in love with you, I have to tell you.'

'Do you know, I watched some old film or other I was in on the television recently, and do you know, I don't even remember making it. That's how memorable most of my films were.'

'*All At Sea*? I bet you remember making that

473

one. You had a smashing love scene with that rather dishy dark-haired bloke.'

'Who would have been a great deal happier kissing the actor who played my fiancé, I can assure you.'

'Yes, I have to say we were all in love with you, my friends and I.' Anthony sighed. 'Before I was married, of course.'

'I don't think you need get upset about this, Connie,' Rory said, having finished reading the item in the paper.

'And then when I married it turned out that my darling wife said she'd modelled herself on you.'

'I shall certainly look forward to meeting your wife, then.'

'Alas not,' Anthony said with a sad shake of his head, turning to look at his late wife's photograph in her Court presentation dress. 'I lost her some years ago now.'

'I'm very sorry to hear that.'

'Thank you, Constance. She was a wonderful woman.'

'Then that makes it all the sadder.'

'No, this is all water under the bridge, Connie.' Rory threw the paper into the log basket, and shrugged. 'I don't see the point in bringing it all up again.' He sat down on the sofa beside Constance. 'Although I agree with my father – smashing photo.'

'Once upon a long time ago.' It was Constance's turn to shrug her shoulders. 'Yes, indeed a long,

long time ago. But this.' She pointed at the crumpled newspaper. 'This is ridiculous, this piece. Hardly one word of truth in it. For a start I most certainly did not have an affair with that awful blackshirt Bolton. I hardly even knew the fellow. And I did not flee abroad. I said at the time I was determined to stay here and prove my innocence—'

'Which you did?'

'Yes, and when I did go abroad it was only on the advice of the Home Office. The way that horrid little gossip merchant, that peddler of the misery of others has written it up, it makes it sound as though I vanished at the same time as my wretch of a husband, when in fact it was a long time after. Ages after, in fact.'

'They shouldn't publish such an inaccurate piece.' Anthony frowned. 'Like me to do something about it?'

'I would love it, of course,' Constance said. 'But what can you do?'

'The chap who's the editor,' Anthony told her, reaching for his telephone book. 'When he was something else – features editor, I think – he had a horse with me. He'd had it with someone else who shall be nameless, but he got fed up and sent it to me – and he won a couple of races while he was here. Three, in fact. He's always said if there was anything he could do in return, so now seems to be a very good time to call in the favour.'

Anthony excused himself and took himself off to his study to telephone his journalistic contact.

'This is very good of your father, Rory,' Constance said. 'He doesn't have to do this, you know.'

'That's my father. A friend of his told him the reason he'd had a heart attack was that his heart was too big.'

'How is he now? He looks very well.'

'He's much better; be even more so if we could find some way of getting him to America. According to his specialist, they have a procedure there which would be just the job. But it's very expensive and Dad thinks he isn't worth it.'

'While you obviously think he is.'

'Of course. But try telling him that. Besides, we're a bit short of beans at the moment.'

'I know it's really none of my business,' Constance said after a moment, 'but what if he doesn't have the operation?'

Rory pulled a wry face. 'Your guess is as good as mine.'

'All done and dusted,' Anthony told them on his return. 'Apology in tomorrow, and he's promised it won't be hidden down the bottom of page two either. They wanted to ring you for a quote but I said I didn't know where you were.'

'I very much appreciate that, Anthony. Thank you.'

'It's nothing. Glad to be able to help. So . . .' He looked at the snowscape outside the drawing-room window, and then at Constance. 'It looks as though we shall be having the pleasure of your company for a day or so.'

'Afraid so,' Constance said, fishing in her bag for her cheroots. 'Sorry about that.'

'I dare say we'll manage,' Anthony replied. 'Long as we don't run out of Scotch.'

It turned out they were snowed in for six days. The weather was so bad they were unable to do anything with the horses other than walk them round a track they had cleared and kept having to clear round the yard. After the initial two days of heavy snow the blizzard stopped, but then it froze, which made any horse exercise impossible. So the string were confined to their boxes and their diet changed from a full training and heating one to half-rations supplemented by plenty of fresh, damp hay.

'If this goes on, Pop,' Rory said to his father, 'if we have another week of this, it'll be the equivalent of losing a month's work. And you know what that means better than I. If the owners are even vaguely thinking of Cheltenham we've got to get another run into the horse, but to get him fit enough for that would take at least three weeks' full work. So suppose the weather doesn't relent until late January? We wouldn't be able to run him till near the end of February, which would only leave us about a fortnight to the race itself. And I don't think that would be enough.'

'You're talking in ifs and ands here, old chap,' his father replied. 'It all depends when the thaw comes and how hard it thaws when it does come.'

Having talked to his owners and made sure they had all seen a recording of the big Kempton race so they knew exactly the sort of opposition they might face at Cheltenham, Rory had done as requested and at least made an initial entry for The Enchanted in the big race, feeling a little happier to do so since the handicapper had raised the little horse's rating another five points. Rory knew a lot could happen between early January and the second week of March, so while not particularly happy about entering the horse he knew that so far there was no commitment other than the financial one the owners had been prepared to shoulder when they requested the entry in the first place. When the list of first entries was duly published, as far as non-combatants went there were no surprises. All the top cup horses had been entered, as had the top half a dozen or so handicappers, while there were only two novices in the list, a little heard of Irish horse and The Enchanted. But as the weather showed no signs of breaking, Rory began to feel that time might be on his side, since the longer it froze the less time he would have to prepare such a young and inexperienced horse, which would give him every reason to opt the horse out and save both his own and his father's faces, convinced as he was that the whole professional racing world would be laughing at him.

The only other good thing to come out of the freeze was Kathleen's continued presence at the yard. When she was unable to make the journey back to Ireland on the day she had planned to do so, Rory had been only too happy to agree to her staying on.

'Not that I ever wanted you to go in the first place,' he'd told her.

'You did not?' Kathleen had replied with a frown. 'You said there was nothing left for me to do here.'

'No. No, *you* said that, Kathleen. I didn't say anything.'

'Comes to the same thing though, does it not?' she had asked in return, turning a pair of large green eyes on him. 'Your saying nothing told me there was no point in staying.'

'Don't let's start all that business up again, shall we?'

'I'm not starting anything up, Mr Rawlins,' Kathleen had replied, walking away from him, before calling back over her shoulder, 'You were the one who said nothing!'

Afraid to go up that particular dark alley again, Rory had given her best, just happy that she wasn't leaving.

Then the thaw came, and when it did, it did so as dramatically as it had snowed. Just six nights after the first blizzard, they all went to bed in sub-zero temperatures and woke in the morning to find water everywhere. Thawed snow was pouring in wide rivulets off the stables roofs into gutters quite unable to cope with the torrent. The yard was ankle deep in slush, and the paddocks themselves were beginning to resemble small lakes.

'At least the gallops will be rideable,' Rory observed as he lent a hand sweeping water into the yard drains. 'Although judging from the amount of slush we're facing we'll probably have to swim up there.'

But in another two days the last of the snow and slush had completely disappeared, the yard was back in business, and Constance was on a train to London, her newly formed friendship with Anthony foremost in her mind.

First thing every morning for three days the horses were walked for five miles on the roads before breakfast and then another five miles in the early afternoon, before anyone was allowed near the gallops, and when they were finally allowed up the hill it was only for a couple of long steady canters. After such a long lay-off the last thing anyone wanted was to have a horse pulling a muscle or doing a leg, so caution was the byword.

'Slow and steady!' Rory would remind his work riders as they left the yard. 'I don't want anyone going on. I just want to see you all swing up and by. OK?'

Blaze, who had returned from hospital and was now completely recovered from his fall, thanks largely to Kathleen's tender care, was given the leg up on Boyo and rode him exactly to orders. As far as anyone could tell the horse was as fit as he had been before the snow arrived. Every morning he would appear at the crest of the gallops cantering over his stablemates, only to thunder past Rory with his head in his chest and his big ears pricked, full of premature joys of spring, a season which to judge from the bitter winds on the downland was still a long way off.

'I'm entering him at Devon and Exeter, Ludlow and Towcester, all three-mile races, and since all the races have good prize money and everyone with a decent horse is looking for at least one more run before March, we can expect good fields everywhere – which is what we want if we're all being serious about this.'

Rory had called a meeting of the owners to discuss their strategy, and now it was Alice who spoke up. 'I don't understand why we shouldn't be being serious about it,' she said. 'We all think – no, sorry. We all *know* Boyo is special and we all of us believe he deserves to run in one of the special races, if not the most special race.'

'I know, Alice. And I'm not trying to talk any of you out of it.'

'Oh, but you are, Rory. Of course you are. Millie said you would, because trainers are infinitely more sensible than owners, she said.'

'I'm not sure I want to be remembered for being sensible.'

'Very well, more knowledgeable then. More pragmatic, if you like.'

'I don't think I want to be remembered for being either of those either.'

'It's your job to be realistic,' Alice persisted. 'Not ours. Our job is to dream, and we all dream the same, the four of us. We all dream of The Enchanted winning at Cheltenham.'

'You wouldn't prefer to put it on hold for say another year? Just to see how right or how wrong we all are? Another year on the horse could make a whole lot of difference.'

'Another year on the horse could see him injured or worse,' Grenville said. 'There's nothing to say he'll be any better next year than he is now. He's six. Six-year-olds often win these sorts of races.'

'But he's not very big, Grenville. He's not really built for this.'

'He's not going to get any bigger in a year, Rory. Who knows? He might be at his very best now, and if he is, there's nothing to stop us running him.'

'As long as he's qualified.'

'He's practically qualified already, and any-way—'

'Grenville—'

'No, seriously, old man, do hear me out on this,' Grenville insisted. 'A chum of mine who was at school with the handicapper had a private word on our behalf. It's all right, it won't go any further. The handicapper's also married to my chum's sister, if you get my drift. Anyway, he had a word in the old ear, and *el handicapper* said that even if the little horse's rating stayed the same – which it will not – but even if it does, and we want to run him, he would let us do so, which he can if he thinks the horse jumps and races well enough.'

'As long as you all know what it means.' Rory sighed, finally getting the feeling that he was being strong-armed into doing what they all wanted. 'We could be a laughing stock, you know that?'

'You mustn't mind what people might say,' Lynne said. 'Grenville says you're worried because people are already saying novices have no place in Gold Cups.'

'It could well be so, Lynne. It's not really a race designed for novices.'

'Not novice novices, it isn't,' Lynne agreed. 'Sorry – I mean, that is according to Grenville. I'm only quoting Grenville here. But since we all of us think that The Enchanted isn't a novice novice, that answers that, really.'

'And I've just had a long talk with your father,' Constance chimed in. 'Because frankly I wouldn't know one race from another. As far as I'm concerned they go hoppity-hoppity-hoppity for a few miles while Alice and I close our eyes—'

'You don't close your eyes, Connie. You watched every inch of the race at Huntingdon, when we all thought Eddie Rampton was going to murder you.'

'That wasn't Boyo's race, clever dick. That was another race, the race I had a bet on. Ever since he won his first race at wherever it was I haven't been able to watch a thing. Anyway, beside the point, I fear – all I want to say is that I listened to what your dear father had to say.'

'And?'

'And I didn't understand a word of it. But I do so love talking to your father. He's a very good listener, and he has such a lovely voice.'

Rory smiled and left it at that. As far as he was concerned the little horse was entered up but no decisions were to be made until it was seen how he ran in his next contest. As for other matters at Fulford Farm, another decision seemed already to have been made concerning Constance, for it now appeared that although the brief freeze was over and the brouhaha in the newspapers concerning her had quickly and completely died down, at the express invitation of Anthony, Constance was back at Fulford Farm not just for a meeting, but to take up residence in one of the farm cottages, where she said she would be out of everyone's way, everyone, that was, other than Anthony, who judging from the increasing amount of time he spent with Constance in the cottage seemed also to be changing his place of residence.

But of course, as Rory well knew, there was a downside to the change in the weather. Now that the freeze was over and road and rail were all but back to normal, there really was nothing to keep Kathleen at the yard any more – nothing, that was, except the horse.

Chapter Twenty-three

Re-enter My Pal Joey

The horse hadn't run as planned in the big race on Boxing Day, the King George VI Gold Cup, even though he had been the firm co-favourite in all the ante-post betting lists and in spite of Eddie Rampton and his connections maintaining he would. Instead he was withdrawn on the morning of the race, the veterinary certificate stating that a foreign body had been found under a shoe, the result being an infection. Naturally the punters who had taken the price on offer ante-post were not best pleased, although the majority of them, as they tore up their vouchers, might have been heard to mutter a more colourful version of *that's racing*.

The truth of the matter was that the trainer liked to play the waiting game to unsettle the opposition. He was also a gambler who liked to take the odds ante-post, and he also particularly enjoyed winning valuable races for his owners, most of whom also enjoyed a tilt at the ring. But what really rocked Eddie Rampton's boat was beating those trainers whom he perceived as belonging to the Smart Set, the loud-talking, party-going, arrogant young men most of whom had inherited the family stables and whom, Rampton had long ago decided, looked down their noses at the likes of him, and him in particular. So he derived a peculiar pleasure from rattling their cages. And, it had to be faced, having the favourite for the Gold Cup offered him ample opportunity to indulge his chip. He knew most of his rivals preferred to avoid taking on any of his good horses before the big Cheltenham meeting in March so he took great delight in spreading as much misinformation about intended and non-intended runners as possible, after which he would sit back to watch his rivals getting into flat spins as they tried to decide whether or not to run their own charges.

This was by far his favourite time of year – the run-up to Cheltenham, and yet another chance to win the most coveted racing trophy of them all, the Gold Cup. So far Eddie Rampton had been twice denied a triumph he thought was his as two of his horses, on separate occasions, had galloped up the famous hill after the last fence looking certain to win, only to tire and be caught at the post by horses trained by two of his most despised rivals. But this year was different: this year he knew he had a worthy favourite in My Pal Joey, who had won his two preparatory races this year with the sort of consummate ease that is the hallmark of an exceptional horse.

My Pal Joey was a large horse, standing at a full seventeen hands, and for his size he was blessed with stamina, an exceptional cruising speed, and a prodigious jumping ability. Such was his presence that he normally had his rivals beaten a long way out simply by dominating the race with his sheer physical presence. Given a trouble-free run-up to March, Rampton considered he had his best chance yet to triumph in the Gold Cup. His only regret was that the horse's terminally ill owner had known that he himself wasn't going to make it to Cheltenham and so had sold his horse in order that someone else could enjoy the thrill of having not only a runner in the Gold Cup but possibly the favourite and perhaps even the winner. But even though he had lost an owner of long standing, Rampton very soon realised that My Pal Joey's new owner was a man after his own heart. A real go-getter, someone determined to win at all costs. There was no coming second in this man's book – it was win, and win whatever the cost.

So as soon as the entries were published in January the favourite's new owner and his trainer put their heads together to hatch various stratagems, shortly after which Eddie Rampton initiated his campaign of disseminating misinformation, a process that began with the last-minute withdrawal of My Pal Joey from the big race on Boxing Day.

On the other hand, Rory and his four owners put all their cards on the table as far as their horse was concerned. Not that there was a lot of undue interest in his possible participation in March even when his name appeared among the initial entries. To the racing and betting public he was a largely unknown and hard to rate quantity, certainly a promising novice steeplechaser but one whom the cognoscenti were ready to dismiss because of his size, his lack of breeding, his relatively inexperienced trainer and the fact that the horse had only run on what they liked to call the gaffe tracks, the smaller and less fashionable country racecourses. So when the bookmakers made their first ante-post lists it was no surprise that the price quoted against The Enchanted to win the Grade One Cheltenham Gold Cup on 13 March, to be run over three miles two and a half furlongs for five-year-olds and upwards, was a hundred and fifty to one.

When Alice noted the apparent generosity of the odds, she began to fashion a plan of her own, and once she had considered it carefully she made two telephone calls, one to her bank for information on the state of her current account and the other to her friend Millie for advice on a certain bit of protocol.

As far as the owners of The Enchanted went, no one had yet realised who the new owner of the star of Eddie Rampton's yard was. Rory's secretary Maureen so far had been the only person to spell out the name, but since she had no idea that Lynne had once been Mrs Fortune, and not so very long ago at that, the name of the new owner did not mean anything to her. The Enchanted's owners were not always glued to racing on the television or reading every item of gossip in the racing papers, and by the time they turned their attentions to any other horse that might be taking on their own in March the story about My Pal Joey's changing hands had long gone cold. So it was not until Grenville and Lynne happened to be sitting in front of the television in Lynne's now fully furnished apartment one wet Saturday afternoon that the penny finally dropped.

The racing was from Ascot where one of the contests, according to Grenville, was looked upon as being a good trial for any Gold Cup candidates who wanted to pit themselves against stiff well-made fences on what was reckoned to be a seriously testing course. Before the race was run, to kill time as the horses were cantering down to the start, one of the presenters informed the viewers that he was about to interview the owner of a horse which had been one of the favourites for the Gold Cup until recently, when it had suffered an injury that had, according to the interviewer, indeed prevented the animal from running in this prestigious Ascot race this very afternoon.

Whereupon the new owner was introduced to the public.

'Bloody hell – will you look at who it is?' Lynne exclaimed. 'By all that's Satanic and evil, it's only my bloody ex!'

And sure enough, there was Gerry, wearing a fashionably overlong black overcoat with matching fedora, Maddy by his side, dressed in a red leather overcoat and a Dr Zhivago-style fur hat.

'What do they look like?'

'I'm too much of a gentleman to say,' Grenville murmured. 'An updated Bonnie and Clyde, perhaps?'

'But he doesn't know any more than I do about racing! All he knows about is blooming dodgy motor cars!'

'I've always been mad about racing and horses,' Gerry was saying, smiling urbanely into the camera. 'Ever since I was a nipper.'

'Baloney,' said Lynne. 'First time he ever went racing was with me.'

'My dad always had horses,' Gerry went on.

'And they pulled carts,' Lynne retorted.

'So, you know, horses have always been part of my life.'

'Mine as well,' Maddy simpered, tightening her grip on Gerry's arm. 'I had my first pony when I was seven. He was a little skewbald called Paintbox.'

'And it lived in a toy cupboard,' Lynne hissed.

'Now, now, Linnet,' Grenville remonstrated. 'One mustn't speak ill of the brain dead.'

'Course I'm sad that the guy who owned the horse previously won't be here to see him run,'

Gerry continued. 'But I think he'll be watching anyway. From his cloud up there.'

'He'll be taking Holy Orders next,' Lynne said.

'Or holding up banks,' Grenville remarked. 'Particularly in that coat.'

'So what's the news on your horse, Gerry?' the interviewer was asking. 'Is he over the setback that prevented him from running in the King George?'

'He's certainly back in work,' Gerry replied, returning to the script Eddie Rampton had prepared for him. 'It's a bit early to say whether he's fully over it. It was a real nasty infection.'

'Got right in between his poor toes,' Maddy added helpfully.

'Right in his hoof,' Gerry corrected her as quickly as he could. 'Right in the – you know. The outside bit.'

'Inside the outside bit.' Maddy again.

'The bit right under the shoe,' Gerry said with a nod. 'Very painful. Anyway, as I said, he's back in work now but we're taking it day by day.'

'And if he does make it to Cheltenham,' the interviewer said, 'which of course we are all hoping he does, which horses do you most fear?'

'You would have to say County Gent,' Gerry replied, looking at his most knowledgeable. 'County Gent, certainly.'

'Yeah,' Maddy agreed. 'You would have to say County Gent.'

'And the Irish horse,' Gerry added. 'Spun Silk.'

'Right.' Maddy nodded. 'And the Irish horse, Spun Silk. Course.'

'I think most of all you'd have to say County Gent,' Gerry said, summarising. 'And the Irish horse Spun Silk.'

'Good. Thank you both very much,' the interviewer concluded. 'Hope to see you both again in March.'

'You bet!' Maddy said, leaning to camera and holding up her free hand clenched in a fist. 'Cheltenham here we come!'

'They really should give them a show of their own,' Grenville said, lying back on the sofa with a deep sigh. 'One of those in-depth chat shows.'

'Must be because of us,' Lynne said, sitting back on the sofa. 'Only reason Gerry muscles in on something is when he thinks his precious nose is out of joint.'

'Really?' Grenville pulled a face. 'Rather an expensive get-you, isn't it?'

'You don't know Gerry, Grenville,' Lynne said, still staring at the screen. 'And you certainly don't know Maddy. Hold on – isn't that that American's horse? Fly The Flag? You know, that nice bloke we met at Huntingdon.'

Grenville checked the runners in the paper just as the odds were being flashed up on the screen.

'Right, it is,' he said. 'Should be favourite.'

'It is favourite,' Lynne replied. 'Two to one.'

They watched the race, a three-mile handicap with Fly The Flag carrying top weight of 11st 9lb, a burden that certainly didn't stop him winning as he liked, sauntering home in the soft going by an easy four lengths.

'Another one for the notebook,' Grenville observed. 'He also holds an entry for the Gold Cup.'

'But we're not sure we'll go to Cheltenham,' Harrington Lovell said when he was interviewed in the unsaddling enclosure. 'If the ground dries up, which it usually does, he might be found out in the speed department. There are some fast horses entered, and really our fella's bred to stay, so we might be looking at Aintree instead. It's always been on the wish list, the Grand National, and you know, from the way he ran today, he could go close.'

'Yes,' Grenville agreed from his armchair. 'But we did beat him somewhat easily at Huntingdon, so although he has to come into the reckoning he's not my major worry.'

'Who is, sweetheart?' Lynne wondered, getting up to go and make them both some tea.

'Your ex's horse, I suppose,' Grenville replied. 'A little bird told me they'd laid him out to win.'

Kathleen turned the television off in her cottage and sat back in her chair. In front of her on the floor stood her bags, already packed ready for the journey she intended to make that evening, a journey she had been intending to undertake in fact for the past three days, but having warned Rory of her intention she had found herself finding plenty of reasons for delaying her departure, all of them concerning Boyo, who she kept discovering needed just a little bit more care

493

and supervision with every day that passed.

She had hoped that Rory would notice her increased diligence and invite her to stay on just in case Boyo needed her, even though they both knew there was nothing about the horse to cause even the slightest concern. But he had said nothing at all, not one word. In fact, if she didn't know Rory for the kind-heart that he was, she would have said he was doing his best to ignore her altogether. So finally, now that Saturday had arrived, the day, she had told Rory, on which she simply had to leave because of pressing matters at home, Kathleen realised that she was going to have to be as good as her word and take her leave of the place where she knew she had found true happiness.

Of course, what she had just seen televised from Ascot racecourse was only making her job harder. Most of the talk had been about the Gold Cup, and although no mention was made of The Enchanted in the entire broadcast the fact that the chances and merits of all the favoured horses were being so readily discussed and compared only served to make her departure more of a terrible wrench. For a moment she had even seriously contemplated going to find Rory to ask him directly if perhaps she could stay, pleading her special relationship with Boyo as her reason, only to remember it was too late, since Rory was at Ascot and Blaze was coming to pick her up in half an hour to take her to the station.

'You sure you know what you're doing, Kate?'

Blaze asked her yet again as he drove her off to Salisbury.

'Just leave it alone, will you?' Kathleen replied, turning away from him. 'And leave me alone as well.'

'You're mad,' Blaze said. 'You've completely lost it.'

'That's my business,' Kathleen insisted. 'The whole thing is a lot of baloney anyway. Boyo'll be fine, and so too will everyone else involved.'

'Sure,' Blaze said. 'Everyone, that is, except you.'

All the way back from the race meeting, which he left early, Rory found he could do nothing but think of Kathleen. The main reason he had gone to Ascot was not to see the competition but to be away from the yard when Kathleen left it, thinking that if he remained he would only do what he had resolved not to do, namely beg her to stay. Now, as he was driving back in more than a slight panic, he knew that was exactly what he should have done and never minded the consequences. Life at the yard was not going to be the same without the beautiful Kathleen and he had let her go. Worse, he had let her go without having made any really serious attempt even to interest her, let alone win her heart, and when he realised this he felt ashamed of himself for making such a feeble fist of it.

Leaving before the second last race, he reckoned, gave him an outside chance of getting home before she left, but thanks to an accident on the motorway slip road his journey took him half an hour longer than usual and so he missed her.

'You haven't missed her by that much, Guv,' Teddy told him when he asked. 'She can't have left more than twenty minutes ago.'

Without stopping to think, Rory got back into his car at once and headed fast for the station. He didn't know what he was going to say to her, but since Salisbury was a good fifty minutes' drive away he reckoned he'd have time enough to come up with a good reason for asking her to change her mind – that is, if he managed to get there before her train left. Motoring faster than he had ever driven, he made it – by the time he had hurled himself out of the car and run into the station – with a minute to spare.

He saw her just about to get into the train and started to run along the platform waving frantically at her, hoping to catch her eye before it was too late, but she wasn't looking his way. She had turned away to embrace the man who had come to see her off, to throw her arms round his neck and lay her head on his shoulder. Rory recognised the man immediately and stopped dead in his tracks, about to turn tail and leave when she looked up and saw him. Rory froze, unable to move or think. They stared at each other and then after a moment Kathleen put up one hand and slowly waved to him over Blaze's shoulder. Absurdly enough, Rory found himself waving back.

As they watched each other without moving,

people arriving to catch the train at the last minute hurried down the platform, pushing their way through the throng and into the nearest available carriage, while Rory and Kathleen remained exactly where they were, until Blaze finally turned round and saw the man who was also his employer staring at the girl in his arms.

Finally, as the guard blew his whistle and the train prepared to leave the station, Rory began to walk towards Blaze and Kathleen, pointing at the train, which was now starting to move.

'You'll miss it!' he called, beginning to run. 'You'll miss your train!'

By the time he reached her the train was moving too fast for her to get on it – not that Kathleen showed the slightest intention of trying to do so. Instead she waited calmly for Rory to reach her.

'Your train,' he gasped. 'You've missed it.'

'So I have,' Kathleen said, looking round at the departing transport. 'I have so.'

'Well, now you'll m-miss everything!' Rory shouted over the increasing noise. 'You'll n-never catch your ferry now!'

'Ah no, she won't do that either,' Blaze agreed with a smile.

'I don't know what you're both looking so pleased about,' Rory yelled. 'I thought the whole intention was for K-K-Kathleen here to return h-h-home.'

'That was her intention, guv'nor, not mine,' Blaze assured him.

'No. No, it wouldn't be, would it?'

'No, it would not indeed. No, sir.'

'But even so,' Rory stuttered, turning his attention to Kathleen, who was still staring at him. 'I don't understand why y-you didn't get on the train.'

'Because I saw you, Mr Rawlins,' Kathleen said, as if it were obvious. 'When I saw you running on to the platform, sure I thought there must be something wrong back at the yard which would explain why you were here. What else was I to think now?'

'There's nothing wr-wrong,' Rory assured her through gritted teeth, realising that the whole thing had now gone seriously pear-shaped. 'At least not at the yard, there isn't.'

'So what is it, then?' Kathleen enquired earnestly, as Blaze picked up her bag and began to saunter back down the platform. 'Something must have happened to bring you here.'

'It's nothing,' Rory said in haste, turning his attention to Blaze. 'And where does he think he's going with your bags?'

'There's precious little point in staying here, boss!' Blaze called over his shoulder. 'The horse has long bolted.'

'So what was it, Mr Rawlins?' Kathleen enquired once more, catching up with Rory. 'What exactly's the matter?'

'There's nothing the m-matter, Kathleen,' Rory said slowly, trying to mind what he said, knowing Kathleen's propensity for taking things wrong.

'It's just—' He stopped to scratch his head. 'It's just – it's j-just – it's jer – *just* – it's just that I don't w-wan— I don't think you should go, that's all.'

'Why?' Kathleen wondered, shaking her head so that a thick lock of dark hair fell across her eyes. 'Why ever not?' she asked again, brushing the hair slowly aside and looking right at him. 'Is it something in particular? Or just nothing really at all? Just a whim?'

'It is *not* a wh-whim,' Rory said, almost crossly. 'I just don't happen to think you should go, that's all. That's all there is to it. All right?'

'Because?' Kathleen wondered, widening her eyes at him.

'Because – because of the horse, that's what!' Rory retorted. 'Because of the Gold Cup! You know he's running in the Gold Cup—'

'I didn't know for definite, Mr Rawlins.'

'Well he is. It's definite – and I'm s-sorry for shouting. It's just that I got a bit – I was a bit thrown when I realised you'd gone and that they want to run him definitely in the Gold Cup and so I thought if anyone should be there – that is, if anyone shouldn't be here – no, I mean if anyone *should* – if anyone should be here then that someone would be yer-yer-yer—' Rory came to a standstill, word-bound, staring back into the pair of green eyes that were staring so solemnly at him.

'Me?'

'Yes,' Rory said. 'You l-looked.' He smiled at her while frowning at the same time.

'OK,' Kathleen said, clasping her hands behind her and nodding. 'That seems only sensible. In that case, 'tis just as well I missed the train.'

'Yes,' Rory agreed, his frown deepening. ''Tis just as well you did.'

Shortly after teatime on the same day, Alice's telephone rang.

'Harry?' she said in wonder. 'This is a surprise.'

'I got your number from Rory,' Harry replied. 'I hope that was all right?'

'Well, of course,' Alice replied. 'And congratulations. I just watched your horse winning. Well done. He won jolly easily.'

'Thank you. I'd sort of hoped you might be there – except when I saw the runners, I thought no chance.'

'I think we're headed for Devon and Exeter next. And that'll probably be his last race.'

'I'm sorry?' Harry sounded startled. 'You don't mean for the season, surely?'

'Oh, no.' Alice laughed. 'No, of course not. I meant before Cheltenham.'

'You're really intending to run there, then?'

'It rather depends on how we do at Devon, I think. Why? Don't you think we should? You sounded doubtful.'

'My, Alice,' Harry replied, 'that really wouldn't be my place, and anyway it's absolutely not what I'm thinking. I think if you want to go run, so you should. Your horse has earned a place in the line-up, whatever they say.'

'You've heard, have you?' Alice asked. 'Even the other side of the pond, as you call it? A lot of the wiseacres are saying the race is no place for novices.'

'Don't listen to them. Listen to your trainer and to yourselves. He's your horse, and you run him where you like. It's a sport, not a religion.'

'Thank you, Harry. I shall treasure that advice. And what about you? Cheltenham or Aintree?'

'Tell you what,' Harry replied, 'why don't we discuss that over lunch? Or even dinner? I'm coming down to London tonight to stay for a couple of days. I would love it if you came out for a meal.'

'You would?' Alice was unable to stop the catch in her breath.

'I really would. But if it's too much of a slog, you know – for you to get up to town – I don't mind a day out in the country.'

'No, Harry.'

'Please don't say no, Alice.'

'No, Harry,' Alice assured him. 'I wasn't going to say no. At least not to you. I was about to say no don't worry about coming down here. I'd actually like a day in London. I have some things to do.'

'Lunch or dinner?'

'I think dinner.'

'Better by the minute. I'm staying at Claridges. Let's meet in the bar at around eight tomorrow, OK?'

'Of course. I shall be there.'

Before she left to go to London to meet Harry,

Alice wrote two brief but affectionate notes to both her children, enclosed the two vouchers that she had received that morning in the post and then drove into the village to send the letters recorded delivery. After that she drove to the station, parked her car and caught the train to Waterloo.

From Waterloo she took a taxi to Sloane Square, spent an hour shopping at Peter Jones, had her hair done, checked into a small hotel off Lower Sloane Street that offered special rates for country visitors, changed into her new clothes, then took a taxi to Mayfair, arriving at one minute to eight o'clock. Harry was waiting for her in the bar, dressed in an immaculate dark suit, handmade white shirt and dark red silk tie. He stood, took her hand as if to shake it, and then decided to kiss it instead.

'My. You look beautiful.'

'And you look very handsome.'

'A mutual admiration society it is, then.'

Offering her a chair, he asked her if champagne would be all right, and after Alice had accepted the offer he sat down opposite her, started to speak and promptly fell to silence. As they waited for their champagne to arrive, neither of them spoke. They just looked at each other and after a moment smiled. Finally Harry breathed in deeply, and shook his head slowly, while Alice smiled once more and putting her hands together leaned forward slightly to speak to him.

'Don't let's waste time at our age, Harry,' she

said. 'I think I feel exactly the way you do.'

'You do?' Harry's eyes widened. 'You really think so?'

'Absolutely,' Alice replied with a nod of her head. 'And if I'm right, if that's the case, we don't have to say another thing. All we have to do is enjoy ourselves.'

Which is exactly what they both did, and after a fine dinner and long and wonderful conversation, rather than take a taxi Alice and Harry decided to take a walk on what was a fine, albeit frosty, winter night, the two of them strolling arm in arm out into Park Lane, down round Hyde Park Corner and into the Brompton Road, stopping now and then to look into the brightly lit shop windows in Knightsbridge, before cutting down the side of Harrods to Alice's small hotel, where Harry wished her a very good night, kissed her once, but only briefly, and then with a wave of his hand walked all the way back to his own hotel.

When they all arrived at Devon and Exeter race-course, set high on Haldon Hill, the rumours were of abandonment, so heavy was the mist that enveloped the track.

'It's always like this,' Rory said, taking them all to the bar. 'Nearly always. This course is famous for its mists and fogs, as well as for being the longest oval track in the country.'

'I don't understand, Rory,' Alice said. 'How can one track be longer than the others when the races are the same length – no, I see what you mean.' She laughed. 'You mean longest all the way round.'

'With most other tracks – well, all other tracks really –' Rory replied, 'for a three-mile chase you have to go round at least twice, sometimes near enough three times. But here – if you look at your racecard, the three-mile chase starts here . . .' Rory pointed out the spot on a map on the card. 'The circuit being two miles, you just go round one and a half times, and although it looks flat there's quite a steep pull up the back straight, which at the moment you can't see at all, so it calls for not only speed but stamina.'

Half an hour later a breeze got up and began to shift the fret that had all but obliterated the course, and after a further short delay it was announced that racing would go ahead.

By the time they got to the three-mile chase in which The Enchanted was running, the mist had thickened again, making it once more impossible to make out what was happening on the far side of the course. Even so, the runners went to post, with The Enchanted second favourite at five to two, the market leader being another of the season's most promising novices, an athletic-looking grey called Mossman, from the same yard as County Gent. Once off, and past the stands for the first time, the field of ten runners disappeared into the mist, the commentary petered out, and nothing more was heard or seen of the action until the horses reappeared coming off the bend on the home turn to head for the two fences in the straight.

There were three horses in a line, well clear of the rest of the field, which remained invisible, but at first the race reader was unable to call them with any certainty, finally naming them as Mossman, Pondarosa and Penny Off.

'Where's Boyo?' Lynne cried, turning to Grenville. 'Where's our horse gone?'

'What do you mean?' Alice cried from behind Rory's back, where, as usual, she was hiding. 'What do you mean, where is he?'

'Something must have happened out in the country,' Grenville said, adjusting his race glasses in an attempt to get a better and more focused view. 'Except – wait a minute . . .'

'And as they land after the second last it's still Mossman in the lead, but only just, and now with Pondarosa beaten and dropping back it's Penny Off who's laying down the challenge – except . . .'

'Except that isn't Penny Off,' Grenville cried.

'Except it isn't Penny Off!' the commentator agreed. 'My mistake – it's The Enchanted!'

'It's Boyo!' Lynne cried joyfully. 'Come on, Boyo! Come on, our little horse!'

'Yes, it's not Penny Off, it's The Enchanted who's now laying down a serious challenge to the favourite – and on the run to the last there's nothing in it between Mossman and The Enchanted – whose rider Blaze Molloy appears still to have a double handful—'

'Come on, Boyo!' Alice yelled from behind Rory.

'Come on, The Enchanted!' Grenville shouted. 'Come on, Boyo! Go for it!'

'And as they jump the last it's the two market leaders neck and neck,' the commentator called. 'But as they land Mossman pecks, but it's too late anyway because The Enchanted has landed flying – and as they run from the fence The Enchanted has already opened up a two-length lead . . .'

'Come on, Boyo!' his owners shouted, Lynne jumping up and down as always, and Alice now daring to peep out from her hiding place. 'Come on, the little horse!'

'It's OK,' Rory managed to say, the first words he had spoken since the horses had disappeared into the fog. 'He's home and hosed.'

'And it's The Enchanted who is first past the post,' the commentator announced, 'by what looks like a good five or maybe six lengths, with a very tired Mossman just hanging on to second from what looks like an equally exhausted Penny Off.'

'First number five, The Enchanted,' came the official announcement. 'Second number three, Mossman, and third number four, Penny Off.'

'If you want to know, guv'nor,' Blaze said after he had hopped off the horse in the winners' enclosure, 'don't ask me, because you weren't the only ones who couldn't see a thing.' Blaze looked round him in case the journalists had arrived yet, but seeing they were still alone except for the owners the jockey dropped his voice and continued, 'We'd have won by a street if we hadn't been all but knocked out of it – four from home, I reckon it was. Don't ask me which horse it was either, because I hardly saw it, but Jeeze – it barged right into us and oh so nearly carried us out. I had to take a huge hook, but this little horse is something else. We were into the bottom of the fence but he still managed to pick up and jump it – no, fly it. But whichever horse it was took two others out, and one of them had the unholiest of falls. I hope to God he's all right.'

With a tip to his cap Blaze was gone to weigh in, the thanks of the owners ringing in his ears.

'Wonder which horse it was? I didn't see the Rampton horse come in. But then we're never going to be any the wiser, since nobody could possibly have seen anything that happened in the back straight any-old-how.'

'There's a horse coming back now,' Grenville pointed out. 'Someone caught him over there. By the last fence.'

They all watched through their binoculars as the loose horse was brought in, minus its saddle but otherwise seemingly unharmed, unlike, they soon discovered, its trainer, none other than Eddie Rampton, who had all but broken a blood vessel himself in his rage.

'You!' he yelled, stomping across the paddock with a thick finger pointed at Rory. 'You. Rawlins or whatever your name is!'

'Sorry? Are you talking to me, Mr Rampton?' Rory wondered, pulling a help-me face.

'What the hell do you think you're playing at?'

Rampton continued, pushing Grenville, who had stepped in front of Rory, out of his way. 'Or rather what does that idiot of a boy you allow to ride your horses think he's playing at? Eh?'

'Matter of fact your guess is as good as mine, Mr Rampton,' Rory replied, retreating from the thick finger that was attempting to stab him in the chest. 'Or rather it's probably a lot more creative.'

'Don't you get fancy with me, Rawlins,' Rampton warned him. 'Your boy apprentice rode my horse off out there! I've just heard it all from my jock!'

'Ah yes, Kevin Billings, right?' Rory asked, consulting his card with a studied frown. 'Yes, I gather he always has a tale to tell.'

'I said don't get fancy with me, d'you hear?' Rampton roared, attracting the attention of several racegoers. 'Your blasted learner jockey – for want of a better word – rode my horse off! Cut right across him five from home and ran my horse out! And I'll tell you something else, shall I? We were cantering all over your stupid little horse! And furthermore it wouldn't surprise me in the least if he and his idiot pilot missed out a couple in the back straight!'

'Careful what you say, Mr Rampton,' Grenville said, in his gravest voice. 'I happen to be a lawyer.'

Eddie Rampton spun round and stared at him, his mouth opening and closing like an oversize carp's at feeding time.

'We'll soon see about that.'

'Yes, we no doubt will,' Grenville replied. 'Whatever that may mean.'

'I'm off to see the stewards,' Rampton shouted. 'I am off to lodge a formal complaint! You just wait, Rawlins! You haven't heard the last of this yet!'

'I have a feeling we might have,' Rory turned to his startled owners. 'The patrol cameras out there won't have been able to pick up much, you see, but if they have, I bet they'll find we're completely in the clear. And if they haven't been able to pick anything up then old Eddie won't have a leg to stand on.'

'Thank heavens he didn't shout like that at me,' Constance sighed from under her large hat. 'I might have been forced to teach him a lesson.'

In the event, the stewards threw out Eddie Rampton's complaint without even calling in any jockeys, since the far-seeing senior steward had positioned several of his staff at all the fences in the back straight to keep an eye on things in view of the lack of visibility and two of them had already reported an incident at the fifth fence from home where it appeared the horse trained by Eddie Rampton and ridden by Kevin Billings had been seen to dive and cut across the horse on its outside, the horse believed to be The Enchanted. The only thing the witnesses had to add to their official report was a commendation to the young jockey riding The Enchanted for managing his horse so well at the fence in question that an accident had unquestionably been avoided.

'Don't think you've heard the last of this, Rawlins,' a furious Eddie Rampton warned Rory later in the car park when he passed him.

'On the contrary, Mr Rampton,' Grenville replied, stepping in front of Rory. 'If you do not desist, you can expect a formal letter of complaint from my client. I hope that is understood. Good afternoon to you.'

'Don't you just love that? "Good afternoon, to you!"' Lynne laughed, catching at Grenville's arm. 'Talk about old-fashioned cool.'

The call Alice had been expecting came that evening when she got back from the races.

'Mum?' Georgina said down the telephone. 'Mum – please – *what* is this?'

'What is what, dear?' Alice enquired. 'I can't see down the telephone.'

'This – this *thing* that's arrived in the post. From some bookmaker or other. I don't want to open a bookmaker's account, thank you.'

'It isn't a bookmaker's account, Georgie. If you look properly—'

'Mum?' Georgina interrupted. 'There is this thing that says quite clearly on the top the name of a well-known bookmaker. OK?'

'Yes. And what else does it say?'

'I really don't know. I have only just got in from a seriously exhausting day – I've got Will in bed with a sore throat and I think Finty is now sickening for it, Joe has got problems at work, and I come home and find this. This bookmaker's thing.'

'Your tone seems to have changed, Georgie.' Alice smiled to herself. 'Have you noticed something?'

'I don't understand, Mum,' Georgina returned, her tone indeed changed. 'It seems to be some sort of betting slip. For rather a lot of money.'

'That's exactly what it is, darling.'

'Why? What's this about? Do you want us to hang on to this for you for safe keeping or something?'

'Why don't you just read the note I wrote? In fact if you'd read the note first instead of just grabbing the telephone . . .'

'Mum?' All at once her daughter sounded just how she used to sound, before she had decided life was turning against her. 'Mum, I really don't understand. This is for a thousand pounds.'

'No, it's not, not really,' Alice explained. 'It's not worth a thing, unless the horse wins, which probably won't happen. It's what's called an ante-post voucher.'

'For a thousand pounds?'

'Yes,' was all Alice could think of to say. She had been about to go into a long explanation of the whys and wherefores, but had quickly thought better of it. The deed had been done and now everyone concerned just had to go along with it.

'I still don't understand, Mum.' The edge was beginning to creep back into Georgina's voice, and, hearing it, Alice took a long, steady and deep breath. 'No, OK, I think I do. You have bet a thousand pounds on your horse? A *thousand pounds*?'

'Georgina darling, it is my money. And yes, I have bet a thousand pounds on our horse.'

'And you want me to have the voucher – for safe keeping.'

'No, you silly daft girl!' Alice found herself suddenly laughing at the ludicrousness of the situation. Here she was having given her daughter the chance – albeit an outside one – of making a lot of money without raising a finger, and here was her daughter criticising her for it. 'No, I want you to have the voucher! It's for you – for what you're always so worried about. School fees. But look, if you don't want it—'

'No, hang on.' Georgina stopped her. 'It says here – it says one thousand pounds bet at odds of one hundred and fifty to one.'

'Sounds about right.'

'So if the horse won—'

'If,' Alice interrupted. 'And you must understand it's a very big *if* we're talking about here. That's why the odds are so very long, apparently. Anyway, the point is I haven't got enough money to give you anywhere near the amount you say you need to educate your children – my grandchildren – but this at least gives you an outside chance. And before you say anything else I've done exactly the same for your brother. For Christian. Not for school fees, obviously, but to help him out. But you're not to tell anybody. Not a soul. It's bad luck, right? And chances of its happening are not only extremely slim but probably non-existent. Anyway.'

'Mum?'

'Yes?' Alice asked carefully, wondering what the objection might be this time.

'Mum, I really don't know what to say,' Georgina said, her voice dropping almost to a whisper. 'Except – except sorry.'

'Sorry? What on earth for, Georgie darling?'

'For being such an A1 prat.'

'You have been nothing of the sort. Nonsense. Now all we have to do is hope he runs. And if he does run, I understand he won't start at anything like that price. I'll keep you posted.'

'You'd jolly well better, Mum. And Mum?'

'Georgie?'

'Love you.'

'I know, darling. The feeling is entirely reciprocated. 'Bye, darling.'

Dear old Mum, Georgina thought to herself as she put down the telephone. *Still can't say it. Oh well . . .*

While as she was putting down the phone her end Alice was thinking *And now all we can do is get out the prayer mats, light the votive candles, keep everything crossed and not walk under any ladders. In other words, just hope and pray the little horse stays in one piece and gets to the races.*

*   *   *

513

Different hopes and desires entirely were entertained by a certain other person who, as Alice was busy praying and hoping, was equally busy scheming and plotting, trying to imagine every single possible way she could thwart the aspirations of all her rivals, real and imagined.

Chapter Twenty-four

Creeping Murmur and the
Poring Dark

It was Kathleen who saved the day.

With the big race now only a week away and the owners in full agreement about running The Enchanted and the horse going from strength to strength in his work, the security blanket round Fulford Farm was pulled even tighter than before, particularly after a couple of alarms and excursions when both Teddy and Kathleen had sworn they had heard the sound of would-be intruders late at night when they were on watch. Dunkum gave chase on both occasions, only for the prowlers to escape over the perimeter fencing. Kathleen then came up with a plan with which Rory immediately agreed and put in motion at once.

The horse was due to have only one more piece of fast work before the big day so what was proposed was eminently feasible, relying only on the discretion of the staff at Fulford Farm and the assistance of Rory's friend Henry Carmichael, a keen horseman who trained his point to pointers and hunter chasers from a yard on a farm less than five miles away. Oddly enough, despite its risks, the very simplicity of the plan was its strength.

'I thought we were going to have to hire some muscle, p-p-perhaps,' Rory told Kathleen the first night the plan was put into effect, when he came down at midnight to take over her watch. 'Yet here we are, quiet and safe as can be, and it's all really th-thanks to you.'

'Not a bit of it,' Kathleen replied, getting up from her seat at Rory's desk from where she had been keeping an eagle eye on the yard and on the all-important stable directly in front of her. 'Anyway – your shift.'

'My shift,' Rory agreed. 'Ab-ab-absolutely.'

'Might I ask you something now?' Kathleen enquired. 'Without upsetting you, that is.'

'From what I know of life, when a w-woman asks you that sort of question – you know – ther-ther-the would-you-mind-if-I sort of question – they're going to anyhow. So yes – f-f-fire ahead.'

'It's just I was wondering,' Kathleen said, hesitating by the door. 'I was just wondering if I – do I make you nervous?'

'N-n-nervous?' Rory returned, doing his best to laugh lightly. 'Y-you? M-make me nervous? Why on earth – wh-what on earth would make you ther-ther-ther-*think* ther-that? H-heavens above.'

'It's just that I couldn't help noticing you only seem to have trouble when I'm around,' Kathleen persisted. 'You know – you don't seem to stammer so much with other people. If at all. Not as much as you do when I'm around.'

'I don't know what you m-mean,' Rory lied, pinching the fleshy part of one of his thumbs between thumb and index fingernails to try to control his speech. 'I don't know what you're talking about, actually.'

'That's all right then,' Kathleen said with a polite smile. 'I best be getting along now.'

'Did you see the l-latest ratings?' Rory said, calling her back with a wave of a sheet of print. 'They arrived this morning.' Unable to resist getting an update, Kathleen came back and stood just behind Rory's shoulder while he pored over the figures. 'Better than you might think,' Rory continued, glad of her return. 'They put County Gent top obviously, with a rating of 156, but our horse has gone right up and n-now they rate him 132. With a plus mark, d-denoting his improvement.'

'If racing were all done be ratings, Mr Rawlins—'

'Yes I know, Kathleen,' Rory interrupted her, turning round and finding her face considerably closer to his than he had been expecting, a sight that stopped him midstream. He swallowed hard and frowned at her.

'Yes? Something the matter?'

'Yes – no. No,' Rory corrected himself again. 'Form also notices his jumping, is what I was about to say. They make special – you know. They remark on his j-jumping.'

'And so they should, too,' Kathleen replied, now standing away from Rory. 'He's more than earned the right to be in the line-up. None of the others jump like him.'

'You're not alone in th-thinking that,' Rory added. 'There's been money for him.'

'That wouldn't surprise me a bit, Mr Rawlins.'

'The first shows had him at a hundred and fifty to one, if you remember. He's now a sixty-six to one chance, which one would h-have to say – ther-ther-that's quite a reduction.'

'He won't start at that on the day either, you can be sure of that,' Kathleen said, with a stretch and a yawn. 'I'd say you won't be able to get better than twenties on him for a starting price.'

'Who am I to argue with the Oracle of Cronagh?' Rory replied. 'Anyway – th-thanks. I'll take over now.'

'Have you had a stammer all your life?' Kathleen asked out of the air. 'If you don't mind my asking, that is.'

'I thought the Irish axed rather than asked,' Rory replied, trying to work around the question.

'Have you?'

Rory drummed his fingers lightly on the desk as he tried to prepare his answer. No one had ever asked him directly about his stammer, no one except his therapist, the woman who had taught him the coping mechanisms that had gradually fallen out of use as his control had increased, to the point where he had thought he was completely cured – until Kathleen came into his life.

She put a hand on his shoulder, making him start. 'That was very tactless of me. I'm sorry.'

'It wasn't at all tactless, as it happens, Kathleen,' Rory said, sitting back in his chair and closing his eyes while Kathleen's hand remained still on his shoulder. It took all his emotional strength not to reach up and hold it in return. 'Actually I wish more people had asked rather than pretend it wasn't happening. Might have helped me cope with it better. I haven't stammered for years, not really. Not since I played Henry the Fifth – at school, of course. Of all things – I mean, I was still stammering fit to bust then – but I had this great English teacher who'd sussed that I hardly stuttered at all when I was reading and took this huge risk of getting me to play Henry Five.'

'End of stammer, was it? Being onstage? I'd have thought that would have made it worse.'

'Yes,' Rory agreed. 'Me too. But it didn't, believe it or not. Soon as I started being someone else, that was it.'

'And after the play was over?'

'Yes – well, it came a bit, but not nearly so badly. Course, when my therapist heard – and saw – when she realised this could be a key she changed her treatment and besides giving me key words and finger clicks and all that, she suggested that

519

when I hit a bad patch I pretended to be someone else. Sounds a bit facile, but it worked.'

'So why do you think you—' Kathleen began, then stopped.

'Go on,' Rory said.

'It's none of my business.'

'I think it is actually, Kathleen.'

'Not a bit of it,' Kathleen said crisply. 'Now I must to bed – leave you in peace.'

'Kathleen—'

'If I'm to be of any use in the morning, which it is now, I have to get some sleep,' she insisted. 'Now if you're OK? I rather enjoy this, don't you? Sitting up on watch.'

'Yes, I do actually,' Rory agreed. 'As it happens it always makes me think of the play – of *Henry the Fifth*. It's a bit like the night before Agincourt. *Now entertain conjecture of a time when creeping murmur and the poring dark fills the wide vessel of the universe. From camp to camp, through the foul womb of night, the hum of either army stilly sounds, that the fix'd sentinels almost receive the secret whispers of each other's watch.*'

'What was that?' Kathleen suddenly asked, looking out of the window in front of them. 'Didn't I hear something just then? I could swear I did.'

Rory was on his feet and at the office door. Whistling for Dunkum, he picked up the heavy knobkerrie he kept in his office as a precaution and went out into the yard. With one hand on his dog's collar and his stick in the other, and

520

Kathleen carrying a searchlight torch, the two of them made a tour of inspection, but found nothing amiss. All the horses were either fast asleep or idly munching at their hay, while all the gates and doors were shut and locked. Happy there had been no intrusion, Kathleen finally took herself off to her bed, leaving Rory to settle down in his office to his own spell of duty.

Rather than read, Rory sat and drew, something that allowed him to keep an ear out and also helped him keep his eyes open. The first night watch he had ended up reading, only finally to fall fast asleep, so he decided he would use the time instead to do some sketching. He had started a series of horse studies and the concentration needed to work on these kept the adrenalin flowing enough for him to stay on full alert. Two hours later, when it was time for Teddy to come and take over, Rory had no idea of where the time had gone.

Each night up to the eve of the race the procedure was the same, and each night – nothing. Two nights before the big day, however, when Rory came down to take over from Kathleen he found her closely studying the sketchbooks he had left on his desk.

'I take it these are yours?' she asked, apparently unashamed to have been caught in the act. 'They're wonderful. Really. I hope you don't mind – I'm a dreadful snooper.'

'It'd be a bit late if I did,' Rory replied. 'Mind, that is. Of course I don't. Mind that is.'

521

'They are wonderful,' Kathleen said once more. 'They are really beautiful.'

'They're only sketches,' Rory insisted, suddenly feeling shy. 'It's only work in progress, as they say. Which is a terrible expression. Sounds as if you're digging a road up.'

'You have an amazing talent,' Kathleen said, taking no notice of his protestations. 'And surely isn't this something you should be doing seriously?'

'You mean rather than falling about laughing?'

'I mean seriously,' Kathleen chided him. 'You know what I mean. People who can draw like this—'

'It's nothing,' Rory said, wanting to dismiss the subject, and trying to close the sketchbook. 'It's just something I do.'

'This isn't something anyone just does. This is a gift.'

Kathleen looked round at him with something in her eyes Rory didn't think he'd ever seen before. Then she returned her attention to the next and largest sketchbook, opening it carefully at the page on which Rory had last been working.

'Look at this now,' she said. 'This one of Boyo. It catches everything about him, including—' She stopped, and frowned.

'Including? What? Yes? Including what?'

'The special thing he has,' Kathleen said slowly and quietly. 'His magic.'

'Do you really like it?'

'Like it? This is just brilliant.'

'OK,' Rory decided. 'Then it's yours.'

He took a small penknife from the desk and carefully cut the drawing out of the sketchbook.

'No,' Kathleen protested. 'No, please. Please. What are you doing?'

'I want you to have it.'

'I couldn't. I couldn't take it – I simply couldn't.'

'If you don't . . .' Rory said, holding the drawing up. 'If you don't . . .' He moved as if to tear it in two.

'Are you crazy?' Kathleen said, grabbing hold of his hands to stop him. As she held them in hers, they both fell silent and looked at each other. This time Kathleen was the first to drop her eyes.

'Good,' Rory said finally, setting the drawing down and covering it with a sheet of tissue paper. 'It isn't fixed. I'll do that in the morning.'

'Fixed?'

'Stuff you spray on to stop smudging. A fixative.'

'I don't think you should give this to me at all,' Kathleen muttered behind his back as he finished covering the drawing. 'I really don't.'

'Why not?' Rory shook his head in bewilderment. 'I want you to have it. Because of the horse. Because of everything you've done here with him. Because I just – look, I just want you to have it. Knowing that you have it, that you love it – well.' Rory stopped and swallowed. 'That's great.'

'Rory?' Kathleen said after a moment.

'Rory?' Rory repeated, genuinely astonished. 'I can't have heard right.'

'The thing is, Rory,' Kathleen began, lowering her eyes. 'I really don't feel right – not you giving me this, but me taking it. I really don't.'

'Because?'

'I'd rather not say.'

'Oh, and why would that be?' Rory wondered with an exaggerated sigh. 'Let me guess. Could this be something to do with Blaze Molloy, I wonder?'

'Well – yes. Yes and no. Both really. Yes and no.'

'What a surprise,' Rory said, giving his head a quick scratch. 'Well, it doesn't matter. I'm not taking the drawing back. I still want you to have it – in spite of Mr Blaze Molloy.'

'In spite of—'

'Yes. In spite of. In spite of Mr Blazes Molloy.'

'Oh, I see. Of course.' Kathleen sighed all of a sudden. 'What an idiot. *What* a total idiot.'

'Who – me?'

'No, you fool – me!' Kathleen returned, her eyes flashing. 'Why didn't I see? Of course there was you thinking—'

'What am I meant to think?' Rory demanded. 'Every time I look he has his arm round you, or you're holding hands – or you're in his arms at the railway station, or you're . . . oh, I don't know – so I really don't see what else I'm meant to think.'

'But it isn't like that, Rory,' Kathleen assured him. 'I know that's what it must look like—'

'That's exactly what it looks like.'

'OK,' Kathleen said, changing her tone. 'So suppose it did. So what? I mean, so why should it matter? Why should it matter to you?'

Rory said nothing. He just stood looking at her, scratching the side of his head.

'Rory?'

'Did I say it mattered?' he asked all but inaudibly.

'You started pulling it-matters faces as soon as you mentioned Blaze. *Oh, I suppose this is all to do with Mr Blaze Molloy.* Remember?'

'So?' Rory shrugged, feeling the rug being pulled slowly but surely from under his feet.

'And you know something else?' Kathleen started to smile. 'You haven't stammered or stuttered for a while. Not since you got all hot under the collar about you-know-who.'

'Of course I have,' Rory protested. 'Don't be silly. Of course I – I must have done.'

'Well, you haven't so.'

'Look – Kathleen,' Rory began again, wondering how best to regain the lost ground. 'What you feel about Blaze really – it's really no skin off my nose.'

'I've never known what that meant exactly.'

'Does it matter? Anyway, it isn't – whatever it may mean. Whatever you and Blaze are – whatever you feel about each other—'

'Blaze is my half-brother,' Kathleen interrupted quietly, putting a hand on his. 'I know. I should have told you—'

525

'Your half-brother?'

'Yes, my half-brother – and yes, I told him to come over. I lied to you, and God forgive me for it, but I only did it for the best.'

'The best being? Not that I mind,' Rory added hastily. 'I don't mind if you lied. Not that sort of lie. I really don't. Your half-brother? Can I ask how come?'

'After my mother died, and not that long after – because my dad went completely to pieces and people do the strangest things when they're like that, you know – when they're deep in their grief. Anyway, the long and short of it is, he and this woman . . . Da had a child be her, and of course he couldn't – not that he would have anyway – he couldn't marry her because of the way he is and the way my mother and he were . . . and the result was Blaze. Blaze grew up in a village not far away with this woman and her brother, and everyone thought they were man and wife, but that was only because they pretended to be, for Blaze. Then one day Da told me. He said you have another brother, or should we say half-brother, and it was Blaze. And young Blaze be then was making a bit of a name for himself – even though he was still a nipper – pony racing. On the strands. He went on doing just that for a while, then he started riding points – then he came over here.'

'At your instigation.'

'I admit that quite readily. Yes.'

'So why didn't you say? Why the need for subterfuge?'

'Now we didn't know how you'd take it,' Kathleen argued. 'How could we? I'd been as bold as brass anyway, the way I came here, the way I just elbowed me way in. So can you imagine? Imagine if I said *Oh and by the way, here's a relative of mine. I want him riding for you as well.* No, I don't think so, Rory. I don't think that would have been the best way at all.'

'So you pretended he was your boyfriend instead.'

'I never did! Didn't I say we'd never met before?'

'And weren't you off with him the very next minute? Do you think I never smelt the tiniest bit of rat there?'

'I'm devoted to Blaze,' Kathleen said quietly. 'He's a very special boy.'

'He's certainly a very talented one.'

'Anyway. Enough of that,' Kathleen decided. 'As I said earlier, what's the fuss? Why should it matter?'

'Oh, because it does,' Rory groaned. 'Because it does matter. What do you think? Why do you think it matters? Of course it matters.'

'I can't imagine why it should.'

'Are you fishing? Because of course that's something else the Irish are dab hands at.'

'Fishing for what, pray?'

'Fishing to find out why it matters!' Rory mock-glared at her, then groaned again. 'Why do you think it matters? One person being – well. One person minding that another person seems

527

to be – seems to be – well. Attached to another person.'

'You were . . . jealous?' Kathleen finally asked, visibly amazed. 'You?'

'Yes,' Rory insisted. 'Yes, all right. Yes I was jealous. Does that surprise you?'

'Yes.'

'Yes?'

'Yes.'

'Why should it surprise you? You're surprised that I – that I was jealous about you and Blaze?'

'Yes.'

'Why?'

Dumbfounded, for once Kathleen found herself all but speechless.

'Kathleen?' Rory prompted her.

'Because never for one moment did I imagine that someone like you could possibly be in the slightest bit interested in someone like me, that's why,' she finally replied in a near whisper. 'That's why.'

'Someone like me?'

'Yes! And do stop repeating everything I say! Yes, someone like you!'

Rory stared at her. 'I don't know what someone like me seems like. Not to someone like you.'

'Different. Rich. Sophisticated. Successful. And now, as we gather, a brilliant artist.'

'While you, of course – and by the way you can forget the rich bit – in fact you can forget all the other bits too because it's complete nonsense, your assessment of me – particularly when compared to you.'

'Me as?'

'Well,' Rory said, shrugging hopelessly. 'You as in by far and away the most beautiful girl I have ever seen—'

'Me?'

'Don't start that. You're doing it again. Yes, you. You are . . . you are beautiful. In fact I would go so far as to say ravishingly – no, that's a terrible word. What's wrong with just beautiful? You are the most beautiful girl I have ever seen, as well as the liveliest, the most warm-hearted and just about the sweetest and funniest—'

'Funny? I'm not at all funny.'

'Ah, but you agree with the rest of it, right?' Rory teased her.

'I most certainly do not. It's a load of cod.'

'No, it is not. You're all of those things and more – and you're a brilliant horsewoman as well as everything else.'

Kathleen just looked at him, at an utter loss for words.

'And do you want to know something else, Kathleen Flanagan?'

'If it's worth hearing,' Kathleen replied, tongue in cheek, 'then certainly.'

'I'm very glad you didn't get on that train,' Rory said. 'I really am.'

'And do you want to hear something as well, Rory Rawlins?' she asked in return.

'If it's worth hearing, then certainly.'

'I'm very glad I didn't get on that train as well,' Kathleen said. 'Sure as eggs.'

But all the time they were beginning to declare their true feelings for each other, and explore their hopes for the future, in the yard outside – so very close to where they were standing – there were others who knew exactly what they hoped for the future and were in the process of making sure it happened.

It wasn't until the next morning that everyone found out how close they had been to disaster. No one knew when it had happened exactly, nor at first did anyone know how. Teddy was the first to blame himself, but it was no fault of his. He was just finishing his watch, dawn was breaking, and even though it had been yet another quiet night he thought he would check all the boxes once more before the stable woke up and clicked into its normal routine.

As always Teddy went straight to Boyo's box. This morning he found the horse standing on three legs. Initially he thought the animal was still half asleep and only resting a leg, until he picked up the limb in question, looked at the hoof and found a rusty two-inch nail driven into the sole of the horse's foot.

'Mother of God,' Kathleen sighed when she arrived and saw the damage. 'He never stepped on that, so he didn't. As sure as anything that nail was driven in.'

'And no one heard anything,' Rory repeated,

just in case any of his team had overlooked or forgotten anything. 'No one dropped off, or went to spend a penny or anything? So they could have missed something?'

But no one had, and Teddy insisted on blaming himself because according to both Rory and Kathleen, when they had checked the horses at the end of their respective watches, all were apparently sound and healthy.

'But whoever it was would have had to get through the stable door, which is right slap bang in front of the office window,' Rory said. 'Yet nobody saw or heard anything.'

'Boss?' Teddy called from the back of the stable. 'Look.' He pointed up to the roof above him. 'That's how they got in. They lifted the sheeting on the back of the roof. They must have climbed across the other stable roofs and dropped down into this one.'

'OK,' Rory said, having eased the nail out of the horse's hoof as carefully as he could. 'I'm going to call the vet, and Kathleen's going to poultice this hoof, and we're all going to thank our stars and Kathleen here that it wasn't Boyo's hoof they nailed, but dear old Flibberty Gibbet's.'

He shook his head and went off to telephone for the vet.

It had been as easy as that.

After the first suspicion that they were going to attract the wrong kind of attention from intruders, Kathleen had suggested stabling Boyo somewhere anonymous, which was where Rory's friend and neighbour Henry Carmichael had come in. Henry rented Fulford Farm gallops, so the morning after their first nocturnal alarm, once Boyo had finished his piece of work, Rory and Kathleen boxed him up in Henry's horsebox and Henry took him down to his own modest yard, along with the couple of hunter chasers he had been exercising.

Since it was a matter of only a few miles away, Kathleen could easily commute between the two yards to feed, look after and ride the horse in his road work which, aside from one last long easy canter before the race, was all that was planned.

And no one suspected a thing.

The only ongoing argument that still remained unsolved was who was to ride the horse in the race, the diehards insisting that the best and most experienced jockey should be put up, while the owners lobbied insistently for their own so far faultless rider. Rory, who was still keen to listen to both sides, once again consulted his father.

'Look, Rory, this is a case for common sense. If you could utilise the boy's weight claim then I could see why you would still be considering it, but since that doesn't come into the equation, what's the point in risking using someone who after all is nothing more than an apprentice? He's ridden once round Cheltenham in a hunter chase, which to my mind is not enough. Nor is it the same thing as the hottest Group One race in the calendar, and you know as well as I do that Cheltenham takes all the riding there is, and then some more. You have the breakneck pace of the race to contend with, you have to be able to deal with the tactics of the best and the toughest jockeys in the land, you have to be able to handle that terrible downhill run, keeping your horse balanced at all times so he doesn't take those two fences by their roots, and then you have to know how to ride a finish up that heartbreaking final hill. Now if you think young Molloy is up to that, fine, but if I were you – and the boy will understand it, sooner or later – you'll offer one of the top lads the mount. I see there are quite a few without rides still, and if I really was you, old boy—'

'Which at this very moment you are.'

'—I'd offer the ride to Richard Durden. His intended has just been withdrawn with a leg.'

'I already did, Dad.'

'And what did he say?'

'He said he wanted to sit on him first.'

Since Rory had given the horse his last piece of fast work at the weekend, before this final argument had really come to a head, all he could offer Richard Durden was the chance to ride the horse in an exercise canter. However since Boyo was the type of horse who told you as soon as you sat on him exactly what you had in your hands and under you, Rory was confident that a horseman as skilled and as experienced as Durden would be happy enough just to work the horse at half-speed. Boyo had other ideas.

533

As soon as he was saddled up and brought out of his box it seemed he knew something was afoot, and laying his ears flat he began to swish his tail ominously. Having walked round the horse a couple of times to get his measure, Richard Durden then asked for a leg up from Rory, and as soon as he was in the saddle he was out of it again, decanted summarily.

Kathleen got a firm hold of the horse's bridle and they tried again. They tried twice more, but Boyo was having none of it.

'Bad-tempered bugger, isn't he?' Durden said, dusting himself down grimly. 'Well, we'll have to show him who's boss then.'

And he promptly vaulted up unaided on to the horse and raised his whip, but it got no further than shoulder height before Boyo bucked him off again, this time so hard that the jockey was flung far further, into the muck heap.

'This horse got a cold back or something? Or is he just some sort of nutcase?'

'There's really nothing the matter with the horse, Mr Durden,' Kathleen informed him.

'Then let's see you sit him,' the jockey said, handing Kathleen the reins.

'Sure thing,' Kathleen said, and vaulted up herself. As soon as he saw who was about to mount him, Boyo had pricked his ears and stopped swishing his tail.

'Fine,' Durden said, staring. 'Obviously a cold back.'

Next time Rory tried to leg Durden into the

534

plate, the horse simply stepped smartly away and swung himself round, leaving his would-be rider with nowhere to go but the ground.

'Thank you,' Durden said, picking himself up for the last time. 'I hope you all enjoyed that. I'd say this horse is unfit for anything except a tin.'

'You got a fan there all right, Guv,' Kathleen laughed as they watched the stained and furious figure disappearing into his car and driving off. 'He'll ride for you any time.'

'I think that certainly answers the question as to who's going to be riding. By the time this gets round the weighing room there won't be a fee big enough to tempt anyone. Anyone good, that is.'

The decision reached, Blaze was informed he had the ride. There was a long silence at the other end of the telephone, broken finally by a quiet voice in Rory's ear.

'You'll not regret it, boss,' he said. 'God bless you.'

Everything was set fair until the next morning, when they all woke up and found everything outside once more frozen hard.

535

Chapter Twenty-five

Come the Hour

The freeze continued into the weekend, giving
the racing Jeremiahs endless pleasure as they all
prophesied the cancellation of the great National
Hunt meeting scheduled to open on the Tuesday,
and when by Monday morning the course was
still frozen there was every indication that at
the very best they would have to forfeit the
opening day and hope to fit in and run all the
cancelled races on the next two days, weather
permitting.

But then, shortly after seven thirty that very
morning, it being the fickle and changeable month
of March, the temperature suddenly rose and the
heavens opened, deluging the whole of the south
of England in thunderous showers followed by an
afternoon of strong wind and spasmodic March
sunshine. By eight o'clock that evening, Edwin
Armstrong, the diligent and urbane clerk of the
course, announced that subject to a 6.30 a.m.

inspection the following morning the meeting would go ahead, and with Tuesday dawning dry, bright and blustery every road to Cheltenham was choked with traffic and every train headed west was packed with punters.

With no other runners at the meeting, Rory and his staff stayed at Fulford Farm for both the Tuesday and the Wednesday, not taking their eye off the ball for a moment. The little horse was still at Henry Carmichael's, eating and looking as well as ever, and yet in spite of a total shut-down on any information coming from the stables, a rumour – among many rumours that week – began to circulate that The Enchanted had met with a setback. His price began to drift, the ante-post market showing twenty-five to one across the board by midday.

'If you ask me,' an ex-jockey who was one of the experts on one of the preview programmes opined, 'horses such as The Enchanted have no real place in a Gold Cup line-up. Rumour has it that Dick Durden went down to have a look-see after he'd lost the ride on Sportsmaster, and that he said not only is the horse a pony, but he's got several screws loose.'

'Oh dear,' Grenville had remarked when he had watched the programme with Lynne before setting off for the course. 'Another little soul off the Christmas card list.'

Having never been to Cheltenham before, when she got her first proper view of the wonderful Cotswolds racecourse set in the bowl of Prestbury Park, Alice was impressed. In spite of the vagaries of the weather the track looked in superb condition. It was as if the grass had just been planted and grown for this one occasion. The sun was shining with the particular March light that brings hope and spiritual refreshment to the long wintered soul, the sky was blue, the clouds were high, and the place was packed.

'It's all right,' Grenville assured them as he led Alice, Constance and Lynne along a concourse thronged with racegoers and past packed bars. 'Rory's got a box for us all – belongs to a friend of his old man. The box's owner can't be here today which is tough on him, but lovely for some, namely us.'

Once they were safely ensconced in their private box, which directly overlooked the home straight and from which they could see the whole of the racecourse, the party began to try to relax a little, but the atmosphere was far from the seemingly light-hearted ones that had accompanied their horse's previous appearances. Although naturally nervous on those occasions, they had had nothing to lose. Boyo was unknown, nobody was risking real money on him, the pundits had little or no interest in him and their ambitions had consisted of little more than seeing the horse get round and come home safely. The fact that he had won his first race and then his second was nothing short of miraculous, and at that point they might perhaps all quite happily have drawn a line under it and called it a day. Only their wildest dreams had brought them this far, to have their horse running in the most prestigious National Hunt race not just in the country but in the world.

'If anyone's nursing any second thoughts,' Grenville said as he handed out the racecards, 'I'm afraid it's way too late now. Here are the runners for the Gold Cup,' he explained, opening the card, 'and here is our horse.'

'Isn't this odd?' Alice stared at the details of their horse and the colours he would be carrying. 'What is it – a bit less than six months ago? About six months ago we didn't even know each other, and yet here we all are.'

'And what a thing, too,' Millie remarked, her invitation earned by the fact that if it hadn't been for Millie in the first place none of this would have happened.

'But it is extraordinary, really, when you think about it,' Alice continued. 'And never mind what happens or doesn't happen, because rather like Humphrey Bogart in *Casablanca*, we shall always have this. Always.'

'I'll certainly drink to that,' Grenville said, handing round the champagne. 'Mind you, today I shall drink to most things, but first to what Alice has just said. To The Enchanted Partnership.'

They all raised their glasses to make the toast. 'The Enchanted Partnership.'

'And may the best horse win,' Grenville added.

'And let that one be ours,' Constance said firmly. 'I need the money.'

'Don't say you still haven't paid for your share, Constance,' Grenville teased her.

'Cheque's in the post, Glanville,' Constance replied, with a wink to Alice. 'First-class stamp, too.'

'Only pity is Anthony couldn't be here today,' Alice said. 'But, of course, too much excitement would not be good news.'

'There's going to be too much excitement anyway,' Constance told her. 'Anthony said he's had what he calls a bit of a tilt. Says if the horse wins it'll pay for his op and a recuperative cruise. For two,' she added with another wink. 'I told him I'd stay home and try to keep his lid on, but he insisted I didn't miss the race – and anyway, what chance would I have with someone who escaped from Colditz twice? We locked him up in his bedroom without even a telephone, in case he rang one of those racing line things. We also gave him an old klaxon horn Rory found in the garage which he can sound in case of an emergency, because Maureen's on watch. And she's been told to keep an eye on him and to tell him the result. So now. What are the chances of us all becoming squillionaires, please?'

'The prize money's excellent,' Grenville told her, pointing to the figures on the card. 'A hundred and twenty thousand pounds to the winner, but since anything has to be divided by four less Rory's percentage, even if we did win I don't think we'd be sailing the Mediterranean in our private yachts, right?'

'Don't be so vulgar, Grenville,' Constance repri-

quietly taken away by a tall and beautiful young man with eyes the colour of coral, to be returned to the kingdom under the seas where his heart had always belonged.

THE END

If you enjoyed THE ENCHANTED, look out for Charlotte Bingham's next novel, THE LAND OF SUMMER

Charlotte Bingham would like to invite you to visit her website at www.charlottebingham.com

Depend upon it, Sir, when a man knows he is to be hanged in a fortnight, it concentrates his mind wonderfully.

—Samuel Johnson
September 19, 1777

To my mother, who has never stopped striving to do her best and to make sure her children were able to do the same.

Copyright © Walter Walker, 1989

First published in the USA in 1989 by Viking Penguin Inc.

Coronet edition 1990

British Library C.I.P.

Walker, Walter
  The immediate prospect of being hanged.
  I. Title
  813.54[F]

ISBN 0 340 53030 8

Printed and bound in Great Britain for Hodder and Stoughton Paperbacks, a division of Hodder and Stoughton Ltd., Mill Road, Dunton Green, Sevenoaks, Kent TN13 2YA (Editorial Office: 47 Bedford Square, London WC1B 3DP) by Cox & Wyman Ltd., Reading, Berks.

The Immediate Prospect of Being Hanged

Walter Walker

CORONET BOOKS
Hodder and Stoughton

About the Author

Walter Walker is the author of three highly
acclaimed thrillers, A DIME TO DANCE BY,
THE TWO DUDE DEFENSE and RULES OF
THE KNIFE FIGHT. He was born and raised in
Quincy, Massachusetts, and now practises
law in San Francisco.

THE IMMEDIATE
BEING HANGED

The file had been prepared over the course of the night by the Woodedge police department. It contained a sketch of the scene, a detailed listing of photographs and prints taken and evidence inventoried, and a lengthy note of what the investigating officer (a Roland Tagget) had observed. Officer Tagget was meticulous in detailing that the victim showed no visible signs of having been raped or sexually molested, other than the fact her stockings were torn above the thigh.

"There's some reason why a woman like this would be in a place like that, and whatever it is, it stinks," John Michael said. He turned from his books. He looked at me with a fiery glint of pleasure in his eye. "That's the part I want you going after, Patt. The part that stinks. We'll let Chief Tuttle worry about the dusting and the tracking and the fibers on the seat covers. I want you finding out what kind of woman this was, what kind of man her husband is, how she could have let herself get in the position she was in. You follow me?"

"You want the dirt."

"I want the dirt."

JHS
BURY
NOV/91

manded him. 'I'm not talking money money. I'm talking about just supposing we won. Winning something like this makes you a squillionaire, which is nothing to do with money. Winning a race like this must be something money can't possibly buy. This sort of thing can stand life on its head. So here's *hoping*,' Constance concluded, raising her glass, 'and here's *toping*.'

Rory put his head round the door of the box just before the second race.

'Horse is fine, everyone,' he said, trying not to sound breathless. 'Travelled fine, looks fine. Anyone know where I can be sick?'

'You do look a little pale.'

'I feel a little pale, Alice.' Rory breathed slowly in and out. 'No, I'm fine really. And everything's fine. The horse is fine, so there we are, and here we are. Everything will be fine. Don't worry. See you all down in the paddock.'

Down in the pre-parade ring, with less than forty minutes now to go to the off, Kathleen kept her charge walking round in an easy swinging rhythm, talking quietly to him all the time and sometimes singing to him. Then, shortly before she was due to take Boyo into the main parade ring, she happened to look up and away from her horse for the first time for a long time and saw her father and brother leaning on the rails smiling at her.

'Looks a picture, Kathleen,' Padraig said with a whistle and a tilt of his head. 'You've done him proud, my girl, you have so.'

'Everyone's over,' Liam told her the next time she came past them. 'Practically the whole of Cronagh.'

'The church is clean out of candles!' Padraig called after her, on her last lap. 'Good luck, now, girl!'

'Good luck, Katie!' Liam shouted. 'And to the little horse, God bless him!'

The parade ring was packed to the very top with everyone anxious to get a closer look at the contenders for the Gold Cup. Kathleen could hardly believe that she was here and this was really happening. The atmosphere was electric, the buzz around the ring making her flesh turn to goose bumps. She put a hand up to stroke Boyo's neck. But the gesture was more to calm herself than to soothe her horse, who wasn't turning a hair, even though the animal in front of him was beginning to boil over already, swishing its tail and kicking out now and then with a hind foot. She glanced up at the huge electronic price board that showed the approximate odds and saw to her astonishment that the price of twenty-five to one that had been on offer some ten to fifteen minutes ago for The Enchanted was now as little as fourteen to one.

Now the parade ring was filling up with trainers and connections – owners, officials, television commentators and reporters, and finally the jockeys, streaming out from the weighing room in their brilliant colours, some of them joking with their colleagues in order to allay the nerves

they were feeling, others careless of showing their tension, tapping their boots with their whips as they made their way to touch caps to their owners and take their last instructions from their trainers. Then they were mounting, legged up by trainers, some of whom walked with their mounted horses round the last couple of circuits of the parade ring, calling up their last thoughts, while some of the horses began to prance and play up, others started to break into a slight sweat, and some were as calm as police horses facing a riot. Racegoers abandoned their positions by the ring to hurry to the Tote windows or the bookmakers, while others rushed back to the stands to get the best vantage point possible, as a now orderly line of horses made their way from the paddock to parade in front of the grandstands, lads and lasses at their heads, some assistants following out on to the course in case of any accident or mishap. Red-coated huntsmen on strapping horses waited to escort the parade, and cheers were already rising from the jam-packed stands as the line of horses and handlers walked and jogged in front of them.

'The runners are parading in racecard order,' the course commentator called. 'At the head is the favourite, County Gent, followed by number two, Duke's Biscuit, three, Jenrich, followed by number four, Jenuflecked, five the French challenger, Le Corbeau, six the second favourite, My Pal Joey, number seven one of the Irish, Na Shonaca, followed by Rumbledumble, number

eight. Out of order at nine for some reason is number ten, Stopdat – then number nine, another Irish challenger, Spun Silk, number eleven is The Enchanted, followed by the raider from north of the border, Ticketpleez, number twelve, thirteen is Tyron, fourteen is Vulcan Flyer, fifteen is Welsh Harebit and last but not least the only mare in the field, Moosey.'

A great roar went up as, with the parade over, the horses, released by their lads, about-faced to the left and began to canter down to the start at the bottom left-hand corner of the track.

'My,' Alice sighed, standing at the front of the box and watching the spectacle. 'What excitement.'

'Don't tell me you're actually going to watch the race, Alice?' Grenville laughed.

'Of course not,' Alice replied, heading for the door. 'I shall be out here if anyone wants me.'

'Did he go down all right, Grenville?' Lynne asked, still watching through her race glasses. 'I don't know the difference between going down well and going down badly.'

'He's nice and calm, if that's what you're worried about,' Millie told her. 'One or two of the others have got pretty hot, even though there's quite a cold wind.'

'I'd have thought horses would run better hot than cold,' Constance said, lighting a cheroot. 'I was always better for the sun on my back.'

'Hot as in sweating up, Connie,' Grenville said. 'Means they start taking it out of themselves.'

544

'Of course, horses can sweat, can't they?' Constance mused. 'It's only we ladies who glow.' She thought she felt and looked calm. It was only when she put her glasses to her eyes that she realised she was having difficulty keeping them steady, to say the least.

'They're under starter's orders!' the course commentator called, as the horses got into line by the starting tape, only for two of them to break the formation and so necessitate another call-in from the starter.

'He's squeezed right up on the rails,' Lynne observed. 'Hope he's OK.'

'Rory's told Blaze to try to get an inside berth first time round, and also to kick on if he can and make it,' Grenville put in.

'No – a horse has come right in front of him!' Lynne exclaimed. 'Practically pushed him through the rails!'

'They're in line . . .' called the commentator.

'It's number thirteen,' Millie observed. 'Eddie Rampton's other runner.'

'And they're off!' the commentator announced, his proclamation almost drowned by the almighty roar that rose from the grandstands and enclosures as the race began.

'They're away to a good level start – except for Vulcan Flyer who's wheeled round, and The Enchanted who must have lost a good six lengths as they set off.'

'Blast,' Grenville cried. 'That looked quite deliberate to me.'

Blaze knew it was deliberate. He'd had Kevin Billings's mount Tyron in his own horse's face ever since they filed out on to the racecourse proper, Billings shadowing Blaze's every move and leaning his horse on Boyo at every opportunity, so Blaze knew something was up. He kept trying to avoid Billings, and then just before the tape was released Blaze and Boyo were all but knocked sideways through the guard rail by Tyron. Seeing the field charge off without him, Blaze thought better than to panic his horse by kicking and flapping at him, so once he had got him straight he jumped him off just as if he hadn't missed the break at all. Boyo picked up at once, deciding for himself to cut down the distance between himself and the back markers, an objective that by the time they cleared the first fence to all intents and purposes he had achieved. In the run from the second fence to the next, Blaze and Boyo made up more ground, going from tenth place into seventh, only to have Billings on Tyron loom up on their outside.

'Going somewhere, Mick?' Billings yelled at him, over the thunder of hooves, the slapping of leather and the shouts of the other riders. 'Because if you are, I'm coming with you!'

'What's going on out there?' Grenville wondered, race glasses trained hard on the action. 'It's that horse again – Tyron. He's crowding Boyo!'

'What?' Lynne cried. 'God, he is too! Look – he's running into him!'

'And as they approach the third,' the commentator

called, 'My Pal Joey continues to make the running a good two lengths clear of Le Corbeau, while behind there seem to be some traffic problems with Tyron, The Enchanted and Duke's Biscuit – and Duke's Biscuit has gone at that one! Tyron appeared to cannon into him and Duke's Biscuit has gone – leaving The Enchanted now third with Tyron ranging once more up alongside him as the rest of the field have all flown that fence – with Le Corbeau still in second, Tyron now third, The Enchanted fourth, followed by Spun Silk, County Gent, Jenuflecked, Na Shonaca, Rumbledumble and the mare Moosey.'

'He's trying to break his rhythm,' Grenville said over the commentator. 'Look! Every time Boyo goes to pass him, the other horse cuts in front of him and then slows down. What a dirty trick. What a simply filthy trick!'

'Is it allowed?' Constance wondered. 'Should they not perhaps stop the race?'

'They can hardly do that, Connie!' Grenville called back, glasses still trained on the action. 'Blaze is just going to have to find a way of dealing with it!'

At the first of the line of fences in the back straight, having forced Blaze to take a pull on The Enchanted to avoid being run into the wing of the fence, Billings straightened his horse and did his best to run into the back of the French horse that was still lying second. Disturbed by the proximity of the animal all but jumping up on him, Le Corbeau made a mistake, went through

547

the top of the fence and down on to his nose on the landing side. His jockey made a fine recovery to get his horse racing again, but by then Billings had pushed Tyron past Le Corbeau so that he was lying in second place, some four lengths off My Pal Joey, exactly where it had been planned he should be. As soon as he slotted himself in behind the leader, Billings kept his mount in hand, all the time glancing over his shoulder at what was coming at him, then riding across any horse that tried to overtake him. At the last fence along the back straight Tyron ran Na Shonaca out, to the sound of a huge roar of disappointment from the enormous Irish contingent, many of whom, knowing a thing or two, had backed the horse in from twenty-five to one to sixteens.

Swinging out of the back straight and heading now downhill for the first time the field faced two of the most formidable fences on the course, both downhill, the second one being the harder since the ground on the landing side fell away while the running rail into the straight suddenly came into play, bowed as it was into the course so as to carry the horses out before they swung left-handed into the home straight.

Blaze knew what was going on. He had ridden in far too many bareback, rope-bridled pony races on the strands of Cork and Kerry not to know a dirty trick when he saw one, so the slow, slow, quick-quick slow tactic employed by the broken-nosed Billings came as nothing new to him. But what it did mean was that Blaze could not now

allow Boyo to run his usual race, which was of course the whole point of the exercise. Rory, Blaze and Anthony had gone through every possible aspect of the event the previous evening, a discussion that had left nothing to chance and so had included possible spoiling tactics, the sort of so-called jockeymanship that had previously marred several of the more prestigious races, particularly those with a lively ante-post market.

'Which is why I always say we should have a Tote monopoly, like the French,' Anthony had pronounced. 'About the only thing I like about the French, though.'

'Besides their wine, their food, their women, their cities, their bread, and practically everything else,' Rory had replied.

And so now here it was happening to Blaze and Boyo as the race unfolded, a horse entered deliberately as a spoiler, a horse whose jockey was riding under strict instructions to do everything he could within a certain amount of reason to put off the opposition and allow the stable's favoured horse the best and most trouble-free run possible. So Blaze and Boyo's only hope of salvation lay in running a race that was the opposite of those they had run so far, a dangerous tactic which could easily backfire, since it meant dropping the horse out of the race – and often when a rider did that the horse switched off and the day was lost.

But there was nothing else Blaze could now do. Ahead of him he saw Billings perched up on his tall and burly horse's neck, taking good looks

around him as they approached the first of the downhill fences. It was clear this was not going to be a short-lived diversion, so Blaze knew he had to start steadying his horse without for a moment allowing him to become unbalanced – and all of this at the most dangerous part of the course. Any loss of momentum coming downhill could easily result in the horse's not having enough power to take off safely as it ran towards the intimidating obstacle, and that would mean end of story. So Blaze chose to decelerate not going into these two downhill fences but after them, as he and Boyo turned into the home straight for the first time – if they got that far. This meant he now had to outsmart Billings, and once again his pony-racing skills came to the fore as he feinted to come up on the inside of Tyron, only at the last moment, as Tyron closed the gap, to switch to the outside, hoping and praying that in doing so he hadn't broken The Enchanted's fine rhythm.

He hadn't. Swinging right of Tyron at the first downhill fence Boyo jumped fast and immaculately, landing running, but not quite fast enough to get clear of Tyron, on whom Billings was now hard at work, beating the horse and turning the air blue with his curses against Blaze and Boyo. Dropping down faster and faster to the second downhill fence, again Blaze pre-guessed his adversary, reckoning that Billings, predictably enough, would think Blaze was about to do the same thing at this next fence – go round the outside – which indeed Blaze feinted to do.

Billings immediately pulled Tyron wide to cut off all sight of the fence whereupon Blaze at once shortened his left rein to cut inside and safely up and over, using to the full the deftness and agility of the little horse.

'What is happening, please?' Alice asked, putting her head round the box door for the first time. 'Are we still in one piece?'

'Just about, Alice,' Grenville called back to her. 'You ought to come and see this. This promises to be the race of a lifetime.'

Alice crept into the box and half hid herself against the wall at the edge of the open window, peering round through half-closed eyes as the race continued.

'But this I don't understand,' Grenville continued. 'Just as he appeared to have the measure of that horse, Blaze seems to be taking a pull.'

'Yes, he does,' Millie agreed. 'I hope everything's all right. I hope the horse hasn't gone wrong.'

What Blaze was hoping was that the horse wouldn't go wrong, that he wouldn't switch off and go to sleep. Knowing Boyo he somehow doubted it, but equally well did he know that horses have minds and moods of their own, and that the one thing a really good horse hates is being disappointed. So somehow – and he didn't know quite how – he had to keep the horse sweet. He had to keep him believing. So as he eased him ever so slightly back off the pace, Blaze began to sing to him. As he turned the horse into the home

straight, in a fine lyric tenor voice Blaze sang 'The Minstrel Boy' to his horse, to the slack-jawed astonishment of other jockeys now ranging up alongside them.

He saw Billings looking round again, and guessed that seeing Boyo dropping right back through the field, the mean-minded rider would turn his attention to more ready dangers, which indeed he did as the field jumped the two fences in the straight for the second time. Billings now proceeded to try to disrupt the rhythm and racing flow of what now appeared to be My Pal Joey's closest rivals, Jenrich, who had made a move up through the field, Spun Silk, who was going exceptionally well and the bay mare Moosey who as always was running her gallant heart out.

'So as they go out into the country for the last time,' the commentator called, 'and with Stopdat and The Enchanted going backwards through the field, both appearing to have run their races, it's still My Pal Joey taking them along at a really good gallop, My Pal Joey, Jenrich, Spun Silk, Moosey the four leading horses with Tyron still in close attention and now moving up to jump into third place at that one, almost carrying Moosey out through the wing there . . .'

With the hill in the straight climbed and now behind him, to everyone watching it might seem as though The Enchanted had indeed shot his bolt, and yet even as he began another verse of his song Blaze felt the horse come back on the bridle, which was what he had been praying for

all the way up the stiff climb past the grandstands. Of all places to choose on the course, switching a horse off when it was going uphill was the most dangerous, as passing the winning post the horse could easily think his work for the day was over. So when Blaze asked the horse to pick up he half expected Boyo not to do so. Instead, to his delight, Boyo took a hold once more of the bit and swung back out into the country full of running and – Blaze suddenly felt – determination.

At the first open ditch in the back straight Rumbledumble fell, the horse simply failing to pick up and crashing through the fence, sending his jockey spinning over his head and also bringing down Welsh Harebit, who seemed to be going particularly well at the time. The falls happened in front of Boyo but by then Blaze had tracked to the inside and so had a good, clear and unimpeded run at the line of fences, a row of obstacles that finished before the turn downhill with another ditch where the horizon lay so far below as horse and jockey jumped that it appeared as if they were jumping off the edge of the world. Boyo flew it, landing full of himself and swinging left downhill with only the lightest of instruction from Blaze.

Ahead, with four fences to jump, they had only five horses now in their sights, Boyo having moved up easily but not overly quickly through a fast depleting field, past other horses beaten now but not fallen, more or less running on empty, two of them looking as though they might be pulled

up at the top of the hill, so murderous had been the gallop. Blaze wasn't exactly sure which horses were ahead of him, although he could make out My Pal Joey's colours, and those of Spun Silk and the mare Moosey, who was still somehow hanging in there, in spite of the regular interference she was suffering from the horse in the hands of Billings. The leading quartet, or maybe quintet, Blaze thought, seemed to be coming back to him, or else Boyo was even more full running than he had thought, but whatever was happening he knew if he hugged the rail down the hill and into the home turn he could come off it at speed, pick up the best of the ground and give it his best shot.

It was then that he heard the sound of a horse behind him, the noise of its rhythmic breathing, the powerful thrumming of its great hooves, and up alongside him, on the very inside of him, up through a gap Blaze had carelessly left, moved the forgotten man of the race, County Gent. As he galloped past The Enchanted, his rider not moving, Blaze felt his blood change. He felt himself suddenly grow cold and he felt suddenly dense and very stupid. For the one thing he had not thought about since he had dropped his own horse back was the chance of some other horse picking him off, having done exactly the same thing.

He remembered seeing Dennis Maloney as he had eased his way back to the pack of chasing horses, sitting as still as a mouse on the big black

horse from Lambourn, the easy winner of the King George VI chase. He should have known then to watch for the horse, to trail him if necessary, for the big horse had one weakness. He liked to come from behind and he did not like to be challenged once he had made his move.

Twice before when this had happened the horse had simply downed tools and lost races he was winning easily. Blaze should have remembered this and he knew he should have done so, because during his pre-race briefing the fact had been dunned into him. And now the big horse was through.

Over the first downhill fence they both flew, Boyo now a good length down on a horse that still seemed to be only in third gear. Knowing he couldn't take his rival here, Blaze did some quick thinking, and then on the run to the next fence he thought some more, but nothing occurred to him until they were flying the most dangerous fence on the course for the second time, the third from home, the last of the downhill fences, where just ahead of them Blaze saw Spun Silk make a mistake that cost him half a dozen lengths and meant Moosey's pilot had to check her and pull her round the still stumbling Irish horse.

Roars and cries and cheers rose from the stands as the field turned for home, a great wall of sound, a noise that had so intrigued the mighty Arkle long ago that he had turned to stare at where the noise was coming from and nearly fallen for doing so. But today the noise thrilled

and inspired not only Blaze but the brave horse under him, who all at once quickened, well before Blaze had even thought of asking him to do so, hugging the rail on his left so tightly that he could have been running on tracks.

'And now as they turn for home it's still My Pal Joey!' the commentator called. 'My Pal Joey who has made every inch of the running then Jenrich, who will not be shaken off, Tyron, who at last seems to be weakening, Moosey whose task now seems impossible, with Spun Silk, who made that serious blunder at the last dropping back fast – but County Gent is starting his run! County Gent who has been making ground hand over fist downhill is now swinging wide into the straight – followed by The Enchanted! The Enchanted is tight on the rails – The Enchanted, who has also made up an enormous amount of ground to get back into the reckoning – there's only half a length between County Gent and The Enchanted – and now the two of them are only three or four lengths behind the leaders as they approach the second last!'

First of all Blaze wanted to see where Tyron was, in case the horse was still in the reckoning, and on the run to the second last he could see him only a length or so ahead of him, zigzagging across the course from sheer exhaustion, being severely beaten up by his jockey. Someone behind Blaze yelled at Billings to pull his horse up, but Billings took no notice, driving his semi-conscious horse on in the hope of carrying out yet another

challenger. Again Blaze had only a split second to make up his mind about where to jump and how, yet it seemed Boyo made up his mind for him, jinking first to the right then changing legs and heading left of a horse too tired to be able to obey the wilful demands of his rider even if he had wanted to do so. Tyron staggered as Boyo ranged alongside him and in that moment Blaze saw his opportunity and asked Boyo for a big one. At once the horse came up in his hands and they were airborne, yards outside where the leading horses had left the ground, but as they flew Billings took one last chance, sticking his left leg out as Blaze and Boyo sailed by him and catching Blaze's right foot, knocking it clean out of its stirrup.

How the blow didn't knock Blaze completely from the saddle he would never know. Perhaps it was due to his legendary 'stick' or perhaps it was due to Boyo's beautiful balance. Whatever the reason, Blaze's right foot was out of the pedal and swinging loose and in a flash, he pulled his left foot free as well, all at once realising that if he landed acey-deucy, one foot in and one foot out, the odds were one hundred to one on that he would be catapulted out of the saddle and out of the Gold Cup.

So he landed with his horse on the far side of the fence sitting right back in his saddle with both legs stuck out in front of him and reins as long as curtain pulls. Yet he stayed there, he stuck on the horse, and even as Boyo began to power away from the fence the nimble Blaze, blessing his

days as the champion pony racer in the west of Ireland, was already slotting his feet back into the irons and gathering his reins for one last fight.

'Dear God above us!' Grenville cried to the rest of the box. 'Did you ever see anything like that!'

'I didn't!' Alice shouted back over the tumult her hands in front of her eyes. 'I didn't see a thing! What's happening, someone?'

Then she looked and what she saw was what everyone that day saw, one of the very best and most inspiring finishes to a horse race any of them had ever seen.

'There really is very little in it now!' the commentator was shouting over the tannoy and above the ever growing crescendo of sound. 'As the field runs to the last My Pal Joey has finally surrendered the lead to Jenrich! But County Gent is not finished with yet – nor is The Enchanted in spite of the rider's losing his irons at the last fence! So on the run to the last there are four horses together – Jenrich, My Pal Joey – the still improving County Gent, who seems to have timed his run just right – and The Enchanted! The Enchanted, who seems to have caught his third if not his fourth wind! And at the last they all rise together – Jenrich landing first and My Pal Joey now making a mistake! The horse's first mistake and he's all but down on his knees – and now he's passed by County Gent who landed yards the other side of the fence – then The Enchanted! The Enchanted lands third, a length down, and still running on – but they both have to face the

hill now! The famous Cheltenham hill now faces both these brave horses – and it's County Gent now! It's County Gent who is lengthening his stride and beginning to put daylight between him and The Enchanted, who doesn't seem to have anything left!'

'Damn, damn, damn,' Grenville said to himself through gritted teeth.

'Oh, Geoffrey Alcott Wilson!' Alice shouted, watching the finish unfolding. 'Hell and dam's ladders!'

'I'm afraid we're roasted,' Constance observed sadly, putting her binoculars down.

'Hang on, everyone,' Millie said. 'Hang on – hang on in there!'

Blaze knew he had to wait his moment. If he moved too soon there might not be enough gas left in the tank to complete his challenge, and if he moved too late the huge-striding County Gent would have swallowed the ground up and galloped past the post. He had to time it just right. He knew there was something left in his horse because he felt it still there in his hands, but he also knew he couldn't and wouldn't beat the effort out of him, so he waited. And waited. And waited.

And then he pounced.

He was only a length down but there were only a hundred and fifty yards to run and he waited for a sign and when he saw the sign he pounced. They both did.

There were in fact two signs. First County

Gent's head went up – only marginally, but one thing young Blaze had learned on the sands of Kerry and of Cork is that the very second an animal's head goes up is the moment it is beat; and the other sign was from Dennis Maloney, from the champion jockey in person, who could not resist a quick look round. It was only a very quick look, but he looked over the wrong shoulder. Expecting the young thruster to be coming up on his inner, he took a split-second look over his left shoulder and when he saw it Blaze knew he had got him.

Down in the drive position he sat, down he went and hard he drove, throwing the reins at the back of Boyo's head, shouting battle cries of victory at him in Gaelic, thrusting and driving the horse up the final lung-bursting, heart-popping hundred yards, the two horses now neck and neck, Dennis Maloney throwing everything at his horse, producing all his great skills, riding one of his greatest finishes ever – but it just wasn't enough. It just wasn't enough to beat the horse racing at his side, sticking out his proud head, all but leaving the ground to fly home the winner, finally by no more than a head.

For a moment no one knew who had won. The crowds that had been roaring a sound that could be heard for miles fell all but silent as the two gallant horses slowed to a canter then to a trot and finally to a leg-weary walk as they too awaited the result.

'Did you get up, lad?' Dennis Maloney gasped,

barely able to catch his breath. 'God, I don't even know who you are.'

'Blaze Molloy, Mr Maloney sir.' Blaze grinned at him, sticking out a muddy hand, which Dennis shook.

'There's a thing,' the other Irishman grinned. 'They'll all be saying – *look at those two fine sportsmen* – when little will they know all we're doing is introducing ourselves!'

'Here is the result!' the official announcement rang out. 'First number eleven – The Enchanted—'

Boyo's name was hardly heard, such was the roar from the stands.

'First number eleven – The Enchanted!' the official repeated. 'Second number one, County Gent—'

Drowned by another mighty cheer.

'And third number three, Jenrich! The fourth horse was number nine, Spun Silk.'

'Well done, Blaze,' Dennis said, this time putting an arm round the young tyro's shoulders. 'Say what you like about old Mother Erin, but she doesn't half turn us out.'

Blaze touched his cap to one of his great heroes, thanked him, then turned Boyo round to face the stands and the long walk back into the unsaddling enclosure. He had never even imagined this moment, not in his wildest dreams, so he had no idea of what it might be like. In spite of his bravura, the most Blaze had ever hoped and prayed for was that one day he would just ride in a race at Cheltenham, and now that it had happened he still

561

didn't know how. Nor had it really sunk in that not only had he ridden in a race, he had ridden in the greatest steeplechase of them all. And not only that – it seemed he had won it.

Kathleen was waiting for him at the entrance to the track that leads past the stands and into the unsaddling enclosure. She had watched the entire race away from everyone she knew. Once she had turned Boyo away to the start she had taken up her selected position, and simply prayed. Now she was proudly leading in her horse, the horse she had helped deliver into the world, the horse she had reared herself. The people in the enclosures she and her horse passed by were still beside themselves with the power and magic of the great race, showering love, compliments and congratulations on horse and jockey alike. Television crews with cameras on their shoulders and microphones stuck on sticks ran backwards before them, twenty thousand flash bulbs burst around them, hands were clapped sore, throats were roared red. Yet nothing could match the noise and tumult that awaited them in the unsaddling enclosure.

Rory was there, waiting at the last turn in the path before it opened to reveal the packed enclosure. Kathleen put out her free arm and hugged Rory to her and he hugged her to him. He slapped Blaze on the thigh and Blaze took Rory's cap and threw it into the crowds. As soon as the people saw the horse and rider a roar went up that was loud enough to have announced victory in a great

battle. Eyes filled with tears, hats were thrown in the air and the police had to link arms to cordon off what looked as if it might be a stampede to greet the victors in what would go down as one of the most enthralling Gold Cups ever run. And there in the paddock were waiting Boyo's faithful band of ecstatic owners: Constance, Alice, Lynne and Grenville, transformed by the horse, transformed by the moment.

As things began to calm down and the snappers came forward to take their pictures, a most beautiful Irish tenor voice was raised somewhere in the middle of the throng. And at the sound of it, everyone stopped to look and to listen.

'Bless this horse, O Lord we pray!' the singer sang, and when they heard the words the crowd roared once again, before the song was taken up by a whole choir of racegoers from Ireland.

> 'Bless this horse, O Lord we pray –
> Make it win a race each day!
> Bless the jockey, chimney thin –
> Bless his mum for feedin' him gin!
> Bless this horse that we may be
> Richer for each victor – eee!'

'Three cheers now!' another Irish voice commanded. 'Three cheers for Blaze Molloy – and three more for a great racehorse!'

'Well,' Constance said when the cheers had died down. 'I think that's the last we'll ever hear of his being little, don't you?'

Then all at once, as the sound of the cheering died away, the odd and quite unexpected sound of the very opposite was heard coming from a crowd that had gathered round the unmistakable figures of Eddie Rampton and the owners of My Pal Joey.

'Well I'll be blowed,' Lynne said, having caught sight of the objects of the crowd's derision. 'If it isn't my ex and my ex.'

'Ex and ex what, precisely, Lynne dear?' Constance wondered, putting up her race glasses and directing them at what seemed now about to be a skirmish.

'Ex-old man and ex-best friend.' Lynne grinned. 'Seems they're getting the bird.'

'You're going to enjoy this, Rory,' a tall, languid man remarked, joining the group by the winners' enclosure. 'You should be there, rubbing your hands in glee. And by the way, one and all, well done with your horse. What a champion, eh? James Roderick from the *Sporting Life*.' He shook all their hands and gave The Enchanted a well earned pat on his steaming neck.

'What's going on exactly, Jim?' Rory asked. 'It seems the people are taking against Eddie Rampton. Right?'

'Spot on, cocky.' James laughed. 'He can never shut it, can he? Starting mouthing off his owners, saying his jockeys' race tactics were all their idea. At which the owner, whatever his name is—'

'Gerry Fortune,' Lynne volunteered. 'He can never shut it either.'

'Too right, my lovely. Mr Fortune started slamming back at old Eddie, saying he'd cooked it all up and that he never knew a thing about it. Whereupon all hell broke loose, and . . .' He stopped to look round at the crowd surrounding the still wildly gesticulating figure of Eddie Rampton. 'And to judge from the sound of it,' he continued, 'is breaking even more loose. Not the sort of thing one wants to see here in the Holy of Holies.'

At that moment a tall, well-dressed figure with a pair of large race glasses slung over one shoulder appeared on the scene, followed by a retinue of assistants, reporters and policemen, all headed for the skirmish.

'Ah,' James said. 'The cavalry have arrived. I would say any moment now the connections will be called in to have a quiet word with the stewards – or, seeing it's old Eddie, not so quiet will be more the order of the day.'

'And what will happen to them, do you think, James?' Lynne asked, giving him her very best smile, much to the discomfort of Grenville, who began slapping the side of his leg with his racing hat. 'I do hope they'll all be clapped in irons and set adrift.'

'Very possibly, Miss . . . ?'

'Faraday,' Lynne replied. 'Lynne Faraday.'

'Soon to be Lynne Fielding,' Grenville said with a smile and a nod. 'Very soon to be Lynne Fielding.'

'Well, Miss Faraday soon to be Mrs Fielding,'

James said with a grin, 'I would say there's every chance of that happening. Mr Rampton is forever getting himself into trouble, and having seen that race I doubt if this time he'll get off with just a warning, I don't think any of them will. One thing racing's powers-that-be most certainly do not like is anything that brings the sport into disrepute – and there's no doubt that the way they ran that second horse did exactly that.'

'Goody.' Lynne laughed. 'I shall stand outside wherever it is—'

'Portman Square,' Rory volunteered.

'I shall stand outside Portman Square and throw rotten eggs at all of them.'

'And I shall be there right by your side, my dear,' Constance assured her. 'What an awful lot of flotsam.'

'Oh, my,' Alice said as they all waited to be presented with the Gold Cup. 'I've just remembered the children.'

'I didn't know your kids were here, Alice,' Lynne said, as Edwin Armstrong beckoned them to come forward to receive the most coveted trophy in National Hunt racing.

'They're not.' Alice smiled. 'But I do hope they were watching.'

One of them had been. Although Joe and Georgina were unable to get to the course itself because of Joe's work and the children's schooling, Joe watched it in a betting shop round the corner from his office while Georgina managed to

watch at home, having persuaded her friend and neighbour to do the return school run. By the time The Enchanted was making his effort up the hill Georgina was standing on the sofa screaming so loudly that two passers-by – thinking someone was being murdered – rang her doorbell to make sure everything was all right.

'Yes! Yes!' Georgina laughed. 'God, I'm sorry – it's just – it doesn't matter. Yes it does!' she suddenly shouted at the two utterly nonplussed strangers standing staring slack-jawed at her. 'Yes it does matter! My mum's horse has just won the Cheltenham Gold Cup!'

As she tried to persuade the bewildered but now beaming young couple to come in for a celebratory drink Georgina's phone rang.

'Hi!' she said happily as she answered it. 'Hi – Chris! Chris – were you watching? You were watching, weren't you?'

'Yeah, well, no actually,' Christian confessed with an embarrassed laugh. 'I mean I actually forgot.'

'You what? You forgot?' Georgina repeated in disbelief.

'Yeah, I know, sis. But honestly, at that price – like one hundred and fifty to one? I thought, *Come on – what sort of a no-hope is that*? So I forgot – yeah.'

'But he won, Chris! Mum's horse won!'

'I know, I know,' Chris laughed. 'Why I'm ringing. I was in Horrids – in the audio and television department looking at stuff and there was Mum

all over the screen. Getting this little gold cup. I mean – what? But he wasn't anywhere near one hundred and fifty to one, sis.'

'No, you dibbock!' Georgina laughed. 'But you had him at a hundred and fifty to one! Like me! That's what an ante-post voucher is, apparently – that's the price we had him at. You realise how much money you have just won?'

'You are kidding me,' Christian said, his whole tone of voice changed. 'Seriously? You really are kidding me.'

'I am not kidding you, Chris,' Georgina assured him. 'You are a rich young man.'

'Fantastic.'

'You can say that again.'

'No – *fantastic*, sis. I mean wow.'

'You bet, bro. So too do I.'

'Hey!' Christian said, as if suddenly realising something. 'This is cool – because you know what this means, right? This is cool because it means I can pay Mum back what I owe her.'

'No, I don't think so, Chris,' Georgina replied. 'I don't think either of us is ever going to be able to do that.'

Epilogue

MAY

Turned Away

Summer came early. April was fine and warm, with little rain, but May simply burst into spring which in two weeks became summer. Kathleen and Rory roughed their newly crowned champion off as soon as the celebrations had died down and turned him out in his favourite paddock with plenty of company. At first, as if back home in Ireland, he had hardly strayed from the area around the gate, happy to graze on the fresh spring grass that was already full of goodness but seemingly loath to turn his back on human company. But a week or so later he was gone from the gate, and when Kathleen went to check his welfare morning, noon and night she would find him in what had fast become his favourite spot, a shady oasis afforded by two enormous horse chestnut trees under which lay

a shallow spring-fed pond from which Boyo and his playmates could drink and in whose mud they could lazily roll and cool.

The oddest thing was that he no longer looked smaller than his companions. It was as if the race had made him grow taller, and when Rory and Kathleen had put a measuring stick to him, something they had never done in fact, just in case he turned out to be as small as his critics would have him be, they found to their delight and astonishment that in his shoes he now stood at a full sixteen hands, no longer the size of a milk pony. His six months as a racehorse had certainly brought him on, although nothing did so to such purpose as his magnificent, heroic and famous run in the Gold Cup. When the four owners and their trainer had stood admiring him in the unsaddling enclosure they had all remarked on how much more of a horse he seemed to have become, which they say is often the way with winning horses. They look like winners. They look stronger for their race. They look altogether bigger for their victory – and Boyo was no exception. As he had stood there proudly in the enclosure with the steam of his efforts rising from his heaving flanks and the breath of his labours steaming from his flared nostrils, he had looked mighty. Not tall, not huge, not statuesque, but strong and mighty, as if his victory had already transformed him from a good athletic and burly sort of racehorse into the near mythic creature he was to become, the winner of twenty-eight races including two

Cheltenham Gold Cups, three King George VI Steeplechases, one Whitbread Gold Cup and an Irish Grand National, the last two named races being the only two handicaps in which he ever ran, notable contests he won carrying top weight, the Whitbread by an easy four lengths and the Irish National by a jaw-dropping ten. But now as his first summer at Fulford Farm unfolded, and as if mindful of the battles that lay ahead of him, Boyo switched himself off and grew fat on the fine farm grasses, coming back into his stable to sleep the day away when the sun got too hot and being turned out in the fields at night when all was cool and the flies had gone.

As for his human friends, all was as well with them as it was with himself. Constance insisted on accompanying Anthony to America for his operation, flown there in Harrington Lovell's private jet and back again after the procedure had been successfully completed. Meanwhile, Harrington and Alice, his soon to be wife, found a fine but manageable house in a little-known part of Somerset where they would spend the rest of their days in peace, quiet and deep contentment. Grenville and Lynne married but went on living exactly as they had been, happy to keep Grenville's elegant Knightsbridge flat for their London life and Lynne's spacious country apartment for their rural days. Grenville ceased his dabbling in the world of investments, on Lynne's suggestion founding a racing club for people who could not afford to buy horses or even legs of horses but

wanted the fun of ownership. In the first season the club had fifty subscribers, a membership that ten years later had swelled to over twenty thousand happy punters. The Fieldings had two children, neither of whom had the slightest interest in horses, their daughter becoming an opera singer and their son a chef.

As for the boys across the wather, there was never a race The Enchanted ran when the money wasn't down. Cronagh prospered, and the citizen who prospered most was Padraig Flanagan, thanks initially to the fact that Rory credited him with the breeding of his Gold Cup winner in his post-race press conferences, a credit that soon brought the dealers, bloodstock agents, pin-hookers and well-heeled owners to the door of his modest smallholding in south-west Cork, an establishment that thanks to the continued wondrous success of The Enchanted, ten years later had grown into one of the most successful small stud farms in Ireland. The fact that neither the so-called sire or dam of The Enchanted had lived to see their son's first success had no bearing on the events whatsoever, for all the horse people wanted was to be privy to the skills and the magic of a man already rumoured to be a singular breeder of outstanding national hunt horses. This was a reputation that Padraig very quickly and truly deserved, himself and Liam going on to breed the dual winner of an Irish Champion Hurdle and three fine and strong steeplechasers that all went on to win at the Cheltenham Festival,

which perhaps only goes to show that as far as equine breeding goes, very often the stud book is as much use as a tuning fork is to the tone deaf.

When Anthony returned from America with his life expectancy greatly increased, decisions had to be made about the future of Fulford Farm.

'The first thing I would like to do and intend to do, as it happens, Dad, is to get married,' Rory told him.

'I would have to say that is one of your better ideas, Rory,' Anthony replied. 'And after that, what then?'

'That rather depends on what you're going to do.'

'Well, I'm going to enjoy myself,' Anthony told him. 'Connie and I have got one or two things we'd like to do and a couple of places we'd like to go and see, but before I can do that, I have to know what's to become of the yard.'

'I can go on running it, if it's all right with you. Or rather we can. Kathleen and I, that is,' Rory said, taking Kathleen by the hand.

'And that's all? That's it, is it?' Anthony sighed. 'You're just going to train horses for the rest of your days and do nothing else.'

'No, of course he's going to do something else, Mr Rawlins,' Kathleen reassured him. 'In fact, if I have anything to do with it, soon he'll not be training the horses at all.'

'Is that so, Katie?' Anthony laughed. 'Mind you, I rather thought it might be.'

'He's to spend the rest of the summer painting,' Kathleen said.

'Are you going to Florence after all, old man?'

'And no, he's not,' Kathleen chipped in. 'That has been decided against.'

'By herself here,' Rory said, indicating Kathleen with a nod of his head.

'Rory can paint horses like nobody's business,' Kathleen continued. 'Haven't I already got him half a dozen commissions, and in a couple of years won't Mr Rory Rawlins here only be one of the top equine artists in the country?'

'With no time to look after the yard,' Anthony commented.

'Go on.' Kathleen laughed. 'Now you know well enough who'll be doing that, Mr Rawlins. And if it's all right with you, I can't think of anything I would want to do more.'

'It's very all right by me,' Anthony said mock-seriously, 'as long as you stay as beautiful as you are and don't turn into another Eddie Rampton.'

'Fat chance,' said Rory.

So while Kathleen trained, Rory drew and painted, and in time they had three children, two daughters and a son, their son's most notable achievement being the riding to victory of one of his parents' horses at Aintree in the Foxhunter's Steeplechase, otherwise known as the Amateurs' Grand National.

And all this time Boyo continued to run his heart out and to enjoy doing so.

'When he stops enjoying it, that's the day

574

we retire him on the spot,' Rory and Kathleen agreed, and indeed the day finally dawned when the great horse was retired to grass, though not because he was no longer enjoying his races, but because he developed arthritis. He spent the rest of his days being as mollycoddled as he would allow, which wasn't very much since even though his legs were stiffening and his back was aching the one thing Boyo could not abide was being shut in his stable doing nothing. So whenever the weather allowed, the horse was given the freedom of the field, well rugged up in winter and always brought in when the flies became bothersome. Never short of company, he ran with the youngsters Kathleen introduced to him and taught them his ways, and he tended to the older racehorses, making sure their well-earned holidays were spent with as few interruptions from the youngsters as possible. He was parent and nanny goat, guardian and grandfather, a perfectly tempered animal who looked after his pastoral kingdom with great care and compassion.

His favourite spot to lie was a fold in the home paddock just under the shade of the biggest of the chestnut trees, a haven to which he would take himself off to sleep when the aches in his bones became too much and finally when the sun could do his discomforts no more good. It was there that Kathleen and Rory found him late one summer evening, fast asleep for ever now, his life over, his great and indomitable spirit having been

THE
IMMEDIATE
PROSPECT
OF
BEING
HANGED

The body of Rebecca Carpenter was found late one October night at an overlook in Woodedge that was popular with teenage neckers who drove there from Nestor or Walmouth. But Rebecca Carpenter was from neither of those places. She was from Woodedge. And she was not a teenager. She was forty years old and had been married for sixteen of those years to a prominent local golfer named Wylie S. Carpenter.

When found, Rebecca Carpenter was propped upright in the front passenger's seat of her Mercedes SEL. There were few signs of struggle inside the car—and that was thought to be a little puzzling because Mrs. Carpenter's pantyhose were torn and her $150 silk scarf had been twisted so tightly around her neck that she had died of asphyxiation, which is neither a quick nor a passive way of dying.

This was not the only unusual death ever to occur in Woodedge. It was not even the only one to involve me. It was merely the first in many years that anybody seemed to think important.

1

The town of Woodedge, Massachusetts, was founded in 1640. Founded may be too strong a word, but the town's inception dates from that year, when a group of nine colonial families were given permission from the leaders of the Watertowne plantation to seek "fresh woods and pastures new" by pushing their way further up the Charles River. The names of those nine lucky families were Pendleton, Eire, Stowers, Browne, Whitney, How, Norcross, Mayhew, and Patterson.

They traveled until they reached the edge of a great wood, and then they spread out individually, each seeking the best possible farmland and claiming whatever they saw in the name of the Watertowne plantation. Homesteads were established, paths were beaten from one to the other, and a community of sorts was formed. By 1685 there were 118 inhabitants of what had become known as Woodedge, and the largest contingency by far was the Patterson family. It was in that year that there appeared the first recorded instance of the penchant for isolationism that would mark Woodedgians for the next three centuries.

It seems the frontiersmen were tired of journeying all the way back to Watertowne for their church services and they petitioned to be relieved of the taxation imposed on them to support the ministry in Watertowne. There followed a debate which lasted thirteen years. The debate no doubt was taken seriously by those involved, since on at least one occasion a meeting to discuss the issue had to be adjourned in order "to prevent such inconvenience

as might justly be feared by reason of the heat of the spirit that
seemed to prevail."

In any event, permission was ultimately granted for Woodedge
to build its own church, or meetinghouse, and in 1700 the town
applied to the Reverend President Mather of Harvard College for
advice as to choice of a minister. What Reverend President
Mather gave them was Thomas Chesley. What Woodedge gave
Mr. Chesley was a home and firewood and 125 acres of land
tax-free. What Woodedge got was the inception of a mini-
dynasty.

By 1757 there were 156 names on the Woodedge tax lists, and
more of those names were Chesley than Patterson or anything
else. There are no surviving official records between that year
and 1896, and so demographics have to be pieced together from
other sources. Some people have done that, using church records,
gravestones, and the insides of family Bibles; but the conclusions
I have seen, published in town "histories," vary on every point
except the prominence of the Chesley family.

In 1860 Woodedge's first town hall was built, or consecrated
if the plaque that marks the ruins of the foundation is to be
believed. Five years after that a statue of a Union soldier resting
his hands on the open-barreled end of his rifle was erected in the
middle of the lawn of the town hall. The base of the statue lists
the names of the twelve Woodedge residents "who gave their
lives in the holy cause of freedom." One of those men was named
Chesley. Two were named Patterson.

Among the things controlled by the Chesley family at this point
in time were half a dozen taverns that lined the Boston Post Road,
which served as the main thoroughfare linking Boston to Worces-
ter, Hartford, and New York. Although this road ran through
the heart of Woodedge, it brought Boston no closer than a two-
hour ride to the east for Woodedgians, who preferred to satisfy
their commercial needs at the string of shops that flanked their
town hall and Civil War memorial.

There were other alternatives, of course. If they wanted, Woodedgians could follow the Post Road over the bridge that spanned

the Charles to the already industrialized city of Walmouth, or they could ferry across the river to one of the villages in the city of Nestor, where they could board a train and "take the cars" to Boston. But like their predecessors, the townsfolk of this era took pride in keeping their distance, both literally and figuratively, from their neighbors.

An 1890 autobiography by one William Francis Chesley entitled *Life of a Yankee Squire,* while primarily a paean to the author's ability to breed horses, green plants, and children, nevertheless sheds some light on attitudes of the time. It makes a strong, if grandiloquent, plea for self-reliance and appreciation of nature by extolling the beauty of Woodedge's wooded hillsides, hidden ponds, and sylvan glens. But after painstakingly describing the virtues of his beloved hometown to his somewhat obscurely targeted audience, Squire Chesley was then forced to concede that the vast majority of people are, lamentably, simply not capable of either self-reliance or appreciation of nature.

Such people, the book explains, are simply better off living together. The closer together the better. The problem recognized by the squire was that these people often do not recognize their need to live together and so persist in the mistaken belief that each and every one of them deserves his own plot of land. The squire's book is dedicated to correcting that. It argues that if all men got their own plots of land, the majority would only be made to feel lonely and inadequate. They would, inevitably, end up destroying the very thing they thought they wanted. They would sell off whatever space they were not actively using. They would cut down their trees so that they could see what was being done with the land they had sold, and they would start building and not stop until they had made of Woodedge exactly what they had left behind in places like Walmouth—thus destroying it for those who really deserved it. The only solution, besides barring residency to all non-natives (which Squire Chesley, being a graduate of the Harvard Law School, suspected would be unconstitutional), was to limit ownership in Woodedge to ten acres per household.

Again, no record exists today as to whether the Woodedge board of selectmen, of whom Squire Chesley was one, ever considered this proposal. The loss of records is due to the fact that in 1896 Mr. Chesley's son, William Francis Chesley, II, also known as "Wild Bill," burned down the town hall, and only a handful of books survived. Woodedge had not, as of that time, deemed it necessary to have a fire department.

Wild Bill, whose motive for such an anarchistic act is not recorded in any documents I have seen, did not get off unpunished. Although he was not prosecuted, he was forced to leave town and spend the next several years roaming around Europe. A gravestone behind St. Mark's Episcopal Church indicates that Wild Bill was killed in action in 1918, at the age of forty-four. Where he died, how he died, and on whose behalf he was fighting at that rather advanced age are not indicated.

Wild Bill's banishment aside, the Chesleys were repentent enough to build Woodedge a new town hall on land donated by the Chesley family not more than a mile and a half from the site of the previous town hall. At this point the records become complete again, and among the earliest to be found at "the new town hall," as it is still occasionally called, are those of the town clerk showing the sales of Chesley land along a five-block strip running due west from the new town hall. Most of these sales seemed to have been made to the merchants who formerly had been located in the immediate vicinity of the old town hall. One, however, was a little different. It involved one-third of an acre of Chesley land immediately adjacent to the new town hall and sold to the town itself. Board of selectmen minutes for April 10 of that year show the sale was approved by a vote of four to nothing, Mr. Chesley abstaining. The purpose of the sale was to provide Woodedge with the location for a firehouse.

The hold the Chesley family had on the town diminished over the next twenty-five years as Woodedge got its own train service and became more accessible to certain Boston types who brought with them their own sources of money, power, and social contacts. A Mr. Clare Ransom built the town's first $100,000 estate on land he bought from the last of the Pendleton heirs. Mr. Ransom owned a series of textile mills in Georgia, Rhode Island, and Maine. He belonged to the Longwood Cricket Club and the Brae Burn Country Club, sent his children to the Fessenden School, Groton or Miss Porter's, Harvard University or Wellesley College, and cared not a fig whether any of the Chesleys invited him and his wife to dinner—which, of course, they fell all over themselves doing.

William Francis Chesley's proposal of ten-acre zoning was never enacted, but by the early 1930s Woodedge had scores of estates of at least that size. They were owned by industrialists and bankers and other financial types whose only connections with the founding families came when they wrote them checks.

The Pattersons, what was left of them, sold fast and, at least in the case of my great-uncle Frank, often. Frank Patterson pled guilty to fraud and was forced to live under the pains of probation for three years. It was not the family scandal that it might have been only because by then my grandmother Emily had already brought shame on the Patterson clan by fleeing to Gloucester and marrying a common fisherman named Jared Starbuck. By the time my father was born, the Frank and Emily branch had simply slipped away from the rest of the Pattersons, with Frank selling real estate in Florida and Emily remaining on the North Shore painting seascapes.

To the best of my knowledge, Emily Starbuck never expressed any regret at leaving Woodedge. My father, however, was no-where near so willing to let the family heritage pass. It was his idea to give me the Christian name of Patterson as a means of reestablishing ourselves. It was his goal, often voiced during Sunday drives through the town, to return "to the land that was rightfully his." It was his constant frustration never to be able to do so. His announcements of my birth and baptism went unacknowledged. His Christmas cards, addressed, I suspect, to people whom he had never met, went unanswered. His pursuit of fortune went unrealized to the point that, on his death, after twenty-two years in the insurance business, he had been able to move my mother and me no closer to Woodedge than the village of West Nestor, several miles and a social world away from where he wanted to be.

My father's irrational and increasingly bitter longing for the town in which he had never lived was probably the central theme in our house while I was growing up. He would, with regularity, rant about his second cousins Parker and Frost Patterson, Yale men whom he claimed had never worked a day in their lives and yet lived in splendor on Woodedge's shady hills. Parker, who called himself a writer, occasionally had an article published in *Reader's Digest,* and my father maintained a subscription to the magazine for no other reason than to ridicule, line by line, whatever Parker wrote. But even worse than Parker, according to my father, was the reprobate Frost, who did nothing more than play the stock market.

They were men of about my father's age and, as he constantly reminded my mother and me, they were not one bit smarter than he was. It was just that they had not had to take a job straight out of high school and stay with it day after day to make ends meet. My mother, who as a teenager had been a waitress at a lunch counter my father used to frequent, who had never been ten miles from Gloucester until she met my father, would dutifully agree and damn Parker and Frost right along with him. My mother generally supported my father whenever he railed against the raw deal life had given him. She generally defended him, even when he wasted all his weekends working on short magazine articles that never got published, or when he lost all our money dabbling in the stock market.

So it was that I spent most of the years of my youth being vaguely convinced that the Pattersons of Woodedge, and Parker and Frost in particular, had somehow robbed my father and me of our rightful inheritance. But whereas my father would constantly complain of his lost opportunities to buy or be whatever struck his fancy at a given moment, I remained blissfully confident that somehow, some way, the Patterson family fortune (millions, as I understood it) would sooner or later descend to me. That fortune, once lodged in my name, would allow me the green Jag with the tan interior I saw on Route 128, the trip to Jamaica advertised in the travel magazine I was flipping through at the dentist's office, the girl ahead of me in line at the bank who was pretending I didn't exist. That fortune, and all it inevitably brought with it, made it unimportant if I studied hard or got into a good college.

It was, for a while, a comforting inspiration and on occasion I even managed to put it to good use, as when I was able to talk Mary Marie Gastonatto into taking down her pants while we were making out in the front seat of my mother's Ford. Mary Marie, unfortunately, was so carried away by her misperceived prospect of being married to an heir that she told her sister Angeljean about my impending wealth, and Angeljean told half the high school.

Not wanting to jeopardize Mary Marie's affections, I did nothing to discourage the story. It swelled and spawned rumors that became increasingly ridiculous. That was okay as far as my friends were concerned. They knew what it took to score with a girl like Mary Marie and they understood my inheritance to be simply a line I had used. But among people who didn't know me so well, who didn't know Mary Marie so well, the rumors persisted. They continued right up to the day the article appeared in the *Courier* about my father's body being found in the woods behind the Patterson family home. After that I didn't hear them anymore.

John Michael Keough was thirty-six years old, which made him two years younger than I. He was also district attorney of Exeter County, which made him my boss. As near as I can tell, John Michael, although born with that name in Walmouth General Hospital, did not become known as John Michael until he started practicing law. His yearbook at Walmouth High, which I made a point of finding, simply identifies him as John M., nickname "Jack." His yearbook biography, run out beneath the picture of a very serious young man sporting a hairstyle noticeably shorter than those of his classmates, says he lettered one year in football and was a member of the debating team. It also says he was president of the junior class. It says nothing about him being a class officer in his senior year, nor is his unsmiling face included in the picture of that year's class officers.

After graduation from high school, John Michael commuted to Boston College. His campaign bio, now his "official bio," says he worked in a laundry to help pay his tuition. When I asked him what laundry it was he told me it was the Pilgrim. When I went down to the Pilgrim nobody could remember him; although, to be fair, the Pilgrim is a big place and not that many of the workers speak English.

John Michael also went to Boston College Law School. His campaign bio says that he was a member of the team that won the National Moot Court competition. He has a round medal bearing the engraved image of Supreme Court Justice Powell to prove it and he keeps the medal on his desk at the Exeter County Courthouse.

John Michael took a job with the Commonwealth attorney general upon receiving his law degree, and it appears he did quite well. He was in the organized crime division and the newspaper clipping he has framed on his wall shows he was instrumental in putting a local Mafia chieftain in prison.

John Michael then became deputy district attorney for Exeter County. With just four or five years of legal experience behind him he was put in charge of criminal litigation. That was when I met him. He hired me as an office investigator. It was a bold move on his part because D.A.'s investigators are supposed to be members of the state police force. But the chief investigator for the office was an affable detective lieutenant named Libby and John Michael told me in confidence that he did not trust Libby because he was part of the "old boy" system. He was going to phase Libby out, he said. Bring in new people, his own people, people he could trust. People like me. I needed a job. I told him that was great.

Three years later I was still working and John Michael wasn't. He had fallen into disfavor with the then district attorney, a man named Phil Burns. "Burnsie" was liked by most everyone who is supposed to like a D.A. He could drink with the best of them. John Michael didn't drink. He made allies in other ways. One day Mr. Burns sobered up long enough to realize that John Michael had developed as many allies as he, Burnsie, had friends. The next day John Michael was fired.

This proved to be a mistake for Phil Burns. John Michael held a press conference. Whereas Burnsie had seen nothing newsworthy about letting one of his deputies go, John Michael turned the incident into the lead story on the six-o'clock news. With cameras snapping and whirring, he sat in his dark blue suit, blue shirt, and red tie, like some implacable John Dean, and gave straightforward, noteless testimony for fifteen minutes about the corruption and incompetence in the Exeter County district attorney's office.

Taken by themselves, the Keough revelations were not that remarkable—a dismissed drunk-driving charge against one of Burnsie's Knights of Columbus buddies, a reduction of a burglary charge against the son of another buddy, some lost evidence in a construction-fraud case against the contractor who built Burnsie's swimming pool—but orchestrated as they were by John Michael, the cumulative effect was quite disturbing.

John Michael explained that the morale of the office was devastatingly low, and that all but a few fawning toadies were incapacitated in their ability to do the people's work. Cleverly, he named no names, thus mitigating the willingness to rebut his charges by anyone who did not want to be accused of being a fawning toadie. Piously, he announced that as a public officer he could take Mr. Burns's abuses of power no longer, and that it was his ultimatum to Burns to stop running his office as a private fiefdom that had caused him to be dismissed.

KEOUGH BLOWS WHISTLE, belched the headline in the *Walmouth-Nestor Courier*, which had always liked Burnsie but was nevertheless obliged to play up the story to keep from getting scooped on its own turf by the Boston papers. The *Globe* and the *Herald* had squadrons of young reporters foraging through the file rooms at the county courthouse, and the *Courier* was reluctantly forced to tap its own sources. All these newspapers found dirt, of course, and in their eagerness to outdo each other they managed to keep the story going for a couple of weeks.

Under such competitive scrutiny, Burnsie's most endearing little qualities, like his willingness to show up at any gathering of two or more people where liquor was being served, became cause for criticism. A felony trial of no particular interest to anyone other than the people involved was lost by a very capable member of Burnsie's staff, and the *Courier* said, NO WONDER.

Stung, Burnsie went out and tried a slam-dunk murder case himself. He had not tried a case in years and he should not have tried this one. He should especially not have tried a case in which the outcome was thought to be a foregone conclusion. His every move was criticized, his every mistake magnified. John Michael stood on the sidelines like a color commentator, somberly and almost patriotically providing the *Courier* with a running analysis that made the daily reports of the trial sound like law review articles.

The jurors, who were prohibited from reading the newspapers' accounts, returned a verdict not of first-degree murder, as Burnsie demanded, but of voluntary manslaughter. One of the jurors, when interviewed after the verdict, spoke of mens rea, a term never once used in the courtroom but discussed at length in one news article. It did not matter. Burnsie's career as D.A. was over. The public, even those who did not know who he was, had lost confidence in him.

John Michael, meanwhile, had taken a job with the county's largest law firm. His name was added to the firm's letterhead and then he was essentially freed to go off and orchestrate a campaign for the next year's election, where he beat Phil Burns in a runaway and became Exeter County's youngest district attorney in a century. This should have made John Michael happy. But John Michael, as I came to find out, was not easily given to happiness.

Among the things that displeased John Michael once he became D.A. was that he was not president of the United States, or even a senator or a congressman. He also did not like the fact that he was not wealthy, famous, absolutely respected, and right in his opinions one hundred percent of the time.

John Michael, however, did like me. This was in no small part due to the fact that it had been his idea to create my position as "litigation coordinator" and the success I had experienced in that role reflected favorably on him. It was also due to my willingness to tell him he was famous, brilliant, infallible, and ought to be president-senator-congressman.

There were other people, of course, who told John Michael these same things. But there were only three of us whose words he really believed. One was Royster Hansen, whom, like me, he had brought into the office and on whose legal advice he was dependent. For all his accomplishments, John Michael Keough at thirty-six was not a tower of legal knowledge. Hansen, ten years older, had been John Michael's mentor in the attorney general's office. John Michael's first move as D.A. was to make him chief deputy in charge of the criminal division.

The third member of John Michael's triumvirate of advisers was his wife, Jessica. People in the office had many names for Jessica. One was the Bitch. Another was the Ice Queen. She is a platinum blonde who would be beautiful if only her features were not so rigid. Still, she photographs well.

The dynamics were interesting. Royster pretended to like me and really did not. Jessica pretended not to like me and really did.

We would meet regularly, the three of us and John Michael. We would meet in John Michael's paneled office on Friday evenings or whenever Jessica happened to streak in. Sometimes I would be summoned to the lounge at the Roadhouse Restaurant; and sometimes we would gather at the Keoughs' house in Nestor Heights. The home meetings would usually be characterized in their invitations as a dinner or a cookout, and Royster would usually bring his wife, Patty. I would be encouraged to bring a date so that Patty would have someone to talk to while the rest of us discussed important things. If I didn't bring a date then Patty would have nothing to do. She would get sloshed in relative silence while the rest of us discussed important things around her. We were a fun group.

Sometimes the important things we discussed had to do with other people, such as a bombastic Waterford city councilor named George Constantinis who was always stirring up the blue-collar folk of that fair city with his demands for a new dump or a new senior-citizen recreation center or resident parking permits or whatever seemed politically opportune at the time. George Constantinis was a hack, but he was young and aggressive and he had a knack for generating publicity, and John Michael worried about him constantly.

Sometimes our concerns would be rather exotic, as when we would fret over the latest rumor that one of the Kennedy children was moving into the area and would soon be seeking the congressional seat. We knew there were plenty of Kennedy children out there and their possible arrival was a fear the Keoughs had to live with from day to day.

And sometimes the concerns of the moment were more personal, as when an editorial appeared in the *Courier* on the use and abuse of plea bargaining. Any publicity that was not absolutely favorable tended to spawn rage, gloom, and intricate plans for vindication in our little gatherings.

"The voting public is fickle," John Michael would constantly remind us. "They'll turn on me in a minute if I give them the chance."

And then Jessica would tell us, "What we really need, what John has to have, is a big case. Something that will give him some exposure."

At this point John Michael might say something like, "Wouldn't it be great if we could catch some Russian spy stealing secrets from one of the defense contractors out on 128?" And if Royster, being more experienced in dealing with that sort of thing, pointed out that a spy case would probably be a federal matter and handled by those assholes in the U.S. Attorney's Office, it would be up to Jessica or me to modify John Michael's wish accordingly. The Route 128 belt of contractors and computer companies was arguably the leading high-tech spot in the nation, and much of it lay in our county. John Michael was always trying to figure out ways to cash in on the attention the Route 128 companies generated.

Jessica, however, preferred to think in more basic terms. Her constant refrain was that what the American people love is scandal. "Sex, wealth, and foul play," she would urge.

We had plenty of cases dealing with those subjects in the office. But the sex usually came in the form of rapes and child molestations, the wealth in the form of corporate fraud, and the foul play in the same mind-numbing forms experienced by every other

county in the country. What we were looking for, what John
Michael and Jessica were looking for, was one case involving all
three elements. What we got was the death of Rebecca Carpenter.

My first knowledge of the Carpenter slaying came on a beautiful mid-October morning when I arrived in John Michael's office
and found him parading from wall to wall and happily waving
a file over his head. John Michael looked young to begin with,
but when he smiled he looked even younger. On this particular
day he looked like a Boy Scout. "This," he crooned, "is it."

The file had been prepared over the course of the night by the
Woodedge police department. It contained a sketch of the scene,
a detailed listing of photographs and prints taken and evidence
inventoried, and a lengthy note of what the investigating officer
(a Roland Tagget) had observed. Officer Tagget was meticulous
in detailing that the victim showed no visible signs of having been
raped or sexually molested, other than the fact her stockings were
torn above the thigh.

Officer Tagget had contacted his watch commander, a Sergeant
Roselli; and the Sergeant had gone first to the scene and then
directly to the Carpenter home, where he had interviewed the
new widower at one a.m. Sergeant Roselli's report was considerably less detailed than that of Officer Tagget. One gathered, on
reading it, that Mr. Carpenter was quite surprised to learn that
his wife was dead. Other than a notation that Mrs. Carpenter's
pocketbook was missing, it contained little of interest.

The part about the interview read:

Proceeded to home of victim, 6 Bulham Road. Engaged husb.
of vict., Wylie S. Carpenter, in pajamas. Infd. him of event.
Became distraught. Thought wife was with friends. Had been
at Stonegate C.C. until 10:00 p.m.

I agreed with John Michael. I told him this was it.

John Michael clasped his hands behind his back and strode
across his office. "And I don't," he said, addressing me while he

faced his rows of bookshelves, "want those palookas out there fucking it up."

I was not sure what he meant. Not much happened of a serious criminal nature in Woodedge, and I had no particular reason, other than the lack of information in Roselli's note, to think that the Woodedge police department was any more incompetent than any other in the county.

"There's some reason why a woman like this would be in a place like that, and whatever it is, it stinks," John Michael said. He turned from his books. He looked at me with a fiery glint of pleasure in his eye. "That's the part I want you going after, Patt. The part that stinks. We'll let Chief Tuttle worry about the dusting and the tracking and the fibers on the seat covers. I want you finding out what kind of woman this was, what kind of man her husband is, how she could have let herself get in the position she was in. You follow me?"

"You want the dirt."

"I want the dirt."

"Where do you want me to start?"

"Friends, neighbors, fellow club members. Start with the husband, of course, and work your way out from there."

I tucked the file under my arm and headed for the door. As I reached it my boss stopped me with one more remark.

"This time we're really going to get them."

I turned, knotted my fist, and pantomimed a short punch to the gut. I did not even bother asking who "them" was.

3

There are several roads that lead from Walmouth to Woodedge, but the main one emerges from the traffic lights of Walmouth's busy downtown shopping area, runs past a former movie theater that is now a Pentecostal church, and then past a bowling alley and a McDonald's, a Papa Gino's pizzeria, a bar or two, and a string of glass-fronted shops that sell doughnuts or insurance or windowshades. Gradually it leads into a neighborhood of single-family homes with overgrown hedges and bare spots in their front yards. The houses have mongrel dogs that bark, and large American cars that back dangerously out of their driveways, and posted sidewalk signs that say CAUTION CHILDREN AT PLAY.

If you follow this main road, which appropriately is called Main Street, you will eventually come to the river. The bridge over the river is, in fact, a traffic circle. You can exit the traffic circle onto 128 going north or south, or you can go exactly halfway around the circle from Walmouth and enter Woodedge. At this point Main Street becomes Old Boston Post Road.

There is a very old, partially broken, stone wall that runs along the Old Boston Post Road, and for the first mile or so there are simply no houses at all. Then there is the hint of one, a dark spot in the trees on the other side of the wall. A few more houses appear, well camouflaged if they are old, intrusive if they are not. There is a roadside farm stand, where, depending on the season, the world's best corn and apples can be purchased. There is a

florist with a greenhouse and a gravel turnoff in front of his door.
The road goes deep into the woods after that and then emerges
into a meadow that begins with an old Presbyterian church and
ends with a fairly new Catholic church. The latter has a long
paved driveway that runs between planted trees, and a fifteen-
foot crucifix at the junction of the driveway and the road. The
Presbyterian church, however, divides the road itself. The right-
hand fork becomes Woodedge's Main Street. It rises uphill to the
town hall—fire station—police station complex, and then runs
gradually downhill for two miles until it rejoins the Post Road.

For several blocks Main Street goes past a row of shops selling
fabrics, apothecaries, women's dresses, books, hardware supplies,
pastries, and real estate. The string of shops ends at the post
office, and since Woodedgians pride themselves on having no
home mail delivery, the post office has the largest parking lot in
town.

Next to the post office is a restaurant called Adolfo's, a converted home with patio dining and white table umbrellas that
are used more to keep leaves and twigs out of the food than to
ward off sunshine. Across the street from Adolfo's is the town
library, a three-room affair patronized by no one between the
ages of fifteen and sixty; and next to that is the Woodedge Woman's Club, its function and membership as much a mystery to me
once I became a county investigator as it had been when I was
a child and used to cruise this street with my father.

Beyond the Woodedge Woman's Club are a few more houses
that, like Adolfo's, have been converted into business establishments, most of them travel agents' or realtors' offices. Then there
is the original town cemetery, with its eighteenth-century head-
stones and its haphazardly mown lawn. There is a Christian
Science church and a Congregational church and then there is
nothing until the statue of the Union soldier standing forlornly
on what used to be the grounds of the old town hall. When I
drove past there on my first trip to the Carpenter home I noticed
a yellow wreath on a wire stand jammed into the earth in front
of the statue. It looked as if it had been there for some time and

I wondered why it was there at all. I wondered if it was the work of the elusive Woodedge Woman's Club, perhaps some one hundred neofeminists strong, marching ten abreast down the center of Main Street in their tartan skirts and sensible shoes to plant a lousy wreath in front of an obscure memorial as part of their cryptic annual rites.

There was no particular reason why I was driving down Main Street on my way to the Carpenters' house, it was just something I had not had reason to do in a number of years and I felt the urge to see if anything had changed. Once Main rejoined the Post Road I turned right and followed that west to Rotten Row, a country lane with a name that supposedly had honorable English derivations.

Rotten Row led me south onto Highland Street, which is lined with horse farms; and then the horse farms ended and the wood thickened. I passed Whitehall Road leading to the old Patterson place and a half mile beyond that I turned off of Highland Street and entered Bulham Road. The number 6 was set into each of a pair of stone pillars that stood on either side of the entrance to a twisty driveway that ran uphill past a couple of hundred fruit trees. The drive ended by bending into an elipse at the Carpenters' front door.

Just outside the door a young cop whom I did not recognize was seated in a Woodedge police cruiser with the door open and his feet on the ground. He eyed my little Alfa Romeo suspiciously. He eyed me suspiciously as I got out. He eyed me as if he thought I might be the killer.

"Starbuck," I said, walking directly up to him and showing him my I.D. "D.A.'s office."

The young cop went from eyeing me suspiciously to eyeing my I.D. suspiciously. Nothing was going to escape his scrutiny.

I knew how to handle guys like this. "What's your name?" I demanded.

"Griffin," he said.

"What are you doing here?"

Surprised, Griffin said, "I'm with the chief." He pitched his head toward the house.

I grunted and simply walked in the front door without Officer Griffin asking me anything at all.

It was, of course, a very large house. It had three stories, although the top story tapered with the roof. There was an attached three-car garage. There was a separate cottage off to one side, a grape arbor and a gazebo and a murky little fish pond. Everything was in place and everything was painted the same off-yellow color that probably had some fancy name like Mojave.

I guessed the main house had about fifteen rooms, but I didn't get a chance to count them because Chief Tuttle was sitting in the very first one I entered. Sitting with him was a well-tanned, slim fellow in a Ralph Lauren knit shirt, khaki slacks, and deck shoes with no socks. He was, in an aging and vaguely unappealing sort of way, quite handsome. I figured if he wasn't Wylie Carpenter, local golf hero, he should have been.

Chief Wembley Tuttle had gotten dressed for the occasion. He had on his full police uniform. His plastic brimmed hat lay next to him on the sofa, turned upside down. His stomach was launching the buttons of a jacket he probably had not worn since the last parade. On the table in front of him was an empty coffee cup. He looked both relieved and a little upset to see me.

"Patt," he said, without getting up. The chief was in his late fifties and on the home stretch. He knew the easy part of being chief of police in a small town and he knew the hard part. He had grown comfortable with the easy part.

Carpenter was leaning forward in his overstuffed chair. His knees were apart, his hands were together as he waited to be introduced.

I had to do it myself. "Patt Starbuck," I said. "D.A.'s office."

Tuttle realized then that he had missed his cue. He waved his plump hand in my direction. "Patt's the D.A.'s personal investigator," he said. "We don't usually have the pleasure of his company in a case this early. We don't usually have the D.A.'s

investigators involved in our little town too much at all." He still
did not give me the man's name.

"You're Wylie Carpenter?" I asked.

The man nodded.

"You have my condolences."

The man said thank you because he assumed I was talking
about his wife.

Tuttle was still speaking. "They're usually spending all their
time out in Waterford or Walmouth, that's where the real crimes
are. Even Nestor, get some good crimes out there once in
a while. Not too often we get much around here except the
occasional burglary. Not too often we get anything like this."

I stood in the center of the room and looked around. It was
some sort of den, and while everything in it was reddish or brown-
ish in color, I couldn't help but think it was all rather a mishmash.
There was a small bar built into a set of bookshelves and there
was an elaborate set of cabinets, which I suspected hid a large-
screen television set.

Chief Tuttle stopped rambling and we exchanged looks with
each other. I noticed he did not have any notepaper in front of
him. He just had the coffee cup, and that told me he must have
gone through all the preliminaries, all the niceties. I looked from
him to Carpenter. "So who do you think did it?"

Carpenter's head snapped back. He turned to Chief Tuttle for
help and Tuttle said, "That's what we're trying to find out, Patt."

"Uh-huh." I walked over to one wall and inspected the pictures
I saw there. One was a signed Meyerowitz photograph of a Cape
Cod scene. I had the same scene on my wall calendar. Next to
it was a small, overly green oil painting of a golfer teeing off in
front of a large gallery. Then there was a set of three antique
hunting prints. As I said, things were a mishmash.

"This seems to be a man's room," I commented.

"We called it our sitting room," Carpenter said. "It was . . .
it was both of ours. We tended to close it off when we were
entertaining, I suppose."

I turned and saw that he was pointing to a pair of wood-paneled sliding doors. "Reason I'm asking, Mr. Carpenter, is I don't see much that reflects Mrs. Carpenter's personality in here. What was she like?"

Wylie Carpenter waved his hands. "She was kind," he said.

The chief was surreptitiously shaking his head at me.

I pressed on, even though Carpenter had now covered his eyes. "I'm more interested in her activities. Was she, for example, a golfer, like you?"

Carpenter shook his head. His hand stayed on his brow and moved as his head moved. "Not really. She played, but . . ."

"Yachting? Was she a yachter, Mr. Carpenter? Or a tennis player?"

"Tennis occasionally, when the weather was good. She swam, she skied—"

"In good shape, was she?"

Carpenter was giving me a list and he stayed with it. "—rode horses, danced."

"Where would she do all those things, Mr. Carpenter?"

He sniffed and dabbed at his eyes with the pads of his fingers. "Well, at the club, mostly, or with friends. It depends, I guess."

"What club are you talking about?"

"Bollingbrook. It's our country club. We've been members ever since we got married—or I have, at any rate. Becky's family have always been members."

"Mrs. Carpenter grew up around here?"

The chief spoke up. This was something he felt qualified to handle. "She's a Chesley, Patt."

"I see. They're well known, are they? The Chesleys?"

The chief bubbled over on the couch. If his breath had been spittle it would have dribbled down his chin.

"They go back to the *Mayflower*," said Carpenter; and even though I knew from my father's research that that was not quite true, I let it go by.

"What other clubs did she belong to? What did she do with her days? Did she work outside the home? Can you help me with any kind of information like that, Mr. Carpenter?"

"Oh, the usual," Carpenter said. "Junior League, League of Women Voters, Woodedge Historical Society, I suppose. But she wasn't really active in any of them except Bollingbrook. How did she spend her days? Oh, I don't know. The same things all women do, I suppose. Go out with friends, take care of the grounds—she was very concerned about the grounds lately because she was just breaking in a new caretaker—I don't know. We have a place down the Cape in Osterville and another up at Stratton Mountain, and there always seemed to be something that had to be done at one or the other. I don't know, Mr. Starbuck. I don't know what she did."

Chief Tuttle sighed heavily.

"You mentioned Bollingbrook, Mr. Carpenter, but I saw in the police report that you spent last night at Stonegate Country Club. Did they have that right?"

Carpenter nodded. "Yes, I belong to both and I played yesterday at Stonegate. I tend to do that, you see, if I just have a golf game. It's a lot less formal than Bollingbrook. I had some snacks at the bar, a few drinks, and then played cards with the fellows until about ten." He smiled, or came close to it. "You wouldn't do that at Bollingbrook."

The chief smiled with him. The chief had probably never been to Bollingbrook in his life.

"You mentioned that when you got home you thought your wife was with friends. Who were you thinking about?"

Carpenter had his thumb and his forefinger pinched over the bridge of his nose. He answered with his eyes closed. "Oh, Molly Barr, Hannah Babcock, Gretchen Patterson."

"Males? Any male friends you're aware of?"

On the couch the chief started, doing untold damage to the timing of my question.

Carpenter said, "Oh, their husbands, I suppose. Dickie Barr, Dodge Patterson. Um, Jim Babcock."

"You've got a picture of your wife, do you?"

He made a half-point toward the chief, who got something out of the inside of his jacket and handed it to me. It was a photograph of Rebecca Carpenter standing next to a magnificent-looking horse. Rebecca's blond hair was pulled back and her brown eyes were steady on the camera. She was a good-looking woman, if you liked the kind that stared right through you. I gave the picture back.

"No children?"

He shook his head. "We wanted to, but . . . no. None."

I got out my notebook and took the names and addresses of the three couples he had mentioned. I asked about the help the Carpenters employed. He waved in the direction of the cottage I had noticed when I was coming into the house.

"We had a couple living there, Dominic and Gina, but we had to let them go. We caught her stealing our liquor." He snorted and wiped quickly at his nose. "Big deal, huh?"

"Last name?"

"Marconi. I don't know where they went, if that's what you're going to ask next."

"That's it for help?"

"We have a black gal who comes in Monday through Friday to do housekeeping. Sarah Mitchell. She's been with us for years."

"And you said there was a new caretaker?"

"Oh, that's right. What's his name? Doug Rasmussin, from Walmouth. He's been working here since the Marconis left. Becky took care of all the arrangements with him, so I never paid much attention."

Wylie Carpenter was covering his brow again and the chief was glowering at me when I switched to the subject of the missing pocketbook. "Any idea what was in it?" I asked.

"Near as we can figure, a few hundred dollars," the chief said.

"No jewelry missing?"

"None that Mr. Carpenter is aware of."

I nodded as though that was significant. I narrowed my eyes just to make the chief nervous and then I thanked the new widower and headed for the door with a promise that I would be in touch.

I was just starting my Alfa when the chief came bustling out after me. His white hair was blowing in the breeze and his chubby cheeks were red from the effort of running. I smiled up at him as he planted fingerprints all over the side of my car.

He made an effort to compose himself before he spoke. "Did Keough send you out here?"

"Of course."

"Did he think we couldn't handle it? Is that why?"

"He didn't say anything of the sort. He wants me handling a parallel investigation because he knows you're going to find the murderer and he wants to get a jump on trial preparation."

The chief made his last pant for air. He cleared his throat and tried to smooth his hair. "Yeah," he said, "well, if that's the way you're going to go about it we're going to be stepping all over each other's feet. The way you were talking to Mr. Carpenter in there, that may be okay for your common criminals out in Waterford or Walmouth, but it isn't right with people in this town. You gotta be more respectful." He put his hand on my shoulder. He gave me a fatherly smile. "Believe me," he said. "I know these people. They're different from you and me."

Inadvertently, I gunned my engine. Startled, the chief withdrew his hand. Nothing further was said as I let the car roll forward. Apparently I missed his toes.

Rebecca Carpenter's car had been towed to a garage known as Samuels, which the Woodedge police used for an impound center. There was precious little impounding that went on in Woodedge, and so the police simply contracted with Samuels to do both the towing and the storage. Samuels's tow trucks were painted yellow and had the AAA insignia all over them.

The Mercedes was silver in color and appeared to be in perfect condition. It looked thick and strong; as handsome and potentially dangerous as a sleeping lion. The police had secured it by isolating one corner of the garage with a yellow ribbon of tape.

Four cops were gathered in and around the car when I arrived. I saw little Lester, Woodedge's lone inspector, standing like a movie director with a clipboard and pen in his hand. I saw Browning, Woodedge's lone policewoman, perched in the front passenger seat, the focus of everyone's attention. The other two people were young men in uniform, neither of whom I recognized. One of the young men had a camera and stood outside the car. The other sat behind the steering wheel. Up close, all four people looked very excited by what they were doing. Their excitement was manifested by the quickness of their movements.

Browning, I saw, had a long scarf around her neck.

"Okay, lean over slowly, Tompkins," Lester called out in his rapid-fire, heavily accented voice; and the young uniform behind the wheel dutifully inclined toward Browning, who was positioned with her back between the door and her seat.

"Okay, hands on her shoulders."

Tompkins did as he was told. Lester yelled, "Okay, snap it, Morrison," and the flash of the camera held by the second uniform went off.

"You across that console? You can do it, Tommie? Okay, both hands on the bloody scarf. Okay, snap it, Mo. Now knot it, Tommie. One time, hup, that's it: over, round about, up, and through. That's it. Pull it now. That's it, lad. Not too tight. Snap it, Mo."

The flash went off on command. Lester noticed me and pretended he didn't. I moved behind him so I could get a good angle on the proceedings and stood with my arms folded.

"All right, Elizabeth, what are you doing now, you bloody cow?" Lester was from Zimbabwe (Rhodesia, he would tell you), by way of England; and because he was he could get away with a lot that nobody else would dare.

"I'm fighting," Browning shouted, and crooked both her arms at the elbow to pummel poor Tompkins.

"Not bloody well yet, you're not. Put your arms around him. Tommie's hand goes on your thigh. All in the name of the law now, children. That's it. Snap it, Mo."

The actors hung frozen, waiting for the next direction from their tyrannical director. I noticed what appeared to be a growing area of wetness under Browning's outstretched arm and suspected that of the four she least liked her role.

"Now, let's give this a think, shall we?" Lester said, moving up and resting his hand on the roof of the car. "The two of you are embracing. The bugger wants that pot of honey. He's moving his hand ever closer. Move it, Tommie. That's quite enough. You don't want him touching it, Elizabeth, so what do you do?"

Browning raised her fist as if to crush Tompkins' skull.

"No," cried Lester, slapping his clipboard against his leg. "You wiggle that bloody big arse of yours, that's what. You're struggling with him. But you wouldn't have come here in the first place, him driving your car, you over here in the passenger seat, if you didn't like him a little bit. So you're not going to bloody crown him, you're just going to try to keep him away."

Browning promptly pushed Tompkins to arms' length. Lester barked at Tompkins to get closer, and Tompkins, who was a big but rather lardy-looking lug, whose face would have resembled nothing so much as a marshmallow if it were not for the fact that it was transected by a mustache, leaned in until Browning quite clearly was straining to keep him away. Her position began to crumble and Lester ecstatically leaped out of camera range. "Snap it, Morrison, you bastard. Snap it."

The flash went off. Lester rushed forward to inspect his subjects and then jumped back again. "Now, go for the scarf, Tommie. What are you going to do, Elizabeth? Righto, now maybe you'd hit him. Where, now? On the side of the face. Snap it, Mo. But now he's tightening the scarf. And again, Mo. What are you going to do, Bessie? You push his shoulders. You rake his face. You punch him in the stomach. You're slipping down. Keep shooting, Mo. Keep leaning in Tommie. Now you've got it. Where are your feet going? Kick them, Elizabeth. The bugger's trying to kill you, isn't he? Get the feet, Mo. Get 'em now, lad."

Finally, Elizabeth Browning screamed and everything came to a sudden halt. Tompkins sat up straight, a look of surprise on his simpleton's face. Officer Browning shoved open the door and emerged from the car coughing, hacking actually, her face and neck bright red as her fingers tore at the scarf on which Tompkins had been tugging. She was a good-sized woman, about five foot nine and 140 pounds, and she made quite a sight as she bent over and grabbed her knees and struggled for air. I noticed that the tops and toes of her shoes were covered with white chalk.

Lester nearly knocked her over in his effort to get to the car and stick his head in the well where her feet had been a moment before. "Balls!" he yelled.

He stood up angrily and glared at Morrison, the photographer. He did not pay the slightest attention to Browning, who was still bent over and was now gobbing drool onto the floor of the garage.

"Shoot it all," he ordered. "And see if you can get the white marks and the green marks in the same bloody frame, will you?"

At last Lester turned to me. "Starbuck," he said as he patted his shirt pocket and went inside his rust-colored double-knit sport coat for a cigarette.

I stood with my arms folded and nodded at him.

"Figured somebody from your office would show up sooner or later. Didn't figure it would be you, though."

I let Lester have his moment of superiority. I knew what he made for a living. "What else do you figure?" I asked.

"I figure," Lester said, making me wait while he lit his cigarette, sucked on it, and waved it at the car, "that there's no bleeding way this woman got strangled in there."

Officer Browning dropped to her hands and knees. Her head was down close to the floor. By the change in the sounds she was making she seemed to be getting better.

I walked over to where Morrison was working and looked inside the car. I could see the white marks of Browning's shoes all over the dash and the console. I could see lines of phosphorescent green as well, but they were only on the underside of the dash. I said, calling back over my shoulder, "You see the body, Les?"

"What a godawful sight that was. Lips and ears purple. Tongue hanging out, white stuff all over her nose and mouth."

I asked if he saw any petechiae and Lester looked confused.

"Burst blood vessels. Little red spots?"

"Oh, that. All over the face. Eyeballs, too."

"Then what makes you think it wasn't strangulation?"

"Oh, it was strangulation all right. They took an X ray first thing and she had a broken bone right there in her neck." Lester checked his clipboard. He turned a page of notepaper. "The hyoid, I think it's called. What I'm saying, if you open your ears, Patt, is that she didn't get strangled in there." He thrust a pointing finger at the car.

Browning switched over to a seated position and was at last breathing close to normally. Lester stepped around her and came up to where he could jab with the eraser end of his pencil at the green marks. "If she was, she didn't put up much of a struggle. These things we've colored here are the only marks we've found."

Somehow, I wasn't that impressed with Lester's evidence. I looked over at Browning and said, "Elizabeth's a big woman. How big was Mrs. Carpenter?"

Lester put the cigarette between his lips so he could blow smoke while he talked. "Well, I haven't seen the autopsy and I didn't exactly get out my own tape measure, but I'd wager she was about five six, five seven." He, too, looked at Officer Browning. "About half the size of that one, I'd say."

We both looked at the green marks again, doing our silent approximations.

"The guy leans over," I said. "He's being amorous. He puts his hand under her skirt. She pushes him away. He grabs her scarf . . . and then what? Does he knot it?"

Lester shook his head. "It was a simple over-and-under. She probably did it herself when she put it on and he just grabbed the ends."

"Okay, can he do that?" I demonstrated what I imagined to be the maneuver. It called for me to spread my hands apart. "She could be whacking away at him. Tearing at his face. Was there any flesh under her nails?"

"I didn't see anything. Maybe the autopsy . . ." He shrugged and let the sentence dangle.

We continued to stare at the car. "So you think the murderer killed her someplace else and then put her in her own car and drove her out to lovers' lane and abandoned her there?"

Lester was silent. This was, after all, his investigation. It was up to him to write the report.

"That would mean that the killer then would have had to manipulate her legs after she was dead to make her feet put the marks on the dash."

Lester shrugged again. "It's possible."

I opened the back door on the passenger side and slid onto the seat. There was a moveable headrest on the top of the front seat where Mrs. Carpenter's body was found, but it still could have been possible to get around it. Lester saw what I was considering and ordered Officer Browning back into action. Taking a deep breath, she stood up and replaced the scarf. Then she silently assumed the position.

I patted her shoulder and whispered thank you. She nodded without turning around.

"Place the knot exactly where you saw it, Les," I asked.

Lester didn't move. He glanced at where Browning had the knot, in the middle of her throat, and said, "It's there."

I reached forward and took one end of the scarf in each hand. Browning tensed, but I did little more than move my hands apart. I watched as her back arched and her feet pushed deep into the well beneath the dash. Lester saw what I saw and I dropped the ends of the scarf.

"It's just a thought, Les," I said, getting out. "I assume, before you started creating evidence of your own, you scoured both the front and back to see what the killer might have left behind."

Lester was still staring into the car. He kept staring even when I asked who was performing the autopsy.

"Dr. Havens is doing it at Filbert and Tweed mortuary."

"Let me know when you get the results, will you?"

I took his grunt as an assent and headed out to my own car. As I reached the door to the garage I looked back and saw that Lester had Tompkins in the rear seat and Morrison kneeling with his camera on the outside edge of the driver's seat. I suspected that poor Browning was in for another bad time of it.

I had an apartment in Boston. It wasn't the smartest thing to do, renting an apartment in Boston—paying big-city rates and commuting to and from work—but I liked the anonymity it provided me.

My building was on Commonwealth Avenue. It was a renovated mansion with a wood-paneled entranceway and none of my neighbors knew, or apparently cared, anything about me. We would nod when we bumped into each other. We would say such things as, "It's going to be tough driving today" when it snowed and "Looks like a beautiful day" when the sun shone. Like the single women in the building, I had my name posted on the mailbox, but not next to my doorbell, so it was quite possible that nobody other than the manager even knew who I was.

On days when, for one reason or another, I could not make the commute to Boston, I would stay at my mother's house in West Nestor. It was the house I grew up in, and in that neighborhood everyone knew me. The kids playing football in the streets would temporarily halt their game when my car approached and yell "Hi, Patt," when I passed by. If Mrs. Graham in the house next door to my mother's was sitting on her porch when I pulled into the driveway I would be obliged to go over and exchange a few meaningless sentences with her. I was always anxious to avoid seeing Mrs. Graham, and yet I almost always would go over to speak with her. While she was as sweet and kind as she could be, usually there was a slight note of desperation in her voice, a tacit admission that she knew I wanted to get on to someone or somewhere else. And so she would do her best to rapid-fire her questions or stories at me, and I, in turn, would answer or listen, mostly because of that note in her voice.

Mrs. Graham was not visible when I went to my mother's house on the evening of my first day's investigation into the Carpenter slaying, but Kelsey was. Kelsey was a friend of my mother's, although he was much younger than she. He was, indeed, closer to my age than to hers, and she was very sensitive about that. She did not want me to think they had any sort of relationship, and I went along with that because I told myself it was none of my business whether they did or not. Still, I remained uncertain as to what my mother and Kelsey managed to see in each other.

My mother had gotten married to my father when she was twenty years old. For their honeymoon they went to Boston and my mother took along her Brownie camera so that she could snap pictures of all the tall buildings. Even now, when she knows Boston intimately, she remembers that trip as a wondrous adventure. From what I can tell, there were few points of comparison during her twenty-year marriage.

Widowed at forty, she inherited a ten-thousand-dollar life insurance payment from her husband, the insurance salesman, and a sixteen-thousand-dollar mortgage. She set out to find work for the first time since my father had swept her away from the lunch counter in Gloucester and came home with a job as a sales clerk at Van Dyne's department store, the pride and joy of Walmouth's downtown shopping area.

She regarded working at Van Dyne's as a privilege, and someone there recognized that. She was made a floor walker and then promoted upstairs to the corporate offices. She was made assistant personnel manager and, eventually, personnel manager itself. All the while, she viewed this progression rather distrustfully, as though she was the mistaken recipient of someone else's good luck and soon would be skittering back to where she belonged—

selling ties or cookware or handkerchiefs with initials on them.

This reluctance to accept her own accomplishments may account in part for Kelsey, who seemed to have none of the refinements, none of the ambitions, and of course none of the troubles of my father. Kelsey was head of shipping and receiving at my mother's store, and while that was no small position, it meant he worked in laborer's clothes and spent his days on the docks checking invoices and bills of lading and making sure trucks were loaded and unloaded correctly. Still, he seemed content with his job, content with my mother, and generally content with everyone and everything except me.

When I walked into the house and found him sitting alone at the kitchen table playing solitaire he grinned uncertainly at me as if he was afraid I had come to kick him out.

I said "Hi," as I went past him to the refrigerator.

"I've got beer in there," he said.

I nodded. I could see it and I knew it wasn't my mother's.

"If you'd like one."

I drew two bottles out and slid one over to him. He took it gratefully, as if I were the giver.

"Your mother's upstairs exercising. You want to sit here?" he said, half-rising from his seat.

It was a foolishly sincere gesture and I answered it simply by pulling out another chair and dropping into it. Very faintly I could hear the whir of my mother's stationary bicycle coming through the floorboards. She had taken what we used to call the spare bedroom and transformed it into her own gym. In addition to the bicycle she had a small Nautilus bench attached to various pulleys and weights and a big mat on the floor that she used when she worked out to a series of Jane Fonda tapes that she played on her VCR.

"She's getting real strong," Kelsey said.

I said that she was, even though I did not know that for a fact. Like her relationship with Kelsey, my mother's recent devotion to physical fitness was more a subject of denial than discussion between us. "Oh, I just fool around," she would tell me whenever I asked her about it.

"Tough day at the office?" Kelsey asked.

"Yeah."

"Yeah." He drank his beer. "What were you up to?"

"I was working on that Carpenter murder over in Woodedge."

Kelsey's pleasant face lit up. "Oh, yeah, I was reading about that. Boy, that must be kind of interesting, going around to all those big Woodedge houses asking questions."

I said, "I'd appreciate it if you don't mention it to my mother."

Kelsey looked surprised. Then he grunted. "Yeah, I guess she doesn't need to hear any more about that place if she can help it."

Kelsey grew up in Walmouth, where he developed a reputation as a fine baseball player. He made it into the minor leagues, got kicked around for a while, and then was sent back home, a washout in his chosen profession at the age of twenty-two. Some time after that Kelsey got involved in softball and became a legitimate star in the local leagues. Even now, in his middle forties, he still played regularly and well. That tended to put him in touch with a lot of people, and in my search for a subject of conversation I suddenly wondered if that couldn't be put to use.

"I'm told the caretaker of this lady's estate was a kid from Walmouth named Rasmussin. You wouldn't know him, would you?"

Kelsey rolled the name around in his mouth. He rolled his eyes around in his head. "There's a guy, used to play outfield for Balducci's, I think."

"Balducci's Tavern?"

"I think. I seem to remember that guy's name on the back of a uniform and the reason I remember it was we were razzing him, calling him Rasputin. 'Course, it could be his brother or something." Kelsey shrugged. He smiled. He wanted very much to be helpful, if only to keep us from having nothing else to say to one another.

He need not have worried. At that moment there was a footstep on the stairs and I turned. My mother came into the kitchen wearing a gray leotard that nearly matched the color of her hair. Beneath the leotard she was wearing a white body stocking. She had a towel around her neck and a sheen of perspiration on her forehead.

"Oh, hi, Patt," she said. "I didn't know you were here."

She touched me lightly on the shoulder as she went to the refrigerator and got out some kind of whipped drink she had cooling in a blender jar. "Kelsey just dropped by a few minutes ago."

I looked at Kelsey, who no doubt had been there since he got off work, and he nodded solemnly.

"Working out?" I asked.

"Naw," she said. "Just fooling around."

I nodded solemnly, just like Kelsey. The two of us sat there with our heads going up and down while my mother asked what I was working on.

"Nothing," I told her, and Kelsey and I bobbed our heads some more.

John Michael was delighted with my first day's progress. He liked especially my report of my visit to the home of Molly and Dickie Barr. Sitting in his overly large leather swivel chair, his ankle crossed over his knee, his fingers steepled, he practically had me act out the scene.

"Big house," I said. "Not an estate, like the Carpenters', but a big place on a corner lot, set on top of a knoll. White with green shutters, and the lawn just kind of rolls away from the front door, going down the hill to a thick stand of pines that separates the yard from their street."

"Dead end street?"

"Oh, but of course, monsieur. Leetle black maid in maid's clothes answers the door." I did a curtsy, even though the maid had not done one to me. "She says Mr. Barr isn't home,

Mizz Barr can't be disturbed. I let her know that I'm the law and she goes scurrying off to disturb Mizz Barr just as I asked.

"A few minutes later Molly Barr comes toward me from the back of the house. She's got blond hair that must cost her a fortune to get colored and fluffed. She's got white sunglasses and what looks like a bathrobe and tennis shoes with half-socks that have little bobbins on them. The robe's tightened, but it's cut so you can see the tan on her neck and upper chest and it only comes about three-quarters of the way down her thighs.

"I'm standing there looking as studly as I can in my tweed sport coat and she greets me like I'm the plumber or something. 'Yessss?' I'm starting to explain to her about Rebecca Carpenter and then I realize she already knows. That's what the dark glasses are for. She's in mourning.

"The whole conversation takes place in the little entranceway. She says her husband heard about Becky on the radio on his way to work. Called her on the car phone. She hasn't known what to do since. She's not asking me or anything. I mean, I'm only the professional investigator, who you would think has dealt with this situation before.

"I ask her how long she's known Mrs. Carpenter and she tells me they went to school together at Wheaton."

"Where?"

"Rich girls' school. I just asked how come they both ended up living in Woodedge. The sunglasses go down. She peers at me over the top. 'Becky was a Chesley,' she says."

"What's a Chesley?" asked the man who would be the congressman for Woodedge, who was already the elected district attorney for that town.

I explained that they were a leading family.

"How about the Barrs? They a leading family too?"

I said that I believed they were. I said that Becky grew up with Dickie Barr and Becky introduced Molly to Dickie while Molly was working in Boston after college.

"How nice. Becky and Dickie and Molly. And the Carpenters, they a leading family, too?"

I shook my head. "Wylie S. was a trust officer at Boston Union, where Becky had her trust fund. That's how they met. He grew up in western Mass and went to Bowdoin."

"Bowdoin?"

I threw up my hands. "Hey, that's the way these people identify each other. I ask Molly Barr to tell me about Wylie and she tells me where he went to school twenty-five or so years ago."

"He's not still with Boston Union, is he?"

"Resigned while he was going out with Becky. Took a job with First Yankee and eventually became an investment banker. Quit that some years ago and became one of the directors of Woodedge Savings and Loan. Molly was vague as to times and details, and when I was pressing her—this was the fun part. She's in mourning, right? Got the sunglasses, the little ball of tissue pressed to her nose, the catch in her voice. This is the scene when all of a sudden Mr. Tall-Dark-and-Handsome appears at the end of the hallway coming from the back of the house. Not only is he dressed in full tennis whites, but he's got a goddamn Prince racket in his hand. 'Molly,' he calls out. 'Are you coming back? There's only twenty minutes left before I have to go to my next appointment.' "

A smile crept over John Michael's face. These Woodedgians were turning out just as he suspected.

"She says, 'I'll only be a minute, Cliff,' and turns back to me. But for all intents and purposes the interview's over. Old Cliff is standing there swatting the palm of his hand with the edge of his racket, and she's in effect told me to wrap this thing up."

"So what did you do?"

"So I did. I asked her one more question. I asked her how long the Carpenters have lived on the estate. 'Oh, that,' she says. 'That's Becky's family home. She grew up there, and then when her mother died about four years ago she and Wylie moved in.' "

John Michael leaned forward in his chair. He carefully placed his elbow on his desk and waved a finger back and forth at me.

"So when she dies the estate goes to him, the man who was in charge of her trust and who has had no ownership in anything up to now."

I raised my shoulders and held them for a count or two before dropping them. It was always best to let John Michael think he was figuring things out for himself.

"I think we've got our suspect," he said.

Jessica Keough had her own ideas about how I should conduct her husband's investigation. They were conveyed to me at a hastily convened cocktail meeting at the Keoughs' house on the evening of my second day's effort. I got the order to appear when I called in to the office switchboard late in the afternoon.

Given the hour of my notice and the fact that dinner was not included in the invitation, I made no effort to get a date; and when I arrived at the Keoughs' I could see the disappointment in Patty Hansen's eyes. Already she was halfway through a tall glass of amber-colored liquid.

Her husband was there in his suit, swirling some sort of high-ball, but John Michael had changed from his office clothes into jeans and a short-sleeved shirt. He was seated in the middle of a huge couch, with his ankle crossed over his knee just as it had been when I reported to him that morning.

"Good news," was Jessica's greeting when she opened the front door for me. "Autopsy report is in. Point one eight blood alcohol and enough Valium to sedate a horse."

She was very serious about her good news and so I was very serious about receiving it. In the living room, however, both John Michael and Royster were grinning, so I grinned back at them.

"Don't you just love it?" John Michael asked.

I nodded enthusiastically.

"Fix him a drink, will you, honey? What do you want, Patt?

Beer? I got some Beck's on ice for you." John Michael rolled onto his hip and began addressing me with both hands in motion. "Can't you just see it? He loads her up on Valium and liquor, piles her into the car when she barely knows what she's doing, drives her out to the overlook, throttles her when she can barely resist, and then sneaks away on foot so that it looks like anybody but him did it."

I wondered which of the three of them had put this together. The theatrics quite obviously were John Michael's, but big Royster was standing there with a self-satisfied look on his face as if he had done something well and was trying to be modest about it. Jessica's degree of gravity showed more than a touch of smugness. Only Patty Hansen showed no proprietary interest in the theory that had just been put forward. Her chestnut-colored hair hung straight and limp as her dark eyes stared transfixedly into her glass.

I took a cold green bottle and a drinking mug from Jessica and stood with what was left of my grin. "Why anybody but him?" I asked.

Jessica sat down next to her husband. Instinctively he put his arm around her. "The only person you would not expect a married woman to go with to a lovers' lane would be her husband," she explained. "No need to."

I poured the beer and everybody waited, knowing that my failure to say "Oh, yeah," meant that I was going to be trouble. "What's the story on clothing fibers?" I asked. "Were there any?"

Royster spoke up. Like Patty and me, he was standing. "A few. They're still being checked out."

"And fingerprints, they provide any help?"

"Wiped clean on the steering wheel, shift, and hand brake, but in other places they found some latents of hers and a couple of his."

"And those were to be expected, weren't they?"

Nobody answered. John Michael was no longer grinning.

I said, "Stanley Lester told me he thought she wasn't killed in the car. That maybe she was put there after she was dead and then had her feet manipulated by the killer."

"That's not what he put in his report," snapped John Michael. "He put in his report that he thought she was strangled from behind, by somebody in the back seat." He snorted and withdrew his arm from its resting spot on the back of the couch. "The idiot. He thinks, what?, she's sitting snockered by herself in the front passenger's seat of her own car and the killer gets in the back to do her in? Does that make sense to you?"

I agreed it sounded preposterous.

Everybody except Patty grumbled for a few moments.

"Unless maybe there was more than one person," I offered.

John Michael's eyes flicked like a pair of headlights turning on high beam. "A guy in front and another in back?"

"It would be one way to commit a robbery. The police report noted her pocketbook was missing."

"Her husband could have thrown it out," Royster said quickly. He demonstrated what he meant by flinging his arm to one side, and when he did his drink spilled on the front of Patty's dress.

It was, I felt certain, not a dress Patty Hansen was wearing when she got the call to muster at the Keoughs' for cocktails. It was black with a burnt umber print and a roll collar, and it looked new. The liquid from Royster's glass had gone almost entirely on her right breast and as she stared down at the wet spot it seemed she was on the verge of tears. Although Royster said "Sorry," he did nothing other than wave his free hand in-effectually in front of her, as though he wished to rub the spot dry but dared not.

We were all staring at Patty's right breast and somebody should have said something to make light of the moment, but nobody did. We were discussing important things, and her wet breast was merely a distraction to the discussion.

"If Carpenter was going to fake a robbery, he would have at least covered that detail," said John Michael, still staring.

Patty looked about helplessly.

"There's some club soda on the table," Jessica said, pointing to where she had set up a little bar. "Use a towel from the guest bath." She pointed toward the opposite end of the house, where there was a half-bath in an alcove beneath the stairs leading to the second floor. She made no other move to help, and Patty went wandering off in the direction indicated.

"Well, which is it?" I said. "Was Carpenter faking a robbery or a lovers' tryst?"

"It doesn't make any difference," said Royster, as though he really wanted me to understand and thought I was being just a bit too obtuse. "See, that's the beauty of it. Maybe the cops go looking for some punks who jumped her while she was getting into her car somewhere, or maybe they go looking for a suitor or somebody who was obsessed with her. Either way, they're not going to be looking at him."

I finished my beer in a swallow that was too large for mixed company. I had to wipe my mouth with my fingers. "What time did the medical examiner say she died?"

"Can't tell exactly, but based on the rectal temperature he took around one A.M. he thinks she was dead between nine and ten."

"Anybody know where she was supposed to be at that time?"

Royster Hansen struck quickly. "That's what you're supposed to be telling us."

I gave an expansive shrug and headed for where the beers were kept. Hansen would zing me whenever he could and I had to be careful not to react to it. "Nobody I've talked to seems to know," I called back over my shoulder.

"That's because she was at home," Jessica pronounced, and I felt a little twinge in my chest.

I snapped the top of a fresh Beck's and poured myself a second glass. "I talked to the maid today," I said casually. "Housekeeper, I guess she's called. Said she left at six. Made a light dinner for Mrs. Carpenter to eat alone. Said nobody was expected to visit and she knew of no plans to go out."

"So we know she was alive at six—" Hansen started.

"You knew that already from the medical examiner."

THE IMMEDIATE PROSPECT OF BEING HANGED 45

"—and alone," he concluded with exasperation.

I smiled at him. "Maid says Mrs. Carpenter was alone at six in the house. Husband—realizing he's a possible suspect and all—says he goes home at ten and she's not there. He's not even alibiing after that."

"So what we need to find out," snapped Royster, "is what she was doing between six and ten."

It was my turn to pay Royster back. "And what you're thinking, Roy, is that if she wasn't doing anything at all, then that means her husband must have killed her. Is that it?" We were playing subtle games here, getting our digs in before the boss, but my question was enough to make Royster blush.

It was the district attorney himself who spoke next, and it was me to whom he spoke. "Hey, we're not putting on the trial here, you know. We're trying to ascertain which way we go with this investigation. If Wylie Carpenter didn't do it, he didn't do it. But until we figure that out for certain let's use our brains and our experience to try to anticipate what we can. We're working on suspicion here, and suspicion doesn't require any due process that I'm aware of."

Now I was embarrassed, and because I was embarrassed I imagined how John Michael would look with that quote on his campaign posters: SUSPICION DOESN'T REQUIRE ANY DUE PROCESS.

Jessica tried to resolve things. "What we really need is to find out what Wylie was doing between six and ten."

"That much I can tell you," I said. "The starter at Stonegate confirmed that Wylie came in from the course at about six. Guy said Carpenter played eighteen with three people named Whitman, Teasdale, and Patterson. Checked in his golf cart just before dark."

Royster smiled his most vicious smile. "Sergeant Roselli talked with the bartender in the clubhouse this morning and already got that information. The bartender said Teasdale, Carpenter, Whitman, and Patterson came in. They bought some drinks, some sandwiches, and they spent the evening playing gin. Them and a guy named Butcher. People were coming and going all night, but the bartender remembered Carpenter and his buddies being there when he closed up at ten."

"So Carpenter's covered until then," said John Michael disappointedly. "Plus whatever time it would have taken him to get home."

"Not exactly," I said.

"Why?" asked John Michael.

"Because I located Mr. Butcher and interviewed him about three hours ago. He swears he left the clubhouse before eight. Even told me about the show he watched on television at nine."

I tried not to look at Royster. I tried not to look as though I had just kicked ass in the points-with-your-boss department.

"So the bartender can't be relied upon," said Jessica, summing things up nicely.

"This Patterson, is he the same one who's married to one of Rebecca Carpenter's friends?" asked John Michael, surprising me as he sometimes did with his excellent memory for details.

"D. Dodge Patterson, yes."

"Have you interviewed him yet?"

"No."

Royster charged back into the fray. "Then I'd say he's your next step."

"My next step," I said, "is to go to the bathroom."

It had been a long time since Patty Hansen had gone off and, frankly, I had forgotten she was even in the house. I remembered only when I got to the bathroom and saw it was closed. I stood outside the door for a minute or two waiting for it to open and when I started to get uncomfortable I knocked and called her name. There was no answer, so I tried the door and it opened. There was no one inside.

I shut the door behind me and went to the toilet and lifted the seat. I was thinking petty thoughts while I urinated into the bowl. I was wondering why the district attorney of Exeter County had flocked pink and white striped wallpaper in his guest bathroom. I was imagining pissing on Royster Hansen's head.

Suddenly the door opened again and a woman's voice said softly, "Patty?"

I turned. Half-turned.

Jessica Keough's head and shoulders were inside the room. She was looking directly at me and she was not looking at my face.

I turned back, thinking she would excuse herself, thinking she would close the door. She did both, but she stepped inside before she did either one.

I cut off in midstream, but I was still standing there holding myself. "Jessica," I said. "I'm not done."

"Never mind that. We have to talk."

I shook, dressed, and hit the flusher. As I moved to the sink I could see Jessica in the mirror. She was standing with her arms behind her waist and her shoulders against the door. "About what?" I asked.

"About what we need to do."

I wasn't sure what she meant. She seemed a little breathless. I nodded and continued to watch her in the mirror while I spent an unnecessarily long time washing my hands.

"John told me he wanted me to get the dirt."

"That's good," she said, and this time I was sure she was breathless.

I wondered if she knew that the way she was standing emphasized the fullness of her breasts, and decided that she did. I shut the water and turned for a hand towel from the rack on the wall next to where she was standing. Our eyes met. "Anything else?" I said.

She hesitated and then changed her position. The floor space in the bathroom was small, no more than seven feet from the door to the far wall, where the room's only window was located. Part of the ceiling sloped because the stairs leading to the second floor ran directly above our heads. With the sink and the toilet and the green leafy plants that Jessica had hanging from the ceiling, there was not much room for the two of us to maneuver.

"I think you ought to go back to Wylie Carpenter's hometown. I think you ought to trace his life as much as you can. Up to

Maine, down to Boston, out to Woodedge. I think you're going to find this man is the ultimate golddigger. I think you're going to find he's spent years plotting to get his hands on the Chesley fortune."

"You knew Rebecca Carpenter was a Chesley?" I said, taken aback.

"You mentioned it to John and John asked Chief Tuttle about them. He said the Chesleys were the oldest and richest family in town and she was the last of them. You see, it's a natural. And that's what's going to give us the hook we need to get some national attention. The richer she is, the longer and more intricately he plotted to get her money, the more fascinating everyone will think the case is."

"You're forgetting a couple of things."

Jessica looked as though she didn't believe me.

"He already had access to her money. He was living on her estate, working a couple-of-hours-a-week job, playing golf all the time—this guy had everything he could possibly need already."

"What he had was another woman."

For the second time that evening I felt a twinge in my chest because I thought Jessica knew something I didn't. "How do you know?" I asked cautiously.

"Because that's the way it always is in these situations. Look at all the great rich-wife murders in this country. It's always the social-climbing husband who kills his wife so he can get her money and marry some young beautiful woman."

"Rebecca Carpenter wasn't exactly a dog, you know, and she was only forty."

"Look," Jessica said a trifle impatiently, "I guarantee you that if the other woman's not more beautiful she's at least a whole lot younger than forty."

I tried to imagine what had made Jessica so cynical. She herself was only in her mid-thirties. She had been married to John Michael for ten years and had no reason of which I was aware to doubt his fidelity. Yet here she was, nodding at me with total conviction as she explained the rotten core of man's nature. Men cheat, she was saying. Men take what they can get and it is best to understand that and live with it and attempt to use it to your own advantage, because that's the way it is.

A knock broke against the door and both of us, each about to say something, froze.

"Honey?" a husky voice called softly, and by process of elimination I knew it had to be Royster.

"It's me," Jessica called back sharply, loudly. "I'll be out in a minute or two, Roy."

"Oh," he said, and I suppose we expected him to take that news and go away. But he didn't. "I'll wait."

"Use the bathroom upstairs, Roy," she told him, her eyes a little wide and fixed on mine.

"No, no, that's fine. Take your time. I wanted to speak to you anyway, Jess."

This tiny bathroom seemed to bring out the words in people. Both Jessica and I looked at the window. I had to get close to her to ask about it. I had to put my mouth next to her ear. My body touched hers and she rested her hand softly on my arm as she strained to hear what I was saying.

"Where does it go?"

"To the side yard."

"I'll do it."

Jessica hit the flush and I pushed upward on the opaque glass. It did not move as far as I would have liked, but I stood on the toilet seat cover and put my head and arms through the opening as best I could. It did not work.

Panic was now coursing through me, panic that far outstripped the situation. It wasn't my fault Jessica had come into the bathroom while I was using it. If her intention was innocent we both should have been able to walk out together with a smile and an explanation. But now she had spoken as though she were alone. Now she had flushed the toilet. I thrust my right arm and right shoulder outside. Jessica hit the water faucet and turned it on full. I got my head through and wiggled. I had my left shoulder and my left arm far enough along so that I was more out than in. My feet had to leave the toilet seat and Jessica, reacting quickly, grabbed my legs to keep them from banging against the wall. She held them, lifted them, guided them, and clipped them of one shoe as I went headfirst, straight down the outside wall.

I landed in the grass with my hands out in front of me and did a forward roll onto my back. A moment later my shoe came flying out and landed on the turf next to me. The window slid softly shut and the light I was getting was cut by at least half.

I lay in the darkness, trying to catch my breath, trying to feel for my shoe, and only gradually realizing that something else was wrong. Slowly I sat up and squinted around until I saw what it was.

Patty Hansen was standing in the shadows of the hedges that marked the property line between the Keoughs and their neighbors. We stared at each other in silence as I continued to pat the ground blindly for my shoe. We could have, perhaps, exchanged greetings, but there were questions neither one of us wanted to have to answer. When my hand at last touched my shoe I looked down to secure it, to put it on my foot. When I looked up again she was gone.

The funeral for Rebecca Carpenter was held on a Friday morning. Her casket was closed and the service was private. I stood in the street across from St. Mark's Episcopal, wearing a blue blazer because it was the closest thing I had to black, and watched the people arrive. There were nowhere near as many as I would have expected for the services of the last survivor of the leading family in Woodedge history, and in that small a crowd it was hard for me to look inconspicuous. But I, at least, was trying—which is more than can be said for Stanley Lester of the Woodedge Police Department.

Lester was wearing a sport coat that was a vicious shade of lime green. It would have been appropriate to wear on Arbor Day in the New Hampshire woods, but Lester acted as though it was the perfect disguise as he stood at the base of the steps to St. Mark's and gave everyone a thorough beady-eyed going over. The purpose of this exercise was not readily apparent to me, and it was made even less so when I happened to observe an unmarked Woodedge police vehicle on my side of the street containing one un-uniformed Officer Morrison with a video camera and a long-range lens.

Seeing the police in action made me feel silly. It had been my intention to watch for single men between twenty and fifty years of age, to look for anyone who appeared to be out of step with the rest of the crowd, to try to identify what I could about those who were invited to the ceremony. But I determined relatively quickly to abandon the field to Lester.

By the time the last of the invitees arrived I had already slipped away to Brigham's to buy an ice cream. Mocha almond fudge with jimmies. I took off my blazer to eat it and waited for the mourners to head for their homes.

Rebecca Carpenter's friend Hannah Babcock was blond and chubby. Her eyes were very blue, her face was very round, she smoked long cigarettes, and seemed to have more than a passing acquaintance with demon gin. She and her husband and their two children lived in a brand-new house in an area that had been nothing but woods the last time I had seen it. The house had a brick front and a bay window that gave it a middle-class air, but inside it proved to be expensively appointed and much larger than it appeared from the street.

She greeted me at the door in a distinctly unsorrowful orange blouse and a pair of fresh white cotton slacks that would have looked much better on a smaller woman. She acted annoyed, even angry, that I had come to ask her questions on the afternoon of Rebecca's funeral, but I was polite and I had the force of law printed on my card and so we spoke across the threshhold until gradually she relented and invited me to come in and sit in the sun room.

It was a beautiful room, beautifully planned. It was built onto the rear of the house and was almost entirely glass-enclosed. It faced a back yard of lush green grass manicured to a long but uniform height and surrounded on three sides by a crescent garden of hardy flowers. Beyond the crescent were the lucky survivors of a grove of ancient oaks that had been cut back far enough to minimize the amount of leaves that would blow onto the lawn.

As I glanced around the sun room my eye fell on a plate containing a fork and the remains of a very large slice of multilayered cake. Hannah Babcock saw me see the cake and said,

"Oh, I eat when I get depressed." Then, to be polite, she added, "Would you like some?"

She was obviously surprised when I said yes, but after fluttering for a second or two she went and got me a piece that was nearly as large as her own. She directed me to a white wicker chair and she herself moved to a chaise longue. We ate in silence except for the click of our forks against the china. When she was done she put her plate on the floor and lit a cigarette, inhaling deeply as if she had just undergone a long sexual workout. Even though I was not done I put my plate on the floor as well. The experience of shared confection seemed to relax her and I chose to wait to see what she was going to say before I resumed my questioning.

"Do you cook?" she asked.

"No."

"But you like to eat."

"I like good food."

"Me, too. That's my problem."

I didn't say anything.

"How do you stay in shape?"

"I work out."

"Where?"

"At a fitness club, near where I work."

"You use weights, that sort of thing?"

"Nautilus, mostly."

She took another long drag on her cigarette. She was not looking at me. "Why do you do it?"

I could have told her my job required it. I could have said something zenlike, told her it made me feel better about myself. Instead, I said, "Because it makes me more attractive to women."

This particular woman, only hours from the funeral of her friend, wearing orange and white and binging on cake, looked at me appraisingly. "Chesley would have liked you," she said.

"Why?"

"She liked men who take care of themselves."

"Her husband's an athlete."

"Maybe that was the attraction."

"You weren't sure what it was?"

Hannah Babcock shrugged as though she begrudged the effort.

"You don't like Wylie." There was no inflection in my voice, no question mark at the end of my sentence.

"Wylie is"—she waved her cigarette around—"different."

"What I had heard, I thought you were old friends—you and your husband, Wylie and Rebecca."

"Chesley and I were old friends. She was my best friend when we were little tiny girls in ruffled dresses. Our parents were best friends and so we were, too. We grew up together, like cousins."

"Can I ask you a very sensitive question, then? One that I could only ask someone who knew her as well as you did?"

Hannah rested her head on top of the longue's back cushion and fixed her eyes on the ceiling.

"Would you say," I hesitated, waiting until she looked down at me, "that she was a happy person?"

"Chesley?" Hannah Babcock's eyes opened wide. For a moment I thought she was going to tell me that Rebecca Chesley Carpenter was the happiest woman who ever lived. But then she tilted her head back once again and said, "Ches was not really what you would call the happy sort. I mean, that's not the way you would describe her."

"Was she always that way?"

"Oh, who knows when you're little kids? There was always something planned for us back then, always so much going on that you didn't have time to figure out if you were unhappy or not. I mean, Ches and I went to summer camp together in Switzerland, we went to Rosemary Hall together, we did show riding, our parents took us skiing and sailing. You know how it is."

I nodded. "Sure."

"She seemed to me to be happy enough back then."

"So what happened?"

Hannah stubbed out her cigarette even though there was still an inch of tobacco above the filter. It was a very long cigarette. "I don't know," she said. "Maybe she ran out of things to do."

I nodded again. "What about in the past few months? Would you say she was more happy, less happy, or about the same happy?"

Hannah Babcock answered promptly, without smiling. "About the same happy."

"And her husband, would you say the same about him?"

"Of course."

"Why 'of course'?"

"Because," she said indignantly. She shifted her heft. "Because why shouldn't he be?"

The white wicker chair in which I was sitting almost required me to rest my arms on its arms. I sat forward and clasped my hands down low between my calves. "You have no reason to believe they were having marital problems?"

Hannah flipped her hand. "Not really."

"Then"—I sat back, slumped back, as though I had to think this problem through—"can you think of any reason why Rebecca would have been where she was on the night she was killed?"

"There could have been any number of reasons."

I responded appreciatively. "Really?" I said. "Can you tell me one?"

Hannah Babcock swung her feet around to the floor and flattened both her hands on the cushion beneath her oversized buttocks. "Look, I know what you're getting at. Chesley was an attractive woman and I'm sure she was perfectly capable of having affairs, but she would hardly need to have one in the front seat of her car, now would she?"

"Was she having any affairs that you knew of?"

"No." The answer was emphatic.

"Was Wylie?"

"Wylie? Wylie has an affair with his golf clubs." She said it as though she had come to grips with human perversity in its purest form.

"Is that what you don't like about him?"

"I didn't say I didn't like him. I said he was different and, yes,

that's part of the reason why he's different. If Ches wanted to
have an affair she could have had it right in her house because
the chances are nine out of ten that Wylie would have been off
at one of his silly country clubs."

We were staring at each other now. All my various efforts to
be charming, convivial, honest, and inoffensive had come down
to this. "Can you think of any reason why Wylie would want
his wife dead?"

Hannah Babcock did not so much as blink. "Not a single one,"
she said. "He had it made."

Gerard Whitman also could not think of a reason why Wylie
Carpenter would want his wife dead; although I did not put the
question to him in quite the same way as I had to Mrs. Babcock.

"Hell of a guy," said Gerard from behind the big desk that he
used to run the Whitman Orthopedic Supply Company. "On his
worst day he's a scratch golfer. He could make money on the
seniors tour, not a doubt in my mind about it. I'm out there twice
a week, three times if I can get away, and I can't come within
ten strokes of him. That's what he's giving me now, ten. And I
still can't beat him." Whitman shook his head sadly.

"Usually play for money, do you?"

Whitman grinned a bit. He held out his freckled hand and
tilted it one way and then the other. He recognized me as a
sporting kind of guy, but he wasn't sure how far the long arm
of the law extended.

"Other than that, did you ever get involved in any financial
transactions with Wylie Carpenter?"

"Wish I had," said the man whose wholly owned company
had a forty-eight-state map on the wall in its main lobby showing
distributors in 112 locations. "Wylie's a financial genius."

I smiled indulgently. "How do you know that?"

Whitman raised the stakes on indulgent smiles. "Let's just say
that if Wylie Carpenter had been doing for Whitman Orthopedics
what he was doing for First Yankee Bank and Trust at the time
they were putting together the financing for Quincy Market,

there'd be a statue of yours truly right behind Faneuil Hall at this moment."

I made sounds designed to indicate that I knew what Whitman meant. Then I asked him, "If he was so successful at First Yankee, why did he leave?"

"Exactly because he was so successful. He had made his mark and he didn't feel the need to go any further. So he bought into that little S and L of his and went home to do what he wanted."

"Play golf, you mean."

Whitman shrugged. Then he drew himself up straighter in his chair and looked at me sincerely. "I hate to think what this is going to do to his game."

I agreed that it was a tragedy.

"Nice girl," he said. "His wife. Lovely funeral service."

"Did he say anything about her during your golf game that day? Anything about having to be home at a certain time?"

"No," said Whitman, pushing out his chin and scratching it with one delicate finger. "He didn't say anything like that before he left."

"Left? You mean he left before you did?"

"Oh, sure. The only one still there when I left was Dodge."

"What time did he go? Wylie, I mean."

"Can't tell you that because I wasn't playing him. Gin rummy, you know. You go one on one. It's where we duffers get Wylie back. He always loses, always goes out early." Whitman chuckled. "Let me see, there was me, him, Dodge, Ben Butcher, and Bud Teasdale—five of us. So we played round robin. Started off I played Dodge and Wylie played Ben . . . Is that right? Yes, because then Ben and I played winners while Wylie played Bud. Then Bud and I played and then Dodge came back and challenged the pot." He chuckled harder, wanting me to ask who won.

Instead, I asked, "And you don't remember Wylie being there after the second game?"

"Well, I don't, but that doesn't mean he wasn't."

"Bartender seemed to think he was there at closing."

"He'd know, I guess. Unless he got Wylie mixed up with

Dodge—who was staying around to drown his sorrows." The chuckling this time was accompanied by an eyebrow raised in anticipation of my congratulations.

"Why would he do that? Mix them up, I mean?"

"Well . . ." Whitman paused. "They were both wearing club sweaters, as I recall. White V-neck jobs with the club emblem on the breast. But, look," he let his face soften a bit to show me that he meant no harm. "Obviously you can't expect the bartender to be the brightest kid in the world."

"Obviously," I said, and this time Whitman and I chuckled together. It seemed a small price to pay.

There was no reason for my mother to expect me on a Friday night. She knew that Friday nights usually meant office meetings with John Michael and Jessica and Royster. But John Michael wasn't going to be around this Friday evening and it was nearly dinner time when I got out of Whitman's office and I thought my mother might have something on the stove.

The house, however, was dark when I got there. I only stopped because Mrs. Graham saw my car and waved me down. I only went in because it was a way to escape from Mrs. Graham. I went over and chatted first, of course, just to be polite.

"Have a date tonight, Patt?" she asked, leaning forward in her chair so that she could talk to me over the porch rail.

"Yes, I do, Mrs. Graham," I fibbed. "Just coming by to grab a bite to eat and then I'm off."

"Anybody special, Patt?"

"Not really. Just someone I met."

"Big strapping boy like you, I can't believe you haven't stolen someone's heart yet."

I sighed. This was a little ritual I had to go through with Mrs. Graham, who had a tendency to forget past conversations.

"Still," she said, nodding in consolation, "at least you've got a job. That's something."

She gestured toward Charlie Curren's house, catty-cornered

THE IMMEDIATE PROSPECT OF BEING HANGED

from her own. "I guess young Charlie's still having a hard time of it."

"Young Charlie" was nearly my age. To the best of my knowledge, the one and only job he had ever had was boosting cars for an outfit that stripped them down in Providence. He had gotten caught once and I had put in a good word for him with the arresting officers. I owed him that much. He was home a lot during the day and he was always willing to do lawn mowing and minor maintenance for my mother and Mrs. Graham.

"And that little Sharon down the street, she's pregnant again, by the looks of her."

I knew the girl Mrs. Graham was talking about. I remembered when she herself was born. Her mother had been a schoolmate of mine and had introduced Danny Spinelli and me to the joys of manual sex in the woods behind the junior high. Later, she had married a kid from the trade school and moved into my neighborhood. I always waved when I saw her, but we never spoke. I always looked at her hand when she waved back.

"Is Sharon married this time?" I asked; and Mrs. Graham said she wasn't sure.

"I sit here sometimes, Patt, and everything just blurs together. I've been in this house now forty-nine years and I've seen so many young people come and go, I get them all mixed up. Was it Sharon that used to play that rope game in the street, or was she the one that had all the boys who used to leave their car radios on?" Mrs. Graham's voice trailed off. "I don't know."

I murmured a meaningless response because I knew that Sharon was both but I did not want to get into a discussion about it.

"I remember your father, though, Patt. Always such a serious look on his face. You're a lot like him, you know."

"I'm really not, Mrs. Graham," I said. "I'm really not serious at all."

"I'm still blessed with good eyes," she said. "I think it comes from not reading."

"I guess I'm going to have to go now, Mrs. Graham."

"I used to see him come and go. Always as if the weight of the world was on his shoulders. That wasn't good, you know. That's what caused him to do what he did."

I was turning, I was trying to say good-bye.

"This one she's got now," Mrs. Graham said, pointing to the house, "he's better for her. They get along just fine."

"Yes, Mrs. Graham. Well, I have to go in there now. Lots of things I have to do."

"That's good, Patt. A young man like you should have lots of things to do."

I hurried across the lawn before she could think of something else to tell me. I went up the stairs and through the door as quickly as I could get it unlocked. Then I went straight to the kitchen and drew one of Kelsey's beers from the refrigerator. I unscrewed the cap and stood drinking from the bottle in the middle of the kitchen floor.

Aside from the beer, there was no sign of my mother's friend; but from up on the second floor came the sounds of movement and I assumed they were coming from my mother's exercise room. I assumed they were the sounds of her Nautilus machine. I finished the beer about the time they stopped and went up to say hello.

The second-floor hallway was relatively small. At one end was a door leading to the attic stairs. Then there was my room, then the little gym, and then my mother's room at the opposite end from the attic door. The bathroom was at my mother's end of the hall, directly across from the gym.

As I reached the top of the stairs I started to turn in that direction just as the door to my mother's room opened. Kelsey walked out, shirtless and fumbling with his belt. I was too stunned to move and Kelsey did not even notice me until he was into his second step. He froze without completing it. Behind him the door was semi-closed, the room was dark.

What I wanted more than anything else that moment was to disappear, to slip silently down the stairs and out of the house without my mother ever knowing I was there. I even had my index finger halfway raised to my lips, but apparently Kelsey didn't see it because he was not quiet about my exit. He was not quiet at all.

"Hey, Patt," he said, and already I was heading back down the stairs. My cover blown, I was trying to get out of there as quickly as I could.

I was taking the steps two and three at a time and Kelsey was still calling after me. "Patt, I found out about that Rasmussin guy."

I had the door open and Kelsey was calling louder. "A kid on his team told me he took off for California the other day. He's not around anymore."

By the time Kelsey got out those last words, I wasn't around anymore either. I could hear his voice, I could hear Mrs. Graham calling good-bye to me, I could hear one of the neighborhood kids saying "Hi, Patt," and I was flat out running for my car.

My father was arrested in Woodedge once. Wembley Tuttle was on the police force then, although he was not yet chief, and since he never mentioned the incident I assumed he either had forgotten about it or did not associate me with the wild man named Starbuck who had broken into the Patterson family home on Whitehall Road. I also assumed he did not associate me with the stunned little boy who had watched four squad cars of Woodedge policemen surround the Patterson home and forcibly evict him and his mother and father from the property. I would have thought Wembley Tuttle would have remembered. For it was not just the break-in that was bizarre, it was the fact that my father had moved his family into the house and refused to let any of us leave until he was taken away in handcuffs.

I had not been back to that house since that day, but I had not forgotten anything about it. Most particularly, I had not forgotten the view from the living room window, where my mother and I had stood as the police cars assembled, their blue lights flashing and their radios snapping warlike messages, while my father shouted defiance from an upstairs bedroom.

The police did not know if he had a gun. They did not know he was only my father. All they knew was that Mr. and Mrs. Gordon Patterson, parents of Frost and Parker, grandparents of D. Dodge, had returned home from their Palm Beach vacation to find the house occupied. And so they assembled behind their squad cars with rifles and canisters of tear gas, ready for a full-scale assault if need be.

My father's claim to the house was based on no legally recognized concept, even though the house had been built by his great-grandfather Frederick. Frederick had passed it to his son Alfred and Alfred had passed it to his son Gordon, who ultimately would pass it to his son Frost, the reprobate stock marketeer. My father, however, was descended from Alfred's brother John, who had his own property, which he had passed to my father's uncle Frank, who of course had sold it several times over.

The Pattersons had made numerous additions to Frederick's house over the decades, and it had come to form a layout that comported with no commonly used descriptive phrase in the English language. In my brief time there it had seemed labyrinthian, with each wing presenting its own mystery and sense of adventure. Now, as I approached it, the house conveyed the same potential but little of the majesty with which my memory had endowed it. The paint on the front door was peeling and the stone lions that guarded it were crusted with bird droppings and barnaclelike shells that indicated the statuary had not been tended in some time. I assumed, as I drove up, that the front door was not the entrance of choice for the family, but it sat at the crest of the semi-circular driveway and it deserved more attention than it reflected.

The driveway itself was unmarked and began as a break in a stone wall. It swept behind a small grove of trees, past the front of the house and past the entrance to a detached garage barn. After that it forked: a left turn returning to Whitehall Road, and a right turn running behind the barn and along the rear wing of the house. Beyond the wing the yard was filled with leaves and branches and small stands of decaying firewood. Beyond the yard were the woods, and in the woods was a path that if followed long enough would lead all the way to the Charles River. Or at least it did when I was a kid.

The rear wing contained an entrance that looked used. Parked near it were a battered Country Squire station wagon and a dusty

Mercedes sedan of a similar color and model to Rebecca Carpenter's. As I pulled up behind those cars a Bedlington terrier began barking madly from behind the screen door of the entrance. As I got out of my car a man appeared behind the screen. The mesh obscured his features somewhat, but I could still tell it was my father's hated second cousin Frost Patterson.

He stared at me through the screen and made no move to stop the antics of the beast at his feet. His stare was not exactly imperious, but I had the feeling that if I turned around and walked away it would have no effect whatsoever on his expression.

I had a moment's fantasy of yelling, "Cousin Frost, it's me, Patterson Starbuck," and rushing the door with my arms thrown open. But what came out of my mouth instead was an almost obsequious, "Pardon me, but I'm looking for Dodge Patterson."

Frost's ice-cold blue eyes measured me as I approached. Age had robbed those eyes of their sharpness, made them soft around the edges, but the loss of his hair and the sweep of his spotted scalp gave them a background that enhanced both their size and color. "He's not here."

I stood on the doorstep looking down at the frantically yapping dog and thinking he needed a good kick, either a gentle one by Frost or a hard one by me. "When do you expect him back?"

"Don't know."

It was Saturday morning. It wasn't unreasonable to think that D. Dodge might be around or that his father might know when he would be back. I decided that it was probably Frost who needed the good kick. "I'm from the district attorney's office," I said.

The old man said nothing.

"It's kind of important I speak with him right away."

The old man still said nothing.

I extracted a card, one that said "Patt Starbuck, Litigation Coordinator, Office of the District Attorney for Exeter County," and held it out to him. He did not open the door. He tried to read it through the screen.

I was wondering if the name was going to mean anything to

him and my hand was beginning to shake a little more than the weight of the card required when there came the sound of a woman's voice from inside the house. "Dad? What's going on out there? What's Tennyson making such a racket about?"

Frost Patterson turned, a maneuver that seemed to require several distinct movements on his part. The dog barked even louder and hurled itself against the tin base of the screen door. Behind man and dog appeared a woman's shape. I saw a head of luxuriously thick black hair; a face of smooth, naturally dark skin; a pair of huge dark eyes that looked friendly and sultry and intelligent and vulnerable—and whatever I was about to say strangled in my throat.

Frost took a half-step out of the way and the woman reached down and hushed the dog with a single stroke of her hand. She opened the door with one long, beautiful, slender arm bared by a loose-fitting, short-sleeved white blouse, and said, "Can I help you?"

She was bent, holding the dog's collar with one hand and holding the door open with the other. I wanted not to look down the top of her blouse. I wanted to be professional. But I looked anyway. Quickly. Her breasts were small but rounded and incredibly firm, and they weren't covered by any bra.

I stammered. I tore my eyes away. I was looking at the side of the house, staring intently at an oleander bush.

"Pardon me?" she said, changing her position so that now she was propping open the door with her hip and more or less looking at me over her shoulder while she held down the dog.

I was able to look back. "I'm Patt Starbuck of the D.A.'s office," I said, handing her the card I had tried to give Frost Patterson.

She read it and cocked her head as if to say she did not understand. Her black hair fell with the tilt of her head, falling front and back and springing up again.

"I'm looking for Dodge Patterson." I was beginning to perspire. I was wishing I could start this process all over again, appearing at the door cool, calm, and collected, the way I had intended.

"Well—stop it, Tennyson—he's out playing golf right now,

but I'm his wife . . . if there's anything I can help you with."

Frost Patterson stood to the side watching the two of us with what struck me as a faintly disgruntled interest.

"Are you Gretchen Patterson?"

"I am."

"It's about the death of Rebecca Carpenter. She was a friend of yours, wasn't she?"

Gretchen's lower lip tucked beneath her brilliant white teeth. She glanced at her father-in-law, who discreetly looked away. "She was," she said. "But what does that have to do with Dodge?"

"We've got some leads, Mrs. Patterson. What we're trying to do now is develop a big circle of information so that we can get an idea of everything that would possibly be relevant. See what's in the circle and what isn't."

I wasn't fooling Gretchen Patterson. She knew I had just given her gibberish for an answer. I smiled, and it changed nothing. I waited, and finally she invited me in.

She and her father-in-law had been standing inside a small porch that served as a bootroom. To get to the main part of the house we had to step around a child's vehicle. "My son's," Gretchen said simply.

She led the way and I followed. She was wearing pale pink pants that were of such thin material and fit so snugly around her hips that they molded her buttocks and showed the skimpy lines of panties worn very, very low. The shape of the pink pants may have exaggerated the narrowness of her waist, the slimness of her hips, the length of her legs, but I was trying not to inspect those things too closely.

We went into a paneled room occupied with bookshelves, a desk, a few pieces of overstuffed furniture, and a large stone fireplace. I knew the story of those panels. They had come from one of the Chesley taverns that had served as a coach stop along the Post Road in the eighteenth and nineteenth centuries. They had, as I understood it, been a source of pride to my great-great-grandfather. In my memory of my brief childhood stay in this house, those panels were extremely imposing—almost holy relics. "George Washington looked at these very panels on his way to Boston to take command of the Continental Army," my father had told me; and I believed him. Now, in the sunshine of my cynical adulthood, I could see that the panels were marked and chipped and desperately in need of oiling. Their importance had been so lightly regarded that someone had actually verithaned a map onto that portion of them that was above the desk. I found it shocking and tried to pretend the map wasn't there.

In general, the whole room was in a state of disrepair. The carpet, an antique Oriental, was threadbare. Books were piled sideways in the shelves. The fireplace was filled with ashes. The desk was overflowing with papers, and a black cat occupied the single best chair. I recognized that chair. It was on a list of antiques that my father had cataloged when he was in the house, a list that was still in a cabinet drawer in West Nestor.

Gretchen directed me to a seat on the couch and sat herself in a rocker that could have used some extensive restoration. "My father-in-law's study," she said, gesturing toward the man who had followed us to the room and who now stood in the doorway resting his weight on a carved walking stick that I had not noticed previously. "This is his house," she said, and I accepted that as an explanation for the condition of things.

I nodded. I looked around as if I had never seen it before. "Our understanding," I said when I was done looking, "is that Dodge, your husband, was playing golf with Wylie Carpenter on the day Rebecca was killed."

She nodded, her dark brows arching slightly.

"Do you remember what time your husband got home?"

She turned to her father-in-law. She shook her head. "No . . . well, I mean, it wasn't anything I thought about."

"You remember the night, don't you?"

Again, Gretchen Patterson looked at her father-in-law. I liked when she looked at me. I liked looking at her.

"From what I understand," I said, drawing back her attention, "Dodge played golf and then stayed at the clubhouse to play cards. He might have gotten home around ten."

She spread her hands. "I think I was upstairs in bed reading. Ian, that's our son, would have been asleep already. That's right, because Dodge stuck his head in Ian's room before he came in to see me."

"Is that what he usually does when he comes in late from golf?"

She nodded her head once. Her dark eyes spoke wondrous messages to me that I could not really understand. She struck me as being innocent and inviting and desperately in need of protection from someone like me.

I forged ahead. "And Dodge acted as though everything was usual that night, did he?"

"Is my son a suspect, Mr. Starbuck?" rumbled the old man, chilling me by the fact that he used my name.

"No, sir, he's not."

"Because if you're trying to tie him in with her, you can forget about it." He grunted with a great deal of ugly self-satisfaction.

"Dad," Gretchen said, moving her fingers on the arm of her chair and looking at him worriedly.

"Well, I know these policemen fellows," he said, poking his stick in my direction. "They operate on old gossip and rumors. That's what fuels 'em. Keeps 'em running from one place to another."

"Is there a rumor I should know about?" I asked brightly.

"No," said Gretchen.

The old man smacked his lips and looked away.

Gretchen Patterson was fidgeting, trying to ignore both Frost and his noises. I looked from one to the other and asked, "When was the last time you saw Rebecca Carpenter, Mrs. Patterson?"

"Saw her? Well, saw her, I don't know. We talked on the phone at some point not too long ago."

"This is Saturday. The murder was Tuesday night. Any idea what she was supposed to be doing that night?"

Gretchen Patterson shook her head.

I waited, expecting something more.

"You don't have any reason to believe my husband was not playing golf that day, do you?" she asked, trying to sound casual.

Now the old man leaned in, his face twisting unpleasantly.

"No," I said, looking at him.

Frost Patterson twitched as though he had not heard right. Then he leaned back patiently.

"Dodge and Wylie played regularly, didn't they?" I asked.

"Golf?" croaked Frost Patterson.

"Golf," I affirmed.

"They played," Gretchen said, "They played."

"Golf?"

Gretchen's eyes heated up quickly and I was instantly sorry I was such a clown. I went to put up my hand to tell her I was just making a joke, but already she was flicking her glance between her father-in-law and me and already she was snapping, "Look, everyone has probably made a mistake at some time or other. And I don't see where there's any sense trying to make something out of ancient history just because certain people don't have anything better to do than go around stirring up old trouble."

I cleared my throat. My heart picked up its pace. "This mistake you're referring to, did it involve Rebecca Carpenter?"

Mrs. Patterson stared her answer.

I was wondering what kind of man D. Dodge Patterson could possibly be to mess around with Rebecca Carpenter when he had this exquisite creature available to him, but I asked the next question anyway. "Do you have any reason to believe a mistake was still being made?"

"None," she said firmly.

I let my eyes wander to the old man, but his expression was now stoic.

"Do you," I said, throwing the question to either one of them, "have any reason to believe Dodge was not playing golf on Tuesday—not playing cards Tuesday night?"

"None," Gretchen Patterson said, virtually challenging me to ask another impertinent question.

I chose not to do that. I chose to get to my feet instead. I said I was sorry I had intruded on them, but I was going to have to come back at some point and speak to Dodge.

"Should my son have counsel here when you return?" asked Frost. "He's a lawyer himself, you know."

"I don't think so. I'm neither a lawyer nor a cop, so I don't see where I'll be any real threat to him."

He nodded as though keen for the confrontation between his son and me. I looked back at his daughter-in-law and she nodded without any encouragement whatsoever.

"Thank you again," I said and turned to leave. Frost Patterson stepped out of the doorway and let his walking stick flare upward in a half-point toward my exit. As I squeezed by him I said, "Nice place you've got here, Mr. Patterson."

It's possible Cousin Frost's head would have snapped even if I had not said anything. It's possible he was just being informative when he said, "Yes. It's been in my family for generations."

There was a message on my telephone answering machine when I got home. It was from my mother. She said she had made a huge tray of lasagna and she wanted to know if I was interested in coming by to help her eat it. She did not mention Kelsey.

I, however, had other plans. I wanted to spend the evening with a dark-haired woman with wondrous eyes. I thought of calling a friend of mine named Deirdre, who had neither dark hair nor wondrous eyes but who was available. I liked Deirdre all right. She had an impressive body that she held in place with clothes that were always a little too tight. But Deirdre was also a divorcee with two kids and if I failed to give her enough advance notice she would be unlikely to get a baby-sitter and we would end up sitting around watching television until the kids went to bed.

Then she and I would have a glass or two of wine and make

mad, silent love on her living room couch. By eleven thirty I
would be anxious to leave and she would know it.

I never thought of calling Deirdre except when it was too late
to call anyone else, and I chose not to call her this time. I called
Robert instead.

9

"Rule number one," said Robert, who figured to
know about such things, "is always look for a woman with small
hands."

We were in a fashionable singles bar called Hadley V. Bax-
endale's and I found myself looking at the size of women's hands
as we made our way through the crowd in search of an open
place to stand. "Why?" I said at last.

"Makes it look bigger when they hold it," Robert called back
over his shoulder.

He was obviously a familiar figure in this bar. The doorman
knew him, called him by his first name, and let us in immediately
even though there was a long line of people waiting on the sidewalk. One of the waitresses knew him, pushed him gently on the
chest as he walked by and meaningfully smiled at him as if they
had some secret in which he had been naughty and she was being
forgiving. A young woman in a low-cut blouse knew him. She
stopped him and kissed him on the cheek. She introduced him
to her friend and he introduced me to both of them and I tried
to act as though I was not feeling awkward about the fact that
I was at least fifteen years older than they were.

I should not have felt awkward. Robert was older than I was
and he was feeling plenty comfortable. This was his turf. Nowhere
on earth did Robert look better or function so well as he did in
singles bars.

THE IMMEDIATE PROSPECT OF BEING HANGED 73

I had known him when he was called Bobby and aspired to nothing more than a job as a printer. He had left that career when he was in his early twenties because he was having difficulty getting the ink off his hands and because he found it immensely better for his social life to sell drugs. By the time he was thirty, Bobby had turned his marketing skills to real estate and before long he was transformed into Robert.

We were friends because we had grown up together in West Nestor and because we now lived four blocks away from each other in Boston. We were friends because I had once advised Bobby that it was no longer very wise for him to visit the home of a certain Colombian art dealer, regardless of how much interest he had in that gentleman's pottery. Bobby Greenberg, now known as Robert, considered me a very good friend indeed, and he was more than happy to have me accompany him on his Friday-night rounds.

"Rule number two," he said when he had returned from getting us a couple of wallbangers from the bar, "is never stand next to a guy who's more than three inches taller than you." He motioned with his head toward the man standing directly behind me, and then he motioned me away.

As we moved along, Robert was scanning in every direction for likely prospects. He bestowed a lingering smile on a very young, rather Rubenesque woman who responded by sticking out her hand and introducing herself as Chrissie.

As Robert traded intimacies with his new friend I began to regret that I had called him. I regretted I was not with Deirdre. I regretted I had not stayed home alone. And while I was in the middle of all these regrets I glanced across the room and saw the most unlikely sight I could ever possibly see.

There was a woman who looked amazingly like Jessica Keough. She was sitting at a booth in a corner with several other women, all in their thirties, all attractive, all well dressed, and all seemingly out of place.

I did not want it to be Jessica Keough who was sitting there and I did not keep looking for fear it would be. I let Robert drag me into the conversation with Chrissie, even though she was far more interested in Robert than she was in me.

"Patt's a private investigator," said Robert.

"Oooh, maybe he could investigate us!"

"He only investigates privates."

"Robert! I don't believe you said that!"

Robert laughed silkily. He took Chrissie's plump arm and directed her attention to me. "Tell her the kinds of things you really investigate, Patt."

"I specialize in the theft of eggs from fish hatcheries."

"What?" she said, the word coming out like the sound of metal brakes being applied. She looked to Robert for help.

Robert, however, was doubled over with laughter. He thought I was funny. It was another reason we were friends.

Suddenly she was standing there at my elbow, the woman who looked like Jessica Keough. The woman who was Jessica Keough.

"Thank God you've come," she said. "Now I can escape."

I stared at her and her expression changed.

"Didn't John send you?" Her eyebrows rose. Her forehead tilted back.

"Jessica, it's Saturday night. I don't work around the clock, you know."

She watched me as though registering what I was saying for future use. I looked at my drink and sensed, rather than saw, that Robert was waiting for an introduction.

I said, "Jessica, this is Robert, Chrissie."

Chrissie said hello and looked away. Robert said hello and waited for something more. An explanation, perhaps.

"I'm here for a bachelorette party," Jessica blurted. "Karen Coe, do you know her?"

Of course I knew her. She was one of the better attorneys in the office. I looked again at the booth in the corner and realized that not only did I recognize Karen, but I also recognized a couple of others. I recognized all the ones who were waving to me. I recognized Patty Hansen, who was not waving.

Jessica said, "If you really didn't come to get me, will you at least say you did so I can get out of here?" She moved her head in close to mine, close enough that I could smell her perfume. "It's really not my kind of place," she confessed.

Somehow the option of saying no did not seem available. I told Robert I had to go.

He regarded me as if I was crazy. He excused us from the two women and pulled me off to one side. "Hey," he said, "she's not bad, but there's all kinds of young stuff here. We've just gotten started."

"She's a friend," I said, finding myself irrationally wanting to defend Jessica against the "young stuff."

"Well," sniffed Robert, studying her, "she looks rich anyway." He clapped me on the shoulder, as though bestowing his blessing, and I went back to free Jessica from the strains of trying to make conversation with Chrissie, who was a word processor but was hoping to become a travel agent.

Jessica slid into my Alfa as though she were slipping into a comfortable Japanese tub. "Whew," she said, throwing back her head, "that was quite an experience."

I was mad at her, mad at myself, mad at the course of the night's events. I said nothing.

"Where would you like to go now?" she asked.

I had been attempting to put my car into reverse. Something failed, either my hand or my foot, and the gears made a horrible noise. "I thought you wanted to go home."

"I just wanted to get out of there, plastic-people-land."

"They're not plastic people. They're just different from what you're used to, that's all."

"Oh," she said, meaning the same as "Have it your way." Then she asked me again where I wanted to go.

"Isn't John expecting you?"

"Oh, he's at a dinner tonight for Mayor Mackey in Waterford."

"Will Constantinis be there?"

"You think he'd pass up a chance to make a speech? Can't

you just hear him? 'Mayor Mackey has fought long and hard over the course of his distinguished career to bring public transportation to the point where it is today. We must make sure that we carry his torch forward, that we provide appropriate shelters for the poor, the lame, the halt, the mentally deficient who wish to use that transportation.' By the time he's done everyone will think they're at a retirement dinner rather than a fund-raiser."

We had swung onto Commonwealth Avenue and I was heading for the Turnpike.

"Oh, don't take me home, Patt. It's so rare that I get to be out on an unofficial sort of thing."

"What is it you want me to do with you, Jessica?"

There was a good deal more silence than the question required. "Stop somewhere," she said at last, and it was up to me to figure out what she meant.

"A drink? Would you like a drink?"

"Sure, that would be all right, although I've really had about all I can handle."

"How about some dessert? Some ice cream, something like that?" I was thinking of an ice cream parlor in Cleveland Circle. I was thinking we could get in and get out of there and it would not be any big deal.

"I don't really feel like eating," she said. "Why don't we just go somewhere where we can talk?" She put down the window and filled the car's cockpit with cold air. She tilted her head back. "I love your little car. It makes you feel so close to the road. It makes you feel so . . . almost wild. Take me somewhere in it."

"I am."

"Take me to Newport or down the Cape. Take me to the beach. That's what I feel like doing. I feel like hearing the waves crash and feeling the sand between my toes."

I could not believe she was serious. We were heading in completely the wrong direction and there was no beach even reasonably close. I took her to the Charles River instead.

We got off the Turnpike near the Marriott River Inn at the Nestor-Woodedge line and I drove in a big semicircle that took us to the base of what had once been a small bridge. The bridge had stood burned and broken throughout my childhood, a relic of wooden construction that had not been designed to carry multi-ton metal vehicles. Now all that was left was the foundation on either side.

I had been to that same spot numerous times, and not once in more than twenty-five years. I had smoked my first cigarette there, perhaps heard my first dirty joke there, launched half a dozen ill-fated rafts and homemade boats from there. I remembered it as being a much prettier spot.

But Jessica acted as though it was wonderful. "Patt," she said, her eyes sparkling in the darkness, "where have you brought me?"

"You said you wanted to go to the beach and this was the closest thing I could think of. The waves aren't much, but they lap against the shore. There's no sand, but we can walk along the embankment if you want."

She did not immediately accept my invitation. "It looks muddy," she said. "How did you know about this place?"

"There used to be an abandoned bridge here and my father used to walk across it to get to Woodedge."

"Whatever for?"

"He wasn't supposed to be going where he was going."

Jessica waited.

"He was afraid if he drove the main roads someone might recognize him or his car and so he used to walk overland."

We were both staring at the river and I was awaiting the next question when she said, "I'd probably ruin either my shoes or my pantyhose."

I looked down. She was wearing a thin gray leather jacket, a pink striped blouse, gray slacks, and narrow gray shoes. I asked her what she was talking about.

"If we got out and walked along the river."

"What were you planning to do if we went to the beach?"

"If you had a blanket or something I could put it over me. Then I could take off my slacks and my pantyhose, put my slacks back on and walk barefoot."

The thought of the district attorney's wife removing her pants in my car, however briefly, brought back the memory of Mary Marie Gastonatto and the last time I had been parking—eighteen or a hundred years ago. I reached behind Jessica's seat and pulled out a neatly folded plaid blanket. She may or may not have seen it when she got in the car, but it was something I had to keep passengers' legs warm at night if I drove with the top down.

Jessica reached out her hand and for two seconds we both held the blanket, our eyes locked on each other. Then she took it. She faced forward and slid off her shoes.

She flipped open the blanket so that it covered her lap and her knees. She put her hands under the blanket and undid the snaps to her slacks. I heard a zipper open. Her hands moved slightly apart. "Don't look at me," she said.

I looked straight ahead again. My fingers tapped against the steering wheel. Jessica pulled the blanket up higher and tucked it under her chin. She was starting to wiggle, trying to get her slacks or her pantyhose or both down over her hips.

Suddenly she stopped. "I can't do this," she said.

I didn't turn, but my fingers ceased their tapping. "You see how easy it is, though," I said.

"How easy what is?" An edge crept into her voice.

"If I just turned now. If I put my arm around your waist, brought my face close to yours, would you resist me? What if I—knowing your bare ass is on my seat and not being able to control myself—reached down under that blanket, would you push me away?"

She did not try to get her slacks or her pantyhose back in place. She did not rush to say or do anything. "What are you talking about, Patt?"

"I'm just trying to tell you how it could have happened with Mrs. Carpenter."

Mrs. Keough exhaled slowly. "Oh," she said.

"She was with somebody—they could have run into each other or they could have been riding together innocently enough, and they stopped just like we did. Then the guy got the wrong impres-

sion because of where they were and the way they were talking.
He tried to kiss her, he tried to put his hand between her thighs
and she resisted him. Maybe he got angry, maybe he felt misled
or he couldn't understand. Maybe he was a jerk. Maybe all of
the above . . ."

Jessica said nothing.

"Or it could have been, you know, that she really wanted to
be with somebody—this person she was with. She's a married
woman with a big old house, but she has no idea what time her
husband is coming home. He's out, that much is clear. He's
playing golf and she knows he'll have a snack or a drink and
play some cards, so she's got no problem getting out of the house
without any questions being asked, but she can't meet with her
friend inside the house because her husband could come walking
in at any moment."

"She could have gone to her friend's house," Jessica said softly.

"Of course. Unless the friend was married himself or something
like that. Maybe all it was, she didn't really want to go to his
house. She wasn't that committed. Maybe she was attracted or
interested, but she wanted to see how things developed. Maybe
this guy was just a little fantasy she had and she didn't really
want to go through with anything, she just wanted to get as close
as she could to see what it would be like. A guy can't always tell
those things, you know."

There was just enough light to distinguish the various ripples
across the surface of the water. It gave us something to look at
as we sat.

"Should I start the engine or do you still want to get out and
walk around?"

"I think," she said, "it must be getting pretty late."

I nodded. I reached for the ignition key.

Jessica let the blanket drop away from the upper part of her
body. It bunched in her lap. She straightened her legs and arched
her hips and the blanket fell away from her legs. She was reaching
beneath her thighs and I saw that both her pantyhose and her
slacks were much lower than I had thought. I saw a brief glimpse

of a thick triangle of blond hair and then she was covered again. Her slacks were snapped shut.

"I guess you can start it up now," she said, without looking at me.

I flicked the key and the engine roared to life. I let it warm for a little while, even though it was not necessary, and then I backed out of our parking space. Jessica rolled up her window. On the way back to her house she took the blanket and covered her legs.

10

On Monday morning I was asked to step into Royster's office by Anita, Royster's secretary. Anita wore very short skirts, had very muscular legs, chewed gum, and generally acted as though being Royster's secretary was the second or third most important job in the office. Anita abhorred typing. She loved clicking around in her heels dispensing orders.

Royster had a high-backed leather swivel chair like John Michael's. He had a large desk like John Michael's. His office, however, was a good deal smaller than his boss's and so its furnishings tended to throw things out of perspective. If you were in front of Royster's desk and he was seated behind it, it was virtually impossible not to focus your attention on him.

When I opened Royster's door on Monday morning I saw that Ralphie Libby had taken up the one position in the room where he did not have to look directly into Royster's face. He was standing behind and slightly to the side of Royster's chair. He was standing at parade rest, with his forearms bulging and a crooked smile on his cracked and lined face. Ralphie was the state police detective lieutenant who had been assigned to our office as an investigator for more years than anyone could remember. He was the one whom John Michael had wanted to replace with me when John Michael had been a deputy in charge of criminal litigation. It was, indeed, the inability to get rid of

Ralphie that had caused John Michael to create for me the parallel position of "litigation coordinator."

Everyone, of course, knew that I functioned as John Michael's chief investigator, and had Ralphie Libby been of a different temperment he never would have allowed the situation to exist. But Ralphie had little ambition and even less interest in getting his skinny old butt out of the office in the heat of summer or the cold of winter. He liked drinking coffee, reading the *Herald* from cover to cover, intricately planning his picks at the dog track, and bantering inanely with the office personnel about whatever had been on television the night before. The unwritten agreement that everyone followed was to call Detective Libby our office investigator and to let me do the work. That was what made it disturbing to find Libby in Royster's office in the middle of a big investigation.

"So," said Royster, by way of greeting, "how was your weekend?" Like Ralphie, he was in shirtsleeves; but his were long where Ralphie's were short.

I chose to focus on Sunday in my response. "Not bad. I watched the Patriots get the shit kicked out of them down in New York. Then I went out and ran about five miles along the Charles until I didn't care anymore."

"Wasn't that awful?" said Ralphie, who may already have forgotten the reason he was there to meet with Royster and me.

Royster smiled impatiently. He had a pencil intertwined among his fingers and was tapping it on the glass top of his desk, first one end and then the other. "You didn't get a chance to do any work on the Carpenter case, did you?" He asked me.

"Yeah, as a matter of fact," I said, to Royster's obvious disappointment. "I was out to the Patterson house on Saturday and interviewed the last of Rebecca Carpenter's close friends. You remember, you thought that should be my next step."

"Learn anything?"

"I'm not sure. They're all pieces in a puzzle, Roy."

Tap-tap-tap went the pencil. "What was he like?"

"Gretchen Patterson was the one I talked to. Her husband wasn't there."

The pencil beat faster. "He was the one I said you should interview." Royster was excited now. He had found something about which he could complain. "Patterson's our key to learning what Carpenter was doing between six and ten Tuesday night."

"I'm working on it."

"And what have you done to learn what the victim was doing between six and ten that night?"

"Since we last talked? Nothing."

Royster silently threw down his pencil and looked at Ralphie. His look was obviously a cue for Ralphie to say something, but Ralphie was into the ceremonial aspect of his role and he was busy grinning and trying to look sharp.

Royster did a double-take. "Ralph here's been working on the case himself. Tell him what you've been doing, Ralph."

Put on the spot, it took Ralph a moment to remember. He broke parade rest, scratched his arm a bit, and said, "Well, I located the gardener."

"Rasmussin?" I said in surprise. "I heard he split."

Ralphie's brow crushed under the weight of his thoughts. "Rasmussin? No, this guy's name was Marconi."

"Oh, the old caretakers, Dominic and Gina."

"That's right," Ralphie said, brightening.

"Tell him about them," Royster ordered.

"Well," Ralphie said, holding out his hands, palms inward. "You should see the guy's wife. Tits out to here. I'm not kidding you."

I made a show of getting my notebook out of my jacket pocket. Royster shoved his chair back from his desk and delivered a glare that even Ralphie could interpret.

"Well, all right," he said, scratching some more. "They're sort of a middle-aged couple. The guy's about five-five and speaks broken English. The woman's got the heavy accent, but she speaks better, you know? I guess they both come over from Italy about ten, twenty years ago. Right now, they're living in a room at their daughter's house in Waterford and they're pretty pissed off about it, if you know what I mean." He waited for some sort of affirmation that I did, indeed, know what he meant.

When I nodded to his satisfaction, he went on. "It seems they'd been living on the Carpenter estate since Rebecca Carpenter's mother had the place, doing all the gardening, all the landscaping, tending to the orchards—even hiring all the fruit-pickers. It wasn't just him, it was her, too. Both of them working and never any complaints, according to them. And they sort of thought of the place as home, you know? I mean, they lived there and all. Then one day a couple of weeks ago Mrs. Carpenter comes to them and tells them they're fired. Three days notice, month's severance pay, and boom, they're gone."

"Thing is," Royster said, trying to move Ralphie along, "Mrs. Carpenter won't give them a reason. She just says their services won't be needed anymore."

"Wylie Carpenter said they caught Gina Marconi stealing liquor."

"Stealing liquor, huh?" Ralphie hitched up his belt as though contemplating whether stealing liquor was a firing offense. "Well, they claim they don't got the slightest idea what it's for. So they wait to see who replaces them."

"Doug Rasmussin."

"They don't got his name, but what they can plainly see is he's a young kid. Good-looking, early twenties. And they're saying, 'Hey, the property's so big the two of us could barely do it all before, and now we're getting replaced by one young kid?' Now, remember, these guys are Italian and all, but they think they know why. They say Mr. Carpenter, he's not home a lot." Ralphie leered, giving us a hint as to what was to come. "They get to this part and the two of them really start getting excited. They're both waving their arms around and yelling, some's in English, some's in Italian, and some's somewheres in between. But I get the sign language, you know?"

With that, Ralphie put his hands on his hips and began thrusting his pelvis in and out while he grinned unabashedly at Royster and me. As performed by Ralphie, it was the single most obscene gesture I had ever witnessed. Royster must have felt the same way because he waved violently at Ralphie and told him to cut it out.

For one moment Royster and I looked at each other in communication of unspoken, sympathetic misery. Then Royster blinked and we resumed our old adverserial positions.

"Get the picture?" Royster asked me. "She sees this young hardbody and wants him. She hires him to replace the faithful family retainers, starts a little thing going with him, husband finds out about it and kills her."

"Let's arrest him right away, Royster," I said.

Royster Hansen stared at me with eyes that were as blank as a wall. Perhaps inside his head he was counting to ten. "What I suggest," he said at last, "is that this is a new lead. If you don't want to follow up on it, I can have Ralph, here, do it. He can go find this new yardboy—"

"Caretaker. Rasmussin."

"—Rasmussin, and have the pleasure of learning whether he was sticking Mrs. Carpenter in between tree trims."

"Rasmussin's disappeared. I'm told he went to California."

"When?"

"A few days ago."

"A few days ago. Like, you mean, right after Mrs. Carpenter was killed?"

I shrugged. I tried not to look happy at Royster's sudden consternation.

"I'd like you to follow up on that," he said slowly.

John Michael and I played squash at the fitness club down the block from our office. We had a regularly scheduled time of Monday at six, but more often than not John Michael was unable to keep the date. On this Monday, he made it.

John Michael did not look good on a squash court. He wore matching wristbands and headband. He wore white sneakers, high white socks with horizontal stripes at the top, and white shorts that emphasized the whiteness of his skinny legs. He wore a gray T-shirt that bragged about the fact that Boston College had gone to the Cotton Bowl. He looked as though he was eighteen years old and undergoing a fraternity hazing obligation. He also was not a very accomplished squash player.

For a while John Michael had played racquetball. It was something he heard everyone was doing. Then he observed that there seemed to be a class distinction between those who played racquetball and those who played squash and so he took up the latter. Where John Michael went, I was sure to follow—because I was the person with whom he played. I suppose I could have refused to switch from one sport to the other, but the matter never came up for discussion.

So now on Mondays at six, whenever John Michael could make it, we met on a little wooden court where he would flail away at a little black ball and sweat and curse and generally drive himself into a provoked state of anger and frustration that he mistook for the fun of competitive athletics. On this particular Monday I beat him two straight, 15–12 both times. The score was not coincidental. I could have beaten him by almost any amount I chose.

As his last shot blasted into the tin base of the front wall he let out a roar of pain and drew back his arm as if he were going to throw his racket. Then he thought better of it and slumped into a corner. I slumped down next to him.

"You almost caught me there at the end," I lied.

"My foot slipped as I was hitting that last one," he claimed.

"Maybe you ought to try a new pair of court shoes," I suggested. "Maybe they have special ones just for squash."

John Michael grimaced at the soles of the sneakers he was wearing as though considering whether he could get away with blaming the outcome on them. "Jessica tells me you've got some new ideas about the case," he said.

Unsure as to the detail with which Jessica might have described our conversation, I said nothing.

"She tells me that you think Rebecca Carpenter could have voluntarily gone to that lovers' lane with her killer. Then Roy tells me you're thinking it might have been the gardener who killed her. Is all that true?"

"I haven't come to any conclusions of any sort, John."

"Reason I'm pressing you is that public attention seems to have already passed on this baby. You see what's on the front page of the *Courier* today? The whole thing's taken up with the latest brainstorm of Constantinis, that nitwit."

I had seen it. At Mayor Mackey's dinner on Saturday night Constantinis had unveiled a sweeping proposal for the gentrification of Waterford. He wanted the city to issue a bond which would allow it to buy up a huge section of riverfront property in order to re-create the original Watertowne plantation of the 1600s. The newspaper carried artist's drawings replete with little figures wearing Pilgrim-era costumes. It also had economic projections indicating that such a tourist attraction could bring tens of millions of new dollars a year to the city.

"Poor Neil Mackey thinks everybody's there to put feathers in his cap, and goddamn George sharpens his quill to a stiletto point and drives it right into Mackey's skull. 'The mayor,' he says, 'has worked tirelessly to bolster the economy of this great city of ours.' I'd like to know what the hell's so great about it. You ever heard of anybody who was born in this country who wanted to move to Waterford?" John Michael resumed his imitation. " 'But the Mayor cannot do it alone. Like any great craftsman, he must have the tools he needs to work with. He cannot spin gold out of straw. But if we give him those tools there is no telling what Mayor Mackey might do. One of the tools we must give him is increased funding. Where can we get the increased funding our city government so desperately needs? Not from our citizenry.

They have been taxed to death. They spoke out years ago on Proposition 2½ and said "No more." The funding must come from outside our great city. How? By giving the people outside our city something they can get nowhere else. What can they get nowhere else? Our history. Our heritage. That's what. It is as unique to Waterford as a fingerprint. How can we give it to them? Well, I have a proposal . . .' and out comes this whole stupid plan about turning the city into a theme park.

"I'm telling you, Patt, all around the room people are barfing into their tapioca. Anybody who knows anything, that is. Of course, they've got some yahoos there, the people maybe who're friends of a building contractor who's bought a table for ten, and they're applauding like crazy. That's what the press picks up on. 'Constantinis Proposal Greeted Enthusiastically,' that's what the headline said today. You have to read two paragraphs to find out it was Neil's dinner."

The district attorney got to his feet and looked down at me. "That's why I'm concerned about where we're going with this Carpenter thing. We don't come up with something fast everybody's going to forget we're working on it."

"Well," I said, getting up to stand alongside him, "the murder didn't get all that much attention to start with. What happens in Woodedge tends to stay in Woodedge. It doesn't affect anybody other than Woodedgians."

"You think anything that happens in Waterford affects anybody anywhere? But look what Constantinis is able to do with his harebrained schemes. You have to catch the public's fantasy. That's the key, Patt. In his position he can get people to fantasize about what can happen in the future. Me, I've got to get them fantasizing about what happened in the past. If I get everyone believing that the rich people up in Woodedge have been fornicating and plotting and killing each other, then I've got something they're interested in. Otherwise, you tell me this is some stickup artist whose gun goes off accidentally, or some handyman shoots his boss, you don't give me much to go with in terms of fantasy. That kind of crap can happen anyplace. I've gotta have something that can only happen in Woodedge. You know what I'm saying?"

"I'm working on it, John."

"Well," John Michael said, and he gave me a grin that was meant to indicate he was not really a bad guy, "work a little harder."

Mrs. Violet Rasmussin of 1429 Merrymount Avenue in Walmouth had already been interviewed regarding the disappearance of her son. A nice little man had come by, she said. Had an English accent. Reminded her of a pint-size Prince Charles.

"Inspector Lester?" I asked.

"That's the ticket," she said, and promptly lay down on the couch.

Mrs. Rasmussin had a headache. She also had a backache. She didn't mind being interviewed again, but she only wanted to talk from the prone position. I accepted her hand gesture as an invitation to sit in a modified rocker with a fixed base and a cheap colonial print cover on its cushions. I left the front door open even though Merrymount Avenue was the main thoroughfare between Walmouth and Waterford and the noise from the passing traffic was terrific.

Fourteen twenty-nine Merrymount Avenue was a small red brick house perched very high on a cement foundation. It was separated from the street by a sidewalk, a short hurricane fence, fifteen feet of grass and cement walkway, and six fairly steep cement stairs. The house had an air of wanting to be cozy and neat and modern, and that made it sad. The front door opened directly into the living room, where there was a fake fireplace and a picture window that looked out onto the traffic.

The fake fireplace was useful because it had a mantel. The

mantel was useful because it held several framed pictures and several elfin figurines that were either Hummels or imitation Hummels. Either way, the figurines, in their supposed jollity, were every bit as sad as the house they decorated. I pictured one of them being hurled against the wall, breaking into pieces, and still maintaining its sickly little smile on its glazed face.

The house made me feel claustrophobic. It reminded me of a hospital room. I had to take deep breaths, but when I did I inhaled the otherwise abeyant smell of heavy ethnic food—boiled cabbage, perhaps. So I kept the front door open and we talked over the noise.

Doug, Mrs. Rasmussin said, had indeed gone to California. No, it wasn't anything sudden. He'd been talking about doing it for some time. "So finally I said to him, 'Why don't you stop your yapping and just go?' "

"When was this, Mrs. Rasmussin?"

She was lying on the couch with her head closest to me and her feet propped on the distant arm. It was not a very becoming position. It made her patterned dress fall away at the knees and revealed the varicose veins in her lower legs. The back of the couch was to her right. She took the arm that was next to it and crooked it so that she could cover her brow with her hand.

"I know what you're thinking," she said, "but you're wrong. That little Mr. Lester told me all about how that lady who got strangled was the one Doug worked for, but Dougie couldn'ta had nothing to do with that because that happened on Tuesday night and he was already gone by then. I already went over that with Mr. Lester."

"I'm confused, Mrs. Rasmussin. When did you have your talk with Inspector Lester?"

"What's today?"

"Today's Tuesday."

"So he's been gone a week, Dougie. Lester was here, I don't know, maybe two, three days after that."

"Do you know why Doug chose to leave on the day he did?"

"Well, he was planning to all along, you know. That was his

plan, he was going to leave at the end of the summer. After the kids went back to school and the pool closed down. And then they offered him this job, just until he got all the leaves up and everything, but he told them from the start he wanted to be outa here before the snow came. What's the date now?"

"October twenty-second."

"So he told them he was going to leave around the middle of October. That was the deal. Me, I get so one month looks pretty much like another. You got your hot months and your cold months and your in-between months going one way or the other. That's all that really counts. You know, is it hot or is it cold? What else is there?"

I didn't tell her. Instead, I said, "Mrs. Rasmussin, let me go back over a few things. What was it you were saying about the pool closing down?"

"The pool where he was a lifeguard. At the club."

"What club?"

"The country club. Stonegate Country Club over there in Woodedge. You gotta know that place. Dougie was the lifeguard there during the summer. Taught the little kids to swim. But it, you know, it closes down September sometime. He coulda gotten another job at the club for the fall, but he said, 'Nope. This year I'm going to California.' So he went. It didn't have nothing to do with that lady dying. You can ask anybody."

"But before he went he did take the job with Mr. and Mrs. Carpenter."

Mrs. Rasmussin took her hand away from her brow and twisted around to get a look at me. She quite clearly thought I was dense. I smiled at her.

"You woulda too," she said, "if they offered you what they offered him. Twice what he was making at the club. But I guess they were desperate, you know? So he said, 'What the heck? It don't make any difference if I go in September or October and I can use all the money I can get.' I mean, he'd saved up, but if he's moving out there for good then he couldn't have too much, could he? So this was the deal, he'd work for them for a few weeks, get things ready for winter and all, pick up a few extra bucks, and then he'd take off."

"And your understanding was that he was going to take care of the property all by himself?"

"What's to picking up a few leaves? Pruning a few bushes?"

"Have you seen the size of the Carpenters' property?"

Mrs. Rasmussin returned to her previous position, feet up, hand on her brow. "Doug's a big strong boy. He could do it."

"He say anything about the orchards the Carpenters had?"

"He didn't say nothing about orchards. Why, did they have orchards?" From the tone of her voice, she might have been asking if they had bunions.

"Would you have a picture of Doug, by any chance, Mrs. Rasmussin?"

She pointed with one of her feet at the mantelpiece. I got up and walked over to look at the array of framed photographs. One was a black-and-white of an unhappy looking young man in an army uniform. "Not him. That's my husband," Mrs. Rasmussin said. "He's dead."

One was a color photo of a bull-necked grinning blond man in a chief petty officer's uniform. "That's my son Alex," she said. "He's in the navy. Goes all around the world in submarines."

Next was a high-school graduation picture of a young man blond and grinning like Alex, but decidedly more slim and handsome. He had a perfect set of white teeth and one charming dimple that told you he was delighted to be photographed and made you feel delighted along with him.

"Good-looking boy," I said.

"Doug could be a movie star," she told me. "If he wasn't so soft in the head."

I asked if there was a picture I could have to take with me and Mrs. Rasmussin suddenly sat up.

"Why?" she said, clinging to the top of the couch with one hand, the bottom with the other.

"Because I may need it as part of our investigation."

"Oh, no. I told you, I already had this talk with that inspector guy and I explained to him how it couldn't have been Doug had anything to do with this. You just go talk with him, you don't believe me."

I told her I would do that and she nodded as though I had damn well better. I asked if she had heard from Doug since he left and if she had any address where I could reach him out in California.

She told me no on both counts. "Dougie's hitchhiking out there and I don't expect to hear from him until he gets settled in. If he's anything like his brother I don't even expect to hear then."

I propped a card against Doug's photograph. I said, "Since Doug didn't have anything to do with what happened, you'll have him call me as soon as you hear from him, won't you? Have him call collect, or at least get a number where I can reach him."

She thought about it for a moment and then told me what she knew I wanted to hear. "Sure," she said, and flopped back onto the cushions.

I closed the door behind me on my way out, knowing I wouldn't hear from her again.

Chief Wembley Tuttle's office was too small for its accumulation. It had a desk covered with papers; a credenza covered with papers; a tall set of bookshelves that contained half a dozen large books, twice as many manuals, some syllabi from various law enforcement conferences, and more papers. The chief had a swivel chair with a cushion on it. There were two other wooden chairs and a blue couch. About half the blue couch was covered with papers.

Hanging on the wall were photographs of Chief Tuttle shaking hands with various people. There must have been a dozen such photographs and most of them hung crookedly. In one he was shaking hands with Willie Mays. Willie was wearing a golf hat and looking at the camera. The chief was wearing plaid pants pulled high on his belly and he was looking at Willie. In another picture the chief was standing with Burnsie, my former boss. Burnsie's mouth was open, his tie was loose, and his eyes were glazed. The chief had his hand on Burnsie's back and might have been holding him upright for the photographer.

"I thought it was time we compared notes on the Carpenter investigation," I said when the chief, Inspector Lester, Detective Lieutenant Libby, and I were all seated.

The chief was in the chair behind the desk, the one with the cushion. Lester was on the couch smoking a cigarette. They exchanged looks.

I was in one of the wooden chairs, penned in by a couple of heavily loaded cardboard boxes. The chief's desk was on my left, the couch was on my right, and I was facing Libby, whom I had brought with me and who was leaning forward in his wooden chair with his elbows on his knees, his feet spread, his hands loosely clasped. Alone among the four of us Libby did not have out a pen and a notepad.

"How are you guys coming?" I asked when enough time had passed without anybody saying anything.

"Good," said the chief, nodding wide-eyed and blank-faced at Lester.

"Good," responded Lester quickly. "Good, good."

"Good," said Libby as though it were a password to get into the conversation.

"Figured out who did it yet, Chief?" I asked with my pen in my mouth.

"We're working on it," he said, unknowingly echoing what I had told Royster the day before.

"That's right. We're working on it," said his able inspector.

Libby nodded. He was ready to leave now that we had gotten all the essential information.

"Got a list of suspects?" I asked.

The chief again looked at Lester. All he had to do was stare straight ahead.

"Everybody's a suspect," cracked Lester.

Libby kept nodding. This all made sense to him.

"Ralphie, here, did some digging and located Mr. and Mrs. Marconi, the former caretakers at the Carpenter place. After talking with them he's come up with a theory. Tell the chief what it is, Ralph."

Libby looked confused for a second. Then he straightened his back and I had a flash of fear that he was going to put his hands on his hips and start that horrible pelvis-thrusting thing again. I moved quickly to head him off.

"The information he got from the Marconis leads him to believe that Mrs. Carpenter might have been the philandering sort, that she might have hired this young guy Rasmussin for reasons other than his gardening ability, that maybe Mr. Carpenter found out about this and didn't take kindly to it. You guys looked into this possibility?"

"Well . . ." The chief spread his hands.

Lester waved his cigarette. He did it by holding the cigarette at the bottom between his thumb and other four fingers. "The kid's a suspect," he said.

"Everybody's a suspect."

"That's right."

"Including Wylie."

The chief's hands and the inspector's cigarette did their little dance again.

"I was out to Rasmussin's house today," I said. "You're aware he's gone, aren't you, Les?"

"Hitchhiking out west." He looked the conversation back toward his boss, who picked it up from there.

"We've notified the state police in Nebraska and Kansas to be on the lookout for him. You knew that, didn't you, Patt? Ralph did it last Friday."

It must have been readily apparent that I had not known that. Ralphie and I had just driven from Walmouth to Woodedge without him ever mentioning anything about it.

"You been in touch with the FBI or anything?" I said. "Done anything about trying to get a warrant issued? Anything else I should know about so I can do my job?"

The chief regarded me contemplatively. "No, nothing you should know about."

"We figured, chances were he'd be going through one of those states," offered Libby. "And he could be picked up for vagrancy or something until we got out there to question him."

"We told 'em he's a suspect in a murder. But obviously they can't arrest him for just being a suspect," explained the chief.

"Just hold the bugger, that's all we want them to do," added Lester. "Let us have a go at him."

I doodled ugly pictures on my pad. "What about Ralph's theory?"

The chief looked at Ralph for several seconds. Ralphie responded as though he were waiting to be selected by the captain of a sandlot baseball team.

"We'll consider that, Ralph," he said, and Ralphie beamed.

"Let's consider it now, Wem," I said. I pointed at Lester. "As Stanley has no doubt told you, the young Mr. Rasmussin was a former lifeguard at Stonegate Country Club. As you'll recall from our conversation with Wylie Carpenter, he was a member of that country club."

"That's where he was when his wife was killed."

"Well, we're not entirely sure about that, Wem—unless you know something I don't, which you've just indicated to me isn't the case. What we have been told, however, by Wylie himself, is that he didn't pay much attention to the grounds. He left that up to his wife. What Mrs. Marconi told Ralphie was that she and her husband were going along just as they had always been and one day Mrs. Carpenter walks up to them out of the blue and fires them."

"Wylie said Mrs. Marconi was stealing liquor."

"Wembley, look. The Marconis have been there for years. They were living there before Wylie and Rebecca moved in, right on the premises. And suddenly one day they're fired because she supposedly took some liquor? In September? On the eve of the fall season, leaving Mrs. Carpenter so desperate for somebody to pick up the leaves and everything that she's got to hire away the lifeguard from one of their country clubs? Give me a break, will you? The lifeguard's the handsomest kid you ever saw. He goes to work for a couple of weeks and then disappears on the very day Mrs. Carpenter turns up dead. This should at least raise some suspicion in your mind."

"It bloody well does in mine," said Lester, his face long with sincerity, his eyes on Wembley Tuttle's. "Makes me think the kid must have killed the lady, else why would he have disappeared like that?"

"Well," I said calmly, "one reason could be that he was made to disappear."

For a long moment nobody reacted. Then the chief shifted in his chair. "You mean, like, if Wylie killed him?"

"I'm asking if you've looked into that possibility."

The chief looked from one of his fellow officers of the law to the other. None of them spoke.

"Let me give you another possibility," I said. "Les, you talked with Rasmussin's mother, what did you learn about him going away?"

"That he was going to California." Lester gestured with his thumb. "Shank's mare."

"And she made it clear to you that he had already worked that out with the Carpenters, right? He had planned to leave last Tuesday and they knew that beforehand, didn't they?"

Lester's laughter came out in little hacks. "It's his bloody mother, for God's sake. What do you expect her to say after I tell her the lady's been murdered?"

Wembley Tuttle leaned forward. "What are you getting at, Patt?"

"Just this. Wylie could have known that Rasmussin was planning on leaving last Tuesday. He could have known that his wife and Rasmussin were fooling around. He could have figured that Rasmussin would be your main suspect if anything happened to Rebecca on the very night Rasmussin took off."

Tuttle's face became very serious. His voice took on a tone of maximum gravity. "It sounds to me like you're out to get Wylie, Patt."

"I'm not out to *get* anyone, Chief. I'm trying to learn what happened and I just want to know if you've looked into these possibilities, that's all. Since Les talked with Mrs. Rasmussin last week, have you, for example, asked Wylie if he knew her son was leaving? Did you find out if it was all prearranged, like she claims? Is any of this even of any interest to you?"

The silence grew to a point of tension before Tuttle said, "Wylie Carpenter is an important member of this community. His wife was an important member. Around here, we don't just throw accusations at such people. We don't just make up things to investigate, either. Stanley and I are handling this matter as we see fit." He paused for a long moment and looked over at Ralphie. "With Ralph's help," he added.

"We're looking for the caretaker and if we don't find him in the midwest, then we expect he'll be contacting his mother or one of his friends once he gets to California. Or maybe the local authorities there will help us locate him. But right now we've got no reason to believe that he's dead or that Mr. Wylie Carpenter is somehow using his departure as a cover-up for his own crime."

"Besides," muttered Lester, "you've got your basic bloody facts wrong."

I cocked my head. "Oh?"

"Your Mrs. Carpenter that you think recruited this young hardbody wasn't even a member of the Stonegate Country Club. She and her husband had a family membership at Bollingbrook, but he had a single membership at the other place." Lester checked with the chief to see how far he could go. "Unless," he said, "unless you think Mr. Wylie Carpenter brought this fellow into his service just so he could boink his wife."

Lester spoke too fast and his voice was too accented for Ralphie to be able to follow easily, but Ralphie knew a joke of sorts had been made and so he offered a willing, if somewhat uncertain, smile. Chief Tuttle, however, did not think his town's rich people should be held up to even fanciful ridicule. His puffy, double-chinned face remained stern.

"I take it," I said, gazing at each of them, "that someone has asked Wylie if he was the one who offered Rasmussin the job."

The chief cleaned his nose. First he used his thumb and his forefinger, then the side of his thumb, then the back of his hand. "We can do that," he said.

"And I take it that if he admits he's the one who asked Rasmussin if he wanted a job, then you'll ask him why he contrived to give us the impression that he didn't know anything about the guy."

The chief spread his hands.

"Now, let me ask one more question. Who's checked the Carpenters' phone records?"

Lester got permission from Chief Tuttle to answer. "Three calls made from the house on Tuesday. Sarah Mitchell, the housekeeper, verifies two of them as being hers. The other was to the Patterson house at one in the afternoon. Nothing between six and Sergeant Roselli's arrival in the wee hours of the next morning."

"How long was the Patterson call?"

"Short. One minute."

"I think it would be a good idea to obtain the phone records from the Patterson home. Tuesday, Monday, Sunday, Saturday. Also, see if you can get the phone records from Dodge's office. You know where that is, don't you?"

"Law Offices of Hill and Patterson." Lester jerked his head. "Just down the road."

"Now you're saying Dodge Patterson might have had something to do with it? Is that what you're saying, Patt?" The chief sounded disappointed in me.

"Did you ever hear that Dodge Patterson and Rebecca Carpenter might have been more than just good friends, Wem?"

The chief exhaled audibly and slumped back in his chair. "I don't think this is any way to conduct an investigation, Patt."

"Fine," I said, getting to my feet. "I'll have one of the assistant D.A.'s subpoena Patterson's records and I'll review them myself."

As an exit line it had its merit, serving as a none-too-subtle reminder of my position. It was unfortunate, therefore, that most of its effect was lost when I had to return a minute or so later to get Ralphie, who had forgotten to get up and leave when I did, who was still sitting there with his knees spread, his fingers folded, and his prematurely wizened features crossed with bewilderment.

When I got out of high school there did not seem to be any major league teams interested in a slow outfielder who hit .250, and I had not prepared myself for many other options. I thought of joining the merchant marine. Somebody I knew told me you got to see the world and avoid the draft at the same time. Unfortunately, everyone else seemed to have heard the same story and the merchant marine was impossible to get into. I went to junior college instead.

Walmouth J.C. was not a difficult school. Its student body essentially consisted of three types: young men like me who did not feel a patriotic urge to die for our country's policy of Asian containment; women in their late twenties to early forties who had missed college for one reason or another on the first go-round; and some very dumb people of both sexes who could get in nowhere else. The admixture was not inspiring. I soon learned, moreover, that it was not really necessary for me to go to class in order to get the B grades to which I aspired.

That left me with some serious time on my hands. My father eventually noticed this and became quite upset with me. Although he had never mentioned the matter, he told me he had just naturally assumed that I would be going to a "good" college. Yale, he thought, would be nice. He asked me what I was going to do with a Walmouth J.C. education and I told him I didn't know. Shortly after that he arranged for me to be employed with his company as a field adjuster.

It was, I am sure, a move made with the best of intentions by my father. He was certain that a taste of the real world would send me scurrying back to my books and propel me on to the Ivy League education he had previously neglected to discuss with me. Unfortunately, I proved to be fairly adept at insurance adjusting. I started with banged-up cars and did my work quickly and gave my superiors absolutely no indication that I was interested in becoming a claims supervisor, a manager, or anything else. This made them very interested in me. By the time my father took his last walk into the woods of Woodedge, I was already doing residential properties and was pegged by my father's company for the fast track. Company representatives told me so at his funeral.

"Work hard," said a sour-breathed regional supervisor named Winterhalter, as he put his arm around me and rested his sweaty armpit against my shoulder. "Work hard and the world will be your oyster."

I didn't tell Winterhalter how ironic I thought it was for him to be saying that at my father's funeral, but I remembered his words. I remembered them on the day I parked outside the Main Street building of my cousin D. Dodge Patterson. It was three doors down from Adolfo's on the same side of the street, a small gabled house that had been modified to serve as the Law Offices of Hill and Patterson. A new deck and a sturdy flight of stairs had been added to the existing structure to accommodate the hordes of clients who could be expected to park their cars on the vast paved-over space of what had once been somebody's front lawn.

I walked up the stairs and presented myself to the receptionist of Hill and Patterson, who was most disturbed that I wanted to see D. Dodge without an appointment. I had difficulty getting her to be impressed by the information printed on my card. "You will have to wait," she said, spitting out each word as if it were an unpleasant object that had balled in her mouth, "while I see if he is available."

I took a seat on the mini-couch that was there in the reception area for people who had to wait to see if their attorney was available. It was located in the pocket of a bay window, set between a small magazine rack and a tropical fish tank. The fish looked at me. I looked at the magazines. There was nothing in the rack that appealed to me, since I was not interested in sailing, horses, or kitchens.

The receptionist, meanwhile, had turned her back, cupped her hand to the telephone, and whispered into the receiver. When she hung up she pretended I had disappeared.

"Two-person firm?" I asked. I was dangling my right foot over my left knee, showing her that I was comfortable in her frosty presence.

"That's right," she said, without raising her eyes from something she was writing.

"What kind of law does the firm specialize in?"

"General practice of law," she said. A few moments later, perhaps after writing some particularly difficult word, she added, "Mr. Hill does a lot of bank work and some real estate law. Mr. Patterson specializes in real estate law."

"Is Woodedge Savings and Loan one of your clients?"

The woman's voice became singsong. "I'm not at liberty to divulge our clients."

I had nothing else to do. I was killing time until D. Dodge could decide if he was available to see me and I reasoned that this woman probably had not had any good fun since her last kickball game in elementary school. So I asked her why she wasn't at liberty to divulge that information.

She sighed angrily. "Because I'm not, that's why."

"That's no answer," I said.

"I'm not going to argue with you," she told me.

"Why not?" I asked; but she was spared from a further battle of wits by the appearance of Dodge Patterson.

"Mr. Starbuck?" he said as he descended on me with his hand out and a smile of curious greeting spread across his face.

He was wearing neither suit nor tie, but was dressed in a tattersall shirt and a brown crewneck sweater. His thick hair was yellow and wavy and combed straight back. His jaw was rugged, his chin clefted, and his teeth were as uniformly white as a mouthful of Chiclets. He was everything one would expect from the husband of Gretchen and the lover of Rebecca and he seemed abundantly sincere in his welcome. He reminded me of a television game-show host.

"Yeah," I mumbled. "Hi." I withdrew my hand from his as quickly as possible.

"Hold my calls," he said to the receptionist, who either chose that moment to roll her eyes or was experiencing a petit mal seizure. Then he led me down a hallway that took us past a dining room that held a conference table, a galley kitchen that smelled of coffee, a powder room, and a den that held a word processor and a photocopying machine, until at last we entered a room that I assumed had once been a bedroom and was now Dodge Patterson's office. The drapes were drawn and the only light came from the center of the ceiling. The desk looked a little too delicate for a man as big as Dodge, but it had a leather-edged blotter, a gold pen stand, and several little games, including a clown figure on a set of parallel bars and some swinging silver balls that would bang into each other in perpetuity if they were started properly. What was not on the desk was anything that looked like legal work.

I surveyed the four walls before I sat down. There were two large golf trophies and one tennis cup on a shelf. There was a framed bar certificate and two framed degrees announcing that D. Dodge Patterson was a graduate of Amherst College and Boston University Law School. There might have been more items of passing interest, but I stopped scanning when I saw the photograph of Gretchen Patterson. Her face was pressed close to that of a brown-haired, big-eyed little boy who matched her in every way but the darkness of her complexion.

"My wife and son," Dodge said.

"Yes," I said, realizing I had been staring longer than I should have. "I met Mrs. Patterson on Saturday."

"Oh?" Dodge looked puzzled.

"I was out to your house to see you about this Rebecca Carpenter matter."

"That's right," he said, snapping his fingers. "She and Dad did mention something about that." He sat down, his hands folded across his stomach. This was not a man who was greatly on edge as to what I was going to ask him.

"Nice offices," I said. "How long have you been here?"

"Four years."

I glanced at his law degree and saw that he had been out of school eleven years. "Where were you before that, if you don't mind my asking?"

He gave me the name of a firm that sounded prestigious. Crosby, Stills, Nash and Young. Something like that.

"Boston?" I asked.

"Big Boston."

"I guess they don't do criminal law."

Dodge chuckled. He might have been talking to an idiot. "No. They don't do any of that."

"It's a criminal matter I'm here about, you know."

My cousin spread his hands. He smiled. His time was my time.

"You were close with Rebecca Carpenter and her husband, weren't you?"

"Pretty close, yes." A piece of paper caught his eye. He read it, frowned over it, crumpled it into a ball, and lofted it toward his wastebasket. I noticed the wastebasket had a miniature backboard and rim attached to it. "Bird," he said, as the ball of paper dropped cleanly through the hoop.

"You were with Wylie on the night his wife died."

"Yeah. Awful thing. Terrible thing."

"You played golf with him at Stonegate that day."

"That's right."

"And then cards afterward in the clubhouse."

Dodge pushed his hand back over his forehead and held it in his hair. "Did we? I guess we did."

"You and Wylie and Butcher and Teasdale and Whitman."

"Okay."

"You played the last game against Whitman."

"Right. I remember now."

"What time did you leave that night?"

"We closed the place. The bartender was trying to get us out of there, if I remember right."

"Who's we?"

"Wylie and me. I think Gerry Whitman had already gone home."

"Wylie was there when the place closed?"

Dodge hesitated. "I thought he was. Why? Did he say he wasn't?"

"No. He said he was."

"Then he was." Dodge seemed pleased that we had solved that problem. He was playing with a rubber band now.

I looked deep into Dodge's eyes and wondered if he thought this interview was at all strange. To me it was like talking to a stranger who was wearing my shirt.

"How did Wylie get home?"

Dodge's head drew back. "He drove."

"You saw him do that? At the end of the night, I mean."

"Sure. I walked him to his car." Dodge angled his gaze, as if waiting for the trick to emerge from my questions.

"And you, yourself, were in the clubhouse the whole time, six to ten or whatever?"

Dodge nodded slowly, carefully.

"You didn't go home for dinner and then come back, or anything like that, did you?"

"No. In fact, I ate there at the bar in the clubhouse because Gretchen said she wasn't going to be home that evening. She was going shopping or something."

Dodge's rubber band snapped. He looked at it as if it had betrayed him. He looked at me to see if I was through.

"You're a member of that club, aren't you?" I asked.

He nodded. "Ever since they raised the dues at Bollingbrook."

"You know the people who work there."

"At Stonegate? Sure. Most of them."

"Know a fellow named Dougie Rasmussin?"

"The lifeguard at the pool? Taught my son, Ian, to swim."

"You're aware that he left that job to go to work for the Carpenters as their caretaker, aren't you?"

"I think my wife mentioned that, yes."

"But you never discussed it with Wylie."

"Wylie? No. What did I care?"

"You know Dougie Rasmussin left the area just about the same time Rebecca was killed."

Dodge Patterson stopped fiddling with things. His expression changed. He licked his lower lip. "That doesn't make sense, if you're saying what I think you're saying. The Dougie Rasmussin I knew was just a happy-go-lucky sort of kid."

"Good-looking guy?"

"I guess you'd call him that."

"You couldn't see him getting angry or flying off the handle if, say, his advances were rejected by someone like, say, Rebecca Carpenter?"

It took Dodge a moment to answer. "Well, I don't know. I couldn't really see that sort of thing happening."

"Is that because you couldn't really see Rebecca resisting a handsome man's advances?"

"What's that supposed to mean?"

"I'm just trying to learn something about Mrs. Carpenter. Please don't take offense. There's nothing personal about what I'm asking—really, it embarrasses me sometimes—but the circumstances of her death are such that I have to ask some questions that normally would be none of my business."

Dodge pulled at his lower lip with his thumb and forefinger. He could not be a game-show host, I decided. He lacked the resiliency.

"Do you know," I asked, speaking slowly and deliberately, "if Rebecca Carpenter was sexually active outside her marriage?"

Dodge kept his thumb to his lip, but temporarily opened his fingers. "Not that I'm aware of."

"In your opinion, was she the type who might encourage the attentions of a young man like Rasmussin?"

Dodge's eyes narrowed. "I don't think so."

"Do you feel it's more likely she would have rejected his attentions?"

"I mean, that's presuming there are attentions, right? I can't really answer these questions." He smiled. He wanted out of the discussion.

"Didn't you know her pretty well yourself, Mr. Patterson?"

His smile grew broader. He picked up a pewter letter opener and began slicing at some envelopes. "Me? Becky? I've known her all my life."

"Didn't she try telephoning you on the day she died?"

"I don't think so," he said, still slicing, occasionally examining the contents of the envelopes he was opening. "Why would she?"

"Perhaps because you had a relationship with her."

"No," he said. "No. Who told you that?"

"That's not important. I'm not here to gossip or anything. The point is, I was told that you and Rebecca had a relationship at one time."

"A relationship, sure. Like I told you, I've known her all my life. But Becky is, or was, a few years older than me, and if you want to know the truth, she wasn't really my type."

"She seemed very attractive from the pictures I've seen."

Dodge Patterson smiled a between-us-guys sort of smile. His head tilted in a modified shrug. He lowered his voice to just above a whisper. "She was kind of wide in the hips."

"Oh."

He nodded. He apparently understood me to be a guy who could relate to a problem like that.

"So you have no idea why she would have been calling your house that day?"

"My house? I thought you meant she called me here. If she called my house she was looking for my wife. They usually get together, got together, about once a week. Hen party or whatever." He threw me a humorous glance. "Gossip, chew the fat, complain about their husbands." He had found a letter to his liking and he read it as he spoke.

I said, "Well, I guess you've pretty much told me everything you know."

"Hmmn?" Then he realized that I was getting up to go. "Oh, well then, fine. No problem, Pete."

"That's Patt," I snapped, unable to control myself. "Just like your name. Patterson Starbuck."

"Oh, really? How about that?" But already his attention was elsewhere. He was making a note on his letter, he was throwing away the envelope, he was getting up to shake my hand and telling me to come back anytime.

I told him I would do that and tried not to show that I hated him with all my heart.

13

They were all sitting in the corner booth. John Michael felt the corner booth in the lounge at the Roadhouse Restaurant belonged to him, and he had no qualms about asking management to move people if he arrived with any sort of group and found it occupied. Management almost always obliged. They liked having the Roadhouse known as the district attorney's hangout. They liked it so much that when John Michael would send a round of drinks to the displaced persons they often would not charge him.

John Michael had his tie loosened and a tall glass of Coke in front of him. A red plastic straw was still in the drink. Next to him sat Jessica, wearing a dark green blazer and fondling a glass of white wine. Next to her the space was open. Across from her sat Royster, still in his suit, a beer growing warm in his hand; and next to him was his wife, her hair in her face, her eyes hollow, and her drink glass already empty. There was a space next to her as well.

I took the seat beside Jessica and smiled around. No one spoke until I settled in.

"How was your trip?" John Michael asked as he placed his plastic straw between his teeth and chewed it like a toothpick.

"Leaves are still beautiful, although they're going fast. A lot of reds now, not so many oranges."

"What did you learn?"

"That Lee, Massachusetts, is a quaint little Berkshire town just off the pike. A bunch of hotels, motels, and bed-and-breakfasts to take care of the foliage tourists in the fall, the theatergoers and music lovers bound for Stockbridge and Tanglewood in the summer, and the skiers passing through to Vermont in the winter. I learned that Wylie's father was the town doctor and that Wylie did not leave there for lack of room. His old homestead is one of the bigger spreads in town. I was told by one of the local innkeepers, who purported to know about things like that, that Wylie was the smartest kid around until his father sent him off to prep school, where he was president of his student body and a three-sport athlete."

There was silence at the table and then John Michael jabbed his masticated straw at an ice cube in his drink and slopped soda all over the table. "The credit check we ran on him indicated he has seven figures of assets in his own name, not counting anything he gets from his wife," he said glumly.

Jessica, who had not looked at me since I sat down, took a napkin and began mopping up her husband's spill. "His motive had to be jealousy, then."

I glanced up in confusion. "I'm sorry . . . ?"

"He found out his wife was fooling around and so he killed her. Poetic justice. Did it in a lovers' lane."

"I thought we discussed . . ." I hesitated, not sure how much of our discussion I was free to mention. It had, after all, taken place in a locked bathroom. I amended what I was saying. "I thought you felt he might have killed her because he had another woman. A younger woman."

"Either way," said John Michael. "You were supposed to look at both angles. What do you have that would support jealousy?"

The waitress came and took my beer order. She swept the table with the stub of her pencil and only Patty Hansen indicated she wanted a refill.

When she was gone I said, "One possibility is Rebecca might have been having a fling with this Rasmussin, the young stud she hired as a caretaker, who's now disappeared. Word has it that she liked guys in good physical shape and this kid was the lifeguard at Stonegate Country Club before she hired him. Not an unreasonable question to ask why she hired a good-looking young lifeguard to do a caretaker's job."

"Any other possibility?"

"Well," I said, and suddenly my stomach felt funny. I raised my arm as a sort of disclaimer. "She may have once had an affair with Dodge Patterson."

"Her husband's golf partner?" asked John Michael.

"Her friend's husband?" asked Royster.

I told them Dodge denied it.

John Michael thought for a moment. The red plastic straw was back between his teeth. "What's he like?" he asked.

I admitted that he was handsome and athletic-looking.

"A lawyer, isn't he?"

I nodded. "Has a firm called Hill and Patterson right there in Woodedge. Before that he was with a big Boston firm."

"Sort of like Wylie? Made his mark and then moved out to the more leisurely paced life of the idyllic countryside?"

"I don't think so. He's only in his mid-thirties. I gather he was with the Boston firm about seven years."

The two lawyers looked at each other.

"Seven years is the traditional make-it-or-break-it time," said Royster. "You get made a partner or you get pushed out."

"Doesn't make him a killer," I snapped, and all four people turned to look at me in surprise.

"Didn't say it did, Patt," John Michael said softly.

I blushed and looked down at the table.

A minute later the drinks came and while John Michael was signaling to have them put on his tab I told him, "Dodge has been identified by several people as being in the clubhouse that evening."

"What about Wylie? Have you got anything screwed down about how long he was there?"

"It's confusing. Apparently five guys started playing two-man games about six o'clock. I've got Wylie placed for the first two rounds of the games. Then nobody remembers seeing him until about ten, when Dodge confirms that Wylie helped him close the place down."

"What time did the second round end?"

"Well, Butcher played in the second round and he's the one who told me he left around eight. Okay, you say, so Wylie's unaccounted for between eight and ten. Still, that presents us with a logistical problem if we want to make him our killer. You have to figure fifteen minutes to drive from Stonegate to his house and figure another ten minutes from his house to the overlook where Mrs. Carpenter was found. From there he could drive back to Stonegate in about ten minutes, but it would be at least an hour if he walked it in the dark. And I have to figure him walking it because, after all, his wife was left in the car. So that's cutting it pretty close if we want to have Wylie going from one place to the other to the other, killing his wife and wiping off prints along the way."

I looked for my companions to share in the comfort of my logic, but John Michael was staring at me and the rest were staring along with him. I sought to persuade them further. "Also, unless Wylie walked in the first instance from Stonegate to his house, we're left with the question of how he could have had his car at Stonegate at ten. Dodge, you see, says he saw Wylie drive off at closing time."

John Michael had gone from poking at his ice cubes to curling his cocktail napkin. He kept curling until a piece of the napkin tore off. "You know, Patt," he said, "I get the feeling you don't really want to resolve this case. I get the feeling that if you did you'd be looking at the evidence in a whole different light. Is it possible, do you think, just maybe, could the guy have had his wife's Mercedes parked at the overlook all along? Couldn't he have brought her to it? Hey? Wouldn't that be the perfect cover? The guy throws the card game, drives home, dusts his wife, drives her to the parked car, and then drives back to the club. Then he waits for someone like you to come along and conclude that he couldn't have done that. That he had to have driven from his house to the overlook in her car."

I was stunned by John Michael's words. He had never before criticized me in front of others. I looked around the table and saw that Jessica still was not looking at me. Royster was, but he was wearing the blank look he used to hide malicious glee. Patty was looking at me from behind her hair. Then she was looking at Jessica. Then she was looking at me.

"Wembley Tuttle seems to feel that it's far more likely the missing caretaker killed her," I said.

"Wembley Tuttle's an asshole."

"Still, he's got a point, John. The kid is missing."

"Wembley just doesn't want me to get a big hit out of this. He's probably already cut a deal with Constantinis."

"A deal to do what?" I said, genuinely curious, hoping the answer would provide me with some clue as to John Michael's peculiar mood.

"We work on loyalty around here, Patt," he said. "We work on trust and mutual respect. That's why I've always felt comfortable with you, with Roy . . . with Jessica. I know I can depend on you, rely on you, be sure you're not going to cut my balls off the moment I've got my back turned. A man in my position has got to have people like that, somebody I can tell what I want and need without worrying that it's going to get spit back in my face."

John Michael's eyes were probing mine, making me feel guilty of spitting things at him and a myriad of other sins.

He said, "I obviously can't feel that way about Wembley. He's of a different generation, a different school. He's got his loyalties all fucked up. He's like, he's like the head butler in an English manor house. I mean, he's just a poor boy from Nestor Lower Falls." John Michael snickered, a short snicker that brought faint smiles to the faces of his audience. "He thinks it's the height of honor to be working for those rich people. He thinks it's his job to protect them no matter what. To protect their lives, their wealth, their good names. So he's going to do anything he can to keep this thing from blowing up. If that means diverting attention to some non-Woodedge person like the caretaker, then that's exactly what he's going to do. If he thinks it means attacking me because he sees me as the enemy of his charges, then that's what he'll do."

"By attacking you, you mean—"

"I mean giving Constantinis ammunition to attack me. Because that's exactly what will happen if everything comes down the way I think it's going to. I can't have someone like that, Patt. That's why I need you. I know that with you whatever I say or do stays right here in this little group." He swept his hand around the table. "If any of us makes a mistake it stays here. It doesn't get out. Isn't that right?"

The speech was going right through me, but he most definitely wanted some kind of commitment and so I gave it to him. "Yes, that's right," I said.

"Now I told you before I wanted you to find out what you could about Mrs. Carpenter. I see this missing stud, this Rasmussin, as being another angle you should be working. Was something kinky going on there? Did Wylie find out about it? Those are the questions you should be asking. Don't worry so much about where the kid is, Wembley will be looking into that, if nothing else. But I want you to concentrate on digging up whatever relationship there was between Rebecca Carpenter and Rasmussin. Like Jessica said a few minutes ago, we're looking at jealousy at this point if we're going to support what we've got on the husband."

"Have you got something new?" I asked in surprise.

John Michael thumbed Royster, who cleared his throat and said, "The fibers found on the driver's seat have been positively identified as coming from a white wool sweater, just like the one Carpenter was reportedly wearing on the golf course that day."

"The club sweater," I said, my voice flat.

John Michael smiled wickedly. "Think you can get us some evidence on this Rasmussin relationship?"

"I think I can."

"Got an idea of how you're going to go about it?"

"I've got an idea."

"Good."

John Michael took a major swallow from his soda. Jessica and Royster threw back their own drinks. Patty might have joined them, but her glass was already empty.

The scene could not have been more awkward. I tramped hard on the steps and did a lot of unnecessary rattling of the front door. My mother and Kelsey were sitting at the kitchen table playing whist and they immediately put down their cards.

My mother smiled steadily at me, but her eyes were busy searching mine. She offered me chicken soup, French bread, a cup of tea, a bowl of Jell-O with fruit in it. I told her I wasn't hungry. I said I was only there to ask Kelsey to run an errand with me.

Kelsey said "Sure," without waiting to hear what it was. He got to his feet and spared me from having to sit down.

"Are you well, Patt?" my mother asked.

"Yeah, sure. I'm fine." I spoke while I watched Kelsey punch his arms into the sleeves of his plaid L. L. Bean jacket.

"Will you be coming back to spend the night?"

"No, no," I said. "I don't think so. Not tonight."

My mother nodded and turned to Kelsey. "Thank you for coming by, Harry," she said.

Kelsey dipped his head and side-glanced at me and thanked her for having him.

They parted without a kiss or even a touch; and I, feeling guilty, said that I thought I would only need to be borrowing Kelsey for an hour or so. My mother's response was to tell me to keep my coat buttoned. She called me "honey" when she did so, and the term made me flinch in front of her boyfriend.

My mother had always called me things like "honey" and "sweetie" and "dear" when I was a child, and I had taken those words for granted. She and my father were not given to many demonstrations of affection between themselves, and so such names were a mother's prerogative in my family. They were part of the natural order of things in our household, where my mother and I were the closest of allies in dealing with my father and his whims and convictions and illusions. They were part of an order that no longer had the same purpose once my father was gone and we were left, a forty-year-old woman and a nineteen-year-old boy, with barely a clue as to how to proceed without him. Perhaps because it was easiest we made a tacit agreement to try to carry on as though nothing had changed—something that was only possible to do if we never discussed my father or the strange circumstances of his death.

Questions went unasked and unanswered as I continued to live at home and my mother continued to call me "honey" and do my laundry and cook my meals. She went off to work and I returned to school and we would come home at night and tell each other everything had gone well. It was an arrangement made with the best of intentions, and one that no doubt was even worse for my mother than it was for me. I, at least, had buddies and dates and weekend trips and summer vacations. But, at best, my mother's social life consisted of introductions made by others—a field necessarily restricted by the fact that as a couple she and my father had not had many friends. The men to whom she was introduced tended to be older and were prone to wearing hats and inviting her to dinner in places that didn't require reservations. She would go out apprehensively and come back sadly.

And then she met Kelsey, and I was suddenly freed of the responsibility of having to worry about her ability to come to grips with the rest of her life. He was a nice, physical, semi-intelligent, caring man whose company she obviously enjoyed—and he was an apologetic intrusion into our carefully constructed relationship.

I could not look at him as we drove from West Nestor to

Walmouth in his black Jeep Cherokee, even though I talked most
of the way. He did not seem to mind, but concentrated on the
road ahead, as though driving the Cherokee was one of the harder
things a man could do. He listened as I explained generally about
Doug Rasmussin and what I was trying to learn, and he asked
occasional questions about what I expected of him. By the time
we pulled up in front of Balducci's we had the game plan fairly
well set.

Balducci's was not the sort of place that attracted many
strangers. It had a red brick front and a coach lantern hanging
next to its door. It had two windows, but both of them were six
feet off the ground and both were covered with black iron rails.
In one of the windows was a cardboard sign for Schaeffer beer,
in the other was an electric sign for Narragansett.

A green scalloped trim board ran along the top of the building.
It read BALDUCCI'S TAVERN COCKTAILS. But Balducci's was not
the sort of place where you ordered cocktails. Balducci's was beer
and a shot.

Patrons of Balducci's did not limit their activities to the inside
of the bar. Weather permitting, they tended to stand on the sidewalk in front of the door, swinging their arms and swapping
stories and watching the traffic go by. That meant that I would
have been spotted right away as somebody who did not belong
if we had driven up in my gray-green Alfa. The Jeep Cherokee,
however, was okay. It meant we had money to spend, but probably did manly things on the weekends.

Kelsey fit the image perfectly. Besides his L. L. Bean jacket, he
had on work boots and jeans. Emerging from the car, he strode
the sidewalk with confidence and yet nodded in a friendly way
to the two or three guys who were openly checking us out. They
made just enough of a pathway for us to get through the front
door without anyone having to say "Excuse me."

It was dark inside, but I could see two coin-operated pool
tables, a jukebox with a rainbow façade, a couple of sets of tables
and chairs, an oak bar, and a single bartender. One of the pool
tables was being used for a game by a mean-faced man with long

black hair, a long black mustache, and a cigarette dangling from his lips. He was playing against a fat man whose beltless dungarees were slipping far enough down to reveal the crack in his behind. The other pool table was being used as a perch for two women, both of whom had beer bottles and cigarettes in their hands, both of whom had very tight jeans, and one of whom was considerably younger than the other. The women were talking to a group of guys who were seated sideways on their barstools. They all turned to see us. The men and the women.

"You got a pitcher, buddy?" Kelsey asked, leaning onto the end of the bar closest to the door. I did as Kelsey did. I leaned onto the bar with both my forearms, my hands clasping my elbows.

The bartender was a very big guy wearing a white knit shirt that was too small for his arms and that more or less rolled over his belly in little waves. He had a hawklike face with a curlicue scar under his cheekbone. He stopped his walk toward us and said, "Bud or Mich?"

"Bud," said Kelsey.

The bartender, without moving his feet, drew out a pitcher and thumbed on the tap. "Three fifty," he said.

Nearest to us was a man with thick, curly hair, an unruly mustache, and a jersey with a football number on both its front and back. He was watching us over his shoulder.

"How's it going?" I asked, nodding at him.

He tilted his bottle to his mouth and let his eyes slide to his companions while he drank. When he put the bottle down he said, "All right," and cleaned his mouth with the back of his wrist.

Nobody in the place was speaking. The jukebox was carrying the sounds of the Beach Boys singing "Good Vibrations." The pool balls were whacking and whirring and reverberating into rubber pockets. And then the bartender, the pitcher nearly full, said in a very loud voice, "Say, don't I know you from somewheres?"

Kelsey grinned. He put a thumb under his chin and propped

it there. "Not unless you remember every guy who ever took you over the wall at Morrissey Field."

It took a moment for the nickel to drop, but then the bartender's eyes popped wide and he sputtered as the beer he was drawing overflowed the pitcher and ran down his hand. "Kelsey!" he shouted. "I'll be a hot shit." He hit the tap to shut it off and put down the brimming pitcher. "I know this guy," he told everyone in the place. "Harry Kelsey from the Bombardiers." He reached over and slapped the curly-haired guy on the shoulder of his football jersey. "You know him, Billy. Last guy to get cut from the Orioles one year. Only hits the ball about nine hundred fuckin' feet."

Billy tried to say hello, but Kelsey had to pay attention to the bartender, who had rushed over to shake his hand. Kelsey introduced me to Buzzy Balducci and I got a beer-soaked paw thrust at me.

That was all I got. Buzzy was looking around. "Who else is here? Duane, you know this guy? Sure you do." Turning back to Kelsey, he said, "Duane plays the shallowest third base in the league, but he don't play that way against you."

Duane leaned forward from near the other end of the bar. He had short blond hair, a pockmarked face, and tattoos on his forearm and bicep. He waved a stiff-fingered hand and said, "Whadyasay?"

Balducci went back to get our pitcher and a couple of glasses. He said it was on the house. He wanted to know if we were there because Kelsey was thinking of jumping teams.

Kelsey said no, he was a little old to be doing something like that. He claimed he was lucky his own team still let him play.

Buzzy said, "Yeah, I don't know if I'll be coming back myself. Haven't played since I busted my hand against the cops."

"You busted your hand?" said Kelsey, pouring us beers. "I didn't know that."

"Yeah. You didn't know that? We're playing out at that tournament, O'Brien Park? And that douchebag shortstop they got, what's his name? Finnegan? Drives the cruiser? Claims I don't go down fast enough on the doubleplay. He low-bridges me, you know what I mean? I mean, he really low-bridges me. I'm lucky to be a-fuckin'-live. So I says something to him. He says something back. I give him a shot right in the head. Cleaned the cocksucker's clock, 'cept I broke three knuckles doing it." He showed us the damage, but I couldn't see much given the light. "Still can't grip the ball right. And a guy my age, my size, I can't play noplace else but pitch. Then, get this: Finnegan, right? Being the little prick he is, he can't leave the game on the field. Here I am, my hand's all busted up, he still claims he's gonna get me. I catch him one day out here giving parking tickets to my customers. I mean, gimme a break, will ya? Parking tickets? In this neighborhood? What, I pop the guy, he's gonna drive me outa business? I'm the one with the broken bones, for Chrissake."

Balducci grabbed his belt with two hands and hoisted his sagging pants. "First time, you know, I take everybody's ticket. I go down the traffic court to complain. You know what the court says? You know what the fuckin' judge says to me? He says I don't got standing to talk to him about other people's tickets. I goes to him, I goes, 'Standing? I'm standing right here. What are you talking about?' The guy doesn't listen to me. He tells me I raise my voice again he's gonna throw me in the jail. Me. I haven't done nothin' but try to run a barroom and all of a sudden he's gonna throw me in jail. You know what I ended up havin' to do? I ended up having to pay all the tickets myself. I think it's like seventy-five bucks. I can't keep doing that, you know. So now I tell people, 'You got a car out there on the street? Watch out it's not parked illegal because that little bastard Finnegan'll come along and give you a ticket.' "

"He still doing it?" I asked.

Buzzy Balducci looked at me with a trace of irritation. He had, after all, been talking to Kelsey. "Yeah," he said.

"You collect the tickets you got and give them to me. I'll take care of it."

Balducci took a half-step back from the bar. "You a cop?"

"No. But I know people. If you want, I'll take care of the

situation." This was not part of the game plan. This was ad-libbing.

Balducci cleaned his hands on a bar rag and considered me for a moment. Then he looked at Kelsey. "He mean it?"

Kelsey said, "He says he can do it, he can do it."

Balducci still hesitated. "You a ballplayer?" he asked me.

I shook my head.

"You oughta be. You're big enough. What did you say your name was again?"

"Patt Starbuck."

"Used to be a guy by that name played center field for Nestor."

"You've got a good memory if you can remember that far back."

Buzzy Balducci studied me for a minute before grunting. Shouting over his shoulder, he asked if anybody had any Finnegan tickets.

"Tell me about it," shouted back Duane. He was heavily involved in conversation with the younger of the two women on the pool table and he did not bother to look up.

"You got one with you?"

"Fuck no," said Duane. "I threw it away."

"Anybody else?"

The woman speaking with Duane slid to the floor and walked over to us. She said she had gotten one the same night as Duane and thought she still had it in her pocketbook. As she got closer I saw that she was perhaps a hard thirty, maybe a real hard twenty-five. She fished around in a purse that was slightly smaller than a steamer trunk until she came up with the ticket. She handed it to Buzzy and Buzzy handed it to me.

"Guy says he'll fix it," Buzzy said skeptically.

The woman looked at me and shrugged as if she had heard better lines. I watched her go back to her perch and wondered how she had managed to preserve such a nice butt in light of whatever tragedies had ravaged her face.

"I still don't see how you're gonna do that," Buzzy said.

"Hey, Buzzy," I said, putting the ticket in the pocket of my coat, "you don't really care how I do it as long as I do it, right? The way I look at it, you're a friend of Kelsey's and you're getting screwed over. I know some people who can help. I take this ticket to them, I explain about the Finnegan problem, and maybe I can make it go away. If I can't, well, what have you lost?"

Balducci held up his hand. "You can take care of it, you got my gratitude. You know what I mean?"

"No problem," I said. "In fact, you could call it even if you'd just tell me where I can find Doug Rasmussin."

"Dougie's not around no more. He split. Where did he go, Billy, Florida? Someplace like that?"

"Who's that?" demanded Billy.

"Rasmussin."

"He split."

"Right. But where did he go?"

"California. L.A. Hollywood. 'S gonna be a movie star."

"Talk to Billy," said Buzzy Balducci, thumbing in his direction. "He's one of Ras's best friends."

With that introduction, Billy welcomed me onto the stool next to him.

"When did he take off?" I asked.

Billy thought about it. "I don't know. A week or two ago. He should be there by now, but he hasn't sent a card or nothing. I wanted him to send one, you know, with one of those beach chicks on it with their tits hanging out. I like those cards."

"Yeah, those are great. With the Hawaiian chicks and all that? Lying there in the surf?"

"Yeah. I'm surprised they let those go through the mail, you know? I would have thought there'd be laws against that."

"I guess it's all right for the Hawaiian women. They say it's part of their culture. Like the pictures in *National Geographic*."

"Yeah, I guess. So you a friend of Ras's, or what?"

"Not really. I promised a guy I'd look him up. But I went out to this country club where I was told he worked and they said he didn't work there anymore."

"Oh, yeah, he quit there in, like, September."

"He was the lifeguard, wasn't he? What, did the job run out or something?"

"Nah. He wanted, he could have done groundskeeping until they closed for the winter. That's what he did last year. But what happened was, he really wanted to go to California. Only, one thing and another, and he never could get it together until he meets this rich lady from Woodedge who, like, works out the perfect deal for him."

"What, more money?"

"That's only part of it, what I heard," said a voice on the other side of Billy. A guy I hadn't noticed before, a guy with hair combed three inches high, was smirking at Billy.

Billy smirked back. He looked over at the two women on the pool table so that he could make sure they weren't listening and then he leaned in close to me and said, "I heard he had his hand in more than this lady's rosebushes."

"I hear it wasn't his hand," said the interestingly coiffed smirker.

He and Billy had a good laugh over that and I joined in. "You mean," I said, when the laugh was over, "he was working at the country club and some lady hired him to . . . you know?"

"Well," said Billy, "alls I know is that Ras said he got to be friends with this real horny rich bitch who used to go to his club. He said she'd do anything, you know?" Billy's eyebrows soared up and down. "The way I heard it, she offered to pay him, like, in six weeks what he coulda earned in twelve weeks at the club. Promised he'd be outa here before winter. Right, Jack?"

The guy with the hair waved his hand. "Something like that. I think all she wanted him to do was fuck her brains out. Only, maybe she didn't want him to do it forever. She was married, is what I heard."

Billy and I were staring at Jack and he shrugged. "That Ras was a good-looking guy, say what you want about him."

"So," I said, after allowing time for all of us to sip our beer, "he was only planning on working six weeks all along?"

"If you call that working," said Jack.

"The reason she gave him the job, see," said Billy, "was to help him earn the money he needed to go to California."

"That was one reason she gave him the job," said Jack. "The other reason was she wanted to get herself racked up and screaming at the moon." He put back his head and howled into the ceiling.

From down at the pool table came the sound of one of the women howling back at him. She may have just wanted to howl, but she had her head tilted and her eyes closed and her howl was at least as long and loud as Jack's. When she was done somebody else picked up the sound, and pretty soon almost everyone in the bar was howling. Buzzy Balducci beamed at Kelsey, as if he was sure that all this good fun was going to convince Kelsey to jump teams after all.

"So," I said, when the last warbling note had died out, "you guys weren't surprised when Ras left, I take it."

"Cripes, I wouldn't a done it," said Jack, shaking his head. "Get some rich bitch paying me to do that to her, you woulda had to explode me offa her place. But what I heard, this broad he's working for was the one who was encouraging him to go. Always telling him shit like if he was ever going to make something of hisself he had to get as far away from here as possible. Can you imagine anybody believing that?"

Billy, however, gave my question some thought and said, "Well, I sorta was surprised he actually went. I mean, the guy had been talking about going for a long time and he could never quite get it together. There was always some reason, you know? Like, once he couldn't go because the Red Sox were in the pennant race. Can you think of anything more dumber than that? I mean, what the hell, he coulda watched them blow it out in California as good as here. Another time it seems to me he didn't go because somebody offered to take him hunting instead. One weekend, right? So, yeah, I was surprised, I guess."

"So how do you know he really went?"

Billy looked at me as though I was pulling his leg. "Well, he ain't around here no more. Where else could he be?"

I told Billy he had a real good point.

We left shortly after that, Kelsey and I. I gave him the high sign and he broke off his conversation with Buzzy. Kelsey got a chorus of good-byes and I got a big index finger leveled at me along with a reminder to take care of the ticketing.

Kelsey and I walked silently back to the car. It was cold and we were shivering and I sat on my hands while the engine warmed. Then he said, "I didn't know you played ball."

"I didn't know you were the last guy cut by the Orioles."

He snorted. "I never even saw the big club."

"Well," I said, "you fooled them."

Kelsey looked at me for a long time. It was a look he had never given me in my mother's house. "So," he said, "did you."

Thinking about it later, I had to wonder if there wasn't just a trace of disappointment in his voice.

It was easy to imagine Doug Rasmussin. Half the guys I grew up with were like him. Maybe they weren't all good-looking, and maybe some were brighter than others, but they all liked sports and beer and they all lived within the confines of old friendships and familiar places. What I could not imagine was Doug Rasmussin having an affair with Rebecca Carpenter.

She was, after all, about fifteen years older than he was, and probably wealthier than anyone he had ever known. Her attractiveness, or at least what I had seen in her photograph, was not the sort that I suspected would play well in Balducci's Tavern. I could see her offering him a job, I could see him taking it, but I could not see him coming on to her. A guy like Robert, maybe, he would come on to her; but a guy like Dougie Rasmussin would know his place.

On the other hand, after ten days of thinking about her, Rebecca Carpenter remained as elusive to me as she had been when I first learned of her murder. She had a husband who seemed unable to describe her. She had a friend from childhood who seemed unsure as to how well she actually knew her. She had a friend from college who would not let her death interrupt a tennis lesson. She had a friend from adulthood whose husband she may have been screwing. For all I knew, she was a temptress who entranced young men like Doug Rasmussin, enticed them into her Mercedes and forced them to drive her to dark overlooks where she teased them into potentially murderous frenzies. It was time for me to find out more about Rebecca Carpenter.

Once again I started with her husband. On Friday morning, I showed up at Woodedge Savings and Loan and was ushered into a small but expensively furnished office where Wylie Carpenter reluctantly greeted me. He was not dressed to meet customers, but was wearing a pale yellow V-neck sweater over a lime-green polo shirt. He was obviously hoping this interview would not take long because, although he allowed me to be seated in a high-backed, tufted leather chair, he remained standing behind his antique English desk, his hands pushed into the pockets of his moss-green slacks.

No, he said firmly, he did not know Doug Rasmussin when Dougie worked at Stonegate. While Becky did identify Rasmussin as the lifeguard at the pool, he rarely, if ever, used the pool himself. His understanding was that Rasmussin had some landscaping experience and that was the reason he was hired. The subject of him only working until October 15 never came up, but the idea didn't make any sense. "Unless," he cautioned, glancing at his watch, "that's how long Becky gave him as a probationary period."

"Did he do a good job?"

Wylie shrugged. "The summer fruit was all in by the time he started, so what was to do? Cut and rake, and I think he did that well enough. At least I didn't hear any complaints—and that's probably significant. Surely, if my wife was planning on sacking him on the fifteenth she would have said as much to me, and she never did." He was rattling the coins in his pocket when he said that. Then he caught himself. "On the other hand, I asked Becky once if she was planning on having him move into the caretaker's cottage and she said she hadn't decided yet."

After a few seconds of silence the coins began to jingle again. I was strategizing a setup for my next question, but as the jingling grew louder I abandoned the setup. "Do you think," I asked, "it was just a coincidence that Rasmussin disappeared on the day your wife was killed?"

Good old Mr. Carpenter gave me the glare I deserved.

I spread my hands. I opened my eyes wide. I made my expression as innocent as I could. "Have you been able to learn anything about the relationship between Rasmussin and your wife?"

"Oh, Jesus." Carpenter stared out the window, his coins silent. He had a lawn to stare at, and in the far distance he had the town hall. "My wife is dead," he said at last. "The only things missing are her pocketbook and the young caretaker she hired six weeks before. That's what I know, Mr. Starbuck. That and the fact she was found where she was. You want me to speculate? You want me to guess? You want me to torture myself with all kinds of things that might have been going on? I can do that, you know. I can do that or I can try to hold myself together as best I can. Now which is it you want?"

A chill came over me. I could not see the expression on Carpenter's face, but I recognized the tone of his voice and I knew all too well what he meant by holding himself together. It was a phrase with which I felt very familiar.

"I understand what you're going through, Mr. Carpenter," I told him, choosing my words carefully, "and I'm sorry if I've made it more difficult."

There was no response.

"Believe it or not," I tried again, "it can be better to have people ask questions rather than make assumptions."

He nodded this time, but still did not turn. The coin jingling, the watch checking, all the signs of impatience were gone; and I no longer felt like grilling him.

"There's just one more question I have to ask you, Mr. Carpenter," I said, rising to my feet. "And that's a question about what you yourself were doing that night." I hesitated, hoping that would be enough. It wasn't. "I know you were at the club at about eight and I know you were at the club at ten. But I can't seem to account for you in the hours between."

By the time Wylie Carpenter completed his turn from the window to me he was no longer showing a trace of emotion, and whatever feelings of empathy I had been feeling drained away from me.

"I was there," he said calmly.

I asked him if there was somewhere other than the clubhouse he might have been and he insisted there was not. Then he corrected himself. "Well, I might have slipped away to use the facilities."

"But, of course, that wouldn't have taken two hours."

"No. No, it wouldn't."

"Would you keep that in mind, Mr. Carpenter?" I said as I walked toward the door. "That I need help with that one?"

"I'll keep it in mind, Mr. Starbuck."

Feeling somewhat less than pleased with the way things had gone in Wylie's office, I drove to his home, determined to do better with Sarah Mitchell, the housekeeper, an overweight woman whose skin was so dark and smooth it was able to reflect the light of a hallway lamp. I knew from experience that Sarah Mitchell was a very tough interview. She kept her eyes lowered, she spoke very softly, and she hardly ever volunteered information. It was that last trait that made me suspect she had plenty to say and that I had simply failed to ask the right things when I first interviewed her a day or two after the murder.

I started with easy enough questions. I asked her what a typical day was like in the Carpenter household before Rebecca was killed.

"Mr. Carpenter," she said, her voice barely audible, "gets up around seven and putters around with his coffee and his newspapers. Financial pages mostly. He might be on the telephone a lot in the early hours, or he might not. Depending. Then Mrs. Carpenter come downstairs about nine and Mr. Carpenter goes off to work while Mrs. Carpenter has her continental."

"By work you mean Woodedge Savings and Loan?"

"Yes sir."

"What were his work hours?"

"He would usually get there about ten. Then he would go to one of his clubs in the afternoon. Sometimes he would come home for lunch first, sometimes not."

"Did he come home for lunch that day, the day Mrs. Carpenter was killed?"

"I believe he did. Yes sir."

"You don't happen to know if he took the Mercedes anywhere, do you?"

"I don't know. Most of the time he'd drive the other car."

"And Mrs. Carpenter, what was her typical day like?"

"Usually do some things around the house or the grounds."

"And that particular day?"

"I don't remember her doing much of anything special."

"I see. Tell me, did you know Mr. Rasmussin very well?"

"Not really. He's outside. I'm inside."

"Did he and Mrs. Carpenter seem to get along?"

"Pretty well, yes sir."

"Did they seem to enjoy each other's company?"

"Seemed to, yes sir."

"Did he come into the house ever?"

"The house? Once in a while, maybe. Like for lunches, something like that. Uh-huh."

"Would he come in for lunches if Mr. Carpenter was here?"

"Un-unh."

"On those days when Mr. Carpenter was not here, would he eat lunch with Mrs. Carpenter?"

"Mrs. Carpenter? Sometimes she would bring his lunch to him."

"Were lunches the only reason he would come into the house?"

"Maybe to use the bathroom."

"Did you ever see him go up to the second floor?"

"No. There's a bathroom right off the back pantry. No need for him to go upstairs."

"Did Mrs. Carpenter ever invite him upstairs? For any reason?"

A long silence preceded her answer. "No."

"Did you ever have conversations with Mr. Rasmussin?"

"Not really. Just about whether he likes lettuce in his tuna fish sandwiches, something like that."

"Did he ever tell you how long he was planning on working here at the Carpenters'?"

"No. I just assumed, you know, that he took the Marconis' place."

"So you expected him to show up for work the day after Mrs. Carpenter was killed."

"Yes. I did expect that."

"When was the last time you saw him?"

"The only way I remember it is it was payday, okay? And he wanted to get to the bank soon as he could. That was ten, ten thirty, and he come in to wash up before he went. Whether he ever come back after that, I couldn't tell you."

"And you left . . ."

"Around six."

"Was Mrs. Carpenter's Mercedes there when you left?"

"I suppose it was in the garage. I didn't look."

"And you don't know anybody she was supposed to see that evening?"

"I don't. No sir."

"There was a phone call made around one to the Patterson house. Do you know why?"

"Maybe returning a call Mrs. Patterson made earlier."

"I'm told Mrs. Patterson and Mrs. Carpenter used to get together once a week. Is that true?"

"Lately, past couple of months maybe, yes sir."

"What would they do when they got together? Do you know?"

"Drink, I expect."

"You mean, like, get drunk?"

"I don't know what they do."

"Then, if you'll forgive me, how do you know they drank?"

"Because that's how Mrs. Carpenter discovered the Marconis been stealing her liquor. Mrs. Patterson wanted some Scotch, she said, and Mrs. Carpenter told me how they turned the house upside down looking for some and then they thought the Marconis might have some so they went out there. 'Cept the Marconis wasn't home because it was Bingo night and when Mrs. Carpenter opened their door that's when she seen they had all her liquor."

"Did that surprise you?"

"Yes."

"Why?"

"I didn't know what the Marconis would want with all that fancy stuff. I never seen them drink nothing but red wine."

My visit to the Carpenter home improved my spirits immensely. It was a clean, clear, crisp October day and I was cruising the leaf-spattered back lanes of Woodedge, Massachusetts, in my Alfa Romeo driving machine with a whole new set of prospects in front of me.

The enigmatic Mrs. Carpenter had a drinking buddy, and in my experience a drinking buddy was about as likely a candidate to know a person's secrets as you can get. Mrs. Carpenter had a drinking buddy who was going to require my further investigation, and there was nobody I wanted to investigate further than the sultry Gretchen Patterson.

But first I had to get back to the office. It was nearly noon and I wanted to catch Royster before he broke for lunch. Royster was friends with the traffic commissioner and I knew that if he could speak to the commissioner in the time between his double Manhattan and his return to the bench for the afternoon session my chances of wiping out the Balducci ticketing problem would be greatly enhanced. I suspected that a well-placed favor for Buzzy Balducci was my best means of ingratiating myself with anyone likely to be hearing from Dougie Rasmussin, and Dougie was still very much in need of being found.

I wheeled along Highland Street, downshifting at the corners. At Rotten Row I had to be more careful because it was barely wide enough for two cars, but Rotten Row was empty and I drove it the way I wanted. On the Post Road I had to fit in with the speeds of the other cars, but there was no appreciable amount of traffic until I crossed the river and then Main Street was almost bumper-to-bumper. I drove Main to Liberty and Liberty to Court and it took longer than I had expected.

I turned off Court and parked in my usual spot behind the great yellow stone building that housed the criminal courts on the first and second floors, the district attorney's office on the third floor, a branch of the county jail on the fourth floor, and the public defender's office tucked in next to the boiler room and storage area in the basement.

I saw the crowd in front of the elevators and elected to run up the stairs. I took them two at a time, two flights. In the third-floor hallway I bumped into some of our staff people. In our reception area the relief crew was on, and that usually spelled disaster. A woman named Delilah was standing behind the counter ready to give wrong information to anybody and everybody who made inquiries.

There was a door in the wall behind the counter and I was lucky to have Delilah buzz it open for me. Behind the door was a large room that served as the secretarial pool for more than a dozen women who did the work for the various staff attorneys whose offices lined the walls and corridors. Only John Michael's secretary and Royster's secretary had different arrangements. They had doors to their offices and doors behind them to their bosses' offices. Anita, Royster's secretary, had her door closed. I knocked and nobody answered. I opened it and saw nobody inside. The door to Royster's office was also closed and my spirits plummeted.

I stood in the empty room, breathing heavily, and thought about leaving a message on Anita's desk. But Anita's desk was a mess and I thought it would be safer to leave one on Royster's. I thought it would be no big deal to open his door.

I was wrong.

Anita was bent over Royster's desk. She was bent forward and her short red skirt was flipped across her back. She still was in her heels, but her finely muscular legs were spread apart and her white lace panties were hooked around one ankle. Behind her,

wedged against her buttocks, was Royster, fully dressed except
for his suit coat and his open pants. His hands were on Anita's
hips and his skin was slapping against hers.

Anita's own hands were wide across Royster's desk. The side
of her face was pressed into his blotter. Her mouth was making
little gasping sounds, but her eyes were open and she was staring
directly at me. Above her, Royster's head was thrown back and
his eyes were screwed shut as he continued his rhythmical thrusting into his secretary.

I expected a scream or a cry or a break in the action, but there
was none. Royster continued his movements and Anita continued
her staring, and there was nothing for me to do but ease the door
closed, as if hiding the sound of the latch would somehow erase
my presence. Then I turned and fled.

I went out through Anita's office, through the secretarial pool,
and through the reception area. This time, unlike at my mother's
house, no one called after me. Only Delilah seemed to notice
how fast I was moving, and all she wanted to know was if I was
going to lunch.

16

I went to the fitness club. It was in my flight path. I could have returned to my car and driven straight back to the Patterson house, but after seeing Anita and Royster I no longer had quite the same enthusiasm for doing that. It was not that I cared particularly about Anita, with her finely muscular legs and her white lace panties hooked around her ankle, or Royster, with his big mouth and his stringy-haired wife, it was just that I no longer felt prepared to interview Gretchen Patterson. I felt the need to work out instead.

One of the squash courts was open and, although I had not reserved it, I took my racket from my locker and went into the court to bang a few balls off the wall. Playing squash by yourself is not a fun thing to do and some may even question its value. It was, for example, very hard to sustain a volley and practice difficult shots at the same time. But since the only person I ever played was John Michael, it was not really necessary to practice difficult shots. I opted for trying to keep the ball going for as long as possible and working on my rhythm.

A knock on the door interrupted me and I, thinking it was somebody who had reserved the court, started to gather up my balls. The door opened and a man of about my own age poked in his head.

"Excuse me," he said, "but are you waiting for anyone? I thought if you weren't maybe you might like a game. I was watching through the window and I think we're about the same level . . ."

"Fading intermediate, you mean?"

It took a second for the intended humor of my remark to register, but then the man smiled and stepped into the court with me. "Skip," he said, holding out his hand.

"I beg your pardon?"

"Skip. That's my name."

He was a fair-sized man, who looked as if he had been in very good shape at one point in his life and was now battling a softening stomach. His hair was a little long at the ears and in the back, his nose appeared to have been broken on at least one occasion, and he wore a soft brace on one knee. Other than that he looked like a fine fellow. I offered him my hand, my name, and a place on my court.

We warmed up a little and his game appeared to be about the same as mine, a little weak on the backhand, a little erratic on the serve, very physical in terms of establishing position in the center of the court. And then we went at it.

He got out to a six-point lead and then I came back and knotted it at nine. At twelve I put a shot directly into the corner and it dropped like a rock on him. I aced my serves for the thirteenth and fourteenth points and then he jumped in front of me and ricocheted a shot off three walls to take back the serve. He tied me at fourteen and I told him we would play for three.

His chest heaving, Skip lofted a serve off the front wall, the back wall, and into the service box. I scooped it softly forward so that it just kissed the front wall and he had to race for it. He got his shot, but I drilled my return and he never had a chance. My sixteenth point was to his backhand and he returned the ball low, directly into the tin. He got a clean return on my next serve and I played the carom off the back wall. He dinked one, as I had done to him a minute before. This time I had to sprint forward, but my shot was perfect, forcing him to turn his back for the return. I charged for position in center court just as he came up from the other end. We hit head-on, crashing to the floor in a tangle of arms and legs and a clattering of rackets as the ball bounced harmlessly around us.

My head was against his chest. My cheek seemed stuck to his soaking wet T-shirt. My arm was under his back. "Jesus Christ," he said, and when I pulled myself back I saw that he was staring at me incredulously, as if I were a madman.

"Interference?" I asked innocently, and all of a sudden he was laughing. We were both laughing. We were rolling on the floor roaring with laughter, and for that moment I was as sure as I could be that we were both great guys, kindred spirits, and totally without need of worrying about office romances, missing murderers, or misspent lives.

We played for over an hour and then he told me he had to get back to work. We walked to the locker room together, dripping with perspiration, and neither one of us spoke as we stripped and grabbed our towels and went into the showers. There was camaraderie in the silence as we massaged our aching muscles beneath the hard spray of the faucets. We had played as even a match as two men could play, and although I had won two games to one, he had scored more total points than I. When at last we shut off the water we were grinning at each other.

"Have to play you again," he said, before burying his face in his towel.

I told him he would have to give me a week to recover and he laughed.

At this time of the afternoon the locker room was almost empty and we could talk to each other easily across the distance that separated our respective lockers.

"I've been looking for somebody to play with," he said, putting on a pair of tapered boxer shorts. "Nobody in my office seems to be interested."

"Maybe we can set something up," I said. I put on a pair of yellow briefs, tan socks, brown corduroy pants.

"You work around here?" Skip asked.

"District attorney's office," I told him.

"Oh, yeah? I'm an attorney, too."

I glanced up. He was toweling his hair. He wasn't looking at me. He was still bare-chested, but now he was wearing a pair of gray pin-striped trousers and a black leather belt.

"I don't do any criminal law," he said as he threw down his towel and took a white shirt out of his locker, "so I don't suppose our paths will ever cross in court. Where did you go to law school?"

I had a white shirt of my own in my hand. It was a short-sleeved pullover knit with a little insignia over the left breast. It was not the insignia of a polo player or an alligator. "I didn't go to law school," I said. "I'm not a lawyer."

Beneath the button-down collar of Skip's white shirt was a red silk tie with a pattern of little blue diamonds. He had one hand on each end of the tie and was maneuvering it back and forth to make sure it was in place before he began buttoning his shirt. "Oh?" he said. "What do you do at the district attorney's?"

I pulled on my own shirt. I grabbed my black Reeboks off the floor of my locker and thrust my feet into them. "I work as an investigator."

Skip sat down on a wooden bench and drew his own shoes out of his locker. They were black and sleek and each one bore a single small gold adornment. In the expensive stores they were called slip-ons rather than loafers. "Gee," he said, "we're always looking for investigators, even if it's just to serve subpoenas, that sort of thing. You able to do any outside work?"

"I don't serve subpoenas," I said. I could have told him that my title was litigation coordinator. I could have told him that I probably had at least as many years in graduate school as he did, and that I had the job I had because I liked it. But instead I stared into my locker.

"Well," I heard him say, "if you ever think of branching out give me a call. I didn't mean it to sound like it was just subpoenas. My firm does a lot of trial work and there's always something going on. If you're half as good at investigating as you are on the squash court I'm sure we could use you."

The soles of his black shoes slapped against the floor as he approached. "Here," he said, stopping.

I looked up. Skip was fully dressed now. He had his pin-striped jacket to go with his pin-striped pants. He was holding out his card, a card that made no reference to the name "Skip."

"Call me," he said, "and let's get together for another game. Evenings are usually best for me. Today was just sort of a fluke."

"Righto," I said.

He held out his hand and I stood up to take it. In his slip-ons he was taller than I was in my Reeboks.

"See you," he said, removing his hand and turning it into a wave.

"Ciao," I said, doing the same, and waiting till he left the locker room before I crumpled his card and chucked it into the nearest wastebasket.

It was midafternoon by the time I returned to the office. I avoided everyone else and went directly to my desk, where I made phone calls and prepared a report on my interviews with Carpenter and Sarah Mitchell. I was waiting for the Keoughs' weekly Friday-night meeting to begin. I was wondering how Royster would act, and I was envisioning my own possible reactions.

But at five o'clock there was no call from John Michael's secretary, and at five fifteen I was the only one in the office. At five thirty I was on my way into Boston when I impulsively did a U-turn and headed back to the Patterson home. The afternoon had been a waste and the evening promised nothing ahead of me.

It was past six when I arrived at the rear entrance and I had no right to be surprised when my knock was answered by D. Dodge. He was, however, dressed in a cutaway coat and a pair of formal gray trousers, and in the short time since I had last seen him he had grown a pencil-thin mustache and changed his hair from yellow to black. Instead of being wavy, it was now slicked back close to his skull. His Chicletlike teeth now sported a slight gap and he had managed to acquire a pair of extraordinarily large ears. He seemed delighted with his new appearance.

"Dodge Patterson?" I asked, just to be sure.

"You injuh me, suh!" he cried in what was no doubt his best Southern accent. "I believe your attentions are directed elsewhere."

I looked over my shoulder to see what he meant before I said or did anything further. I saw nothing which provided me with any clue. I looked back. Patterson was grinning.

"Clark Gable," he said. "How do I look?" He held out his hands and did a slow spin for me.

I nodded. "Kinky," I said.

"Aw," he said, "it's for the Halloween Ball at Bollingbrook."

"I had the impression you had given up Bollingbrook for Stonegate."

Dodge snapped his fingers. "The guy from the D.A.'s office," he said, pointing.

I said he was uncanny.

"Jesus." He patted his hair. "Didn't we talk enough already?"

"I just had a few more questions to ask of your wife. And as long as I have you here I wonder if maybe I could take a look at that sweater you were wearing the day Rebecca was killed."

"You're going to have to ask Rita Hayworth for that one. She's sent it to the cleaners."

"Is that who Mrs. Patterson is going as, Rita Hayworth?"

"Actually, I'm not sure who she's going as. She thinks a costume party means you try to see how glamorous you can look. I suspect, you know, she's not going to want to talk to you because she's still getting ready and we're supposed to leave here by seven thirty for the processional. It's really quite an event. They announce each couple by their costumes and so you have to give your identifications to the sergeant at arms, who's got to have them all in the right order so he can thump with his truncheon or whatever they call those long poles and say, 'Clark Gable and Rita Hayworth.' "

Dodge Patterson was quite pleased about the evening's prospects.

"So you are members of Bollingbrook."

"Not at all. We're going as guests of Molly and Dickie Barr. You've probably come across them in your travels through the back allies of Woodedge, haven't you? They were friends of Becky's, I guess. I mean, as much as anybody was. Molly and Becky went to school someplace together."

"Wheaton."

"That's right. I went out with some of those Wheaton girls when I was in college."

"At Amherst."

"Right again. Our taxpayers' money is well spent, I see."

"Mrs. Patterson wasn't a Wheaton girl, was she?"

"Gretchen? Hah! Gretchen was a UMass girl, sharing the town of Amherst with me in my wild youth. I picked her up hitchhiking one day. I like to tell her she's been getting a ride off me ever since, but she doesn't always laugh. Anyhow, I mustn't stand here gabbing with you for very much longer and I'm really quite positive she's not going to have time for you herself before we have to leave, so maybe the best thing for you to do is come back another time." He started to close the door. "Call first," he said, and suddenly I was alone on the doorstep.

I walked slowly back to my car, feeling rather like an applicant who has just been turned down for a job. I looked up at the great house and thought of my father and wondered why the two of us always seemed to have such difficulty getting into the place.

My most direct way home was to follow Highland Street to Route 30, turn east on Route 30, and follow it to the entrance to the Mass Pike near the Marriott River Inn. It was also possible for me to get to the same place by turning off Highland at Fox Chase Run, which was a longer and more winding road. By choosing it, however, I was able to drive past the entrance to the Bollingbrook Country Club, and there I found my old friend Officer Browning directing traffic.

It was not a particularly difficult job for her. If she saw a Jag or a Mercedes or a BMW or a Cadillac she would point it through the club's gates. If she saw anything else she would wave it along the road.

She was trying to do that to me, but I insisted on stopping next to her and smiling at her. She was breathing heavily from the exertion of her arm movements and she was pretty annoyed that my little sports car was not responding appropriately to her efforts. Then she saw who I was and said, "Oh, it's you."

"Survived the repeated deaths of Mrs. Carpenter, I see."

She looked at me quizzically for an instant and then remembered. "Oh, God," she said. "That was a piece of work, wasn't it?"

The cars were beginning to back up behind us. Impatient rich people were honking their horns.

"I need a favor," I said.

She waved her hand at a few cars coming from the opposite direction. "Can you ask me later?"

"I need you to get me into this party."

"What, at the Bollingbrook? Are you out of your gourd?"

"It's part of the Carpenter investigation and I've got an idea how you can do it."

There were no more cars coming from the opposite direction and there was now a steady blasting of horns behind me.

"I can't talk to you now," Browning said, starting to move away.

"Wait," I said, thrusting my hand toward her. She glanced back impatiently, worriedly.

I said, "I'll park in the lot and when you're done out here come in and find me."

She nodded, perhaps because it was a way to get rid of me. I made the turn and parked in the most out-of-the-way spot I could find. I shut off the engine, flicked on the radio, and waited.

The clubhouse was built on a rise, overlooking the first and the eighteenth fairways. A paved path ran through a tunnel beneath a portion of the building so that people could drive their golf carts right to the edge of the parking lot. Officer Browning and I strode down that path and through the tunnel and I did my level best to match her pace.

"I'm only doing this because you tell me it's all right, Patt. Nobody said anything to me about any sort of departmental activity except directing traffic from seven to nine o'clock and from ten to one. So whatever it is you're doing, it's your responsibility. You're doing something you're not supposed to, I'm going to say you misled me, you misrepresented your authority to me."

"Now, what do you think, Elizabeth?" I panted. "Think I'll rip off the cake or something? You know what I'm working on. We're working on it together."

"I'm not officially assigned to that investigation. I had special-duty assignment one day, that's all. My job assignment tonight was simply to direct traffic and do street patrol. I have a bad feeling for this, I want you to know, Patt. I'm not in the habit of carrying out unauthorized operations."

She wouldn't look at me. It was enough of a commitment that she was doing what I asked.

We turned the corner at the rear of the building and found the right door. Officer Browning sucked in her breath and opened it. Immediately, we were surrounded by hustling waiters in red jackets and black bow ties. They were being directed by a stocky man in a long white jacket and a black bow tie. We made our way to him.

"Are you the head guy here?" demanded Officer Browning.

"I'm the director," responded the head guy, who was at least four inches shorter than Officer Browning.

"I've been requested by the district attorney's office to solicit your assistance." She looked at me out of the corner of her eye, checking to see if she had delivered her line correctly.

The head guy caught the movement and turned his attention to me. "I'm Patt Starbuck," I said. "We think it's necessary I bodyguard one of the people here tonight, a person whose identity

I can't disclose to you for reasons of legal security." I let the idea sink in. It might have been a rock dropping through water, by the look on the head guy's face. "What the D.A.'s office requests is that you provide me with some minimal form of cover that will allow me access to the event upstairs."

The head guy looked at Officer Browning, who held his gaze admirably. He looked back at me. "You're not going to punch people or anything like that, are you?" he asked. "This is the Bollingbrook Country Club, after all. We have our reputation."

"Mr. Director—"

"Mr. Prince."

"Mr. Prince, the thing about my position is that no one is supposed to know I am here."

"How come nobody told me about this before?" he said, directing his question to Browning.

I answered for her. "Because until just a short time ago we thought we were going to be able to handle this matter in an entirely different way."

The head guy nodded, waiting for the rest. Officer Browning and I stoically gave him nothing. The head guy nodded some more.

I entered the main ballroom of the Bollingbrook Country Club wearing a long white jacket, a black bow tie, a white shirt, black trousers with satin stripes down the sides, and a pair of black Reebok sneakers. Director Prince had not been able to find me a pair of shoes that fit. Tucked into my hip pocket was Officer Browning's home telephone number. It was part of the deal.

The Bollingbrook Country Club was not quite what I had expected. No place outside of Versailles would have been.

My father had told me that his grandfather had been one of the founding officers of the club. He said a picture of his grandfather was on a wall somewhere and he promised to show it to me one day when we were members. I had always had an image of my father and me in matching white flannel pants, blue blazers, and rep ties, approaching the picture with reverence and being greeted by other club members who would exclaim such things as, "I say, you're a dead ringer for old Patterson, wot?"

Less formulated in my imagination was an idea of the layout of the club itself. I had assumed the dining room would be elegant, the ballroom would be the size of a football field, with balconies and gold columns and ballroom stairs cut from the finest Italian marble, but in reality the two rooms turned out to be one and the same. There were no balconies and no ballroom stairs. Walls were simply rolled back to create one elongated room with tasteful gray carpet at either end and an intricately parqueted dance floor in the middle.

The band was arranged on a very low portable stage set against a row of paneled glass doors that extended along the wooden portion of the floor. The band consisted of three black men, and they were the only black men in the room. They wore harlequin costumes that may or may not have been of their own choosing and they were doggedly playing music that might best be described as inoffensive Top 40 tunes of the past thirty years. For the most part, however, the band was being ignored. The Bollingbrookers milled about the round tables that were located everywhere but the dance floor. They formed concentric circles that rotated dynamically as they passed from table to table, commenting on each other's costumes and sipping steadily from glasses of liquor, wine, champagne.

The last Halloween party I had attended had been held at Barnacle Bully's, and the contrast was remarkable. At Bully's a man had come in with a cowboy costume that incorporated a pair of fake legs and made him look as if he were a dwarf riding a pony. Another man had come in wearing a chef's outfit and pushing a table-cart laden with goodies. One of the goodies was the head of his friend lying on a platter, an effect made possible by the long white tablecloth that covered the cart. Not everyone at Bully's had been so imaginative, but almost everyone had made his or her own costume and the overwhelming themes had been humor and creativity. These were not the results for which the Bollingbrookers strove.

Almost all the partygoers on this particular night had chosen to rent their costumes. Almost all the costumes were elaborate and pristine. Gentlemen tended to be dressed as historical figures: Henry VIII, George Patton à la George C. Scott, Emperor Nero, Napoleon, Admiral Nelson (you could tell it was Admiral Nelson because he only had one arm). Ladies were Southern belles, flappers, and all manner of royalty—dependent, it seemed, largely on the cut of their own figures.

And then there was Gretchen Patterson. I found her seated at a table with three other people directly across from the band. One of the people, of course, was Dodge in his Clark Gable disguise. The other two were Molly Barr dressed as a fairy princess with a little halo propped over her head, and a man in wire-rimmed glasses and a great white hunter's suit, whom I presumed to be Dickie Barr. They might have been a group of actors resting between takes at some type of "Hello, Hollywood" production: Rhett Butler, Jungle Jim, the Good Witch of the North, and Gretchen—who was definitely not Rita Hayworth.

Gretchen was Cleopatra. She wore a blue-black wig and a headband with the frontal figure of a gold serpent. She wore a gown that was white and satiny and molded to her body, except in the stomach. Her stomach was flat and smooth and provocatively beautiful as it showed bare through a huge diamond pattern cut in the dress. It was, in many respects, not much of a costume. In other respects it was the best costume there.

The group at Gretchen's table was occasionally chitchatting with passersby, but they were not talking a lot among themselves, and they were drinking heavily. Dickie looked drunk and bored. Molly kept scanning the room. Gretchen looked as if she could have been angry. Dodge just looked drunk.

I had taken up a position from which I could watch them without drawing their attention. I was behind the band's amplifiers, which were far too large for the kind of music that was being played, but which were perfect for my purposes. On the stage, the lead singer was trying gamely not to let it all out on a song by Gary Puckett and Union Gap. On the dance floor, several older couples were flailing away spastically at what they thought were the body motions of rock-and-roll dancing. One of the women, dressed as Queen Victoria, incessantly clapped her hands without ever once catching the beat of the music.

The whole scene was curiously lifeless and it surprised me because Dodge had been so enthusiastic about the party just a few hours before. I had expected wild things to be happening: mass dancing and chandelier swinging. Instead I saw such things as a man in a pirate's costume (cum eye patch) talking to a man in zoot suit about investments. "No, really, Henry, with its current P/E ratio I think Raytheon is vastly undervalued."

I thought, perhaps, the problem had to do with the age of the revelers. The Patterson group were among the youngest people there. Indeed, the majority seemed to be in their forties and fifties, with at least as many people older than that as younger. There was much tinkling laughter from the circulating women, and there were a lot of stationary men who looked as if they hoped their picture was not going to appear in their company's annual report. All in all, it was not much fun. It was not like a party at Barnacle Bully's, where you could be assured that sooner or later at least one of the women was going to lose the top of her costume.

Suddenly a voice at my elbow was telling me that Rollie needed something at the standing bar.

"Excuse me?" I said politely.

A young man in a red waiter's coat grimaced at the task of having to repeat himself. "Rollie," he said, gesturing, his voice rising. "Says he's got no barback. Says he's running outa soda water and champagne glasses."

I glanced at where he was indicating and Officer Roland Tagget of the Woodedge Police Department, wearing a red waiter's coat, acknowledged me with a sharp upward movement of his chin.

"You know him?" I said to the waiter. My eyes were still on

Tagget, but I had not made any attempt to return his acknowledgment.

The waiter was cocky and quick to be annoyed. He could have used a better haircut, his watery eyes slipped around in his head like greasy little pellets, and his mouth hung open when he wasn't speaking. I knew guys like this. I knew them in high school when they used to sit in the back row and shoot paperclips. "A course I do," he said, smoothing his hair, rolling his eyes, letting his mouth smack as he spoke. "He comes in to work all the big parties."

"What else did he say to you about me?"

"He asked me what you were doing here."

"What did you say?"

"I said, 'Beats the shit outa me. I never seen you before.' I never seen a headwaiter standing around staring at one table all night long, either."

I turned away, wondering what I should do next. The waiter helped me with my decision. "So who are you, anyway?"

I moved quickly, grabbing his arm and hustling him toward the paned glass doors behind the band before he had a chance to figure out what was happening. I shoved open one of the doors and we stumbled onto a veranda that overlooked the golf course. Winston Churchill was there already, regaling a dance-hall girl with tales of corporate lust and greed: "And all the time I was exercising my warrants by proxy. Har, har, har."

The dance-hall girl was smoking a long cigarette and did not appear to care much for Winston's proxy, but she and her companion were more than happy to turn their backs on the help and I was able to sling my friend into the farthest, darkest corner.

I got my face real close to his. "Rollie tell you that you're interfering with police work?"

"Oh, God," he said, recoiling, "is that who you are?"

There seemed to be a fear factor associated with the law. I exploited it by wrapping my fingers around his bicep and shaking him for good measure. His head bopped back and forth. "Who you working for?" I demanded.

"What do you mean? I work for the club."

"And Rollie just sent you over to harass me? To try to blow my cover?"

"He sent me over to tell you to order someone to get the stuff he needs."

"Why didn't you do it yourself?"

"It's not in my job description."

I gradually released my hold on him. I asked if he knew the people I was watching.

He tried a shrug, a "you-didn't-hurt-me" kind of shrug. "Sure. Mr. Barr. He's a member."

"How about the other guy?"

"Mr. Patterson."

"How do you know him?"

The waiter was straightening his lapels. "Used to be a member."

"What do you know about him?"

The waiter's loose jaw swung from side to side. He was debating whether to make a smart remark. I could see it in his eyes. He settled for, "He's kind of a legend."

"What's that mean?"

The waiter was as far into the corner as he could go. We were close enough that someone coming onto the porch might have mistaken us for a couple of neckers. I backed off half a step. I stuck a twenty-dollar bill in the breast pocket of his red waiter's coat. A whole new personality blossomed before my eyes.

"For being a sleaze, man. He's like your classic clubhouse rat, you know what I mean?"

"I don't have a clue," I said, but already I was getting prickly heat spots behind my ears.

"The guy . . ." He shook his head. "The guy, the guy was like the worst tipper in the entire world."

My heat spots started to subside.

"But it wasn't just tipping, man. It was anything to do with money. The guy just never seemed to have any."

"How do you know that? Besides the tipping thing, I mean."

"How do I know that? How do you think I know that? I'm a waiter, man. Waiters hear shit. What do you think, we just deliver the drinks and don't listen to what people are saying? C'mon. The guy hangs around long enough and bets enough games, holes, drives—whatever—without paying off when he loses, people start to talk. After a while it was like a joke, you know? People start talking about being Pattersoned. You ask me, that's probably why he left the club. He couldn't get anybody to play with him anymore."

"Not even Wylie Carpenter?"

"Oh, Mr. Carpenter." The waiter brightened. "Sure, he'd play him, I guess. They always seemed to get along real good. Maybe it's because Mr. Carpenter doesn't give a shit about money, I don't know."

"What does Mr. Carpenter give a shit about?"

The waiter hesitated. "This on the same twenty bucks?"

I turned sideways so that instead of facing the man I was standing next to him. I leaned back against the rail with my arms folded, and the waiter did likewise, listening for my response. "It better be," I hissed, startling him.

After a moment of studying the floor in front of my feet the waiter sighed. "Pussy," he said, startling me.

I repeated the word, not sure if I had heard right.

"Pussy," he affirmed, nodding his head. "Best ass man I seen around here. Discreet, though, you know what I mean?"

"Oh, sure."

"Yeah." He had been looking at me to see if I did know what he meant, but now he went back to nodding. "You can tell, though. I mean, you catch the guy coming out of one of the pool cabanas with the tennis instructor, eleven o'clock at night, you don't gotta be any Einstein to figure out what's going on."

I agreed with him about Einstein, but the waiter was on a roll and he liked the power of being able to pass some inside information to someone who cared. Because we were standing side by side he got to speak out of the corner of his mouth, and he liked that too.

"I'd bet that old Mr. Carpenter musta stuck about half the girls who work here. My sister, I'm pretty sure he got her one time." He said that as if he was proud of it, and then explained, "She used to work in accounting."

"Ah, then it all adds up."

"What does?"

I quickly moved the conversation back on track. "What about Mrs. Carpenter, did she know what was going on?"

"What, her?" He dry-spit.

"No?"

"Well, she wasn't around a lot, and when she was, well, she wasn't around much then, either."

"What was wrong with her?"

"Loaded on something. You could ask anybody. I mean, I didn't see her that much, just at a few dinners and stuff, but it always seemed to me that she was in another dimension."

"Like she was on Valium, something like that?"

"Valium? Maybe. Sleeping pills, reds, downers, horse tranquilizers." His voice drifted off into silence.

"Did you ever hear she was playing around, having any affairs of her own?"

"Mrs. Carpenter?" He asked the question as though he were unsure we were talking about the same person.

I had to say yes to get him to continue.

"Nah. You wanna know what she was like? She was sorta like nothing, man. She was like this pretty good-looking lady, little big in the ass, who'd come to something like this thing tonight, drink up a fishbowl of liquor, and then just sit there with her eyes glazed over until it was time to go home. That's why, you know, a lot of people probably didn't blame Mr. Carpenter for all the fooling around he was doing. It was like, you know, everybody was sorta wondering what a great guy like him was doing married to a woman like her anyway."

"She was from one of the richest families in this area."

"Hey," said the waiter, making me look at him, "everybody in this place is from one of the richest families in the area."

Before I could say anything more, the door to the veranda opened and out marched little Mr. Prince.

"Oh, oh," said the waiter, breaking his casual pose and standing upright.

Mr. Prince made straight for us and stopped when he was five feet away. By all appearances, Mr. Prince was steaming mad. "You planning on working anymore tonight, Rodney?"

"Yes, sir," said the waiter, speaking out of the center of his mouth for a change.

"Then come on, come on, come on," cried Mr. Prince, clapping one hand over the other. "And as for you," he said to me, "you told me you weren't going to interfere with anything."

"I'm trying not to. He came up to me and started asking me questions. I didn't want to start a scene."

"You told me you were bodyguarding."

"I told you—"

"How can you bodyguard when you're out here?"

"I'm going right back inside."

Prince, looking at me dubiously, let me go.

From the moment I pushed open the glass door and stepped over the threshhold I could see the scene had changed dramatically. The band had picked up its tempo and was now joyfully working its way through an old Chuck Berry song called "Maybelline." The younger people had moved onto the dance floor and those who were out there seemed to be genuinely having a good time, especially one tall, formally dressed gentleman in big ears and a painted mustache.

D. Dodge Patterson was attempting splits. He was whooping whenever he tried one and he had more than a few admirers who were egging him on. Conspicuous by her lack of inclusion within that group was his wife. Cleopatra was ostensibly dancing with Dodge, but she had allowed several feet of distance between them and she was moving extremely conservatively. When the song ended and Dodge had struggled back to an upright position for the last time, everybody but she broke into rough applause.

The band segued into "My Girl," but Dodge was in the middle

of a group of revelers who seemed to be making their way straight for the bar and Cleopatra was heading back to her table by herself. She was passing by the amplifiers when I stepped out from between them and slipped her into my arms.

She was not expecting the contact. She was not expecting to be grabbed by a man in a headwaiter's coat, but I had a good grip on her and after she said "What? . . . Oh . . . You!" she simply let me glide her around in a small circle. She even rested the heel of her left hand on my shoulder and then she slowly dropped her fingertips until they were touching me. When I looked into her face her eyes melted me and took the bravado out of my performance. Almost immediately I began to perspire and wish I had never been so bold.

"I don't think you're supposed to be here," she said.

I kept up the tatters of my smile.

"Should I scream?"

"Why? I have a disguise, just like you."

"And who are you? Hmmn?"

"Inspector Clouseau?"

"All right, Inspector. Are you here to solve the mystery of the missing chum? Or are you just moonlighting, picking up a little extra cash to supplement your county income?"

"I'm working." It was not much, as lines went, but it was all that came out.

"How disappointing. I thought you might say something romantic, like you had come to see me. Like you had bribed the powers that be, or hit some evil eunuch over the head and stolen his coat, all so you could have this dance."

"You're not far off," I murmured.

"Why? Was it so you could ask me more questions . . . or did you just want to hold me in your arms?"

She moved in closer to me. Her fingers moved a little further across my shoulder. All around us people were taking second and third looks. The band sang, "What could make me feel this way? . . . My girl . . ." And the perspiration rolled down my cheek.

THE IMMEDIATE PROSPECT OF BEING HANGED   157

"Oooh, you're so strong," she said, moving herself even closer to me, slipping her thigh between my legs and then letting it slip out again as if one of us had mildly misstepped, letting me feel how firm and smooth and warm she was beneath that satiny white dress. "And I see you've brought your pistol with you, too."

"I thought maybe you could tell me a few things about Rebecca Carpenter," I said, but the words came out as if I were gasping for air.

"Is that all you want?" she said, moving once more across me, letting her thigh slip once again. Her eyebrows arched.

"Well . . ."

"Catch me another time, Patt," she said, and suddenly she spun out of my grasp. I was alone in the middle of the dance floor in my borrowed waiter's coat and pants and my black Reebok shoes and a bulge that most definitely did not come from any pistol.

A vise clamped on each of my elbows. My head swiveled from side to side and I saw that two of the larger men ever to engage in the food service industry had hold of me. Their expressions reflected a rather determined sadness. As I looked forward again I saw on the very edge of the parqueted dance floor, but not standing directly on it, a very irate Mr. Prince.

Perhaps at any other time or place I would have smiled sweetly at him. As it was, however, I dropped my eyes and let his goons escort me through a parting sea of Woodedgians in fezes and wigs and robes and gowns. "Excuse me, excuse me, excuse me," the goons said, and I was mumbling right along with them. "Excuse me, excuse me, excuse me."

Saturday night I could not get out of going to the Keoughs' house. The invitation came in the form of a Saturday afternoon telephone call to my apartment by Jessica, asking if I would like to join them for Chinese food. Nothing fancy, just the Hansens were coming over and maybe I would like to get a date and come along.

"Sure," I said. "I'll bring Anita."

"Anita D'Orfio? From the office? Whatever for?"

I did not tell Jessica it was because I was feeling mean and nasty and vindictive. I just made noises to that effect.

"What about that redheaded gal . . . Desdemona? The one with the marvelous figure. You know who I'm talking about."

"Deirdre. She can't come. She already has a date."

"Well, there must be somebody you can bring. How about that lovely Asian gal you used to bring? Marilyn?"

"Mai Lin. And she won't come because Patty cornered her the last time and spent the whole night talking about hysterectomies."

"Oh, Patt, just come by yourself then. It'll be fun, I promise. Besides, I have something very special to show you. Something good."

So I went: but in recognition of my single status Jessica allowed me to arrive late and leave early. By the time I got there they were halfway through an eight-course meal, fresh from the cartons.

Jessica began the evening's surprises by answering the door wearing a pair of incredibly tight jeans. She was no teenage bub-blebutt, but the jeans showed she was firm and round and they made me look at her when her back was turned. They made me look at her as I followed her into the dining room, and I knew right away that was a mistake. Suddenly, instead of Royster being embarrassed because I had caught him humping his secretary the day before, I was the one who was blushing because he had seen me eyeing our boss's wife. Patty Hansen must have seen me, too, because already she was doing that crazy thing of looking back and forth from Jessica to me. As for John Michael, he acknowl-edged nothing. He was in the middle of a monologue when we walked in and he kept right on talking until he was done with what he was saying.

I sat and listened to John Michael and ate everything that was put in front of me without asking what it was. And when the food was gone and the plates had been cleared away and John Michael had finally shut up, Jessica pulled out the special thing she had to show us. It was a newspaper.

It was, to be specific, a copy of that day's *Walmouth-Nestor Courier,* and it was turned to the editorial page. "I don't suppose anybody bothered reading this," she said, pointing to a letter that was captioned, A DYNASTY ENDS IN SORDID MYSTERY.

John Michael, as was his due, got to read it first. When he was done he looked thoughtful and passed it to Royster. When Roy-ster was done he looked thoughtful and passed it to me. Patty didn't count in matters that required us to look thoughtful.

The letter read:

A dynasty has ended with the murder of a beautiful and fabulously wealthy woman, and nobody seems to care. In the early morning hours of October 16, the body of Rebecca

Chesley Carpenter was found on the seat of her late model Mercedes at a lonely turnoff in Woodedge. She had been strangled and sexually assaulted, and devoted readers of this newspaper will know little more than that and the fact that she had private funeral services in Woodedge three days later. Yet this woman was the last surviving member of the family that had virtually ruled Woodedge for most of the past 300 years. At least 13 generations of that great name have trod the lands of this town and now all that remains are the structures and grounds of the magnificent Chesley Estate on Bulham Road. One can only hope that Mrs. Carpenter's husband, assuming that's who inherits it, will not allow the estate to be broken up and sold as parcels to suddenly rich hockey players and computer jockeys. And while one is hoping, one may also be wondering why more attention hasn't been paid to this unsolved and exceedingly curious murder. Can it be that there are people even more important in Woodedge these days than Chesleys?

It was signed William Brown, a name that meant nothing to me.

"What do you think?" asked John Michael. He was wearing a white tennis shirt that was supposed to fit tight around his biceps and didn't. His lips were pursed, his pale face was drawn while he awaited my answer.

"It sounds," I said, waving my hand over it, "rather Sherlock Holmesian to me. I read all this 'trod the lands' and 'exceedingly curious' stuff and I want to say, 'Quick, Watson, get the dog cart. The game's afoot.' "

I grinned around the table at my own cleverness, but nobody grinned back. John Michael steepled his fingers in front of his face. Jessica and Royster stared at the tablecloth. Patty looked from me to Jessica and Jessica to me.

"Who is this William Brown, anyway?" I said.

"It's me, for God's sake," said Jessica.

Silence weighed heavily on the group for a moment and then John Michael said, "I kind of like it."

Royster said, "I really like it." He nodded his head at each and every one of us.

"I mean the concept," John Michael added. "When did you do this, Jessie?"

"I sent it in Wednesday."

"I like the Holmesian touch," said Royster, taking the newspaper away from me so he could look at it again. "That sounds the way one of those old Yankees in Woodedge would write. 'Devoted readers of this newspaper,' I like that. Don't you, Patty?"

"What I can do now, you see," John Michael said, reaching out to get the paper from Royster, "is write a letter in response. 'In regard to the letter of Mr. William Brown, published in last Saturday's edition, let me hasten to assure the people of this county that the shocking murder of Rebecca Chesley Carpenter retains the utmost priority in my office. Let me further hasten to assure Mr. Brown that nobody, no matter how rich or influential, famous or well connected, is above the law in Exeter County.' Something like that."

"I like it," said Royster, snapping his fingers.

"Get a little dialogue going," said John Michael. "Get him to write back, maybe."

"Where did you get the name, Jessica?" I asked.

She told me she made it up. "It sounded common enough."

"But if you use it again, somebody might go looking for him," I cautioned.

Everyone looked at me as though I was being purposely annoying.

"I can quote some statistics," said John Michael. "In Massachusetts last year there were one hundred nine murders, of which sixty-nine have been solved. Through the first ten months of this year the Carpenter case is the only murder in Exeter County left unresolved out of some eight that have taken place, a rate considerably better than that in the Commonwealth as a whole."

"You could even put in," said Royster, "that we have a suspect and intend to have the murderer in custody in a matter of, what, weeks?"

"What I thought we could do," said Jessica, leaning onto the table, "is get Miles Bell at the *Courier* to dig out some of the old unresolved murders in Woodedge history. Run a series of articles on them; get the public thinking about murders among the affluent."

"It wouldn't be much of a series," I said, stilling the conversation and immediately regretting that I had spoken out loud.

Jessica, her body still bent, her head turned to face me, demanded to know why not. I was, once again, the focus of everyone's attention.

"There have only been a couple. Around the turn of the century a woman named Mabel Norcross was found dead on the floor of her bedroom in the house she shared with her father and brother on Highland Street. On days when her father and brother were off working she was known to entertain a gentleman caller or two. She was known to do this because she had a neighbor who apparently had nothing better to do all day long than watch her and report what she saw to Mabel's father."

My audience stared.

"One day the brother left, the father left, the milkman was seen entering and leaving the house, one gentleman caller was seen entering and leaving, and a second gentleman caller arrived to find Mabel strangled to death.

"The father and brother claimed she was alive when they were there, the milkman and first gentleman caller claimed they had left without seeing her, and the second gentleman caller was the one who rang for the doctor. Since nobody could figure out which one of them did it they convicted the milkman. He went to the chair protesting his innocence and the story is that Mabel Norcross haunts the house to this day because she was never properly avenged." I offered a tentative shrug in case anybody was wondering if I really believed the story.

Royster took hold of his cup of tea and held it thoughtfully between the table and his lips. "How do you know all this stuff, Patt?" he asked.

I flipped my hand one way and then the other.

"You said there were a couple. What were the others?" He still had not tasted his tea. He still was holding the cup halfway to his mouth.

"A nude body was found in the snow near Bollingbrook about ten years ago. You can ask Ralphie about that one. Most mysterious thing about it was probably his investigation. He decided she was a prostitute from Boston that somebody had brought down the pike and thrown out of his car. Wembley wholeheartedly agreed and that was the end of it. They buried her as a Jane Doe."

"And you disagreed?" Royster said, regarding me curiously.

I shrugged. "What do I know? I wasn't even in this business at the time. Maybe it was the most incisive analysis of Ralphie's career."

Royster put down his tea, untouched. "But you've looked into it. And you looked into the Norcross murder. What, have you made some sort of study of murders in Woodedge?"

"Maybe you could work with Miles Bell directly on this, Patt," Jessica suggested.

"No," I said to both of them.

"I like those two you've told us about, Patt," said John Michael from his position at the head of the table. "Do you know of any more?"

"No."

"They don't necessarily have to be unresolved," he pressed. "I mean, technically, the Norcross one isn't unresolved. Think it would be worthwhile for one of us to go through the *Courier*'s archives?"

"I could do it," Jessica said. "I've got some time this week."

"You won't find anything," I said.

"Well, it won't hurt to look. I mean, between Wembley and Ralph, who knows what's gone down over there? They may have let things go as suicide—"

I spoke quickly, cutting her off. "There was one. About eighteen or nineteen years ago. A body of a man was found on a path that led up from the Charles and it was ruled to be suicide because he had been shot in the head with a small-caliber gun that was lying on the ground next to him."

"Any reason why it wouldn't have been suicide?" Royster asked.

I looked from one person to the other before deciding how to answer. "No note was ever found, the man didn't own a gun and wasn't known to have ever fired one, and the gun that was next to him was untraceable."

I may have spoken sharply. There may have been some edge in my voice that caused the subtle changes I saw in their expressions, that caused them to keep looking at me long after I had finished.

"So you don't think the guy offed himself, Patt?" said Royster, and whatever was in his voice matched whatever was in mine.

I fixed my eyes on his before I answered. "The medical examiner said it was suicide and that was the end of it."

Suddenly John Michael popped his fist into his open palm and we all got distracted. "By God, I like Jessica's idea. But we don't need a whole history. We don't need a series. All we need's that one Norcross story. You see the parallels? Beautiful Woodedge woman, strangled in her own environment while her male guardian is nowhere to be found. Same question in both cases about what the victim could have been doing in the place she was at the time she was killed. Same question as to where the male guardian was. Old Mr. Norcross, was he upset his daughter was whoring around? How about Mr. Carpenter, was he upset his wife may have been climbing aboard the yardman? The milkman took the fall back then, is the yardman taking the fall now?"

John Michael gestured enthusiastically, encouraging us to see what he was seeing. "The husband and the father, the yardman and the milkman . . . and lurking behind everything is the question of steamy, bawdy, untold sex. Huh? I like it, I like it, and I can see Miles Bell liking it, too."

Everybody around the table got into liking it so much that I didn't have the heart to tell them I thought it stunk.

18

To the casual observer, there would have been nothing unusual about a man bumping into a woman with a small child in the parking lot of the Woodedge post office on a Monday morning. If the observer was not so casual, however, he or she might have noticed that the man had been waiting in his little gray-green Alfa for almost two and a half hours, and that he did not get out of his car until a dusty Country Squire station wagon pulled into the lot and lurched into a parking space. He or she might have noticed that the woman sprang from behind the wheel, ran around the car to the passenger's door, quickly unbelted her child, and then started to hurry into the post office with one hand holding onto the child and one hand holding her coat closed—only to draw up short when she saw who was standing in front of her.

"I thought I'd see you sooner or later, Patt," Gretchen Patterson said to me. Her hair was blowing in the wind, blowing away from her head and making her face stand out by itself as a thing of dark and complex beauty.

The sky was overcast in a mishmash of gray colors. The leaves that had been so pretty just the week before were now brown and crisp and blowing past us as if they were late for an appointment. I was cold from my long wait in my little car and I was afraid my nose was starting to run so I kept sniffing and nervously touching it. I was grinning and sniffing and touching my nose and not saying anything.

"You caused quite a stir the other night," she said, with a beguiling flick of her head. "Everybody was so solicitous of me after you left, you'd think I'd been assaulted or something. Old Mrs. Ransom, who usually only talks to me at Christmas, asked me if I wanted to lie down in the women's lounge."

"Did anybody ask who I was?"

"Of course. I told them I didn't know."

"But I must have been recognized. By your husband, perhaps, or Molly Barr."

"Dodge was getting a drink when it happened, and you must not have made much of an impression on Molly."

"She was more interested in a tennis instructor named Cliff the day I saw her."

"Ah, Cliff. Well, that explains it."

"You people in Woodedge seem to live such interesting lives."

"Not really. That's why someone like Molly has a Cliff."

"Is that why someone like Becky had a Dougie Rasmussin?"

"My, we cut right to the bone, don't we?" Gretchen was smiling at me, but her son was pulling away from her. He was also making horrible noises.

Little Ian Patterson was three or four years old and did not deserve criticism, but I was thinking bad thoughts about him nonetheless. I said, "How would the little tyke like a nice cup of hot chocolate while his mommy and I share a little conversation?"

Gretchen looked at her watch. "It's just eleven thirty. Adolfo's will be opening if you want to go there."

I had been thinking of the Brigham's ice cream parlor, but I put on a brave front and told her Adolfo's would be swell. In my mind I was remembering the twenty dollars I had impulsively popped into the waiter's pocket the previous Friday night and I was wondering if I would be able to justify to the office the expense of a lunch for three at Adolfo's.

"Then why don't you go and get us a table," Gretchen said, "and Ian and I will join you after we get the mail."

It was not hard getting a table at Adolfo's at eleven thirty-five on a Monday morning. I was even given one by the window so

I could look out over the patio with its un-used tables and umbrellas. And then I sat alone, sipping from my water goblet and playing with my silverware and trying to decide if the fun-loving Mrs. Patterson had made a fool of me once again. But then, finally, just as I was about to get up and leave, she and her child arrived, and I didn't know whether to be angry that she had taken so long or grateful that she had actually come. I chose to act grateful.

Gretchen brought the freshness of the outdoors with her as she dug her way out of her coat and stripped Ian of his. I watched her shoulders and her breasts move beneath her tan sweater and I found that I actually was grateful.

"Do you come here often?" I asked.

"Adolfo's? Never. The post office? Every day. How about you?"

"The post office? Oh, yeah, sure. I like to be on the spot in case some new commemoratives come in."

Gretchen looked at me strangely, perhaps not realizing what a funny guy I could be. She arranged her napkin on her lap and tried to keep Ian from squirming out of his seat. She buttered him a piece of bread from the basket that had been brought to our table shortly after I sat down, and put it on his plate. When the waiter came within singing distance of us she beckoned him over and quickly ordered Ian a glass of apple juice and herself a Dubonnet. I ordered a vodka grapefruit so I could be one of the party.

"That must have been a terribly humiliating experience for you," she said suddenly. "Friday night, I mean."

"Well . . . ," I said, feigning magnanimity.

"No. It was very cruel of me." She broke off a piece of bread for herself and then broke off a piece of that and buttered it. "Especially since I knew how you would feel."

I laughed. "How could you? We've barely even met."

"I can tell. We're a lot alike, you and I. We both absolutely hate the idea of failure . . . we just go about dealing with it in different ways."

"What is this?" I said, my grin only halfway intact. "Are you trying to psychoanalyze me?"

"You didn't think this was a one-way street, did you? You didn't think you got to go unexplored while you picked my brain?"

"Of course I did. I'm the investigator."

"You don't look at me like you're an investigator." She gave a quick glance at Ian and then leaned across the table and whispered, "You look at me like you want to get in my pants."

I choked. I spit little flecks of bread all over my napkin as I hurried to cover my mouth. I was bent over hacking when the waiter arrived with our drinks and obsequiously asked if he could be of any assistance. I tried to wave him away.

"Does this mean you're not ready to order, sir?" he asked.

Gretchen told him to come back in five minutes. Ian, meanwhile, was in hysterics. He thought it quite funny to see a grown man in such distress.

"Something went down the wrong way," I tried to explain, clearing my throat.

"Sure it did," Gretchen said.

I looked up quickly and she disarmed me with a smile.

"Don't you want to get in my pants?" Her leg touched mine beneath the table.

I dabbed at my mouth.

"I can ask you that, you see, because I know you won't say yes. And even if you did say yes you wouldn't do anything about it. You wouldn't put yourself in that position."

"And why wouldn't I?"

"Because you aren't sure I'm serious. I might turn you down. Reject you." She withdrew her leg. "Your idea of dealing with failure is to keep yourself from ever letting it occur. That's where you and I differ. My idea is to make sure it never does occur."

I took a long sip of my drink and tried to figure out why she was saying these things to me. "Do you really know who I am?"

"Patterson Starbuck. My husband's second cousin, once removed, or something like that. Removed in more ways than one, I might add."

"How did you know?"

"My father-in-law told me. He recognized your name right away. In fact, he told me I shouldn't have let you in the house. 'Once a Starbuck gets in your house,' he said, 'you've got to call the police to get him out.' "

I grimaced. "And Dodge, does he know?"

"Not from me."

"Why not?"

Gretchen toyed with her Dubonnet. She looked at her menu. For the first time she averted her gaze. "I don't know why," she said, not really expecting me to believe her.

"His father must have told him."

"His father and he don't talk, despite whatever appearances they have given you."

"This is where I get to say 'Why not?' again."

Gretchen's smiles came easily when she wanted. She had a way of pointing her chin and catching your eye as she flashed her teeth, and suddenly you were swept away to places you hadn't meant to go. I had almost forgotten my question when she said, "Well, I guess it's no secret that Dodge hasn't quite fit the image that old Frost set for him."

"Image?"

"Sure. Andover, Amherst and all that. Frost expected his only son to come home with a glittering and glorious career and instead he came home with me, the peasant of Lowell."

I wasn't sure if she was putting me on. I couldn't conceive of Gretchen Patterson as a peasant. I couldn't imagine her coming from a working-class city like Lowell. I couldn't understand any man not being exhilarated just to be in her presence and have her smile at him.

"Oh, yes," she said, reading me. "That greatly upset Frost and Florence, Dodge's mother. I was not what they had envisioned at all. They looked at me and saw sex and lust and youthful indiscretion. 'Wait a little while, Dodgie, and you'll grow out of this phase. You'll meet someone of your own kind and you'll realize how transient impetuous infatuation can be with a daughter of immigrants from the mill city.' " Gretchen sang the imitation happily, as though it had been traumatic enough at the time, but did not hurt anymore.

She busied herself for a moment tidying her son. "What they didn't understand," she went on, "was Dodge. The ironic thing is, I didn't understand him either—but for totally different reasons."

The waiter reappeared. Gretchen ordered scallops doré for herself and lobster bisque for her three-year-old son. I ordered coquilles St. Jacques, without being sure what it was, and the waiter bowed as though we had made excellent choices and went away. A busboy immediately took his place and filled our water goblets and placed before us a schooner dish of celery and carrot sticks and black olives. Then he went away.

Gretchen said, "Dodge managed to get himself into law school at B.U. and I took a job as a cocktail waitress in Copley Square so I could be near him." She half-shrugged.

I full-shrugged back.

"Becoming a waitress wasn't exactly why I worked my way through school. But I kept telling myself it was all temporary. That it would all work out in the long run. We lived together the whole three years he was in law school. And that, Florence Patterson would tell you if she were still alive, is where her little Dodgie went wrong. The truth is, of course, that the framework of Dodge's life had been laid long before I came on the scene. It wasn't me who steered him onto the path of penury and frivolity."

"Penury and frivolity?"

My question was meant as a comment on her choice of words. They were not the words of the urban peasant she was claiming herself to be. But her great dark eyes seared me when she heard my slightly mocking tone, and her own voice cracked when she spoke back. "Well, you're the detective, what do you call what you've found out about him?"

I sat whiplashed, unsure of what she meant; feeling a bit like a student who has to come up with an excuse for failing to do his homework.

"What did you think," she pressed, "when you found us all living together in his father's home?"

"I thought," I said, pausing to clear my voice, "that it was a big house with plenty of rooms. I thought that Dodge would be inheriting it anyway when his father dies and that maybe Frost needed you there until then to help him run the place."

"Boy," she said, making a grab for Ian just as he was about to crawl onto the table, "are you misinformed." She managed to get Ian reseated, his nose cleaned, and a stalk of celery and a stick of carrot placed in his hands with an admirable economy of motion. "Dodge's grandfather Gordon left that house to both his sons. Frost got it first because he was the oldest, and Parker was none too pleased because he figured he had the most kids and he should get it. Still, the way it was left, when Frost dies the house goes straight to Parker—and Parker has four daughters who are going to inherit it from him."

"Where's Parker now?"

"Oh, kept up on the relatives, have we?" She was smiling warmly again, ingratiatingly again, sucking me in again. "He's fit as a fiddle in Palm Beach. Living with his third wife and waiting impatiently for his brother to die."

"The house isn't that nice," I said.

"Listen, any house in Woodedge these days is that nice. A house with that much land and that many rooms is worth well more than a million dollars."

I shifted about uncomfortably.

"Besides," Gretchen said, her head cocking to one side, her hair cascading over her shoulder, "as I understand it, the Pattersons put tremendous personal value on the old homestead."

"My father had a lot of emotional reasons for wanting to get in that house," I said, "if that's what you're referring to."

She nodded. "The house, it was originally built by Frederick Patterson, wasn't it?"

"Yeah. Then he built another house for his son John and left this one to his son Alfred. I'm from John's side of the family. Dodge is from Alfred's."

"And what happened to John's house?"

"He left it to my great-uncle Frank, who sold it and moved away." I neglected to mention how many times Frank had sold it.

"Leaving you out in the cold."

"It was long before I was born."

"And yet you're still resentful."

"I'm not resentful."

"Oh."

The bisque came. Gretchen and I received little cups of heated clam broth to prepare us for our main courses.

"You're the one who sounds resentful," I said.

Gretchen put down her cup and stared at me. "Well, can you blame me? Here I am, an outsider in this town full of snobs, trying to go around pretending not only that I'm one of them, but that everything is jim-dandy in my home, which doesn't belong to me, where I'm not wanted, and which is soon going to be taken away from me."

"It seems to me you fit in just fine."

"Oh, c'mon, Patt, be real. Look at my skin coloring. Listen to my accent. I could never be one of these people in a lifetime of trying. But that's not important. What's important is that my son fit in; and as long as we're living here, as long as we keep up the image, he will."

"Why's that important?"

Gretchen dropped her forearm rather loudly on the table. "I can't believe you, of all people, are asking me that, Patt. Wasn't it your father who moved his family into the Patterson place? Wasn't it your father who used to hide in the trees after that, scheming to get back in? Didn't he keep returning even after Gordon Patterson bought a gun and took a shot at him? Even after Frost and Parker chased him through the woods? Why, Patt? Because he knew what it's like to live here and live someplace else. He knew that you live here and you have land and room and privacy and a sense of personal identity. Maybe you look at living in West Nestor differently than he did, but if it's anything like where I come from you share your room and you share your building and you share your street, and your identity comes from being one of the people in the neighborhood. You know what the biggest advantage of that is? It means you don't get your car stolen by somebody who lives on your block."

Gretchen continued to stare at me until she realized I was not going to respond, and then she added, "Like I said, maybe I'm confusing you with what I've been told about your father. But it seems to me I understand what he wanted. He knew the difference between being somebody and not being somebody—and he knew about the arbitrariness that can cause a person to be in one position or the other."

Suddenly her head fell into the palm of her hand. Just as suddenly Ian stopped playing with his soup. "Mommy, are you all right?" he asked, and when he got no answer he looked at me accusingly.

"Hey," I said softly, reaching over to touch her shoulder. She shook me away and I quickly looked around the room to see if anyone was noticing us. No one was. I leaned closer and said, "Gretchen, why are you telling me all this?"

"I suppose," she murmured, "so that you would understand."

"I understand. I understand . . . it's just, I'm not sure why we're talking about it."

"I meant understand what I've done. I meant understand why I'm so scared."

Little pulsations began to race through my body. I sat very still.

Gretchen Patterson's face remained covered by her hand and her hair. She did not appear to be looking at anything other than the white linen tablecloth.

"Are you all right, Mommy?" Ian asked again.

She assured him she was. She straightened up again. She smiled bravely and told Ian to eat his soup. He explained that he didn't like it because it had yucky things in it. In the midst of receiving

THE IMMEDIATE PROSPECT OF BEING HANGED 175

Gretchen's confession I found myself distracted by the nearly full bowl of lobster bisque and feeling pained at the waste of nine dollars and fifty cents.

"Why is it you're scared, Gretchen?"

"What is that, Ian?" she said, directing her son's attention out the window. Ian practically stood on his chair to see, his head tilted back, his eyes scanning. Gretchen quickly turned to me. "Because I've been having an affair with Wylie Carpenter."

She was trying to collect my reaction and I was trying to remain as unreactive as possible. A silly line came into my head. "Oh, yes. Frightfully bad spot, that." But I said nothing. In truth, I was having difficulty knowing what to do with the information.

She shrugged. It was an easy, athletic, undulating motion that swept across her shoulders. "I still am, I suppose, though of course we haven't seen each other since all this happened."

"Is it that bird, Mommy? The one with the thing in its mouth?"

"No, no, sweetheart. Keep looking."

She let her son get up and put his hands on the windowsill so that his back was to us. "You see why I had to tell you before you found out on your own? I mean, I know the types of questions you've been going around asking and I know why you have to do it—to get all the relevant information inside that big circle you were telling me about. But something like this, if it were made public, either Ian and I would be thrown out of the Patterson house or we'd be ostracized from Woodedge society forever."

"Ostrich, Mommy?"

"No, honey. Keep looking."

"Yet it seems to have been all right for your husband to have an affair with Wylie's wife," I said cautiously.

"What was I supposed to do? Leave him? Tell him to pack up and get out of his father's house? This is the very thing I'm worried about, ending up on my own with my son and no place to go. Dodge may have his shortcomings, and I'm sure you've found out about plenty of them if you're doing the job I think you're doing, but he's all I've got. I mean, when I learned what was going on between Dodge and Becky I wanted to kill them both. But what good would that have done me? I lose Dodge, do you think the old man's going to take care of me?"

"You're speaking figuratively, of course. About killing them."

"Of course. Although I was so humiliated when I first found out that the thought crossed my mind. But leaving Dodge, what's that going to gain me? The rest of Woodedge is not going to welcome Ian and me with open arms, even if we could afford to stay here. Dodge is our ticket and we're all perfectly well aware of it. So, again, what could I do? I tried talking about it with my father-in-law, but all he did was make me feel as though it must be my fault. I realized if I was going to protect myself I'd have to do it on my own."

I nodded. I agreed. I was not in control of this conversation.

Gretchen checked on her son, who was still searching the patio and the sidewalk and the street for whatever his mother had told him to find. She said, "So I went to Becky and I insinuated myself with her. And we became friends, she and I, and because Wylie and Dodge were already friends we began to do things as couples. The idea, you know, the idea I had was just to make us all so close that I wouldn't have to worry about Dodge and Becky anymore, but what became clear after not too long was that . . . well, Wylie and Becky didn't have much of a relationship. It probably wasn't even as good as Dodge's and mine. Which, I suppose, is why she was available to Dodge in the first place.

She looked at her glass of Dubonnet, which was only half gone, and said, "Becky, you see, had a bit of a dependency problem. She was always on Valium, Librium, whatever she could get hold of, and when she drank, which was often, she would just sort of zone out. Wylie, on the other hand, is somebody who always wants to be on the go, who always wants to be doing something. And whatever they once had between them, well, it just didn't seem to be there anymore."

"Like with you and Dodge," I said, and then I was ashamed of myself because there was almost a strain of hope in my voice.

"Is it the sign, Mommy? Is that it?"

"No, it's not the sign, Ian." And then she said no to me, too. "Dodge and I haven't reached the point that the Carpenters did. The problems we're having have to do with external things. Neither one of us is very secure about who we are or what we're doing right now. Dodge, as I'm sure you know, hasn't been very successful as a lawyer. His credit, both personal and financial, is pretty much used up. He's tied to his father and yet he almost hates his father. So what he does is, he resorts to the things he does best, that he's most comfortable with. You know, golf, tennis, carousing. And all those things keep him away from his father, away from home, and away from me. I'm left behind, feeling unwanted and out of place, and all of a sudden one of the most prominent men in town is paying a lot of attention to me. He's telling me that I'm beautiful, that I'm intelligent, that I'm interesting." Her voice trailed off.

"And that man is Wylie Carpenter?"

She took a deep breath and sighed. It was a sigh of affirmation.

Our meals arrived. Mine was on a seashell. It was covered with an orange sauce that looked like Welsh rarebit. I gazed at it, only half assimilating what I was seeing.

"Were you," I said, as she started to eat, "with Wylie on the night his wife was killed?"

Gretchen kept her dark eyes on her plate and waited until she was done chewing before she answered. "No. I was out shopping that night. In fact, I was out looking for something for the Halloween Ball."

"Was there someplace special you usually met him?"

Gretchen hesitated. "That's not really important, is it, Patt? I mean, the affair doesn't have anything to do with what you're investigating and I'm only telling you about it so you won't stumble on it and cause my whole marriage to blow up in my face."

"But now that I know about it, I can't just ignore it."

Gretchen had been carving a scallop. Her knife and fork went very still. "Why not? It doesn't have anything to do with anything unless you think Wylie could have killed her because of me." The word "killed" was mouthed silently after a quick glance toward Ian.

She must not have gotten the reaction from me that she wanted. Laying down her utensils, she said, "I'm suddenly sorry I told you anything at all."

I didn't want her to be sorry. I wanted her to look at me again with some kind of indication that she liked what she was seeing. "You know, if a guy is having an affair, it can explain things other than murder."

"What does Wylie need to explain?"

"He's got a couple of hours that night he can't account for."

"If that's the case then I won't have any choice. I'll say I was with him."

I didn't respond. I looked for the good parts of my coquilles St. Jacques.

"Because he didn't do it, Patt. He wouldn't have had any reason to. I mean, he could have walked away from that marriage at any time. He didn't need her money, there weren't any kids . . . What motive would he have for killing her? At a lovers' lane, of all places?"

Suddenly Ian cried out with delight. "I see him, Mommy. I see him." He began pounding on the window with the heel of his hand. "It's Daddy. In here, Daddy. Daddy!"

"Oh, my God," Gretchen said, sliding over quickly to grab Ian's hand before he caused any more commotion. As soon as her fingers closed around her son's arm her expression froze. She waved her hand unenthusiastically. "He's coming in," she said, and her lips barely moved.

She spun back to me. "You won't say anything, will you? Promise me you won't say anything."

Her beautiful features were carved with anxiety. Her voice was desperate with emotion.

"I've got nothing to say."

The tenseness went out of her shoulders. Relief flooded her face. Everything about her told me I was a hell of a guy.

My back was to the door, but I knew when Dodge Patterson

entered the restaurant. Gretchen beckoned him as if she had been saving his seat. Ian called to him. I turned and watched him unbutton his topcoat and smooth back his hair and register only mild surprise when he saw me dining with his wife and son.

"Dodge, you remember Mr. Starbuck," Gretchen said.

"Yes," I said, half-rising and holding out my hand. "Patt Starbuck, D.A.'s office. We've talked a couple of times."

"Sure," he said, giving me a cold hand to shake. "Still investigating?"

It was, I thought, a funny question to ask, but I laughed as though we were both being charming, and said, "Oh, they let us ask our questions over lunch every now and then. Won't you join us?"

I swept my hand toward the empty seat next to me, hoping he would say no and tell me that he had some errand he had to run, someplace he had to be. Instead, he looked at each of our meals and said, "Fine. That would be great."

The waiter, who had been hovering ever since Ian had beaten on the window, moved in for the order as soon as Dodge had taken off his coat and sat down.

"Let me see," Dodge said, "that lobster bisque looks good." And before I could point out that his son's was almost untouched, he had ordered a nice big bowl for himself and the waiter had scurried away like a thief in the night.

On Tuesday morning I went for a walk in the woods beneath the overlook where Rebecca Carpenter's body was found. The overlook itself was a turnoff, a hundred yards wide, bellying out from a little country lane called Ivanhoe Road. It was one of the highest spots in Woodedge and it provided a fine view of the Charles River. This being October, there were a couple of cars from New York at the overlook when I arrived. This being morning, there was fog lifting off the river, obscuring the view for the consequently embittered visitors from the Empire State.

"It always look like this?" one man demanded of me.

"Ay-yuh," I told him, and scrambled over the stone wall that separated the parking area from the wooded slope.

There was a path that was difficult to follow for about twenty yards because of its steepness. Then it went into the trees and spilled onto a cart track that was strewn with leaves and twigs and horse droppings. I had been on this track when I was a boy and I knew that if I followed it one way it would lead to a set of cairns that my father told me were built by the Norsemen hundreds of years before Columbus. If I took it the other way it would lead down to a mud pond, where my father and I had once spent an afternoon digging for buried treasure that he had read about in a book. At the pond the cart track would intersect a path that led up from the river. It was the path my father used to take in order to get from Nestor to Whitehall Road after

THE IMMEDIATE PROSPECT OF BEING HANGED   181

Gordon Patterson obtained a restraining order keeping him from coming within a mile of the family property.

Whoever killed Mrs. Carpenter could have gone downhill to the lake and then followed the path to the river if he wanted to get out of the woods as fast as possible. From the river it would have been a short climb to either Route 128 or the turnpike. I turned the other way and started walking toward the cairns. It was the way Wylie Carpenter would have gone if he was trying to get back to the Stonegate Country Club.

I walked for no more than five minutes and then I stopped. The track was no different now than it had been when I was a child. It twisted and turned and was rutted from horse hooves, and it would have taken an expert woodsman to have followed it all the way to Stonegate in the dark.

I looked in the direction of the pond and memories came back to me as sharp as if I were seeing them in a movie. The path that led by the pond was straight and smooth. I had walked it dozens of times with my father, usually with him lost in thought, gripping the fingers of my hand so hard I wanted to cry out from the pain. I remembered the sounds he made as he walked. His grunting sounded in my ears. It became heavy breathing, and then it became panting and then I realized it was me who was making all those noises. I was standing in the middle of an otherwise deserted trail, surrounded by trees and ferns and bushes, and I was hyperventilating.

There was a conference table in John Michael's office and when it was fully occupied it held eight people. On Tuesday afternoon there was only one seat open. At the head of the table sat John Michael, with his cheek resting against his fist and his arm hooked over the back of his chair. Along one side of the table sat Royster, Detective Lieutenant Libby, and Woodedge Police Sergeant Roselli. Along the other side sat Chief Tuttle in a wrinkled gray business suit, Inspector Lester in a loud check sport coat, and Officer Tagget in a uniform considerably different from the last one I had seen him wearing.

They were waiting for me. They were all unhappy, or uncomfortable, and acting as if it was my fault.

John Michael did his best to lighten up the proceedings. "Jesus, Patt. You look like you just learned Ted Kennedy was going to be driving you to the ferry."

A few of the soldiers dutifully laughed. It was always best to laugh at John Michael's jokes, especially when they dealt with the Kennedys.

"You're not exactly a festive gathering yourselves."

"Yes, well . . ." John Michael let go of the back of his chair and inclined forward so he could rest his arms on the table. "The chief asked for this meeting so he could bring to my attention some of the things you've been doing in connection with the Carpenter investigation."

"You must have been at it for a while."

"About an hour. I left word for you to join us as soon as you came in."

"I was out in the woods behind the overlook."

John Michael shifted his eyes to Chief Tuttle, who looked down the table at Roselli.

"We've combed that whole area," said Roselli. "There's nothing there. No sign of any flight, no pocketbook, no nothing."

The chief turned back to John Michael as though something significant had just been announced. "You see?" he demanded, his jowls flubbering up and down.

John Michael nodded. "Wembley wants me to take you off the investigation, Patt. He says what you're doing is at best duplicative and at worst counterproductive. He says you're upsetting a lot of people in Woodedge."

I waited for some sort of hint as to which way John Michael wanted me to go.

"For example, he says you crashed a fancy dress ball at one of the country clubs last Friday night."

I could feel myself blushing, but I fought the urge to look at Tagget. I fought the urge to look at anything other than John Michael's face.

"Was that part of your investigation?" he asked.

"Yes."

"You didn't tell us anything about that when we met on Saturday night."

"There wasn't anything to tell."

"Wanna tell us now?"

"I was hoping to learn something from people who socialized with the Carpenters. I considered it an undercover operation. Somebody blew my cover."

The looks went around the table: John Michael to Tuttle to Tagget and back to Tuttle. "I understand you blew it yourself," said the chief.

"In any event," John Michael declared quickly, "the chief seems to feel you have your focus a little too narrowly set. There are a couple of reasons why this is important, Patt. One is the general social-political reason, you understand that. The other is that Inspector Lester has just come up with some valuable information that could turn this case around." He pointed at Lester and spoke his name.

The inspector flipped open a little spiral notebook, cleared his throat, and shifted his position so as to address me without looking at me. "On Sunday, the twenty-seventh of October, I located Rasmussin, Douglas A., and spoke to him by telephone. He confirmed that he was hired by Mrs. Rebecca Carpenter on or about the first of September to assume temporary employment at the Carpenters' place of residence, number six Bulham Road, Woodedge. Affirmative that conditions of employment included termination on the fifteenth of October and that was clear to all concerned. Emphasis on 'all,' " he concluded with a flourish.

"How," I asked, "did you locate him, Les?"

"First-class detective work," he said, cutting his eyes away from me and barking out a laugh that sounded like "arf, arf, arf."

"He called his mother and she called you, is that it?"

Lester stopped barking. "Something like that," he said, wiping his mouth.

"Then you called him back."

"Yeah."

"In California."

"Area code 213."

"So you don't even know if it was him you were talking to."

"Oh, it was him all right."

"Is he coming back here?"

"Didn't ask him. Didn't want to scare him till we could get out there to have a go at him face to face."

"That's what we were talking about when you came in, Patt," John Michael said. "We're trying to decide what to do next. Les and the chief would like Les to go out there to interview Rasmussin and talk him into coming back. I'm wondering what you think about that."

"I don't know. Is Les planning on interviewing him as a witness or as a suspect?"

"Well, we bloody well know what you'd do," snorted Lester.

I sighed, showing infinite patience with my pillory. "Les, all we've got on Rasmussin so far is that he disappeared on the day Mrs. Carpenter was killed."

"And she was found in the kind of place only someone like him would take her," chimed in the chief, nodding his great fleshy head.

"Personally," I said, trying to catch John Michael's eye to make sure I was heading in the right direction, "I don't think we've sufficiently explored all our other options."

"Like Wylie Carpenter, you mean," said the chief.

"Not just him."

"Who else is there?" cried Lester. "Mrs. Mitchell?"

"Well," I said, because everyone was waiting for me to come up with a suggestion, "there's Dodge Patterson."

Chief Tuttle sucked in his breath. His face turned red and his meaty jowls began to quiver again.

John Michael put his elbows on the table. He put his hands together and then brought his chin down slowly to rest on his fingertips. He wanted us all to know he was giving full consideration to what I had just said. "You think he might be a suspect because he and Rebecca Carpenter had once been lovers."

The chief groaned. He put his hand to his forehead.

"I was thinking Wylie wasn't the only one wearing a white club sweater that day, and he wasn't the only one missing from the club for a couple of hours that night," I said. "I was thinking Dodge grew up in Woodedge and is as likely as anybody to have an expert knowledge of those woods behind the overlook."

The reaction around the table was palpable. Everyone stirred, adding body movements in support of John Michael's spoken question: "Meaning?"

"That it's possible to use the trail behind the overlook to get to the river, and it's also possible to use it to get to a lot of other places in Woodedge. That's why I was checking it out this morning."

John Michael hesitated. Now it was he who was watching me for signs. He spread his hands. He brought them back together in a soft clap. He smiled, "So what did you learn?"

"Simply that unless the killer was completely familiar with the woods there was no way he could have used them to get back to Stonegate. Not even if there was a full moon, which I understand there wasn't."

"What about using the woods to get to the river?" demanded the chief. "Do you deny the murderer could have done that?"

"It would have been easier," I admitted, and the chief started to look pleased. "On the other hand," I said, putting an end to that reaction, "if it was Rasmussin you're thinking about—indeed, if it was anybody who was robbing Mrs. Carpenter or trying to make it look like a robbery—why didn't your men find the pocketbook somewhere? No thief this side of San Francisco would go running through the woods at night with a pocketbook flopping over his arm. He'd take the wallet out and throw the rest away."

John Michael casually flicked his eyes at Royster, who spoke up for the first time. "Let's put the whole thing into perspective," he said, affecting the voice of reason. "If the kid did it, Rasmussin, what's he going to take her up the overlook for? He can rob her and kill her a whole lot more easily—"

"Unless it was a mistake," interrupted the chief. His eyes were wide. The top of his head was inclined slightly forward. "Unless he took her there for sex, she fought him off, he strangled her by mistake, and then he just grabbed her pocketbook because he knew he would need money in order to make his getaway." He nodded, encouraging others to nod with him.

"Well, what about the sweater fiber we found?" demanded Royster.

"Forget the sweater," the chief snarled back. "Patt's already knocked that out."

John Michael was doing some maneuvering with his lips. They went in and out, over and under each other. He turned to Roselli and Tagget. "How far did you guys search for that pocketbook?"

"All the way to the river," said Roselli, nodding with his boss.

"Beyond that," said Tagget. "All the way to the turnpike. Then all the way along 128 in both directions for a couple of miles. We checked anyplace we thought he could have gone to hitchhike."

John Michael contorted his brow as though he had just come to a difficult decision. "I think I've heard enough for right now, so I'm going to adjourn the meeting and ask the chief and his men to excuse us."

The chief was taken completely by surprise. "What about Patt?" he stammered, pointing a stubby finger at me.

"I'm satisfied for the time being, Wembley. If there are any more incidents like the one Friday night, you be sure to let me know and we'll deal with it then. But I'm going to let him continue with the investigation as he sees fit."

"What about my bloody trip to California?" yelped Lester, and his tone was so sharp that the chief forgot his own problems long enough to lay a trembling hand on Lester's garishly clothed arm.

In a few seconds Lester was pushing back his chair along with the rest of the cops. There were mumbled good-byes and Roselli and Tagget carefully replaced their chairs under the table and then the four men clumped to the door, where the chief turned and made one last appeal.

"I assume I'll be hearing from you?" he said.

"Of course," John Michael said, giving him a smile of blatantly false reassurance.

I watched the door close behind the police entourage and when I turned back I saw that John Michael was studying Ralphie as though trying to remember why he had not booted him out as well. Ralphie hunched forward in his seat, eager to be a part of whatever was about to happen.

"Ralph, tell Patt about the other evidence you boys have just come up with."

Panic streaked across Ralphie's face.

"The credit-card receipt." John Michael made a boosting motion with his hand.

The panic was washed away in a flood of relief. "Oh, yeah," he said, still looking at John Michael. "We traced the murder weapon, the scarf. It was purchased from a place called Burberry's by credit card, signed by Mr. Carpenter on Saturday, the twelfth, three days before she was killed."

I did as Ralphie had done and spoke directly to John Michael. "Now wait a minute," I said. "You think Wylie Carpenter went to the trouble of purchasing 'the murder weapon,' as Ralph calls it, from Burberry's? You think a scarf from Zayre's wouldn't have done the trick just as well? You think he couldn't have used one from the hall closet, maybe?"

Libby spoke up. "We couldn't find any other scarfs in the house. And this one was brand-new. That's what made us suspicious."

I let the remark pass. We all did.

"The fact is, it was done," said John Michael. "Consider what we've got. The man's very wealthy wife is killed. Regardless of how independently wealthy he is, she's got a damn fine piece of property for him to inherit. Okay, that's point one." He held up his index finger. "Point two is, he can't account for his time on the night she was killed." His middle finger went up. "Point three, the weapon, such as it is, was just purchased by him." He waved the three fingers at all of us generally and at me in particular. "So we've got the weapon, we've got the motive, and with his absence we've got the framework for his method."

"Meaning he parks his wife's car at the overlook early in the day, somehow gets himself home and then drives to the club, plays golf, plays cards, leaves the clubhouse to murder his wife and drive her to her own car, and then drives back to the clubhouse and acts as if nothing happened."

John Michael beamed with pleasure that I had remembered and incorporated his theory so exactly. Ralphie, however, was completely lost.

"Does this mean you think Carpenter really did it?" he asked.

John Michael answered him by speaking to me. "I think it's time we took that idea to the grand jury."

Startled, I said, "What about Rasmussin?"

John Michael waved the name away.

"And, well, you haven't even looked into Dodge Patterson."

Royster's booming voice broke the silence that followed. "What possible motive would he have had? What would he possibly have to gain?"

There was more silence. Glances were exchanged between Royster and John Michael.

"I can't answer those questions," I said finally. "I can only tell you that the path behind the overlook also can be followed to the Patterson home by someone who knows what he's doing."

"As well as everywhere else in Woodedge, I think you said."

"Some places easier than others."

John Michael sighed. "All right." He fixed a stare on Ralphie. "Let me talk to these guys alone, will you, Ralph?"

Ralphie looked as if he had just been stabbed, but he did as he was asked and shambled to the door.

When he was gone John Michael put a locker-room grin on his face that did not quite match the burn in his eyes. "Hey, what's the story, Patt? You a little queer for this guy Carpenter, or what? It seems every time we come up with something on him you try to knock it down. Tell me, am I missing some vital point here, or what?"

"It's just, I don't see where we've got enough to prosecute him."

John Michael threw out his hands. His lips opened in a smile that was meant to show a willingness to cast any disagreement in friendly terms. "That's the beauty of the grand jury system. If there's not enough, they'll tell us so. Carpenter's rights are safeguarded by the grand jurors themselves. But it's up to us, hell, it's our duty, to give them the information they need to make that decision. The grand jury's made up of people on the street, Patt. You know that. And right now the people on the street want to know what we have on this case. I think we ought to tell them."

I answered with my eyes pointed at the table. "John, you don't haul a guy before the grand jury unless you're damn sure he's the right man."

"And I'm damn sure of it in this case."

"I think you're moving way too fast."

"I'm not moving fast enough. That's the problem. You see the papers today? I can't get Constantinis off the front page. He wants to have an international architectural competition for his goddamn theme park now. You know what's going on here?" He sat forward, lurched forward. "I've got it figured out. This is a grandstand play he's making, right? He's going for something and he's going for something big. The only big office that's coming up for election next year is the congressional seat. Huh? You see what I'm saying?"

A feeling of amazement slowly spread over me. "You think Jim Kilrain's going to step down? He's only in his fifties, isn't he?"

"Who knows with Jim Kilrain? He and I aren't exactly asshole buddies. I mean, he comes from goddamn Waterford, so who's likely to know what he's got up his sleeve? Constantinis, that's who. And Constantinis isn't pushing that silly Watertowne Plantation out of civic-mindedness, believe me."

Royster shook his head and made clucking noises to show John Michael that he believed him.

"Can you imagine going to Washington, Patt?" John Michael asked, his eyes shining.

"I can't imagine you needing an investigator in Washington, John."

"What do you mean? I'll need something. I'll need you. We're a team, the three of us. Where I go, you guys go."

"And right now where I go is California, is that what you're about to tell me?"

"Hey, and you're gonna complain? The chicks and the sun and the beaches?"

"And Dougie Rasmussin."

"Who's going to turn out to be the key to this case if he's handled right. If I send somebody out there to meet with him I want to be damn sure I know what I'm getting. Follow me?"

He issued penetrating looks that went to both Royster and me.

"Think I can trust Stanley Lester that way?"

He took our silence for the answer he was expecting.

"Not on your life. His loyalty is to that fat shit Tuttle and Tuttle would probably plead guilty himself if he thought it would save one of his precious citizens. You see the way the guy goes crazy because you ruffled a few feathers over there in rich-person's-land, Patt? Well, fuck him. Fuck all those guys. We're gonna do this on our own and we're gonna do it right. If we bring Carpenter before a grand jury we've got to make sure we get an indictment. If we get an indictment we've got to make damn sure we can get a conviction. Now," he paused. "Any reason I can't count on you, Patt?"

"No," I said.

"Good." He paused again, studying me. Then he turned his blue-eyed gaze on Royster. "Any reason I can't count on you, Roy?"

The question surprised me almost as much as it did Royster. He had to clear his throat to get out his denial.

"Good," said John Michael. "Then I want Patt to go out West and if he brings back what I think he will then I want you to handle the grand jury proceedings personally. Snap, Crackle, and Pop. Patt, you, and me, right? We'll take care of this thing from start to finish, right?"

Royster muttered, "Right," and then swiveled his head quickly as if he expected to see some sort of sign pass between John Michael and me.

"Good," said John Michael for the third time. He got to his feet, looking at his watch. "Then that will do for now. Except, Patt, you might want to stick around for a minute or two so we can discuss how we're going to go about approaching Rasmussin." He lowered his watch. He looked at me in all innocence as if it were my feelings he did not want to offend. "That all right?"

I said yes and Royster very slowly and very silently made his way out of the room.

John Michael took a deep breath. He pushed his hands into his pockets and began jingling his keys. He was still staring at the door when he said, "You two don't like each other very much, do you?"

I fought back the urge to say "No shit," and instead told him, "It's not that big a deal, John."

"No," he said, walking around the table toward me. "I think it is. If it's true, I mean. I depend on you two guys one hundred percent and I can't have you backstabbing or bickering or setting each other up. I trust you as much as I trust Jessica, and, believe me, that's a lot of trust. My life's an open book to you. You want something? Let me know. You need something? It's yours. But I expect the same thing from you guys in return. Complete candor. You know what I'm saying?"

"I know what you're saying. I'm not sure why you're saying it."

I was still seated. John was standing next to me, over me,

jingling his keys just a few inches from my face. I was glad when he turned away and walked back to his desk.

"Do you have any reason for believing Roy hasn't been candid in his dealings with you, Patt?" He was bent over, looking through piles of paper.

"Not really." My shoulders were hunched. My voice was on edge. I was not prepared to unload on Royster, not at this time and place, not gratuitously.

John Michael found the piece of paper for which he had been searching. He straightened up while he read it. He spoke without lifting his eyes. "Do you have any reason for believing he's not . . . well, let's use the word 'faithful'?"

The word immediately conjured up images of Royster planted in his secretary, slapping his belly against her bottom; but the context of the question, the tone John Michael was using, told me that he was not asking about Royster's sex life. "No," I said, truthfully. "I think Roy Hansen is a born second-in-command. I think he's your Ed Meese. Your Bob Haldeman."

"The road to my ruin, in other words."

"No. I mean I think he's completely loyal to you. I think he considers your interests his interests. I just don't think he considers my interests to be necessarily the same, that's all."

"Interesting," said John Michael, his brow wrinkled in thought.

After a while I stood up. The motion made John Michael approach me.

"Who," he said, "do you think is most likely to be unfaithful to me?"

When he was close enough, when he saw I wasn't going to answer, he handed me the piece of paper he had retrieved from his desk. It was plain typing paper with no date, no salutation, and no signature. In the middle of the page, in a typical IBM script, it read:

John—
Someone close to you is unfaithful.
Watch out.

"I got that the day you were up in Wylie Carpenter's hometown and I've been holding on to it just to see if there'd be any follow-up. There hasn't. But it's still made me wonder. You don't suppose Roy would be selling us out in any way, do you?"

I remained silent, staring at the typewritten words.

"The only reason I'm asking that, Patt, is because I realize how tricky this Carpenter situation is. It could wipe me out politically if we're not careful. That guy's going to be able to pay for the best defense money can buy and we can't afford to take even the slightest chance."

"I don't think you're taking a chance with Roy, John."

He slipped the letter out of my hand. "And you," he said, holding the letter between us as if it were a Bible on which I was supposed to swear an oath, "the same goes for you, too?"

He looked worried, as if he did not know what my answer would be. I smiled. If he had been a less formal man I would have clapped him on the shoulder. "Yeah," I said.

"You'll go to California and question the kid—Rasmussin, I mean—and you'll get what we need?"

"I'll get what I can."

"We need to know if he was sleeping with Carpenter's wife and we need to know if Carpenter knew about it."

"I understand."

"And once you've got everything you can get I want you to do whatever it takes to convince him to come back here to testify."

"I'll do my best, John."

"Good, Patt. I knew I could trust you."

I stood in a phone booth at Logan Airport with a pen in my mouth. The pen may have been coincidental, but I did not remove it when my call was answered and when a man said "Hello?" I talked around it, using a high-pitched, stuttering, nervous voice that I had not planned on using at all.

"Is Mrs. Patterson there? Mrs. Gretchen Patterson?"

"No, this is Dodge Patterson. May I help you?"

I had had more than enough of Dodge Patterson's help when he crashed our lunch. He had told me nothing of significance and his presence had kept Gretchen and me from communicating on any significant level.

"No, no," I said. "I call back." I used the same high-pitched, stuttering voice.

When I hung up I was sweating profusely. I was sure that he had recognized me, sure that I had made a fool of myself. Thirty-eight years old and I was playing kid tricks, making anonymous phone calls to women and pretending to be somebody I wasn't.

Doug Rasmussin had taken a room in a place called the Apart-Lets in a city called Venice. I rented a little car at the Los Angeles airport, tossed my overnight bag in the trunk, and drove there in a matter of minutes. I was disappointed it was so close.

I had been in California once before. I had gone out to see my high-school girlfriend—girlfriend of sorts—Mary Marie Gastonatto, shortly before I started working for the D.A.'s office. She

THE IMMEDIATE PROSPECT OF BEING HANGED   195

and her sister Angeljean had moved to Newport Beach and, although I had not seen her since my father's death, I had accepted her invitation to visit. It was a mistake. Mary Marie had changed. Her sister had changed. I, apparently, had not.

I had arrived in March and my accent and winter pallor had immediately set me apart from their Southern California friends. I, on the other hand, had failed to appreciate their successes. I had not understood the value of their small condominium within walking distance of the Pacific. I had not admired Mary Marie's breast implants or Angeljean's black boyfriend, who majored in cool and inevitably took Angie, as she was now called, behind closed doors whenever I was around. He was not impressed with my job as an insurance claims supervisor, and neither Angie nor "M" was interested in it either.

"M" was now a sales rep for a sportswear manufacturer. She wore beautiful clothes that emphasized her new cleavage and she drove a little Fiat convertible that looked better than it ran. She was not used to planning where to go or what to do. She was used to having her dates plan for her, and I had no ideas beyond Disneyland and the beach. She said one was too old and the other too cold. I went home early. It seemed better than going to Disneyland alone.

Doug Rasmussin had fared better than I had on his first trip to the West Coast. Venice fit a certain California image for New England guys like us. It had stucco, Spanish-style buildings; elaborate murals painted on public walls; boys towing surfboards behind bicycles, and girls on rollerskates; fancy cars and sporty cars and cars with long sailboards on their roofs.

The building at the address I had been given was boxlike and six stories high. It was ugly, in and of itself, but it was just a few blocks from the ocean and I had learned on my last trip the value of that. I parked my car on the street and did not bother to put any money in the meter since I did not care if the rental company got a ticket, and suspected that neither did the rental company.

I walked through a plain door, over which was painted the word "Apart-Lets," and entered a small lobby. In the lobby was a long unframed mirror that occupied one wall. It was cracked in the lower left-hand corner, cracked clear through so that one piece was separated from the rest. Beneath the mirror were a handful of mismatched chairs arranged around a heavy blond coffee table that bore the marks of a thousand burning cigarettes.

There was a narrow bookcase against another wall. It had four bookshelves and not enough books to fill them. One of the books was volume E of an encyclopedia. Another was entitled *Learn to Swim*.

The only other furnishings in the lobby were an oval braided rug that had lost most of its color, a pay telephone, and a blackboard where someone had written in a large scrawl, "Mitch call home." A different hand had written beneath that, "E.T. wants you."

There was a metal door with a push bar and the word STAIRS stenciled on it. A Bullwinkle sticker obscured the letter I. Another door led to an elevator that was unmarked with words, lights, or floor indicators. Next to that door a reception counter was recessed into the wall. A Japanese lantern hung above the counter. A poster of a middle-aged Ronald Reagan holding a giant sausage was on the wall behind the counter. Taped onto the poster were the words EAT MY MEAT!

A desk clerk looked at me from a chair behind the counter. It was an armchair and because he was sitting down his eyes were barely higher than the countertop. When he wasn't looking at me he was watching a tiny black-and-white television propped on the seat of a straight-back chair.

"Can you tell me what room Mr. Rasmussin is in?" I asked him.

The clerk was dark-haired and dark-skinned and had a jet-black mustache. He concentrated his gaze on the television screen. "Never heard of him."

"Guy's just moved in the past couple of days. Good-looking guy." I pointed a finger to my cheek, where Rasmussin's dimple would be.

"Don't got no guys like that. This a family sort of place."

"This is a family sort of guy. Comes from back east. I think he hitched out here."

"Show me your credentials." The clerk still was not looking at me. He was watching a commercial in which Florence Henderson was pitching Wesson oil. It was a good commercial, I knew, but it lost something on a tiny black-and-white TV.

I said, "I don't got to show you no stinking credentials."

The clerk said, "Try 317."

As I turned to the elevator he said, "It's broken."

As I turned to the metal door with the word STAIRS and the Bullwinkle sticker on it he said, "Don't try to spend the night or I charge the dude twelve bucks."

I walked the two flights of stairs. I found room 317 on a dimly lit hallway that smelled a little of stale cigarette smoke and a lot of cooking tomato sauce. I knocked politely on the door to 317 and nothing happened. I knocked harder and nothing happened. I banged on it once out of frustration and suddenly a voice said, "Yeah, yeah," and pulled it open. Before me was the man in the photo on Mrs. Rasmussin's mantel.

It was after noon, but Doug Rasmussin had still been in bed. I knew this because he answered the door with a sheet wrapped around his otherwise naked body. I also knew it because there was a woman lying in his bed. She had tousled hair, she was still asleep, and, since Dougie had taken her sheet, her bare ass was pointed straight at me. There was a tattoo on one of her cheeks. It was a beautiful ass. It was an admirable tattoo.

The room reeked of alcohol and sex. It was a fairly good-sized room and it contained a kitchenette that had its own mini-refrigerator, two-burnered stove, sink, and linoleum floor. There was some shelf space, a couple of drawers and cabinets, and a breakfast counter that served as a room divider and that had two vinyl-topped stools tucked underneath it. Next to the bed, next to the woman on the bed, was a maple nightstand that held an empty bottle of tequila, some remnants of a lime, a knife, a salt shaker, and two bar glasses. On the floor were some pants and some socks and some panties, a shirt and a blouse. Dougie Rasmussin squinted at me, trying to figure out who I was.

I told him. "Patt Starbuck. I'm from Walmouth."

Dougie's jaw dropped. He rubbed his face. He looked back at his friend, who wasn't moving. He looked at me again. He said, "Walmouth. Jees, that's great," and he seemed to mean it.

I had been prepared for a lot of reactions. I had even been prepared for flight. But Dougie Rasmussin shifted his grip on his sheet and stuck out his right hand for me to shake. "How j'ya know I was from Walmouth?"

"Because I've come out here looking for you." I showed him the card that I had declined to show the desk clerk.

"Shit, what's this mean?" Dougie said, and for a moment he looked worried. It was, however, not the kind of worry that comes from fear.

"You talked with a cop the other day about the death of Rebecca Carpenter, didn't you?"

"Wow! You came all the way out here to see me because of that?"

I was beginning to gather that Dougie did not realize he was a suspect in the murder. "Didn't Inspector Lester tell you someone would be in touch with you?"

Dougie scratched his head. Despite his puffy eyes, unshaven face, and unkempt hair, his appearance was rather appealing. His torso was smooth and muscular, but he carried himself loosely, in an unthreatening, natural sort of manner. He looked like a guy who liked people and expected them to like him. I suspected he would make an excellent salesman.

"He told me, you know, that she died. Listen, you want to come in? Sit down?"

We both glanced around. His naked friend was still on the bed, but there was a black vinyl Danish modern chair in one corner and Dougie pointed to that. "You can sit there and I can sit with her," he said.

We did as he suggested. He shut the door first and then kind of hopped back to the bed. He apologized and said they had had something of a party last night. He pulled a brown blanket over the sleeping woman and sat down on the edge of the bed.

"I just met her," he said. "Imagine that? She asked me to dance. That doesn't happen back in Walmouth, huh?"

I suddenly felt very old, very staid, and very middle-class. But Rasmussin was looking at me as if he and I were two peas in a pod, just a couple of freewheeling young men come out to California to party and seek our fortune.

"She says her name's Laraine. You know what she is? She's a singer in a rock-and-roll band. Look." He got down and scrambled around on his knees until he pulled something up from under the bed. "Leather pants," he said, holding them up for me to admire.

His delight was not the kind you could resent or mock. It was too genuine. He was too anxious to share it. I was beginning to ache in the pit of my stomach.

"How did you get out here?" he asked.

"I flew, Dougie. I just got off the plane."

"That's amazing, isn't it? What did it take, five-six hours? You got up this morning back in Walmouth and now you're sitting here. It took me, what, about twelve days to get out here. But you shoulda seen some of the people I met. Talk about wee-yud. I got picked up by this one guy, he told me he'd just gotten out of jail. You know why? You won't believe this. He got arrested for screwing a dead girl . . . Seriously."

Dougie Rasmussin looked at me with amazement, his eyes reflecting all the wonder of the universe. "You know why he got let go? Because the charge against him was screwing a dead person in the street and the judge says to the D.A., 'What's the evidence this man knew the woman was dead?' And the D.A. said, 'Well, it's against the law to screw anybody in the street.' Judge smashes down his gavel. Says, 'Can't charge him with that. That'd be double jeopardy. Case dismissed.'"

Dougie waited for my reaction.

I shifted my legs so that one was over the other. I said, "Dougie, didn't Inspector Lester tell you that you were wanted for questioning in connection with the death of Mrs. Carpenter?"

Dougie's head bobbed as if he had just been tagged with a glancing blow. He kept a portion of his grin intact. After all, he had just told me a story. "You're shittin' me," he said at last.

"What did he say to you?"

"He asked me if I was the Douglas Rasmussin who came from 1429 Merrymount Ave. and if I had worked for the Carpenters."

I nodded because he wanted me to.

"He asked me when I had left the Carpenters and I told him, you know, whenever it was. Then he asked me when was the last time I seen Mrs. Carpenter. I said the morning of the day I left. She gave me my check and said good-bye and all. There wasn't anything wrong with her then."

"There wouldn't have been, Dougie. She was strangled to death."

Dougie gulped. I could see his Adam's apple move. "How?"

"With a scarf."

"Whose?"

"Her own."

"That's funny. I don't remember her wearing scarfs."

"This was a new scarf."

He nodded. "Oh."

"What else did Inspector Lester ask you?"

"Only, you know, did the Carpenters know when it was I was planning on leaving and I said, 'Yes, of course.'"

"And did he ask you who hired you?"

"Oh, yeah," Dougie said quickly. "Mrs. Carpenter."

The woman on the bed stirred. She lifted her head and peered at Dougie. It seemed to take her a long time to focus. "Arggh," she said, and dropped straight down onto the mattress again. Dougie patted her. He rubbed his hand up and down her back to make her feel better.

I said, "Dougie, why did you leave when you did?"

"Huh? Oh, because it was all planned that way. I mean, Mrs.

Carpenter came to me one day and said she'd heard I'd done some yardwork and she needed somebody, you know, because she'd just had to let her people go." He turned away, checking on his friend again. I had the impression he wanted to get off the subject.

"You told her you could do it?"

"Sort of. Well, for a few weeks anyhow, and she said that was fine. We agreed I'd work until October fifteenth and that would still give me time to get across country before it got too cold."

"You had already decided you were definitely going to come out here?"

"Yeah. Uh-huh."

I said, "How did you know Mrs. Carpenter?"

"Oh, from the pool. At Stonegate."

"Dougie." I unfolded my legs. "She didn't belong to Stonegate."

"Yeah, but she'd come out sometimes. With a friend or somebody."

"Which friend?"

"I don't remember."

"Gretchen Patterson?"

"Yeah. I guess. Sometimes."

"Can you think of anybody else?"

Dougie's eyes were rolling. He was trying. "No," he said at last.

"Were you friends with Gretchen Patterson?"

"Not really. No."

"You taught her son to swim, didn't you?"

"That's how I knew her."

"But Mrs. Carpenter, you were better friends with her, were you?"

"We became friends, yes."

"What kind of things would you talk about with her?"

"Oh, yard things. Property things." He nodded. "Stuff related to my job."

"Did she seem to like the job you were doing for her?"

"Seemed to." Dougie was rubbing his bed companion again. It required him to keep his eyes on her back.

"Did she seem to want you to leave?"

"No. No. She said I was doing good."

"You think she would have kept you on for as long as you wanted?"

"Yeah."

"So it wasn't her idea for you to leave when you did."

"No, it was my idea—you know, October fifteenth."

"Then I'm a little confused, Dougie, because, you see, I talked to some of your buddies at Balducci's, some of the guys on the softball team, and they told me the woman you were working for encouraged you to come out here."

"Oh, yeah." He stopped rubbing. "She did some of that, too."

"These guys said she kept drilling it into your head that you were never going to amount to anything as long as you stayed around Walmouth."

"That's true." He waved an index finger at me, indicating he remembered now.

I cocked my head. I squinted one eye. I asked the next question as though it were a really hard thing for me to do. "What kind of reasons did she give for telling you that?"

Dougie Rasmussin took a moment to tuck in his sheet to make it look more like a toga. "Oh," he said, his chin pressed against his neck as he looked down at his handiwork, "she'd just always tell me how important it is to decide what you want and then go out there and make it happen. She liked to say nothing's ever going to come to you if you sit there dreaming about it."

"And did she explain what she meant by that?"

Dougie blinked, as if he did not understand what was unclear about what he had just said. "She asked me, you know . . . if I could have any job in the world, what would I choose."

I nodded, encouraging him. "What did you tell her?"

"I told her, if I could have any job in the world, I'd like to have Johnny Carson's. Have a job like his, you know?"

"And did she think that was something you could do if you came out here?"

Dougie, to his credit, eyed me closely to see if I was serious. "What it did was, it got us talking. Like, what was it about his job that I liked and could I get to do some of that same stuff in other jobs. And her big thing was—"

"Whose?"

Dougie ran his fingers through his hair. "Mrs. Carpenter's. Her big thing was that I was never going to take the chances I needed to take as long as I kept hanging around with the same guys at the same places. It wasn't the guys or the places so much as it was being comfortable, you know what I mean?" He laughed. "I mean, she told me the one way I could make sure I wasn't never gonna get in movies or television or anything like that was to keep hanging around Balducci's. That's why she said I gotta come out here."

The woman, Laraine, was stirred by Dougie's laughter. She curled her hands into fists and pushed herself into a kneeling position. Her face was thin and her features were rather sharp, but her eyes were an intriguing green and they were set off nicely by the dark, stringy curls that fell into her face. She looked at me as though I had caused her a great deal of pain. "What is this bullshit?" she said.

"Hey, babe," Dougie told her as he slipped his arm around her shoulders, "this is a guy from back home."

He had such an innocent, engaging way about him that I actually found myself angered when Laraine shrugged him away. She crawled to the edge of the bed and stood up, stark naked. Her legs were long and thin. Her breasts were long and thin. Her waist was narrow. Her thatch of hair was very black and obviously sculpted.

"Where the fuck are my pants?" she demanded, and Dougie tossed them to her. She was starting to put them on when she leaned over and picked up her panties. They were red and they were torn. "Jesus," she said to no one, "what happened to these?"

"You want some breakfast?" Dougie asked her.

The woman gave him a withering look. She picked up all her clothes and walked into the bathroom and shut the door.

Dougie turned to me, undiscouraged. "How about you?"

I said, leaning forward, my elbows on my knees, "I'm amazed, Doug. You're the first person I've talked to who actually seemed to have any kind of conversations with Becky Carpenter."

He shrugged. "She was nice enough."

"You're pretty good with women, aren't you?"

He caught my eye. He grinned modestly but quickly looked away again, as though he did not want his secret to get out.

"Was she interested in you?"

We heard the toilet flush. We heard the shower start. Dougie said, "She liked me okay."

"Did your relationship go beyond work?"

There seemed to be something on Doug Rasmussin's knuckles that required his complete attention.

I said, "The woman was killed, Dougie. She died the day you left Massachusetts. She was found at a lovers' lane with her pantyhose ripped and her neck broken and there are people who think you did it."

Dougie's head snapped so fast and so far his own neck could have broken if it hadn't been so muscular. "Cut the shit," he said.

"No shit. This is serious business. I wouldn't be here if it weren't. Rebecca Carpenter was an important woman and somebody killed her and somebody's going to fry for it."

"Well, it won't be me." He was adamant.

"What do I have to prove it wasn't you?"

He had raised his jaw, folded his lips together. He had to unfold them to talk. "I could sleep with her anyplace I wanted. I didn't have to take her to no lovers' lane."

"Where did you sleep with her, Dougie?"

"Outside under the trees. In the caretaker's cottage. In her own bed once when Sarah wasn't around."

"Who knew that you were lovers?"

"Nobody got it offa me."

"What about the boys at Balducci's?"

"Oh, yeah, well . . . I guess I said some things to them."

"Do you think her husband knew?"

"Once I started working there him and me never really spoke. I'd see him sometimes, but he'd just kinda look at me."

"Like he was looking for something?"

"Sorta."

"Had you ever spoken to him before you worked for him?"

"Oh, yeah. We used to talk all the time at the club."

I was digesting this information when the bathroom door opened and Laraine stepped out toweling her hair. She had on her black leather pants and a white blouse of the style where the shoulder seams hung halfway down her arms. She spoke as she walked toward us. "Anybody still up for breakfast?"

We ate at a place that served breakfast around the clock. At three in the afternoon there were a good number of people in need of eggs and pancakes. Most of these people did not look as though they had just gotten off work.

I did my best to be circumspect around Dougie's friend Laraine, but I was not altogether successful. When Dougie got up to go to the men's room she lost no time in asking me the big question.

"You a cop?"

"No."

"You act like a cop."

"I do not."

She shrugged. We were in a booth and she sat back in a two-point position with her arms folded across her breasts, her long thin breasts that I knew were lurking just beneath the surface of her blouse. "Then why're you hassling the poor dude?" she asked.

"I'm not hassling him."

"I heard the questions you were asking him. You think he did something."

"I don't *think* he did anything. I want to know what he did."

"Why?"

"It's my job."

She was enjoying this. I could tell by the smirk that was building on her face. "Just exactly what is your job, if you're not a cop?"

"I coordinate litigation for a bunch of lawyers. I help them prepare their cases."

"What kind of lawyers?"

"Public lawyers."

"You mean like government lawyers? Like district attorney lawyers?"

"Something like that."

"Oh, brother," she said, and her smirk blossomed.

I had been about to take a sip of coffee, but now I put my cup down. "What's that supposed to mean?"

She raised her leg, her knee bent, and put her foot down flat on the bench next to her. It was a provocative way to sit and it made me look at the long leather rise of her calf and the long leather plummet of her thigh. The pants were supple but very tight, and they hugged her as if they were her own skin. "It means," she said, "why would anybody want a job like that?"

I looked down at my plate and what was left of my eggs and hash browns. There are few things uglier than egg yolk on a plate and I smoothed the remnants of my hash browns around to cover the yellow as much as possible. "It can be interesting."

"What, getting involved in other people's misery?"

"I don't look at it that way."

She dropped her hand behind her. She slid further down in her seat. "How do you look at it?"

"I look at it as a job, just a job. Somebody gets hurt, somebody gets killed—somebody's got to figure out who did it, make sure he doesn't do it again."

"But it doesn't work, does it? You capture one person, it doesn't stop someone else from doing the same thing."

"So what's the alternative?" I offered her a smile, not because I felt like it but because I wanted to get out of the conversation. "I don't have any illusions about putting an end to crime, if that's what you're talking about."

"What do you have illusions about?" She was still slouched,

still leaning back. Her foot was still on the bench and her knee was still in the air.

"Nothing," I said.

Now she sat up. Her black leathered leg went beneath the table. "Don't you have illusions about helping people? Saving society? Making the world a better place? Isn't that how you justify going around doing what you're doing—scaring the shit out of everyone, asking them questions, setting them up for arrests?"

"Look . . . Laraine . . . if it's any of your business, I don't do the arresting and I don't make the decisions as to who gets arrested, okay? I try to find evidence as to who did what, and when I get it I bring it to the prosecutors. What they do with it is their business."

"And you don't give a damn what they do with it, is that what you're saying?"

"That's right."

Laraine's mouth opened. Her tongue ran between her parted teeth as she stared at me thoughtfully. "So, then . . . you don't really care whether what you're doing is helping anyone or not."

Exasperated, I answered too loudly. "Hey, if a crime's committed and I come up with the evidence that solves it then I've helped everybody. Everybody."

The conversation stopped at the table next to us. The diners looked over. I looked down at my plate again. "Now, can we talk about something else?" I said softly. "Please?"

But Laraine persisted. "Does it ever bother you, the people you hurt along the way?"

"I told you, I just gather the evidence."

"Would you gather evidence against somebody you knew wasn't guilty?"

"It's not up to me to determine if someone's guilty."

Laraine leaned forward. Her green eyes held mine. I thought she was going to ask me another question and I leaned forward to meet her. "You know what I think?" she whispered. "I think you're a fascist."

I straightened slowly and tried not to look to see if the people at the next table were still watching us. "So," I said calmly, "what do you do for a living?"

She gave my question the time needed to make it perfectly clear that I wasn't getting away with anything. "I heard Dougie tell you," she said. "I'm a singer."

"You, ah, between bands or just between gigs?"

"What makes you think I'm between anything?"

"Because," I said, dropping even the semblance of politeness from my voice, "if you were making any money you wouldn't have spent the night in Rasmussin's shithole of a room."

She swallowed, but other than that she never moved and her eyes were still the green shafts they had been. "Maybe I've got a husband or a boyfriend. Maybe I live too far away to go home. Maybe I was just too drunk to know the difference."

"Maybe," I agreed. "On the other hand, you haven't been in any hurry to leave and the afternoon's almost gone."

Laraine's features, narrow to begin with, took on a pinched appearance. "You know what I think?"

"Yes."

"How could you?"

"Because there's not that much to know."

Suddenly Dougie was back at the table, standing next to us with a big smile on his face. "How're you guys doing?" he asked.

Laraine told him. "Your friend's an asshole."

Dougie looked crestfallen. His loyalties were clearly divided between his girlfriend of one night and his fellow Walmouthian. He wanted us to like each other. He wanted to say just the right thing. "Oh, gee," he declared. It was not enough.

Laraine shoved her way out of the booth. She put her hand on Dougie's chest and shoved him a bit, too. "You want to stay with him, you stay. I'm leaving."

Dougie watched her stride toward the door. Everyone in the place, it seemed, watched her stride toward the door. People were leaning out of their seats to watch her go.

Dougie made up his mind quickly. It may have had something

to do with the exquisiteness of her walk, the perfect sway of her hips in her tight leather pants, but he made a grab for his wallet and told me he had to go after her.

I reached out and caught his wrist before he was able to get the wallet out of his back pocket. "Dougie, I've got to finish with you."

"What do you want?" he said, looking pained.

"I want you to come home to testify."

"But I just got out here."

"We'll provide you with a round-trip plane ticket. You come home, you tell a grand jury what you told me, you can fly back the same day."

Laraine had hit the sidewalk. Through the restaurant's plate-glass window we could see her turn and walk in the opposite direction from the Apart-Lets. "Who'll I be testifying against?"

"I can't tell you that. I can only promise that you won't be the focus of the grand jury's investigation."

"All right," he said, not looking at me. "I'll do it."

"You'll be coming back to the Apart-Lets tonight?"

"Yes . . . no. I don't know. It depends on Laraine."

"But I can reach you there?"

"Yeah. Just leave a message with Zorro at the front desk."

"Good. You run and catch her then. I'll take care of the tab."

"I can pay."

"It's all right. Go. Run."

In a moment I was alone, remembering how much I hated being alone, wondering what it was about me that brought out the worst in the women of California, and deciding that I probably wouldn't carry out any plan I may have had to give Mary Marie Gastonatto a call after all.

John Michael struck quickly. On the Monday following my return from the West Coast he had Wylie S. Carpenter arrested at his place of business, Woodedge Savings and Loan. It was a staged arrest, with the three Boston television stations waiting on the street with their Minicams to record a grim-looking Inspector Stanley Lester, resplendent in a green and yellow plaid sport coat, leading out a handcuffed, ashen-faced Wylie. The cameras on the six- and the eleven-o'clock news clearly showed the horror-stricken employees of the savings and loan gathered at the doors and windows as their boss was guided by his elbow down the walk to a waiting patrol car.

John Michael defended his choice of arrest locations at a little celebratory gathering at his house that evening. "I could have done it at one of his clubs in front of all his hoity-toity friends," he explained. "What do you think he'd rather do, lose a little business or bring shame down on his peers?"

Jessica, who was wearing a low-plunging V-neck cashmere sweater that revealed a hitherto undisclosed array of freckles on her chest, wanted to clink glasses with everyone. She hit mine, she hit her husband's, she hit Royster's, and then she kind of waved her glass in Patty's general direction because Patty was standing behind Royster and looking down at the carpet.

"You could have arrested him at his home, I guess," I said.

I had, everyone knew, argued against an arrest at all. I had suggested that the grand jury be used as an investigative body looking into the murder without a named suspect. "That way," I had said, "we can get Wylie himself to testify without him pulling a lot of Fifth Amendment crap." But John Michael had overruled me. He had said we didn't need Wylie to testify, all we needed was me.

Now John Michael listened to my latest complaint, subtle though it was, and stared into his glass of Pepsi. "That long driveway," he said. "A parade of cars going up there could have tipped him off. I couldn't take any chances on what he might do. It's a lot safer this way."

Inasmuch as Wylie was an accused scarf murderer, I well understood the vast array of household weapons he might have brought to bear on the Woodedge Police Department. I could picture Lester cautioning his mates, "Keep him away from the bureau. That's where he keeps those bloody chokers. And don't let him near his golf bag."

But everyone else was murmuring agreement and Royster suddenly exclaimed, "You know what I can't believe is who he got for a lawyer."

When we had decided to go ahead with the arrest we had spent a good part of Sunday afternoon speculating on who Wylie might get to represent him. Names of all the top Boston attorneys had been thrown out alongside those of the brighter lights of Exeter County. No one had ever once mentioned Phil Burns, and yet that was who showed up at the arraignment.

"He won't keep him," John Michael assured us.

"He was probably the only guy Wylie could get on a moment's notice," Jessica added. "Right now Wylie's probably meeting with Joseph Oteri or F. Lee Bailey."

"I hope he gets Lee," John Michael said, squeezing his face into a little pocket of flesh and shuffling his feet. "Imagine the attention we'd get if Lee came into it?"

"On the other hand," Royster replied, "Burnsie showed up at the arraignment looking reasonably sober. Maybe he'll fool Wylie." He chuckled and showed everybody his white teeth. In a spontaneous gesture that more than anything else revealed the euphoria he was feeling he grabbed his wife around the shoulders and hugged her to him.

Patty rocked stiffly onto one foot, was forced to nuzzle into Royster's neck, and then rocked back again. She looked at me. She looked at John Michael. Her cheeks flushed.

I said, to get everyone's attention away from her, "Old Burnsie didn't do so bad today, getting Carpenter out of there on a hundred thousand dollars' bail. Not really what you'd expect for a rich man and a capital crime."

"Yeah, what did he have to post, a ten-thousand-dollar bond?" said John Michael. "He probably paid for that out of what he had in his wallet."

Royster slurped his grin a little tighter. He was focused on John Michael. "Ah, we didn't really fight Burnsie too hard on that. We knew Wylie Carpenter wouldn't be taking off anywhere. Not a prominent citizen like him."

"Let's hope he's prominent enough to make the goddamn *Courier* forget about Constantinis for a day or so," said John Michael. "But I suppose with my luck the stock market will fold tomorrow or the Russians will invade Maine or the governor will be caught exposing himself to a group of schoolchildren in New Bedford."

"Still," said Jessica, gathering glasses for a new round of drinks, "you don't want Wylie's conviction to be a foregone conclusion. If everybody thinks he's guilty from the moment he's arrested, there'll be no story to tell."

John Michael slapped his forehead. "Oh, my God, I just had an awful thought."

We all turned to him in alarm. The word "What?" came out of all our mouths.

"What if we get him indicted by the grand jury and the son-ofabitch pleads guilty?"

"Then," said Royster, hooking his thumbs in his armpits and mugging around at all of us, "I guess I'll be the one who runs for Congress."

He may have been expecting more laughter than he actually

got; but Patty was too busy watching me, and I was too busy watching John Michael and Jessica. And they were too busy catching each other's eye.

It is entirely possible that there are people charged before grand juries in Massachusetts who are not indicted. I may even have read about some from time to time. The odds, however, are not in favor of the subject of the investigation.

The Exeter County Grand Jury had been impaneled for twenty-seven days of their thirty-day term when Royster Hansen presented them with the case of *Commonwealth* v. *Carpenter*. The grand jurors knew why they were there. They sat, twenty-three of them, in sixteen fixed jurors' chairs and seven broad-bottomed wooden armchairs in a sealed-off corner courtroom on the second floor of our building on Court Street.

They were bored for the most part. They were mostly of retirement age and overwhelmingly working-class in appearance. There were fourteen men and nine women, including one black, but no Asians or other discernible minorities. If any of them came from Woodedge they were doing a good job of disguising it.

I am told that they perked up considerably when Royster informed them of the matter involving Mr. Carpenter. And since Mr. Hansen was ungoverned by any judge and unhampered by any opposing counsel, he could describe the action in pretty much any way he pleased.

The Annotated Laws of Massachusetts provide that the only persons who may be present during a grand jury proceeding are attorneys for the commonwealth who may be convenient to the presentation of evidence, the witness under examination, the attorney for the witness under examination, "and such other persons who are necessary or convenient to the presentation of evidence." In the grand jury proceedings involving the case of *Commonwealth* v. *Carpenter* it was determined by the attorney representing the commonwealth, Royster Hansen, that no other "such persons" except the court reporter were necessary. It was his show and my only knowledge of what actually took place came while I was on the stand being examined under oath by Royster.

The one problem of which I was aware came with respect to Dougie Rasmussin. When I called him several days before he was scheduled to appear, I was told by Zorro, the desk clerk at the Apart-Lets, that he was not there. I had anticipated this situation and had gone out of my way to avoid it by leaving Zorro a ten-dollar bill. Zorro, however, remembered the ten dollars. He remembered me. He would have been more than happy to earn another ten dollars by telling me where Dougie had gone, but he didn't know, because Dougie had simply moved out and had left no forwarding address. He had done it when Zorro was not on duty and there was nothing Zorro could do.

"That's not insurmountable," said John Michael, cracking a pencil between his fingers when he learned of Dougie's disappearance. "You can present hearsay evidence before a grand jury. It doesn't invalidate the indictment."

And so my task, guided by the leading questions of Royster Hansen, was to tell the jurors not only what I had seen and determined, but what I had heard. I was on the stand only ninety minutes, but by the time I was done twenty-three members of the Exeter County Grand Jury had reason to believe that Wylie S. Carpenter's wife was having an affair with Douglas Rasmussin, that Wylie had lied when he told me he did not know Rasmussin was leaving the state on the fifteenth of October, that Wylie's presence could not be accounted for during a period of two hours on the night of the fifteenth, and that my investigation—and my observations of Inspector Lester's investigation—indicated that Rebecca Carpenter had been placed in the front seat of her Mercedes after she had been killed. This last item, of course, was not so much what the investigations had indicated to me as it was what they had indicated to John Michael, but the distinction was not required to be made in my answers to Royster's questions.

Other matters were left to other witnesses, but I apparently did a good job in my role because Royster lost his head for a

moment on the night after my testimony and actually complimented me. In any event, on the thirtieth and final day of the
grand jury's term they handed down a bill of indictment charging
Wylie S. Carpenter with the murder of his wife, Rebecca Chesley
Carpenter.

22

John Michael got the attention he was seeking, or some of it anyway. The *Courier* put the indictment on the front page, but it was put at the bottom and the caption read, WOODEDGE MAN TO STAND TRIAL IN WIFE'S MURDER.

The Keoughs had been hoping for a good deal more. They thought the case should have had enough notoriety to mention Carpenter by name in a headline. They thought the article should have been more explosive and they were quite upset by the negative slant they perceived from the reporter, a woman named Lia Chapin whom none of us knew.

The article read:

> An Exeter County Grand Jury has indicted Wylie S. Carpenter for the October 15th murder of his wife, Rebecca. Mr. Carpenter, 48, reigning golf champion of the Bollingbrook and Stonegate Country Clubs, is a director of Woodedge Savings & Loan and a prominent member of Woodedge society.
>
> According to Deputy District Attorney Royster Hansen, the motive in the killing of Rebecca Carpenter, 40, was a combination of greed and revenge. "Mr. Carpenter discovered that his wife was having an affair," said Hansen. "His method for dealing with that left him in a position to inherit her multi-million dollar estate."
>
> Mrs. Carpenter was the sole child of the late financier and art patron Walter Chesley, and the last survivor of a family whose influence spans the history of Woodedge,

dating back to the arrival of Reverend Thomas Chesley
in the year 1700. Her body was found in the front seat
of her automobile at an overlook off Ivanhoe Road. She
had been strangled with a scarf her husband was known
to have purchased three days before.

Mr. Carpenter, who is currently free on $100,000 bail,
could not be reached for comment. However his lawyer,
former District Attorney Philip Burns, was succinct in
his response to the indictment. "It's bull——," he said.
"Pure and absolute bull——. It is the product of a totally
inept legal system."

Many of those who know Mr. Carpenter appeared
stunned by the charge. "Wylie wouldn't hurt a flea,"
said Gerard Whitman, President of Whitman Orthopedic Supply Company, and one of the town's largest
employers. "He has been devastated by the death of his
wife and I can't believe he had anything to do with it.
The whole thing smacks of a witch hunt to me."

Trial has been set to begin on January 6th and Burns
vowed it would go forward that day. "We're not waiving
Wylie Carpenter's right to a speedy trial," he said. "We
don't think the D.A.'s office has anything on this man
and we want his name cleared as fast as possible."

"The money angle," John Michael screamed, throwing the
newspaper at Royster so that Royster had to raise his hands to
keep from getting hit in the face. "You had specifics you could
have given that reporter, whoever the hell she is. The sixty-three-
million-dollar inheritance. The twenty-five-acre estate on Bulham
Road, the mountaintop retreat in Vermont, and the twelve-room
cottage on the ocean in Osterville. You should have called Freddie
Murray, he would have known how to write the story. But if you
didn't, if you got this broad, you should have at least had enough
sense to give her a hook, something she could use to make her
story better than the next person's story. Give it to her, goddammit, Roy. Give it to her."

Jessica, who had brought the newspaper to us, was trying to
mollify her husband. "I think what John is telling you, Roy, is
that you don't waste an opportunity like this by summing every-

thing up with a phrase like 'multimillion-dollar estate.' Isn't that what you meant, honey?"

Jessica, once again, was dressed differently than I had ever seen her. She was wearing a black sweater with a few colorful horizontal stripes, a black leather skirt that ended above her knees, and black stockings. She had fine legs and she looked good. But I appeared to be the only one who was noticing.

John Michael was carrying his rant around the room. "The reporter's got to fill up her space. You don't give her enough to do it and she's going to keep calling other sources until she's got enough. The more people she calls the less control we have over what she writes. It's as simple as that."

Royster was fuming. When he spoke only his bottom lip moved and only his bottom teeth showed. "I called Miles Bell directly. This is who he had call me back. I gave her the story and this is what she did with it."

John Michael, from across the room, whirled and said, "No written press release?"

Royster drummed his fingers.

"You couldn't manage to write one for the crime of the decade?"

Roy drummed harder. "I figured, I'd give her the story as fast as I could. The indictment comes down at two o'clock, I'm on the phone to Miles at two-oh-five. She's back to me at two-fifteen. I know she's going to talk to Burnsie and it seems to me the most important thing is to get our version to her before the evening edition comes out."

"So it's five o'clock now and the evening edition is out and whosever's version she's got it ain't yours. How do you suppose she got ahold of this other guy that fast? The big shot? Gerard Whitman?"

I spoke up. "He was one of the guys who was playing golf and cards with Wylie that day."

"I know who he is, for Chrissake. But how did she?"

"She's probably one of those gung-ho types," Royster muttered after a long silence. "Thinks she's breaking Watergate or something."

John Michael came back to the table. "We want her to think that way, Roy. We want her digging. But we want her digging up what we know is out there." He was trying to be reasonable now, trying to control his temper. "We don't want her getting blanket statements from us and then having to go elsewhere to get her details. You don't have time to write a press release? Then find out what her favorite booze is, and send her a case of it."

Royster's lips pursed and unpursed.

"Maybe," said Jessica, advancing on us tentatively, "we should call Miles and try to get this girl taken off the story. Ask him to put Freddie on it."

John Michael massaged his jaw a while before saying no. "I don't know. This Lia Chapin may be just what the doctor ordered if we can feed her the right stuff. Let's just play it cool with her for now. Except, Roy, if she contacts you again, you put her right through to me and let me talk to her."

Royster said nothing.

"Got it?"

Royster said yes.

The Keoughs were not the only ones upset about the newspaper article. There was a message waiting for me when I came out of the meeting. Gretchen Patterson had called and wanted a call back.

"Hi," was all I said when I reached her, but she knew right away who it was.

She was trying to modulate her voice. "How could you have done this?" she asked.

I told her I didn't do anything.

"But I explained to you that Wylie couldn't possibly have killed Becky, Patt, and here the newspaper says you've gone and indicted him."

I didn't correct her. I didn't say I didn't indict him. I said, "All you told me was that Wylie didn't do it. You didn't tell me why."

"The why is simple. You just have to know the man."

Once again I had an opportunity to tell Gretchen how little my opinion counted in the office's prosecutorial decisions. Once again I tried to impress her with my silence on the subject.

She caught her breath. "What if I were to tell you that I know where he was during those missing hours you're so concerned about?" The words were said slowly, as if each had been individually selected.

"Are you going to tell me he was with you?"

"Yes."

"You told me before he wasn't."

"I lied. I was afraid." She hesitated. "I told you why I didn't want any of this to come out. I thought, you know, it wouldn't be necessary."

"And now you're willing to testify?"

"Now I'm willing to tell you the truth about that night."

"That may not be good enough."

"I think we should meet."

"When?"

"Now."

"Where?"

"You know where the Marriott is?"

When I was a child growing up in West Nestor, the Marriott River Inn did not exist. The land on which the Marriott River Inn now stands was occupied by Algonquin Park, a very clean and rather leisurely-paced amusement area that offered an array of nonvertical rides, the usual games of chance and competition, boating facilities for the River Charles, an outdoor movie screen that showed mostly free travelogues, a fenced-in bear den, and a number of grassy picnic areas. There was also a ballroom, where teenagers and young couples would go on Friday and Saturday nights to see crooners such as Mario Lanza.

About the time I entered junior high, Algonquin Park was

closed and the rides, the games, the movie screen, the bears, and the ballroom all disappeared in favor of a paved parking lot and a huge multi-unit structure that eventually became the Marriott River Inn. The boating stayed, as did one or two of the picnic areas. Neither kept much of the ambience of Algonquin Park.

By the time I was thirty-eight, however, by the time I approached the River Inn on a cold November night, it looked immensely inviting. Its red neon shimmered its reflection off the water. Its lobby looked busy and affluent. People hurried to and from its doors wearing nice topcoats and wool scarfs. A doorman looked happy to be of service. "Ah," he said, when I told him where I wanted to go, "the apartments!"

He directed me to a separate building, where I rode a wood-paneled and carpeted elevator to the third floor and trudged down a quiet and pleasantly decorated hallway. I found the number 397 and stood for a moment before knocking.

I stood long enough to finish the Velamint I was chewing, to run my hand through my hair, to think weird thoughts: like whether I should have brought a bottle of champagne; like how I was going to react if she was dressed in something revealing, or if she was dressed in nothing at all.

I knocked, the door opened, and Gretchen Patterson was wearing a long cable-knit sweater and a black turtleneck jersey over a pair of plain black slacks. She might have been dressed to go to the supermarket or her son's mighty-tots soccer game. But her dark hair tumbled over one shoulder, her dark face looked at me anxiously, and I found her immensely alluring.

"Patt," she said huskily, and if she had opened her arms I would have moved right into them and swept her off her feet and carried her back to whatever unseen bed lay behind the door she was holding closed against her leg.

"Hi, Gretchen," I said softly.

"I'm glad you came," she said in that same deep, almost breathless voice.

She pushed open the door to reveal a mini-apartment with a

galley kitchen, a small dining area, a living room, a door that led to a bedroom, and a little boy sitting at a desk painstakingly drawing on a piece of paper. "Welcome," she said.

I stepped inside. Ian barely glanced up. The feeling coursing through me was beyond disappointment. It was one of foolishness. "Is this yours?" I asked.

She put her finger to her lips and rolled her eyes back toward her son.

It was a comfortable enough apartment, equipped with everything an American living space requires, as well as a few extras, like a bar and a VCR attached to the TV and a set of wall bookshelves stocked with paperbacks. The furnishings were serviceable and solid and looked fairly expensive, but they were totally undistinguished and there was no artwork or knicknacks or anything other than the paperbacks that reflected a personal touch. I walked into the galley kitchen because Gretchen was directing me that way. It had a coffeemaker and an electric can opener and a Waring blender on otherwise immaculately empty counters. Gretchen walked to the steel sink, turned, and took up a leaning position against it. She put one fingernail between her teeth and looked at me. The light here was brightest, perhaps the brightest in the whole apartment, and it would have been harsh to most women in their mid-thirties, but it only offered Gretchen's skin as a study in perfection.

"What is this?" I said, taking up a lean of my own, my hands in my pockets, the base of my spine against the countertop.

"It's Wylie's place. Woodedge Savings and Loan's place. It's where they keep visitors, special guests, and so forth." She was whispering. "There aren't many of those."

"So this is where you and Wylie meet?"

Her great dark eyes flicked in the direction of her son, sitting behind a wall and out of sight. "Every week . . . for a while." She dropped her voice even lower. "Until Becky died."

"You were able to get away every week without—"

"I'm able to get away when my father-in-law watches Ian. He'll only do that if he knows exactly where I'm going. It was okay to go to Becky's—good family, you know—or maybe to the Woodedge Woman's Club because his wife was a member there."

"What, exactly, is the Woodedge Woman's Club?" I asked, unwilling to let that valuable bit of information pass by no matter how confused I was on every other issue.

But Gretchen waved away my inquiry. "Oh, it's absolutely nothing. Clare Ransom's wife Emily founded it to indulge her philanthropic instincts and guarantee herself a place in heaven."

"But what do you do there?"

"Nothing. They have lectures once a week and an annual antique sale and they plant the flowers in front of town hall and I may be the only active member under fifty."

"Becky wasn't?"

"They don't serve booze."

"Molly, Hannah . . . ?"

"Wouldn't be caught dead there."

"Then why would you?"

"To get me out of the house on Tuesday nights. I'd go to the lecture or whatever they were having, or say I was, and then slip away for two-three-four hours to meet Wylie."

"So that's what happened that night Rebecca was killed. You said you were going to the Woman's Club and Wylie threw his card game and here's where you ended up."

Gretchen raised her fingernail to her lips again. She looked at me for a moment before answering. "Basically."

I shifted my position, nodding, crossing and uncrossing my legs, glancing around the brightly lit kitchen. "What is it, about ten minutes from Stonegate to here? Fifteen maybe? Doesn't leave much time for foreplay."

It was a shot, a dig, and Gretchen took it. She checked to see what she had done to her nail. "Things weren't always ideal," she said. "I don't imagine they ever are."

"Do you love him? Wylie, I mean."

Her eyes stayed on her nail. "I don't know," she said. Suddenly she pushed away from the counter. "I have to go to the bathroom. Will you excuse me for a minute?"

She left without waiting for an answer and I stayed behind, staring at the blank walls and almost blank counters. A little noise, something like a sigh, reminded me of Ian's presence and I wandered into the living room to see what he was doing.

He was working hard with his crayons and paper. He had his little face set seriously and he ignored me even when I was leaning over his shoulder. The scene he was coloring showed trees, lots of them, an oversized red bird, and a big patch of blue that I took for a body of water. It was not bad for a child his age.

I know how to talk to kids. I said, "Whacha got there, Ian?"

"It's the pond my mummy takes me to."

"That's neat, Ian. Is that red bird a cardinal?"

"No. A woodpecker."

"A woodpecker! Do you have woodpeckers in your yard?"

"We see lots of them when Mummy takes me for walks."

"Really?"

The boy tilted his head and stuck his tongue out the corner of his lips to work on a particularly tough coloring spot. "We got lots of places to walk where we live." He lifted his crayon and admired what he had accomplished.

"I guess you're very lucky, then."

"No," he said. "There aren't any other kids around."

His mother came out of the bathroom. She saw us talking and motioned me to return with her to the kitchen.

"I'll see you, Ian," I said, but as I walked away Ian called after me.

"Here's the woodpecker's house."

"Good, Ian," I said without looking.

"My mummy knows where it is."

"Good, Ian."

"It's not far, you know."

I had to call back from the kitchen. "That's good."

"It's on the path behind our house."

This time I did not answer out loud. Gretchen had entered the kitchen from the other side and we exchanged silent smiles about her chatterbox son.

"You take him out in the woods often?"

"What else am I supposed to do with him all day long? I take him with me wherever I go. Like here. I can just see him telling his father now. I'm really going to have to come up with a good one to explain this."

"Why did we come here, Gretchen? Why bring him? Why bring me?"

"I had to bring Ian because it's not Tuesday and I had no excuse to get out of the house without him. You . . . because I don't know what else to do. I tried before, you know, convincing you that Wylie didn't kill her, and it didn't work. I thought maybe if I gave you the evidence, let you see for yourself, you could drop this whole lousy prosecution."

"I'm afraid it's not that easy, Gretchen."

She threw up her hands in a sudden, exasperated gesture. "Why isn't it? It doesn't take any genius to see what's going on here." She froze. The flash went out of her eyes and she slowly lowered her hands. "I'm sorry," she said. "It's just, I thought, coming here and everything I told you before, well, I thought it would be obvious that Wylie's covering up for me."

"With his life, Gretchen? He's covering up your social embarrassment with his life?"

"You don't know Wylie," she said, shaking her head.

"I don't know anybody this side of the Middle Ages who would do that unless he's an idiot."

"Why? Don't you believe in commitments? Doesn't anybody ever depend on you to do what you say you're going to do?"

Now it was my turn to wave my hand. I did it in a rolling motion.

"Because that's what Wylie's doing for me, keeping his commitment. He promised when we first got involved that no matter what he would never let anybody know about our affair. Sure, nobody expected this was going to happen, I grant you that, but if there's any way, Patt, any way that he can be cleared without having to expose me in front of the whole world, he's going to do it. I'm begging you, Patt, begging you for your help." She moved in closer as she spoke and I could smell the sweetness of her breath as she looked up into my face.

"You're asking me to go to the D.A. and get him to drop the charges against Wylie because I have found his alibi—even though Wylie won't admit to it and even though the person he was with won't testify to help him."

Gretchen clasped her hands together. She closed them on my chest. "You can do it, can't you? I mean, you're the one running the investigation—not him. You're the one who's supposed to figure out what happened, who the suspects are, who should be charged. If you don't give him the evidence he's not going to be able to do it on his own. And if you tell him you've learned Wylie couldn't have done it he's got to listen."

I put my hands over hers. She was clutching my shirt and I was trying gently to make her stop.

"They have secret witnesses, don't they? Can't you say you've learned where Wylie was from a secret witness?"

"I'll try, Gretchen. But I don't think he's going to buy it. And if I tell him I've got a witness he's going to want to subpoena you and then one way or another you're going to be blown out in the open."

My words did what my fingers hadn't. She let go of my shirt. "Then you'll have to talk him out of it," she said, backing away only inches. "Now that you know the truth, now that you know what really happened and what will happen to me if the truth gets out, you'll have to convince the D.A. on your own that Wylie didn't do it. You have ways. You can make him believe you."

Her eyes held mine, held me, until I had no doubt what was going to happen next. I leaned just a tiny bit closer and her mouth was under mine, against mine, opening into mine. We didn't put our arms around each other, we just hung there, our lips touching, lingering, and falling away. Both of us looked to see if Ian was still on the other side of the wall and then both of us looked back at each other.

This time when we kissed my arms did go around her, my hands went under her sweater, under her jersey, and slid, glided, across her skin until one of them was in front of her and cupping her small, firm, bare breast. My knees went weak and I pulled her even closer to me. I ran my fingers down to the hard curve of her crotch. "No," she said, but then her tongue was driving into my mouth. She was holding my face between the palms of her hands and I was opening her slacks and peeling them away from her hips. "No," she said again and tore herself away.

She took a step backward, and then another. Her thick dark hair was tossed wildly. Her sweater had fallen so that it was bunched on one hip and her hard, flat belly was exposed all the way down her open zipper until it disappeared beneath the emerald strip of her panties.

I moved toward her and she put up her hand, holding it at bent-arm's length. Her hair was covering half her face and one black eye burned me with a warning to stay back.

"Ian," she called out.

"I'm in here, Mommy."

She looked in his general direction. "Everything okay?"

"Yes."

"Draw me . . . draw me the picture of the fish in the pond. Draw me a lot of pictures and then yell to me when they're ready." Her eye came back to me. She threw her hair away from her face She turned and hit the overhead light. "C'mere," she said.

She had moved to the corner formed by the wall and the refrigerator. "Get behind me," she said, and I, with visions of what I had seen in Royster Hansen's office, did as I was told.

She pushed her slacks and her emerald underwear down her thighs. I wanted to do it myself. I wanted to see how tiny her panties were. I wanted to touch them and take them all the way to the floor. But I was opening my own pants, and it was enough that she was backing into me, pressing her ass against me and letting me feel its cool, rounded firmness against the burning heat of my cock.

"Do it, Patterson," hissed my dark princess as she rose up on the toes of one foot and balanced herself with a hand on top of the refrigerator and a hand pulling down the front of her sweater.

"Do it," she said, flinging her head back against my shoulder, keeping her eyes on the doorway through which Ian could appear at any moment with his latest effort of color and imagination. "I am," I said as she arched her spine. And then suddenly she had let go of her sweater and reached her arm up behind my neck and pulled my head forward until my face was next to hers and her tongue was once again stabbing at my mouth. "Do it," she cried as our bodies twisted in ways they may never have been meant to go. But her lips were against mine and her breath was pouring into my throat and I was promising her that I would. I was promising her anything that she wanted.

John Michael was in his shirtsleeves and his tie was loosened. It was unusual to see him that way in the office. He usually kept on his suit jacket and had his tie knotted and pinching at his neck at all times. But then again, John Michael was not usually in the habit of preparing cases for trial.

He had the transcripts of the grand jury proceedings spread out in front of him. He had the various investigation reports scattered across the floor around his chair. He had a scowl on his face. He was not buying my attempts at subtlety.

"It's a little late in the day to be wondering if maybe we shouldn't be looking for someplace Wylie might have gone instead of killing his wife."

"I'm just saying, John, when you were having the asset check done on him, you didn't try to find out what residential properties his S and L had. You know, maybe they had an apartment or a condo or something where they put up friends and visitors. Maybe that's why Wylie can't or won't account for his time that night. Maybe he was there with somebody's wife or daughter."

"I'm not buying it, Patt."

"Then you better watch out Burnsie doesn't come up with it for a defense, John. Let you set up your whole circumstantial evidence bit and then come in on defense and blow you out of the water with some bimbo who says, 'Oh, yes. Wylie-kins couldn't have been killing his wife because I was humping him for the whole two hours he was out of sight.' "

The blood drained from John Michael's face. "When did you come up with this, Patt?"

"I've been thinking about it."

"When you were supposed to be thinking about where in hell Dougie Rasmussin has gone and how the hell we're going to get him back? Is that what you mean?" John Michael kicked himself away from his desk. His chair rolled over two or three files and a couple of yellow sheets of notes. "This whole fucking case is going down the tubes, Patt, and I'm beginning to wonder whose fault it is." His voice had risen shrilly.

I considered beating a retreat for the door behind my back. I shifted my feet.

John Michael moved faster. He smacked the intercom on his telephone and screamed at his secretary. "Get that asshole Lester in here as fast as you can. Tell him to bring a toothbrush, if he's got one, because he's going on his bloody California trip." He punched off the intercom and thrust a finger at me. "And as for you, pal, you just make sure Burnsie doesn't come up with any bimbo—married, professional, or any other kind. Got it?"

There was not much sense in arguing. "No sweat," I said.

I met Gretchen in the post office parking lot. It was cold enough that windshields were frosted, cold enough to see our breath in front of our faces, cold enough to keep our hands in our pockets while we spoke.

I told her there was no change. The prosecution was going ahead as planned. I told her that it was up to her now, that if she knew Wylie was innocent and he wasn't going to clear himself then she was going to have to come forward and do it for him. I said there wasn't anything more I could do.

"Why?" she asked. The end of her nose was red and her eyes were watery from the wind, and she still was beautiful. "It costs you so little and it would cost me so much."

"Look, it's not enough for one person to say that something happened because somebody else told him it happened. The only one whose testimony counts for anything is the one with the actual knowledge. That's you. If you're going to save Wylie you do it now or you do it at trial—and I've got to know if you're going to do it at trial."

"I can always do it then." She shook her head. "But the moment I do it all else is lost."

"Gretchen, you can't wait till trial. You're playing with Wylie's life by doing that. You'll just be increasing the notoriety of the whole affair. You've got to decide now if you're going to be testifying."

She took a deep breath and looked far off into the distance, to where a row of leafless trees formed a splintered outline against the bleak gray sky. "I won't be testifying, Patt. Like you, I've gone as far as I can." She cut her eyes to me to see if I understood, and then she looked away again. "I lied to you," she said.

The wind picked up. It blew open my coat and made my teeth start to chatter. I plunged my hands into my coat pockets and pulled it tight around me.

"Do you think," she said, "it's okay to lie sometimes? If you know something is right and the only way you can make sure it comes out right is to lie, do you think it's all right then?"

"Are you going to tell me that you really weren't with Wylie after all?"

"I was supposed to be. We were supposed to meet like we usually did on Tuesday nights, but if you'll check you'll see there was no lecture at the Woodedge Woman's Club that night. The speaker canceled and my father-in-law is the one who took the phone message. The only way I could get out alone was to tell Frost that I had to go shopping for a costume and that I couldn't do it with Ian tagging along. That meant I had to buy something. My idea, you know, my idea was that I could get over to Shopper's World in Framingham, get something quick, and then get back to the apartment in time to meet Wylie. But it took longer than I thought. I couldn't find anything and all of a sudden it was nine o'clock and the stores were closing."

"Did you call him and tell him you weren't coming?"

"No, because I kept thinking I'd only be another ten minutes.

You know how that goes. By the time I got there it was nine thirty and he was gone."

"How do you know he'd been there?"

She looked down and pawed a crack in the pavement with the edge of her boot. "I just knew. He'd always been there before when he said he would and there was just, you know, his presence. I could feel that someone had been there a short time before I was."

"Have you asked him?"

"Yes. He told me he waited until after nine and then just assumed I hadn't been able to get away."

"Did he ask you to lie for him?"

Gretchen's attention snapped away from the crack in the pavement. "No! In fact, he forbade even to mention the apartment because he knew we couldn't prove anything about that night and he thought our affair would only make things look worse for him."

"But you decided to tell me anyhow."

"You're the only one." Gretchen's hair blew into her mouth and she had to hold it back with one hand. Her fingers were different colors from the cold, white and pink and red. "I knew that you were the person putting everything together and I thought that if I could just explain it to you . . . show you what really happened . . ."

"Gretchen, you don't know what really happened."

"I do," she protested, releasing her hair and grabbing my arm. She searched my face. "I know he didn't kill her. He couldn't have killed her. I mean, if somebody is absolutely convinced of that it seems to me that she shouldn't just stand by and watch a man get railroaded. It seems to me she ought to pursue every possible option to convince others."

Gretchen's fingers crept downward on my sleeve until they made contact with my bare wrist. They slid then and touched the palm of my hand. They were warmer than I thought they would be. They made my fingertips close over hers. I found myself snorting and saying, "And so you used me."

A little smile came over her face. It was not a friendly smile, just an acknowledging one. "In a strange way, Patt, you were the only one I could trust enough to lie to."

"Well," I said, "I think that option's over. In fact, I think you've about run out of options."

Her smile became braver. It became more fixed. She said she understood that now.

On a Thursday morning in mid-November Wood-
edge Police Inspector Stanley Lester took off for L.A. in search
of the elusive Douglas Rasmussin. On the following day he telephoned the District Attorney's office to inform us that he had
located the Apart-Lets. That was the good news.

He had, of course, not found any trace of Dougie, but that
was only part of the bad news. He had gotten into a fight with
Zorro the desk clerk and Zorro had called the police. The
L.A.P.D. arrived and were not impressed with the fact that Lester
purported to be a brother officer from Woodedge, Massachusetts.
The patrolmen who responded to Zorro's call were unfamiliar
with the concept of reciprocity as it pertained to Woodedge and
they refused to allow Lester to speak with any of their superiors.
Lester wanted John Michael's help.

He also wanted us to know that he was embarking on a search
of L.A.'s rock-and-roll clubs for my friend Laraine. He was worried about the costs of some of these clubs and wanted to make
sure he was going to be reimbursed.

On the evening of the day Lester called, my mother's neighbor
Mrs. Graham was rushed to the hospital with a heart attack.
While she was going down Harry Kelsey was scrambling for his
life across my mother's porch, and before the paramedics had
her out of her house Charlie Curren had chased the cause of their
problems all the way to Balducci's Tavern.

Just before her heart attack Mrs. Graham had been sitting at the table in her kitchen, gazing out the window at the street. It was the warmest room in her house and on cold nights she would often sit there until the "good shows" came on television. She would sit there and drink tea and try to remember who was who and when they had come.

At some point she noticed the large, dark American-model car parked against the curb across the street, but her eyes weren't good enough to be able to tell if anyone was sitting in it. "I wouldn't have expected it," she told us later. "It was so cold."

Kelsey had arrived at my mother's house around six, well after dark. He had waved to Mrs. Graham and she had waved back. She saw him start out of the house at just after seven, on his way to the fish market to get the lobsters he and my mother had on reserve. He opened the front door and pushed open the storm door and then my mother called after him to pick up some extra butter. His head was turned and he was backing onto the porch when the first gunshot exploded and a bullet whacked into the wooden doorframe next to his fingers.

He knew right away, instinctively perhaps, what it was. He dove to the floorboards as a second shot shattered one of my mother's front windows. The bullet would later be found in the back of her sofa. Her divan.

Kelsey, looking for some cover, was crawling on his elbows and knees. He was trying to get behind some rose bushes and vines that could do nothing to stop a bullet but that made him that much harder to see. The porch light was on and Kelsey was a big target, but the shooter kept missing.

Four shots went off before Charlie Curren was out on his front steps firing back. The dark American car turned out to be an old Chevrolet Chevelle, and Charlie, who knew what he was doing, hit it easily. The first bullet that cracked a window caused the driver to leave a thirty-foot strip of rubber in his wake. By the time the Chevelle had found traction, Charlie, in his T-shirt, sweat pants, and wool socks, his .38 police special clutched in his hand, was already running for his Trans-Am. Nobody took shots at anyone in Charlie Curren's neighborhood and got away with it.

For the entire five miles from my mother's house in West Nestor to Balducci's in Walmouth, Charlie chased the Chevelle. He had given it a considerable head start, but Charlie proved to be adept at tailing, a skill that somehow surprised none of us. Charlie managed to guess the right direction, and then he went through stoplights, through stop signs, around cars in intersections and on two-lane roads; and when the Chevelle finally was able to lose him on the back streets near Walmouth Center, Charlie was able to find it again, hidden in a lot behind Balducci's. He did all this with his .38 pressed against the steering wheel. That may not have been too bright, but Charlie was at least smart enough not to go into Balducci's with his gun. Later he told us he would have gone in if he'd had something on his feet besides just his socks, but as it was he contented himself with taking down the license number and calling it in to his mother, who ran it across the street to the investigating Nestor police officers. Charlie was not the sort who would call the police himself.

The license plates turned out to be stolen and the Chevelle unregistered and no one emerged to reclaim it before the police arrived to relieve Charlie from his vigil; whereupon they promptly arrested poor Charlie for possession of an illegal firearm. Once again Charlie called his mother, and his mother called my mother and my mother called me—and that was how I first learned there had been a shooting. Until then she hadn't wanted to worry me.

By the time I arrived on the scene the police had developed a theory. A sergeant on the Nestor force named Mulcahey had been in touch with his Walmouth counterparts to pass along the original information relayed through Charlie's mother about the sniper's vehicle being found behind Balducci's. Mulcahey had then sat down with a somewhat shaken Harry Kelsey and tried to extract from him any connection he might have with Balducci's. What Mulcahey got from Kelsey was softball. What Mulcahey determined was that someone at Balducci's had tried to kill Kelsey because he was a rival softball player.

"You ever slide real hard into one of those guys?" Mulcahey was asking when I showed up.

I handed Mulcahey my identification. He knew my name and picked up the relationship between my mother and me in a remarkably short period of time.

"Do you think," Mulcahey said, his eyes narrowing, his bald dome flushing with thought, "those shots could have been meant for you?"

"Why?" snapped my mother, her face set as if this were an insult, a crazy thing to say. "Why would they be?"

I told her it wasn't such a wild idea, that maybe the shots had come from somebody I had helped to put in jail.

"I was thinking more about the Woodedge murder case I hear you been working on," said Mulcahey, while my mother gaped at me in astonishment.

Just then a call came in to Mulcahey announcing that the Walmouth police had blocked off Balducci's and nobody was getting out unless he could identify himself.

"Let's go," I said, sliding my hand under Mulcahey's elbow.

"What Woodedge murder case?" said my mother.

"C'mon, Mr. Kelsey," ordered Mulcahey.

I put up my palm to keep Kelsey in his chair. "I know the place and I'm damn sure Harry didn't get a look at whoever was doing the shooting. We don't need him."

Kelsey protested because he was not going.

My mother protested because I was.

I was very stern with both of them in front of Sergeant Mulcahey.

Three people had come out of Balducci's since the police had arrived, according to Walmouth Police Sergeant Garimundi. None of them was considered a possible suspect, including the man who was standing in front of the bar waving his arms around in the air and shouting about his civil rights. That was Buzzy Balducci himself.

Garimundi calmly sipped coffee out of a paper cup that bore the logo of Mister Donut. "Claims nobody went running in, nobody went running out. Claims he didn't notice who was in the joint at any time. Claims he don't know the names of any of his customers."

"Well, I know a couple. Let's go in and see what we've got."

Garimundi shook his head. "What d'ya think, I got shit for brains? I went inside as soon as I took care a your friend Curren. Nobody there but this guy. 'Evenin', officer,' he says, like I come in for a couple a wet ones before I finish my rounds." Garimundi snorted. It left his upper lip gleaming in the night light. "A sink fulla dirty glasses, half a rack a balls on the pool table, seats of the barstools still warm, and the only people we seen coming outa there are two broads and this joker."

"There must be another way out."

Garimundi slapped himself in the eye. He let his hand stay there and turned to look at Mulcahey. "This guy," he said, tipping his head at me, "has gotta be a detective."

I walked away from Garimundi and Mulcahey and went over to confront Balducci. The tavern owner was without a jacket, but his arms were moving so rapidly and so frequently that he gave no sign of being cold.

"You," he said, when I got close enough for him to recognize. "I knew you was a cop. Oh yeah, all your talk about fixin' tickets. I knew it. I just knew it."

"I'm not a cop," I said, stopping when I was just outside of arm's length. "I'm a friend of Kelsey's and someone you know just took four shots at him."

"Ooh, slander," said Balducci. He put both hands to his mouth and screamed up and down the street, "Slander. He's slandering my good name."

I waited until he was done. "Tell me how Dougie Rasmussin fits into this, Buzzy."

"Hey," said Balducci, "I'll tell you." He motioned me closer until he was able to speak directly into my ear. "Eat shit, pig," he whispered.

I straightened up slowly as if he had just given me valuable information. I looked him in the eye. His was a triumphant, spiteful look; one that told me he would not mind clouting me, doing serious damage to me for the sheer joy of it. "You don't care that some asshole just tried to kill Kelsey, the best damn softball player in the whole city?"

"Maybe Kelsey should watch who he hangs around with." Balducci checked to see who was near, and then leaned in closer again. "Maybe it wasn't Kelsey he was shooting at."

Now Balducci took his time straightening up. "Yeah," he said, nodding, his near eye bright and unblinking.

"Let's suppose," I said, "that there was some guy who hangs around your bar. Let's suppose he isn't all that smart and he did take a couple of shots at Kelsey thinking it was me . . . why do you think he might do that?"

Balducci's warrior's grin slowly transformed itself into one of smug self-satisfaction. "Maybe," he said, "he was pissed off because you lied to him about the parking tickets."

Jessica Keough was wearing a one-piece red jumpsuit that seemed to have been tailored to her figure. It swelled where she swelled. It was taut where she was taut. I thought it a rather unusual outfit to be wearing in her home at eleven o'clock at night, but I had called to say I was coming and it was possible she had gotten dressed for company.

The two of us were leaning over John Michael's shoulder as he sat at the desk in the study of his house. His desk faced the window and so we had to lean over his shoulder in order to follow the police reports he was reading. Jessica had one hand on the back of his blue leather chair. She had one hand resting lightly on my back as I bent forward with my elbow on the desk. Her right leg was against my left one. The inside of her right leg was against the inside of my left one. I was trying not to make any big thing out of it.

John Michael held up one of the reports. "They ask this woman who came out of the bar, Janice Neeley, why she's covering an attempt to murder somebody in cold blood. 'Hey, those people,' she says, 'what are you going to do?' They ask her doesn't she care that there's a potential killer running around loose. She goes,

'I'm from Walmouth. We keep to ourselves.' " John Michael threw down the report disgustedly. He turned around. Jessica slipped her leg away from mine.

"This is the kind of thing we're up against," he said. "Parochialism. This points up how important it is that the people of Walmouth see me as one of their own. We get the right jury for Carpenter and we can make it a matter of us against them. I see this kind of attitude," he thumped the report, "and I'm thinking, 'You're in trouble, Carpenter. Not only do you come from Woodedge, but you weren't even born around here.' "

"John," I said, pushing all the reports back in front of him. "This was my mother's boyfriend got shot at. On my mother's porch. There's every reason in the world to think he was a mistaken target, that it was me who was supposed to get shot."

John Michael leaned back in his chair. He looked at me with sympathy. "I know."

Jessica stepped around to the other side of her husband's chair so that we could talk across the top of John Michael's head. "How do you figure it, Patt?"

I took my time trying to marshal the words for the jumbled ideas in my mind. "Balducci's is Dougie Rasmussin's place. If he needs somebody back here to do something, that's where he's going to call. The one guy Rasmussin's had direct contact with, face to face I mean, is me. He talks with me, he bullshits me, he splits. It's possible he hears we're back live and in person looking for him on the West Coast and he's afraid we're closing in so he decides to eliminate the guy he thinks is orchestrating everything."

John Michael raised one pale eyebrow in a show of tempered significance.

"Yeah," I said, "I don't buy that either. That brings me to the next possibility, which is that someone wants us to think that Rasmussin is trying to kill me."

"Or maybe even has killed you," John Michael said, his face stretched with concern.

"Yeah."

"And the most likely person that would be," he went on, "is Wylie Carpenter. He knows Rasmussin is our only other suspect. Hell, he set him up that way in the first place, committing the murder on the day Rasmussin left for the Coast. So now he's desperate, see? Desperate times call for desperate measures. If he can get us to make the connection between Rasmussin and you getting shot then maybe he can get himself off the hook."

John Michael began pressing his fingertips together. "So let's think it through. There's no real reason why Rasmussin would panic when Carpenter's already scheduled to stand trial. But let's say Carpenter realizes he's up shit creek without a paddle and is looking for any way he can to create doubt. Hmmn? You with me? Now what would make him think . . . that we'll think . . . that Rasmussin's responsible?"

"The bar?" said Jessica, raising her shoulders and making a silky sound with her jumpsuit as her arms moved against her sides.

"The bar. Consider the cleverness. We don't actually know if anybody from the bar did it. All we know is that the car that was used was found parked near the bar. Whose bar? Rasmussin's bar. What do we assume? One of Rasmussin's buddies must have done it."

Jessica interrupted. "But if nobody from the bar actually did it, why did they all run away?"

John Michael grabbed the police reports, held them up for us to see, and then let them fall back to his desk. "Cops arrive and first thing they do is make a commotion arresting Curren. He starts yelling about the sniper inside. You think it's just a coincidence the two women came out? Bullshit. That's what they do in bars like this. Send the women out to discover what's going on."

I marveled silently at the breadth of John Michael's knowledge of the ways and mores of drinking establishments.

John Michael surveyed us with a professorial eye. "All right, now, any other reason why Carpenter might think we'd blame Rasmussin for this little episode tonight?"

Jessica thought hard. "The timing?" she said.

"Exactly." John Michael's finger soared upward. "And how would Carpenter have known that now, I mean tonight, was the perfect time to get us focusing our attention on Rasmussin? Because there's a bloody little South African in a loud sport coat running around Los Angeles at this very minute making inquiries about Rasmussin. And how does Carpenter know that? Because somebody tipped him off, by God. We have a leak in our organization."

"Wembley Tuttle," I said softly.

"I wonder," said the district attorney of Exeter County. "I wonder if he's the only one being unfaithful."

Almost immediately the inside of my left leg began to burn. For some reason, I dared not look at Jessica and I trusted she was not looking at me.

Down below us John Michael was still speaking. "You know, if it's only Wembley, I can deal with that. Because I know where he's coming from and I don't really depend on him to be any more than what he is. What I couldn't take would be betrayal from somebody I trusted. I mean I really couldn't take that. In fact, I think there's probably no more base crime than to betray somebody who you've encouraged to count on you or trust in you or depend on you. Because that's really a conscious decision, to betray someone, and if you'll do that you'll do anything. You know what I mean?"

He didn't wait for an answer. He sighed instead, and said, "I guess I'm just going to have to be more careful."

My mother's house was placed under twenty-four-hour police surveillance. John Michael offered to arrange the same service for my apartment, but I declined and satisfied whatever fears I had by watching for tails and varying my routes home.

There were no further attacks and no success at learning the identity of Kelsey's assailant. The lack of both served to reinforce John Michael's belief that the shooting at my mother's house had been nothing more than an attempt on Carpenter's part to deflect our attention toward Rasmussin.

"In fact," he said to me one day, "I'm convinced Carpenter wasn't trying to kill you. I'm convinced his plan was to shoot at you and miss just so he could set up the Balducci-Rasmussin connection."

John Michael was smarting from the fact that he had called Lester home early from California. He wanted me to understand that this had been a magnanimous gesture on his part—one made in an abundance of caution and out of the most deep and abiding concern for my mother's safety. He wanted me to know that he regretted it.

Lester, once he returned, made no bones about the fact that he blamed me entirely for his truncated trip through rock-and-roll paradise. He complained to Wembley that I was responsible for his failure to find Dougie Rasmussin, and Wembley took up the matter with Royster, who began to ask me how my mother was doing on a near daily basis.

John Michael, meanwhile, began to prepare for trial in earnest. Unlike his subordinate attorneys, he had the luxury of concentrating on just one case—and the fact that he was concentrating on this one made it far and away the most important thing in the office. He had Libby running in and out and Lester running in and out and me running in and out, and he had us all running at different times.

Monday-evening squash games were canceled, Friday-evening meetings were canceled, no impromptu gatherings were held; and I found myself cranked into an unusual state of anxiety as I watched mysterious assignments being handed out to Lester, who was of no mind to share them with me, and Libby, who acted as though everything he was given to do was the absolute key to salvation. When alone in John Michael's presence I began to search for some sign of approval, or even disapproval, that I could address. I tested him with jokes and concentrated on his eyes when we spoke; but his smiles did not linger, and his expressions remained distant or preoccupied. Occasionally I went so far as to ask him what was wrong, but his answers were uniformly meaningless: "Nothing," or "Everything."

Yet my insecurity as to John Michael's new circumspection was nothing compared to Royster's. He had taken to popping into his boss's office on almost any excuse of news, to laughing boisterously over any remark that vaguely approached the realm of humor, and to staring at me with great concern whenever we happened to cross each other's path.

As for Jessica, her appearances in the office suddenly became very infrequent. On the few occasions when she did appear during the last few weeks of the year I could not help but notice that her recent penchant for tight and shimmery clothes seemed to have been abandoned in favor of a return to more traditional tweeds and wools. The New Year passed without her usual invitation to "join the Keoughs in a glass of holiday cheer," and then I did not see her again until she showed up in court for her husband's opening address to the jury—wearing a conservative dark blue knit suit, gazing with rapt devotion throughout John Michael's spiel, and generally acting as though she had every confidence in the world in what her husband was about to do.

Philip Burns had hair like pumpkin guts. It was a weak and unpleasant orange color and it tended to be stringy and stay plastered close to his round skull. Burnsie's brown eyes floated about in their sockets as if they were not as well tethered as other people's. His skin had a glistening quality to it that made him look as if he was constantly perspiring. These were not the physical characteristics one would expect in a successful trial lawyer.

But Philip Burns's mind, when not pickled, was fairly astute. He also had a wonderful voice, a quick laugh, and a sense of humor that never seemed mean or aggressive. People mocked Burnsie, but he managed to get away with a lot because he was genuinely likable, and those who knew him best did not underestimate him after they told their jokes and did their imitations.

The Keoughs were the exceptions. They believed all the jokes and repeated the ones they did not make up themselves. John Michael regarded Burnsie as an idiot and Jessica reinforced that idea at every opportunity.

John Michael's disrespect for his predecessor was apparent from the outset of the Carpenter trial. It was manifested in eye rollings and quick little tightenings at the corners of his mouth, paper shufflings when Burnsie was talking, and failures to respond when Burnsie was asking him questions.

The two men were a study in contrasts. Burnsie's yellow and brown tie was knotted just below the top button of his slightly rumpled shirt. His brown suit had a slight tear on the seam leading out of the back vent, and his brogans could have used a better shine. He was constantly looking for things, putting on and taking off his reading glasses, licking his fingers whenever he turned pages, being distracted by almost any other noise in the room. John Michael, however, wore an immaculate gray suit, an immaculate white shirt, a bright red silk power tie with fancy little blue figurines, and black calfskin loafers that would have passed a Marine drill sergeant's inspection. He had everything in place and everything under control.

When John Michael needed something he simply extended his hand and a junior attorney named Mary Alice Devon handed it to him. When he wanted a question answered he had only to turn around and Lester and I were right there in the front row, ready to lean forward to the bar and supply him with whatever we could. If he was stuck on some legal nicety he could always send one of the office interns scurrying to the library or, if necessary, to Royster Hansen.

The jury to which these two men were playing was the product of ten days of scrutinous questioning that had eliminated everyone but housewives, retirees, and employees of the phone company, Boston Edison, the post office, and the city, state, and federal governments. Twelve jurors and four alternates, and not one of them was from Woodedge. They looked pleased to have been chosen. They looked happy to be off work or out of the house.

The judge presiding was a little man named Victor LoBianco, and his assignment to the trial had caused John Michael a certain amount of concern. Nobody was ever sure what Victor was up to. He tended to keep his head down and write notes throughout trials. He tended to grin at inappropriate times.

He was grinning when he called the trial to order on the first day after completion of jury selection. He was grinning for the jurors, and for the spectators who filled about three-quarters of the gallery, and for the television camera he had allowed into the courtroom. After his introductory remarks he turned stiffly in his chair and pointed grandly at John Michael. "Are you ready, Mr. Keough?"

John Michael rose carefully to his feet. He gave one last glance at his notepad and then strode out in front of the jury with nothing whatsoever in his hands. He introduced himself for the umpteenth time and explained to the jurors that he was the district attorney for Exeter County and that he was conducting this prosecution on behalf of the people of the county.

The jurors, primed by the long selection process, by the words of the judge, and by the presence of the television camera, were ready to act like jurors. When John Michael thrust his finger at Wylie Carpenter, sitting at the defendant's table next to his lawyer, they turned to stare as if they had never seen him before. When John Michael produced a scale relief model, previously cleared with the defense and showing the relationship of Stonegate Country Club, the overlook off Ivanhoe Road, and the Carpenter estate on Bulham Road, the jurors nearly bolted from their seats to get a better look.

John Michael spoke for an hour. His words rolled, he never repeated himself, he segued from one bit of information to another, and when he was done it was all perfectly obvious that Wylie S. Carpenter, trapped in marriage to an unfaithful wife and trying to secure her fortune for his own, had diabolically plotted and carried out Rebecca's murder to coincide with the disappearance of the family's young caretaker, Douglas Rasmussin.

The change in the prosecution's theory was due entirely to the inability to produce Rasmussin at trial. "You'll see," John Michael had said when I asked how he was going to get around the fact that Wylie was at least a millionaire in his own right; and that, plus a wink and a sly grin, was all that I could get out of him.

The commonwealth's first witness in its case against Wylie Carpenter was Officer Roland Tagget. He identified thirty-six photographs of the scene of the crime and described in scrupulous detail what he had observed. He introduced blow-ups of a couple of the photographs, one of which clearly showed the formerly pretty face of Rebecca Carpenter contorted in the agony of death by strangulation. He made use of the scale model for demonstration purposes. And then he explained how he had accompanied Sergeant Roselli to the Carpenter home to meet with Mr. Carpenter.

It was this last point that Burnsie homed in on. He asked a few questions about whether Tagget had moved the body and whether he had disturbed any evidence at the scene, but mostly he cross-examined on the issue of what Tagget knew about Wylie Carpenter.

"You say you went to his house?"

"Yes sir. Number six Bulham Road."

"You wouldn't really call it a house, would you? More of a mansion?"

"It's pretty big, yes sir."

"And six Bulham Road, that's really an estate, isn't it?"

"I guess it is, yes sir."

"Did you know it was the Chesley family estate?"

"I heard of it, yes sir."

"Uh-huh. And Mr. Carpenter, had you heard of him before?"

"I didn't know him, but I guess I knew there was a Mr. Carpenter."

"Know anything about his background, where he came from, how he happened to marry Rebecca Chesley and move to that house, anything like that?"

"No sir."

"Uh-huh. You certainly didn't immediately suspect Mr. Carpenter when you found his wife's body, did you?"

"No sir."

"Did you even know that was his wife? Did you know right away that was Rebecca Carpenter?"

"No sir."

"How did you find that out, that this woman, this dead body was Rebecca Carpenter?"

"I radioed in the license tag on the vehicle."

"You didn't look at her driver's license, her wallet, anything in her purse?"

"No sir."

"Why not?"

"I didn't find a pocketbook."

"A wallet?"

"Didn't find anything."

"Money?"

"Nothing."

"Uh-huh. I see. When you got to the Carpenter . . . estate, did you check to see if her pocketbook was there?"

"That's correct."

"And was it?"

"Mr. Carpenter couldn't find it."

"Was it there, Officer Tagget?"

"I don't know. I couldn't find it either."

"To your knowledge, has it ever been found?"

"Not to my knowledge."

Burnsie looked as if he were bewildered. He raised his hands halfway from his sides and let them fall back against his flanks. His face was scrunched as if he were about to ask a question that was going to challenge the very heart and soul of everything that Officer Roland Tagget had ever said in his life. But then he backed off. He returned to his seat and almost sat down before he caught himself.

"One final thing, Officer. Now, you've testified that you're a trained policeman, police academy, nine years on the force and so forth . . . You've testified that you examined the body when you found it and that you interviewed Mr. Carpenter that night along with Sergeant Roselli . . . Tell me, based on all that, did you form an opinion that night that Mr. Carpenter had killed his wife?"

Tagget glanced toward John Michael for help, but John Michael did not want to disturb the cool persona in which he had cast himself. He made no motion to object and gave no sign that he cared in the slightest about Tagget's answer.

"No," said Tagget.

Burnsie pressed on. "There was nothing in his demeanor, nothing in his appearance that made you suspect that night that he might have killed his wife?"

"No sir."

"Well, when was it then that you decided he did kill his wife?"

"Objection."

"Sustained," said LoBianco. "Counsel approach the bench."

John Michael rose looking faintly disgusted. Burnsie immediately assumed a perplexed air, as though he was baffled by the consternation he had caused. LoBianco grinned heartily at the jurors, letting them know that this was all part of the great game of law in which we were all engaged.

To say that Wylie Carpenter wore a brown suit to court on the first day of testimony would be like saying Babe Ruth was a ballplayer. Wylie's suit was the deepest, richest brown I had ever seen. It was cut perfectly to his shape and it never seemed to bend, fold or mutilate no matter how he moved. His grayish hair was combed in a longish, yet perfectly neat fashion. His nails looked buffed to my untrained eye, and his skin was as tanned as if he had spent the Christmas holidays in the Caribbean. He remained quiet throughout the day, and his only visible reaction to anything that was said came when he picked up his pencil and occasionally jotted down a casual note.

I noticed the jurors stealing peeks at him from time to time. I noticed that the women jurors tended to let their gaze linger.

Sergeant Francis Roselli described what he had seen when he arrived at the overlook. He confirmed that virtually all prints had been wiped clean. He identified the scarf that had been found wrapped around Rebecca Carpenter's neck. He testified as to its chain of custody and it was admitted into evidence.

Then he explained how he had traced the scarf to its point of purchase from Burberry's just three days before the murder. He identified the charge slip that was used to make the purchase. He read the imprinted name on the charge slip. He read the signature. He read them both as Wylie S. Carpenter.

John Michael let this news sink in while he strode around the courtroom with his hands clasped loosely behind his back. Then he started Roselli in on a new line of questioning. Yes, Roselli affirmed, to his observation this was a death by strangulation. No, he did not think the strangulation had occurred there at the overlook or even in the car in which the body was found.

More blow-up photographs were produced and Roselli used a pointer to go over them with the jury. He explained about the lack of damage to the inside of the car and he walked the edges of expert testimony by describing the expected thrashings of a garotted woman.

Finally, John Michael asked Roselli about any testings he had personally done and the sergeant got out a series of notes and calculations and interpreted them for the jurors. It was exactly 3.6 miles by roadway from the Carpenter home to the overlook. It was exactly 2.5 miles from the overlook to the Stonegate Country Club. The distance from Stonegate to the Carpenter home, by the fastest roadway route, was 4.9 miles. Roselli had driven between all these points, at night, keeping within the speed limit, and it had taken him approximately twenty eight minutes to go from Stonegate to the Carpenters' home to the overlook and back to Stonegate.

John Michael had Roselli make a loose diagram on a large piece of artist's paper and mark off the distances and the times between the three points. Then he offered the diagram into evidence and looked slightly amazed when Burnsie waved it in without objection.

Burnsie was far more interested in finding out what Roselli knew about the missing pocketbook. He wanted to go over Roselli's notes of his interview with Mr. Carpenter. He wanted to know if he suspected Mr. Carpenter right away. He probed Roselli as to what he knew about the Carpenters before the night of the murder, and he seemed satisfied when Roselli said all he knew was that they were rich and lived on a nice piece of property.

"What," demanded John Michael that night as we gathered in his office for the first time in weeks, "is that drunken old bum up to?"

Royster, who had been trying to pour everybody a glass of bourbon, discreetly put down his bottle of Harper's.

Jessica said, "He doesn't know, John. That's what's so wonderful. You're running circles around him."

John Michael, who had taken off his suit jacket, who had his hand wrapped around a warm mug of coffee, and who was getting ready to spend most of the night preparing for the second day's testimony, glanced up eagerly and said, "Do you think so?"

Jessica and Royster answered simultaneously. "Yes," they sang. And John Michael looked very pleased.

26

Dr. Marshall Havens, Exeter County Medical Examiner, led off the second day of testimony. He confirmed that it was death by strangulation and gave his best medical estimate that it had occurred between nine and ten p.m.—closer to nine, he thought. He was given the scarf that had been admitted into evidence and he demonstrated how he thought it had been used. He demonstrated as though the murderer had been face to face with the victim.

Havens confirmed that blood alcohol had tested at .18 and noted that legally drunk in our state was considered to be a .10. He also admitted that toxicology testing had revealed a large amount of Valium in Mrs. Carpenter's system, but he was unable to quantify it. "However," he said, clearing his throat for emphasis, "ten milligrams of Valium, the conventional dose, is generally deemed to be the equivalent of two strong drinks."

"And while you can't quantify exactly how much Valium she had, you can state that it was more than the conventional dose, is that right, Doctor?" asked John Michael.

And Havens, who was a bit of a ham, harrumphed and smiled and said, "Oh, my, yes."

On cross examination, Burnsie, now wearing a herringbone suit so bold it was practically striped, produced a plastic model of a human head and torso. He handed Dr. Havens the scarf again and asked him to strangle the model. Havens knotted the scarf on the model's neck, grabbed it on both sides of the knot, and wrenched it in opposite directions.

"Take much strength, Doctor?"

"Some."

"Doesn't have to be a male athlete's strength to snap that hyoid bone, does it?"

Havens studied the model for too long before saying no.

Burnsie asked him to stand behind the model. He asked him if the model could be strangled from that position. He asked Havens to demonstrate and Havens did, just as I had done for Lester some weeks before. "Any scientific or medical evidence that you're aware of that disproves the killer was behind Mrs. Carpenter as opposed to in front?"

Havens, concerned that he was not doing his best job for the county and John Michael, mumbled his answer.

"What's that, Doctor?"

"No."

"Oh," said Burnsie, as though surprised. He pointed to the torso with his wooden pointing stick. "Your autopsy, it included the liver, did it?"

"It included the liver, yes, Mr. Burns."

"And, in lay terms, how would you describe that liver?"

"In lay terms? Well, in lay terms it was enlarged."

"In an advanced state of cirrhosis, would you say?"

"Advanced state? No. Cirrhotic . . . yes."

"More than you would expect in a woman of forty years?"

"Well, as to what I expect, I have seem some amazing things over the course of my career, Mr. Burns."

"This was a diseased liver, wasn't it, Doctor?"

"Diseased? I guess you would say that."

"Diseased due to a history of alcohol abuse?"

"Due, I would say, to consumption of more alcohol than was good for her liver."

"Over what period of time?"

"It wasn't overnight, Mr. Burns, if that's what you're getting at."

"Yes, Doctor, that's exactly what I'm getting at. No further questions, Your Honor."

Havens was followed to the stand by the bartender from Stonegate. In the afternoon came Teasdale, who among other things identified Wylie as wearing a white V-necked sweater that day; and then Whitman, who turned out to be unexpectedly combative in the defense of his friend. In reality, however, Whitman's attitude did Wylie Carpenter little good. By the time he was off it was clear that every minute of Wylie's life was accounted for between two and eight p.m. on October fifteenth, and none was accounted for from eight until almost ten.

In the normal course of events it did not seem extraordinary that John Michael followed Teasdale and Whitman by having D. Dodge Patterson as his lead witness on the third day of testimony. Still, I was somewhat surprised when Dodge came into the courtroom. He had been part of my sphere of responsibility and I had not been aware that John Michael was planning on calling him. I also was not prepared to see Gretchen accompanying him.

She was wearing a purple hat that was broad-brimmed and almost flat, and when she removed her heavy wool cape I saw that she was wearing a matching purple dress. She was breathtaking in the purity of her beauty and I must have reacted in some way because Jessica wanted to know what it was I was looking at.

She discovered quickly enough, and she did it without me saying anything. "Who's that?" she demanded.

We were standing at the rail, Jessica and I, waiting for things to get started. Jessica was wearing a tweed suit that flattened the curves of her breasts and her buttocks. Her hair was pulled back. Her wool coat was over her arm. She looked exceptionally severe and almost masculine.

"Gretchen Patterson," I said.

The two of us watched her make herself comfortable.

"Dodge's wife?" There was a distinct note of concern in Jessica's voice, one that made me shift my glance to her and wonder why her brow was wrinkling and her eyes were narrowing.

"Yes," I said.

"South American?"

"Beats me. She was born in Lowell."

Jessica's forehead smoothed slowly. A touch of a smile came to her lips. "Pretty," she said, and turned away.

The direct examination of Teasdale had taken only about twenty minutes. The direct examination of Whitman had taken about an hour. John Michael's questioning of D. Dodge, however, covered the entire morning session.

Dodge was not without his charm, and faced with the cool and efficient presence of John Michael he tended to affect a loose and slightly bemused appearance, as though he was very willing to help but didn't know what help he could possibly be. He dipped his head and smiled at the jury and got them to smile back. He sat forward easily at first, and sat back relaxed and comfortable after a while. Every now and then, however, I saw him glance at the courtroom clock on the back wall.

John Michael established Dodge's background, education, and profession, and then established that he had spent the afternoon and evening of October 15 playing golf and cards with Wylie.

"You consider yourself to be a good friend of Mr. Carpenter's, don't you, Mr. Patterson?"

"Yes, I do."

"Known him for a number of years?"

"Pretty much ever since he moved to Woodedge."

"Went to his wedding, didn't you?"

"As a guest of Becky's, I suppose."

"After that you grew close and stayed close."

"I guess that would be fair to say."

"In fact, you could say that Wylie Carpenter has been something of a model for your life, couldn't you?"

"A model? Well, no, I wouldn't say that."

"A mentor?"

Dodge laughed. "On the golf course he has certainly tried to be. But other than that, we're just friends."

"You do admire him, don't you, Mr. Patterson?"

"Sure."

"And wouldn't you say that he has been a major influence on you over the course of, say, the past ten years?"

"This is all very vague, Mr. Keough. A major influence? Sure, like any friend would be. But I'm not clear as to what you're getting at."

"Wouldn't you agree that you have tried to be as much like Wylie Carpenter as you could over the past ten years?"

"Really, you know, I find that impossible to answer." Dodge looked to the jury and gave a very small shrug. "I admire him, I'd like to play golf like he does. . . . He's a smart, generous, personable guy. I could do a whole lot worse than be like him."

"Mr. Patterson, where were you on the night of October fifteenth between the hours of seven and nine o'clock?"

"Playing cards in the clubhouse at Stonegate."

"You played a Mr. Ben Butcher in the first round of cards, and you played Gerard Whitman in the last round. What did you do in between?"

"I don't know. Got something to eat. Watched television. I might have taken a shower."

"You didn't go home to see your wife and child?"

For the first time, Dodge squirmed. "No. Ah, as I recall, my wife was out shopping and my son, ah, probably was in bed. My father would have been watching him."

"You know Rebecca Carpenter was killed that night?"

"I do."

"You knew her from childhood, didn't you?"

"I did. She was a little older than I."

"You regarded her as an attractive woman, didn't you?"

"Very." Dodge folded his hands. His eyes narrowed as he tried to figure out where John Michael was going.

"You were able to observe Rebecca over the course of her sixteen-year marriage. Did you, from your perspective, regard her marriage as a happy one?"

"Objection," said Burnsie. "Calls for speculation or expert opinion, which this witness is not qualified to give."

"Overruled," said Judge LoBianco, grinning.

Dodge said "Yes" in answer to the question.

"Based on what you were able to observe, did you feel that fidelity on the part of both partners was essential to that marriage?"

"Objection."

LoBianco grinned at the ceiling. He grinned at his notes. "Overruled," he said.

Dodge fidgeted. "I don't know," he said.

"Based on what you were able to observe, did you interpret the marriage as being important to Wylie Carpenter?"

"Yes."

"You knew the house, of course. Six Bulham Road?"

"Yes."

"How long had you known them to live there?"

"Couple of years."

"Where did they live before that?"

"Gladstone Road."

"Big house?"

"Mmm—modest. Ten rooms, maybe."

"Not as big as six Bulham Road."

"Not by a long shot."

"Not an estate."

"No."

"How did you refer to six Bulham Road? Does it have another name?"

"I don't know. The Chesley Estate."

"Who lived there before the Carpenters?"

"Rebecca's mother. Rebecca grew up there with her parents. The place dates back to Squire Chesley, I think."

"And so Rebecca and her husband, Wylie, moved onto the estate when Rebecca's last surviving parent died?"

"Rebecca inherited it, yes. They sold the Gladstone Road place."

"And at this time, when they moved onto the estate, was Wylie Carpenter working? To your knowledge?"

"Well, he had an ownership interest in the savings and loan."

John Michael nodded. He waited until all eyes were on him and then, speaking deliberately, said, "Are you aware of any infidelities on the part of Mr. Carpenter over the course of his marriage?"

Burnsie unleashed a torrent of objections. LoBianco quickly summoned the two counsel to the bench and the three men engaged in some animated whispering. I kept my eyes on Dodge and Dodge kept his eyes on the floor of the witness box.

"The objection's overruled," announced LoBianco as Burnsie stormed back to his seat and John Michael, one hand in his pants pocket, meandered over to a spot in front of the jury box.

Dodge opened his hands. "I don't know for certain," he said.

"Is that because you never saw him in the act?"

"That's right."

"But you saw him in situations which led you to conclude that he was having extramarital relations, is that right?"

"Objection."

"Sustained," said LoBianco, pumping his pen as if Burnsie had just said the right word or guessed the right number.

"Mr. Patterson, do you have any personal knowledge of infidelities on the part of Mrs. Carpenter over the course of her marriage?"

"No," said Dodge firmly.

John Michael's chin shot up. He stared hard at Dodge, who stared hard back. "Didn't you yourself have an affair with Rebecca Carpenter?"

"I never did." Dodge was still staring, but a light seemed to come on in his eyes and he slowly twisted his head so that he was no longer looking at John Michael. He was looking at me.

John Michael took a step forward. His voice rose a degree louder. "Mr. Patterson where *were* you on the night of October fifteenth between the hours of seven and nine o'clock?"

"Objection," shouted Burnsie, laboring to his feet. "Asked and answered."

"Sustained," said LoBianco, waving him down.

"Did you see Mrs. Carpenter at any time on that night?"

Dodge was no longer trying to be charming. He was frustrated and angry and suddenly fighting a battle he had never anticipated. "No, I didn't."

"Do you know of anyone who can verify where you were between seven and nine that night?"

Dodge leaned forward. He bit his lip. "I was not with her."

"Did you see Wylie Carpenter at any time between seven and nine o'clock that night?"

"No, I didn't."

"Did you leave the premises of the Stonegate Country Club at any time between seven and nine o'clock? At any time before ten o'clock that night?"

"No."

"Do you know if Wylie Carpenter did?"

"No."

"You did not leave the premises, you did not see Wylie Carpenter, do you agree that Wylie Carpenter could not have been on the premises between seven and nine?"

"No."

"Why not?"

Dodge hesitated. His eyes went from John Michael to Wylie to Gretchen in the back of the courtroom. Then they returned to Wylie and rested there. "Because I wasn't anyplace he could see me. Or I him."

John Michael, who had been all set to bury Dodge, stopped with the words of his next question stuck in his mouth. He walked back to his table. "Where were you, Mr. Patterson?"

This time there was no objection from Burnsie, who was leaning on his elbows, peering over the top of his reading glasses, seemingly as anxious as everyone else for the answer.

It took Dodge a very long while to respond. "There are some rooms at the club," he said. "Some members' rooms. I was in one of them."

Silence followed. Then LoBianco, clearing his throat, said, "Since nobody else seems to be going to ask it, what's a members' room, Mr. Patterson?"

"They're overnight rooms."

LoBianco wrote down that information. "By overnight you mean they have a bed in them?"

"They're basically for use by visiting officials or members who find themselves in sudden need of . . ."

"Overnight accommodation?" offered the judge helpfully.

"Yes sir."

The silence resumed. Nobody, it seemed, was looking directly at anybody else. Finally, the judge asked John Michael if he had any further questions.

John Michael, standing at counsel's table, staring down at his papers, said, "I assume you have some independent corroboration that you were in one of these rooms between seven and nine."

Dodge nodded. Very softly he said yes.

"Who were you with, Mr. Patterson?"

"I was with Shawna . . . I don't know her last name. She's employed in the dining room at Stonegate as a waitress."

John Michael met this revelation head-on. "I think," he said, his voice loud and distinct, "that now would be a good time to break for lunch, Your Honor."

John Michael was mad and he had a very difficult time containing his anger until everyone else was out of the courtroom. He occupied himself by smashing papers into unneeded piles; and then, when he and I and Jessica and Lester and Mary Alice Devon were the only ones left, he wheeled on me. "What kind of bullshit is this, Patt?" he demanded.

"I told you he was missing for a couple of hours. I don't see what difference it makes that he was with some girl—"

"That's not what I'm pissed off about, goddammit." John Michael pushed his face to within inches of mine. The hate in his expression was so unexpected, so intense, that for a moment I had a primitive urge to shove him away.

"You told me," he said, spit flying out of the corner of his mouth, "that Patterson had an affair with Rebecca Carpenter. I counted on that to explain what happened with Rasmussin. How am I going to prove she's a fucking slut whore now?"

"John," I said through clenched teeth, "I just told you what Dodge's wife told me. Just because he denies it now—hell, he denied it when I confronted him."

"But he's under oath now. It's one thing to deny something like that to a stranger, but I've got him up on the stand. He's a goddamn attorney. Think he's going to perjure himself over something like that?"

"His wife was here," I said, gesturing. "Why not?"

"Because"—John Michael drew himself up straight so that we were nearly on eye level with one another—"he just admitted that he was shacked up with some waitress whose last name he doesn't even know as recently as two and a half months ago. You think he's going to admit to that in front of his wife, in front of everyone, practically gratuitously, and then deny something she supposedly already knows about?"

I spent some time clearing my throat.

"Gimme a break, will ya, Patt?" he said, and his voice was almost sad.

Eventually he turned and looked at Stanley Lester. "Go out to Stonegate, find this Shawna woman," he said. "I want a complete statement from her. I want to know if this was a regular thing they had going, or what. I want to know if she also did it with Carpenter that night, or if she ever did it with him. I want to know what she knows about Carpenter's whereabouts and I want to know the name of every other woman who could possibly have been involved in anything like this. Got it?"

Lester practically saluted. But before he bolted for the door as fast as his little immigrant legs could carry him, John Michael held up one hand and asked me a question without looking at me. "I'm assuming this isn't something you've done already, Patt."

I told him it wasn't.

John Michael flicked his hand and Lester was off. His eyes sought out his wife's and he shook his head by moving it to one side and then bringing it back very slowly. His mouth was fixed in a lipless grimace and it stayed that way until he addressed Mary Alice. "This could be the whole ballgame," he said, "if Carpenter's protecting the reputation of some little golf-course slut by refusing to say where he was."

"You want to ask for a recess?" she said. Her square Irish face was worried and sympathetic and ridden with the desire to be of any service she could.

"Not on your life," he told her. "There's still a possibility they don't realize we've been hurt. And even if they do, I'm not going to give them the satisfaction of acknowledging it. We'll play it out for now." He grinned forcefully. "Who knows? When you've got a lemon you can always make lemonade."

"What do you want me to do, John?" I asked.

He stopped grinning. He turned back to the table and began stuffing his little piles into his briefcase. "I told you weeks ago to make sure this kind of surprise didn't happen. 'No sweat,' you said. Remember that? Well, I'm sweating now, Patt." The briefcase slammed shut. He hauled it off the table. "Kind of makes you wonder, doesn't it?"

He started up the aisle with Mary Alice hot on his heels. That left Jessica and me with nobody to look at but each other. She was searching my face and I was searching hers. And then she too turned and followed her husband up the aisle, her heels clicking resolutely on the tiled floor.

27

Gretchen Patterson returned in the afternoon. She sat in the same row, the same seat, but no matter how many times I turned, no matter how long I stared at her, she would not let me catch her eye.

Up on the stand, Dodge Patterson was being gently manipulated by Burnsie. Yes, during the nearly four hours they spent out on the course he had had plenty of opportunity to engage in conversation with Wylie Carpenter and he had noticed nothing unusual about his demeanor. Wylie had shot his typical fine game. They had entered the clubhouse together, had a drink together, sat down at the same time to play cards. If Carpenter had acted peculiarly in any way it had escaped Dodge's attention. And yes, Carpenter was definitely back in the clubhouse before ten, or at ten, or near ten—Dodge couldn't be sure of the exact time, but he was sure that Carpenter was acting no differently then than he had earlier in the evening. The thing that stood out in his mind was that they had been bantering back and forth and the bartender had been trying to get them to leave. And then Dodge had walked Wylie to his car.

Dodge volunteered that last bit of information, knowing that it was important.

"You recognized his car?"

"Yes sir. A gray Jaguar XJ-6."

"You saw him get in it? Saw him drive away?"

"That's right."

"No reason to think his car hadn't been sitting right there in the parking lot ever since two o'clock in the afternoon?"

Dodge started to answer and then hesitated. His mouth was open, but his eyes had gone off to one side. John Michael slowly raised his head. He put his pen between his lips and he leaned far back into his chair.

Burnsie, recognizing a mistake, said, "I'll withdraw that question. That's an unfair question. It calls for speculation."

"I object to counsel's argument," said John Michael calmly. "I don't see anything unfair about the question. Mr. Burns has made his bed, now let him lie in it."

"Well, you know, Judge—"

But LoBianco was in full grin. He waved Burnsie quiet and told Dodge he could answer the question.

Dodge said, "I don't know."

"What was that answer?" asked John Michael, turning his ear as if he was a little hard of hearing.

"I don't know."

Burnsie winged the next few questions, trying to get everyone's mind off whatever it was that had caused Dodge's equivocation, trying to restore the sense of synchronization that he had initially established with the witness. Throughout, John Michael sat patiently, twirling his pen between his teeth, until finally Burnsie ran out of questions and sat down awkwardly, his body betraying the uncertainty he felt at turning Dodge back over to John Michael.

"Why," said John Michael, "did you walk Mr. Carpenter to his car?"

"I don't recall."

"Was he too drunk to walk there himself?"

"No."

"Too emotional or distraught?"

"No."

"Didn't he know the way?"

"He knew the way."

"Was his car on the way to your car?"

"Yes."

"Where was his car located?"

"Near the clubhouse."

"How near?"

"Very near."

"The closest space to the clubhouse?"

"I guess."

"Where was your car?"

"Further away."

"How much further?"

"The corner of the lot."

"The back corner?"

"I suppose you'd call it that."

"Why did you park there?"

"It was the only space available when I arrived."

"And what time was that?"

"One forty-five, maybe. Maybe one fifty."

"Was that before or after Mr. Carpenter arrived at the club?"

"Objection!" hollered Burnsie.

LoBianco looked down. "If you know," he instructed Dodge.

Dodge looked at the judge as if he had been hoping he would say something else. He looked back at John Michael, who now had a glint in his eye, a glow to his face, like a predatory animal moving in on his quarry.

"You arrived the same time Mr. Carpenter did, didn't you, Mr. Patterson?"

John Michael could not wait for Dodge's answer. He took a step closer. "You actually saw him arrive and you saw him park his car, didn't you?"

Dodge gripped the end of his chair. "I might have the day confused."

"But what you don't have confused, what you remember now, is that on the afternoon of October fifteenth you saw Wylie Carpenter park his car in a different space than the one it was in when you walked him out at ten o'clock. Isn't that right?"

Dodge Patterson's eyes rocketed to Wylie Carpenter, who sat

at the defendant's table with his own eyes downcast. "I don't remember," he said.

John Michael was happy. John Michael was excited. He was practically raving at Mary Alice Devon, telling her they had to get Lester on the stand right away. "We've got to get the testimony in about the white sweater fibers he took from the driver's seat of Rebecca's car. The jury's going to know then what's going on."

"What about the lab tech?" she said. "Aren't we going to need him to match the fibers in the car with the ones in Wylie's sweater?"

"Of course, of course. But we can put him on after. The jurors are going to know the moment we hold up Les's little baggie. Then we get Mrs. Mitchell up there. She testifies how Wylie came home before he went to the club and we just fill in the gaps. He came home, he took his wife's car up to the overlook, he walked back, he drove his own car to the club. Right? Boom, boom, boom, boom."

Mary Alice began frantically pawing through her notes.

"He plays golf, he plays cards, he takes off at eight to go back to his house. You with me, Mary Alice? Boom, boom, boom . . . gurgle, gurgle, gurgle. Back to the club, shoot the shit with old Dodgie, the moron, and the only mistake he makes is he parks his car in the wrong goddamn place." John Michael beat a drumroll with his open hands on the surface of the counsel's table.

He glanced around the empty courtroom until his eyes came to rest on me. His drumroll slowed to a halt. "Didn't you think to ask him that question, Patt? Didn't it ever occur to you to ask Patterson if Wylie's car had been moved?"

Mary Alice grabbed his sleeve. "But John," she said, reading from her notes, "Sergeant Roselli said it was three point six miles from the overlook to the Carpenter home."

"By roadway, Mary Alice, by roadway." He nodded to me, his face creased peculiarly with a smile that was not a smile. "But that's not the only way to walk from the overlook to the Carpenters', is it, Patt?"

The wooden railing, the fence that is sometimes known as the bar and that separates the audience from the participants in a trial, was between us. I was standing alone on my side and Mary Alice and Jessica and John Michael were all on the other side. My hands were in my pockets and I was not sharing in the general good feeling that was being disseminated as a result of Dodge's unexpected gift of information.

"There's a trail that runs behind the overlook, isn't there, Patt?"

"Yes."

"That trail goes a lot of places, doesn't it?"

"I've told you that before, yes."

"Take it one way and it leads to Stonegate."

"That's right."

"Take it another way and it goes to the Charles."

"Yes. That's what Roselli did."

"But if he had turned west instead of east it would have led him right to the Chesley Estate."

"Not really."

"How long a walk would it be by the trail? Two miles?"

"It's just a path," I said. "It runs from the Charles River to Whitehall Road, but the Chesley Estate is beyond that."

"What are you saying, Patt? That you can't get from Whitehall Road to Bulham Road, where the Chesley Estate is?"

"No. I'm just saying that the path ends there. You want to get from Whitehall to Bulham you've got to walk along Highland Street for another half a mile."

"How come you never told me you could do that, Patt?"

"Do what? Walk from Whitehall to Bulham?"

John Michael shook his head without letting his eyes move. "Walk from the overlook to Wylie Carpenter's home by cutting through the woods. It wouldn't be that hard in the middle of the day, would it?"

"Like I said, the path really doesn't go there."

"How long would it take in daylight for someone like you? For a middle-aged athlete like Wylie Carpenter? Twenty-five, thirty minutes?"

"I haven't been on that path in many years."

"Not even as part of your investigation?"

"That wasn't really what you asked me to do."

"Lester walked it. He discovered the path and found his way to the Chesley Estate using a map and compass."

"He's a helluva man, that Lester."

"Did it in twenty-eight minutes."

"Sounds like Lester has all the qualities of a good dog," I said.

"Like devotion to a task?"

"I suppose."

"Like loyalty to the person he's working for?"

"Lester's switched loyalties from Wembley to you, has he?"

"Like faithfulness?"

"There's that word again."

John Michael's pale brow curled. His tight little mouth became as thin as a pencil line.

"Oh, c'mon, John," I pleaded. "We've been over all this before."

John Michael smacked his way through the gate and came up to where I was standing. He moved rapidly, with his hands hanging straight down by his sides and curled into fists. Mary Alice and Jessica watched us with their mouths open, as if they were ready to start screaming the moment John Michael and I came to blows. But I did not react to John Michael's advance and by the time he came to a halt his expression had changed.

He took a breath and then gently tucked his hand inside my elbow and guided me out to the corridor, where the two of us assumed positions with our backs against the marble wainscoting. "It's times like these I wish I smoked cigarettes," he said, without looking at me.

He put his hands behind him and spread his feet. "I'm under

a lot of pressure these days, as I guess you can tell. A lot of things just aren't quite working out. Almost, you know. Just enough to keep me going. But nothing's quite the way I wanted it."

"Sometimes," I said, "it's best not to want too much."

John Michael's head had been squared to the floor. Now he looked up sharply. "That sort of sums you up, doesn't it, Patt? I mean, a guy like you is not going to sell me out because there's nothing you really want in this life, is there?"

I shrugged. I had not expected my remark to have much significance beyond being a bridge between his thoughts.

"No, really. You're every bit as smart as I am, we're about the same age, we come from the same area—yet look how different our lives have become. I guess you kind of take things as they are, while I'm always out there trying to make them be better. I don't mean that to sound as if I'm putting you down for that, God knows I'm not. I'm just trying to figure out—you know, you get to certain times in your life and you just have to stop and ask yourself if any of what you're doing is worthwhile. Maybe you found the right answer early on. I mean, for each of the things I've accomplished I can think of a hundred reasons why I shouldn't have bothered. This whole thing about being district attorney is a good example. It looks great, it sounds great, but, Jesus, the pressure's never off. A guy doesn't become D.A. in his early thirties and then stay in that position for the next forty years. You've got to move on to something else and get public attention to do it, but meanwhile every little thing you do is open to potshots from the entire community."

John Michael pushed himself off the wall and then let himself fall back again. "That's why I've always valued you and Roy so much. With you guys I could form my own little insular community where I could really be myself. Where I could show my weaknesses, my ignorance. Where I could afford to make mistakes. That's why . . . that's why I'm so sensitive about this anonymous letter I got . . . coming when it did, you know. Coming when I've got this big case in which everything seems to be just slightly off center. All the pegs are just slightly larger than the holes they're supposed to go in. Or slightly smaller."

Some people came walking down the corridor, lawyers with lawyer briefcases. They were talking happily until they saw us and then they cut off in midsentence, perhaps midword. "John," said one of them as he passed by, and the others all nodded and smiled nervously. John had a nice smile for each of them.

As their footsteps drifted away John Michael said, "The combination of things has just naturally made me paranoid. By this point everybody knows I've made a commitment to this case and with the possibility of Kilrain's congressional seat hanging out there, that just ups the stakes to infinity. In other words, if there's one time in my life somebody could screw me up for good it's now. I fall on my face, Kilrain announces his retirement, and fat Constantinis waltzes in."

John Michael shivered at the prospect. He crossed his arms in front of his stomach. "So the case keeps slipping away. And I'm wondering why. And the letter comes. So I start to watch things a little more closely and suddenly the smallest remark, the smallest gesture, the smallest mistake seems to take on added significance. You understand where I'm coming from, Patt?"

"No, not completely, John. I've never liked the case to begin with, you know that. But I'd never do anything to sell you out. And neither, as far as I can tell, would Roy. As for Lester—"

"He's doing what I ask him to, that's all I can say about him."

"Fine. If that's what you want, if that satisfies you, fine. I personally don't trust him, but I don't think he's trying to screw you on this case. I don't think anybody's trying to screw you. I don't know where the letter came from or what it means, but if I were you I'd just forget it."

"Fine," said John Michael, once again pushing off the wall and this time turning to face me. He held out his hand. "Then will you forgive me?"

"Hey," I said, taking the hand in my own, "there's nothing to forgive."

28

Stanley Lester turned out to be an excellent witness for the prosecution, although he did not appear right after Dodge Patterson. John Michael elected to go first with Mrs. Mitchell and then with Mrs. Marconi. Although not making a direct issue out of it, John Michael quite successfully used them to create the impression that the relationship between Mrs. Carpenter and Douglas Rasmussin extended far beyond what would normally be expected between an employer and an employee. And then he called a CPA named Dandurand, who had greasy hair and the personality of a frog, but who nevertheless was able to explain in painstaking detail the multiple millions of dollars of assets, the $63 million of assets, that were about to befall Wylie as a result of the death of his wife.

When Lester did make it to the stand he remained for two full days. Much of what he said was an elaboration, an exaggeration, or simply untrue; but he said everything well and he said it with a mixture of confidence, enthusiasm, and foreign intrigue that made him seem quite credible. Burnsie, with his rumpled suit and his local-boy manner, could not break him, and on more than one occasion his cross-examination technique allowed Lester to enhance his facts with his opinions.

By the time the two counsel had been through direct, cross, redirect, and recross, the story seemed clear enough. The bon-vivant golfer Wylie Carpenter had grown tired of his life with the increasingly reclusive, aging, alcoholic, pill-addicted heiress,

who may or may not have been having affairs right under his
nose. He selected the day when her handsome young yardboy
was leaving for California (to which Lester claimed to have traced
him, trailed him, and lost him). On that day he came home for
lunch, removed his wife's car and drove it to the overlook, walked
back through the woods to get his own car, and then drove off
to the club. That night he sneaked away from his card games,
strangled his wife with the scarf he had recently purchased, delivered her body to her parked car, and then returned to the club
as if nothing had happened. And now he was $63 million richer
and free to frolic with the waitresses at the country club.

John Michael allowed himself to be photographed emerging
from the courthouse and looking triumphant.

In his opening statement, Burnsie had lamented the sad state
of affairs that had caused his client to be made to account for
what he had done simply because of who he was. He had extolled
Wylie as a pillar of the community and had hinted at the dark
forces who were setting up Wylie for their own personal reasons.
A tissue of lies, he called the commonwealth's case, transparent
in its intent and based on nothing more than a desire for sen-
sationalism and character assassination. I naturally assumed
Burnsie was directing his remarks at John Michael, and therefore
was completely taken by surprise when he announced that he
was calling me as his first witness.

I was sitting in the front row between Lester and Jessica Keough
and all three of us reacted as though we had just been bolted to
the backs of our seats. "What the bloody hell?" cracked Lester,
and Jessica, if she didn't use the same words, meant the same
thing.

John Michael literally rushed the bench. He started from his
seat with an objection, but he kept moving closer and closer as
he spoke until he was whispering and gesturing heatedly and
LoBianco had to signal Burns to join them.

The talk at the bench led to talk in the audience. Jessica was
leaning in close to me, so close her hair was touching mine. She

was asking me why Burnsie would possibly be doing this and I was trying to tell her I had no idea when both of us, without a single word to indicate we would do it, turned our heads and looked into the row behind us.

Patty Hansen was sitting only a couple of feet away. Her hair, as always, was hanging over her forehead, dropping in front of her eyes. She was wearing a heavy, fur-collared coat, and she was holding thin brown gloves in one hand.

"Hello, Patty," Jessica said, in a voice that asked what she was doing there when she had never attended a trial before, why she was sitting there without making her presence known, and whether there was any reason why she was looking so furtive as she let her eyes flick back and forth between us.

"Is Mr. Starbuck in the courtroom?" called out Judge LoBianco.

"Yes, sir," I said, turning front and waving my hand.

"Ah." LoBianco grinned and I had the sinking feeling I was in trouble. "You may take the stand, sir."

Burnsie had never been what I would call a friend. When he was district attorney I worked for John Michael and John Michael worked for him and it was a rare occasion when we had direct contact. He never ordered me to do anything, he never praised me, and he never yelled at me either.

Now he was looking at me in that peculiar way attorneys have when they are pretending for the jury they know nothing and yet are almost robotically anticipating certain answers.

"Good afternoon, Mr. Starbuck."

"Good afternoon."

"That's Patterson Starbuck, you said when you were being sworn in?"

"Yes."

"Is Patterson an old family name?"

Burnsie's orange hair was matted down. His face was round and flushed. His mouth was round and it opened like a little hole in his skin when he spoke. Of all the objects in the universe, Burnsie's face looked most like a catcher's mitt.

"Yes," I said.

"Are you, by any chance, related to D. Dodge Patterson, who testified, when was it, last week?"

I looked out at the audience. The benches were about half full. I saw Lester and Jessica and Patty Hansen. I saw Ralphie Libby sitting next to a uniformed Chief Wembley Tuttle. I saw Gerard Whitman, the loyal friend, sitting with Bud Teasdale. I saw the television reporter and the television cameraman, who had not been there since the first day of testimony, and I knew that something was up and that at least a couple of those people knew what it was.

"We're some sort of cousins," I said.

"How are you employed, Mr. Starbuck?"

"I'm what's known as the litigation coordinator for the office of the district attorney for Exeter County."

"And what exactly is the litigation coordinator?"

I nailed Burnsie with my eyes. "Well, Mr. Burns, I'm not exactly sure I'm the right person to define the title since I believe you had a hand in making up the position when you were district attorney, but as I understand it I'm a public investigator employed by Exeter County to investigate crimes and to assist the county attorneys and police in their investigations and presentation of the evidence. In my capacity I assist and supplement the role of the state police, in particular Detective Lieutenant Ralph Libby, who is assigned to the Exeter County office as an investigator."

Burnsie chuckled. It was meant to cover the fact that I had, in a very small way, embarrassed him. It was also meant as a sign to me, a precursor of what was to come.

"As litigation coordinator, do you report directly to Mr. Keough, over here?"

"Sometimes. I report to the attorney assigned to handle the case on which I'm working."

"And you're given a good deal of discretion in your investigations, aren't you? Mr. Keough delegates authority to you in that regard?"

"I guess that's correct."

"And on days when you're not working on a particular case assigned to a particular staff attorney, you regularly report to Mr. Keough, don't you?"

"You could say that."

"In fact, I could say that you and Deputy District Attorney Hansen are part of a sort of kitchen cabinet for Mr. Keough, couldn't I?" Burnsie asked, his voice rising.

"You could . . ." I waited a beat or two until Burnsie had started to milk his self-satisfaction, and then I said, "It wouldn't necessarily be true."

The titters I drew probably did not make the remark worthwhile. Burnsie merely plunged on.

"You assisted in the preparation and investigation of this case, didn't you? Assisted Mr. Keough, I mean?"

"Objection," shouted John Michael in perhaps his loudest voice of the trial.

"Overruled," said LoBianco without looking up.

"Approach the bench, Your Honor?"

"No."

John Michael bit his lip and I answered that I had.

"In fact, you were in charge of the investigation?"

"No. Detective Lieutenant Libby was in charge."

"Did you ever, at any time, receive any direction regarding this particular investigation from Detective Lieutenant Libby?"

I hesitated, wanting everyone to know that the question was ambiguous, but Burnsie bulled ahead without waiting for an answer.

"In fact you never did, and in fact you carried out your investigation right through the indictment of my client by effectively bypassing the state police and Detective Lieutenant Libby, didn't you?"

The first nodules of fear began to cluster inside my chest. "No," I said, but Burnsie didn't care.

"How many times did you question my client without Detective Libby being present?"

"Twice, that I recall."

"How many times did you read him his rights?"

"Objection," said John Michael.

"Overruled."

"None. He wasn't under arrest or even a suspect when I interviewed him."

"When did you determine he was a suspect?"

I needed to think about it and in order to do that I had to remove my eyes from Burnsie. I did not like removing my eyes from him, not until I knew what he was going to do with me up there on the stand. "When at the end of my second interview I ascertained that Mr. Carpenter was unable to account for approximately two hours of his time on the night of his wife's murder."

"Did you ever find out where he was during those two hours, Mr. Starbuck?"

The question pierced me. It made me go cold and clammy. I said, "Not really," and the words did not sound as if they were mine.

"What does that mean, Mr. Starbuck: not really?"

"Well . . . I was told—"

"Objection," said John Michael. "Hearsay."

LoBianco considered his notes, looked down at me and said, "Were you told whatever you are about to say by Mr. Carpenter?"

"No."

"In that case, the objection's sustained. Don't answer what you were told by somebody else."

"I can't answer any other way, Judge."

LoBianco showed me all his teeth. "Then you can't answer at all. Next question, Mr. Burns."

Burnsie held his right elbow in his left hand and ran his right index finger up alongside his cheek. "You conducted interviews of other people besides Mr. Carpenter in carrying out your investigation, didn't you?"

"Yes."

"How many of those people were you told to interview by Detective Lieutenant Libby, the man you said was in charge of the investigation?"

"None."

"Aside from my client, did you at any time consider any of the other people who you interviewed to be a suspect in the killing of Mrs. Carpenter?"

I remembered Lester's line that everybody was a suspect and I probably chose not to use it simply because it had come from Lester. "Yes," I said.

"Who?"

Once again John Michael rose to his feet with an objection and once again there was a lengthy conference at the bench. It ended with John Michael delivering me a quick, unhappy look.

"You may answer, Mr. Starbuck," declared the judge. "However, I caution the jury that any answer this witness is about to give is not evidence of the truth of the matter asserted. In other words, it is not evidence of the guilt or innocence of any person. It is merely being allowed in as part of the defense's case in support of their claim of bias or prejudice on the part of the prosecution."

Involuntarily, my head snapped, my mouth fell open. I was so totally unprepared for such a remark that I compounded its effect. And LoBianco, with a curt nod, simply acted as though he had done me a favor.

"Mr. Starbuck?" said Burnsie. "The judge told you to answer the question."

"Suspects could have been anybody, Mr. Burns. You know that."

"Ah, what I know is beside the point. You didn't, for example, consider Mr. Whitman, sitting back here, to be a suspect, did you?"

I looked at Whitman with his arms folded and his face defiant. "No," I said.

"Or Mrs. Mitchell?"

"I didn't really, no. Not once I met her."

"Well, then. Who did you consider a suspect?"

"Mr. Carpenter."

"Only Mr. Carpenter? Right from the start, is that what you told Mr. Keough? That my client did it?"

"No."

"Then who else did you consider, Mr. Starbuck?"

"Douglas Rasmussin."

"Ah, the missing caretaker. Where was he from?"

"He was from Walmouth."

"I see. And as part of your investigation did you interview Mr. Rasmussin?"

"Yes."

"In Walmouth?"

"In Los Angeles."

"So you found him there?"

"Yes."

"Mr. Starbuck, weren't you working with Inspector Lester on this investigation?"

"We were each conducting investigations."

"And weren't you keeping in contact with each other? Weren't you sharing information with each other?"

"Yes. We were."

"Well, Mr. Starbuck, you were present when Inspector Lester told us how he traced Rasmussin to California and then could not locate him once he got out there. Didn't you tell the inspector where he was?"

"I did. But Mr. Rasmussin apparently had moved without leaving any forwarding address."

"So the only one who ever met with Rasmussin in connection with this investigation—these investigations—was you."

"That's right."

"And you determined on your own . . . what? That he was no longer a suspect?"

"I determined . . . I reported my findings to Mr. Keough and he made whatever determination there was."

"Based on what you told him?"

"Yes."

"And did you tell Mr. Keough that Rasmussin ought to be arrested?"

"No."

"Did you tell him that Rasmussin ought to be let go, disregarded, ignored?"

"I believe I told Mr. Keough he had testimony that may be of use in this trial."

"May be of use in the trial against Wylie Carpenter, is that what you're saying?"

It was and it wasn't. I glanced at John Michael for some indication as to how to answer, but he did not seem to be sensing the danger of this line of questioning. "I meant of use in any trial concerning the murder of Rebecca Carpenter."

Burnsie backed off. He took a walk behind his table and tilted his head to look at the ceiling for a while. "You would agree, wouldn't you, Mr. Starbuck, that at the point the district attorney decided to seek an indictment of my client he had concluded that Douglas Rasmussin was not a suspect?"

"I guess I'd have to, yes."

"And by that point, whenever it was, you had told him your opinion of Douglas Rasmussin, who some time prior to that had been a suspect?"

"Yes."

"And as of that point in time nobody else had interviewed Rasmussin?"

"Actually, Inspector Lester talked to him by phone before I met with him."

"But since then, nobody else has interviewed Rasmussin?"

"As far as I know."

"And nobody knows where he is? Nobody has seen him since you allegedly did some months ago?"

"I can only tell you that I don't know where he is."

Burnsie clenched both fists in front of his chest. "So you would agree then that the dismissal of Douglas Rasmussin as a suspect in the murder of Rebecca Carpenter necessarily had to come as a result of your say-so and your say-so alone?"

John Michael at last saw what Burnsie was doing, but by the time he voiced his objection the damage was done.

Burnsie barely waited until the word "Sustained" was out of the judge's mouth before he was back at me again. "You personally orchestrated the indictment of Wylie Carpenter, didn't you?"

"I don't know what you mean," I said. I wanted to loosen my tie, but I was afraid of how it would look.

John Michael, still seated, was contending that I was being badgered. LoBianco was smiling and telling Burnsie not to badger me. Burnsie was not even listening.

"You didn't care who was found guilty of this murder as long as it was one of the wealthy people of Woodedge, one of the gentry, one of the people you aspired to be. Isn't that right, Mr. Starbuck?"

My feet lost all their feelings. They were empty cylinders at the bottom of my legs. My back was cold. It was nothing but a framework of bones. My facial muscles wouldn't work. I could only stare and listen as John Michael snorted his incredulity at such a question.

"Who first suggested Wylie Carpenter to Mr. Keough as a suspect?" demanded Philip Burns.

John Michael stopped arguing. He looked at me and made no effort to stop my answer.

"Me, I suppose," I said.

"Who first suggested Rasmussin?"

"I don't remember."

"It wasn't you?"

"It may have been Chief Tuttle."

"Did you ever suggest anyone other than Wylie Carpenter?"

"I don't know."

"Oh, really? Well, tell me, Mr. Starbuck, didn't you also propose Dodge Patterson as a suspect?"

My throat was very dry, almost too dry for me to speak. I knew that the defense had a legal right to our investigation files, I assumed Burns had been through them, and I was damn sure they said nothing about me suggesting Dodge as a suspect. I had only mentioned it orally in meetings, in front of people like John Michael, and Jessica Keough, and Ralphie Libby and Royster Hansen. With the exception of Royster, they were all here today. "Yes," I said. "I naturally considered it because—"

"Your cousin?" roared Burns. "Your own cousin?"

"He's a distant cousin and that shouldn't have affected my objectivity."

"No," said Burnsie, adjusting the knot in his tie. "No, it shouldn't."

"I object to counsel's argumentative comments," said John Michael, getting halfway to his feet and pointing at his opponent. He had stopped taking notes. He had stopped looking as though nothing that Burnsie did could possibly faze him.

LoBianco solved the instant complaint easily enough. "Don't argue," he told Burns.

"Just how distant a relation are you, Mr. Starbuck?"

I took a moment, as if calculating what I had known since I was little more than a toddler. "Our great-grandfathers were brothers."

"I see. The Patterson family name is an old one in Woodedge, isn't it?"

"Yes."

"The Patterson family was one of the original founding families, wasn't it?"

"Yes."

"Sixteen forty?"

"That's when they first settled, I believe."

"So you and Dodge trace your roots back a long way together?"

"Yes."

"And did you grow up in Woodedge along with Dodge?"

"No. I was born and raised in West Nestor."

"I see. And where were you educated?"

I asked for and received a cup of water from the bailiff, a weightlifter named Pupulski. He and I knew each other slightly and he made eye contact with me when he handed me the water. The contact was meant to tell me to hang in there.

I drank all the water before I answered. "Nestor High School. I received an associate's degree from Walmouth J.C. and a bachelor's degree from UMass-Boston."

"Anything else?"

Burnsie well knew what else. "I have a master's degree in American civilization from Brown University."

"Anything else?"

"I completed some course work toward my Ph.D. in American civ at Brown, but I didn't write the dissertation."

"Really?" he remarked, as though he had never read my résumé. "And what did you intend to do with a Ph.D.?"

"I was never sure. That's why I dropped out after one year."

"Was that the only reason you dropped out?"

"I had financial reasons, too." I remembered to look at the jury. And to smile. "It cost a lot of money to go there."

No one smiled back.

"You were paying your own way, were you?"

I reached for the water cup again and saw that it was empty. "Yeah," I said, withdrawing my hand.

"That's a rather admirable record, Mr. Starbuck, working your way all the way up from our local junior college to a doctoral program at one of the most prestigious universities in the country. You must have worked very hard."

I said nothing. There was no question, he got no answer.

"Tell me, did that cause you any feelings of resentment that you had to drop out so close to your goal because you didn't have the money to pay the rest of your way?"

"Objection," said John Michael, but he said it as if he did not expect to win the point.

"Same reasons as stated at the bench," responded Burnsie as if he did.

LoBianco nodded. "Overruled."

"It wasn't really my goal, Mr. Burns. That was one of the problems. I had this professor at UMass who more or less sponsored me for the program and I—"

"What was your goal, Mr. Starbuck? To work as an investigator for the district attorney's office?"

"It's an honorable job, Mr. Burns," I said softly.

"Well, what was your job before this one?"

"I was a claims supervisor for Northeast American Way Insurance Company."

"And how did you happen to go to work for Northeast American Way?"

I knew at that moment where Burnsie was going and I wanted to scream at John Michael to stop it. But John Michael was sitting almost in a slouch, his legs stretched out in front of him, saving his precious objections, sparing himself from the mini-defeats of Judge LoBianco's rulings.

"My father," I said, "was an agent for the company."

"I see. A self-made man, was your father?"

"Yeah."

"So he did not inherit any of the Patterson family holdings."

"No."

"And you did not have any inheritance? Nothing to help you pay for schooling at Brown?"

"No."

"Did that cause you any resentment, Mr. Starbuck: the fact that your cousin Dodge grew up in Woodedge in a beautiful home and got to go to Andover and Amherst College and get his law degree from an expensive private university, all without ever having to work?"

"I didn't even know Dodge. I never met him before this investigation."

"And when you did meet him, did you introduce yourself? Did you tell him you were his cousin?"

"No."

"Why not?"

"I didn't think it was relevant."

Burnsie reacted as though this was a very surprising answer. He bent his elbow and touched his finger to his lips and then took it away and gently shook it at me. "Your branch of the family had certain claims to the Patterson holdings, didn't it?"

"I don't know what you mean." But I did. And John Michael still was not moving to help me.

"Didn't your father lay claim to Dodge Patterson's home in Woodedge?"

I looked directly at John Michael. I spoke directly to John Michael. I watched as Mary Alice jostled him with her arm to get him to pay attention to me. "I still don't know what you're talking about, Mr. Burns."

"Didn't your father once occupy that house, Mr. Starbuck? Didn't he, in fact, move his whole family in there while his relatives were away on vacation?"

John Michael threw up his hands. "Your Honor, what does this, even if true, have to do with the facts of this case?"

"I'll tell you," said Burnsie, dropping any pretense of being the innocent questioner. "It has to do with the fact that this man, this Patterson Starbuck, had a motive for everything he did: for orchestrating the investigation, for making his allegations, and for influencing the district attorney to his conclusions. And that motive was, pure and simple, one of revenge, jealousy, and retribution against the whole town of Woodedge for a longstanding family grievance."

John Michael was bellowing indignation at Burnsie's tactic. LoBianco was glaring at both attorneys and slamming his wooden gavel to get their attention. "Gentlemen," he shouted, "get yez both up here." Then he remembered the television Minicam now whirring away and he looked directly into it and clamped his lips grimly together.

The three men were so excited I could hear them as they leaned across the bench and whispered within inches of each other's faces. "But, Your Honor," John Michael was protesting, "this is crazy. Wylie Carpenter isn't even related to him."

"He tried to pin it on his cousin, he couldn't do it, so he turned his venomous attack on his cousin's best buddy," snapped Burns. "He hates 'em all anyway because they're all rich and they all have what he doesn't."

And LoBianco was talking right back at them, stepping on their words, possibly not even listening to what they were saying. "If either one of you makes another outburst like this I'm censuring you. Got me? Because right now I'm on the verge of declaring a mistrial."

"Let me pursue this line, Judge. You'll see—"

"It's not the line, counsel. It's your argument that I'm ripshit about."

"I'll watch it, Judge."

"You do."

Then LoBianco straightened up and smiled into the camera. "The jury is to disregard Mr. Burns's last remarks as they constitute argument and, as I have told you before, what counsel says is not evidence. However, the question may stand and Mr. Starbuck may answer it." He shifted his smile to the jury and regarded them paternally, as though everyone was happy now.

I let the camera continue to roll for a long time before I agreed that my father had once occupied the Patterson house.

"And wasn't your father banned from going near that house for a period of some years after that?"

"A restraining order was issued, yes."

"An order obtained by his mother's cousin Gordon Patterson?"

"Yes."

"Dodge's grandfather?"

"Yes."

"So, would you say there was a family feud between the two branches, the Starbucks and the Pattersons?"

"No, I wouldn't."

Burnsie was rather skilled at getting in his next question before I had any chance to explain my answer to his last. He spoke quickly, saying, "Your father continued to go near the house even though he was restrained by court order, didn't he?"

I wanted the water again. I looked at Pupulski and signaled and he nodded. "I don't know," I said.

"In fact, he used to approach the house on Whitehall Road from the rear, following a path up through the woods; and in fact he was chased away from the grounds at gunpoint on at least one occasion by his relatives—your relatives—wasn't he?"

I watched Pupulski drawing the water from a bubbling cooler. "He may have been," I said.

"What was that?" Burnsie cupped his ear and put a pained expression on his face.

"I said, he may have been."

Philip Burns lowered his hand and stood very still. "And in fact, Mr. Starbuck, your father took a gun to that house himself one day, didn't he?"

Pupulski, starting back, trying not to spill his paper cup of water, stopped cold.

"No," I said, but I did not hear the word come out of my mouth.

"And that day he was found shot to death on the path behind the Patterson house, wasn't he?"

The courtroom was very, very still. Everyone in it seemed to understand my answer even before I gave it.

Burns, his voice now nearly as soft as mine, said, "And although it was ruled a suicide, you always thought that your father's death was brought about by one of the Pattersons, didn't you?"

As though he was a caring physician whose only concern was my interest, Philip Burns leaned in closer. "What's your answer, Mr. Starbuck?"

"The answer," I said, the words catching in my mouth, "is that what you're asking, what you're implying, is disgusting. I think it's so far beneath normal standards of human conduct, what you're doing, that you've made me sick to my stomach."

Somebody, somewhere, suppressed a nervous giggle. It wasn't John Michael. He was staring at me in shock. Most everyone else was not looking at me at all.

"I see," said Burns, leaning back again. His arms were folded, his hands were tucked under his biceps. "Well, then. Let's go back to a different area. Wouldn't you consider yourself, Mr. Starbuck, to be the single greatest influence on Mr. Keough's decision to prosecute my client?"

Pupulski delivered my water. There was apology written all over his face.

"No."

"Who was then? Jessica Keough?"

John Michael's head popped up. A look of disbelief crossed his boyish features. "What's he doing bringing my wife into this?" he demanded.

"It's relevant, Judge," said Burnsie quickly.

"No," said John Michael, bouncing his pencil off his table. "I want to know what he's doing bringing my wife into this." He had gotten to his feet and Burnsie instinctively moved away from him.

"Explain, Mr. Burns," ordered LoBianco.

"Let me withdraw the question, Judge, and ask this. Mr. Starbuck, you didn't protest when I used the term 'kitchen cabinet' a while back. You understood that to refer to John Michael Keough's little informal group of closest advisers, didn't you?"

"I suppose."

"And that group consists of you, Roy Hansen, and Mr. Keough's wife, Jessica, am I right?"

"There he goes again, Judge."

"The questions so far are all right, Mr. Keough. Let's just see where he's going with this."

I said, "Insofar as I know what you're talking about, Mr. Keough has on occasion called the three of us together for advice."

"And you were present when Mrs. Keough advised her husband with respect to this case, weren't you?"

"Your Honor, this is outrageous."

"Sit down, Mr. Keough."

"You would agree she had an influence on him in his decision to prosecute Wylie Carpenter."

"I can't agree or disagree. I don't know."

"And you had an influence over Mrs. Keough, didn't you?"

John Michael was too stunned by the question to object. I looked to the audience, where Jessica's eyes were as big as Christmas ornaments. Then, behind her, I saw the twitch of a head, a sweep of stringy brown hair; and by leaning to one side I was able to see the face of Patty Hansen, and I was able to see that her expression was one of pure glee.

"I don't think so," I said slowly.

"Weren't you . . ." Burnsie hesitated. His mouth formed a circle, closed, and opened again. ". . . In fact having an affair with Mrs. Keough—"

Whatever his last words were they were drowned out by John Michael. With a sudden shot of his arm he knocked half his files and papers and books to the floor. "Is that outrageous enough for you, Judge?" he said shrilly. "Accusing my wife of adultery in the middle of a goddamn murder trial?"

Mary Alice Devon was unable to keep her hold on John Michael's coattails and it is possible he would have gone after Philip Burns in front of everyone if Pupulski's muscle-bulging frame had not magically appeared between them.

Burnsie, now that he could see he was safe, was trying to explain himself to the judge. "But why can't I ask a question like that? It's the same thing he asked of Dodge Patterson."

"He's gotta be drunk," shouted John Michael over Pupulski's shoulder. "Everybody knows he's a drunk. That's how come I've got his job."

Pupulski slipped his massive arm around John Michael's waist and lifted his feet off the floor. The judge was pointing the handle end of his gavel at Burns and telling him that he was censured.

"Just make him answer the question," Burnsie was pleading,

his sweaty hands spread wide. "And then if he says no you can censure me."

"You're censured now," LoBianco hollered. "You're censured, you're in contempt, and you're going to jail because this is a mistrial, Mr. Burns, and you have caused it."

His gavel smashed down on the bench. Burnsie kept arguing, John Michael kept hollering, and all the while the television Minicam kept rolling.

29

It is best not to want too much. John Michael had said that was my creed. It is best not to want. My father wanted. Too much. John Michael wanted and now I was suffering the consequences. Betrayed by everything I never stood for.

I lay on my bed in my anonymous Commonwealth Avenue apartment listening to the sounds of late-night Boston pass beneath my window. Snow tires made squishing noises as they rolled over salt-marked pavement. Occasionally a radio would crackle. Rarer still was the cry of a human voice. I could hear them, those human voices, but in the hours I lay awake they only drifted my way once or twice or maybe three times. Just enough to remind me that there were people out there in the darkness, people with jobs and families and problems that had nothing to do with me and my humiliation. Just enough to remind me of my favorite sound ever, the sound of children playing outside as night was coming on.

That was the sound of my childhood, when the world was mine, when I was going to grow up to be a great ballplayer—or at least rich and secure, honored and honorable. It was an indistinct memory, but the strongest one I had: my friends' voices calling to me in the growing darkness, our ways lit by the last vestiges of twilight, by the occasional streetlight, by the glow of familiarity of everything in the neighborhood. And when it was finally too dark to stay out I would rush into the house, still full of energy but ready to be made safe and warm and full by my mother.

She had never wanted too much, my mother, and I had always believed her to be the most stable person I knew. When my father was with us she made the best of the situation by adopting his dreams and complaints as her own. When he was gone she put them behind her, as though they had never existed, and there was no further reason to speak of Woodedge or Pattersons or suicide, estates or heirlooms or inheritances. From then on she only mentioned my father's name in connection with good things or simple things, such as the way he laughed or the foods he liked; and I would listen and say nothing because she seemed happiest keeping memories on that level and because neither of us wanted to open the doors to the world of hurt he had left behind.

She had called me after the evening news and she had asked me if there was anything she could do. I thought of a hundred funny lines: make me a bowl of chicken soup, yell at mean old Phil Burns, ask Kelsey if he can get me a job on the loading dock. Remind me in the future to pay more attention to miserable women like Patty Hansen. "No," I said, "there's nothing you can do." And she had said, "Well, at least they kept you in the background."

I had, of course, been in the background throughout. Yet that had not kept me from serving as the means by which the Keoughs sought to achieve their fame, Carpenter and Burns their defense, Patty Hansen her revenge. All of them had exploited me because they had wanted so much more than I. Or perhaps they had done it simply because I had let them—because I had confused wanting with caring and had told myself I had no need of either. Or perhaps they had recognized what I had not: that there were things that I wanted, things that I had wanted so much they had made me blind.

That last thought bothered me more than any other. It made me unable to sleep no matter how long I lay in bed.

*   *   *

It was still pitch dark when I got dressed. I put on wool socks and blue jeans, a T-shirt, a flannel shirt, and rubber-soled boots. I splashed water on my face and brushed my teeth and then I put on a parka and gloves and went downstairs to warm up my Alfa. I sat sipping instant coffee and listening to the good morning voices of the radio news readers and when the coffee was gone and the car was warm I drove out to Woodedge and parked by the side of the road before the sun came up.

At seven o'clock there was enough gray light for me to be able to get out. The snow on the sides of the road and beneath the trees was covered with a breakable crust that looked like ground glass. The driveway on which I started walking was rutted with ice, some of it blue, some of it almost yellow. I followed it to the old wooden barn, slip-sliding even on my rubber soles.

When I was a boy I thought that the barn must hold wondrous things. Viewed from the path at the rear of the property it had the potential for haylofts and rope swings and horse stalls. In reality it proved to be a makeshift garage and storage area, occupied in the middle by the two family automobiles and on the sides by the wreckage of the sixties and seventies and perhaps the eighties: an old refrigerator, a sink, a broken couch, crates of moldering books, empty oil cans, and rusting machinery parts. There were other things, more modern things, things that looked new enough to work, like a riding lawnmower and a snowblower and shovels and garden utensils; but I was interested in trunks and cabinets and cartons and whatever would make a good hiding place.

I found it in a cardboard barrel choked with strands of metal and broken chunks of Sheetrock. The metal strands were probably part of an old bedframe. I had to hold them out of my way with the back of my arm and shoulder so I could reach to the bottom, so I could move aside the pieces of Sheetrock. I was bent over, almost handcuffed by what I was doing, and I did not hear the doors move or the footsteps behind me. I only heard a voice tell me to straighten up slowly with my hands empty.

I did as I was told, my hands held high.

"It's you, isn't it, Mr. Starbuck?"

I admitted that it was.

"Give me one good reason why I shouldn't shoot you."

"Because then people might start asking questions you don't want to answer." I turned very slowly. "Particularly if you leave your gun next to my body."

Frost Patterson was dressed for the cold. He was wearing a three-quarter-length coat that would have allowed him to survive an Arctic night. It's fur-lined hood peaked above his bald head and shadowed the colorlessness of his haughty, unforgiving face. In one hand he held a gnarled cane, and the only thing that made him look dangerous was the pistol he held in his other hand. It was a medium-caliber automatic, the kind that a frail person like Frost could use with some accuracy over the distance of twenty feet or so that separated us.

There was a slight tremor to his body, one that I could not remember seeing before, but his voice was flat, almost resigned. "Your father was a pest, Mr. Starbuck. A pain in the ass. But I didn't shoot him. He did that himself, and I always suspected he did it on our property as a final little element of whatever game he thought he was playing with us. I suspect he did it hoping somebody would think it was one of us. My brother or me, maybe. But it wasn't."

"People will never know, though, will they?"

He laughed harshly. "People don't care."

"They might if you shoot me now."

"On the contrary. They'd know exactly why I had to shoot you now. You've come here to do my family harm because you've got this crazy idea that I shot your father. It all came out in court yesterday, didn't it?" There was nothing pleasurable about the grin on Frost Patterson's face. It may not even have been a grin. "The news didn't bother to show it all. It was only interested in covering the sex and violence angle, the question about your affair with the district attorney's wife and Keough's assault on that other lawyer there. But Wem Tuttle came by last night and told me what really happened. He told me what led up to that farrago. He told me to watch out for you, that you might be coming out here after Dodge next." He grunted at Wembley's prescience.

I slackened my hands. "What would I be doing out here in the barn that could possibly harm Dodge?"

"Planting something."

"What if I wasn't planting anything? What if there was something that was already here that would be evidence as to who killed Rebecca Carpenter? What if there was something here that would help to clear Wylie and make sure he isn't retried for the murder?"

"Wembley says there's no way Keough will try him a second time. He says the whole case is in shambles, that Wylie's lawyer discredited you and proved it was just some kind of a vendetta on your part. He says Keough's publicly disgraced himself and the judge actually did him a favor by declaring a mistrial." Frost paused and I could hear him wheezing until he got his rhythm going again. "He says the only thing we have to be careful of is you trying to pull something. That's why I was watching for you. Been up all night."

"Frost, what if Rebecca's pocketbook is in this barn? What if it's in that barrel I was just looking in? Wouldn't that mean anything to you?"

"It would mean that you put it there. It would mean that you're twice as dangerous as I thought you were because now I have to wonder how you got it."

"What if I didn't put it there, though? What would that mean to you?"

"You did put it there," he said, his voice rising, cracking, making me instinctively thrust my hands higher. "You put it there to frame my boy. You're going to say he did it to get money to pay off his gambling debts, or maybe because of the affair he had—"

"Your son didn't have an affair with Rebecca. That was just something your daughter-in-law told you to cover up her own affair with Wylie."

Frost's tremor became a shimmer. His gun moved up and down, but it stayed trained on me. "Gretchen?" he said.

"Why are you so surprised? Did you think she and your son had such a wonderful marriage? Dodge may have looked darn good when he was a twenty-year-old preppie, but not when he's an indebted thirty-five-year-old with no inheritance and no future. What did you think, that a woman like Gretchen was going to be satisfied forever just because she got the Patterson name? Think again, Frost. The Patterson name doesn't mean shit in this day and age."

Frost was thinking. I could tell by the trembles.

"She and Wylie used to meet on Tuesday nights at the River Inn. You remember Tuesday nights, that's when she told you she was going to the Woodedge Woman's Club. Only she didn't go to either the club or the inn on the Tuesday night that Rebecca was killed."

"She went shopping," Frost mumbled.

"Maybe. But she also went to the Carpenters' house. Maybe she told Rebecca they were going to go together. They talked earlier that day on the phone, you know, and Rebecca probably needed a costume, too. It would make sense that Rebecca would have put on her new scarf if she thought she was going out. People don't tend to wear scarfs if they are staying home alone, do they? But I don't know exactly what went on, Frost. I can only tell you what I think happened: that Gretchen went to the house, that either Rebecca was loaded or Gretchen got her loaded, and that Gretchen strangled her with her scarf—probably from behind, probably while she was sitting in a chair somewhere so that when she kicked out or fought back she wouldn't leave any marks on Gretchen or anything else."

Frost cleared his throat with a rattling noise that I took as a sign to continue.

"She hauled Rebecca out to her own car and manipulated her feet to make it look as if that's where she died. Then she drove her up to the overlook and walked back to the Carpenter house by way of the woods. We were stumped by that part for a while, but then I remembered what your grandson had told me about taking walks in the woods with his mother. Ian even had a picture of the pond you have to go by if you walk from the overlook to your house. Gretchen could have done it with a flashlight if she knew the trail. Once she got here it was just a matter of walking along the road to the Carpenters', picking up her car, and getting back home to bed before Dodge returned from the club."

"You're guessing, Mr. Starbuck," Frost said, but there was not a great deal of conviction in the way he said it.

I lowered my hands. I put them all the way down. "Perhaps on some things. Not on everything. If that pocketbook is here it's going to substantiate a lot. You see, as long as it's missing the possibility exists that the killer took it because he needed the cash that was in it. It helps make a logical suspect out of the caretaker who disappeared the day Rebecca was killed.

"Gretchen knew that caretaker very well, Frost. She orchestrated his hiring by the Carpenters. She knew Rebecca liked good-looking, athletic men, and that Rebecca was lonely and unhappy and being ignored by her husband. Gretchen set up the dismissal of the Marconis, who had been with the Chesley family for years, and she convinced the lifeguard at Stonegate to go to work in their place until the fifteenth of October and then take off for California. The Carpenters probably never knew he was leaving. He probably never knew why he couldn't tell them, but Douglas Rasmussin's a stupid kid and he would do whatever Gretchen wanted because Gretchen knows how to manipulate men—all sorts of men. Even now I imagine he's been in touch with her and she's responsible for him making himself scarce. And this is the point, Frost . . . her plan was to set up Rasmussin as the suspect, even the scapegoat if necessary, so that her lover Wylie wouldn't be in any jeopardy for what she did. Taking the pocketbook was part of the plan."

Frost said nothing. He just stared.

"The police have combed the woods looking for it and can't find a trace—which makes sense because she wouldn't have wanted to have thrown it away along the trail leading here. But once the trail ended, once she had to walk along Highland Street, she wouldn't want to be seen carrying a dead woman's purse, would she? And she had to pass right by this barn to get to the Carpenters', didn't she?"

The old man's eyes flicked to the barrel behind me.

"I've got more, Frost," I said. "It's all circumstantial, but I think it'll mean something to you."

Frost licked his lips. It was an ugly sight.

"I don't know how much Wembley said to you, but the cross examination of me yesterday was based on a lot of inside information, information Phil Burns shouldn't have had. Some of it came from a leak inside the prosecution team, but not all of it—not the personal stuff about me. There were things brought up that I've never talked about with anyone—that nobody else would know, or suspect, or put into words except you, Frost. And you didn't call up Wylie's lawyer and tell him, did you? You wouldn't have had any reason to. I mean, you weren't planning on marrying Wylie and sharing his newly inherited sixty-three-million-dollar estate, were you?"

Frost blinked. It was something that seemed to take him an extraordinarily long time to do. "Gretchen's married to my son," he said weakly.

"She'd asked you a lot of questions about me, hadn't she? Starting with that day I first came here to interview her, when you told her never to let a Starbuck in the house, you gave her all the dirt about my father, I bet."

"She asked me some questions." The skinny old tongue came out and went around his lips again. "I told her some things."

"Did you tell her where I lived?"

He moved the gun from side to side. It was a way of shrugging. "I told her your father lived in West Nestor. I told her your parents' names and she could have looked the address up in the phone book, I suppose."

"And she could have sent a hit man there, too, couldn't she?"

Frost Patterson's head drew back. "That's preposterous," he snorted, and the old contempt returned to his eyes.

"Why?" I said, speaking quickly in case he was deciding he did not have to listen to me anymore. "Somebody went out to my mother's house in November and put four bullets into the front of it in an attempt to shoot me. I don't know if I was supposed to get killed or not, but I know everyone was supposed to think Dougie Rasmussin was responsible because the gunman used a stolen car that was abandoned behind Dougie's favorite watering hole in Walmouth. The one thing I can be certain about, Frost, is that Dougie didn't have any reason to shoot me—not then, anyhow. Not just after Wylie had been indicted. So who else is there at that point? Not Wylie. The time to take out an investigator is before he hands in his evidence. Doesn't do you very much good to eliminate him after you've already been indicted. The only one who still had reason to fear the investigator, who knew the investigator had information about her that nobody else had, was Gretchen."

"Sounds to me," Frost said, clearing his throat with a rattling sound, "as though you're throwing mud against the wall, Mr. Starbuck."

"I don't imagine she ever gave you the spiel about how tough it was growing up in Lowell, about how you had to get to know your neighbors just to keep them from stealing your car, but she gave it to me. If she needed a stolen car she knew where to go. She might have gotten the driver along with it, or she might have just gotten the car and taken the shots herself. She might even have used that gun you've got in your hand."

There was an added tremble in Frost's arm as he glanced at the gun. His glance became a stare, as if he was remembering something or seeing something that he was not sharing. "How," he said at last, "are you going to prove that it was my daughter-in-law who did any of these things?"

"I can't prove it. Like you said a few minutes ago, my credibility is shot. But find the pocketbook and you can judge for yourself."

The old man thought about what I was saying. "And if I find it, I should tell Wylie, is that what you want me to do?"

"I suspect he already knows. I suspect that's why he refuses to tell anybody where he was for those two hours on the night of the fifteenth. Wylie, from everything I've been able to learn, considers himself an honorable man. But he's got a confused sense of honor. It's all bundled up with notions of chivalry and machismo and dignity. He's not going to be making accusations or offering up someone else to save himself. But he has to know. If he and Gretchen ever professed love for each other, if they ever talked about marrying, then he has to wonder why she never joined him at the River Inn on the night his wife was killed."

"Is it possible . . ." Frost hesitated, trying to decide if he should say the next words. I helped him.

"That he was involved? I don't know. There are some things that point to it even now. The scarf, for example. Was it just a coincidence he bought it three days before it was used to kill Rebecca? The police haven't been able to find any other scarfs in her wardrobe, her house. How did she happen to be wearing one that night? Was it something he told Gretchen would be there? Or did he even give it to Rebecca? It cost a hundred and fifty dollars, maybe he gave it to Gretchen. He wouldn't necessarily have intended her to use it the way she did, but at the very least it would mean he knows she did it.

"There's something else that troubles me about Wylie. He claims not to have known Rasmussin before he started work, but he did. Maybe he helped Gretchen set up Rasmussin. Maybe, on the other hand, he's just figured out how she set the kid up and he's trying to protect her. These are things I can't possibly know for sure.

"That's the dilemma I have, Frost. People shouldn't be able to get away with murder. Not even beautiful people or talented people or rich people. Not even if their victims are murdering themselves with alcohol or drugs or self-pity. Not even if the victims are obsessive or emotionally disturbed. But at the same time someone who is charged with enforcing the law is not supposed to be going around trying to convict people unless he can prove beyond a reasonable doubt that they did it. There has to be something in the middle. There has to be some kind of pain and punishment in other people knowing that you did it even if the law can't prove it.

"It's all in degrees, Frost. If Wylie won't explain himself, that's not enough to put him on trial, but he has to suffer the doubts and suspicions that go along with keeping silent. And if you know somebody did something as awful as murder, then you either make other people know it as well as you or you share in the guilt."

Frost started to clear his throat again. He started deep down in his chest and by the time it came out of his mouth it had become a cough. Being the well-mannered Yalie that he was, he covered his mouth with his gun hand. But I didn't move. "And you think," he said, looking at what he had done with the gun, "that if the pocketbook, Becky's pocketbook, is in here we'll know for certain?"

"I would. Whether it's enough for you isn't for me to say. But I'm giving you the opportunity to find out. And I'm giving you the opportunity to watch Gretchen and Wylie to see what happens between them. And if nothing does, then I'm still giving you the opportunity to watch Gretchen. Whether you decide to discuss it with Dodge is your decision."

Frost thought it over. His blue eyes flicked once more between me and the barrel. "Tip it over, Mr. Starbuck," he said.

I turned. I walked around so that the barrel was between Frost and me. I carefully lifted out the metal pieces and dropped them so that they clanged onto the wooden floor. The noise made Frost jump, but he kept his attention on the barrel. I squatted and pushed and the barrel tipped over and its contents spilled onto the floor. Sheetrock and bolts and odd-size pieces of wood tumbled out. There was no pocketbook. I looked inside. I swept the barrel with my hand, but it was not there.

"It's somewhere, Frost," I said. "Maybe she loaded it with rocks and threw it into the pond that night. Maybe it's been destroyed between October and now. But I doubt it. I think it's still here and I'm willing to keep looking if you are."

Frost Patterson stared at the mess on the floor for a long time.

Little clouds of Sheetrock dust were still swirling around our feet and I was still squatting. "I think," he said, "you've done enough, Mr. Starbuck. I think you should go now."

I got to my feet, nowhere near as thrilled as I should have been at being freed from the immediate prospect of dying; and knowing, too, that I had nothing more to argue with Cousin Frost. I walked outside, but I made it only as far as the yard, where I stood for several minutes staring at the house with all its branches and additions, all the twists and turns that had never been contemplated by the original builder. It once had been a beautiful place, I suppose. Now, like the Patterson family itself, it was showing its age.

I was starting to turn away when I saw a figure appear at an upstairs window. I saw what looked like a sleeveless cotton undershirt and for an instant I thought it was Dodge. Then I saw the outline of the breasts, the smooth flow of the neck, the dark skin, and I knew it was Gretchen.

She moved closer, until she was right against the window and I could see the look of surprise, of disbelief, on her face. She started to raise her hand as if to wave and then slowly her eyes shifted to the barn behind me. I had been listening to the sounds of Frost Patterson moving things around, opening and closing doors, but those sounds had gone silent now.

I looked over my shoulder just as Frost emerged into the early-morning light. His gun was out of sight, his cane was tucked under his arm, he was limping along on arthritic joints. And cradled in his arms like a newborn baby was a woman's black leather purse.

M. DAVID POHLMAN

THE PROBLEM OF VIRTUE

Barney Fowler didn't expect to be made welcome in the small California town where he'd once taught — before the conviction on a morals charge.

The son of a mob boss, he had a message to deliver that could leave a local businessman walking funny and talking high. But it was Verna's suicide that forced him back. He'd been very close to Verna, who nonetheless refused to divorce her estranged husband. And if divorce was out on religious grounds, suicide was even more so.

Something didn't add up and Barney owed it to her memory to find out the truth.

'Gripping . . . complex and credible. Tops most first novels and introduces an empathetic hero-narrator'
Publishers Weekly

'A deeply satisfying mix of deep emotion and driving action'
Mystery News

Post·A·Book

A Royal Mail service in association with the Book Marketing Council & The Booksellers Association.

Post-A-Book is a Post Office trademark.

LINDA BARNES

THE SNAKE TATTOO

Find the woman with the snake tattoo.

A hooker, she'd witnessed the bar-room fight that had ended with one man in a coma and Lieutenant Mooney of the Boston Police Department suspended from duty.

Carlotta Carlyle owed it to long time friend and mentor, Mooney. Then there was the second commission: a poor little rich runaway who'd gone for a walk on the wild side. Which was why Carlotta, moonlighting as a cabbie, was cruising the red light district by night and by day, prowling round a very expensive private school with a reputation to protect.

Two can-of-worms jobs for a private eye who, like anyone with the builders in, was fleeing the chaos at home.

'Delightful — taut, engaging action with three-dimensional characters'
Sara Paretsky

'Another stunner from the inspired Ms Barnes'
The Sunday Times

'The dialogue bubbles, the action is strong and serious, and the climax is both shocking and intelligent'
The Times

'A warm welcome on second appearance to leggy, red-head Carlotta Carlyle'
The Observer

HODDER AND STOUGHTON PAPERBACKS

K.C. CONSTANTINE

THE DOUBLE DETECTIVE

The Blank Page

A Fix Like This

Two Mario Balzic Mysteries by
K.C. Constantine

The Blank Page

'K.C. Constantine's Mario Balzic series gets better with each instalment. In *The Blank Page*, Balzic investigates the murder of a co-ed at the local community college. For all of Balzic's beer drinking and profanity, the reader always knows there's *mensch* behind the badge. Balzic and his cronies, in and out of the Rocksburg bars, are an entirely diverting bunch'

Newsday

A Fix Like This

'Constantine's specialty is a kind of ethno-psychology: the violence, in other words, that erupts (usually within families) when inflexible, Old World tradition runs up against shopping-mall culture...Constantine's fourth and best shot is *A Fix Like This*'

The Boston Phoenix

'Constantine is a marvelous writer. May Mario Balzic thrive'

The New York Times Book Review

HODDER AND STOUGHTON PAPERBACKS

K.C. CONSTANTINE

THE ROCKSBURG RAILROAD MURDERS

A Mario Balzic Mystery

Mario Balzic, Chief of Police of Rocksburg, Pa, is a cop who knows his town. Nothing moves – or even sits still – without him knowing why and how.

Rocksburg is a small mining town where the coal has mostly run out, where times are hard and tempers a little frayed. So Mario Balzic is already somewhat wearied when the call comes through.

A man beaten to death down at the railroad depot. A decent, hard-working man, killed while waiting for the late local to his night-shift job at Knox Steel. The sort of inoffensive citizen Chief Balzic cares about . . .

'Constantine has created some very personable characters'

Saturday Review

'Mario Balzic is one of mystery fiction's great characters'

Ellery Queen Mystery Magazine

'Carries a tremendous wallop'
New York Times Book Review

HODDER AND STOUGHTON PAPERBACKS

KEITH PETERSON

THE TRAPDOOR

A John Wells Mystery

John Wells, *New York Star*. Ace crime reporter and journalistic dinosaur. Refusing to trade in his battered manual for a word-processor or his old-fashioned ethics for a flashy headline. A man at odds with his new editor who's learnt the business at journo-school and babbles in California-speak of relatability and on-line inputting.

One bright editorial idea: take John Wells off the corruption-in-the-city beat and pack him off upstate to cover a very local teen suicide story. An act of simple sadism since Wells is still haunted by his own daughter's suicide.

He grits his teeth, takes his typewriter and his professionalism and sets to work in his dogged way. And begins to discover that nothing in Grant County is quite what it seems and that what looked like suicide might just turn out to be murder . . .

'An impressive and important debut'
Stephen Greenleaf

'A promising new talent on the literary scene'
Tony Hillerman

HODDER AND STOUGHTON PAPERBACKS

MORE TITLES AVAILABLE FROM
CORONET CRIME

LINDA BARNES
☐ 50919 8 A Trouble of Fools   £3.50
☐ 53538 5 The Snake Tattoo   £3.99

M. DAVID POHLMAN
☐ 53025 1 The Problem of Virtue   £3.50

K.C. CONSTANTINE
☐ 50823 X The Double Detective   £4.99
☐ 50234 7 The Rocksburg Railroad Murders £2.99
☐ 43052 4 Upon Some Midnight Clear   £2.50

KEITH PETERSON
☐ 52121 X The Trapdoor   £2.99
☐ 52122 8 There Fell a Shadow   £2.99

*All these books are available at your local bookshop or newsagent,
or can be ordered direct from the publisher. Just tick the titles you
want and fill in the form below.*

Prices and availability subject to change without notice.

Hodder & Stoughton Paperbacks, P.O. Box 11, Falmouth, Cornwall.

Please send cheque or postal order, and allow the following for
postage and packing:

U.K. – 80p for one book and 20p for each additional book ordered
up to a £2.00 maximum.

B.F.P.O. – 80p for the first book, plus 20p for each additional book.

OVERSEAS INCLUDING EIRE – £1.50 for the first book, plus £1.00
for the second book, and 30p for each additional book ordered.

Name ....

Address ....

....